The Money Makers

Harry Bingham was born in England in 1967. After graduating from Oxford University, he worked for ten years as a London-based investment banker. He spent time in major American, Japanese and European banks where he gained first hand knowledge of the world of billion dollar deals, hostile takeovers, and company bankruptcy. In 1997, he left banking to care for his disabled wife and to write this book. He lives in Oxford with his wife and an increasing number of dogs. He now writes full time.

THE

MONEY MAKERS

HARRY BINGHAM

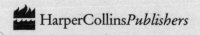 **HarperCollins**Publishers

HarperCollins*Publishers*
77–85 Fulham Palace Road,
Hammersmith, London W6 8JB

www.**fire**and**water**.com

A Paperback Original 2000
1 2 3 4 5 6 7 8 9

A catalogue record for this book
is available from the British Library

ISBN 0 00 651354 9

Typeset in Palatino by
Palimpsest Book Production Limited,
Polmont, Stirlingshire

Printed and bound in Great Britain by
Caledonian International Book Manufacturing Ltd, Glasgow

Dedicated to
my beloved wife, N.

'Who think the same thoughts without need of speech
And babble the same speech without need of meaning'

Acknowledgements

This book is better than it would have been thanks to Rosemarie McSweeney's thirst for vengeance, Lorraine Frances-Rees' red eyes, Jeremy Wilson's desire for warmth, Jesse Norman's flattery in high places, and the boundless enthusiasm of my family. Daniel, Phil, Joshua, Rachel and Hammond all encouraged me to believe the book would find an audience. Thanks also to Felicity, the queen of agents and to all at HarperCollins, especially Fiona, who have been wonderful people to work with. My wife, Nule, has simply been the best possible companion throughout this endeavour: supportive, insightful and wise, encouraging me down paths I might never otherwise have found. My greatest thanks are to her.

And finally a word to my friends in the libel trade. Contrary to the bland little piece of blurb at the front of the book, three of the characters and one of the names in this novel are strictly non-fictional. The name is Nick Draper's (who isn't an ogre and scarcely even a billionaire). Of the three characters, two have been portrayed with such remarkable (though unflattering) fidelity that no grounds for action are conceivable. The third individual, however, has been deliberately, savagely and gratuitously defamed, and would make an ideal plaintiff in any libel suit. Happy hunting!

THE
MONEY MAKERS

The Beginning
Leeds, Yorkshire, 1998

There are a million ways to torment your kids, but from beyond the grave Bernard Gradley had found a new one.

Technically, of course, he was within his rights. Every legal aspect had been considered, the document drafted and redrafted under Gradley's dictatorial eye. Augustus Earle had resisted every change. He knew the difference between right and wrong, and he fought to preserve the family's disintegrating rights. But Gradley was unforgiving. He demanded a document 'watertight as a Scotsman's wallet' and wouldn't rest until he had it. And once he did, he signed it, then put it away from him for ever, a document hard and mean as the dead man's heart.

Earle pitied the family. The mother, who had for so long defended her kids from their father's severity, had done nothing to merit this. And if the kids weren't perfect, their punishment would far outweigh their faults.

They would come in hope. Their father had built a mighty fortune, and isn't wealth supposed to pass down the generations more reliably than genes? Well, hope might bring them, but other emotions would send them away. Grief, sorrow, anger, rage.

The clock readied itself to strike twelve noon. The family would be here any minute. With tension mounting in the pit of his stomach, Earle patted the documents nervously into line, beneath his desk lamp: the will and the letter, heavy as a curse and more certain.

Leeds, Yorkshire, 1959

You don't find too many saints on a construction site, but Bernard Gradley was in a class of his own. It wasn't just the night of the accident that he'd 'borrowed' one of the site's dumper trucks for a private job, it had been pretty much every night for the past eight months, cash in hand every time. Plus it turned out that Gradley had three pieces of heavy equipment as well as numerous cement mixers and the like 'on lease' to local building firms. Given how hard he worked by day and the extent of his extra-curricular activities at night, it was hardly surprising that he dozed off once when he shouldn't. He was found in the morning, badly concussed, wandering the site. The dumper truck, wheels still spinning, was lying upside down on the remains of the site engineer's cabin. With his foreman's insults boiling in his ears, Gradley left the site for ever, saved from prosecution only by the company's embarrassment at its own negligence.

Gradley was seventeen years of age. His father was dead, his mother alcoholic, his numerous brothers and sisters all of school age, his job prospects all but annihilated by the accident and its aftermath. It was, as he told his children later, the morning when his career took flight.

Before even returning to his lodgings to bathe his head, he walked to the centre of town to make some purchases: a suit and tie, white shirt and decent shoes, a briefcase, some stationery, and, costing as much as everything else together, a pair of binoculars with lenses hand-ground in East Germany.

His routine was quick to develop. On the first day he would get up, put on his dust-stained working clothes and set out on foot to do the round of construction sites in the area. His first move was to find himself a vantage point from which he could watch the activity on site. He took no notes and drew no pictures, but his eyes, glued to the binoculars, never left the scene. He spent several hours in that way, sometimes a whole day if the site was large. Finally, and only when he had seen enough, did he make his way to the nearest working man's café or pub.

There he ordered food and drink and unfolded a copy of the *Racing Post* on the table in front of him. As he always took care to arrive at peak hours, however, there was no chance of him being left alone for long, and with an air of reluctance he'd put away his paper and begin to engage in the talk swirling all around him.

Posing as an unemployed labourer seeking work, he probed for the information he needed. What equipment did they use? What worked well, what didn't? What were the foremen like? The site engineer? The construction manager? How many people were on the site altogether? Were they ahead of schedule or behind? He took care never to look inquisitive. He avoided direct questions, cracked a lot of jokes, slagged off bosses in general, told tall stories about bits of equipment he'd worked with in the past, encouraged even shy men to open up about their jobs, to complain about the idiocies they were forced to endure. He bought oceans of tea, laughed inordinately, and forgot nothing.

The next morning he returned to the site unrecognisable. This time he wore his suit and tie, his hair shone with Brylcreem and his shoes looked as if their owner had never heard of builders' dust. He sought out the construction manager whom he already knew by description and usually also by sight. His pitch was simple. From his briefcase he took out a sheet of paper entitled 'Site Costings: Current'. On it he had written carefully in pencil a complete list of the workforce and equipment employed on the site. By each item on the list were three columns showing the number of units, the cost per unit, and the total cost. He spent some time explaining rather elaborately that of course such an analysis was only illustrative and no doubt the manager had his site much better arranged than 'the chaos typical around here'. The manager would look away, agree that the site was better managed than that, but encourage Gradley to continue 'just supposing that things were that bad, but only for the sake of argument, mind'. At that point, Gradley knew he was home and dry, but still he took his time.

He talked about different construction routines, analysed them with equipment and without, and costed them out to show how the labour saving more than paid for the extra cost of the equipment. Every time he started, he hesitated, saying ''Course, I don't know why I'm telling you this, it's obviously second nature to someone like yourself.' Each time, however, he could be coaxed back into his patter, knowing that every routine he analysed was used on site and in most cases was even more inefficient than those he described. Eventually, and only after protestations, he pulled out a second sheet of paper from his case. This one was entitled 'Site Costings: Potential'. There was the same list, and the same three columns. But this time the workforce was dramatically smaller, the need for construction equipment much bigger, and the total site costs a full third lower than they had been. Beneath the total was a number neatly written in pencil and underlined twice, labelled 'Percentage Saving'.

The closer he came to landing his fish, the slower he wound the reel. 'I feel like a complete bloody fool teaching my grandmother to suck eggs,' he'd say, 'I should be getting you to teach me my business instead.' He got the site manager to walk with him around the site, making sure the manager watched every activity with new eyes whilst not appearing to see a single thing himself. Instead, he told stories about mythical site managers fired for incompetence when their bosses saw how ineptly things were being run, and others who had been promoted and given company cars for finishing impossible projects under budget and ahead of schedule. He larded his talk with things he had heard in the café the day before: the things the workers complained about, the ridicule they directed at their bosses, the petty cheating which goes on everywhere.

As the time for leaving drew near, Gradley almost seemed to forget that he had introduced himself as a construction equipment rental agent. He needed the site manager to bring his attention back to the equipment available, the pieces of machinery needed to bring the site's costs from the first list to the second. Once they did get stuck in though, it was amazing how quickly the site's equipment needs grew. No point in having just one bulldozer when a second could be used to clear the rubble. No purpose in using just one mechanical hoist when there were workers enough to be busy with two. Whenever the manager suggested another piece of kit, Gradley would pause with a little frown, before exclaiming: 'Bloody brilliant! I would never have thought a site like this would need one of those, but you're absolutely right. Bloody visionary, you are. Just like that sod I was telling you about who was promoted twice in two years just when everyone thought he was going to be fired for being pissed morning, noon and night. Mind you, while you're at it, you may as well have another of them to cover the north end. No point in skimping.'

And by the time Bernard Gradley left the site, smiling at the workers who had entertained him the day before and who would be losing their jobs within a matter of weeks, he swung in his briefcase a lengthy order for construction equipment not a single item of which did he possess.

The next stage was easier. The construction industry has always been one of boom and bust, and while one firm is so busy with orders that no customer is attended to properly, another firm only a short distance away may be laying workers off and leaving equipment idle for want of work. Gradley had a knack for finding companies of the second sort. For them it was a godsend to have Gradley appear off the street and offer to take their surplus gear for long enough to tide them over until the next burst of activity. The rates he offered were not great, of course, nothing in fact compared with what he charged his own customers, but anything was better than nothing.

The business did well. The sixties was a time of renewal and change, and nobody benefited more than the construction industry. Slums were cleared. New tower blocks and housing developments rose in their place. Go-go businesses heady with twenty years of unbroken peace and growth built glitzy new head-quarters of glass and cement. Even Britain's creaking manufacturers, like geriatrics in the sun, forgot their weaknesses and spent money on factories and ware-houses. Gradley Plant Hire Limited, as the company was called, took on staff and expanded from Leeds out into Yorkshire, and from Yorkshire out into the counties beyond.

As the business grew and strengthened, Gradley found the time to marry, have kids, to divorce acrimoniously when the marriage went bad. He was a rich man now, worth thirty million by some accounts, forty or more by others. His business wasn't just successful, it was one of the biggest of its kind in the country, so strong it no longer depended on him, its father, for its prosperity. Instead of making him happy, the fact left him discontented. He longed for the old days, back when it had been just him, no money, and ambition as big as the sky. A man of some leisure now, he experimented with buying racehorses but had no luck. He then discovered motoring and began to build up a collection of cars, all British.

The hobby killed him. One day in mid-July, he was driving at speed when he suffered a minor heart attack. The attack itself was not fatal but he briefly lost con-sciousness. At a bend in the road the car carried straight on. It bounced off a stone wall into a tree. Gradley died instantly.

All that remained now was to divide up his fortune.

Leeds, Yorkshire, 1998

1

The sweep of tyres, the jerk of a handbrake, a clatter of car doors, then a knock at the door. The family arrived, swept into his room and now waited, silently, eager for money.

'Welcome,' said Earle. 'Welcome to you all.'

It was a poor welcome he had to give. There were five of them, of whom Earle recognised only the mother, Helen Gradley, a nervous, pale woman, mid-fifties but a decade older in appearance. As Bernard's divorce solicitor, Earle had threatened her with every trick in the book to win a favourable settlement. In theory, Helen had been the party at fault. She'd had an affair and admitted as much. Hers wasn't such a great crime, not when her husband's relationship with his business was more passionate, more permanent and more exclusive than anything she had done. But Bernard hadn't seen it like that, of course. He'd wanted to give her 'what she deserves – nothing'. He threatened a custody battle, on grounds that Earle was obliged to fabricate, and the friendless woman gave way. She got the kids, he kept the money. She settled for a small London house and an allowance which would terminate once the youngest child, Josephine, reached eighteen.

In the years after the divorce, Gradley had thrown money at his kids, hoping to win them from their mother. They were to be indulged, she to be kept poor. The strategy had worked up to a point. The kids, especially the three sons, George, Zachary and Matthew, had taken the money and been spoiled by it. They had grown used to their life of fast cars, jet travel, nice flats in the right parts of London. Their mother's house in Kilburn struck them as grotty, too embarrassing to show their friends. But if Gradley had wanted to win their love, he'd failed entirely. His sons loved the cheques, but despised the chequebook. They knew the gifts were motivated more by bitterness than by love, and Gradley himself couldn't help but resent his own generosity. He reminded his kids of how useless they were, how indolent. He told them repeatedly how he had made his fortune, conjuring an empire from the desert sand.

And now the emperor was dead, what was left but to divide the empire? The five inheritors – the tense mother, the stony-faced sons, the grave and serious daughter – waited in silence.

'Welcome,' said Earle again, 'though I can only regret the sad occasion which has brought us together.' He felt the tension again, more strongly this time. Why? He alone knew what the will contained. He alone was unaffected. His voice rose a little as he continued. 'You know, of course, why we're here. The deceased, Bernard Gradley, told me that none of you had any knowledge of his will. Perhaps I should begin by confirming that this is indeed the case.'

He looked around, but he already knew the answer. The hungry faces of the three sons and their mother's agitation told him. They knew nothing and wanted everything.

'While it would be wrong of me to speak ill of the dead, especially when the deceased has been such an important client of this firm's,' Earle paused. His words sounded crass and for a moment he was stuck. He had a weak voice which became high, almost falsetto, when he was nervous. He fought to regain his control, to drop back an octave. 'While, er, it would be wrong to do so, this will, I'm afraid, is not a document which, er, was a pleasant one to draft. And, er –' He tailed off, his voice trailing into a squeak.

'D'you want me to read it?' drawled one of the sons, dark and lean, frightening somehow.

'That won't be necessary,' said Earle sharply, and – thank goodness – deeply. The challenge got him restarted. 'You may read the will yourself in due course and you may well wish to show it to your own legal advisers. In summary, however, the desires of the deceased are as follows. His mother, Mrs Victoria Gradley, will receive a sum of three hundred thousand pounds to be held in trust on her behalf by certain trustees. His brothers and sisters will each receive, on top of certain small personal bequests, the sum of one hundred thousand pounds.'

Earle's listeners registered these facts tersely, hungering for what was to come. In their minds, their father's company was already sold, the money counted and divided. A few hundred thousand quid to their granny, aunts and uncles wasn't much to give up. They shifted forward. The punch line was drawing near.

'The residual estate is hard to value,' Earle continued. 'The principal asset, of course, is the one hundred percent ownership of Gradley Plant Hire Limited, though there will naturally be a considerable liability in the form of

11

inheritance tax. We have estimated the residual estate to be worth some thirty to thirty-five million pounds after payment of tax. Out of this sum, you, Mrs Gradley,' and he nodded at Helen, whose nervousness had grown rounder and harder with each passing minute, 'you will receive a sum of five thousand pounds per annum payable until your death. I am sorry, I am very sorry, that I was not able to prevail on my client to be more generous.'

Helen Gradley was white faced, but otherwise blank. There was shock, certainly, but Earle guessed that none of them had expected Gradley to be generous towards his ex-wife. The real issue was how the money was to be divided amongst the kids. Helen didn't need the money herself, just so long as the kids were fairly treated. Nobody said anything, all of them willing Earle to continue.

'And as for you,' Earle said, looking at the four children, the flinty men and the expressionless girl. 'As for you, Mr Gradley expressly required me to read the following letter.'

Earle picked up the letter which lay by the will and broke open the seal. Gradley's writing was clear and heavy. Earle read slowly and distinctly, master of his voice once more:

To my children,

I'm dead now, proud of some things, ashamed of others. I'm proudest of my business, of course. I loved Gradley Plant Hire. I gave it everything and it rewarded me for it. With my business, things worked just as they were meant to. You lot think profit is just another name for money, but you're wrong. Profit means health. It means rosy cheeks and a happy smile. Gradley Plant Hire was a bouncing baby and its father loved it.

With you lot, things were never so simple. I wanted to teach you about life. I wanted to teach you about work and pride and discipline. I wanted you all to love my business the way I did.

And I failed, didn't I? God knows what you lot really think, but I swear to you I only ever saw you think about the business when you wanted to cadge money from me. My eldest son George is the crown prince of idleness; Zack's a bloody philosopher; and Matthew and Josie will probably drop out just as soon as they've got anything to drop from. If I tell you that I wanted to be a good dad to you, you probably won't believe me, but for what it's worth, I swear to you I did. I still don't know what went wrong. I don't know if it was your fault or mine. But don't accuse me of not wanting things to work out better, because I did, I really did.

Maybe it doesn't matter now. You're not here to worry about our family failures, you're here to see how much I've left you. Well, I wouldn't want to disappoint you, so I've come up with a way of giving each of you what you most want.

Josephine first. I had the most trouble with you. You never minded spending my money on clothes and parties, but you never really wanted to be rich, did you? Being nice to people was more your thing. Swotting away at school and do-gooding. I thought of getting you a truckload of designer clothes, but of course they'd all have been the wrong colour or too bloody short or too bloody long. If it came from me there was always a problem, wasn't there? Then I had a brainwave. You remember how you used to come into my office when you were little? You used to tidy my pens and play at being my secretary. You didn't grumble about my business then. You didn't want to try to change me from what I am. You know what I think now? I think that was the last time we were ever happy together, like a dad and his little girl are meant to be.

Very well then. To you, Josephine Gradley, I give an enrolment at a secretarial college of your choice plus five hundred quids' worth of Marks & Spencer's vouchers to get yourself properly kitted out. If I'm wrong and you're more ambitious than I've realised, then you've got the brains and looks to get yourself whatever it is you want. I don't need to worry. You'll be OK.

As for my sons, George, Zack and Matthew, well you were easier to deal with. You only ever wanted money and your only ambition was to get your hands on mine as soon as you could. Fair enough. But there's one condition. I worked my balls off to get my money, while you lot haven't done a day's work in your lives. Maybe that's my fault. Maybe I didn't bring you up right. If so, I'm sorry. I hope there's time to make amends.

The rest of my estate – Gradley Plant Hire mostly – will be put into a trust. The trustees will look after things for three years, keep the company ticking over and that sort of thing. Then in three years' time, three years from today, we'll see what you've achieved. If any of you can produce the sum of one million pounds in a bank account under your name and your exclusive control, then you get the lot. Everything. You'll have to show, of course, that you haven't just borrowed the money or anything like that. It needs to be yours and only yours and not owed to a bank or the taxman or the man in the moon. But don't worry, the lawyers have gone into all that and the rules should be perfectly clear. If more than one of you kids has come up with the million, then the one with the most gets everything. I like winners, not runners-up. You can do what you like then. You can sell the company and spend the rest of your life on a tropical island for all I care. You'll have earned it.

If, by any chance, you don't come up with the million, then I've obviously misjudged you and you don't truly want my money. In that case it will all go to charity and you can each make your own way in the world, just like I did. At least you'll have the knowledge that anything you do get has come your way through your own hard work and honesty.

Good luck. I really mean it. Make me proud of you.

Love from your father, Bernard.

Helen Gradley was weeping copiously now, cocooned in Josephine's arms. Her tears were not just tears of grief, they were tears of shock, tears of ultimate defeat. Josephine was crying too, but her grief was different. She was hurt by her father's viciousness towards her. She was upset at finding what her privileged life was about to turn into. But most of all she was upset that her father's last act should be one of spite and unkindness. He'd deserved a better memorial.

Earle brought his attention back. He had been staring, and staring at pretty, vulnerable young women is not recommended behaviour for family solicitors. The three young men remained almost expressionless. Only a tightening of their lips and a hardening of their eyes betrayed any emotion. Zachary, the dark one, had his eyes almost completely narrowed, his hand over his lips, concealing his feelings, appraising the situation, planning the next step.

Earle shivered.

'Gradley Plant Hire and your father's other assets are now held in trust, and they will be looked after for you by a group of very able trustees. Should any of you meet your father's conditions, you will find everything in very good order in three years' time. The will goes into all these matters in greater detail, and you may of course read it at your leisure. You may also wish to consult your own legal advisers, but I regret to say that in my opinion there should be no difficulty in enforcing the terms of the will. I'm really very sorry.'

2

Helen Gradley had lost the key to her own front door. Standing on the step outside, she rummaged uselessly through the rubbish in her handbag and began to cry.

'Don't worry, Mum,' said Josephine. 'I've got it.'

On the long drive home Helen's shock had dissolved repeatedly into tears, but the hard centre of her pain had, if anything, grown. Since the divorce, she had never quite brought herself to believe in the permanence of her poverty. Though she had been in work, she was a poor housekeeper, prone to surges of extravagance she could ill afford. A few years back, she was diagnosed as suffering from repetitive stress injury caused by poor typing posture, and she had invalided herself from the workforce with a speed and decisiveness none of her kids had been able to overcome. On hearing the news of her ex-husband's death, she had been openly delighted.

16

'At least his money will be of some use now,' she'd said. The will devastated her. Her worn carpets, her threadbare curtains, her hopeless dreams of a better life were all here to stay. The cavalry wasn't coming. Rescue was impossible.

Josephine unlocked the door, took her mum upstairs to bed, and left her there with a hot-water bottle and a promise to look in soon. The kids needed to speak openly with each other and weren't able to do so in their mother's grief-stricken presence.

By the time Josephine emerged, her three brothers were sitting at the kitchen table round a pot of tea. Zachary, named after his grandfather, but always known simply as Zack, had arrived that morning with a bottle of champagne, expecting to celebrate later, but nobody felt like it now. With their mother quiet, they could turn at last to the thing on all their minds.

'Poor Mum,' said Josie. 'It's awful for her. She'd so relied on the will to make everything better.'

'Don't be silly, Josie. It's awful for all of us. The old bastard's probably laughing himself sick,' said Matthew. He had sympathy for his mother, but his sympathy for himself was very much greater. Matthew's broad, good-looking face was puckered up into a boyish scowl. His cupid's-bow mouth pouted in an eight-year-old's sulk.

'He's not an old bastard. He's our dead father,' said Josephine.

'Of course he's our father,' said Matthew. 'None of us wished him dead and all of us would bring him back if we could. But we all know that he was a bastard when alive, and he certainly acted the bastard in his death. And face it. He's succeeded. He's screwed up my life. He's screwed up your life. He's screwed things up for all of us, not just Mum.'

'You mean we'll all have to earn a living like every

17

other person in the world.' Josephine's voice was high and tense. She knew Matthew spoke the truth, yet she thought it wrong to speak ill of their dead father only days after laying him in his grave. And, despite everything, in his own infuriating way, he had loved them.

'Oh come on, Josie,' said Matthew, unable to keep his voice from whining. 'It's like being imprisoned. None of us has ever really expected to earn our livings, and now we're going to be locked up like everyone else in tedious jobs, suits, mortgages, pension plans, and all the rest of it. It's a life sentence.'

'You've got a job with that American investment bank, Madison, haven't you? That's not so bad.'

'It's not a proper job, just a summer job. I need to finish my economics degree before I look for anything permanent. And Madison won't have me back. I only took the job because Dad made me, and I haven't done a stroke of work since arriving.'

'You're talented enough –'

'Of course I'll find something eventually, but that's not what I expected, or any of us. It's a life sentence, Josie, and it's what that bastard wanted.'

Tears rose to Matthew's eyes as he spoke. He had a vision of his future as it should have been – leisured, pleasured and easy – and of his future as it now was: leaden, penniless and hard. He'd toil away for forty years and his reward would be this: that he'd have enough cash to avoid cold and hunger in his old age. George saw Matthew's tears and moved the conversation forwards, giving his brother the opportunity to wipe his eyes with the back of his hand.

'You're right,' grunted George. 'But I'm worse off. I've got seven lousy O-Levels. I was chucked out of school. I've never done a day's work in my life. I've got a couple of thousand quid in my current account, I've got my car, and that's it. My flat's rented. If I look for a job, I'll be lucky to get something stacking shelves.'

He wasn't exaggerating. George had been expelled from Sedbergh for holding a champagne party for a dozen friends, mostly female, in his housemaster's sitting room. His housemaster had arrived back early from a weekend away to find the music blaring, the lights blazing, and champagne ringmarks all over the fine antiques it had been his life's passion to collect. George's education had finished that very night and, without regrets, he'd plunged straight into the life of the international playboy. He mixed with the young, rich and idle from Europe and the States, rotating between the ski slopes of Gstaad, the yacht clubs of the Riviera, the grouse moors of Scotland, and the glittering parties of London, Paris and New York. The one talent that George had developed to the full was getting money out of his father. For some reason, Bernard Gradley paid up for George's extravagances with a freedom none of the others enjoyed. The others put it down to their physical similarity: the same heavy build, the same ginger hair and piggy eyes. George himself didn't bother to question his father's generosity. He just took the money, endured the criticism, and took off for the next party.

'Can't we get the will overturned or something?' he added. 'I mean there must be a law against this kind of thing.'

'Oh grow up,' snapped Zack. 'Of course there isn't a law against it. It was Dad's money and he's allowed to give it to whoever he wants. We can get a lawyer to look at the will, but it's bound to be watertight. Dad wouldn't screw up something like that. He was a bastard, but he was a competent bastard.'

Zack scowled, dark and intense, silencing the room. Brilliant, abrasive and arrogant, he had always been the boys' natural leader, despite George's three year advantage in age, and Zack's assessment carried complete authority.

'At least you've got a proper job,' sulked Matthew.

This was true up to a point. Zack had gone to Oxford to study law, but had grown quickly bored and switched to philosophy. The move had enraged his father. 'You show me somebody who's made any money studying the meaning of life and I'll sell him my business for a tenner,' he roared, and obstructed Zack at every turn. But Zack could be as stubborn as his father and, having completed his degree with flying colours, went on to pursue a doctorate in a particularly obscure area of philosophy. Unfortunately, just as he was close to finishing his thesis, some new work published in the United States seemed to overturn the conclusion he was trying to prove, and he abandoned his work in a fit of annoyance.

At his dad's insistence, he'd looked for a job and reluctantly signed up with a big London accountancy firm. He'd been there for four months and hated every minute. A week ago, a simmering quarrel with a senior partner exploded into a major row and Zack fully expected to be fired upon his return to work.

Zack shrugged. 'I may have a job, but that's the point. I don't want a job. I want to be rich enough not to need one. Same as you.'

Matthew reached for the teapot and poured himself tea. He swigged it and breathed out with a sigh. 'Let's have a minute's silence out of respect for the poor sods in hell who'll have to put up with Dad for the next million billion years.'

'Matthew! Honestly!' exclaimed Josephine, shocked.

'Hear, hear,' said George, lifting his mug in a mock toast. 'Here's to the late and unlamented Bernard Gradley.

May he enjoy as much kindness and generosity in the life hereafter as he showered upon one and all in his time on earth.'

Matthew and George looked at Zack for his support. Zack was the leader and the two brothers needed him. Zack held their gaze in agonising silence. Nothing in his face moved. The dark pools of his eyes had narrowed to slots, guarding the secrets within. Matthew and George searched his expression for an answer but found nothing.

'Well?' asked Matthew at length, the whine returning to his voice. George was calmer, but equally intent, perhaps already guessing the turn Zack's thoughts had taken.

'Well what?' replied Zack, with a slight tremor. He slowly rose, walked to the fridge and took out the champagne. He uncorked the bottle and carefully poured himself a glass. 'I don't know about you guys, but I'm quite happy.'

'Happy? How can you be happy?' Matthew and George spoke as one.

'Well, the most I'd been expecting was a quarter of Dad's fortune. Today I've discovered I can have all of it.'

'What the hell do you mean?'

'Just what I say,' said Zack calmly. 'I'll make a million. In three years. Then I'll have everything. I couldn't have hoped for more.'

'How are you going to make the money?'

'I don't know yet. But I will. And in three years' time, I'll be very rich indeed.'

Matthew and George were stunned. If Zack said he would do something they both believed he'd do it. But Zack said nothing about sharing the money out, and neither of his brothers wanted to bet a whole lot on his generosity.

Matthew's boyish features gathered in a frown. Zack might be the brilliant one, but Matthew was deeply competitive. He could seldom resist a challenge, and on this occasion he wasn't going to try.

'You may make a million, Zack. But I'll make more. I'll beat you to Dad's money. I'll get it. Not you.'

The two brothers, one dark and angular, the other broad and fair, gazed at each other like gladiators before bloodshed. George spread his hands in despair.

'You'll share out the money, guys, won't you? I mean whoever wins. I'm sure you will.'

Neither Zack nor Matthew spoke, but their faces gave George his answer. If he wanted his father's cash, there was only one way to get it.

'Oh Jesus,' he said. 'I don't believe it. Alright. I'll have to make my million too, I suppose. Oh, Jesus.'

'You babies,' said Josephine. 'You stupid babies.'

Upstairs Helen Gradley began to cry again in deep sobs that racked the little house.

Summer 1998

1

As morning broke over London four young people awoke to face the day.

First was Matthew, who, as on so many mornings, awoke to find himself in a bed not his own. Beside him there slept an attractive girl, naked. He brushed her hair away from her face. Alison? Amanda? No, Amelia. He'd met her at a party the night before and they'd left together. She was pretty but mediocre in bed, he remembered. No, that was unfair. It was Matthew who'd been off form. The will had got to him, as had Zack's aggressive response. Amelia had been just fine, and her skin looked lovely in the morning light. Matthew tweaked the duvet up over her bare shoulder and crept out of bed.

He dressed silently in front of the mirror. His light fluffy hair needed to be damped and combed, but he didn't want to run the bathroom taps in case he woke the sleeper. He patted his hair ineffectually into place. He looked like a stubbly choirboy with untidy hair. Matthew grimaced at his reflection but it didn't help. It just made him look like a sulky choirboy.

He crept downstairs and found a bit of paper and a pen. He searched a bit further and found an envelope in the dustbin addressed to Miss Amelia Somebody-or-other. Good. Amelia, then, not Amanda.

'Dear Amelia,' he wrote. 'Thank you for a wonderful night last night. I thought you were absolutely terrific. Sorry I had to rush off this morning – urgent business elsewhere, and I didn't want to wake you. All the very best, Matthew.'

He was practised in such notes and had stopped signing off with 'love from' or 'we must get together again'. His one-night stands were mostly with partners who were no more looking for true love than he was, but on occasion he had been caught out and the word 'love' had come back to haunt him. So now he aimed to be generous, warm-hearted but final. As far as he could remember, Amelia wouldn't have a problem with that, but in any case she didn't have his phone number. He closed the front door quietly and walked across the park towards his Chelsea flat.

Once there, he showered properly and dressed again with care. He was a good-looking chap, Matthew, and fussy as a showgirl over his appearance. He got himself some coffee, a pad of paper and a pen. Across the top of the page he wrote in block capitals: 'Plan: One million pounds in three years.' He underlined it.

Then he paused. He wasn't going to list all the things he was missing, he believed in a positive approach. Underneath his heading he wrote, 'Assets: temporary job on Madison trading floor.' Then he was stuck. He had no money, no qualifications, and his job was already half-lost. He thought for a long time.

At school he had always been Zack's younger brother. Zack had seldom appeared to work, but ended up with a string of A grades and a scholarship to Oxford. Matthew had worked hard, his exam results were peppered with B grades and worse, and his teachers thought him lucky to have won his place at Cambridge. Never once had Zack made things easier by showing humility or understanding. Matthew had a point to prove, and prove it he would.

His coffee went cold. He got himself another and thought some more. Eventually, he picked up his pen again and wrote: 'Plan A: Get a permanent job at Madison. Become the best trader ever to hit the trading floor. Get a million pounds in bonuses – after tax!! Comment: very hard to achieve but worth a try.'

Then shaking his head, he continued: 'Plan B: Get a permanent job at Madison. Become a very skilful trader. Get some big bonuses. Then –' But he broke off. He knew what he had in mind but it would be foolish to put it into writing. It was going to be a challenging three years.

2

Just as Matthew was throwing away his sheet of paper, his elder brother Zack was at the office getting one out. He'd been happy enough to fling down a challenge to his brothers yesterday, but this morning it didn't seem so smart. A week earlier Zack had told his senior audit partner to shove his head somewhere it would neither reach nor fit, there to entertain himself by auditing his kidneys. Predictably, the partner had stormed off, put in a request for Zack's dismissal, and the firm's disciplinary machinery ground into action. The final review meeting was tomorrow and it was a near certainty that Zack would get the sack.

Accountants don't become millionaires. They may, of course, if they work hard, do well, and save prudently, but not in three years. Not aged twenty-six. On the other hand, ex-philosophy students with no job, no references, and no capital aren't exactly in the millionaire bracket themselves. Zack needed a job – a proper job – but to do that he needed not to be fired. Scowling and gritting his teeth, he wrote out a grovelling letter of apology. Zack blamed 'my extreme grief following the death of my father' and begged 'to be given a second chance to show my deep commitment to the firm'.

Zack tucked the letter into an envelope, addressed it, then pretended to spit on it. Along with tact, modesty, patience, kindness and a few other virtues, the art of apology was one Zack had yet to master. He dumped the envelope into the internal mail system and snapped at a secretary to check it was collected and delivered. That was that. No more to be done on that front.

Meantime, there was a larger problem to be solved. How was Zack to make his million? Right now he couldn't say, but there was only one place to try: the City of London, one of the world's great financial centres, and home to more banks than any other city in the world. But how to gain entry? His accountancy firm would give him a terrible reference, and he had nothing else to show except a failed doctorate and a useless philosophy degree. Good banks don't hire losers.

Zack scowled again, adding to the natural intensity of his narrow face. Matthew was the best looking of the three brothers, but many women found Zack's darkly brooding looks irresistible. Matthew was always baffled that Zack didn't appear to notice, let alone take proper advantage, his only serious romance to date being a long and stormy one with a girl at college. Zack picked up the phone and dialled an Oxford number.

'Ichabod Bell speaking.'

'Ichabod, it's Zack. Zack Gradley.'

'Zack, my boy, nice to hear from you.' Zack's old

philosophy tutor was genuinely enthusiastic. 'What can I do for you? Are you coming back to finish your doctorate? I can't believe you're going to be a godforsaken accountant all your life.'

'No, actually, I wanted to ask a favour.' And Zack explained what was on his mind.

Ichabod Bell thought for a moment in silence, then said, 'Come to dinner in two weeks. College High Table. There's someone I'd like you to meet.'

'Who?'

'Jolly good. Saturday, in two weeks, then. Seven thirty for eight. Look forward to it.'

'Who am I meeting?'

'Oh, you'll love him. Give you a chance to catch up on all your rowing gossip. Glittering mornings on the water, the thrill of the race, all that stuff.'

'Ichabod, you know perfectly well I've never sat in a rowing boat in my life.'

'Nonsense, Zack, you've been a lifelong fan of the sport. Nobody quite like you for memorising race statistics and all that rubbish. Just come to dinner.'

And he rang off. Zack had no idea what Bell was planning. All he knew was that he had two weeks to become expert in the noble sport of rowing.

3

George was woken shortly before midday by a loud thumping. He tried ignoring it but the noise wouldn't go away. He pulled on a dressing gown and went to the door.

A group of beautiful young people stood in the hall outside. Beautifully dressed, beautifully tanned, slim, athletic and many-accented, they were among the wealthiest, laziest, most easily bored young people in

Europe, George's friends of the last eleven years. A petite, bird-like French girl headed the deputation.

'Georges!' she exclaimed, using the French pronunciation of his name. 'You aren't even up and we're already late. You need to be ready this moment or we'll miss the races. Papa's horse is running at two-thirty, remember.'

'Oh God, Kiki. Is it Deauville today? I'd completely forgotten.'

In his previous life four centuries ago – or was it only four days? – George had suggested chartering a plane to take them to the races at the French casino town of Deauville. The plane had been due to leave at midday, so they were already holding it up and incurring extra charges.

'But Georges, of course it is Deauville today. And we are due at the casino this evening. You can't have forgotten because, look, I have remembered, and I have even got up early, and I never get up early and I never remember anything, so you must have remembered, except you haven't.'

Kiki's illogical proof tumbled out in a single breathless flurry. Her dark brown hair fell down her slim neck in artful wisps, positively inviting male touch. She wasn't beautiful, Kiki, but she was pretty.

And she spoke the truth. It was a minor miracle that she had remembered an appointment and been ready on time, something George had never known before. Damn! He fancied Kiki desperately and had arranged the trip mostly to be with her. If she had got herself ready, did that mean she returned his affection? Possibly, possibly not. But if he jumped on the plane to Deauville he could hardly get out of paying his share, and the last thing he needed was an evening of champagne and roulette at five hundred francs a chip.

'Kiki, I'm so sorry. I've been terribly ill. Stomach upset. I don't think I'm up to flying. You go on anyway. I'll come another time.'

'Oh, poor Georges! You don't look well at all. Very pale and your hair is all stuck down one way and sticking up the other way. You should be in bed.'

'I was in bed.'

George didn't look ill, or at least no iller than normal. Of the four kids, he'd drawn the short straw in the genetic sweepstakes and ended up every inch his father's son. He had Bernard Gradley's pale English skin, his piggy little eyes, his stockiness, his uncontrollable ginger hair. The sick-as-a-dog look came naturally.

'Well you must go straight back and eat a lot of chicken broth.'

'OK, Kiki. Have a good time.'

Kiki left in a swirl of the young and beautiful. A handsome young man, playboy son of an Italian billionaire, positioned himself next to her as they left. George crawled back into bed, pulled the covers over his head and groaned.

4

And as George lay in bed groaning, Josephine was making grunting sounds of her own. She had rummaged round in the attic of her mother's Kilburn house and found something she'd remembered playing with as a child. She grunted as she lugged the heavy typewriter downstairs into the kitchen. It weighed a ton and the attic had covered her in dust.

Never mind. There are worse things in life than dust. She sat down at the ancient keyboard and opened a battered textbook. 'ASDF are the home keys for the left hand.' She spread her fingertips over the dusty keys, thumbs resting lightly on the space bar. It's a new feeling, but one she'll need to get used to. She can forget about A Levels. She can forget about Oxbridge.

It is Wednesday 15 July 1998. There are three years less one day to go until Bernard Gradley's deadline: 1095 days.

5

Thursday morning. The red lights of digital clocks display the times around the world's financial centres. News messages roll incessantly across a dot matrix wall panel while the glow from banks of computer screens fights back the dark. Every now and then a phone rings briefly in the silence. But apart from a few early-morning cleaners there is no one here to check the screens or answer the phones. No one except Matthew. It is five fifteen am.

Matthew was attached to a group of four traders dealing in the smaller European currencies: the Swiss franc, the lira, the Dutch guilder, the Swedish krona, the peseta, a few others. Between them his four traders mustered six passports, thirteen languages, and a shared passion for dealing.

Matthew's job was to support the group in any way it wanted. He was meant to forage for information, calculate spreadsheets, run errands, and get the coffees. So far the only job he'd done at all was getting the coffees. He couldn't stand the trashy coffees from the vending machines, so four times a day he went to the Blue Mountain Coffee Company's boutique to get the world's most heavenly cappuccinos at £1.80 a cup. If it weren't for this unaccustomed service, the traders would have had Matthew fired weeks before. As it was, they rated his survival chances at just about zero. As Luigi

Cuneberti, the Swiss-Italian who traded Swiss francs and lire, put it: 'Matteo, we give you a job when Italy has paid its national debt and the lira is worth more than the dollar.'

That needed to change.

All banks have the same information from Reuters, Bloomberg, Telerate. A million computer screens can be accessed with a few key strokes. Data is updated every second, news reported as it happens. It's not information that makes the difference but judgement. And judgement requires the right facts in the right format at the right time.

Matthew set to work. He scrolled through the overnight news stories on Reuters, printed off the full list of headlines plus the handful of stories he thought important. Next, he called the bank's main Far Eastern offices: Tokyo, Hong Kong, Singapore, Sydney. Some markets were quiet, others not. After every call, he made detailed notes.

Then, he went out on to the street to an international paper stand, where he bought eight European newspapers plus the European edition of the *Wall Street Journal*. He wasn't fluent in any language other than English, but he had spent enough time skiing in Courcheval and Zermatt, enough time in the bars of Tuscany and the beaches of Mallorca, and enough time with girls in all these places to get the gist of what he read. He made clippings of the articles he thought important, and added them to his growing stack.

He looked at his watch. Six forty-five am. He had more to do, but was out of time. He collected up his work and ran it through the copier five times: once for each of his traders, once for himself.

As the pages copied, Matthew realised three things.

First, he had absorbed a surprising amount since being

at the bank, despite his weeks of indolence. Second, there was an almost infinite amount of research he could do. Today's effort was only a start. And third, he had eight weeks of his summer job remaining. At the end of those weeks, he had to convince Madison not just to hire him, but to hire him right away without waiting for him to complete his degree. That was unheard of. But if Madison turned him down and forced him to return to Cambridge in October, he'd have failed to meet his father's goal before he'd even started.

6

Through the glass doors at the end of the room, Luigi came in. He exchanged insults with the Italians working in fixed income and blew a kiss at a secretary he was trying to seduce. Then he arrived at his desk, banged down a coffee and bagel, and stared at Matthew.

'*Santa Maria!*' said Luigi. 'You have the time wrong, my friend, no? Or a brain disease? It is serious, I hope? Hey, what is this?' Luigi held the neatly stacked papers on his desk at arms' length.

'It looks like work. It smells like work,' he said, sniffing, 'but, there is nobody here except Matteo.' Luigi's face grew sombre. He swept some clutter off his desk and knelt on it. He raised his eyes to heaven and added, '*Grazie a Dio*! A miracle has happened and I am unworthy.' He got back to his feet, scanning the package more seriously now.

'You've spoken with Tokyo about the trade surplus overshoot?'

'Yes,' said Matthew. 'The figures look enormous and are well above the consensus, but the Tokyo market seems to have shrugged it off. Our economist out there tells me that if you dig into the data, it's mostly one-off items. There's a reasonable summary in the *Wall Street Journal* actually.'

Luigi stared at Matthew, then flipped through his package to the article which was highlighted. His eyes scanned it briefly.

'Hmm. So no issue then.'

Matthew hesitated a moment. 'I'm not sure that's right,' he said. 'If I made out the headlines properly, I think the Italian press is a bit more excitable.'

Luigi followed his train of thought. It wasn't the data itself which mattered, it was other people's interpretation of it. If Italian investors got the wrong end of the stick because of bad reporting, then they might misjudge their trading strategy until they wised up. Luigi turned to the articles from the Italian press. Again, he scanned the articles in a few seconds.

'Interesting. I know the Banca di Roma needs to close out a short yen position at the moment. Be interesting to see how they react.' Luigi meant that the Banca di Roma needed to buy some yen. If it thought the price of yen was going to soar, they'd want to buy quickly before the price had moved.

Luigi was a good trader. He scanned the rest of the documents and picked up his phone. He wouldn't put it down for more than a few minutes until the end of the day. Right now, he was checking facts, sensing attitudes, exchanging banter with traders and investors, trying to sense the mood of the market. One idea always leads to a dozen others, and when Luigi picked up an interesting lead, he pursued it. He said not another word to Matthew.

The market was in full swing by eight thirty by which time the other traders – Anders, Cristina, and Jean-François – were in and busy. Each of them reacted the way Luigi had to the new-look Matthew. But they were restrained in their praise, waiting to see how long his new work ethic would last.

Luigi called the Banca di Roma, letting the conversation play from his speakerphone. The two men bantered briefly before switching to business.

'Hey, you better be getting out of that giant short position you've got on the yen. Did you see the trade numbers? You're going to get toasted today unless some kindly person takes you out of it.'

'Bullshit, Luigi,' said the Banca di Roma guy. 'We couldn't care less about the yen. We don't have a short position and anyway a month's data is neither here nor there. The Tokyo market didn't move much.'

This already told Luigi a lot. If Banca di Roma really didn't care what happened to the yen, their trader wouldn't have prompted Luigi to keep the discussion going. Luigi now had a choice. He hesitated so briefly that Matthew, who was following the conversation intently, only just noticed.

'*Amico mio*,' said Luigi, 'the market didn't move because the data was bullshit.' He quickly summarised the reasons why the yen hadn't moved. 'If you try to get out of your position too quickly, my friends in the market here will stiff you. You do need to close out your position because there are more big numbers coming out in Tokyo and Rome next week and God knows where rates will be by Friday. But you need to go slowly and use your head.'

The Banca di Roma guy almost audibly relaxed. He asked a couple more questions about last night's number and then a whole lot more about how to exit his position, which was in fact very large. Luigi talked him through it and promised to stay in touch through the day. Then a call came in on another line and Luigi hung up to take it.

Matthew spent the day doing what he could to sift out the nuggets which mattered from the flood of information which roared through the bank. As he picked them out, he made sure that his increasingly frenzied team of traders got them quickly and clearly. He worked so intently that it had got to eleven thirty without him going out for the coffees. When Luigi noticed, he picked his half-eaten bagel from the dustbin and threw it accurately at Matthew's head.

'You're still only here for the coffees.'

At five thirty that afternoon the market fell quiet. The frenzy which had raged across London for nine hours had moved on to New York. New York would pass the baton to Chicago and San Francisco. Then the West Coast would hand the baton on to Tokyo and just a little later to Hong Kong and Singapore. The Asians kept long and lonely watch as the sun rolled over the endless miles until once again European traders woke up to play the everlasting game.

Matthew helped his traders tidy up after the day, making sure each trade was properly documented with a complete and legible trading note. Thanks to his help, Matthew's team finished its paperwork fifteen minutes after the close of the market. All around other traders were cursing and fidgeting as they grappled with the unwelcome slips of paper.

Luigi had to rush off to a dinner date, or so he said. The crude comments thrown at him by Anders and Cristina suggested that anything he wanted to do in the hour and a half before dinner time was likely to be done lying down, and not by himself. Matthew grabbed Luigi before he left.

'I'd like to ask you a question. Why didn't you stiff the Banca di Roma guy earlier on today? I could see he'd have let you if you'd wanted to.'

'Matteo, Matteo,' said Luigi, patting his cheek, 'if he wanted to get out of his position quickly, he would have tried to spread his trades among as many banks as possible. We'd all have stiffed him, but he'd have felt better about it that way. As it was, he trusted me. I did maybe sixty percent of his trades today at a rate which was fair to me and fair to him. He is grateful to me because he was scared this morning and I didn't shit on him when I could have done. The Banca di Roma does a lot of business, and right now they love me. Signor Matteo, you can make a lot of money by stiffing people, but you only make it once. Give your clients a good service and they come back.'

Luigi started to walk off to his 'dinner date', then turned and added with a wink, 'And you never know. If you stiff even your best clients perhaps once a year, they are probably too stupid to notice.'

7

Ichabod Bell greeted Zack with a glass of sherry.

'Decided to drop all that tripe about money, I take it. Damned if I can name a single ancient Greek millionaire, but I can think of a good few philosophers whose credit is still good today. Anyway, blast you, you're nowhere near good enough to make the grade. You want to be an accountant, right? I forget. No, silly me. Too exciting. An actuary. Much better. Less stressful. Very reliable pension arrangements. How's your rowing?'

'I've studied nothing else for two weeks. Am I allowed to know why?'

Ichabod ignored him.

'Gong's already sounded. Let's go in to dinner. Mind you taste the wine. Tonight's a fund-raiser and the Dean's serving only the best.'

Upstairs in the dining hall, panelled in six-hundred-year-old oak, Zack found his place in between a history lecturer he had liked when a student, and a Sir Robert Grossman, whose name rang a bell but nothing more. Once everyone was seated, the chaplain rose.

'*Surgete*,' he said in Latin, indicating with his hands that the company should rise for grace.

Everybody did so except for Ichabod, a fierce atheist. A long Latin grace followed. Zack took the opportunity, as did most others, to squint downwards at the menu card on his plate. Trout, beef, chocolate mousse, cheese. The ingredients would be good enough, but Zack knew that the college kitchens were of the traditional British school. The chef's idea of a luxurious gravy was to stir a bit of wine in with the stock granules. Vegetables would be boiled into surrender, the beef roasted into submission. At least the wine would be first-rate.

The first two courses passed in agreeable banter with the history lecturer, who brought Zack up-to-date on college politics and scandal. As the plates were being cleared, Zack turned to the man on his left, Grossman, who had also turned.

'Well, young man, are you enjoying the wine?'

Zack hated nothing more than a patronising old fool, but tonight he was on his best behaviour.

'The wine's great,' he said. Then, a snippet from his two weeks' research suddenly falling like a silver penny into his lap, he added: 'Do I remember you used to row for the college eight?'

Grossman was instantly transfixed.

'Yes, indeed! Captained it, actually. We had a damn good season and damn near went Head of the River. You're a rower are you? Best sport in the world, I always say. Clever of you to remember my name. Still, I suppose I did have quite a reputation in my day.'

Rowing was the great love of Grossman's life. At Oxford he'd been a bit too dumb to make it academically and a bit too ugly to have much luck romantically. In a bright and talented world, Grossman felt marooned. Then he discovered rowing. Rowing gave him friends and an activity at which he excelled. In his memory at least, his time at Oxford had been a succession of bright mornings and golden afternoons, racing triumphs and disasters, drinking feats, puking and songs.

Zack left his previous conversation partner dangling as Grossman rattled away like a racing commentator. He and Zack talked rowing right through to the end of dinner, comparing techniques, race statistics, competitors, anecdotes. Zack boasted a photographic memory, and his research bore up easily under the barrage. Pudding, cheese, wines and port passed in an increasingly alcoholic haze. Rowers, it seemed, were heavy drinkers.

When the time came to move downstairs for the cigars and more drinks, the Dean appeared silently at Grossman's elbow. Time for a chat about leaking roofs and vacant fellowships. Grossman understood the hint, and, firing a few last sentences at Zack, walked off in the Dean's wake. Zack grabbed Ichabod as they went downstairs.

'OK. I've talked rowing for two hours without a break and I still don't know why. Who is Grossman, anyway? And I warn you, I'm three quarters dead with boredom.'

Ichabod grinned. 'I knew you'd love him.'

Back in the senior common room they helped themselves to cigars and more alcohol. Zack's head was spinning. He was glugging down wines worth twenty pounds a glass, enjoying them but not tasting them.

'Grossman is your future employer,' said Ichabod.

'Deputy Chief Executive at Coburg's, the merchant bank. A fading light there, but still a big hitter. Worst rowing bore I've ever met, and I've met a few. I'll never understand how second-raters get to the top in business. It must be surprisingly easy.'

Zack looked at the gentle don in his corduroy jacket. Bell's financial acumen stretched no further than remembering (most of the time) where he'd left his wallet. It was hard to picture him as an international mogul. The pair chatted a little longer. Then the Dean came into the common room with Grossman in tow. The Dean looked serious, while Grossman beamed in delight. The Dean had the happy gift of being able to take a very large cheque from people and leave them feeling like they'd won the lottery.

Ichabod left Zack and walked over to Grossman. Zack felt two pairs of eyes on him and he buried himself in conversation with his historian friend. Later, as dons and guests began to disperse into the warm summer night, Ichabod and Grossman, who was obviously the worse for drink, approached Zack.

'You're heading off to London, aren't you, Zack? Perhaps Sir Robert could give you a lift?'

Grossman and Zack compared addresses and found they lived only three blocks from each other. The deal was swiftly done and Zack soon found himself sliding out of Oxford in the banker's chauffeur-driven BMW. If possible, Grossman drunk was more boring than Grossman merely tipsy, and Zack had to endure another barrage of anecdotes, most of them missing a punch line and many of which he'd already heard at dinner. At one point, Zack managed, as it were, to put his oar in, mentioning that he was looking for a job in corporate finance, preferably with a good British bank.

Grossman looked at the younger man.

'Corporate finance, eh? You're the sort of fellow we're always on the lookout for. I'm at Coburg's, you know. Deputy Chief Executive.'

Zack tried to look surprised.

'Coburg's? Really? I've always so admired the bank. I was hoping . . .'

'Hoping to join, eh? Well, come in for an interview. I'm sure you'll do well.' Grossman said, slurring his words. 'I'm a sharp judge of character, y'know, and I've had my eye on you this evening.' Zack had watched Grossman drink the best part of three bottles of wine at dinner, not to mention sherry before and port after, and had listened to him talk virtually non-stop. What Grossman was like when he didn't have his eye on someone, Zack couldn't imagine. 'Besides,' added Grossman, 'that man Bell with the funny name –'

'Ichabod. Ichabod Bell.'

'Quite right. Itchy-dog Bell. Fellow told me you were one of his best ever students. I wasn't surprised. Not a bit. I could tell you had a good head on you. Anyway, come in to Coburg's for an interview. I'll tell 'em to look out for you.'

And so he did. When Zack called Coburg's, the man from personnel said, 'Ah, yes, Grossman's friend,' and scheduled a day of interviews for Zack then and there. The interviews were strange, dream-like affairs. The interviewers went through the motions, but both sides knew that the important thing had already been decided. Two weeks following dinner with Grossman, Zack received an offer of employment. The post paid twenty-seven thousand pounds per annum plus a January bonus. Peanuts, of course. Less than the rent on his flat. But that wasn't the point.

The point was he'd done it. He'd been admitted. He was a season ticket holder to the City of London, the enchanted forest where money really does grow on trees.

8

'D'you know what Josie wants to talk about?' asked Matthew.

'Not me,' said Zack. 'Probably just wants to escape Mum for the evening. I'd go nuts in that grotty little house with Mum crying away all the time.'

'Poor Mum. She certainly took the will terribly hard. I should visit her, but I'm working all hours at the moment.'

'Mmm,' said Zack, who was in between finishing at his accountancy firm and starting at Coburg's. Despite his leisure time, he hadn't called on his ailing mother. A silence began to grow, filled only by the rumble of traffic from Camden High Street. 'Where's George, d'you know?' he said, changing the subject.

'No, no one knows. Josie left loads of messages at his flat, but he's either not there or not responding.'

'I wonder what he's up to. He's going to have a bit of a job financing his lifestyle now.'

That was true enough. George's playboy life had been paid for by huge dollops of cash from their father. No more cash, no more jet-setting.

'You never know,' said Matthew. 'He's probably persuaded a billionaire friend of his to give him a couple of million to tide him over. He was always good at getting cash out of Dad. Better than us.'

Zack shrugged. 'I don't think we need worry. George would get through a million in a matter of months.'

Both men laughed. They weren't worried about George getting his million. Zack was the cleverest of the brothers, Matthew the most determined. George wasn't smart and he hated work. Both brothers had always vaguely resented the ease with which George had taken cash from their father, but now it was payback time. Zack knew that Matthew was his only serious rival, and he was Matthew's. The two men looked at each other warily. They were tense, defensive, nervous.

When the doorbell rang, Zack stood up quickly. 'That'll be her now. If you get the door, I'll get her a drink.'

Matthew opened the door and found a stranger. It was Josephine alright, but as he'd never seen her. She wore a navy blue skirt with a white cotton blouse. A single gold chain was her only jewellery. Her long, dark, naturally curly hair was pulled back and pinned up. A few weeks before, Josephine had been a slim, pretty, lively girl with a passion for dance and parties. Today, she was professional, competent, unobtrusive. For maybe the first time, her mouth was tucked down, not up, at the corners.

'Jesus Christ, Josie,' murmured Matthew. 'So soon?'

'Yes, I was lucky. I got a last minute place at the Cavendish Secretarial School and I've been there a week now. It's going OK.'

'And this stuff – from M & S, I suppose?'

'Yes. I'd never realised how much £500 could buy. I'm all set up now as you see.'

She gave a half-twirl as though to show off a party frock, but her heart wasn't in it.

'It's not right, Josie. It's not right.'

She looked away, not wanting to let Matthew see her quivering eyes.

'I haven't many options, have I? Besides, it's how most girls my age get by.'

Matthew raised his arm, offering her a cuddle, but she gently pushed it away. She'd cry if he cuddled her and she wasn't here to cry. Once inside, Josephine took a tumbler of gin and tonic with a sigh of relief. She stretched out her legs on Zack's gleaming glass coffee table, uncomfortable beneath her brother's dark unemotional scrutiny.

'M & S, huh?'

'That's right.'

Zack just nodded. Josie saw his eyes pass the information to his brain, which stored the fact as just another item to be memorised and filed. He cut to the chase.

'Well, Josie, are you going to reveal why you've got us together or shall we guess?'

'I don't think it should be all that hard to guess,' she said, keeping her voice steady and reasonable. 'Mummy's shocked, she's depressed. Even after a month, she's showing no sign of improvement. I think we need to do something.'

'She needs to get out,' said Zack. 'Get a job.'

'She can't. She can't type any more, and secretarial work is all she'll do.'

'Oh, come on. We all know she could type if she wanted. She could do anything if she just pulled herself together.'

'Zack! She's in a bad way. She's finding things hard.'

'What are you suggesting? We take it in turns to sing her lullabies?'

Josie's temper began to rise despite herself, despite her foreknowledge that Zack would be difficult.

'I'm saying that she needs help. From all of us. Now.'

Zack snorted and threw himself back in his chair, leaving it to Matthew to ask more gently, 'What? What did you have in mind?'

'Mum had relied on the will to make her comfortable. Dad failed her, but we don't have to. We can all get jobs. I'm hoping to find work as soon as I finish my course. We

43

can all put as much as we can towards a regular income for Mum, maybe club together to get her somewhere decent to live. She's never liked it where she is now.'

'She's perfectly capable of going out to work herself,' snapped Zack.

'How would you know? When did you last see her?'

Matthew once again sought to make peace.

'Have you thought about taking her to the doctor's? Trying her out on antidepressants? She probably just needs snapping out of it.'

'I have taken her to the doctor's, yes,' said Josie, still taut. 'He spent three minutes with her, then wrote out a prescription for Prozac, which stopped her from getting to sleep, then gave her nightmares. If you want her to see another doctor, then it's a private specialist she needs, paid for by us.'

Matthew lapsed into silence. He didn't like the thought of leaving his mum without help, but he didn't like the idea of offering his money before Zack had offered any of his. Zack lay slumped in his chair, swilling his whisky round his tumbler, then sat forward, alert again.

'No,' he said.

'No? What do you mean, no?'

'No, Josie. I've got three years to make a million pounds. I'm not going to work my knackers off only to miss the target by a few quid at the end, because Mum was too lazy to go out to work for herself.'

'It's not laziness!'

'What else do you call it? The moment you start giving in to these sort of people, they learn to do less and less.'

'These sort of people, Zack? She's –'

'And there's no need to worry about money. In three years' time, we'll see to her properly. Either one of us wins Dad's money, in which case he'll see her right.

Or none of us wins, in which case we'll certainly have enough between us to look after her. It's not a problem.' Zack looked at Matthew for his agreement, which he gave with a nod. 'I'm sure George would agree too. Stop worrying.'

'She needs help now.'

'Josie, you're out of the will anyway. You may as well use your salary to look after Mum. It's not as though she eats much or spends anything on clothes and stuff. We'll pay you back in three years. If there's a shortfall, you can always mortgage the house. Christ, in three years we just won't have any problems. We'll send you back to school for a start, and chuck that Miss Moneypenny outfit of yours in the incinerator.'

Josephine was furious. Angry and upset. She put her drink down on the table, hands shaking badly. She stood up.

'For your information, this Miss Moneypenny outfit is what I expect to wear when I start to earn my living. And if you think I'm going to mortgage Mum's home on the off chance that one of you three babies wins the Lottery in the next three years then you must be nuts. And if you think that it's OK, now that she really needs you, to ignore her completely, then you're totally out of line.'

Zack made no answer, but contempt was written on his face in lines of white.

'Matthew, tell him.' Josie appealed to her brother.

Matthew sat like a five-year-old, hoping that by keeping silent he could stay out of trouble. He didn't have Zack's abrasive selfishness, but he didn't have his sister's warm-hearted sense of justice either. He swallowed, but shook his head.

'For God's sake, you two. She's not just some batty old cow. She's your mother.'

Zack sat forward and opened his mouth. The others

45

knew what Zack was thinking. He was thinking of saying that she was a batty old cow as well as his mother. Josephine was ready to throw her tumbler at him if he said it, but Matthew beat them both to the draw, interjecting quickly: 'Josie, of course she's our mum. But Zack's right, you know. It makes no sense at all for us to devote our time or money to looking after her right now, when that could mean that we lose Gradley Plant Hire and all the money held in trust. Everybody is better off if we make sure that Dad's money comes into the family instead of going to some godawful charity.'

'So you'll cooperate will you? Pool the money you make at the end of three years and divide up Dad's money into quarters?'

It was a question addressed to both of them, but Matthew deferred to Zack, and Zack's silence was implacable.

'And now? What happens now?' persisted Josie.

'Well, I can see it's going to be tight for the next three years,' Matthew answered. 'It'll be hard for all of us. But we need to think of the future. And Zack's right, you don't want to be a secretary for the rest of your life. You will need a way out of that, you know.'

'I'll need a way out of that,' repeated Josephine distantly. 'So the answer's no? You won't help? Nothing?'

'Of course we'll do what we can.' Matthew looked at Zack, who was adding to his whisky and looking away. 'But realistically it won't be much. But we'll do what we can.'

'I see.'

Josephine put down her drink. Her hands had stopped shaking. She picked up a heavy bronze statuette on a polished granite base from the glass coffee table in front of her. She turned it over in her hands. The statue was of a racing car. It had been a gift from Bernard Gradley to Zack, who had never liked it, but had never thrown it away either. She looked at it. It reminded her of her father's campaign to win allegiance with money, and of his failure to do so. Love buys love, money buys money.

She held out the statuette and dropped it. It fell heavily and landed in the dead centre of the table, shattering the glass. Two diagonal cracks running from corner to corner split it into four pieces. Half the glass slid from its mounting and crashed on to the thickly carpeted floor. The remaining bits of glass stayed sticking out, suspended. The statuette lay on the floor surrounded by debris.

'So sorry,' she said, and left.

9

Where was George and what was he up to? Those were questions he was asking himself right now. He was somewhere in Cornwall, he knew that much. His car was parked in a lay-by off the A30 somewhere close to Bodmin Moor. It was late evening in mid-August and George watched as the last blue light surrendered to the gathering stars.

Somewhere in the car was an insect which George wouldn't find until it bit him. He wound his seat back as far as it would go. It wasn't far. A Lotus Esprit is not designed for men of stocky build to camp out in, as George had by now proved many times over. But his first attempt outside in a tent had been a disaster, with a summer storm leaving him soaked and desperate and since then he had preferred the car's cramped interior to any tent, no matter how spacious.

He closed his eyes with a sort of fantasy idea that

closing his eyes would send him to sleep. It didn't. His legs sent him a message which he mostly ignored, but it had to do with bucket seats, feather beds, and their relative merits. Somewhere outside the car, an animal screamed. George remembered seeing video footage of a puma loose on Bodmin Moor, apparently still not caught. But they couldn't attack Lotuses, could they? He wound up the window, just in case.

As he slumped back into his seat, the insect found George, and slap around though he did, George failed to find the insect. He struggled for the light switch, found it, and swatted round aimlessly for a minute or two, using the copy of the *Financial Times* which lay rolled up beside him.

As the light was on and the paper in his hand, George looked again at the familiar page. A section of classified ads, all but a few of them with blue lines through them. He'd carry on with the rest tomorrow, then it would be time for the next paper and the next set of ads, and so it would be until his last dribble of cash ran out, leaving him stranded in his Lotus Esprit, too poor to afford a gallon of petrol.

Zack and Matthew might laugh about his billionaire friends, but George knew the rules of the international jet set better than they did. If you wanted to be part of it, you either had to pay your way or be young enough and pretty enough to sleep your way. George hadn't the cash or the body for it. As soon as people found out his wallet was empty, he'd be dumped faster than last season's clothes. He'd sooner do the dumping himself.

He threw the paper down. On his answering machine at the flat, there had been three messages from his sister and one from Kiki. He missed them both.

He turned off the light again and tried to sleep.

10

Matthew emerged on to the floor of the deserted trading room. Except for the red digital wall-clocks and the flicker of screens, the room was in darkness. Matthew turned on an Anglepoise lamp over his desk. He liked the dark and the hour of silence before the cleaners arrived at five am. He fetched a cup of black coffee and got to work.

In the five weeks since he had really got started, Matthew had his routine well developed. By the time Luigi came in with fresh coffee at seven, Matthew would have prepared five neat piles of painstakingly referenced and highlighted bundles of research. At first the piles had been a welcome luxury. They had since become little short of essential: the Saint Matthew Gospel, as Luigi put it.

The fictional lira which marked Matthew's progress with Luigi had nudged up to nearly one dollar. In practice, Matthew knew, Luigi would vote in favour of Madison's offering him a full-time job to start once he had completed his degree. But that wouldn't do. He had three years to make a million, and he wasn't going to spend one of them studying economics. Matthew needed a job and he needed it now.

Later that day, Matthew was to have an interview with Brian McAllister. The son of a Glaswegian truck driver, McAllister ruled the trading floor with quiet voice and omniscient eye. By reputation, he knew each trader's market better than they did themselves. He was willing, as most traders were, to take large risks in search of profit. Less commonly, he was also willing to refrain from risk whenever he judged the conditions were wrong. Many people had made bigger profits than Brian McAllister, but none had made smaller losses.

McAllister's judgement would decide Matthew's fate, and there was no court of appeal.

Just after nine, Luigi came by his desk. 'Matteo, where does ze lira stand today?'

Matthew pretended to check his screen. 'Hey, Luigi, what d'you know? The lira equals one dollar exactly.'

'And how is the Italian deficit, please?'

Matthew touched some buttons on his keyboard. A new screen flashed up. 'Well, look at that. Rupert Murdoch's just bought the Italian government for a zillion dollars and the deficit's been eliminated.'

Luigi grinned. 'Seriously, Matteo, Big Mac will ask me why you suddenly work, when before you were the most goddamn lazy prick I have ever seen. How do we know which one we're buying?'

'My dad died six weeks ago,' said Matthew, who had said nothing about it earlier. 'About five weeks ago, I realised I needed to look after myself now. So I did.'

Luigi nodded seriously. His trader's eyes scanned Matthew's face, looking for the truth behind his words. 'I'm sorry, Matteo, I didn't know.'

Luigi walked off to find Big Mac, as McAllister was known behind his back, never to his face.

Luigi's conversation lasted perhaps five minutes. Given the number of demands on McAllister's time, that counted as a long interview. Matthew drummed nervously on his desk and felt inside his jacket pocket to reassure himself that a certain document was still there. Luigi returned, and one by one Anders, Cristina, and Jean-François went to speak with McAllister. Matthew believed they would support him. Each of them had said to him privately that his support over the last weeks had really given them an edge in the free-for-all of the market. Their trading profits still depended on their daily judgements, but Matthew had helped them and they were grateful.

Jean-François came back. He patted Matthew on the back. '*Allez*,' he said, and gave a wink of support.

Matthew walked over to McAllister's office. McAllister had taken advantage of the thirty second gap between Jean-François's departure and Matthew's arrival to take a call from his counterpart in the Paris office. The phone call blared from a speaker on McAllister's desk. The subject of the conversation appeared to be how the French bond markets would react to a European summit being held the following day.

McAllister saw Matthew come in and signed him to sit. Privacy was unheard of on the trading floor. Conversations were yelled across the room. Phone calls were recorded. Pierre d'Avignon, on the phone to McAllister, wouldn't raise an eyebrow if he knew that somebody else had just come in to sit in on his call. D'Avignon asked McAllister a question, something to do with the European summit.

'An interesting question,' said McAllister, in his strong Scots accent. 'I'll get our analyst here to do some research on that point and we'll get back to you tomorrow.'

'OK, but it needs to be tomorrow first thing, before the markets open.'

'Aye. First thing tomorrow.'

'And put one of your best guys on this, eh, Brian?' said d'Avignon. 'We've got five hundred million dollars' worth of bonds on our books at the moment, and we don't want to make a mess.'

'Don't worry. You'll have the best.'

D'Avignon hung up. McAllister looked at Matthew. 'Got that?'

'You want me to do the research?'

McAllister nodded.

'Yes. No problem,' croaked Matthew. He knew virtually nothing about the European summit which d'Avignon was on about, but if he screwed up, he could wave his job goodbye. His mouth turned dry.

'Good. We'll talk about your job after your conversation with d'Avignon tomorrow morning.'

Matthew was dismissed, but he continued to hold McAllister's gaze. The Scotsman's eyes were pale blue and piercing. It was like gazing into the eyes of God.

'Thank you,' said Matthew. 'There's just one thing I'd like to ask you.' He paused. McAllister said nothing, waiting. God, he was intimidating. 'I don't want to finish my degree. The last few weeks have made me realise that I love trading. I don't believe that completing my degree will make me a better trader. I want to work hard and I want to start now. I like Madison and I'd like to work here if I possibly can.'

Matthew paused to review the effect of his words, but McAllister's face was as empty as granite. Matthew decided he might as well play his only trump card and drew a letter from his pocket. He gave it to the Scotsman.

'I've been offered a job by Coburg's. I don't want to work there. I want to work here. I know as well as you do that Madison is going to wipe the floor with Coburg's, and I want to be part of that. But above all I want to trade and I want to start now. And if that means I need to start at a second-rate firm, then I will.'

McAllister barely glanced at the photocopied letter in front of him. Matthew had pinched the letter from Zack's flat the evening Josie smashed his coffee table. Except for a couple of initials and the name of the department, he'd hardly needed to alter it. 'Dear Mr Gradley, We are pleased to be able to offer you a job as Assistant

Manager in our Global Markets Department. We are keen that you should start with us directly, and I would ask you to confirm your start date with us as soon as possible.' The letter continued with banalities. Matthew had photocopied the doctored original, then inspected it under a magnifying glass. He was confident that the changes were virtually undetectable.

McAllister tapped the letter lightly with his finger to indicate that Matthew should take it back.

'Don't write off Coburg's,' he said softly. 'They've been around for more than two hundred years, twice as long as we have. We'll be doing well to last that long ourselves.'

The interview was over.

11

George drove away from the little cluster of buildings. Once out of sight, he pulled out his *Financial Times* and put a line through another box. This was getting ridiculous. He'd try for another two weeks – three at most – then give it all up. Zack or Matthew could try to win their father's fortune. He'd apply for a job stacking shelves. He'd make new friends, find new things to do. Maybe in time he'd go back to school and get some exam results and a proper job. He'd live the way most people lived. But for now he'd go on trying, just a little longer.

He looked back at his newspaper. Next on the list was Gissings, based in the village of Sawley Bridge up near Ilkley in Yorkshire. He phoned a number and was put through to somebody who put him through to somebody else. George explained his interest and asked if there were any documents he could have a look at. Yes, there were documents. Would he like them posted?

Yes, please, said George, but it wasn't convenient to post them to his business address at present. Perhaps they could send them to the hotel he'd be staying at – The Devonshire Arms near Skipton. That was fine. They'd send the documents out right away. Did he want to make an appointment for a site visit now? No, that was fine, he'd look through the documents first.

George switched his phone off. He was headed north anyway to view some Scottish outfit, a long shot. He'd pass by the Devonshire Arms, apologise for changing his plans and pick up the documents from a mystified receptionist. He was getting good at doing that. Just like he was getting pretty good at keeping himself pretty much respectable while living mostly in a two-seater Lotus Esprit with an engine capacity bigger than its luggage hold.

He looked back at the ad. Gissings, eh? He didn't feel hopeful, but he didn't feel ready to stack shelves either.

He drove off, wearily.

12

First step, gather information.

Matthew dug into the bank's news database to get the dates of all European summits over the last ten years, then printed articles from Europe's leading papers in the run-up to and aftermath of each summit. Then, switching to a new database, he collected bond market data around the key dates. Then, finally, he called up relevant research reports published by the major investment banks and printed about thirty reports of a few pages each. The database was charged at twenty-five dollars a sheet and he ran up a bill of a couple of thousand dollars in an hour and a half. It didn't bother Matthew and it wouldn't bother anyone else either.

When a single trade, even a small one, can easily win or lose five thousand dollars for the bank, cost control is a game reserved strictly for losers.

By this point it was four in the afternoon and Matthew had a vast pile of paper by his desk, of which he'd read almost nothing.

Matthew worked his way swiftly through the pile. Most of it was dross, but amidst the rubbish were diamonds scattered and he needed to find them. He skimmed document after document and built a shorter stack of those he thought important.

Then he started to crunch some numbers. He printed graphs. He looked at the markets for bonds, currencies and shares. He categorised the previous summits in a dozen different ways and reran his numbers searching for a pattern.

By eleven in the evening, Matthew knew what he wanted to say. He also knew how he was going to say it and prove it to an audience much more knowledgeable than himself.

He got more coffee and started to build a presentation. His presentation had a dozen slides, five appendices containing sixty graphs and another two appendices with some of the most interesting statistics and research comments he'd unearthed. The whole document was around a hundred and twenty pages long. He stepped wearily over to the fax machine. It was one thirty in the morning. Matthew had been in the bank nigh on twenty-two hours.

He wrote out a cover page and punched d'Avignon's number into the fax. It rang a couple of times and then started to pull the first page through the scanner. Matthew walked off to get another coffee. Something had gone wrong with the vending machine and the coffee tasted like metal. He drank it anyway.

When he came back, the fax had stopped. An error message slowly printed out. D'Avignon's machine was out of paper. By the time anybody was in the office to refill it, it would be far too late to send the documents across. Damn. He tried a different number, of a machine he thought would be somewhere close to d'Avignon's office. Five pages ticked their way slowly through. Then, the same result. Damn, damn, damn. It was now two o'clock, three o'clock Paris time.

Matthew considered his options briefly. They were few and far between. Matthew copied the presentation and dropped it on to McAllister's desk with a scribbled note on the front cover. He walked downstairs and hailed a cab from the rank across the street.

'Where you going, mate?' asked the driver.

'Paris,' said Matthew, 'rue de la Colonne.'

They made it to Paris in four hours flat, which would have been impossible but for the cabbie's conviction that there was no speed limit on French autoroutes. Matthew kept silent about the difference between autoroutes and autobahns and snoozed in the back as the flat French countryside slipped past in the gathering dawn.

They entered Paris before rush hour and drew up outside Madison's elegant Paris office. Matthew asked the driver to wait and dashed inside.

D'Avignon had arrived only shortly before. Mildly startled to see Matthew in person, he apologised for his empty fax machine and waved Matthew into a seat. Matthew handed over the presentation, d'Avignon called McAllister on the speaker phone, and the conference call began. Matthew led them through his work. He reckoned the discussion might last for twenty minutes all told and that he might speak for perhaps seven minutes of that. In the cab on the way across, he had run through his introduction a dozen times, until falling asleep somewhere after the turn-off to Lille.

Matthew felt confident of his conclusions. All the evidence seemed to confirm that after a few days of thinking that the end of the world had happened (or alternatively that the millennium had arrived early) the bond markets would turn their attention to something else. Matthew ran through the relevant data and summarised his conclusions. He spoke without interruption for six and a half minutes exactly. There were a couple of questions on points of detail, as McAllister and d'Avignon flipped through the charts and other material in the appendices. Neither trader challenged Matthew. After a brief discussion about how best to place the firm's bets, d'Avignon rang off. He thanked Matthew for coming over and invited him unenthusiastically to tour the building. Matthew declined. D'Avignon looked relieved and dived off to take a call coming in from Milan. Matthew went downstairs to his waiting cab and they crept out of Paris in swelling traffic, heading north to Calais and London.

Back at his desk, Matthew came in for a bit of stick.

'Go to Paris for breakfast but don't even bring me back a bloody croissant,' complained Luigi. 'It's a good job I tell Big Mac to fire you yesterday.'

'*Oui*, but it was an expensive breakfast,' said Jean-François. 'I don't think the firm pays for taxi rides outside London, so I think you pay, no, Matthieu?'

'I don't know if I can afford to. Big Mac still hasn't told me if I've got a job.'

Matthew glanced over towards McAllister's office to see if this was a good time to interrupt. The door was closed, and the lights were off. Luigi followed Matthew's glance.

'Big Mac's away on holiday, Matteo. He only came in

57

this morning for an hour or so. He'll be back a week on Monday.'

Matthew had been too tired to be nervous earlier, but now that changed. Matthew stared at the empty office. It would be ten days before he got a decision. Ten days, and meantime he didn't know if he was still in the running for his million or if he'd fallen at the first hurdle. Anxiety took its first long feed from Matthew's stomach lining. He turned away unhappily, aimlessly. As he did so, a bagel crust flew through the air and struck him on the neck. Luigi.

'How much longer you keep us waiting for cappuccino?'

Autumn 1998

Autumn in England, and nothing to report. Leaves are just starting to give up their greens in favour of a sickly yellow, which will soon give way to a matt and uninteresting brown. After this brief show of what is politely known as colour, the leaves will fall to make a slimy brown carpet beneath the bare trees and boys will fight for the shiniest conkers. Meanwhile, after a sodden August bank holiday, the usual parade of crying children and stationary traffic, the skies have turned an iron grey.

Bid farewell to the sun. It is 1 September 1998, and there are 1046 days to go until Bernard Gradley's deadline.

1

'Good morning, sir.'

The red-coated doorman held the door open. Zack walked through with a shudder. In an age of automatic doors, revolving doors, doors you could just push through, Coburg's had to employ some ancient flunkey in a red tail coat to do the job. That said it all. Coburg's is one of Britain's biggest merchant banks, but its glory days are long gone. The big American banks – Goldman Sachs, Merrill Lynch, Morgan Stanley, Madison, Weinstein Lukes – bestride the globe, while Coburg's, a village beauty in a world of supermodels, clings to its past and tries not to look.

Zack knew this. He knew that Coburg's wouldn't make his fortune. But it was a doorway into international finance, the only industry in the world where millionaires aren't rare, they're commonplace. Even amidst Coburg's dilapidated glories, Zack could smell the money and he loved it.

His boss was a posh nonentity called Fabian Slater, who collected him from reception and took him on a quick tour of the bank. Zack shook hands, exchanged greetings, and avoided saying anything he felt. Slater said, 'In my opinion, the best way to get ahead is to lie low for a couple of years, soak up as much as you can.' Zack smiled and said nothing. He had other ideas. He shook more hands, met more people in more departments: mergers and acquisitions, equity capital markets, debt capital markets, credit.

There wasn't much to see. On a trading floor, you can smell the marketplace. On a busy day, when the markets are roaring, a well-run trading floor looks and sounds like barely organised mayhem. You can hear the flood of money pouring through the room. But that's Matthew's world, not Zack's.

Zack belongs to the quieter world of corporate finance. To its unremarkable offices, the world's biggest businesses come to sort out their financial needs. Some come to raise money, in the hundreds of millions, billions even. Some come to play safe, to protect against the risks that a difficult world is full of. Others come to play fast and loose, taking dangerous bets concealed from their shareholders by a paragraph of flim-flam in an annual report. Best of all, this is where companies come when they're in the mood for attack. Scared of your competitor? Buy him. Noticed an outfit with faster growth? Grab it. Think you could run that guy's business better than him? Buy him up, push him out, rip up his company and flog it.

Traders think testosterone is all about how loud you can shout, and how big are the risks you take with other people's cash. Zack knew different. The quiet world of corporate finance, where bankers and company executives talk in whispers, has its own testosterone load. It doesn't shout. It isn't flashy. But it's just as greedy, just as ruthless, just as hard.

'Just one more person you ought to meet,' drawled Slater. 'Girl called Sarah Havercoombe. D'you know her by any chance? You must have overlapped at Oxford, I think.'

'Sarah? Sarah Havercoombe? Yes. I know her.'

By God, he knew her. At Oxford, he and Sarah had had a stormy on-and-off relationship for three years. She was blisteringly well-connected and rich with it. Her father was a viscount with an ancestral seat in Devon. Unlike most aristocratic families, the Havercoombes had nurtured their wealth prudently and amassed it buccaneeringly. The family stake in a Hong Kong company, Hatherleigh Pacific, made them one of the two hundred or so wealthiest families in the country.

'Sarah,' called Slater, as he walked up to a young woman, faced away from them, mannishly dressed in a pink cotton shirt and a plain navy skirt, 'I think you know our latest recruit. I'll leave you together, shall I?'

Slater left them, while Sarah Havercoombe looked round and started in surprise. She hadn't changed. Short brown hair, nearly blonde, worn with the inevitable hairband. Wide, strong face, clear-complexioned, but a bit too solid to count as beautiful. Minimal make-up, but plenty of confidence. Her widely spaced eyes lit up in surprise.

'Sarah! Hi!' said Zack, 'I didn't know you worked here.'

'Well, I do.'

'So I see. I've just joined. Less than an hour ago, actually.'

'Welcome aboard, I suppose.'

Zack could feel the electricity already starting to rise behind this inane exchange, and wondered if she felt it too. Their relationship had been the most passionate either of them had ever known. It had been passionate in a sexual sense for sure. Scarcely a day had passed without their making love at least once and usually two or three times or more. But it had also been passionate in a worse sense. They had argued incessantly. They were strong-willed and had nothing in common. She loved balls, parties, horses, country houses. He loved philosophy, cynicism, and hating the things she liked. They had argued, stormed, and made love. Their friends had told them they didn't belong together. Their heads had agreed but were powerless in the teeth of their bodies' overwhelming mutual longing. Only when Sarah had finally left Oxford did distance allow the inevitable to happen.

'What's new?' asked Zack.

'I'm engaged,' she said, 'to a chap you might know. Robert Leighton.'

Sarah sounded like she expected Zack to know who she meant, but he didn't. He raised his eyebrows.

'He was at Eton while you were there, but I wouldn't expect you to remember him . . . He's nice and kind, he likes what I like, he loves me very much.'

Zack hadn't meant anything by his question. He just asked it to say something and to defuse the electricity rising in the air. But her answer told him something. She felt the crackle of static too and she thrust her engagement at him as a defence.

'That's great news. I'm delighted. I hope everything works out really well for you both. I'm sure it will.'

'Yes, I'm sure it will. And thanks.' Their eyes met briefly then moved away. 'Here, have you met the equity origination group yet?'

Zack walked off to shake more hands and grin at another set of people whose jobs he didn't understand. Their voices were firm with each other now, just pleasant, nothing too familiar. But all along his right-hand side, where she walked beside him, he felt a prickle beneath his skin. Careful as he was to remind himself to keep guard, to step back, to break contact, two thoughts persisted.

First, he remembered just how good their sex had been. It had puzzled both of them that their sex could be quite so good when their relationship was such a disaster. It was almost as though their bodies understood something the rest of them had yet to grasp.

Second, it occurred to him for the first time that the future husband of Miss Sarah Havercoombe would step right into one of England's richest families. For Miss Sarah Havercoombe, a million pounds would be small change indeed.

2

The sign must have been painted thirty years ago. 'The Gissings Modern Furniture Company (Ltd)', it boasted in giant pink lettering. 'Our *modern* furniture means *modern* style but *modest* prices!' The feeble pun was complemented by a picture of a secretary, complete with miniskirt and beehive hairdo, gesturing inanely at a suite of office furniture. No doubt it had looked cool in 1963, but in the late 1990s prices would have to be very modest indeed to tempt the average buyer.

George slowed his Lotus and turned in between the factory gates. Beyond the factory, there were a few fields of rough grazing, then open moor. It would be a bleak place to work in winter, comfortless in summer. A couple of men dawdling across the yard glanced at the newcomer, then stared. Not many Lotuses came to The Gissings Modern Furniture Company nowadays.

George turned the engine off and listened to its musical notes dying away. The yard which doubled as a car-park was covered with a mixture of rainwater, gravel, wood chippings, and machine oil. George poked his beautifully shod foot out of the car and stood up carefully, making sure his turn-ups weren't dirtied by contact with the ground. He drew his Dior sunglasses from his jacket pocket, put them on and walked over to the door marked 'Reception'.

A listless woman at the reception desk put down her copy of *Puzzler* magazine and stared at the apparition. George stared back. 'Tom Gissing, please.'

The receptionist gestured towards a hideous suite of furniture in the corner of the small lobby. 'Please sit down,' she said. 'I'll let Mr Gissing know you're here.' George sat on one of the Gissings chairs in the corner, which wheezed and creaked as he lowered himself. Just for a moment, George wondered why he'd come.

In time, an elderly man limped over to George.

'Mr Gradley? George Gradley?' he said shaking George's hand. 'I knew your father, you know, back in the sixties when he was starting up. Tried to have him join our Chamber of Commerce and Rotary Club, but I fear he was a little fast for our ways. Still, he did well for himself and we'd have liked to have had him. You do look like him, you know. Everyone must tell you that. I'm very sorry, of course, to have learned of his, er, accident' – the old man couldn't bring himself to use the word death – 'I always feel these things are terribly hard on the young. So much less experience of loss, you see. Nothing, really.'

As the old man rambled on, he led George to the proudly named executive office. A secretary, only about thirty but already ageless, watched them grimly.

'D'you want tea?' she asked.

'Coffee, please,' said George.

'The machine's knackered, so you'd best have tea,' she said and left the room. She was short and squarely built, much as George himself was, and much as Bernard Gradley had been too. The ginger hair which crowned George's head was there on hers too, worn in a bob. Her face was a bit wonky and her chin was too broad to be quite feminine. But George's face was crooked too and his features were hardly delicate. To a stranger, the two of them would look like brother and sister. The old man took George to a table at one end of the room and twitched at some papers which lay there.

'Mr Ballard from the bank told me you would be coming. It's a relief to see you, not the receiver. I am afraid we had more or less resigned ourselves to that fate.'

'Yeah, well, I haven't made any decision yet.'

'No, of course not. Well, you couldn't. I mean, you'll want to see the shop floor, and the cutting room, and the paint shop. And we have some wonderful designs on the drawing board right now. All we really need is a bit of a cash injection and I really believe we'd get ourselves going properly again. And our workers are

65

excellent, you know. We've always kept the traditional craft methods here, and all our lads are properly trained. Lord, some of them must have forty years' experience and I know there's a round dozen of them who have been here longer than I have. Quality. That's what we've never sacrificed. Our buyers don't always recognise it these days. Don't really care whether a joint is dovetailed or glued, you know. But if you do things the right way, it'll tell in the end. Quality never goes out of fashion. That's my motto. Well, my father's actually. But he was right about that.'

A mug of tea slapped down in front of George.

'Ye didn't tell me how ye liked it, so I gave you two sugars.'

'Thank you, Val,' said the old man.

George didn't like tea much, but the day before he'd enjoyed a rare day in London celebrating a friend's new racehorse at the Café Royal in Regent Street. The meal had been served on the whitest china. The bergamot scent of Earl Grey tea had mingled with the smell of freshly baked cakes, warm napkins, women's perfume, polished wood, and the promise of smoked salmon and brown bread. Kiki had been there, petite and elfin in a pale blue dress, gorgeous and inaccessible. She'd complained because 'I had to fly to Paris two times for the dress fitting, then go back again because I swear there aren't any nice shoes in London.' As she complained, she'd twirled around angling for compliments which George and others had willingly supplied.

The smell of the tea steaming in front of him brought him back to reality. The tea was strong enough to poleaxe a navvy and the sugar had been added with a shovel. Jesus Christ. George was penniless. In a month or so's time when his cash ran out, George wouldn't even be able to afford a mug of tea like this one. And as for mingling with the likes of Kiki, the thought was absurd. The only way she knew how to have a cheap day out was to forget her purse, and that only meant somebody else picked up the bills. George shoved his mug away.

'Let's take a look around,' he said.

The old man led him around the factory. A sawmill operated at one end of the complex. Logs came in, were sawn and treated, and lay stacked in neat rows. Right now it was clear that the sawmill was not exactly busy. The few men who were there made no pretence of working when they saw their boss. Instead they stared bluntly at George and George was not left in much doubt whether they approved of what they saw. The day was dull with rain on the moors, but George tucked his sunglasses more firmly on to his nose.

The factory floor was busier. Around half the men glanced up and continued to work, the rest gave George the same candid appraisal he had received in the saw-mill. The verdict, he guessed rightly, was the same.

The old man hadn't lied when he spoke of craft methods. The factory used machine tools, of course, but each piece of furniture was sawn and assembled by hand. Gissing showed George how they had been forced to compromise standards by the imperative of cutting costs. Dovetailed joints had given way to tongue-and-groove, tongue-and-groove to nails and glue. Old man Gissing seemed to want to lament each nail until George dragged him off. The tour finished with the paint shop, the warehouse, and a totally absurd factory shop, whose last customer had died in the shock of the Profumo scandal.

Back in the executive office, the old man pulled out the company's accounts. It was a relief to see they had been run off using a computer, not a quill pen. George pored over the papers. Until a little over two months ago, he'd never looked at a balance sheet in his life and vaguely thought that double-entry book-keeping was something practised by the shadier sort of bookmaker. He'd had plenty to learn.

He looked at the annual accounts for every year since 1980. He looked at the monthly reports for each of the last thirty-six months. He had Tom Gissing explain to him in laborious detail the intricacies of the 'LIFO' inventory reporting system, the reducing balance method of depreciation, the acronyms used to identify the machine tools logged on the register of assets. He even drank two mugs of peaty tea.

After eight solid hours he understood the story. Back in the early eighties, recession had actually been kind to Gissings. Larger competitors had seen their export markets wither and hadn't chopped their costs quickly enough. Gissings, without an export market to lose, had trimmed costs, redesigned its products, and made money. It had earned revenues of £1.9 million on costs of £1.7 million. Mr Gissing, as managing director, had elected to pay the shareholder, Mr Gissing, a handsome dividend of £50,000. But that was a long time ago.

The profit spurt of the early eighties dwindled away as other companies found their feet. For the last part of the decade, the company had bumped along at break-even, squeezing capital expenditure here, trimming marketing budgets there, forsaking product development in favour of cosmetic changes which came too little, too late.

The recession of the nineties had been cruel. In the last year before the economy tanked, old Tom Gissing had somehow persuaded his bank to approve a loan of £400,000. The idea was to provide the impetus for a major renewal. The production area was to be expanded and modernised, and new computer design systems would be introduced. Perhaps – just perhaps – if all had gone according to plan, The Gissings Modern Furniture Company would have found a new lease of life.

But recession came. Gissings' markets trembled and collapsed. The money from the loan went to meet the company's losses. Worse still, the prime contractor on the construction work went bust with the job half done and Gissings' advance payments in his pocket. Redesign of the product range was halted. Costs were trimmed when they should have been slashed. The £400,000 loan ballooned into £550,000, with arrears of interest. Penalty interest was now being charged and the dangerous snowball gathered momentum at a compound rate.

Meanwhile, old man Gissing had lost his will to fight. He spent his time sorting through the company archives and threw his remaining energies into setting up a 'museum' to lure visitors to the factory shop.

The bank had been tolerant, but its patience was at an end. Three weeks ago the bank had called in its loan. Gissings had thirty days to find the cash. If it failed, the official receiver – a cross between a bailiff and an undertaker – would step in. He would auction the company for whatever he could get, and if he thought the company would fetch nothing, he'd close it down and sell the assets piece by piece. Either way, Tom Gissing wouldn't end up with a brass farthing.

The thought terrified the old man. Losing the company to someone else would be hard, but watching the firm die would probably kill him. That was why he had called in the accountants. The accountants had come in, drawn up a report, and stuck an ad in the 'Businesses for Sale' page of the *Financial Times*. That was where George had found the name, and where he'd obtained the report which had encouraged him to make the visit. But whatever rosy words the accountants used, the company was in a desperate plight.

It was now eight days before the deadline and the evening was drawing on. George had read everything, examined everything. He had seen all he wanted and still had no idea whether this walking dead company could ever live again. On the other hand, there were some simple facts he hadn't lost sight of. He had no money, so buying anything at all would be a triumph of sorts. Also, he had traipsed across Britain for two months in search of a company he could buy for next to nothing. So far he'd found nothing at all. The good companies were totally unaffordable. The bad ones much worse than hopeless. And Gissings, for all its faults, had one major advantage: it still sold one and a half million quids' worth of furniture each year. That meant there was something to work with.

The old man came back into the room. In the deserted factory buildings only George, the old man and his secretary were left. In the course of the day Tom Gissing had floated away from reality altogether. At times he seemed to think he was selling his company for a small fortune. At other times he treated George like a business partner and spoke of how they would develop the business together. Sometimes it was as though George were a historian, there to record the proudest moments of the company's glorious past. It was pathetic. George wanted out.

Gissing dumped another load of papers on to the table.

'I expect you'll be wanting to see these next. Some of our very earliest brochures. See this? *The Thunderer*! What a name for a desk, eh? Very daring at the time, I can tell you.'

George interrupted rudely.

'I've come to buy your company.'

The old man sank into a chair.

'Yes. Yes, of course. Quite right.'

'Have you had any other offers?'

The old man shook his head. 'No.'

'It's not worth much right now, is it? Not with half a million quid of debt. Not when you haven't made a profit for six years.'

'No, well, I suppose you're right. Still you never know. Things look a bit rough, but we've never lost hope.'

'Yeah, well, whatever,' said George. 'I want to make an offer for the lot. Factory, designs, inventory. The lot.'

The old man licked his lips, which had gone suddenly dry. 'How much?' he croaked, his voice barely audible.

The question threw George. He'd only just made up his mind to make an offer, and it hadn't occurred to him to think of a price. He shoved his hands into his pockets for inspiration.

'I'll give you a pound,' he said, tossing a coin on to the table. It spun for a moment then fell over. 'If you give me the company, I can recapitalise it and make it live. If you don't, the company and all your hard work will die. The bank will kill it. You know it will.'

George hadn't intended to be cruel, but he was feeling awkward, and awkwardness made him tactless. He wondered whether he should say something, an apology maybe or something to try and buck the old man up, but he was held fast in the room's gathering silence. For an infinite moment, the old man stared down at the golden disc. His rheumy blue eyes filled suddenly with tears. His lips opened and closed without sound. Finally his hand, shaking violently, closed over the glittering coin.

'Good luck,' he said. 'Take care of things. You will take care, won't you?' The old man began to shuffle from the room. The pound coin was clenched so tightly in his hand that George feared he would cut himself. Then at the door he turned and added, 'Oh – the name. It's yours to do as you please with now – but I've always liked the name. Gissings Furniture. It's got a ring to it. Anyway, best of luck.'

His footsteps moved hesitantly away down the dark corridor which then fell silent.

The old man's secretary had watched the whole scene. Her eyes blazed with contempt.

'Delighted to have you on board, sir,' she spat.

She held George's eyes a moment, then she too turned and walked away, her face angry and complex, her deep eyes invisible. Minutes passed, and George was left, the only person in the whole factory.

His factory. His headache. His problem. His key to a million pounds.

3

McAllister's ten days were up, but he was busy. Matthew watched his office like a hawk. McAllister was either in meetings or on the phone all day. Anxiety continued to chew at Matthew's stomach. Get off the phone. Give me the answer.

Eventually, at four o'clock, McAllister caught Matthew's glance and signalled him over. Matthew hurried across and was about to take his seat when McAllister asked him to close the door. That door was never closed. It was never closed, except, if rumour was true, when McAllister fired people. Matthew shut the door and sat down awkwardly.

'I've three things to say to you, Matt. First, you did a fine job on that piece of work the other day. Too many traders, not just in this bank but everywhere, think that their market feel is so good that they don't need to understand the facts. That's bullshit. Every good trader has market feel, but a fine trader is a salesman, an economist and a diplomat as well. I think you understand that and I like it.

'Secondly, we are going to give you a job here. You can finish your present assignment and then we'll send you off to New York for the training programme. If you flunk that, or if your teachers there think you need to complete your degree, then we'll chuck you out and that's that. But I don't see why you should fail. I think you will make a good trader.

'The third thing is this. My good friend, Bob Landau, who runs the trading floor at Coburg's, tells me that your brother is expected to do well in the corporate finance department there. They've never heard of you, and it's pretty clear that you don't know much about them. There are rules which matter a lot in banks and they matter most of all on the trading floor. At some point most traders break them. They don't record a trade when they should do. They exceed a position limit. They tell a lie or conceal the truth from a client. I regret that this game is what it is. But I know that paying young men what we pay them and motivating them as we motivate them will encourage mistakes. What I tell traders in this firm is this: you can make one mistake and usually we will forgive it. But if you make two, it suggests you're not capable of learning from your errors and we don't want you here. You, Matthew, have used up your mistake.'

4

Home late after a party. The music had been excellent, the drink OK, the men crap. Josie tittered to herself, releasing a belch into the gentle autumn night, not walking quite straight as she turned into the street for home.

But beneath her giggles and her party dress, she was

sad. Her best friends had been planning their skiing holiday and chatting about their fast approaching university life. Josie hadn't the money to go skiing and she wasn't going to university. She'd joined in, but sadly. Before the party broke up in a familiar scurry for taxis, mobile phones and sports cars, Josie had left, needing to catch the last tube.

She was annoyed with her mum. She knew, as Zack had said, that their mother's plight was in part self-inflicted. But what was she to do? Ignore her? Leave her without an income? Tell her to get on her bike, get a job, get on with life? Roll up her increasing depression and put it out with the garbage? Her seventeen-year-old self wanted life now, skiing now, A levels, university, career, everything. She wanted the life she'd been promised and was angry at whatever stood in its way.

She unlocked the front door. In the living room, a light was on. Helen Gradley sat in the armchair, head slumped, a needle of saliva hanging from her mouth. Her hands were blue.

'Mum? Mum! Jesus Christ.' Josie leaped to the phone, dialling 999. 'Ambulance, please.' She reached for her mother's mouth. There was no flow of breath that she could feel. 'It's my mum. Please come quickly. I think she's dead.'

5

Buying a company is no different from buying a used car. You can go for a test drive, you can lift the bonnet, you can haggle on price. But once you've handed over your money and driven away, there's no comeback. When the car overheats, when the big end blows, when the hydraulic system escapes the engine in a cloud of steam, it's tough.

Some people are experts. They can spot a repainted panel from twenty yards and a dodgy dealer from twenty miles. They don't need help. They can do the whole job – inspect the car, negotiate a price, agree the deal – by themselves. Lucky them. But most people aren't like that. We either call in experts to inspect the car – the AA, the RAC or whoever – or we get used to clouds of steam, expensive call-outs, and handing money over to people who burst out laughing as soon as we've left the forecourt.

It's the same with companies. If you want to buy a company, then, before you scribble out your cheque, you'll lift the bonnet and have a damn good look. And, unless you're very smart or very foolish, you'll want to have an expert with you when you do. What's more, if you're about to write a cheque for a hundred million pounds, or a billion, or more, you probably won't mind writing a little tiny one – not more than one percent of the purchase price – to the expert who looks after you so well. The experts in company takeovers are called corporate financiers, and if the good ones aren't always happy you can be sure it's not for want of money. One percent of a billion is ten million pounds.

Right now, two corporate financiers from Coburg's had the bonnet up and yawned with tedium.

The room they sat in was twenty foot by fifteen. One side was wall-to-wall windows with a view out over the sweeping roofs of Liverpool Street station. One wall held the door and a low side-table for coffees and suchlike. The other two walls were covered in pale beech shelving stacked with eighty-eight lever-arch files. A further six files lay open on the table in the middle. Each file was thick with documents. The index to the files was fifty-five pages long, plus a three-page 'Guide to Additional Material'. Zack rubbed his eyes.

'Jesus Christ. Is it always as dull as this?'

The two men from Tominto Oil had gone off for lunch, so Zack and Sarah could speak freely. It was weird working together. She was engaged to be married, he was as attracted to her as ever. They weren't even friends, really, just colleagues. Perhaps they had never been friends, just lovers who argued. So now they kept themselves to themselves, talked about work, tried to be polite, to ignore the electricity which filled the air.

'We've got ninety-four files to cover. That's not so bad. I once saw a data room with three hundred and seventy files, for a deal that lasted a year and a half then never happened. That was bad.'

Sarah spoke dismissively. She felt uncomfortable. Putting the two of them in the same project team was like mixing air and petrol and hoping there wouldn't be a spark. But Piers St George Hanbury, the project leader, didn't know their history, and Sarah did her best to muffle the possibility of any real contact, let alone a spark.

They were part of a Coburg's team helping a Texan oil company, Tominto Oil, buy a Scottish one. The Scottish one, Aberdeen Drilling, was being auctioned off by its parent company, which was currently talking to four serious bidders, including Tominto. Zack and Sarah and the two men from Tominto Oil were in the Aberdeen Drilling data room: the room which held every important document to do with the company. This was the Aberdeen Drilling engine, and the bonnet was up. Each bidder was allowed one week to look. They were allowed to read everything, take as many notes as they wanted, but they were allowed to copy nothing.

At the end of the week the bonnet would be brought down again and Tominto and Coburg's would need to go away, discuss what they'd seen, and work out a price they'd be prepared to offer. If their bid was the highest of the four submitted, they'd sign a contract, buy the company, and drive it off into a happy, and hopefully breakdown-free, future. If their bid was one of the three lowest, the seller would shake his head, say so sorry, and leave them to watch all their work go swirling down the plughole. The Tominto people would go back to running their company and the Coburg's corporate financiers would go chasing the next deal.

And what if the data room wasn't complete? What if, amongst the myriad documents – management accounts, tax filings, statutory accounts, environmental reports, supply contracts, customer analyses, and a thousand other things – what if one or two nasty surprises were carefully left out, so that the poor old buyers didn't have a clue? Well, it's like the better end of the car trade. When you buy a company, you sign a contract which gives you a limited warranty. The warranty protects against any nasty surprises which you *haven't* been told about. If something should have been in the data room and wasn't, and it ends up costing you money, then you can go to the seller and demand a refund.

So sellers have a different strategy. Sellers put every-thing into the data room. *Everything*. They fill it as full as they possibly can. If they have time bombs, they bury them. They bury them under a mountain of detail so dull, that Buddha himself would kick the walls and scream. Every time Zack and Sarah were tempted to skip a page, they were stopped sharply by the thought that as they flicked forward they might miss it. The time bomb. The thing they were in the data room to find.

There were the two guys from Tominto Oil as well, but they weren't the experts. In its forty-year life, Tominto Oil had purchased only about five companies worth more than a few million dollars. Coburg's closed more deals than that every two or three months. The guys from Tominto are like you looking under the bonnet. 'The thingamajig looks dirty,' you say. 'Is that doodah meant to have that bend in it?' Stand back, sucker. Get out of the light and let the experts look.

Zack and Sarah went back to their files. Sarah was tapping notes into a portable computer. Zack had a laptop too but he wasn't using it, he was using something more powerful: his memory. Since early boyhood, Zack had developed a pretty much photographic memory. He could look at a page, take it in, then just move on, knowing that he could bring it back to mind as clearly as if he had it in front of him. They weren't allowed to copy stuff, but Zack didn't need to. He was photographing it.

The silence settled again: Sarah tapping keys, both of them turning pages, looking for trouble, feeling strange in each other's presence. Page, after page, after page.

6

Terminal 4 at Heathrow is the most exciting of them all. Long-haul destinations flick up on departure screens like locations in a Bond movie. African chiefs in full tribal regalia rub shoulders and crash trolleys with neat Japanese businessmen. Arabs travelling with enough baggage to fill a jeep mix with students holding a single battered rucksack and a passport crammed with visas. This is a true melting pot, the world in chaos. It is exhilarating.

But amidst the confusion, a silent but complete apartheid rules. Economy travellers to the left. Business travellers to the right. And to the very far right, in their own quiet corner, first class and Concorde passengers are massaged gently through the inconvenience of having to walk to the plane at all. In that land of whispers, the rich, the famous and the powerful disappear down their own gangways, flattered, pampered and attended every step of the way.

Matthew was standing in the economy queue, and he wasn't enjoying it.

In the days when his father had paid for his airline tickets, Matthew had usually travelled business class, even first class if he could stand the inevitable argument. Today, with an economy ticket, Matthew gazed at the long queue stretching ahead of him and looked again at his watch. It was now only fifty minutes to takeoff and the queue seemed to be stuck. Only the rear view of a particularly attractive French girl kept him from losing his temper altogether. She was casually dressed in jeans and a crisp white cotton shirt, but the designer look was unmistakable and her figure was a pleasure to behold. She pushed a single large suitcase and carried a soft white leather bag on her shoulder. Matthew wanted to see her face but was half afraid that if she turned her head she would disappoint him. Right now, she looked perfect.

Just then the queue which had been stuck broke into a confusion at the far end by the check-in desk. The neat line of people dissolved into a scrum. Like everybody else, Matthew pushed forward to see what was happening.

The plane due to leave for New York at six that evening had developed some mechanical failure. They had found a replacement, but the replacement was a smaller 767, instead of the scheduled jumbo. The remaining passengers would not be able to travel that night. All passengers would be given a choice of accommodation at a nearby airport hotel or cash to allow them to travel home. All passengers would be able to travel out first thing the next day on a plane arranged especially for them. British Airways apologised profusely for any inconvenience caused. Passengers should contact the ground staff if they required help.

Matthew was apoplectic. He was flying to New York to join Madison's notoriously tough training programme, which started tomorrow. On the first morning, the bank's president was to give an introductory talk famous for its brevity. 'Take a good look at the students on either side of you,' he was reputed to say. 'Chances are that by the end of the programme, one of those students, or you, will have flunked the course. And there is no second chance, so do your best. And remember: in times to come, your fellow students may be your friends and colleagues. Right now they are also your competitors.'

It wouldn't be his fault if he were late. Brian McAllister had kept him in over the weekend on some dumb project that needed finishing and this was the last flight to get him there on time. Because he was a trainee, he had to fly economy, a saving which now threatened to tip him off the flight. But Madison wanted results not hard-luck stories, and Matthew looked set to be the first student not even to arrive on the first day.

'*Merde!*'

The thought was Matthew's, but the words came from elsewhere. It was the French girl in the white shirt. Her face was no disappointment at all. Long, dark brown hair fell smoothly from a centre parting, beautifully framing her oval face. She had clear fair skin, a slight pink blush, high cheekbones. She looked like a madonna, travelling light. Though obviously annoyed, she remained entirely composed. She was perfect, thought Matthew, absolutely perfect. Just for a moment the flight was forgotten.

80

The French girl wasn't really talking to anyone, just announcing her feelings, but Matthew felt he might as well respond.

'Unbelievable, isn't it?' he said, brilliantly.

'Terrible. I need to be in New York tonight. I have changed my booking twice already.'

'Me too. Let's see if we can get any joy here,' said Matthew, throwing his weight into the mêlée ahead.

'I don't think you will have any fun there. Not unless you have something which the fifty people ahead of you don't have. Come.'

She turned and set off rightwards to the serene world of business class. Matthew hesitated a moment, then followed. When he caught up with her a few yards from the check-in counter, she was in tears and her hands twisted round her handkerchief in agitation. He hurried to keep alongside her. At the desk she threw down her passport and her ticket. Between sobs she gasped, 'We have to go to New York tonight. We have to.'

She then seemed to break down completely, and in an instant had nestled herself inside Matthew's startled embrace. She was beautiful, beautiful, beautiful. Her body melted into his, seeking protection. He held her. He didn't mind.

Then, with a further convulsion, she jerked free. Tugging at the ring finger of her left hand, she pulled off two rings and flung them on to the counter. One held a simple sapphire surrounded by a circle of tiny diamonds. The other was a plain gold band.

'If you are going to ruin our honeymoon, you may as well have these as well!' she cried.

The rings skittered across the counter. One of them fell into the stewardess's lap, while the other flew on to the conveyor belt taking luggage to the cargo hall. The stewardess made a cricketer's leap and snatched the ring up before it was carried away.

The diversion was enough for Matthew to regain his cool. As the stewardess grabbed the ring, he stole a glance at the passport on the counter in front of him. Sophie Clemenceau. As the stewardess resurfaced again, red-faced but holding both rings, Matthew stepped in. Drawing his companion further into his arms, he said, 'I do apologise. Sophie doesn't mean that at all. She knows it's not your fault. She's just upset.'

'This is your honeymoon?' asked the stewardess.

'That's right. You're looking at the brand new Mr and Mrs Matthew Gradley.' A squeeze below the level of the counter thanked him for the information.

'Oh, it seems a terrible shame to spend your first night on honeymoon in the airport hotel. It's not very nice, to be honest.'

'Well, I suppose we don't have much of a choice. I'm sure Sophie will be OK after a few days, though she is very superstitious.'

Sophie did a good job pretending that she wouldn't get over the shock in a few months, let alone a few days. Matthew felt his shirt sticking to his chest where it was soaked from her tears.

'Just a second. Let me see what I can do. I wouldn't have wanted my honeymoon to be spoiled by anything like this.'

The stewardess whisked away. Matthew went on petting the sobbing Sophie. It was no torture. He hoped the stewardess would take her time. With her gone, Sophie held herself away from Matthew's body but she stayed put.

'Good thinking,' he whispered into her hair.

'Good job,' she responded before getting on with more heavy-duty sobbing.

He stroked and she sobbed for a few minutes more. She was heaven, better than perfect. Matthew, her pretend husband, was virtually ready to marry her for real on the spot. All too soon the stewardess returned, smiling.

'Luckily we have a couple of seats available in first class. They were booked, but nobody has shown up for them. I'll book you in right away with the compliments of the airline.'

Within a minute they slipped away, hand in hand down the fast-track passport channel. A happy glance behind told them that the fifty or sixty frantic passengers they'd left screaming and shouting at the check-in desk were still there, still yelling. Matthew turned to Sophie.

'Do tell me about our wedding. I seem to have forgotten it.'

She laughed. Her teeth were very white.

'Tsk. Forgotten already? I have a good mind to divorce you.'

'Better wait till we're airborne. We wouldn't want them to change their minds. That was quite a show you put on.'

'I've been able to make myself cry since I was seven. I used it to make sure I never got in trouble for starting a fight, even when I had.'

They parted after passport control, she to the Harrods boutique, he to the newsagent for magazines. But their seats were together, and the armrest between them was already adorned with a bottle of champagne and flowers. Matthew, arriving first, was obliged to describe the happy day in exact detail to the inquisitive cabin crew until Sophie's arrival rescued him.

They were left alone for a while as they made themselves at home in the luxurious seats. Matthew stretched out his legs and felt with difficulty for the seat a long way ahead of him. The menu promised good things, and a video library exclusively for first class assured him of a good evening's entertainment. He glanced sideways again at Sophie. She had pulled a navy lambswool jumper out of her bag and had thrown it over her shoulders. She was casual, assured and beautiful. She wore her two rings on her ring finger, but Matthew could see the faint circles of pale skin which betrayed their normal positions. So she wasn't married.

Matthew urgently wished he was more to her than a casual accomplice in a petty fraud. One of the stewardesses came over again.

'We don't have details of your destination address on arrival in New York. We have a complimentary limousine service to take you wherever you're going to.'

Matthew paused. The gentlemanly thing would be to allow Sophie to give her address. He could get a cab from the airport. He already felt a sense of loss at their approaching parting. He had made up his mind to get to know her as well as he could on the flight over. If she was as great as she seemed, he'd do his utmost to mix pleasure with business during his five-month stay in New York.

Sophie pulled out an address slip. 'It's the intersection of Park Avenue and 75th Street. Upper East Side.'

It was the same block as Matthew was going to. The sheet of paper on which the address was printed had a familiar look to it. Hudson House. A small hotel with one very large corporate client. When the stewardess was out of earshot again, Matthew leaned over to Sophie.

'Are you with Madison by any chance?'

She looked at him sharply.

'I'm beginning the training programme tomorrow. That's why I was so keen to make the plane.'

'Me too. On both counts.'

'Pleased to meet you.'

They formally shook hands, carefully so none of the cabin staff could see. It was only forty minutes after the moment that her tears had been gluing his shirt to his chest, and about thirty-nine minutes after Matthew had decided to see more of her.

Now he was both relieved and tense. Relieved because he would see her every single day for the next five months. Tense because he remembered the famous speech he was due to hear tomorrow. The beautiful Sophie Clemenceau might become a friend and colleague. If Matthew had his way she would also become his lover. But for five months she was also to be a competitor.

7

George had found a solicitor in Ilkley to draw up the Sale Agreement which would legally transfer Gissings into his name. He had instructed the solicitor to make the document totally one-sided and sent two copies round to Gissing. He assumed he'd have to make some concessions to get the old man's consent, but one copy of the contract came back by return signed in a shaky hand, 'Thomas Gissing, Proprietor and Managing Director, 1963–98'. There were no amendments.

Eleven weeks since hearing his father's will, George owned a company. Its annual turnover was £1.5 million. Excluding the bank loan, its assets were valued in the accounts at around £350,000. So far, George had spent one pound plus a few hundred in solicitor's fees. He should be feeling good.

He wasn't. It was now Monday. On Friday, The Gissings Modern Furniture Company was required to repay more than half a million pounds to the bank. Val

Bartlett, old Tom Gissing's secretary and now his, was able to find about fifteen quid in the company's petty cash tin. There was a float of perhaps five pounds in a decaying vending machine. George's car would fetch twenty grand second-hand. And that was it.

George made an appointment to see David Ballard, the company's bank manager.

As luck would have it, Ballard had been Bernard Gradley's bank manager when Gradley had first opened an account, and they'd done good business together. Both men's empires expanded. Ballard took over responsibility for all lending to mid-sized companies in Yorkshire and the North West, while Gradley's business spread across the nation. Despite their different paths, the two men had maintained a respectful friendship. If George needed a favour to get him started, Ballard should be the ideal man to grant it.

Ballard's office overlooked the old market square in Richmond, a well-to-do market town in North Yorkshire. The room was furnished by Ballard himself, not his employer, and the result was welcoming and warm. Ballard had been offered promotions, but he refused anything which took him away from Yorkshire. His clients loved him and his bosses left him alone. He welcomed George with coffee and biscuits.

'Well, well, George. It's a while since I've seen you. Very sorry to hear about your father's death. Very sorry indeed. You must be very cut up, I suppose. How's poor Helen taking it?'

Ballard munched on the biscuits as he spoke. He was a fat man with greying hair and moustache. He had the no-nonsense mouth of the tough banker and the twinkly eyes of a kind and humorous man. Crumbs from his biscuits lodged inside his moustache.

George shrugged. According to Josie, their mother was

in a very bad way indeed, having teetered on the brink of following their father into the night. As it was now . . . but Ballard didn't need to know the real, gloomy story. A brightly-coloured fairy tale would do for him.

'Mum's taken it OK to be honest,' said George. 'As you know, there wasn't much love lost between Mum and Dad by the end. She's just pleased that the money's coming into the family proper after being under lock and key for so long.'

The will was secret, but Ballard knew as well as anyone how much Bernard Gradley was worth. If George could con him into believing he was about to inherit millions, then getting him to show a bit of grace with Gissings shouldn't be so tough.

'Yes. A few million must dull the edge of pain I suppose. Especially if you couldn't stand the old bastard – and I speak as a friend of the old bastard, as you know. Still you haven't come here to talk about that, I guess. Proud proprietor of old Tom Gissing's shop, eh? Wouldn't quite guess it. Not from the look of you. Still, stranger things have happened. How can I help?'

'Well I owe you half a million quid, give or take.'

'That's right. But it's give not take. Five hundred and forty-eight thousand, seven hundred and eighty-two pounds. Due close of business on Friday.'

'That's fine, but I wonder if we could sort out an extension. Two or three months perhaps?'

'An extension? With all that cash from your dad?'

There was a twinkle in Ballard's eye, but his mouth was unforgiving, and it was the mouth talking.

'Nothing has yet been released by the estate's executors,' said George truthfully. 'There are death duties, valuation of the business, all the rest of it. Until I get my slice of the pie, I'm as poor as a church mouse. What I want is to defer the loan until I can recapitalise the business, write off the debt, give it a healthy balance sheet once again.'

'You have a letter from the executors? I might be able to grant a deferral if you had a letter.'

George stuttered for a moment. He could get a letter. It just wouldn't say what he needed it to say.

'Er – I guess so. What I don't know is whether I can get it in time. There's a whole bunch of executors and the legal palaver seems to take for ever.'

Ballard checked some figures on his desk.

'The interest payment due on Friday is around six grand. If you get that to us plus another thirty grand as an advance on the next series of interest payments, then I'll give you a temporary extension. Let's say three months, shall we?'

George nodded without being able to speak. In his mind's eye, he'd expected Ballard to nod the whole thing through without a hint of difficulty. As it was, Ballard had hardly helped at all.

Emerging blinking into the market square, George chased a traffic warden from his illegally parked car, pulled out his mobile phone and started to dial. He had five days to find thirty-six grand. If he couldn't, he would be the shortest lived proprietor The Gissings Modern Furniture Company (Limited) would ever know.

8

Not dead, thank God, but very, very ill.

An ambulance had come quickly. A kind paramedic had been swift to reassure a distraught Josephine that her mother's pulse was steady, her breathing weak but constant. The journey to hospital was an unremembered rush of sirens and flashing lights. Once there, Helen Gradley was thrust fast and unemotionally on to the processing line of the modern NHS. Her case was serious and, queue-jumping the groaning hordes in casualty, she was placed immediately into intensive care. Through that night and the days that followed, diagnosis and prognosis became clearer.

Helen Gradley had had a stroke, a stoppage of blood to the brain. The consequences were hard to predict, even for a specialist. Some people lost speech, lost coordination, lost memory, then recovered the lot within weeks and months. Others might lose less, but lose it for good. With Helen, whose stroke had been severe, only time would tell.

And Josephine? That first night at the hospital she had sat up all night with her mother. Doctors had come and gone, giving conflicting advice, rushing off at the command of a pager, too busy to do their job. Josie, in her party dress still, held her mother's hand, whispering encouragement. She remembered the mood she'd been in, climbing the hill towards home: her anger, her passionate demands for her old life back. That was all gone now. Helen Gradley, for so long the shield between her children and their father, the victim of an unfair divorce and a cruel will, lay in bed, helpless as a baby, looking to her daughter for help.

Josephine was just seventeen. She had never expected to earn a living, let alone care for a disabled parent, but she knew her duty. 'It's OK, Mum. I'm here,' she said.

9

It's a common problem amongst bankers. You work hard all day. You come home tired as a dog in a heatwave. Then when at last you collapse into bed, you can't even sleep. Worse still, you do sleep and your dreams are full of the rubbish you've spent your day with. Numbers walk past in an endless stupid procession. You're no longer you. You're just a cursor flashing in a crowded spreadsheet, roving up and down, sorting out numbers, the last traffic cop left alive in Gridlock City.

It was three o'clock in the morning and Zack threw off the covers. He groaned. Outside there was a distant whistle of traffic from Camden High Street and the sound of a milk float clinking. Zack tried to let the sounds drift in and over the clickety-click of marching numbers.

He put the light on, splashed water on his face, then decided to have a shower. Maybe that would wash the rubbish away. He stood under the jet of water and scrubbed himself with the Boots aromatherapy shower gel which Josephine had given him for his birthday. It was a rather pointed present, bought for less than a tenner – Josie's way of reminding him that she was struggling to cope. Damn her. She'd quit complaining when Zack saved their father's fortune single-handedly. When she had a few million quid in her pocket – money which Zack would have put there – she could buy him a decent present. The purple gel ('Refreshing and Relaxing') dripped off Zack's bony figure under the spray. Numbers still chattered, but not as much.

He threw on a dressing gown stolen from the New York Plaza in happier days, and padded into the kitchen. Nothing in the fridge except a yoghurt past its sell-by date. He opened it and sniffed it. It smelled OK. What's the difference between a yoghurt pot and Australia? The yoghurt's got a living culture. Ha, ha. Zack ate the yoghurt and stared at the lid. The sell-by date. More numbers. He'd be dreaming about the bar code next. If he scrabbled around in the dustbin he could probably find a till receipt to read.

He went back into the bedroom and sat on the edge of

the bed. Sarah Havercoombe seemed completely indifferent to him and, besides, she was engaged to be married. Coburg's was beginning to bore him and he wasn't close to his million pounds. He didn't even know how he was going to make it. Meanwhile, Matthew was on Wall Street learning to trade, and George was god-knows-where doing god-knows-what. Maybe Josie was right, maybe they were all a pack of fools. Still, there didn't seem to be much else to do except try. Go on trying until they'd reached their sell-by date.

Why was that phrase in his head so much? Sell-by date. The numbers had gone, but the phrase stayed. Probably something to do with that blasted Aberdeen Drilling data room. All those piles of contracts and accounts. Random phrases stuck around just like the numbers. Zack got into bed again and turned off the light. The yoghurt sat in his stomach feeling funny. It probably had been off. He tried to sleep. Sell-by date. Sell-by date.

Five minutes later, he threw off the covers and turned the light back on. Frowning with concentration, he began to bring a page from the data room into his mind's eye. The page came, blurry at first, then in sharp focus: 'Standard Warranties for Consultancy-type Agreements'. Zack read the words below the title. It was drafted in legal language so dense you could saw it into blocks and build with it, but to Zack the meaning was clear. He brought another page to mind. It appeared, then cleared, like the one before: 'Insurance Arrangements: Provisions and Exclusions'. Zack gazed at the remembered page. Things were becoming clear. No wonder he couldn't sleep. Just one more check to make: 'Schedule of Principal Consultancy Projects, 1988–98'. The page began to clear, but Zack hardly needed to look at it to know what it said.

He turned off the light and slept like a baby.

10

Through the slatted blinds behind the students, the Hudson River emptied into the Atlantic Ocean. The waters were crowded with traffic and in the late summer sun, the Statue of Liberty waved her torch, calling order to the congested skies. The gateway to the free world isn't too keen on the weary and dispossessed these days, but it sure has time for anything which can be packaged, shipped and sold. Away to the south west, too far to be seen in the haze, the port authority's cranes kept the flood of goods moving swiftly on.

None of the students had their eyes on the scene. You could stack up all the cargo passing through the air and sea ports of New Jersey and New York in a year and you'd have a mountain big enough to boast a skiing industry. But the whole enormous pile wouldn't be worth a thousandth part of the invisible cargo which passes noiselessly down the electronic thoroughfares of Wall Street.

The market for US government bonds is worth over six trillion dollars. The foreign exchange market turns over a trillion dollars each and every working day. The US stockmarkets are capitalised at fourteen trillion bucks. The market for corporate bonds and bills, and certificates of deposit, and a hundred other varieties of security add trillions more to the total. And each of these bits of paper belongs to investors, skilled and unskilled, wise and foolish, twisting and turning to dodge losses and snuffle out profit.

Wall Street does various things, some good for the world, others not so good. But its main function is simple: it's a bureau de change where investors can sell one bit of paper and buy another. And every time a bit of paper changes hands, leaving an investor happy and excited about the future, there is another person even happier. That person is the Wall Street trader who did the trade. For every dollar that changes hands, a tiny amount of change stays in the hands of the trader. In some markets, the amount of change is almost microscopic. In the foreign exchange markets, the Wall Streeter might keep just a few hundredths of a cent. In the stockmarket it might be half a cent, sometimes as much as two or three.

But traders don't care that their take is small. If you multiply by a million dollars, one tenth of a cent is worth a thousand bucks. Multiply by a billion, and that tenth of a cent is worth a million dollars. And if you're sharp enough and smart enough to squeeze out two tenths of a cent, then the investor still hardly cares – what's two tenths of a cent to him? – but you've doubled your take to two million bucks. Keep at it and before long you'll have your nice house in Long Island, your German sports car and your decent sized yacht. Your kids will go to the right schools, your wife will be invited to the right parties, and you will no longer keep in touch with your pals from college who got better grades than you but who made the life-destroying error of opting for a career in engineering or civic service.

Life as a Wall Street trader can be very sweet. And that, of course, is why the students were there.

Matthew looked around. Sophie was sitting diagonally in front of him. He caught her eye and smiled at her. She smiled back. It hadn't been his imagination. She was still gorgeous, with her perfect figure and a complexion so nice you wanted to sing to it. Matthew definitely wanted to get to know her.

A tall blond Californian barged along the row of seats and sat down next to Matthew.

'Mind if I sit here? My name's Scott Petersen. Nice to meet you.'

Scott Petersen was an inch or two taller than Matthew, an inch or two broader and maybe an inch or two better looking. Matthew disliked him at once.

'Hi. Matthew Gradley.'

They shook hands.

'From England, right?'

'Right.'

'At least that's easy,' said Petersen, looking round the room. 'We've got twenty-two North Americans, same number of Europeans, then maybe fifteen or twenty from everywhere else. Mostly Pacific Rim, I guess, but I bumped into a couple of South Americans earlier and I know there's a Russian and some kind of Middle Eastern oil princess.'

Matthew nudged his neighbour. Down the row to Matthew's right came a plump dark-skinned girl, her hair piled up and fastened with a couple of heavy gold clips. Gold glittered and clunked at her fingers, wrist and neck. She walked looking straight ahead, her heavy-set face impassive.

'That's her,' whispered Petersen. 'I've heard she only just managed to graduate from college and her English is none too good either. But her family controls oil reserves worth tens of billions of dollars and –'

Petersen shrugged. He understood it, but he didn't like it. At Madison merit is the only way to get ahead, but merit comes in different shapes, and the podgy figure of the oil princess was one of them. Matthew turned to her.

'How do you do,' he said. 'Matthew Gradley.'

'Yes. How do you do,' replied the girl in a heavy accent. 'Fareshti Al Shahrani –'

Anything further she had intended to say was interrupted as the entrance door opened and a man strode across to the podium. The students fell silent. The man was Dan Kramer, the Lion of Wall Street.

The old-fashioned walnut podium concealed a battery of switches controlling the sound system, lights, blinds, screens, projectors – everything. But Kramer stood away from the podium. He hadn't any slides, and his voice needed no amplification. He was not a large man, but with a mane of dusty blond hair bristling round a granite face, he didn't need to be large to be awe-inspiring. When *Time* magazine had done a cover story on Kramer entitled 'The Lion of Wall Street', the nickname became permanent. When he was calm, he looked fierce. When he was angry, he was terrifying. Today Kramer was not angry, but he was emphatic.

'My name is Daniel Kramer. I am the Chairman and Chief Executive of Madison. I would like to welcome you all to this training programme today.'

He grinned, but his smile cheered no one. It showed too many teeth and lasted a few seconds too long.

'You succeeded in obtaining a job here because the people who interviewed you believed that you have what it takes. We try hard to be right because it's a waste of our time being wrong. But we do get it wrong, about one time in three. When we screw up, we say sorry and ask you to leave. We don't want you to have a nasty life, but we want you to lead it outside of this organisation.

'Those of you who remain with us will sometimes wonder if you made the right choice. The work is hard, the pressure is relentless. Each time you think you've mastered a task, we will increase your responsibilities, demand more from you. You will meet every challenge or you will leave the firm. If you continue to succeed, you will earn sums of money that are unimaginable to all but a tiny fraction of the population. You will also have the satisfaction of knowing that you've made it in one of the world's most demanding workplaces. So much for your rewards.

'More important to me are the rewards for the firm. I am sometimes asked to define our strategy. That's easy. In every country where we operate, we recruit the best. Once we've recruited them, we retain them. Then we just get on with our jobs, as best we can. That's it. The rewards for the firm will follow.'

Kramer continued to prowl to and fro across the floor of the amphitheatre.

'Are there any questions?'

Coming from him, this wasn't a question. It was a joke. Nobody asked a question, nobody ever had since Kramer started giving these speeches. He smiled once more. Too many teeth again and the smile lasted long after the light had vanished. Without another word, the Lion of Wall Street stalked from the room.

Matthew knew beforehand that Kramer wasn't exactly a touchy-feely kind of guy. And Matthew didn't just cope with competition; he thrived on it. All the same, Kramer was genuinely menacing, and Matthew's mouth felt dry. He glanced downwards and across to where Sophie was sitting. She looked completely composed. She wasn't licking her lips, or shifting in her seat, or fiddling with her pencils, or doing any of the other things that the other students were doing. She just looked beautiful and desirable. Matthew forgot Kramer.

He opened his folder and took out a card which he'd bought that morning. He scrawled something inside, scribbled Sophie's name on the envelope, and tossed it accurately on to her desk.

She looked round to see where it had come from and

sent Matthew a polite smile. She opened the envelope and read the card. She smiled, not politely this time, and sent Matthew a look, which meant 'Yes'. With a bit of luck it even meant, 'Yes, please, I'd be delighted'.

The inscription inside the card was brief. It ran: 'Dear Mrs Gradley, as today is the first day of our honeymoon, perhaps you would care to dine with me this evening? Eight at The Riverside. Your loving husband, Mr Gradley.'

11

Hank Daggert, the Chief Executive of Tominto Oil, didn't care too much for the mother country. He liked some things, of course. He liked Maggie Thatcher, the flexible labour market and North Sea Oil. But the list of things he didn't like was much longer. He disliked the Queen, trade unions, New Labour, John Lennon, unarmed policemen, the BBC, hot tea, warm beer, and cold rooms. He didn't like the bunch of old Etonians who were helping him buy Aberdeen Drilling but he hadn't much choice. He was buying a British company and he figured that picking Coburg's, the biggest independent British bank, was the best way to succeed. All the same, Daggert listened to Piers St George Hanbury with growing irritation.

'You're telling me there was a time bomb in that data room all along?'

'Yes. We believe you should reduce your bid by ten million pounds or insist that the seller insures you against any liability you might be taking on.'

'Jesus. We're only a fortnight away from making our final offer. Couldn't you have told me this sooner?'

'Yes, I understand. The problem was very carefully hidden, and it took us some time to spot it.

But we thought you would sooner know late than not at all.'

'You're telling me,' growled Daggert. Tominto Oil was worth about a billion dollars and Daggert owned about five percent of it. Hank Daggert wasn't exactly a sweet old man, but if you were a shareholder in Tominto Oil you loved him just the same. 'Just take me through the problem one more time. I want to be sure I understand.'

Piers Hanbury was too important to care much about details. He was one of the biggest deal-makers in the City of London and he wasn't unduly fussed over a hundred million pound deal with a miserable little million pound fee. He was there to look distinguished and make the client feel happy.

'Zack, why don't you walk us through this?' said Hanbury smoothly. 'It's your discovery, after all.'

Hanbury was polite in front of a client, but he'd been absolutely furious with Zack the day before. 'Why the hell didn't you bring this up sooner? We don't stand a chance of doing the deal now.' Hanbury was sore.

One thing about buying companies is different from buying a car. With a car, when you call out the AA to inspect it, you pay the AA a flat fee irrespective of whether you end up buying the car. That way you can be sure of getting impartial advice. If you agreed to pay only if the inspection was clean, you'd find yourself with clean reports for cars only a tow-ride away from the breakers' yard.

For some reason, which no one on earth can explain, it doesn't work like that when it comes to buying companies. Corporate financiers only get paid if they win the deal, if their client beats the other bidders. The temptation to encourage the client to bid too much is almost overwhelming – and every now and then, there are those who don't try so hard to resist. Piers St George Hanbury was one of them. If Zack had found the problem when they were in the data room a couple of weeks back, Hanbury would have found other reasons for getting Tominto Oil to pay up for Aberdeen. But now they'd debated the price and fixed it, when bloody Zack Gradley comes along with a ten million pound hole. The deal was running into the sand.

'OK,' said Zack. 'The seller had a problem. They were all ready to sell Aberdeen Drilling, when along comes a major headache. A Norwegian consultancy project they'd worked on returned to haunt them. They'd advised on the construction of a North Sea pipeline into Bergen. They did their work, got paid, and forgot about it. But to win the contract, they had offered a guarantee. Either the work's OK or they'd pay to put it right. That was the deal.

'Now, just as they were getting ready to invite you guys into the data room, the Norwegians come along. It turns out there was a major foul-up which the Norwegians say is the fault of Aberdeen Drilling. Well, maybe, maybe not. It hasn't been tested in a court of law, but let's just suppose the Norwegians are right and Aberdeen did screw up.

'Normally, that wouldn't be too bad. They've got insurance. If they have to pay out to the Norwegians, they just get the cash back from the insurers. But here's the problem. When they signed the Norway contract, they weren't insured. There was a cock-up in accounts and they were a week late in making a premium payment, something to do with staff sickness, I think. Anyway, the week the contract was signed, they weren't insured. The sellers are desperate to sell before the liability hits, plus they want to make sure the buyers don't see what's coming.'

'But you said all this was in the data room? Why would they go and tell us if they wanted to keep it quiet?'

Zack smiled.

'They had to put it in the data room or else you could claim the money back on the warranty. So what they did was smart. They dismantled their time bomb. They broke it into four little pieces and hid three of them in the data room and one in the press. Any of those bits on their own is harmless. But the four of them together stand to make a very loud bang.'

'Go on.'

'The first part of the bomb was concealed in some standardised consultancy agreements. That's where they told us that all their consultancy work was guaranteed. Any problems down the line would need to be paid for. The second part of the bomb was buried in a footnote way down in a mountain of stuff to do with insurance contracts. The footnote pointed out that there was a period of a few days where these insurance arrangements didn't apply. The third part of the bomb was a note mentioning when the Norwegian contract had been signed, which was – surprise, surprise – bang in the middle of the time when the insurance was on the blink. If you like, the deal was signed after the insurance had passed its sell-by date.

'And here's the clever bit. The most dangerous part of the bomb – the bit which would have aroused our suspicions instantly and sent us hunting down all the other parts – they didn't even put inside the data room.'

'But I thought –' began Daggert.

Zack cut him off. 'Yes. You thought that if they didn't put something in the data room, then we were covered by the warranty. That's true – unless that thing was already public knowledge, defined as something already

100

being in the press. So what they do is, they take their bomb's most dangerous part to a Norwegian journalist. A journalist who works for a Norwegian oil industry magazine with a circulation of about five thousand. They say what they have to say. The journalist writes a couple of paragraphs, in Norwegian of course, and bungs it in the magazine. Hey presto. It's public knowledge. The story's not big enough to be picked up elsewhere, and if it is, it'll probably hit the English-language journals too late for the deal. After all, there aren't all that many people with fluent Norwegian and an avid interest in the offshore oil business.'

Daggert shook his head. 'So how the hell did you guys find this bomb? You read Norwegian oil industry magazines for fun?'

Zack shook his head. 'Thinking about the data room afterwards, I realised that they'd concealed the first three pieces very carefully. They were a long way apart. Each one was buried in documents almost too boring to read. I realised that they had a perfect bomb, all they needed was some explosive. So then I started looking for the explosive. We used our databases to search the English-language press, then the press worldwide. Up pops this Norwegian article which mentions a sum of ten million pounds. And there we had it: a bomb, primed and ticking.'

Zack tossed the article across the desk with a translation. Daggert scanned it. It didn't say much: just that there was a problem and that the Norwegians would be putting in a claim for the money. But it was enough.

'You got notes on the other stuff, the other parts of the bomb?' Zack shook his head. Daggert looked at his two subordinates: the ones who had been with Zack and Sarah in the data room. 'Did you pick up this stuff?' They both shook their heads and the more senior guy glowered at the junior guy, as though it was his fault. Daggert's voice grew sharper. 'You don't have any record of this and you want me to drop my bid by ten million pounds?'

Hanbury leaned forward. Here was a chink of light. They could be honest with the client, but still maybe encourage the client not to change his bid. That would be the best of all worlds. He began to speak, but the arrogant young Gradley beat him to it.

'I do have records, just not written ones.'

'What?' Daggert was pissed off. Was Gradley playing games?

'I have a good memory. I don't forget a fact.'

Daggert gave a sharp laugh. 'That's easily tested.' He reached for the yellow legal pad of one of his subordinates. It was crowded with notes from the data room. Daggert flicked through the pages and looked at Gradley, his eyes openly challenging. 'OK. File fifty-seven. Tab eight. Tell me what it says.'

Zack brought the file to mind, then the tab, then turned the tab to find the first page. He let the page swim out of memory into focus.

'Employee grievance procedures,' he said. 'Disciplinary committees. First and second warnings. That kind of thing.'

Daggert nodded and flicked forward again through the notes. He smiled. This would be a good test. 'File ninety-one. Tab four. There are some numbers on that page. Read them to me.'

Zack found the page and let it swim into view. Then he smiled and began to go red.

'What's up?' said Daggert. 'Something amuse you?'

'Er, well, no not exactly,' said Zack, his red deepening. This file hadn't been one of his. It had been one of Sarah's and he hadn't looked at it fully. But as he tried to bring

102

the picture to mind, he realised he had seen it after all. He had been standing up, getting a cup of coffee from the table at the side of the room. Sarah had been sitting in front of him, leaning over the file. Her light brown hair fell down either side of her neck, leaving it exposed, vulnerable, kissable – Zack had stared at her with yearning and found himself staring also at the file open in front of her: file ninety-one, tab four. 'Sorry,' continued Zack. 'I was smiling because I remember Sarah – er – walking into the room about that time. I guess that must have been a nice experience for me.'

'Nice to see a good team spirit,' growled Daggert, glancing at Sarah, who went red in turn herself. But she wasn't angry, just embarrassed. 'Did you get a chance to look at the numbers too?'

'Yes. Of course. The numbers you wanted were eighteen point six, fourteen point eight . . .' He continued flawlessly. Daggert followed from the notes in front of him. Zack was perfect.

'OK. Stop. You've proved your point. Good catch, young man. Piers, we'll drop our bid by ten million pounds. Is that clear? We offer a hundred and fifteen million only.'

Hanbury swallowed. Damn Gradley. Damn him.

'That's perfectly clear. You do of course remember our advice that the winning bid is unlikely to be less than one twenty-five. I must warn you that your revised bid is most unlikely to win.'

The oilman glared at the aristocratic Hanbury.

'Damn right. And we won't overpay either.'

12

'Kiki? It's me. George.'

'Georges, darling, how are you?' Kiki's English was

excellent but she knew that a French accent sounded sexier and she exploited the fact for all it was worth.

'I'm OK. Look, can you come over to my flat right away? I need to see you.'

'Now darling? I'm going out right now. I have my hat on.'

'You're always just going out. I've ordered you a cab and it's waiting outside your hotel now. Kiki, I need to see you.'

She paused for a moment, wondering whether to provoke him with a longer refusal.

'OK, Georges. But you will need to admire my new suit very much. It is new today.'

George promised.

'And I really am going out, so I will only be able to stay with you for two minutes.'

'That's OK.'

'Maybe only one minute, if I have to spend time getting ready.' Getting ready for Kiki meant fussing over her immaculate make-up and leaving expensive brand name cosmetics in other people's bathrooms.

'Kiki, I'll give you a personal pedicure if I have to. Just get a move on.'

She came. An hour and a half late, of course, and carrying a bag from Harvey Nichols. But she came. Her new suit was stunning. Coral pink and perfectly fitted, it was as eye-catching as its price tag. George gave it as much praise as it deserved and almost as much as Kiki demanded.

Nobody annoyed George more than Kiki, but nor had any girl ever attracted him as much. Other than a kiss one New Year's Eve in Monaco – which had meant a lot to George, but nothing at all, it appeared, to Kiki – nothing had passed between them. He was heavily built and, dressed differently, could easily have passed as a

Yorkshire farmer: slow-talking, stolid, strong. She, in contrast, was petite, pretty, brightly coloured, fluttering constantly from one thing to another like a bird hopping from twig to twig. They were unlikely friends, but George kept her doggedly in his sight, as she skipped from Gstaad to Monaco to London to New York to Palm Beach to Milan and back home to her chateau in the Loire valley.

As for her, she showed no outward sign of attraction to George – or at least no more to him than to anyone else in her wide circle of friends. Yet it was noticeable that, wherever she went, her path always circled back to George's flat in London. She sat on his sofas, showed him her latest purchases, scattered her make-up, showed him photos of the party she'd just come from, agonised with him about what to wear for the next one, patted his cheeks, called him darling, rumpled his hair and left him in a frenzy for the next visit.

At length Kiki stepped down from the coffee table where she had been pirouetting.

'OK, Georges, my darling, you have been a very good boy. But I think you wanted to see me not just because of my nice new suit. No?'

George seized the moment. In a few sentences, he told Kiki the story about his father's will, the challenge it threw down, how George and his brothers accepted the challenge, how George now had just three days to find thirty-six grand.

'Kiki,' he finished, 'I have a question. You've always told me that you love this flat and how fed up you are staying in hotels whenever you come to London. Well, there's about nine months rent prepaid on this flat and I'm ready to move out tomorrow. If you can take the flat off my hands, I'll be eternally grateful.'

Kiki had listened very quietly and seriously to George's

narration. Now that he came to the end, she said, 'But Georges, this flat is so *masculin*. I need something a little more *feminin*, you know. All this blue and gold, it is good for you and it was *très* fashionable last year, but this year the colours are lighter, you know.'

She waved her hand around but her speech tapered off. Despite her words, her face was solemn.

'Georges, you really need this money, no?'

George nodded.

'And if I give you the money, then you will give it to some bank manager who will take it away and not give it back to you, no? And you say that this business of yours is a very bad business, no? That it will probably go down the hole? Oh Georges, and then you will have no money and then I will not be able to see you because you will have holes in your shoes and I do not like men who have holes in their shoes.'

There were tears in her eyes.

'But I suppose you need to have this stupid money because you are a man and because your brothers are men too I suppose and because you have to look tough with them and so I will have to give you the money and then you will lose it all but you will be a very tough man and you won't mind and then I will hate you because you have no money and you don't mind even though you have holes in your shoes so I cannot see you.'

She was crying now. Big tears fell soundlessly from her trembling eyes. George stood up to find her a tissue. In an instant she was in his arms, her face buried in his chest. After a while, she stopped weeping and looked up at him. He held her gaze and bent down towards her. Who kissed whom first? Who knows? But, within a second, each was kissing the other, first on the mouth, then inside. Kiki's lips and tongue burned with passion. Her tiny body pressed into George's bulky frame. George hugged her with all the passion that years of longing had given him.

After a time, how long neither knew, they stepped back to look at one another. Kiki had stopped crying, but her cheeks were flushed and damp. George stepped forward again seeking to gather her up with renewed passion but she moved away.

'Now look what you have done, you beastly man,' she said, dabbing her face. 'I will have to start over now. Then we have to go and find your stupid money. Then we have to go and find some proper curtains. What do you think? Maybe pink? I have seen some oh-so-nice ones in that gorgeous little shop on the Fulham Road, but they are silk of course, so then we would need to get rid of these funny old sofas which would be all wrong. Oh, Georges, you are nothing but a problem to me.'

She whisked off into the bathroom. He was molten with feeling for her. But already he could sense her tripping away again, a kingfisher pursued by a bear.

In due course she emerged from the bathroom looking immaculate. She took George off to see her '*avocat*'. The avocat was a London solicitor retained under the terms of Kiki's trust fund with the near impossible responsibility for keeping some sort of hold over Kiki's purse strings. The solicitor approved the proposal gratefully. Kiki's London hotel bills were astronomical. There was, however, a problem. The solicitor was more or less obliged to meet any bills which Kiki ran up as long as the goods purchased were bought at a 'fair market value'. Unfortunately the nine months rent remaining on George's flat were valued at only £27,000 under the existing tenancy agreement. The solicitor, despite Kiki's despairing wails, insisted that he would be in breach of trust if he paid any more than this for the flat.

There was only one solution. George asked Kiki if she

wanted his car. Of course she wanted his car. She berated
him for ever having considered that she might not want
his car. She had no driver's licence (she admitted in
response to the solicitor's enquiry) but how could she
ever learn to drive if she wasn't even allowed a car?

And so the deal was done. George gave up his flat
and sold his car in exchange for a total of £47,000. The
money flew from Kiki's trust fund into George's account.
From George's account £36,000 sped into the Gissings
company account and from Gissings straight to David
Ballard's bank. The final transaction was cleared at four
o'clock on the Friday afternoon.

Kiki told George off for ruining her week, making
her see that beastly *avocat*, spending so long on the
telephone and making all the wrong choices when he'd
had his flat decorated the year before. George and Kiki
swept around the most expensive boutiques in Sloane
Street, the Kings Road and the Fulham Road ordering
items for the flat. At the rate she spent money, she
would get through another £50,000 within a matter of
weeks.

At two o'clock on Saturday afternoon, Kiki remembered she was meant to be at a cocktail party in New
York that evening and she shot off to the airport to
jump on the next Concorde. George saw her off. At the
fast-track customs channel, they stopped. They couldn't
delay a goodbye any further. Kiki turned to her companion, her face showing the signs of passionate struggle.

'Goodbye, Georges.'

'Kiki.'

George wanted to kiss again properly, as they had
done before. He couldn't believe that she didn't want to
too, but she shook her head and her troubled eyes were
begging him 'No'. She reached up to kiss him high up

on the cheek and hugged him as she hugged practically everyone she knew.

'Good luck with your horrid factory.'

'Bye. Don't . . . don't lose touch.'

She left him there, watching till she passed out of sight. George ached with longing. He wondered if he would ever see her again. He also wondered where he was going to spend the night.

13

Zack was depressed. He was working hard on stuff so boring it hurt. The Aberdeen Drilling deal, as expected, had run into the sand. Tominto Oil had put in a bid of £115 million and been politely told that its bid was too low but thanks so much for trying. It was goodbye and good riddance. The winning bidder hadn't yet closed the deal, but it hardly mattered. Whoever won, it wasn't Tominto. Zack's first deal was a washout. In climbing the ladder to a million quid he still hadn't put his foot on the first rung.

What was worse, he was beginning to realise something about his chosen profession. To make money in corporate finance you don't just have to be good, you have to be old. Chief executives making life and death decisions don't simply want wise heads, they want old ones. Forced to choose between the two, they'd pick the old one every time. It's not like that on the trading floor. In the markets, you can be old and grey, but if you bet wrong and the office boy bets right, then, before you know it, you'll be sweeping the floors and the office boy will be on the phone to the Long Island estate agents. Zack could be the most brilliant mind in the City of London, but without long years of experience he'd never make bonuses big enough to release his father's fortune. If he weren't careful, Zack wouldn't just be beaten by Matthew. He'd be humiliated.

And there was one final irritation. Every day he had to see Sarah, work with her, be professional, keep his hands off, not make love. He was as hopelessly in lust as he'd always been and he was being forced to sit and watch politely as she and her millions got married to some aristocratic lumphead. Zack was depressed.

It was eight o'clock in the evening and he was finishing up for the night. On his way out he walked by Sarah's desk. She was still there working, bent over a presentation, hair tucked behind her ears.

'Hi, Sarah.'

'Zack. Hi. On your way out?'

'Yes. I wondered if you'd like to come out for a beer?'

This was the first time either of them had suggested moving beyond careful professionalism into something like friendship. Sarah hesitated.

'Um. I'd like to, but I've some stuff to finish up. Robert's coming to pick me up in forty-five minutes.'

Robert Leighton, the fiancé. The obstacle. Zack sighed.

'OK. Some other time? Tomorrow? It's stupid you and me working together so closely and pretending we hardly know each other.'

'Yes, but let's be realistic. You would never have chosen me as your colleague and I wouldn't have chosen you. But that's how it is and so far it's worked. Why mess things up?'

Zack spread his hands. He didn't tell her, 'Because I'm filled with lust and I want your money.' Instead he said, 'A drink can't hurt. It's been years now. I've changed. I know I was difficult then, but it doesn't have to be that way now.'

'Not difficult, Zack. You were impossible.'

She was pushing him. In the old days, he would never have let himself be pushed. They were already on the brink of an argument. Zack defused things carefully.

'OK. I was impossible. I apologise. I was impossible and you were stubborn.'

His turn to challenge her. Would she acknowledge any fault? She nodded.

'Yes. I was stubborn. I still am. I haven't changed. I still like all the things I used to like. Hunting, balls, everything you loathe.'

'That's OK. You can murder every furry thing in England for all I care. It doesn't bother me now. It's Robert you have to share a life with. I'm just inviting you to share a drink.'

Sarah took a deep breath and looked at Zack. It felt like the first time they'd properly looked at each other in all this time. They hadn't changed much. He was tall, angular, dark, intense. She was fair, square-chinned, athletic, honest-looking. Physically, everything had always worked between them, the only thing that ever had.

'OK. A drink sometime. That'd be nice.'

'Good. Great. I'll hold you to that.'

They nodded at each other, Zack's cue to leave. But he couldn't tear himself away. His body fizzed with desire. Sarah had pulled her hair from behind her left ear and was fiddling absent-mindedly with the short brown strands. Zack watched. He knew Sarah. Playing with her hair meant she was thinking about sex.

'Working on anything interesting?' he asked, not because he wanted to know but because he wanted to stay.

Sarah laughed. 'Not unless you count tax loopholes as interesting. It's the sort of thing you'd probably be good at.'

'I'm interested already.'

111

'Well then, you'd better take a copy of this presentation and read as much as you want to. It's as boring as hell to me.'

Zack took the presentation that Sarah gave him and riffled through it. He felt a sense of gathering excitement.

'What's the idea?'

'It's all in there,' said Sarah, but Zack wasn't leaving. She pushed her chair back and began to explain. 'In every tax law, there's a loophole. The point of this game is to find ways of passing as much money through the loopholes as fast as you can, until the tax authorities catch you at it and stop you doing it.'

'And if they catch you?'

'Well, you're not doing anything illegal. In fact, you're following the law to the letter, you're just doing something completely different to what was originally intended. So when the taxmen discover their tax revenues are vanishing out of sight, they get a new law passed to block up the loophole. Then our tax experts put their twisted minds to work thinking up new ways to subvert the law. That's why you'd be good at it. You've got the most twisted mind of anyone I know.'

'And I can take a copy?' asked Zack, waving the presentation.

'Yes,' replied Sarah laughing. 'I've already said so. Just bring it back.'

Zack impulsively moved forward. He wasn't sure if he was trying to kiss Sarah on the cheek or on the mouth, but anyhow she moved in surprise and he ended up kissing her half on the mouth, half on her upper lip. It was awkward and stupid. He apologised for his clumsiness and rushed off to copy the presentation, excited as a six-year-old.

Corporate financiers need to be old and wise and grey. Tax dodgers don't. They just need to be right.

14

The factory shop had been cleared out. The museum exhibits which old Tom Gissing had lovingly pieced together lay shoved to one side, roughly covered by a dustsheet. George watched silently as the last of the workers filed in. There were no seats and the workforce, mostly men, stood, arms folded and muttering. Gissings wasn't just the biggest employer in Sawley Bridge, it was pretty much the only one. George didn't just own a factory. He controlled a community.

There was no platform, so George had had a Gissings desk pushed up against the wall. He sat on it and looked out at the sea of faces. Next to him stood Val Bartlett, old Tom Gissing's secretary, with a sheaf of papers they had spent six long weeks putting together. Her mouth was taut and thin-lipped, turned down at the corners. The muttering from the assembled workers had an aggressive edge. George felt nervous.

When everybody was present, the murmur died away. All eyes were on George, who clambered heavily on to the desk. At least the old-style Gissings quality should bear his weight. He had some notes in his pocket, but he didn't take them out. He knew what he wanted to say.

'Thank you all for coming. My name is George Gradley and I am the new owner of this company. What I want to do is to tell you how things stand and what needs to change.

'First, the good news. In the last twelve months, this company has sold one and a half million quids' worth of furniture. That means there are still plenty of people who like what we do enough to fork out for it.

'Now the bad news. We sold less last year than we did the year before, and less that year than the one

113

before that. In fact, sales have fallen every year for five years.

'I wouldn't mind too much if our costs had come down. But they haven't. They've gone up or stayed the same. As you all know, our costs are higher than our revenues. Much higher in fact. About two hundred thousand a year, and that's before interest.

'There might be some consolation if Gissings had been building for the future. But it hasn't. It's been building for the past. The factory extension is half-finished, but there's no cash to finish it. Meanwhile our product line hasn't changed in three years and it's a decade out of date. Our marketing brochures are terrible and our prices are uncompetitive. Our most loyal customers are starting to look elsewhere, and I don't blame them.

'All this would be bad, but not disastrous if we had time to put things right. But we don't. We owe the bank more than half a million pounds and we've got just under two months before the money's due. We don't have a chance of getting that much cash together in that space of time. But we do have a chance – a tiny one – of doing enough to persuade the bank that it should give us more time.

'I know none of you knows me. Probably nobody in this room likes me or wants me here. But I want you to know that I'm speaking the truth. You all know Val, my secretary. I've asked her to show those of you who are interested all the facts and figures. You can see anything you want to. Our sales, our costs, our debts, everything. She understands all of this as well as anyone. Better than me, in fact. So talk to her. This is your company. You have a right to understand what's going on.

'Any questions so far?'

George looked around. Nobody moved. It had been obvious to everybody that Gissings was in trouble, but nobody had ever told them how bad. George could tell that the workforce believed him. But trust was a different matter and the toughest part of the speech was still to come. He felt nervous but committed.

'So what are we going to do about it? Well, in the long term, if we get there, we're going to turn Gissings into a thriving, expanding company, with a healthy balance sheet, a bloody good product line and a fat order book. But right now, our aim is to survive and we can't do that with our costs the way they are. As of today, I am suspending thirty-five of you. Val will read out the names in a moment. I say suspending because I hope to take you back on as soon as I can. But that won't be much comfort to you because your pay cheques are stopping as of now and in all probability we'll go bust within a matter of months anyway. I owe you some redundancy money. Some of you, who have been with us longest, are owed quite a lot. Well, you're not going to get it, because we don't have it. You can take us to court if you want, and you'll win. But you won't get your money because by the time you get your award, this company will have been picked bare. I'm sorry, but that's how it is.'

Val stood beside him with the thirty-five names. Everybody in the sawmill would go. There was no point in a sawmill, when you could get better quality product delivered more cheaply. On the factory floor, everyone who had looked up and dawdled on George's first tour of inspection was going. Those who had stayed working were the lucky ones.

'As for the rest of you, I'm cutting your pay by fifteen percent. If any of you want to give up more than that for the good of the company, then I'll write your name in gold on the factory gates just as soon as we can afford the paint. I'm not allowed to cut your pay like that. Once again, you can take me to court, and you'll win. But you won't get any cash back and you won't have a job, because the company will be as dead as a doornail. For what it's worth, I don't intend to take one penny in pay, until this company has made enough money to cover its costs including interest. And I'm going to work my tits off to see that it does.

'Are there any questions?'

There was silence from the assembled company. Weak sunshine threaded its way through the dirty plate-glass windows. The yard beyond looked grey and empty. Standing on his desk, George felt exposed and vulnerable, but also renewed. He had said what needed saying, done what needed doing. He stayed standing. 'Any questions at all?'

The silence lasted half a minute or so. Then somebody at the back of the room cleared his throat.

'Why the fuck don't you just write a cheque to the fucking bank for the fucking money and leave us poor bastards alone?'

15

'Now try without the rails. Use your stick if you need to.'

The nurse was patient and kind. Helen Gradley let go of the wooden rail that ran along the wall towards the mirror and stepped forwards, her stick thrust in front of her, not for support so much as proof that the ground in front continued solid. One step. Two step. Three step. The nurse and Josephine counted them out as Helen watched her reflection grow larger.

'Well done, Mum. You can do it. Four more steps.'

It was an encouragement too far. Helen leaned forwards, letting the point of her cane slide away from her. There was a moment of suspense as competing forces tussled for supremacy, then gravity played the ace of trumps and Helen Gradley and her stick fell crashing to the floor. She began to cry. A rising smell warned that her bladder control had come tumbling down as well.

'Oh, dear,' said the nurse. 'Bumps-a-daisy. Best call it a day.' To Josephine she added: 'You often get incontinence with a stroke, I'm afraid. I'll get some stuff to clean up.'

She left the room, briskly efficient. Josephine let her mum continue sitting, just rubbed the back of her neck for reassurance. Her mother's recovery was proving painfully slow. No one at the physical therapy centre had suggested it directly, but Josie caught an undertone which hinted that Helen could be trying harder. She didn't disagree. One of the doctors had proposed a further trial of antidepressants and Josephine had readily agreed.

She looked at her watch. Time to go, back to her job as secretary in a big London bank. Her employers were amazingly generous, giving her time off to be with her mum when she needed it, but there were limits. Josie picked up the cane from the floor and tossed it from hand to hand. Part of her handled it as it was meant to be handled: a cane, a mobility aid, a support for the weak. But part of her felt the stick as a man might feel it: a hockey stick, a baseball bat, a sword.

Winter 1998–99

Two months into the training programme. Long days of economics, bond maths, computer analysis. Evenings of study and developing friendships. Manhattan cold, but getting colder. The park empty of leaves, stores crowded with merchandise. The weekends are full of skating, window-shopping, Christmas lights, phone calls home.

It is 14 December 1998. There are 942 days to go until Bernard Gradley's deadline.

1

Could it be that Matthew was falling in love? If so, it would be a first. Until now, Matthew's love life had been like dining off sushi: plenty of variety, but nothing more than a mouthful. And now? Well, it was too soon to say and they were still just friends, but Sophie was charming, clever, ambitious, cool-headed and she liked Matthew. What was more, she was beautiful and dressed like a dream, enough to satisfy – more than satisfy – Matthew's not inconsiderable vanity. He wooed her carefully, attentive but not pushy.

Tonight he was taking her to a trattoria in Little Italy.

He'd make his move then. And for the first time in his prolific romantic career, he really felt anxious about the outcome. Could it be love?

Perhaps love or perhaps just nerves. Because before evening came, Matthew was to face the toughest test of the course so far, when the first of the trading games took place. Calling them games was a joke, really. They were more serious than any exam. You'd never make an outstanding trader without knowing the bond maths, the economics and all the rest of it. But if you got one hundred percent in all of that and still couldn't trade, you could kiss your dream home in Long Island goodbye.

The game was simple enough. The students were divided into three groups. One group were investors, the second salespeople, the third traders. The investors each had a pile of fictional money and fictional government bonds. Their aim was to invest their assets to make as much money as they could. The investors worked alone and competed against each other.

The salespeople and traders worked in pairs. Each pair represented an investment bank. The banks started with no government bonds and just a small amount of money. Their object, too, was to make money. As much as they could, as fast as they could. These are the rules of Wall Street.

As it happened, Matthew was to be a trader, Sophie a salesperson. They teamed up, to Matthew's delight, calling themselves the Banque Entente Cordiale. They were competing against each of the twenty or so other investment bank pairs in the game.

There were just a couple of other rules. Investors were not allowed to trade with each other, only with the banks. Suppose, for instance, that Fareshti (the podgy oil princess who played an investor) wanted to buy a particular government bond – say, the bond falling due

119

in 2017. She'd need to contact a number of salespeople to check the price they were selling at. When she found a good price, she'd agree the deal and scribble out a ticket to record it.

And where did Sophie get her prices from? Simple. She got them from Matthew. And where did Matthew get his prices? Simple again: he made them up. But when Matthew quoted a price, he had to try to pick a price fine enough to win the deal, but fat enough to leave a margin for the Banque Entente Cordiale. Remember: any trading floor is just a glorified bureau de change. If Matthew thought he could sell a bond at $103, he'd be happy to buy it at $102. He didn't care that he was only making a buck. The biggest houses on Long Island belong to people who just skim a few tenths of a cent on every trade. They just do a lot of trades.

There was one other ingredient. A course tutor sat by a flip-chart, and every now and then turned a page to reveal a news item. It might be about consumer spending, an election result, or the death of a president. With each announcement, the market reacted. Investors who were sitting pretty one moment could watch their assets tumble or soar as prices shifted.

And that was that. No other rules. At the end of the game, everyone's assets were counted up. And, as the T-shirt philosophers of New York put it, he who dies with the most wins. Roses and champagne were awarded to the winning investor and the winning investment bank. There were no penalties for failure, except one. The penalty was that the trading games were the most important tests of the course, and the course had a failure rate of one in three. The Lion of Wall Street would not go hungry.

The game was about to start. Sophie and Matthew had worked out some ground rules, but it wasn't like an exam, you couldn't revise for the future. Matthew put his mouth to Sophie's ear.

'Good luck,' he whispered.

'Bonne chance, Monsieur Gradley. Good luck.'

A whistle blew and the game began.

The students were arranged in three rows. The investors sat along one side of the room, while the salespeople sat in another row down the middle. The traders sat opposite their salespeople, but they weren't required to stay there. If they wanted to get up, to mix with the other traders in search of a deal, they were welcome to do so.

At first though, there was no movement and not much noise. The students had been brought up to be polite and, for a while, decorum reigned. A few investors, thinking they should invest some of their cash in bonds, asked a couple of salespeople for prices. The salespeople sorted out a price with their traders. Any haggling was done with apologies and laughter. The traders stayed seated.

Then the tutor in charge of the flip-chart turned a page. The announcement was visible to everybody. GREENSPAN BULLISH ON INFLATION PROSPECTS. Alan Greenspan was the head of the powerful US Federal Reserve. If he thought inflation would stay low, then bonds should rise as investors bought into positive economic prospects.

The traders quickly changed the prices they were giving their salespeople, but not all traders thought alike. The quiet equilibrium changed. Investors started shouting out their requirements to the salespeople. The noise increased.

The salespeople now asked their traders for prices several times a minute. The traders knew that prices were constantly shifting and worried about getting out of line. They began to leave their seats to check out what others were doing or to deal directly with other traders. When their salespeople needed a new price, they had to yell to get their attention. The volume of trades increased. The room grew noisier.

Then, unannounced and unnoticed by half the room, the flip-chart was turned to reveal another message. CONSUMER SPENDING SIGNIFICANTLY HIGHER THAN EXPECTED. So perhaps Greenspan had been wrong. Perhaps inflation was more of a risk. Bond prices needed to come down again. By how much? There was no right answer, no wrong answer. There was only the answer of the market.

Sophie shouted at Matthew to check he had seen the message. He had, but he hollered his thanks for the tip-off. Sophie was taking more orders now, building up the flow of deals. It was good business, but demanding. Matthew wanted to avoid sitting on a big stack of bonds in case he was caught short by a change in the market. So for every deal that Sophie brought him, he had to do one or two more to square his position again.

The flip-chart messages came faster now.

'Give me a price to buy the 2017s and a price to sell the 2012s,' shouted Sophie.

Matthew thought on his feet. Investors didn't wait long when the market was moving so fast.

'I'll buy the 2017s at $99. I don't want to sell the 2012s, because I'm short of them as it is. Ask $105 for them. No one in their right mind will take that price.'

Matthew knew that a decent investor could get the 2012 bonds much cheaper from elsewhere.

'OK. 2017s to buy at $99. 2012s to sell at $105.'

Matthew raised his thumb in agreement. Another rule of theirs: always confirm the price. Other pairs hadn't agreed to do this and got into arguments as misunderstandings spread.

Meanwhile Matthew plunged back into the throng

of traders. By acting fast he could buy bonds off one trader and sell them back to another at a slightly higher price. It was tough to do. Decent traders understood the market and cut out the middleman, but not everyone was that slick. Matthew noticed a couple of the Japanese in particular were struggling.

He tried to remember their names. Sophie prompted him: Takashi and Atsuo. Matthew greeted them warmly amidst the frenzy and made some little joke about the swelling chaos. He stayed close and helped them out a couple of times in small ways. In the bond markets, real or fictional, no friend is better than a stupid friend.

He was interrupted again by Sophie.

'Matthew. We've done both deals. Bought 100 lots of 2017s at $99. Sold 200 lots of the 2012s at $105. I've updated the accounts.'

Matthew broke off what he was doing and leaped across to Sophie's desk.

'Jesus, Sophie. Who did these trades? The 2012s are trading at $100. We've made $5 clear profit on each bond.'

In a game where the profit margin seldom rose above a dollar, $5 was wealth indeed.

'Fareshti,' said Sophie. 'I think she's finding it tough.'

They looked across to Fareshti, who was sitting bolt upright in her chair. Her face was pale and her eyes open in a blank stare. Her pad of paper lay face down on the desk and she clearly hadn't a clue what her position was. While Matthew and Sophie watched, she pulled off her heavy gold earrings and laid them next to the thick gold necklace which already lay on the desk. She looked as though the jewellery had been weighing down on her, crushing her even.

'I spy with my little eye an investor who needs the help of the Banque Entente Cordiale,' said Matthew.

Sophie glanced at him.

'That's not fair. She doesn't know what she's doing any more.'

'I don't know about you, but my nearest and dearest forgot to provide me with a few billion dollars' worth of oil. I propose to earn my living as a trader instead.'

Sophie half-smiled in incomplete agreement. '*C'est vrai. D'accord*. But I don't like it.'

She called to Fareshti, who woke up pleased to hear a friendly voice amidst the din.

'Give me your pad,' said Sophie. 'Let me help you get up-to-date.'

A grateful Fareshti tossed her pad over to Sophie who bent over it with her calculator. The princess, meanwhile, put her hands to her neck and massaged it, staring down at the heap of gold in front of her. Drilling a few metres down into the desert sands was simpler than this. But her parents thought she should have a Western business education and this was it. She watched Sophie gratefully.

After a while, Sophie rose and handed the pad back to Fareshti, who held it uncertainly and without looking at it.

'I think you may have too many of the long bonds and you're short of the shorter maturities,' said Sophie.

Fareshti was totally blank.

'I think you should sell 150 units each of the 2012s and 2017s and buy a similar number of 1999s and 2005s. We can do that for you if you want.'

Fareshti nodded. Sophie was so kind and she didn't shout. Sophie turned back to find Matthew who was lost again in the hubbub.

'Fareshti would like . . .' Sophie began.

She was hinting that Matthew's prices could be way off market. He pretended to think deeply and called back some prices which would allow him $10 of profit on each bond.

'But that's the very best I can do,' he yelled. 'And I can't hold those prices for long.'

Fareshti was oblivious to the charade. She nodded through the trades which Sophie proposed and let her write them down. The princess removed her thick gold bangles and watch and laid them down on the mounting pile of gold. She massaged her wrists.

The game went on. The flip-chart turned. The chaos rose to a crescendo and hung there.

Fareshti mostly held back from doing any more trades. But every now and then she shook herself and did another trade as though to prove she could play the game as well as anyone. Every trade she did, she did through Sophie. Every time, Matthew took $10 or $15 profit on each bond. At one point, Sophie protested.

'We've done enough.'

'Sophie, for Fareshti this is only a game. For us, it's life or death. You won't be feeling sorry for her if you're kicked off this course for underperforming. Besides, Fareshti's not the only one to be taken for a ride here.'

Matthew spoke with some certainty on this last point. Takashi-san and Atsuo-san were also contributing handsomely to the Banque Entente Cordiale's profits.

'OK. But remember, we're already doing very nicely. We don't need to gouge the last dollar.'

Finally, three hours after the game had started, a second whistle blew. Game over.

A stunned Fareshti put her hand to her head and withdrew her last remaining ornament, a heavy gold hair clip. It joined the rest of the glittering pile on her desk. Otherwise, she hardly moved.

The course tutors gathered up all the trading tickets, which would be processed by a clerical team over the next few hours. Around four o'clock, the results would be announced and prizes awarded. But Matthew and Sophie already knew their result. They had started the game with $5000. They had ended with $32,420.

And Sophie, as Fareshti's trusted advisor, knew her result too. As an investor, Fareshti had started the game with a much larger amount of money – $100,000 to be precise. She had finished with $68,920. The Banque Entente Cordiale had by no means pocketed all of Fareshti's missing $31,080, but it had had more than its fair share.

Takashi and Atsuo left the room congratulating themselves on their first taste of trading. On their way out, they took care to thank Matthew profusely for his help. Neither of the two Japanese was aware that they had lost considerably more money than they had started with. Nor were they aware how much of it had ended in Matthew's pocket.

As the room cleared and the noise died away, Matthew and Sophie looked at each other properly. It seemed ages since they had done more than glance at each other or yell messages across the din.

Even after three hours of mayhem, Sophie looked flawless. Even in the thick of the game, she had kept her cool. She had dealt calmly with the questions that flew at her from all sides, while at the same time accurately updating the bank's accounts. She had been the only person in the room, male or female, to have kept their jacket on throughout the game. But now the turmoil was over, she threw her jacket on to the ground beside her. She leaned her head back as far as it would go and ran her hands through her hair. Then she whirled forwards again and grabbed Matthew by the arms.

'We've won, Matthew. I think we've won.'

'I think we have.'

She stayed holding on to his arms. Matthew moved his hands gently, ever so gently, to her waist. Her lips parted, but not in reproof.

They kissed. If the whole world had folded away around them, they wouldn't have noticed or cared. They kissed again and again.

'Oh, Mrs Gradley. We must win more often.'

'Indeed, Mr Gradley, I think we should.'

The Banque Entente Cordiale did win the champagne and the roses, notching up $11,250 more than its nearest rival. Scott Petersen, the tall Californian, was the winning investor, with $121,870. The worst performing investor was Fareshti Al Shahrani. Her eyes were full of tears, but she sat upright and proud, as a princess should. She continued to believe that Sophie had rescued her from a worse fate, and she thanked her again as the class disbanded.

Matthew and Sophie did not visit Little Italy that night. They returned to Matthew's apartment, called out for pizza and celebrated their win in a way that satisfied even Matthew's most ardent dreams.

2

Zack burst into Hanbury's office. Hanbury, who was married, was on the phone to his mistress and was less than pleased to be interrupted. He waved Zack out of the room, but Zack, typically, took this as a signal to sit down. Hanbury finished his call abruptly, 'Look, I'll see you at the opera tonight. Don't be late,' then turned to Zack. 'What do you want?'

'I've got a way to rescue the Aberdeen Drilling deal. I think we can get back into it.'

'We've already lost. The deal's over. And I don't want you bursting in –'

'Yes, but we bid too low. I know it's late, but if we came back with a bid, say ten million higher, even twelve –'

'Oh, don't be stupid. We've lost. The other guys won. Our fee went down the pan. It's over. Now, will you –'

'But you haven't heard my idea. Listen. Tominto Oil lost a lot of money drilling unsuccessfully for oil in Nigeria. In total, it threw away sixty million bucks without tax relief. Aberdeen Drilling, on the other hand, has a profitable subsidiary out there –'

'I don't want to know. Shut up and get out.'

'What do you mean, you don't want to know? I'm bringing you the solution here.'

Hanbury had a quick temper and Zack's mistimed intrusion guaranteed a vintage display. The senior banker stood up, incensed.

'This is the last time I'm going to tell you. The deal is dead and I don't need your kindergarten tax scams. Now get out of my room and stay out.'

Zack had worked hard on his tax idea. His concept was that under Nigerian tax laws, Tominto's losses could be used to offset Aberdeen Drilling's profits. After intensive research, he was pretty sure it could be done, and had fondly imagined that Hanbury would be only too pleased to get back into the race. Zack was suddenly angry. Angry, and out of control.

'Jesus Christ! I come in here with a good idea – an idea to save a deal and earn a fee – and you are too pompous, too arrogant, too fucking stupid to even hear it. I don't know why I bothered.'

Zack turned to go, but Hanbury flew to the door and flung it shut. Hanbury put his face a couple of inches away from Zack's and hissed at him.

'How dare you say that? How dare you? If you want to continue another day in this bank, you will put a letter of apology on my desk by nine o'clock tomorrow morning. A full and complete apology. If I am satisfied – *if* I am – then we will talk with personnel about getting you transferred to an area where you won't come into contact with clients, because I'm damned if I'll ever trust you with a client again. Is that perfectly clear?'

If Zack had been able to think clearly, he would have been best advised to apologise profusely, to beg forgiveness on his knees if he had to. Piers St George Hanbury was Coburg's most successful dealmaker, and whatever he wanted, the bank would give him. But, as Sarah Havercoombe for one could testify, Zack wasn't the sort to think clearly when he was angry. He leaped to Hanbury's desk.

'I'll give you a letter of apology, right here and right now.'

He grabbed pen and paper, and wrote in capitals: 'DEAR MR HANBURY, I AM VERY SORRY THAT YOU ARE SUCH A POMPOUS DICKHEAD. YOURS MOST SINCERELY, ZACK GRADLEY.'

Leaving the letter on Hanbury's desk and shaking with anger, Zack sped from the room.

He left the bank in a foul mood. The row seemed pretty much fatal. If Hanbury carried out his threat to prevent him from seeing clients – to move him to the so-called back office – then Zack's career would be killed stone dead. At first the gap in pay was small, the difference in responsibility hardly noticeable. But as time moved on, and the front office staff made it to associate director and then just director, their peers in the back office were wondering if they would ever make it beyond manager. A well-regarded thirty-year-old in the front office would be deeply upset if his end-of-year bonus was less than his already generous annual salary. His back office colleague took home a

129

thousand pounds extra at Christmas and was grateful.

Zack left the building, eyes on the ground, collar raised against a thin December sleet, and stepped blindly out on to the zebra crossing leading to Bank tube station. A silver-green Jaguar, which had been driving too fast along the little street, squealed to a halt, skidding in the wet.

'Screw you, you goddamn idiot. Look where you're going.' A distinguished-looking man with swept-back silver hair stuck his head out of the car window, the better to yell at Zack.

'Screw you yourself, you geriatric shit-for-brains,' yelled Zack, pleased to have an opportunity to vent his feelings.

'Next time I won't apply the brakes, you jerk.'

The man in the car was really shouting. His silver hair had come away from his head and shook like an angry mane. His accent was mid-Atlantic. Zack couldn't tell if he was a Brit who had just come back from a long stay in the States, or a Yank who'd been in London too long. Either way, he looked like a viscount and swore like a trooper. Zack couldn't help liking him. Zack yelled something obscene and stomped off.

He felt better for the row. Sod Hanbury. Zack would never apologise. Besides, he'd had a better idea.

3

David Ballard slowed his black BMW. Meeting a herd of sheep on the road up to Sawley Bridge, he had been forced to squeeze up on to a muddy verge, and one side of the car was spattered with heavy clay. It was a freezing afternoon, and by the time Ballard got home, the mud would be frozen solid. The car took a bigger bite out of his salary than he could justify, but he drove twenty-five thousand miles a year visiting clients, and the BMW gave pleasure with every one. He'd wash the paintwork down that evening.

Ballard drove slowly into the factory yard. Armed with ladders and paintpots, a couple of workmen, swearing at the cold, were getting ready to paint over the sign above the gates. Ballard was angry. Very angry.

He brought the car to a stop in the yard, next to the only other vehicle, a Transit van marked 'Gissings Modern Furniture'. They'd be painting over that next, thought Ballard and marched angrily upstairs to George's office.

George was at his desk, immersed in paperwork.

'Hello, there,' he said on seeing his visitor. 'You should have let me know you were coming and I'd have got that five hundred grand ready. As it is, you'll need to wait a little longer.'

Ballard was in no mood for jokes.

'What the bloody hell is this I hear about you changing the name of the company?'

George was taken aback. Ballard was a shrewd but genial man, with twinkling eyes and a chuckle never far from his lips. He usually looked and acted like everyone's favourite uncle. Not now. George responded coldly.

'I don't see what that's got to do with you, as long as we comply with the terms of our loan.'

'Don't give me that shit. Is it true or isn't it?'

'For your information, yes, it is true.'

Ballard was seething. The red of his face contrasted oddly with the iron grey of his hair. His voice was furious, but controlled.

'I saw Tom Gissing last night at the Rotary Christmas shindig. He told me you were changing the company's name. It was the only thing that still mattered to him and you knew it. I honestly think he wouldn't have minded the insulting way you bought the company, if you had brought it back to life with his name on it. In fact, he'd have been the first to thank you. As it was, he spent the whole damn evening crying on my shoulder. I called him this morning to check he was OK. No answer. I went round to see him and found him dead. Heart attack.' Ballard paused, before delivering the final accusation. 'That attack was your fault and God damn you for it.'

White-faced, George rose, went to a filing cabinet and drew out a piece of paper. He tossed it across the table to Ballard.

'Here's our application to change the company name. We're changing the name from The Gissings Modern Furniture Company (Limited) to Gissings Furniture Limited. The original name is hopelessly out-of date, but I've never even dreamt of getting rid of the founder's name. Nor will I now he's dead.'

'And what about the sign above the gates? That just says Gissings Furniture as it is.'

George shook his head.

'I cut everybody's wages by fifteen percent and said if anyone gave up more than that, I'd write their names in gold up above the gates. My secretary gave up thirty percent, so her name's going up, just like I said. The Gissings Furniture bit is staying put.'

Ballard breathed out heavily and stroked his moustache with his hand. His face changed back from red to pink.

'I'm sorry,' he said. 'I shouldn't have accused you until I knew the facts. I take it back and I apologise.'

He extended a hand, which George accepted. 'Don't worry about it. I don't blame you for being upset. I'm sorry to hear about Tom Gissing. I still hope to make him proud.'

'Yes. I hope you do too. I do apologise, George. It was hasty of me.'

'Yeah, well, I suppose I am partly to blame,' said George. 'I've been playing my cards fairly close to my chest here, so it's only natural that rumours get started. Fact is, I'd like to get more people involved with waking up this corpse, because it's more than one man can do by himself. The trouble is, I don't seem to have anyone's trust. It's like pulling teeth all day long and I honestly don't know what's the matter.'

'Bit of advice to you, George,' said Ballard, winking. 'Never tell your bank manager when you're having a hard time. He might get scared and call in his loan. But you're alright. I assume you'll be getting your hands on your dad's cash any day now. Good job, given that your loan extension runs out in less than a month.'

Ballard's face had changed and George could no longer read his expression. There was something odd about it. George didn't spend time wondering. He'd felt bad about deceiving Ballard and now seemed as good a time as any to come clean.

'David, there's something I need to tell you.'

'Not bad news, I hope.' Ballard's face was secretive, laughing.

'Well . . . it's not good.'

'Don't mind what it is, so long as you pay the loan off in a month. That's what we agreed, isn't it?'

'Yes that's what we agreed –'

'Well, that's OK then.'

'David, I'm not getting the money. The will . . . it's a long story. But there's no money.'

'No money?'

'Not a penny piece. I suppose you'll have to close us down, will you?'

Ballard's expression was emerging into the open now. He was chuckling.

'Don't worry. If there's a delay, just get me a letter from the executors.'

'I can't . . . what's funny? This isn't bloody funny.'

'D'you know who your dad's executors are?'

'The solicitor, Earle, is one of them, I think. I don't know about the others.'

'You think your dad might have thought of his oldest friend in the banking industry perhaps?'

Ballard was laughing at George, as George slowly put two and two together.

'You're an executor? You knew I didn't have any money? Then why did you let me buy the company? Why didn't you put it into receivership as you'd planned?'

'Two reasons. First one is, I got thirty-six grand out of you.'

'And the second?'

'Second, I figured that Gissings was so far gone, it'd take a genius to save it. Your dad would have saved it.' Ballard shrugged. It was the bank's money, after all, not his. 'I thought I'd take a chance on you.'

George was stunned, stunned and flattered. He slowly worked Ballard's logic through to its conclusion.

'So you won't close us down when we can't pay you?'

Ballard shrugged. Once again, the banker had taken over from the genial uncle.

'I may close you down or I may not. It depends on how the business is going and which way I expect to get the most money back. But so far, George, you're doing OK.'

134

4

Nine o'clock came and went and there was no sign of Zack. Hanbury and the two men from personnel looked at their watches and tutted.

Hanbury sat in the corner making incessant phone calls. The two personnel people chatted and fiddled with two pieces of paper which lay in front of them. One was the sheet of A4 on which Zack had written his message of 'apology' to Hanbury the night before. The other was a letter, which began: 'Dear Zachary, we regret to inform you that your employment with Coburg's Bank plc has been terminated with immediate effect.' The letter was not signed.

Finally, forty minutes late, Zack arrived. He hadn't shaved. It looked like he hadn't slept, and he certainly hadn't changed his clothes or showered. He smelled of alcohol. Hanbury, experienced in these things, guessed it was champagne. The older of the two men from personnel waved Zack to a chair.

'Now, Zack, we've had a long talk with Piers here, and heard his version of events yesterday. We also have – er – a document you wrote last night. Now, we want to be reasonable about this . . .'

'Well, I'm sure Piers and I agree on what happened,' said Zack. 'He screwed up a major deal with an important client and refused to listen when I came up with a way to rescue it. I assume he's come to apologise.'

The two men from personnel looked at each other. Hanbury stared into space. He was going to enjoy this. The man from personnel tried again.

'Now, Zack, be sensible. We haven't made any final decisions about your future, and if you behave sensibly now, I'm sure we can find an area suited to your talents.'

'Uh-huh. What did you have in mind? The catering department? Or was it the loo-cleaning team?'

The man from personnel pushed the unsigned redundancy letter across the desk.

'This isn't effective until it's signed. You are at an early stage in your career and you don't want to blow it all up now. A full and frank apology will give you a second chance that you're lucky to have. I doubt whether you're cut out for a front office job, but if you are, we'll give you the chance to prove it. We need somebody to beef up the settlements desk and somebody with your abilities could do very well there. I must warn you though, your last chance is about to expire.'

Hanbury was loving this. The way he saw it, Zack had no choice but to take the offer. He'd urged personnel to make the offer, because he thought Zack's humiliation would be more complete that way, locked up in a dead-end job without prospects. And if Zack stayed with Coburg's, Hanbury could keep an eye on things. He'd make sure Zack never escaped to the front office, make sure Zack was always the last to be promoted, the last to get a bonus.

Zack had been right. Hanbury was not the cooling off type. He planned to imprison Zack for the rest of his working life, and he, Piers Hanbury, would relish every second.

Zack quickly scanned the letter. Immediate termination. Six months' salary tax free. The services of an outplacement agency for up to twelve months. It was a good package. Coburg's hired and fired as much as anyone else these days, but they still aimed to be decent about it. Zack paused for a long while, then turned to look at Hanbury. Hanbury looked straight into the younger man's eyes and gloated openly.

'I withdraw the words I wrote about you yesterday,' began Zack.

'Quite right,' Hanbury smirked. 'Settlements will suit you to a T. I'm sure you'll enjoy the challenge.'

Without altering his expression, Zack continued. 'On second thoughts, I'm not remotely sorry that you're a pompous dickhead. You're such an ugly sod that nothing else would really suit you.'

There was silence round the room. Hanbury was visibly astounded. The man from personnel laboriously withdrew an antique fountain pen and signed the redundancy letter. He shook it dry and slipped it across to Zack.

'You are a very foolish young man. You will live to regret this.'

Zack grabbed the letter.

'This is binding, right? Irrevocable?'

'That's right.'

'Six months' salary, tax free, no questions asked?'

The man from personnel nodded.

'Good. Then you won't be needing this. Merry Christmas.'

So saying, Zack took a sheet of paper from his pocket. He tore it in two, down the fold. He dropped both halves on the table and walked out of the room, without so much as glancing back.

Piers Hanbury put the two torn pieces of paper together. It was a letter from Zack to personnel. The text read simply:

As I have just been offered a superior job in a superior bank on a superior salary and with a significant signing bonus, I feel obliged to tender my resignation with immediate effect. For the record, I have not enjoyed working with Coburg's. I do not respect its leadership. And I shall look forward to competing vigorously and successfully against it in years to come.

The letter was not signed. Piers Hanbury read it through slowly, then walked out of the room without a word. The two men from personnel read it through, too. They read it a second time, then the older man picked up the two pieces of paper, walked over to the dustbin and dropped them in. Really! Sometimes he felt he no longer understood the City these days.

5

It was a vile December morning. Cloud wrapped the village and the factory with it. Everything was clammy and cold. The gunge covering the factory yard was frozen with a sort of oily crust. From the moors, a north wind whipped down and snuck its way through Gissings' decaying windows. It was a grim and depressing place to work. A grim and depressing way to earn a living, especially if you didn't draw a salary and your current account was written in shrill red capitals.

George started work early, and punctually at eight thirty loud footsteps down the corridor alerted him to Val's return. She marched in, dressed in the kind of tweed they wrap horses in. Square and crudely cut, her suit brought out her shape to perfection, thought George unkindly. The contrast between her and Kiki was so extreme, George could hardly help comparing them mentally every time he saw Val or thought of Kiki. Nowadays, both happened often.

'Are you taking the piss?' she asked George directly. She'd seen her name above the gate, then.

'No,' said George. 'Anyone with your degree of loyalty to this company deserves recognition. If this company had any cash, I'd happily give you some of it. But since I can't do that, I'll do what else I can.'

'I don't want your pathetic little gifts,' spat Val. 'Anything I do isn't for your benefit and it certainly isn't so that I can win gold stars like some schoolchild.'

'I know, Val. I don't want to fight. If you ask me to, I'll have them paint over the sign again right away. I just wanted to keep my promise first. But there's something more important. I don't know whether you've heard, but you ought to know. Tom Gissing died of a heart attack the night before last. He died quietly, it seems. I'm very sorry.'

George wasn't prepared for the reaction he got to this news. Val's normally strong features collapsed. She sat down on George's desk, knocking papers to the floor, and wept, her deep-set eyes flooding her wonky face. George offered her a handkerchief, which she took.

After a while, she stood up. She struggled to compose herself, but George interrupted her. 'Don't worry about today, Val. Do whatever you need to do. Take time off. Come back when you're ready. Just let me know when to expect you.'

'Probably never,' she responded distantly. 'There's no reason for me to stay here on a stupid salary working to save a three-quarters dead company, if Tom Gissing isn't even around to appreciate the results.'

'How can you say that? What about all the workers here who rely on the place for work? What about their families? What about the company itself?' George was genuinely appalled. Christ, if even Val Bartlett was deserting him, he hadn't much hope with the rest.

Val jerked as though stung. 'How dare you? How dare

you?' she hissed. 'When Tom Gissing said that sort of thing he meant it from the bottom of his well-meaning heart. When you say that, it makes me puke.'

'Jesus, Val. What have I done that's so bad? Don't I work hard enough? Aren't I trying to do the right things here? Is there anything more that I could possibly do for this place?'

'Of course there bloody is. Why don't you open your wallet, pay off the bank, restore people's salaries and give jobs back to the people you've fired? I know costs need to be cut, but the way you've done it is just revolting for a man as rich as you.'

'As rich as me? Are you off your head?'

'As rich as Bernard Gradley's son. That's right. I don't know how many millions you're worth. And I don't know why you're pissing your life away here. But you make me sick and I'm not coming back.'

She turned to go, but George grabbed her by the arm. She would have protested, but George's face was stone and his grip steel. He pulled her out of the office.

They walked downstairs, through the reception area and out into the frozen yard. The only vehicle there was the Gissings Transit van, which George had commandeered shortly after taking over. The van hardly ever left the yard, but George refused everybody the use of it all the same. George went to the back of the van, unlocked its doors and flung them open.

Inside was a mattress and bedding. A paraffin lamp swung from a hook in the ceiling. A camping stove and utensils lay next to a few tins of food and an elderly loaf of bread. A jerry can of water and an enamel bowl marked the beginning and end of the van's sanitary arrangements. A furniture rail behind the driver's seat carried a rack of George's designer kit. Suits, jackets, trousers and shirts. The place had the look and the smell of long occupation. A water spill from the morning had turned to ice on the floor.

'As rich as Bernard Gradley's son,' he said. 'Welcome to the castle.'

He swung the doors back shut, but, on a gesture from Val, didn't lock them. He turned and walked back upstairs to his office. Val didn't return, and after about half an hour George wandered to the front of the building to see what had become of her.

She was still by the van along with a group of twenty or so workers. More were coming and others leaving on their way back to the factory floor. George realised that for one short hour his van was going to be the region's top-ranking tourist attraction, with Val Bartlett acting as proprietor and guide. He went back to work, but couldn't concentrate.

About fifty minutes later, Val returned. Her broad face was unsmiling, but there was laughter in her eyes.

'I don't think you'll have quite the same problem in getting cooperation from now on,' she said. 'Especially after one of the lads found one of your bank statements underneath your mattress.'

'I hope you charged admission. At fifty pence a peek, I'd have got enough to keep going another week.'

The rest of the day passed busily. For the first time, George sensed real enthusiasm from the workers. A committee working to update the product range was suddenly brimful of ideas and creativity, when previously its meetings had passed in stubborn opposition to every whiff of change. Old Gissing had been right. These people did know their jobs. They loved furniture and it showed. For almost the first time, George felt that buying Gissings had been a pound well spent.

At the end of the day, George and Val walked downstairs. They were, as often, the last to leave, just as they were always among the earliest to arrive. It was a clear night and already freezing. It would be savagely cold. George walked up to the back door of his van. For the first time, he didn't need to pretend he had somewhere else to go. He threw open the rear doors.

'I'd invite you in for a drink,' he said, 'but you know how it is.'

The elves and the pixies had come while George had been at work. The van was tidied top to bottom. Somebody had constructed a bed frame to hold the mattress. Beneath the bed, two drawers held the clobber which had been lying around the floor. A simple table held the camping stove and a tinsel-draped sprig of pine standing in a red-painted pot. There was a six-pack of beer, and beneath a wrapping of newspaper, George could see a pie dish containing something meaty and hot. With a touch of humour, somebody had pinned an old Gissings marketing catalogue to one of the battens running down the side of the van. 'The Thunderer! A desk for today!'

George was moved to the point of tears. It had been a hard and lonely time since his father died, and for the first time someone had stretched out a helping hand. He turned to Val to see if this had been done at her instigation, but she was as surprised as he was.

'Well,' George commented, once he had found his voice. 'Someone's keen to show off their carpentry skills. Gissings' spirit and all that.'

'Gissings' spirit or not,' said Val, 'you're not stopping here any longer.'

'I beg your pardon?'

'Think I want to work for a gypsy? You're coming home with me, especially as it's Christmas soon. You can park yourself in my lounge until you think of somewhere better to go.'

George would have protested, but he couldn't. Val had grasped his upper arm in a formidable grip of her own and frog-marched him to her battered Metro. They drove off leaving the Transit door swinging open in the wind.

6

It was a dingy Christmas, that first Christmas. Helen was in a worse way than usual. She'd managed to swallow half a dozen Valium a couple of days earlier because she liked the lift they gave her. But the biochemical pendulum was relentless and by Christmas Day itself she was experiencing all the withdrawal symptoms of one of the world's most immediately addictive substances. She wept and was irritable and exaggerated the extent of her disability.

Josie sat in the front room playing patience with her, as George and Matthew contrived to burn the roast potatoes (George through forgetfulness, Matthew from jet lag), while Zack, unbelievably, was on the phone to work.

'Your new employers . . .' said George, searching for the name.

'Weinstein Lukes,' said Zack.

'Yeah, whatever. Do they ever give you a day off?'

'Not so far, but you never know. Besides, these days I'm working mostly on oil and gas deals, so a lot of our clients are Middle Eastern. They like to get a call on Christmas Day. It makes them feel special to know they're screwing up an investment banker's holiday.'

'How the hell did you get the job?' asked Matthew, who had been dying to ask the question ever since hearing of Zack's switch, but had been trying to restrain himself, for fear of giving away his envy.

143

Zack shrugged. 'Natural genius,' he said, and began to make another call. Matthew bit his lip while George went back to scraping the burnt bits off the potatoes.

George felt deeply outclassed. Matthew had jetted in the day before, Virgin Atlantic Upper Class, and was going back the next day the same way. Zack was all mobile phones and multinational business deals. Meanwhile what had he, George, the eldest, made of his first five months cut off from his father's pocket book? He was dependent on his secretary's charity. He had no income. And his one remaining asset – a clapped-out furniture factory – threatened to be a complete waste of the pound he'd spent on it. Meanwhile, Kiki was inaccessible, his mother was a wreck, and his brothers were bent on humiliating him with their phones and their salaries and their million dollar mouths. George left Matthew with the potatoes while he went next door to sit with Josephine.

'You burned the potatoes? You'd better stay with Mum, while I check what's happening through there. You have remembered to baste the turkey haven't you?'

'Baste the turkey?'

But George was speaking to a retreating back. Josephine slung Zack out of the kitchen and he sat on the stairs with his phone, muttering about the signal weakness and getting impatient with a junior analyst, who, it seems, was actually in the office that day getting something finished. Matthew and Josie between them sorted out a Christmas lunch and put it on the table. George went to help his mother up and into the dining room, when he noticed that she had wet herself, just a dribble, but more than George wanted to deal with.

'Oh, Jesus. Josie, can you help?'

'What is it? . . . Oh, God, George. I thought I asked you to look after her.'

'Well, what did you want me to do? Sit her on a potty?'

'Can you two be quiet, please? I'm on the phone.' Zack's voice from the hallway.

Josie went into the hall and, before Zack could put his hand over the mouthpiece, said loudly and clearly: 'Zack, your mother's just peed herself. Can you come and help change her, please?'

Looking daggers at his sister, he bounded out into the street to finish his call. The signal faded somewhere between the hallway and the pavement and the door slammed shut behind him. Zack began to curse as he stamped his feet for warmth and stabbed the redial button to reconnect.

From the dining room, Matthew called, 'Is anyone coming? The food's getting cold.'

By the time the others came, he was slumped over the table fast asleep, a prisoner of his jet lag. It was a dingy Christmas, that first Christmas, and it made no one happy.

7

The bears, doom-mongers of the financial markets, had predicted a crash, but no one had guessed that Japan would lead the way. The immediate cause was trivial. Yet another Japanese bank was caught handing over bribes to organised crime. Some of the individuals involved were linked to the ruling party. There was a fine, some arrests, some resignations. Nothing out of the ordinary.

The early reaction was subdued. A mild correction moved bond prices down about half a percent. The Japanese stockmarket seemed unperturbed and even rose a little. There was a holiday coming up, and, even in Japan, people's minds wander.

But the first day was just a tremor, the earthquake had yet to come. Exactly why it came will remain a mystery. Perhaps investors were bothered by the evening news footage of disgraced dignitaries being slapped into handcuffs. Maybe it was the thundering speech of denunciation by an opposition leader. But whatever the reason, when the market opened the following day, bond prices began to tumble and the stockmarket followed suit. A slip became a landslide. By the end of the day, the bond market had fallen three percent, the stockmarket fifteen.

European investors saw the chaos in Japan and wondered if they would be affected. Trading was anxious and indecisive. If New York opened strongly, there was nothing to fear. If American investors took fright, there could be catastrophe. It was an edgy morning.

The headline in the *Wall Street Journal* that day read: 'Fifteen percent fall in Nikkei index – US investors nervous'. The best-known TV pundit filmed his morning comment from a mock-up of a Wall Street window ledge. He predicted calamity, then jumped. It was only a stunt, but hardly calming.

The market opened quietly. Nobody wanted to make the first move. But then, one by one, investors decided to play safe. Playing safe means selling out, and when everyone sells, there's no one to buy. Bit by bit, the screens glowed red. Bond market nerves tipped over into the stockmarket, which made up for lost time by falling even faster. By the end of the day, the bond market was down three percent, the stockmarket eighteen.

Soaked in sweat, traders left their desks and stumbled outside for a drink. Eighteen percent. Some traders had cause for celebration. These were the ones who had started the day 'short' – owing securities instead of owning them. Their debts had collapsed in value and their profit on the day looked incredible. Many more were as miserable as these traders were happy. Even careful traders were reporting huge losses. These unhappy souls watched their hard-won annual profits blown away in a single day. Their bonuses had certainly gone, their jobs in doubt. They pondered the injustice and avoided the bars where winners drifted on rivers of champagne.

And on an upper floor of a Wall Street skyscraper, a committee sat down to think. This was the Madison Market Risk Committee, chaired by Dan Kramer, Chief Executive and Lion of Wall Street.

The bank had had a bad day. It had chosen to bet on a rally in US markets. It hadn't bet much, but even a small wrong bet produced a big loss. The bank's computers indicated that Madison had lost around $80 million, before tax.

Nobody on the committee was too upset. Next to annual profits of way more than a billion, eighty million wasn't much more than a blip. These things happen. But there were other things to consider. In the wake of a violent upset, business goes quiet for banks like Madison. Firms on the point of issuing bonds or equity pull out of the deal. Investors trade less. Phones fall silent.

Until nine in the evening, the committee deliberated. Madison was famed for its prompt and decisive management, and it wanted to issue a press release in time for the morning news. In the end the verdict was unanimous. A press release was quickly drafted and approved.

The key paragraphs ran as follows:

Madison reports that today's correction in the financial markets has resulted in a pre-tax loss

of approximately $80 million. The bank is confi-
dent that no further losses of any magnitude are
expected and the bank continues to believe that
the long-term outlook for the financial markets is
positive.

Nevertheless, to ensure that costs remain firmly
under control during the adjustment period, the
bank intends to implement an immediate review
of staffing levels throughout the firm. Significant
down-sizing is anticipated. A further announcement will be released in due course.

The announcement was covered extensively in the press
the next morning. It was taken as a very positive sign
that Madison had publicly stated its confidence in the
markets. Once again, the bank's management was held
up as a shining example of leadership and decisiveness.
One of the popular papers covered the story under
the caption 'Markets breathe easy as Lion roars'. The
battered markets nudged upwards once again.

On the training programme, the students were less
enthusiastic. Rumour had it they would all be dismissed
that very day. The American students left their desks
to lobby the people they hoped to work for after the
course. The foreign students hung on the phones, trying
to find out the mood in Tokyo and Buenos Aires, Paris
and London.

Matthew and Sophie, happily and publicly in love,
dived downstairs for coffee after coffee. They talked
about the news, the rumours, the gossip from home.
Matthew had called Luigi Cuneberti, who sounded
despondent. Matthew tried to laugh it off as Italian
overreaction, but Luigi corrected him.

'Hey, Matteo. I'm Italian-Swiss you know, and when
we Swiss get depressed we really mean it. This is bad

news and especially tough for you new guys. But don't do anything dumb. If you don't make it this time, you'll always get another chance next year.'

Matthew didn't have a year to spare, but he could hardly tell Luigi, let alone use it to plead with McAllister. Sophie was anxious too. The Paris office had been in the midst of a major expansion, and it looked as though all that would be put on hold. New recruits would be distinctly unwelcome.

Matthew and Sophie held hands across the table, kissed, and worried. At least they had each other.

8

The bagpiper finished playing. A champagne cork popped and there was a round of applause. Hank Daggert, Chief Executive of Tominto Oil, and now Chairman of Aberdeen Drilling too, raised his glass.

'Here's to our newest subsidiary and to a long and profitable future as part of Tominto Oil.'

Douglas Mackenzie, Chief Executive of Aberdeen Drilling, beamed, resplendent in his kilt. In place of the dirk traditionally worn on the leg, he wore a miniature drill bit complete with diamond tip. Daggert loved the idea, and Mackenzie had ordered him one from the same silversmith as a present.

'And here's to young Gradley,' added Daggert after everyone had drunk, 'without whom, none of this would have been possible.'

Everyone lifted their glasses again and drank. There was a sprinkling of applause, which he acknowledged with his usual thin smile.

The evening following his row with Hanbury had been an eventful one. Once Zack had decided not to apologise, he had to move fast. From his mobile phone, he called a few numbers. The first person he reached was the head of the energy group at Weinstein Lukes.

Weinstein Lukes is a big league investment bank, one of a handful of global big-hitters. This group of banks – Goldman Sachs, Madison, Morgan Stanley, Merrill Lynch, maybe a couple of others – dominates the financial world. Whenever and wherever a major corporate upheaval takes place, whenever companies are born, married or die, you may be sure that one of this select band will be hovering at the bedside or altar, sickly smile and can-do attitude firmly in place.

Zack told his contact, a businesslike American called Amy-Lou Mazowiecki, what he wanted and what he had to offer. Mazowiecki listened to Zack and answered briefly.

'OK. Get over here now.'

Zack leaped into a cab, arriving at eight in the evening. A secretary whisked him up to the tenth floor, which was given over to meeting rooms. She left him in one with a view of the river and a tray of tea and coffee. Mazowiecki came in soon after.

'OK. Shoot,' she said.

Zack said his piece. He was currently an employee of Coburg's. Coburg's had been advising an oil company on an acquisition. The project leader had failed to identify a major liability and Zack had done so instead. He had also thought of a tax scheme to make good the liability and had been laughed out of the room by his boss at Coburg's. In his view, however, the client was as keen as ever to complete the deal at the right price. He furthermore believed the client would be happy to work with a bank other than Coburg's.

'What are you offering?'

'I'll introduce you to the client. I'll give you the specifics on the tax scheme. If you play your cards right, you'll have a new client, a nice deal, and a decent fee.'

'And what do you want from us?'

'A job.'

Mazowiecki drummed her fingers on the table. She explored Zack's intense, angular face. Interesting. He didn't play the usual interviewee's game of smiling too much, trying to get you to like them. She made up her mind.

'OK. We may be able to do a deal, but first a few points. One, we never hire anyone unless we think they're going to be good long-term hires. That means we insist on a tough interview process and you're no exception.

'Second, if we're to do anything for your client, we need to move quickly. It may already be too late. That means you need to tell us everything you can about this tax scheme, and we'll get working on it right away. I know you won't want to give us any confidential information until the client's given authorisation. But these are special circumstances. I give you my word that we will not misuse any information you give us.

'Finally, I hope you're prepared for a long night. Our aim is to spend a couple of hours working on the tax angle, then spend the rest of the night on interviews. We'll give you our final decision in the morning. OK?'

Zack thought for a moment. This was a different world from Coburg's, and he longed to be a part of it. But still he hesitated.

'That's great,' he said, 'but I'm afraid I can't accept an oral commitment not to misuse the information I give you. I'm still an employee of Coburg's.'

Zack didn't give a monkey's about the ethics, but he wanted to appear trustworthy. He wasn't sure that he'd made the right choice and stopped short. He needn't have worried. Mazowiecki smiled.

'Good. You've passed the first test. We don't hire people who are casual with their clients' secrets.' She took a letter from her attaché case, signed and dated. She passed it across to Zack. The letter promised, on behalf of Weinstein Lukes, to make no use of any information given them by Zack Gradley, unless and until he gave them written permission to do so. 'Here's one we did earlier. We put it together on your way over, just in case we decided you weren't a bullshitter.'

Then passed one of the strangest nights of Zack's life. He spent the next three hours with Mazowiecki and a bleary-eyed Weinstein Lukes tax specialist called Hal Gillingham. Zack explained his idea and outlined the things he thought needed to be done. Gillingham quickly understood the scheme. He spotted a couple of technical problems that Zack hadn't seen, but also thought of ways round them. He looked like something the cat had dragged in, but his mind was as sharp as a razor. At midnight, he sat back.

'Let's call a halt. I'm convinced we have a workable scheme. If we work nonstop we should have it in reasonable shape by Friday. Frankly, I rather like it.'

Then the interviewing began.

Ordinary firms would find it difficult to arrange an unscheduled series of interviews running from midnight to six in the morning. Not so Weinstein Lukes. Across the building, lights burned late as bankers rushed to meet critical deadlines. Mazowiecki collared half a dozen of her colleagues and told them to fit in a full forty-five minute interview with Zack before reporting back with a detailed appraisal. It was an unusual request, but unusual requests were commonplace. Nobody was put out.

The interviews were searching and rigorous. Any weakness identified by one interviewer was mentioned to the next, who then tested Zack on it as thoroughly as possible. At Coburg's, Zack felt himself a cut above the rest. Here he was unsure of himself. He felt like a schoolboy trialling for the Olympics. When asked for the fourth time how many languages he spoke and he was forced to say just English, he began to wonder whether he should have apologised to Hanbury after all.

At four in the morning, Zack realised he hadn't eaten since lunch the day before and asked timidly if there was a vending machine anywhere. His interviewer, a Spaniard who looked every inch like the Castilian aristocrat he was, looked at Zack puzzled.

'Do you want crisps or do you want food?' he asked. 'I will not recommend hiring you if you give the wrong answer.'

Zack laughed and asked for food. The Spaniard dialled four digits on the phone on the desk, and fifteen minutes later a waitress entered with an enormous club sandwich loaded with treats.

'Some of us pretty much live in this building, so it is important to have the necessary conveniences. In New York, it is all diet Coke and microwave pizza.' The Spaniard shrugged. A rival firm had recently offered him a guaranteed bonus of $2 million a year for two years to head up their Latin American business based in New York. He hadn't even spent a minute considering the offer.

Finally, a little after six, Zack's last interview was over. Out of the window, the River Thames lay like a dark band between the banks of offices and cranes strung with inane Christmas lights. Zack felt battered and exhausted. This had better be worth it. Finally, at six forty-eight, Mazowiecki returned.

'Congratulations. We'd like to offer you a job. We propose to make you a vice president in corporate finance, reporting to me. Your starting salary will be forty thousand pounds. You will also be entitled to an annual bonus, payable in June, based on your performance over the last year. Since it's now January, we will not have had sufficient time to appraise your performance in the ordinary way. However, if the deal we are discussing comes off, we will pay you a signing bonus of fifty thousand. What do you say?'

'Yes. Yes, please. That's absolutely wonderful. I'm delighted.' Club sandwich or no, Zack was light-headed.

'OK. We've drawn up your contract, but we can't formalise it until we get clearance from Dixon Banderman. Dixon is the head of corporate finance in London and insists on seeing every new hire. I've never known him overturn a decision, but it's a hoop we have to jump through.'

'OK. When do I get to see him?'

'Right away. He'll be down in our health club now. We'll go find him.'

Mazowiecki and Zack took the lift down to the basement. At this time in the morning, the place was mostly empty, but a thrumming sound indicated that some of the cardio-vascular machines were busy. Mazowiecki, more than a few pounds overweight, walked the aisles of the body beautiful, following the sound. Her pace picked up as she saw who she'd come for. Zack followed a couple of steps behind.

An elderly man, his back turned, pounded a treadmill. Dixon Banderman.

'Hi, Dixon,' said Mazowiecki, handing him the draft contract. 'Can I introduce Zack Gradley?'

'Amy-Lou. Hi. For you, anything.'

The man's voice sounded familiar. Mid-Atlantic. An

American who had been in London too long. Banderman's silvery head turned to look at Zack. He looked like a viscount, but Zack knew he didn't always behave like one. Oh, Jesus. It was the man he'd had a screaming match with on the zebra crossing the evening before. Recognition dawned in Banderman's face. Zack half-closed his eyes. If he was going to be executed, he didn't want to look.

'Jesus Christ, Amy. Have you lost your marbles? You seriously want to offer this foul-mouthed jerk a fifty grand signing fee?'

Zack's eyes closed completely. How unlucky could he get? He began to compose the most offensive possible riposte in his mind. If he was going to be sacked by Coburg's and rejected by Weinstein Lukes, then somebody would feel his tongue. He only dimly heard what Banderman said next.

'From what you told me before, Amy, this guy's bringing us a deal worth millions and he's already proved he's got a hell of a brain for tax structures. I know from my own experience that he looks after himself in a fight. The bugger deserves a hundred grand if the deal comes good. Go get this thing seen to.'

So saying, he flung the contract at Mazowiecki who caught it, startled. She didn't often miss a trick, but something had happened here she didn't understand.

'Welcome on board,' said Banderman, extending a sweaty hand.

The rest of the week passed in a daze. Zack and Mazowiecki called Daggert. Zack said he believed Aberdeen Drilling was still available and that they could find a way to make the price acceptable. The only condition was that Weinstein Lukes was hired immediately.

Daggert was surprised by the call but he listened carefully.

155

'You're positive we can utilise our tax losses?'

'Ninety percent.'

'And you're sure Aberdeen Drilling's still available?'

'Ninety percent.'

'And what fees are you guys asking?'

Mazowiecki proposed a fee based on how much Weinstein Lukes saved Tominto Oil. Coburg's had suggested paying one hundred and twenty-five million for Aberdeen Drilling. For every pound Mazowiecki saved, Weinstein Lukes would keep twenty pence. It was pricey but Daggert was in no mood to haggle.

'Fine. Fax me a contract and I'll sign it.'

They hung up and Mazowiecki produced some champagne.

'Your job and our deal,' she said.

It was now eight forty. Zack remembered his meeting with personnel at Coburg's. He couldn't work for Weinstein Lukes while still an employee at Coburg's. He assumed he'd be fired, but he took a letter of resignation along just in case. Getting a fat redundancy payment was an unexpected plus, but the best thing had been Hanbury's face when Zack delivered his parting shot.

For the rest of the week, Zack worked an average of twenty hours a day making sure that the tax scam worked. By Friday night, Hal Gillingham said they were done. Mazowiecki just said, 'Great. Have a good weekend, guys.'

'Aren't we going to call the seller?' asked Zack.

Mazowiecki told him to relax, she had a call to make to 'a friend of mine, a journalist'.

Zack took her advice, puzzled, but when on Sunday he picked up a newspaper, he discovered that the deal was front-page news in the business section. The article – 'Black hole in accounts threatens Aberdeen sale' – blew the auction apart. The other buyers vanished. Tominto

156

shuffled its feet. The seller grew desperate and virtually threw the business at Tominto.

Once everything was added up – the price, the tax relief, the Norwegian liability – Tominto got Aberdeen Drilling for one hundred million pounds exactly, twenty-five million less than Coburg's had recommended. Weinstein Lukes' fee was one fifth of that, or five million. The assignment had lasted twenty-two days from start to finish. Daggert agreed the fee but shook his head.

'If I didn't love oil better than money, I'd be damn sure I'm in the wrong business,' he complained.

The bagpiper was playing faster now, and champagne had given way to whisky. Douglas Mackenzie had grabbed Mazowiecki and was teaching her how to reel to the bagpipes. Daggert grabbed his Chief Financial Officer, an earnest-looking woman of thirty-five, and joined in. Zack felt relaxed and happy. It was his first deal.

9

You couldn't blame Matthew.

He was working late, no harm in that. He needed to check something in the reference books kept in the course tutor's office, Gillian McCutcheon. No harm in that either. While digging out what he needed, he happened to glance at a binder on her desk. Again, he was hardly to blame for that. He wasn't some Victorian schoolgirl, obliged to keep his eyes modestly downcast. The binder lay there plain as day, labelled: 'Course Tutor Notes for Final Trading Game.' Matthew picked it up.

The final trading game was unquestionably the most important test of the course. In deciding who should pass and who should fail, this one last brutal game had enormous weight. If Matthew had been more sure of his position, perhaps he could have left the binder alone. But it was now confirmed that, following Dan Kramer's decision to slash costs, the sixty-three students on the course were competing for just five jobs.

Two of the lucky winners were already known. One was Adam Campbell, an unimpressive Englishman with little hair and less dress sense. He looked like a nerd, but he was expert in a branch of mathematics that the bank's London options desk badly needed. The second lucky man was an Argentine, Diego Burelli. The man was handsome as a movie star, impeccably connected with the leading families of Argentina, and possessed of a commercial instinct second to none. He was destined to head up the Buenos Aires office and would do it well.

So that left sixty-one students and three places. Matthew was a strong contender, as was Sophie. There were probably only four other serious contenders: Scott Petersen, the golden-haired Californian; Heinz Schiffer, a blustering German with heavyweight supporters in Frankfurt; Karen Onsley, a skilful trader, who had two parents, three uncles, a brother and a sister already working on Wall Street; and Fujimoto Takako, a dapper Japanese with an uncanny capacity for alcohol and a sixth sense for the Asian markets.

What should Matthew do? Put the binder down and go on his way pretending not to have seen it? But why should he? He had worked late, unlike his colleagues. In a way, this was a just reward for his diligence. What's more, how did Matthew even know that the others hadn't already found, read and copied the binder? He wouldn't put it past Karen Onsley, or Heinz Schiffer for that matter.

Whatever the rights and wrongs of the situation, the fact was that Matthew reached for the binder, opened it, and began to read. He began to read it standing up. Then he continued to read it sitting down. Then, realising that a single sitting wouldn't do justice to the excellence of his discovery, he took it to the photocopier and copied every page.

He put the binder back where he'd found it, and walked out of the bank with the thirty-five photocopied pages in his briefcase. Each one was gold, pure gold.

10

'This is good. Very good.' It was Sally Dummett speaking, head of Gissings' tiny design team. She held a drawing of an office suite and turned it so that the others could see it. 'Every piece has a superb finish. The design is very up-to-date, very crisp. It's like a really good sports car, clean, sharp and functional.' She checked herself before she got too carried away. 'But at the same time, the construction is dead simple and the materials are as cheap as anything. First class.'

The others round the table nodded gloomily. It was first class, but it wasn't Gissings'. The drawing came from a brochure put out by one of their major competitors, Asperton Holdings. Andrew Walters, the sedate head of production, responded.

'Well, I grant you that it looks very well to the untrained eye, but there are still plenty of customers who want the traditional construction methods. And we have to face the fact that with our equipment we simply can't produce stuff like that at the right price. Maybe not at any price.'

'I'm not saying what we can or can't produce. All I know is that George is right. We're getting further and further behind the game.'

Dummett looked at George for his support, but none was forthcoming. George hadn't done a day's work in his life before coming to Gissings and a few months of hard work now didn't make him an expert. He just did what he could with common sense and Val's encyclopaedic knowledge.

'What we really need is a bit of capital,' said Walters. 'It wouldn't cost all that much to bring our tooling up to minimum modern standards. A hundred thousand or so should cover it.'

'No. No, no.' It was Jeff Wilmot who interrupted, the mousy accountant who had the nerve-racking job of keeping Gissings' accounts in order. 'We simply can't . . . we can't even contemplate . . . begin to contemplate that magnitude of expenditure. Unless . . . I mean, of course, unless . . .' he looked nervously at George to see if by any chance George was going to toss a hundred grand on the table. George didn't. 'Well, I mean, we simply can't afford anything which isn't absolutely critical.'

Ballard had agreed to a further extension on the loan, but it hung above them still, a boulder capable of crushing them at any moment. The debate meandered on, without conclusion. Sally Dummett was right: Gissings' products were hopelessly out-of-date. Walters was right: the factory was decaying as it stood. And Wilmot was right: there was no money to spend. The discussion had a lost and hopeless feel.

After a while George intervened. 'Look, we all know there's truth in everything that you lot are saying. So we can either give up now or we can at least have a go at saving things. If we have a go, then the starting point has got to be a decent product, and at the moment our stuff is overpriced and out-of-date. Sally, would you be able to design us some completely new product ranges? It would need to look great and we'd need to be able to produce it in our clapped-out factory.'

'I can have a go.'

160

'You mean "Yes, definitely," don't you, Sally?'

'Yes, alright. I mean, definitely.'

'It'll look as good as that Asperton stuff?'

'Yes.'

'Better?'

'Yes, better.' Dummett was enthusiastic. She had a thousand designs in her head, which, in Tom Gissing's time, had stayed right there. Now they could start to pour out.

'Good. Now, Andrew, how are we going to produce the stuff?'

Andrew Walters spread his hands. In Gissing's day, the boss had always been sympathetic to Walters' preference 'for doing things right or not at all'. George wasn't like that. He didn't understand the first thing about production and he hadn't a clue about traditional furniture construction.

'Our new products are going to be cheap and easy to produce, right, Sally?'

'Right.'

'But we need to make sure that the production side is involved from very early on to make sure that the designs are adapted to what our factory can do. So, Andrew, I want you to be involved in Sally's work from now on.'

Walters was less than thrilled with the idea of being a junior sidekick to Sally Dummett of all people.

'OK,' he grunted, 'but obviously, I'll need to give priority to keeping the shop floor running properly.'

'Mmm,' said George. 'I guess that's a pretty much full-time responsibility?'

'Well, with our machines in the state they're in . . .'

'Fair enough. In that case let's nominate someone else from the production side to support Sally. I'd suggest that young man, Darren, from the cutting room.'

'No,' interjected Walters quickly. 'I'm not sure that Darren has the necessary maturity. Let me think about who would be more suitable. Perhaps I might be able to find some time . . .'

'Good. That's settled then,' said George, selectively deaf. 'Val, would you mind fetching Darren for us?'

Andrew Walters continued to protest, as George turned to Wilmot.

'And I want you to be involved too, Jeff. I want you to cost out all of Sally's designs and I want you to get estimated sales prices from marketing. If there's not enough profit, then you send Sally back to her drawing board. Right?'

'Yes, indeed,' said Wilmot. He had long harboured resentment that Tom Gissing had never involved him in anything more than book-keeping. For Gissing, making furniture had always come first, making money had come a long way behind. The philosophy was an attractive one, but it had almost killed the company. Wilmot would be glad to be involved.

Just then, Val came back into the room with a scruffy young man in tow. He had more hair on his stubbly chin than on his shaven skull. He wore an earring in one ear and a pair of trainers so dirty you could farm them.

'Alright?' he asked, nodding greetings to the room.

'Good morning,' said Andrew Walters.

'Good morning, Darren,' said George. 'Andrew and I would like you to do something for us. Andrew?'

Andrew Walters began, pompously, to explain what was required. When Walters' explanation started to sound like an order to obstruct change of any sort, George interjected gently with his own explanation. Darren wiped his nose and listened.

'Yeah, alright. Shouldn't be a problem,' he said.

Darren had come to George's attention when a hoist

in the warehouse had broken. Walters said it needed replacing, but Darren, who was in there bumming a tenner off the warehouse operative, had interjected. 'Bet I can fix that,' he'd said.

Walters said it was dangerous to attempt a patched-up job on anything load-bearing, but George invited Darren to do as he said. By the end of the day, Darren had fixed the hoist using nothing more complex than an ordinary car tool-kit and a length of steel wire. Walters examined the job, said it was temporary, insisted that the hoist be used for half-loads only, but couldn't find anything seriously the matter. Val said that Darren was the most natural engineer she'd ever seen at the factory, and his best mate Dave ran a good second.

'OK, then. Sally, Jeff, Darren, Andrew – you all know what we're doing?'

Everyone nodded.

'Yeah. We're alright, eh, Sally?' said Darren.

'Oh, yes! Just raring to get going.'

'Good. Just one other thing. As you know, the annual British Furniture Showcase is being held at the Olympia exhibition centre in three months' time. We've got a stand booked, and of course it's a huge event for us. All the big national buyers are there, all our customers, everybody. We've got to have our products ready by then. Not drawing board ready, but production ready. In fact, I want to have our warehouse well stocked with products, so we can start shipping the day we get the orders.'

Wilmot and Walters both began to shake their heads.

'Frankly, we'll be doing well to have a set of designs by then. We can always show the drawings to buyers and promise to keep them in touch with developments,' said Walters.

Wilmot nodded vigorously.

'I don't think our cash position will allow us the luxury of building prior to receipt of orders,' he said, but George was having one of his bouts of deafness.

'Good, so that's agreed,' he said.

11

The victoria sponge wouldn't have held the fifty-three candles which Helen's age demanded, but she took a grave pleasure in the five it did have and she sat over them, her face lighted and warmed by the flames beneath.

'Careful, Mum,' said Josie.

She took her own hairband off and settled it on her mother's head, to keep her hair back from the burning candles. Helen was quiet today and uncertain in her movements, but behind her eyes there was a self-aware adult intelligence, watching the world and her own fumbling part in it. She smiled at her daughter, finding with effort the words for 'Thank you'. Josie smiled back. Zack watched briefly, impatiently.

'For Christ's sake,' he said. 'Can't you just blow out the candles and get on with it?'

It was six thirty in the evening. Zack had landed at Heathrow an hour ago and was stopping off at his mum's birthday party on his way back into work. Matthew had already phoned from New York to send his love. George couldn't come down from Yorkshire midweek, but he'd be here at the weekend. Helen looked anxiously at her daughter, disturbed by Zack's interjection.

'When Mum's ready,' said Josie. 'This is her party, not yours.'

She was tired, but determined not to let Zack spoil things. She'd defend her mum from his snappiness, just as she'd protect her from the candle flames. She could manage it all, she knew that now. Earn a living, look after Mum, keep the house, even find space to enjoy the good times.

She glanced at Zack, seeing him suddenly as he was. Not as the obstreperous elder brother she had always known, but as the investment banker he had now become, travel-weary in his Jermyn Street suit, mind still engaged on business. How would he be if she were his secretary? He wouldn't notice her. He'd remember her name and be polite for just as long as she managed to take his calls, sort out his meetings, and handle his paperwork without error. The minute she failed, he'd snap. Even if she got it right and he felt snappish, he'd snap.

Brother and sister, banker and secretary, watched a little longer. The candles burned down to stumps and the flames began to gutter.

'There, now –' began Zack.

'There you go, Mum,' said Josie. 'Let's see if we can blow them out.'

Helen rounded her lips into an O and blew. The action which had once been unthinking now demanded painful concentration, reconstructing every neural command from a blank template. The damaged bits of her brain would remain damaged and new parts had to learn unfamiliar roles. It was tough, a harder challenge than the one faced by her sons. Helen produced a draught of air, but one nowhere strong enough to blow out a candle.

'Well done, Mum!' exclaimed Josie, finishing the job. 'Well done.'

'Oh, for God's sake,' muttered Zack.

The cake was a shop-bought one with icing sugar sprinkled on top and a layer of artificial cream and cheap jam smeared meanly through the middle. Zack took his slice and, without tasting it, set it down away from him.

'I've got you presents. I'm afraid I haven't had time to wrap them.'

He rummaged in his duty-free shopping bag. He brought out perfume and chocolates, both expensive, and handed them to his sister.

'Here, Mum. Look at this,' said Josephine, helping her mother's hands to find and hold the gifts. 'Can you smell that? Isn't that lovely? Do you want a chocolate?'

'Lovely,' said Helen. 'Thank you.'

Zack acknowledged his mother's thanks with a minuscule smile. 'I've got something for you too, Josie.'

Zack poured out the contents of his bag on to his lap. There was a shirt from Pinks, three Hermès ties and a silk scarf, also from Hermès. Zack passed the scarf over to Josephine. She shook it out to see the design, then knotted it round her shoulders. It was gorgeous and suited her well.

'It's beautiful, Zack. Thanks.'

'You're welcome.'

Josie looked at the pile of goods still on Zack's lap. He'd remembered to take the price off the scarf, but he hadn't bothered with his ties, and the tags made their discreet little boasts as clearly as if they'd used trumpets. Fifty pounds each. The shirt would be another forty or fifty, minimum.

'It is beautiful, Zack, but . . . well, if you ever have any spare cash, Mum and I could really use it. The daycare's really expensive.'

'Oh Christ, you're not going to start whingeing, are you?' Zack was tired.

'No. I am not going to start whingeing,' said Josie angrily. 'It isn't –'

'I come out of my way to get here –'

'Heathrow to Kilburn by taxi. That's hardly a pilgrimage –'

'I give you some bloody nice presents and all you can do –'

'Things aren't easy and –'

'Oh that's right. It's not easy being a secretary. First you've got to paint your nails, then it's gossiping in the Ladies, then what? A bit of strenuous photocopying?'

'Stop it.' Josie was white-faced. She didn't want to hear this from Zack. She was an eighteen-year-old girl coping well with a difficult world, and being angry at Zack would use up more energy than she had to spare. 'Stop it!'

'And Mum. Playing nursery games with a middle-aged woman. That must really strain the brain cells.'

Zack got up to go. Josephine was crying, hot tears burning her cheeks. She was furious with Zack and furious with herself for letting him get to her.

'Get out.'

'I'm going. I've got work to do. Real work. Work for adults.'

'Get out.'

Josephine half-shoved her brother out of the front door, sobbing without restraint now. Damn him. Damn him! She wiped her eyes on the Hermès silk. No one was allowed to talk to her like that. No one.

Spring 1999

Spring doesn't mean much on Wall Street. January is traditionally a good month for the stockmarket, as fools forget the lessons of the year before and rush in optimistically with minds as blank as new-minted chequebooks. But that's January. By February, the holiday season is long over. The bonuses have been cashed and saved, or committed to boring but sensible projects like the kids' education, or paying down the mortgage, or refurbishing the yacht. The markets are busy and serious. Corporate financiers work crazy hours on mega-deals which will cause job losses in Wichita and giant bonuses on Wall Street. By March, people are already looking ahead. Will I meet my revenue target? Will the markets let me keep the profit I've made? What bonus will I get this time around?

On the training course, the students are tense and unhappy. They don't want bonuses. They want jobs. It is 4 March 1999. There are 862 days to go until Bernard Gradley's deadline.

* * *

1

Somewhere below Wall Street, the Consolidated Edison Power Company had a problem. Even now, on the cusp of the millennium, New York's buildings are heated by steam carried through Con-Ed's network of underground pipes. Most of the time the system works but, as with all old things, from time to time things go wrong. Today was one of those times.

A large vertical pipe, placed like a chimney in the street, belched forth torrents of steam. Beneath it, workmen scurried round an open manhole.

To the commuters emerging from the subway at the top of Wall Street, the scene was like something from the Civil War. Behind them a blackened church spoke of God and duty. Before them, in a dazzle of morning sun, clouds of steam, like gun smoke, filled the deep canyon of the street. You could just about see as far as the former Federal Reserve where old man Washington still presides, an iron statue on his stone pedestal. Beyond that, nothing but dense smoke and blinding sunlight. Amidst the clouds, here and there, a few flags flew – the Stars and Stripes by the dawn's early light. The commuters hurrying to work could have been the defeated in flight or the victors on the rampage. Matthew moistened his lips.

This was Wall Street. The most famous street on earth. More money moved down this short alleyway than any finance minister in the world had under his control. Here was wealth. Here was power. Here was everything.

Matthew was ready for it all. He bought a coffee from one of the stalls lining Wall Street and walked on into Madison's glittering skyscraper. Above his head as he entered, the Stars and Stripes fluttered in the billowing steam.

Today was the day of the final, critical trading game: sixty-three students fighting for five jobs. Matthew was nervous but excited. He enjoyed the games and was good at them. And this time he began with an advantage, the advantage of having read and memorised the binder he'd found in Gillian McCutcheon's office.

If the binder was right, the game they were about to play was different from all the others they had played so far. Instead of bonds or shares, the students were to trade lottery tickets. Each student would start with a thousand tickets. Each ticket would offer the chance to compete in a lottery with a theoretical million dollar prize. Various news items, each of which had been spelled out in an appendix, would be released throughout the game. The price of the lottery tickets would, of course, go up and down as the market digested the new information.

Every trader dreams of knowing the future. If you only knew one stupid statistic each day – say the price of the US government long bond – you could forget your big house in Long Island and go buy yourself an island someplace sunny. Give yourself time and you could trade up again, from an island to a country, from a country to a continent. Today, just for the day, Matthew knew the future.

The binder didn't give him the price of lottery tickets, but it gave him something just as good. In previous games there wasn't a right answer to where prices should be; there was only the answer of the market. In this game, however, you could work out the price a lottery ticket ought to have by simple maths. For instance, if there were a million lottery tickets in circulation, competing for a single million dollar prize, each ticket was worth $1 exactly. If you could buy a ticket at 99½ cents you were getting a bargain. If you sold a ticket at $1.00½, you were making a profit.

So, early in the mornings while Sophie slept, Matthew sat over his notes, calculating to the nearest sixteenth of a cent how prices ought to move. He made himself practise the calculations again and again. He timed himself for speed and set himself ever more complex puzzles. He was not going to allow himself to be caught out. This was his chance.

Sophie came in and slid alongside Matthew at his desk. Usually they had breakfast together, but not today. Matthew was too preoccupied.

'You look nervous, *mon cher*,' said Sophie.

'Yeah. I do feel queasy. You look alright.'

As ever with Sophie, this was an understatement. She wore an ash-grey suit with green trim and a brilliant white silk blouse beneath. Her skirt would have been considered conservative, almost frumpy, in the daringly dressed Paris office. Here in New York, however, she showed a length of leg that her American coursemates exposed only in the shower. Her complexion glowed with health and there wasn't a glimmer of uncertainty in her bearing. Matthew felt bad about his secret, but he knew Sophie wouldn't cheat with him and it was too late to confide in her now.

Sophie kissed him.

'Don't worry, dearest. You'll do fine. Either you win and get your precious job or you don't win, don't get the job, and get another one just as good next year. Either way you'll be fine. What difference does a year make?'

'More than you think,' said Matthew grumpily.

Sophie tugged his hair in mock rebuke.

'You're twenty-two, you *imbecile*. You could always go back and finish your degree, you know. I don't much care for uneducated men.'

'And if you lose?'

'*Que sera, sera.* I'll do something else.'

'It's alright for you. Supermodel. Movie star. Financial mogul. The world's your oyster.'

'Don't mention oysters. They make me come over all sexy.'

The conversation descended into lovers' nonsense. And as the time came to move through into the big conference room where the game was due to begin, Matthew was certain of only two things. The first thing was that he desperately wanted a job at Madison. The second was that he had never felt about a woman the way he felt about Sophie.

The students assembled. Half of them were obviously nervous. The other half were either resigned – like Princess Fareshti, who seemed on the verge of sleep already – or, like Sophie and Scott Petersen, were apparently immune to nerves. The enviable Diego Burelli, soon to take up his new job in Buenos Aires, cracked jokes in Spanish on his mobile phone as Matthew's nerves danced the jitterbug.

Gillian McCutcheon was already there, as were a scattering of senior traders, there to inspect the proceedings.

'That's Coniston, isn't it? Head of the corporate fixed income desk.'

'And that woman next to him. Maria Hernandez. The junk bond queen.'

To the students trembling for their future, the ordinary-looking figures of Fred Coniston and Maria Hernandez were like gods descended to earth. Gillian McCutcheon began to outline the game.

'Unlike previous games, you will not be trading financial instruments. You will be trading lottery tickets. Each of you will own a thousand lottery tickets to begin with.

172

Each ticket gives you a one in a million chance to win a jackpot worth a million dollars.'

She rambled on. It was exactly what Matthew had been expecting. Exact to the details of the wording. His tiny fear that his precious document would prove to be misleading vanished. He really did know the future. The game got underway, and the first news announcement went up. Lottery fraud in Wisconsin, murmured Matthew under his breath. Five thousand tickets scrapped. Sure enough, the placard announced that a counterfeit ring had been exposed in Wisconsin. Five thousand tickets were being impounded.

Matthew knew the prices he should be quoting. He pretended to do a calculation to check, but he was quick to position himself in the middle of the throng. He sang out his prices and asked others for theirs. It was a rule of the game that everybody had to quote a price when asked and had to stick to their quote if the other person wanted to deal. That meant there was nowhere to hide. You couldn't simply sit in a corner and keep your head down. In fact, there could hardly be a worse strategy. You might as well string a balloon round your neck saying 'I'm a sucker – please take advantage'. Everyone would cluster round you, ask you for your prices and hit your bid every time you offered to buy high or sell low.

Matthew liked to be asked for his prices. He knew his prices included a profit margin whether he was buying or selling, and the more trades he did, the more money he made. But he was even happier when he was able to ask others for their prices. He sought out the least able students, asked their prices and bought or sold in bulk whenever he spotted an opportunity. He dived around the room seeking out ignorance and profiting.

Then at his shoulder a familiar voice whispered, *'Bonjour, Monsieur Gradley*. Your prices, please?'

He turned and found himself looking into Sophie's ever-beautiful face.

'To anyone else, I'd sell at eighty-eight, buy at eighty-seven,' he said. 'But you, my dear, can have all the lottery tickets in the world for a dollar and a kiss.'

Matthew tore out a trading ticket for her. He signed it and left the rest for her to fill in. It was a blank cheque. If she wanted to buy all of Matthew's tickets for a penny, she only had to fill out the ticket. His signature would authenticate the trade beyond dispute.

Sophie raised her eyebrows and filled the ticket out with mock seriousness:

Trader's name	*Matthew Gradley*
Type of deal	*Sell*
Buyer/seller	*Sophie Clemenceau*
Number of units	*10,000*
Price per unit	*$0.01*
Total deal value	*$100*
Deal time	*09.46*

The ticket stated that Matthew was selling Sophie ten thousand tickets at one cent each. If Sophie chose to enforce the deal, Matthew would be bankrupted out of the game, dead in the water. Not even Fareshti Al Shahrani would be able to lose that much money.

'Voilà,' said Sophie. 'That should put paid to your ambition.' So saying she stepped close to Matthew, where no one but they could see what happened next. She threaded the ticket between the buttons at the front of her shirt, and tucked the ticket into her bra. It was a snug fit. 'You can take it back, if you wish,' she murmured.

Matthew smiled. He stepped even closer to her and felt for the ticket with his fingers.

'*Fais attention*! You're only allowed the ticket, you know.'

'Maybe I'll leave the ticket for now and see what else I can find.'

But Matthew was impatient. He'd have as much time as he wanted to explore the contents of Sophie's shirt front on other occasions. He pulled away, gave Sophie a perfunctory kiss and dived back into the throng. She shook her head. She tried to withdraw the ticket from its resting place, but it had made itself at home and resisted disturbance. She left it and got on with her own trading.

Matthew watched his rivals to see how they fared. Scott Petersen stood head and shoulders taller than a throng of Japanese around him. Tickets flashed to and fro as the frenzy continued. He heard Petersen's voice calling out prices. Damn the man. His prices were spot on. Exactly the same as those Matthew was offering. He checked out Karen Onsley and Heinz Schiffer. Both of them were busy. Both of them were dealing at the correct prices.

Damn! Matthew knew that he wasn't as mentally agile as either Petersen or Schiffer. He certainly wasn't as smart as Sophie, whose own trading was doubtless impeccable. The whole advantage he had obtained from the illicit notes amounted to this: he'd been able to bring himself up to the level that Petersen and the others reached by their own merit. And Petersen, in particular, looked very busy with trades, as did Karen Onsley. Matthew wasn't especially popular on the course, as he was well aware. He had no time for popularity for its own sake and divided his energies equally between work and Sophie. But now, while he had to yank people away from whatever they were doing to get a trade done, Petersen just stood and watched customers stream towards him.

Double damn!

He left the mêlée for a few minutes to update his accounts and to grab a cup of coffee. He sat with his back to the wall and worked quickly. The table he sat at was draped with a floor-length baize cloth. Sophie saw him leave the throng and slipped over towards him.

She sat down beside him and, in the shelter of the green baize, moved her hand down to his trousers, tucking a slip of paper neatly into his underpants. 'My turn to return the compliment, *Monsieur*. If you need help in removing it, please don't hesitate to ask.'

She kissed him and moved off. Matthew heard her, calling out accurate prices to all who asked. Sophie was popular too. People moved towards her when they saw her. They moved away from him. Triple damn!

Matthew took the piece of paper from his trousers. It was a blank trading ticket, signed by Sophie. He smiled, but his mind was elsewhere.

2

Amy-Lou Mazowiecki wasn't built to run fast, but she was doing a good job of it now. They ran from the taxi to the check-in counter, Zack arriving narrowly in front.

'Can you get us on the London flight? No bags.'

'Take-off in twenty minutes.' The SAS check-in attendant was dubious. 'I'll call the gate.'

She dialled the gate and said something in Swedish. Her face registered neither pleasure nor displeasure at the answer. She replaced the handset.

'OK. Please show your tickets at the gate and collect your boarding passes there. But you'll need to run.'

176

They ran. There was no wait at passport control, no line at security. At the gate, twenty or thirty people were still waiting to board. Seeing them, Mazowiecki stopped.

'Heaps of time. I wish they wouldn't tell you to run when the plane's not even full.'

If everyone in the world lined up according to their consumption of fossil fuel, at the very head of the queue, jostling rudely for position, would stand the world's corporate financiers. It's perfectly common for London-based bankers to take a hundred and fifty flights a year or more, many of them intercontinental, many of them just for a single meeting. In his brief career, Zack had already flown to Houston for a meeting, to Dubai for a day-trip, and to Tokyo for no reason at all that he could remember. Distance is no barrier to business. Airplane seats are beds, jet lag a way of life. To such people – and Mazowiecki had long since stopped collecting air miles for holidays she rarely took – the idea of stepping on to a plane more than a couple of minutes before take-off is anathema.

They ambled on to the plane. Zack had some documents to read, while Mazowiecki had come in from New York the day before and intended to catch up on her sleep. But before settling down, she said, 'Zack, we should have a quick chat about the firm and your future and stuff. I should have done it when you joined, but I guess we've been kind of busy.'

'Busy? Call this busy?' said Zack. This was his nineteenth working day in a row.

Mazowiecki smiled feebly. Humour is one of the first things to go when a bunch of highly able and competitive people work together for eighty hours a week.

'OK. Here's the beef. What is Weinstein Lukes? Well, it's an investment bank, but it's something else as well. It's a partnership. Not metaphorically, literally. At Weinstein Lukes there are about a hundred partners currently employed. There are a few hundred more retired partners. Between them, these guys own the firm. When we make a billion and a half dollars in profit, those guys get to share it. The ones who are still employed get most of it, of course, but the retirees still get a cut. If you stay at Weinstein Lukes and make it to partner, you will be very wealthy indeed. Last year, the worst paid partner took home around four and a half million bucks. The highest paid partners – well, they find enough for their heating bills.

'And that's it. That's the secret. That's how come we can work people so hard. That's how come people put up with the job insecurity, the absence of a social life, the relentless pressure. We stick it, Zack, you and me both stick it because one day we hope to make it to partner.'

'You ever think of quitting?'

'Sure I do. Everyone does. I get called by headhunters maybe six times a year with real offers. Nice ones. Less work, more money. But I'm a senior vice president. Either I make it to partner in the next year or two, or the firm tells me ever so gently that they don't need me. If I'm not wanted, I can go and work in an easier firm. Enjoy the money, the respect, see if I can patch together my wreck of a personal life. But if I'm invited to partner, then I've got it made, financially at least.'

'And the pressure eases, right?'

Mazowiecki laughed out loud. 'No way. The pressure never eases. Listen.' She snatched a napkin from the tray in front of her and scribbled on it, drawing a rough triangle. 'This is how the firm works. At the bottom we have analysts. They work eighteen-hour days, six-day weeks, for two, maybe three years. After that, we fire most of them. We keep about one in three. Those who make it go on to the next level, associate. Our associates are the engine room of the firm, the slave drivers for the analysts. After associate comes vice presidents, like you. It's a big-sounding title, but the firm has over a thousand VPs. The main difference between you guys and the associates is that you actually have to market the firm's services. You have to be able to meet a chief executive old enough to be your father, and convince that guy that he needs – *needs* – to hire you for what could be one of the most important events in his company's life. An awful lot of our associates can't make the transition and we lose a lot of associates and VPs because of it. But that's fine.' Her pen jabbed again at the scrawled triangle on the napkin. 'We need to lose people to keep our pyramid structure. We need to be thin at the top, fat on the bottom if we're going to pay our top people as we do.

'As a first-year vice president, Zack, you need to bring in revenues of six million dollars for the firm. Next year, it'll be eight. The year after that, twelve. If you miss your targets, we'll hear you out. Sometimes even good deals go wrong. We'll be sympathetic. But if you get in the habit of missing targets, you'll soon be looking for a job elsewhere. Remember the pyramid. As a senior vice president, I face the same challenge but my targets are higher. Quite soon I need to be convincing people I'm good enough to make partner, or again, I'll be out on the street.'

'And how much do you need to earn for the firm to make partner?'

Amy-Lou smiled at the question. Zack was a little young to be worrying about that, but she liked his directness. Here was a guy comfortable with money.

'There's no set target. Not at that level. But if you

bring in revenues of thirty-five million bucks or more, then they have to consider you. If you make a habit of it, you're as good as in.'

'And after that?'

'And after that, the pyramid continues. You have to continue to perform, or they push you out. If you don't keep bringing in a little more each year, they worry that you're getting soft and they bring in someone younger. But though the pressure's the same, you know you've made it professionally. There's nothing better than being a partner of Weinstein Lukes. Not on Wall Street. Not anywhere else. And, as I say, you don't need to worry about your heating bills.'

Zack's face was almost expressionless. If anything, his short mouth was a little tighter than usual, his narrow eyes still narrower. But little as he showed, he was lost in wonder. Weinstein Lukes was in a different league from Coburg's, a different world. This truly was the Olympic squad, and, for the first time in his life, he felt it a privilege to be a part of something instead of feeling that that something was privileged to have him in it.

But that wasn't his main thought. His main thought was this. If he made thirty-five million dollars for the bank, he'd be in line for partnership. A partnership would net him millions of dollars in the first year alone, millions of dollars which would unlock his father's fortune. If Zack had ten years to do it, he'd be as certain as anyone could be that he'd make the grade. But he didn't have ten years, he had just two and a half.

3

George's belch rose from his stomach like a whale fart. His hand leaped to his mouth, but dropped back before reaching target. He could be himself here. His belch emptied itself cavernously into the room.

'Sorry. Great tea, Val. Thanks.'

'My pleasure. You'll do tea tomorrow, will you?'

'Yeah, OK. Can you leave me a recipe and a shopping list?'

'If I'm going to do that, I might as well do it myself.'

George was silent. This was a familiar routine of theirs. After a short pause, Val conceded.

'If you want, you can mulch the garden and I'll fix the tea.'

'What's mulching?'

'Spreading manure. Just pretend it's your dirty washing and the garden's my lounge and you'll do fine.'

'OK.'

'And you do the washing up.'

'OK.'

'And one day you can learn how to use a saucepan.'

'Alright. If you like, I'll do you my liver and onions one day.'

'Idiot,' said Val. He knew she hated liver. She knew he couldn't cook it. 'I'll wash up now if you tidy up next door. Tea?'

'Please.'

George went next door and lugged the sofa into position. He made a pile of his laundry, shoved his dirty socks at the bottom and threw a towel over the mound. Oddly enough, George hardly missed his Chelsea flat with its twice-a-week cleaner and acres of pale carpet. He didn't miss the playboy crowd either. He didn't phone them or write to them. Only Kiki did he miss. His infatuation had grown with absence and he thought about her incessantly, day and night. Many images recurred to him in his dreams and daydreams, but three above all. The two times they'd kissed – once in Monaco, once in his flat back in October – and the time he saw her off at the airport for the last time. She was so lovely, so fragile; so removed from this dirty, plain Yorkshire world. Whatever happened to Gissings and his father's fortune, George seriously doubted whether he could ever be happy without her. Val interrupted him.

'Take this, and mind, it's hot.'

George took the mug of tea. Val had only one way of making the stuff – hot, strong and sweet – but George had grown to like it. He had his father's heavy build, which, in his previous life, had been kept in check by women friends who twittered with horror if they saw him eating the wrong thing. Those days were gone. Nowadays George let himself eat what he wanted – mixed grills, pork pies, chips from the chip shop – and he took no exercise beyond walking around the factory. He had outgrown his old suits and he needed to find new holes on his belts. He was getting fat.

George and Val sat down for a rare evening in front of the telly. The film looked cruddy, but neither of them were fussy and they slurped their tea, watched the film, and ruined it by talking. Val was in good spirits, laughing a lot and teasing him about his growing belly. He laughed too, feeling comfortable. Once he sighed. His hand fell against her leg. He let it lie there and she didn't move. It was a pleasant evening.

When it was over, George took the mugs through into the kitchen.

'I'll get breakfast in the morning,' he called, assuming Val was still next door.

'Thanks,' she said right behind him. Then: 'Are you happy?'

'Happy? What, with Gissings and stuff? It's going alright, I suppose. I don't really know.'

'I didn't mean that. I mean with living on the floor of my lounge.'

'Yes. I don't mind. Sorry. I must be in your way a lot. Perhaps I should roll my bed away in the mornings.'

'Do you want to come upstairs?'

Val was looking directly at him, the colour high on her cheeks.

'There's no space is there? I thought –'

'George, if you want, you can sleep with me. I'd like to sleep with you.'

George was speechless, but it wasn't speech that was called for. He became aware of his body and its desire for Val. Her warmth and strength made sense to him, welcome after the long months of loneliness, the long aching nights spent on the seat of his car, the floor of his van, a mattress on his secretary's floor. He looked at her, meeting her gaze and smiling.

'Yes, Val,' he said, putting his hand to her cheek. 'I'd like that, I really would.'

They walked upstairs and did what people do when their bellies are full and their work is done. Next morning, George rolled up his bed in the living room and put it away for ever.

4

The results of the trading game were announced in a monotone, an unemotional roll call of destiny. Petersen, Onsley, Schiffer, Takako had all done well. Schiffer was impassive, Petersen and Takako were pleased, Karen Onsley split by a grin so broad it threatened structural damage.

'Sophie Clemenceau.'

Sitting beside Matthew, Sophie looked as beautiful and calm as ever, the madonna of the trading floor, the brown-haired beauty Matthew was still learning to appreciate. He looked sideways at her, taking in her untroubled face, her perfect skin, the sweet curl of her ears. He was Adam in the Garden of Eden, taking his last look at perfection.

'Sophie Clemenceau.' Her result was read out. It was appalling. Not one of the very lowest, but bad enough that it marked her out as a loser, bad enough to cost her her job.

'*Non!*' she cried.

She started from her seat. The trading slips were in boxes, filed by trader. Sophie seized her stack of slips and, under the eyes of the class, searched among them till she found what she wanted. It was the blank trading slip she'd signed and given to Matthew. It was blank no more. The ticket was filled out with the details of the trade that had blown her away, broken her bank, stolen her job. It was only a piece of paper, but it felt like a dagger through her heart, a dagger set there by the man she'd loved.

She stared wildly at Matthew. Colour left her face, her mouth and eyes wide open in an impossible question. Her look implored him, begged the world to be other than it was, but the evidence was unmistakable. Without collecting her things, with one last agonising look at her betrayer, she ran from the room.

Matthew should have been elated. His own result would be read out in a moment. It would be stupendous. Better than Petersen's, better than Schiffer's, better than Onsley's, better than Takako's. It was his passport to the Madison trading floor, another milestone on the road to his father's fortune. But, far from being elated, Matthew was scarcely able to breathe. By a trick of lovers' magic, the dagger he had thrust into Sophie's heart now pierced his own. She wouldn't forgive him. She couldn't. He couldn't even ask her to. He had won what he most wanted, and lost what he held most dear. It was too late to wonder if the bargain was a good one.

He was never to see or hear from Sophie again.

5

Zack found Sarah at a table already strewn with champagne glasses. This was the John Peel Ball, an annual get-together for the sons and daughters of the British aristocracy. This year, the ball was at Syon House, a stately home juddering beneath the Heathrow flight paths, but set in gardens a developer would kill for. Like the other women, Sarah was dressed in pearls and a ball gown, hers a billowing concoction in red taffeta.

'Sarah! You look fantastic.'

'Zack! Hi! Thanks. Lovely to see you. Everybody, this is Zack Gradley, an old friend of mine from college. Zack, this is Charlotte . . .'

Sarah sat him next to Charlotte, who said she was dead impressed by him being an investment banker. 'I'm just a nursery-school teacher, I'm afraid,' she admitted, though her accent told Zack as surely as her diamonds, that she didn't depend on her salary to scrape by. Zack struggled to make conversation and stay polite.

Sarah watched him. In the old days, Zack would have made a scene. He'd have upset Charlotte and, when he had her in tears, he'd have stormed off and had a row with Sarah when they were alone. But that was then. This time he was on his best behaviour. He struggled on until Sarah rescued him.

'Charlotte, do you know Dominic? Apparently you were in the same pony club as his sister.' Charlotte went off to squeak about horses with Dominic. 'How are you getting on, Zack?'

'OK, I think. Charlotte seemed nice.'

'Yes, isn't she?' Sarah paused. She was wondering whether to trust him with her fiancé, then impulsively hauled him to another part of the table, adding, 'You haven't met Robert yet, have you? Robert, this is Zack Gradley.'

Robert Leighton was just exactly as Zack had imagined him. Solidly built, a bit short, a bit red in the face, decent enough looking. Zack felt he already knew everything there was to be known about him. Eton. Farming college. A big house and an estate somewhere in the West Country. The intellectual curiosity of a horse. The commercial nous of a leg of mutton. Zack used to tell Sarah she would marry someone like this. The two men shook hands.

'Pleased to meet you,' said Leighton affably. 'I've heard all about you, as they say.'

'Not all good things, I expect. I was pretty disagreeable at times.'

'All water under the bridge now, eh? Couldn't have been that bad if you're still friends.'

Zack shrugged and Sarah smiled. It had been that bad. Much of the time, it had been worse than bad. Even now, they weren't sure they were friends. The evening was an experiment, a dangerous one, with the possibility of a sudden bang. Leighton noticed nothing amiss and continued.

'Sarah tells me you're one of these high-powered banking whizz kids. Don't understand a thing about it myself. Terribly impressive, though.'

'Not at all. It's as dull as everyone thinks. But I should congratulate you. It's a lucky man who marries Sarah.'

Zack's lips smiled, but his hand curled round a tube in his pocket. The way he planned it, luck wouldn't come into it.

'Yes, she's terrific, isn't she? Don't know what she sees in me. Ha, ha.'

Sarah drifted away. She let her ex-lover and her future husband talk, but stayed close enough to keep an eye on them. Robert Leighton was pleasant and dull. He would chase hounds, throw house parties, attend balls, manage his estates, and grow ever redder in the face until he dropped dead. Zack knew that Sarah wanted that lifestyle. She had been born to it and loved it.

But was it enough? Zack didn't think so. As Leighton's wife, Sarah would divide her time between throwing parties and breeding children. She was worth more than that. She was clever. She had a decent career. And she had once belonged to Zack.

Dinner was a crab mousse wrapped in slivers of Scottish smoked salmon, followed by Welsh lamb chops with all the trimmings, and a choice of puddings – either summer fruits in a red wine jelly, or a treacle sponge with *crème anglaise*. The caterers had underestimated the appetite of English public schoolboys for heavy puddings, and only the summer fruits were left by the time the waitresses reached Zack's table. Robert Leighton was deeply disappointed and sent one of the waitresses off in search of a spare treacle sponge, then started praising the lumpy Bird's Eye custard they'd had at Eton. Sarah admonished him, but she'd have done better to get used to it, thought Zack. If Robert Leighton were cut open, they'd probably find treacle sponge. Zack was jealous. Jealous but prepared.

As the port came round, Zack knocked Robert's glass, caught it and restored it to its owner. Robert Leighton drank it happily. Twenty milligrams of powdered melatonin doesn't taste of much, not even to palates more sensitive than Leighton's.

The evening wore on. Balls are not as they used to

be. No waltzes. No dance cards. No debutantes waiting modestly for a chap to appear from the throng, bow from the neck, and beg the honour of a dance. The string quartets have given way to rock music. A couple of live bands in one hall competed noisily with a DJ playing Oasis, Verve and Madonna in another. The dancers were enthusiastic but incompetent. Elsewhere, bouncy castles, tarot readings, fire-eaters, hypnotists and comedians destroyed any lingering resemblance to the gracious balls of old. The flower of England's aristocracy swarmed around like kiddies in a cake shop.

Zack danced for a while with Sarah, Robert Leighton and a few of the others. He was a hopeless dancer and he hated it, but no one else was any better. Leighton complained of feeling queasy and went out to get some air. Zack, Sarah and two of the other girls went along to watch the hypnotist. One of the girls was tempted to go up as a volunteer, but Sarah, who had seen him perform elsewhere, restrained her. They left just as the hypnotist was getting his volunteers to imagine themselves in bed with a blow-up doll of Prince Charles.

As they walked away, Zack caught Sarah's arm. The soft touch of her skin jolted him. Once she had been his and his alone. He wasn't sure he loved her, but his body craved her. He kept his voice steady and pleasant.

'Any chance of a stroll in the garden? Just to clear our heads before the next act.'

The next act was Wulf the Regurgitator.

'Yes, alright,' said Sarah, looking at him sideways, trying to read him, deciding to risk it. 'We haven't had a proper talk for ages.'

'I'm not sure we've ever had one. Not unless you count our rows or our sex. My fault, probably.'

'That's very sweet of you. I hope you're not going to go and turn over a new leaf.'

188

'Don't be silly. You're all set up now.'

'Yes. Rob's nice, isn't he? I'm pleased you two met.'

'Yes. Yes, he is nice, really. Congratulations.'

Sarah looked hard at Zack. Her gaze asked what her voice couldn't. Zack answered her.

'Well, OK. I think you're much brighter than him. I think you have a real opportunity to do well at Coburg's. I don't know what happens to that part of you when you marry him. But I don't mean to criticise. I completely failed to make you happy, and if Robert can do it then so much the better for him.'

Sarah didn't reply immediately. She turned and walked away from the brightly lit rooms into an avenue of towering plane trees. Zack walked beside her, shoes crunching in the gravel. They walked for a moment in silence.

'No, you did make me happy,' said Sarah after a pause. 'It's just that you drove me mad as well. I couldn't live with that. Robert is – I don't know – milkier than you. He's no superbrain, but he likes what I like and he admires me and loves me. Ours is hardly a love without compromise, but what relationship is?'

She looked at him as though genuinely wanting an answer.

'Don't look to me for advice,' laughed Zack. 'You were the only woman who's ever mattered to me and look what happened there. My track record's a lot worse than yours.'

'And you're not famous for your ability to compromise.'

'No.'

She was needling him, to see if he would react. He mustn't. He turned and went on walking. In the distance behind them, pop music wailed and boomed. Coloured lights spilled from the crowded rooms, painting the mild night-time air.

'Thanks, Zack. I was so worried you'd make a scene tonight, and now I feel mean for worrying. I never thought you could be so sweet.'

Just then, from the darkness in front of them, a woman came running. She wore a dress of midnight blue trimmed with velvet and black lace. She was crying and running. One of her shoes was missing and her dress was torn at the sleeve. She sobbed and ran, her one remaining shoe causing her to lurch as she sobbed.

She passed them. Sarah started to walk forwards faster. Zack followed. Beneath a tree, there was a glimmer of white. Sarah started to run. The white patch resolved itself into the shape of a man's starched shirt. The man was Robert Leighton.

He was fast asleep, breathing with a thunderous snore. His flies were undone and his trousers partly lowered. On the ground beside him there was a woman's shoe. In his right hand, tightly clenched, there was a small scrap of fabric, black lace trimmed with velvet. He stank of alcohol.

Sarah's face emptied. She made no move towards her snoring fiancé. There was nothing to say. Zack let her watch for a moment, then pulled her away.

'I'll take you home,' he said. 'I'll speak to the medical staff on the way out and get someone to check on him.'

He put his arm round her and she went with him, unresisting. Through the black cloth of his dinner jacket, he could feel her bare shoulders rising and falling in heavy sobs. His hand wanted to move inwards, to feel the skin on her neck, to touch her properly once again. But it was too soon.

They took a taxi home. Zack took her door key and let them both into her flat. She insisted on undressing by herself, but when she had finished, he put her to bed with a mug of cocoa. He hung her dress up and found a hot-water bottle from somewhere. Sarah weakly smiled her thanks, but Zack brushed them aside. Neither of them said anything about what had happened.

Zack took a spare door key and promised to pop in the next morning to check on her. Don't treat shock lightly, he advised.

He went home elated. He was in a full flood of feeling for Sarah and he urgently wanted to be naked in bed with her again. For Leighton he had no sympathy. He was a fool and deserved what he got.

Back at his flat, the lights were burning and a woman dressed in bra and knickers was sitting on one of his sofas. On her lap, a ball gown was spread out, midnight blue silk trimmed with velvet and lace. The woman was sewing a sleeve back on.

'Unless you've got my other shoe, you owe me a pair of new shoes,' she said.

'You can have a dozen pairs,' said Zack. 'Oscar-winning performance back there. The audience was deeply moved.'

'What did you put in his booze? He keeled over before I could get him into the trees. I had to drag him the last bit.'

'Melatonin. The human sleep hormone. It's totally harmless. My dad used to take it all the time for jet lag.'

'Well, it worked alright. Just don't tell me what the charade was all about. Whatever it was, I'll probably wish I hadn't done it.'

'Oh, no. You virtually saved the planet single-handed. Besides what are old friends for?'

They were close to each other now. Close enough to kiss. They kissed.

No woman was equal to Sarah in Zack's eyes, but

191

while he was waiting for the real thing, he'd take whatever was going. And with his close friend, Annabel Queensferry, their occasional nights of sex had never complicated their long-standing and ever-reliable friendship. They kissed again, and the midnight blue ball gown dropped silently to the floor.

6

One month to go before the trade fair. Sally Dummett had produced her designs. Darren had managed to persuade a reluctant Andrew Walters that the designs could be manufactured, and Jeff Wilmot had been pleasantly surprised to find how low the unit costs would be. George was pleased, and said so.

'Great stuff, you guys. Anyone would think there's life in the old firm yet.'

'We're all off to Wem-ber-leee,' chanted Darren.

'Can we start making this stuff right away?'

This wasn't really a question. Walters and Wilmot had initially said no – Walters because of the problems involved in running too many product lines simultaneously and Wilmot because there wasn't the cash to pay for supplies. But George had started refusing to sign cheques except when he had to, and when there really wasn't an alternative, it was amazing how often he put the wrong date on the cheque, or Val misaddressed the envelope, or forgot to put a stamp on. Val, normally so efficient, had even managed to make a complete hash of copying the returns needed by the VAT office, so it was weeks before the mess was sorted out and the VAT men could submit their claim. So, since there was almost no cash leaving Gissings and still a trickle of revenue coming in, it turned out that Wilmot was wrong and there was enough money to start production.

As for the technical challenges, Andrew Walters, of course, had a point. Gissings, with its antiquated equipment and incomplete production area, was going to be hard-pressed to replicate the techniques of a modern factory. It was like a Spitfire fighting F-111s. But that was where Darren and Dave came into their own. For every problem Walters raised, Darren and Dave found at least one solution and usually two or three. If Gissings was a Spitfire, then Darren and Dave were mechanics determined to get it airborne. If something was broken, they'd fix it. If they had to use string, they'd use string. If they were out of string, they'd use a shoelace. And if the shoelace was broken, they'd use chewing gum and a prayer. One way or another, they'd get the bugger to fly.

At first, Andrew Walters resisted. What the two young men wanted was bad practice and in some cases was bluntly contrary to health and safety regulations. But George was not Tom Gissing, and he approved every suggestion which Walters didn't rule out as impossible. And eventually Walters' pride was piqued. He wouldn't let Darren and Dave steal the show in front of the boss. So he counterattacked. He had technical qualifications and experience far beyond what the two young men could muster. He took their suggestions and improved them. He peeled off their chewing gum and showed them how to arc weld. He didn't want the Spitfire to fly. He wanted it to soar.

So when George asked if they were ready to go, he already knew the answer. Solemn nods from Wilmot and Walters. Unconcerned grunts from the ever-scruffy Darren and Dave. A blithe wave from Sally Dummett.

'Good. Then we'll get started tomorrow. But now there's something else I want to talk about. Or rather, Sally, you should tell us about it.'

'Oh, yes, George,' sighed the designer. Sometimes she felt as though George was the first person who truly appreciated her talent and she liked to tell her friends how much she adored him. She meant nothing by it of course, but Val's sharp eyes noticed how Sally always wore make-up if she was meeting George, and her perfumes became more obtrusive. Val pursed her lips as Dummett continued.

'I wanted to tell you all about some product ideas I've been working on over the past couple of weeks. I call them Bright and Beautiful, because – well, because that's what they are. I got the idea from an Italian designer range, whose cheapest item costs £700. But I think we can produce our own cheap version and really carve out a slice of the market for ourselves. I think –'

'Let's see your drawings, Sally,' said George.

'Of course, George. Here they are.' She emptied her portfolio on the table. In all, there were about fifteen pen-and-ink sketches of different items of furniture: tables, chairs, cupboards, stools, chests, credenzas, and shelves. The shape of the furniture itself was nice enough though nothing out of the ordinary, but the colours were, indeed, bright and beautiful: yellow, red, blue, green. All bright playground colours.

'The idea is brightness, of course, and practicality. These pieces are designed to be completely modular. If you want a bigger table, you just clip a bit on, you don't have to go out and buy a whole new one. Everything is designed to fit into everything else, you can build whatever you want, like a giant multi-coloured Lego kit. Schools will love them. I'm sure there'll be loads of offices who want to cheer things up and who like the flexibility. Children's homework rooms, home offices – the possibilities are endless.'

The others round the table – Walters, Wilmot, Darren

and Dave – picked at the drawings half-heartedly. George and Val, who had seen them before, stayed put. There was no doubting that the products looked fantastic on paper. The question was whether there was any hope of making them.

'Some of these frames are metalwork, are they, Sally? We can't do that,' said Walters. 'We can't deal with materials other than wood.'

'And then there's the paintwork,' said Darren, for once agreeing with his boss.

'Well, absolutely. Our paintshop has trouble dealing with varnish these days, let alone the quantity of paint in this stuff. It's just not realistic.'

George sat silent for a while. Then he turned to Wilmot.

'Tell me how your cash flow projections look for next year, assuming we don't add a whole new product range. Give us your optimistic estimates.'

'Well, on the optimistic estimates, things look OK. We might be making as much as fifty or sixty thousand after interest.'

'So where would the debt be in twelve months' time?'

'With a bit of luck, say four hundred and seventy-five thousand. But I think we should say four nine-five to be on the safe side. Maybe five hundred.'

'Half a million quid,' said George. 'We'll be sitting here with a factory that's a whole year older and a debt that's inched down when it needs to tumble. We need a smash-hit product and, though I love the work you've all done over the past six weeks, it's not a smash-hit. It's a good solid basis for survival, that's all.'

Silence greeted his words. The bright and brilliant furniture stared up from the drawings littering the table. George looked directly at Darren and asked him, 'Are you telling me it's literally impossible to make this stuff at a reasonable price?'

'Ah, no, I mean nothing's absolutely impossible, but, I mean –'

'So, it's possible, then. Right, Darren? Right, Andrew?'

The word impossible didn't exist in Darren's admittedly limited vocabulary, and Andrew Walters refused to appear less capable than Darren in front of George. Both men shrugged unhappily and shook their heads, but they didn't actually say no.

'Good,' said George. 'Then let's get started.'

7

In the lecture theatres of West Point or Sandhurst, you may study the art of war. You will learn at the feet of Hannibal and Napoleon, Caesar and Eisenhower, Marlborough and Grant. You will learn how to beat Wellington at Waterloo and how to have turned Gettysburg for the South. But unless you can stand beneath a hostile sky and feel your courage hold amid the bursting shells, you're no use to your fellow soldiers, you're as useless as pantyhose.

If the training programme was West Point, then the two months following was the march into battle. For those months, Matthew was assigned to shadow a senior trader on Madison's corporate bond desk in New York. His 'big brother' was a tough old New Yorker, Saul Rosenthal, senior enough to have an office and trader enough that he never used it, preferring to sit at his trading station in the middle of the floor. Rosenthal knew the market with bitter intimacy. He spoke as though he were an ill-treated mistress, the market his faithless lover. There was no one better to learn from.

Rosenthal didn't make it easy. Mostly he forgot

Matthew's existence and just got on with whatever he was doing. That was fine. Since Rosenthal kept up a permanent sarcastic commentary on the day's events, Matthew just listened and learned. Every now and then he asked a question. Every now and then he got an answer.

He followed Rosenthal wherever he went and introduced himself to whoever Rosenthal chose to talk to. Most of his future colleagues welcomed him warmly, offering help and advice. Matthew shook innumerable hands and memorised names. So assiduously did he shadow his new boss, that a couple of times Matthew followed him to the john. After all, peeing didn't stop him talking.

Work was a relief, but it was aspirin to an amputee. Matthew missed Sophie constantly and desperately, each day unwrapping new layers of misery. He had no contact number for her and no address. He didn't know what he'd have said if he'd reached her. Sometimes in his dreams, he defended himself. Mostly he begged her forgiveness and asked her desperately to return. She never would. How could she? She was gone for ever and he knew it.

And in the midst of all his pain, one terrible miscalculation injured him almost more than anything. The senior traders who'd watched the final trading game had been impressed. The most senior of them all, Maria Hernandez, apparently insisted to Dan Kramer that all those with 'exceptional trading skills' should be given a job. The Lion of Wall Street had agreed without hesitation. 'Our shareholders like to know we can be decisive when necessary, but we don't need to go overboard. Recruit the best, then retain 'em, right?'

And so it was. Matthew, Scott Petersen, Karen Onsley, Heinz Schiffer, and Fujimoto Takako were each offered jobs. Diego Burelli and Adam Campbell took up their posts, as expected, in Buenos Aires and London. Princess Fareshti Al Shahrani, who ranked next to last in the class, was invited to take up a client marketing post in the Middle East. Her value to the firm had never depended on exam results.

For Madison, there was only one regret: it had wanted to offer Sophie Clemenceau a job as well. As Hernandez put it, 'One bad trade doesn't make you a bad trader and, one lousy trade aside, Sophie's record was outstanding.' Unfortunately it proved impossible to contact her and, after a week, the bank stopped trying. Matthew was left nursing the knowledge that his betrayal had been unnecessary, his cruelty a pointless waste of time.

In the grip of his suffering, Matthew flung himself at work. The US bond markets have a million investors, each with their own set of concerns. A thousand variables affect how investors see things, and there are thousands upon thousands of bonds to allow them to express their views. So for Matthew to know how any given investor would value any given bond at any given time, he just had to get to grips with a few million million permutations.

Boredom was the least of his agonies.

8

As promised, Zack called on Sarah the morning after the ball. He had let himself in with her spare key and prepared a breakfast of croissants, fresh orange juice, bacon, eggs, buttered toast and coffee. He waited until he heard her wake up, then tapped gently at her door and went in. She'd had a terrible night and was pleased to see him. Though she could only nibble at the breakfast Zack had put together, she was grateful for it, and watched

Zack devour her leavings. They kept the curtains drawn and the phone off the hook.

They didn't talk much, but what they did say was final.

'Is there any doubt, Zack? Any doubt about what he did?'

'He was drunk. I'm sure he wouldn't have behaved like that sober.'

'That makes it worse not better.' She paused as her tears overflowed once more. 'We were engaged, Zack. We were going to be married.'

Zack held her hand and was quiet.

The inevitable, of course, took place. Sarah broke off her engagement to Robert Leighton, who had only the very foggiest memory of his supposed crime. Baffled and unhappy, he handed over his Wiltshire estates to a professional farm manager and enlisted in the Coldstream Guards, there to bask in the company of men and horses, neither of which had ever let him down.

Meanwhile, Zack and Sarah cautiously began to make friends. They met for drinks in the City. She invited him to dinner parties, some of which he managed to get to despite his frantic work hours. She talked to him about Robert Leighton. With hindsight, it wasn't just the scene at the ball, she saw that she needed more than Robert could have offered. She had no hard feelings, but it wouldn't have worked out. Zack was generous with his ear, his time and his sympathies.

As time passed, a real friendship began to grow between them. One day, she asked him out of the blue to spend a weekend with her down at Ovenden House, home of her father, Lord Hatherleigh.

'You're not scared I'll throw a tantrum?'

'You'll be out on your ear with the Ovenden Hunt hounds at your backside if you do. But you've grown up a lot, you know. The idea of you meeting my dad used to be my worst nightmare. Now I almost forget to worry.'

'I'll be on my best behaviour.'

'You'd better be.'

'But don't get mad if I start drinking out of the fingerbowls or use the wrong fork.'

'We don't have fingerbowls, unless we're eating something messy,' Sarah began snappishly, then stopped. Zack had been joking. 'Sorry. Just do what I do, bring a decent dinner jacket to wear on Saturday night and don't intentionally annoy my dad.'

It was Zack's turn to be unsure of himself.

'Do you really mean it about bringing a dinner jacket?'

'It's casual most nights, but on Saturdays we like to keep it formal, black tie. Just bring it. Wear it. Then take it off. It won't kill you.'

'No. Don't worry. It's fine. I just didn't know if you meant it, honestly.'

And so it was arranged. Zack sent his dinner jacket to the dry cleaners and did what he could to prepare Weinstein Lukes for the horrible idea that one of its employees might want to stay away from the bank for the whole weekend.

9

For those in the furniture business, trade fairs don't get any bigger than the British Furniture Showcase. Furniture manufacturers, great and small, advertise their wares to buyers from Britain and the world. The product stands are dressed to catch the most fleeting glance: there are desert-scapes, graffiti-spattered New York subways, minimalist backdrops in pure white; even a stand, built on a slant, calling itself 'Ballroom on the *Titanic*'. And always and everywhere, wherever you looked, there were furniture, salesmen, and lists of prices.

And then there is Gissings.

Gissings, of course, couldn't afford one of the giant stands in the main hall. In fact, its budget could only run to a small stand in a room off the hall a little way back from the corridor leading into the main hall. George tried to be upbeat, but the truth was that most of those arriving at the Gissings stand only did so after taking a wrong turn on the way to the loos.

Their products weren't bad. Far from it. Their traditional furniture ranges had been completely overhauled and now looked up-to-the-minute at competitive prices. But unquestionably the star of the show was the Bright and Beautiful collection. Even amidst the clamour of the trade fair, the Bright and Beautiful lived up to their name. They were modern, they were eye-catching, and by God they were cheap. They deserved to sell and to sell well.

'Anything to report?'

George had just come back from a tour of the other stands.

'Nothing, really. We've had a few enquiries, but nothing like an order.'

It was Josephine who answered. George had asked her to help out in an effort to bring a bit of style to the Gissings stand. Val was there too, of course, and knew everything there was to know, but she was hardly a sight for sore eyes. Josephine, on the other hand, wearing one of her designer dresses, was smart enough for venues even more prestigious than this.

'It's always slow the first day,' said Val. 'Buyers look first, buy later.'

'As slow as this?' asked George, but got no answer.

They both knew it shouldn't be this slow. More buyers drifted in, a few of them surprised to see Gissings at all.

'Heard you'd folded. Under new management, are you? You are the new management? Well, good luck to you. Last time I saw old Tom Gissing, he said things were a bit dire.'

Nobody wanted to place an order with a firm which might collapse before fulfilling it. George fretted another hour away, then cut another five percent from their prices.

'It's a really great display,' said Josephine. 'I'm sure things'll come right.'

'Thanks. Yeah. It's OK,' he answered. 'Thanks for coming, by the way. And how are you? How's Mum? Sorry, I hadn't really thought to ask.'

'Well, it's tough,' said Josie. 'Mum's stopped making any real progress and it's a struggle finding the money for daycare. People tell me I ought to put her in a home, but I'm damned if I'm going to.'

'No, Jesus, of course not. I wish I could help, Josie, but I'm not even drawing a salary at the moment.' George paused unhappily and opened his wallet. There was about forty quid there, Val's money really. He hesitated, then handed it all to his sister. 'I'll give you more when I can, I promise. If things get really tough, I can always chuck this in. Get a job that pays.'

'Don't be silly,' said Josie. 'Hold on – buyer alert.'

Josephine put on her widest smile, ready to greet the group of buyers, but it was another false alarm, another group trying to find the loos. Val redirected them, while George and his sister played noughts and crosses on the back of a price list. It was gone midday and sales had been terrible.

Then, unbelievably, a miracle happened. Followed

by a crowd of beautiful young people, Kiki appeared.
Her cream cashmere dress looked stunning against her
tanned skin. A pair of Armani gold-rimmed glasses
teetered on her little turned-up nose.

'Georges, my darling, why do you hide in this funny
little room? It is to be very exclusive, no? Do you like
my new glasses? I bought them so I would look *très*
business. I am very *industrielle*, no?'

The designer frames carried clear glass lenses. Kiki's
eyesight was perfect. She looked about as *industrielle* as a
Versace evening gown. George had left her a message on
the off chance that they might meet for tea or something,
but he hadn't heard back, nor had he expected to. He
longed for her still, despite his continuing relationship
with Val, but he knew that life was carrying him ever
further away.

'Kiki! I'm amazed! How nice of you to come.'

He introduced her to Josephine and Val, whose face
showed what she thought of the newcomer. The beautiful crowd accompanying Kiki milled around the stand,
crowding out any real buyers.

'But Georges, of course I came. My papa is looking for
a new desk and I wanted to get him one as a birthday
present. But he is fond of Louis Quinze antiques. I do
not think these will do. And Georges, where are the
toilettes? We thought they were here or we would never
have found you.'

'You're not the only ones. That's why we're not bloody
selling anything. Nobody comes for us to sell to.'

George's misery flooded out. It was stupid. Nothing
was more certain to drive Kiki away. She left for the
toilets following George's directions, her retinue swarm-
ing after her. The super-rich are pack animals and don't
survive long alone. George thought that was that. No
Louis Quinze writing bureaus. No Kiki. After a quarter

of an hour, he gave up hoping for her return. She'd probably remembered about a party that had to be rushed to
or a dress that had to be bought. His gloom deepened,
unassuaged by Val's companionable presence.

She did come back, though, arms full, loaded with
half a dozen white plastic signs marked 'Toilets'. Her
companions also bore their trophies. They must have
stripped the place bare.

'Sorry we were so long, Georges. Some of these stupid
signs were very high up and so difficult to reach. I hope
it wasn't so bad taking them, but you know they really
weren't working. And I am afraid we might have got
into a tiny bit of a muddle. I think sometimes we might
have put some of these stupid things up again pointing
into this little room. But it is so horrid this place. I do
not think it is nice at all. You see I didn't have very long
to see you and now I have already wasted so much time.
So now I will have to go, but I suppose you will have to
have these,' she added dropping the signs. 'They are not
so clean and my dress is brand new.'

With a last meaningless kiss, she flitted off. George
and Val hid the signs underneath the stand, but it wasn't
long before they needed to straighten up. People began
to drift in, asking for the loos and complaining about
the terrible signing. George agreed, but unfortunately
didn't know where the loos were. For the first time
the room was full, almost crowded. The display drew
a lot of admiring comments, to which George and the
others immediately responded with a price list and
a sales talk. It didn't always work of course, but it
worked often enough. The first orders began to come
in. George began to relax.

That evening, George, Val and Josephine all went
back to Helen's house in Kilburn. George slept with
Val in his old room, but he felt uncomfortable about

it. Sleeping with his landlady-cum-secretary seemed natural enough in Yorkshire, but bringing her to his family home, meeting his mother and sister – well, it made things seem a lot more serious than they were. At least Darren and Dave, who had come down to set up the stand and clear it away again afterwards, weren't there to see them. They had opted to stay with a mate of theirs in Brixton – 'my old dope dealer' as Darren helpfully explained. The two lads had worked like horses to get everything ready, and apart from a few odd jobs to be done at the fair, George had given them the days off. It was less than they deserved.

The evening was a strain. Helen was quite well, with good control over her movements and able to speak fuzzily but fluently.

'Ah, George,' she said, patting Val on the hand. 'Your fiancée? Very nice, dear. Like your grandmother said, always live in Yorkshire, always marry Yorkshire. I did, and . . . and . . .'

Her train of thought led off down the wrong track, and she began to cry. George was killingly embarrassed, too much to notice the flush on Val's cheek, as she leaned forward to explain. For the rest of the evening, Helen was dreamy and peaceful, but she never shook the idea that Val was George's intended.

On the way up to bed, George stopped Josie.

'Er. Tomorrow. Your outfit, you know. Um, do you think it would be OK – I mean, would you mind very much – um –'

He broke off. He didn't know how to say this sort of thing. She laughed at him.

'Longer, shorter, tighter, brighter?' she said.

'Eh?'

'Heels, skirt, top, lipstick,' said Josephine, tapping each in turn. 'Longer, shorter, tighter, brighter?'

'Yes. Yes, please. If that's OK.'

It was OK. The next day Josephine wore an outfit which would have startled a *Sun* editor. It was short. It was pink. It was clingy. It was sexy.

That day, when people came in search of the loos, Josephine said she wasn't able to help, but perhaps they were interested in the products? She bent down low to point out the important features and goggle-eyed buyers were treated to as many important features as they could possibly wish to see. They drank their sparkling wine, ogled Josephine and listened to George's sales pitch. They liked what they saw and orders rolled in.

They sold so much furniture in the morning that George added ten percent to all the prices. Things hotted up even more after lunch, as more people needed the loos. Overnight it seemed that some joker had poured cement into the main toilets at the far end of the complex, so the only ones left functioning were those close to the Gissings stand.

The crowds got so heavy that George raised prices by another five percent. People kept buying. The fact was that people even started coming because they'd heard that Gissings had good stuff at good prices. They sold twice what they had sold the previous day. A journalist from *Furniture Today*, the monthly bible of the furniture trade, came to interview George for a short piece, to be entitled 'Back from the Brink'. George told him that Gissings had been completely recapitalised, and bankruptcy fears were a thing of the past. Buyers could buy with confidence. The journalist swallowed the bait and told George how much he loved the products. George was ecstatic.

The next day was slightly less good. The exhibition authorities had managed to establish some emergency toilets close to the entrance, and the chaos which Kiki had introduced in the signing system had been tidied up, at least a little. All the same, they sold about four fifths of what they had sold the day before, and this time all the sales were at the higher prices.

Going back up the motorway that evening, everyone was exhilarated. Darren drove, claiming to have a valid licence, though Val said the only licence he had was poetic. They counted up the orders and tried to work out how to fill them. It would be tough, but it was a nice problem to have.

As they stopped off for diesel and a cooked tea at a truckers' service station, Darren asked George who that French bird had been on the first day. Apparently, she had seen the Gissings name on the van and had rushed over to Darren and Dave with some bizarre story about toilets and men with holes in their shoes. George deflected the questions. The less Val knew about Kiki the better. And there was another thing too. When they had reloaded the truck for the journey home, George had found five empty bags of cement that hadn't been there on the way down. Perhaps Kiki was more *industrielle* than he had given her credit for.

After getting back on the road, the lads turned the music up and the conversation stilled. George closed his eyes and slept, and his dreams were full of Kiki.

10

Just as Dan Kramer had promised, new responsibilities came fast at Madison, and all too soon Matthew's two-month noviciate came to an end. He was to trade corporate bonds – bits of paper sold by companies to investors, offering a fixed interest rate and a set date for the repayment of capital. His business flow was to come from two salespeople, Alan and Rick, whose job was to bring in the orders. The two men made up the smaller institutions fixed income group, but they looked like a comedy act. Alan was short, fat, and profusely hairy. Rick was tall, thin and bald as a coot. Oddballs or not, they were going to matter. Orders meant trades. Trades meant profits. Profits meant Matthew kept his job, got a bonus and gave him a hope of beating Zack.

Matthew had his desk, his computer screens and his phone in a room where hundreds of other traders had their desks, their screens, their phones. On busy days, the room dinned with two hundred voices roaring deals, exchanging prices, yelling insults. This tumult is the noise of the flood, the flood of money, the largest in the world.

His first day, he returned to his desk from the morning meeting to find his phone flashing. He scooped it up without checking to see who was on the line.

'Good morning, Madison Trading.'

'Hey, Matteo, sell me some bonds,' said a familiar voice. 'I'll have a couple of trillion of Uncle Sam's finest, and a cup of coffee to go.'

'Hey, Luigi, nice of you to call.'

'I was just phoning to wish you luck. I'm going to put you on the squawk-box' – Luigi meant the speaker phone, which would blare Matthew's voice out of a speaker instead of the receiver – 'there are a couple of other guys who want a word.'

Anders, Cristina and Jean-François all came on the line. They abused him and wished him luck in equal measure. Then there was a bit of shuffling and the unmistakable Scottish tones of Brian McAllister came down the phone.

'You've done well, Matthew. I understand only a few people survived the programme, and you did. So that's a credit to you. And Saul Rosenthal tells me you've been learning fast with him and he sets his standards high. So well done so far – and good luck.'

'Thanks,' said Matthew, flattered. He was amazed McAllister had time to think of him – and astonished to find that Rosenthal had even noticed him, let alone formed a favourable impression.

'Remind me who you're working with.'

'I'm on the corporate bond desk, working with the smaller institutions sales team.'

'Indeed. They'll be reporting to Fiona Shepperton, who's been asked to shake up the sales effort over there. She's a fine professional, Matthew. You can learn a lot from her. Don't be put off by her manner. She can be a little sharp.'

Matthew had heard Rosenthal mention Fiona Shepperton with respect as well. She was Alan and Rick's boss, so she'd be worth getting to know. McAllister signed off and Matthew sauntered over to Alan and Rick to discuss the coming day. Alan, already perspiring and with shirtsleeves rolled up, greeted Matthew.

'Jesus Christ, Rick, this guy's hassling us already, and he hasn't even brought us our apples for being nice teachers.'

Matthew dumped a couple of hot coffees on their desks.

'If you wanted apples, you should have said.'

'Aw, real coffee. He's even gone to Starbucks for them. Give the man a kiss, Rick. Show him you love him.'

Rick mopped the top of his gleaming head and took his coffee. His pate reflected the ceiling strip lights in high fidelity.

'Ah. Coffee. Great.' Rick was the quiet one of the duo.

Having introduced himself, Matthew sat down to discuss the day ahead. What were their clients thinking? Were the orders going to be to buy or to sell?

How would the long maturities fare versus the short maturities? What factors would influence the market over the coming week?

The three men quickly gained respect for each other. Alan and Rick had inherited a meagre business from the previous sales team, which had since been fired. Their job was to ramp up business on the basis of good advice and solid execution. However unlikely in appearance, they were true professionals.

For their part, Alan and Rick had dreaded the arrival of a total novice. The trouble with selling to the so-called smaller institutions is that you inevitably end up with the least experienced traders. But Matthew already knew the market well, and he was eager to learn from those who knew more. Alan and Rick had been surprised to get a call from Brian McAllister that morning, but the Scotsman had been right. Matthew did show promise.

When they parted, Matthew knew a lot about what his future clients were thinking and had some ideas on what trades to make to get started. His next visit was to Saul Rosenthal. He found him on the phone to some poor soul on the West Coast, who should have been enjoying a good night's sleep instead of worrying about the bond market.

'Don't worry about it. Get some sleep. You worry too much,' said Rosenthal hypocritically. 'Gimme a call when you wake up, but I tell you Treasuries aren't going anywhere until Friday at the earliest. Trust me.'

Whoever it was on the other end of the line was eventually pacified and hung up.

'Am I a trader or am I a therapist?' complained Rosenthal. It was his way of asking Matthew what he wanted.

'I have some ideas I wanted your input on, please.'

210

'That's right. I'm a therapist. Lie down and tell me about your mother.'

Muttering on, Rosenthal took the pad from Matthew's hand and glowered at Matthew's jotted notes.

'Jesus, those nightmares must be really getting to you if you want to go long at the short end of the curve. And what's this? Your clients want to screw around in zero coupon bonds? Just say no, Matthew. You need to be a big bad man to do that, not the Third National Bank of Banjo Creek or whoever the hell your client is.'

He rambled on, interrupting his own monologue to complain about his bagel – 'no cream cheese today. My fault for breaking the Sabbath' – to take another couple of phone calls – 'Saul Rosenthal, psychoanalyst, at your service. No wacko too crazy, no psycho too nuts' – and to buttonhole a couple of other traders walking past his desk. By the time he'd finished, he had given Matthew a load of useful hints on how to proceed.

'Thanks, Saul. I appreciate it.'

'Don't be grateful. That's your Oedipus complex talking. Tomorrow's rebirthing therapy. Meantime, that'll be four hundred dollars for the session.'

'Cheap at the price,' said Matthew. 'But it's against my religion to give money to Sabbath-breakers.'

The conversation was over.

Shortly after the market opened, Matthew got his first actual order from an actual client. He quoted a price aimed at winning the business. The client hit Matthew's bid and Matthew had sold his first bonds. The next step was to go and buy some bonds in order to meet his obligations. He hit a touch-sensitive screen containing all the phone numbers he would ever need. A string of names came up. Clients, traders, contacts. He selected a name, hit the button, got through to a trader at another bank. Matthew spoke briefly and bought in some bonds, at a price one thirty-second of a percentage point better than the price he'd just sold at.

Matthew had completed his first trade and closed out his position. He'd made a profit of seven hundred and fifty dollars, a nice way to start. The graduate of West Point had fired his first shot.

11

At eight fifteen one Saturday morning, Zack set off in thin traffic for the M4 out of London. He was excited.

It took him three hours to reach Ovenden House, which dominates the little Devonshire village of Ovenden. Zack nosed inside the huge ornamental gates and drove slowly up a long drive. The house wasn't immediately visible. Massive oaks spread their leaves above deer grazing in the park. A lake curved round, its far end out of sight. From a jetty on the further shore, a fisherman cast his rod over the still waters. Then the house itself came into view, pale grey stone floating on the landscape. It was enormous; enormous and beautiful. Better yet, it was enormous, beautiful and immaculately maintained. No tottering statues. No leaking roofs. No parkland dissolving into scrub. The architect was famous, but to Zack, the architecture was less interesting than the wallet which lay behind it. His excitement mounted.

A butler met Zack on arrival and escorted him upstairs.

'You'll find the bed a little tight, sir. It's seventeenth-century, I'm afraid, when gentlemen were shorter. I'll open the windows for you.'

As the butler began to fiddle with the window catches, the door swung open and in strode Sarah, wearing jodhpurs, riding boots and a tweed jacket worn over an old jumper.

'Zack. You made it! We've put you in here, have

212

we? Bed's a bit small, but if you throw that bolster on the floor and sleep cross-ways you should be alright. Seventeenth century, I think, used to belong to some princess or other. The Duke of Wellington once slept in mine, but he was allowed a decent-sized bed. Thanks, Jasper. I'll sort Zack out.'

Jasper, the butler, shoved the windows fully open, then left. The room grew quickly cold. Sarah hurled an antique embroidered bolster from the bed and punched the pillows into position. 'That should do.'

'Great,' said Zack. The bed had looked fine to begin with.

Out in the country, Sarah Havercoombe was louder, posher, horsier than she was in town. Zack winced internally, understanding how Robert Leighton and Sarah had thought they could build a life together. But he kept his self-control. There was more to Sarah than horses and punching pillows. There was her body and her cash for starters, but Zack was thinking of more than that. He wasn't sure if he loved her, but he certainly respected her.

'Riding or fishing?' asked Sarah. 'I'm going out riding. If you want, we'll find you a really quiet horse. Or Dad'll be going down to the lake later. Do you fish? I can't remember.'

'Don't be silly. You know quite well I can't –'

'Oh, I'd forgotten. You're useless, aren't you?'

'– but I think I'll come to less harm with a rod than a rein. Would your dad mind teaching me?'

'Oh, he loves it. He's hopeless, but he loves it. I'll take you down.'

They left the room and began to walk a maze of corridors to the back stairs.

'That's the trouble with these houses,' said Sarah. 'You have to learn them when you're little or you never will.'

At length they emerged on to the ground floor of the main wing. Two spaniel puppies raced out from somewhere and greeted Sarah joyously. She thumped them affectionately, and put her hand in her jacket pocket looking for treats but brought it away empty.

'Sorry, sweethearts. Just carrots for the horses. Nothing nice for you. Bonnie and Smudge, this is Zack. Zack, meet Bonnie and Smudge.'

Zack was nervous of dogs, but he put his hand out to try and pat them. They darted away, but not before Bonnie had given him a huge lick. He wanted to wash it off, but realised that that would be a crime in Sarah's eyes. When she wasn't looking, he wiped his hand on his trousers, but he could still feel – and smell, he'd swear it – the imprint of her tongue. Sarah led the way to her father's study, puppies charging ahead of them, barking.

'Dad's working, but he'll be happy for a break. We'll dig him out.'

She was about to open the door, when Zack grabbed her.

'What do I call him?' he whispered.

'Call him Lord Hatherleigh when you shake hands. He'll tell you to call him Jack. Then call him Jack.'

Zack nodded, and Sarah flung open the door.

'Hi, Dad. Meet Zack Gradley.'

Smudge and Bonnie tore into the room. Lord Hatherleigh, thin as a whippet and as fit, rose from his desk. He moved towards Zack and Sarah, lifting his reading glasses from his nose. Smudge gave a delighted bark and charged between his feet. Hatherleigh tried to avoid the puppy and stepped sideways against a stack of papers on a sidetable. The stack began to totter.

Zack, quicker than Sarah, leaped forwards to steady it, but Bonnie had glimpsed Smudge beneath the desk and was off in pursuit. She tripped Zack, who cannoned forwards. He head-butted the papers and brought the whole lot tumbling down. A heavy glass paperweight which had been sitting on top thumped down on his skull.

'Bloody dogs. Quiet!' shouted Sarah.

'Are you alright?' enquired her noble father.

'Lord Hatherleigh. Pleased to meet you,' said Zack.

12

'We'll have to phone and cancel.'

'We can't cancel. They're customers. They're an endangered species.'

'Well, we can't supply what they've ordered.'

Andrew Walters and George stared at each other. This was a showdown which each had been expecting since George insisted on putting his 'Bright and Beautiful' range on to the stand at Olympia.

The classic and traditional ranges had sold better than expected, but at George's insistence they'd been running the production lines at full tilt over the last four weeks, and by working more long shifts they should be able to meet their commitments. Wilmot was happy too. With the extra ten percent George had slapped on to prices, they were making excellent money on every sale.

But almost half their orders were for the Bright and Beautiful range. George had put prices up once, then twice, then pushed back delivery dates in an attempt to give the creaking factory a chance. If they could meet the orders, they'd have made a huge step towards turning the company around. If they defaulted on their promises, or if the cost of meeting their promises was prohibitive, the company might yet be dead and buried before the end of the year.

There were two main problems. First, they needed a supply of metal frames for the furniture far in excess of what they had already ordered. Second, the paintshop was grinding to a halt about twice a day. It had been designed for varnish only, not paints, and it wasn't much good even with varnish these days. According to Walters, they could simply forget it as a way of painting the furniture Bright and Beautiful.

'How about calling it Naked and Natural, instead? That way we could just send it out without paint or varnish.'

Walters was defeated. George hadn't a clue what to do, but he wasn't defeated. He began to explore the issues one by one with the older man. Just then, footsteps came running down the hall and into the room. It was Darren. Dressed in a hideous brown and purple shirt and dirty hipsters, he was a complete contrast to Andrew Walters' old-fashioned formality. He skipped round like a puppy, waving a bit of paper.

'It's coming home, it's coming home, Gissings' coming home,' he screeched.

He'd have continued, but Walters, with surprising deftness, tweaked the paper from his hand and began to read.

'Well, what do you know?' said Walters, in real admiration. 'The little bleeder's found a place in Sussex which says it can do all the frames we need, on time and under budget.'

'It's coming home, it's coming home,' chanted Darren, wiggling his hips.

Walters passed the paper over to George, who read it slowly. It was a written quote from The Sussex Metal

Workshop. Sure enough, one of their two problems seemed to have been solved.

'Good stuff,' said George. 'Now there's just the paint issue to deal with.'

Darren's chant tailed off. Walters looked grim. Then he remembered Darren's presence and pulled himself together.

'Well, we've basically got about three options. First, we tell all our customers to wait for about a year while we figure out how to fill their order. I assume we're not keen on that one. Second, we buy, beg, borrow or steal a fully equipped paintshop from somebody. Third, we buy a few dozen hand-held sprays, hire enough workers to work round the clock, do everything by hand and stand over the finished articles with umbrellas to keep the rain off while they dry. Remember we can't even dry this stuff with our paintshop configured as it is.'

'Yeah. Let's concentrate on the last two options,' grunted George.

'OK. To do this properly we need a new paintshop, and that would include an expanded drying chamber. My guess is that we would spend, say, two hundred grand on equipment, plus a bit more for installation and all the rest of it. But this isn't the kind of kit you just buy off the shelf. You order it, they make it. It all takes time. If we put in an order today, we'd be doing well to have everything up and running within four months.'

'So we rule that out. What about renting out somebody else's paintshop? Giving them some money for use of their facilities during the night? There must be somebody else with the facilities to do what we want. It's hardly rocket science.'

'I've already called around,' said Walters. 'The trouble is that anyone with the facilities to paint, varnish and dry furniture on a large scale is in the furniture business themselves. And they don't want to give us a leg up. We're competitors, after all.'

'Hmm,' said George. 'Can you give me a list of who you've called? Which companies, and who you spoke to. Oh, and if there are any companies you didn't call, but who you reckon would have the equipment we need, then give me their names too.'

'Yes, if you want. Tell you who'd be best though. Asperton Holdings are the biggest manufacturers in the north of England, and they do a lot of work with paint. But we wouldn't stand a chance with them. They've been dying for us to fold for years.'

'S'true,' said Darren. 'I've got a mate there and he's seen memos and stuff saying they expect us to keel over any day now. They thought about buying us out apparently, but thought, "What the hell. We'll just wait for them to die, then grab their customers for nothing."'

'Lovely,' murmured George. 'Just lovely. Asperton Holdings, you say.' He paused for a moment. 'Now, what about our third option?'

'The spray guns, you mean? That was a joke, George.'

Andrew Walters didn't usually use George's first name. That he did it now was a sign he was being careful with George's feelings. It was as though he worried George's refusal to contemplate defeat was on a par with Tom Gissing's final flight from reality.

'OK. Just tell me your joke at greater length, then.'

Walters sighed.

'Well, the way we got the stuff ready for the trade fair was with hand-held spray guns which you can pick up anywhere. The wood needs undercoat and topcoat, maybe varnish too. Between each stage you need to let it dry. In total it took us about a couple of days per item. We used the museum room as a paint room and let things dry in there. If we had worked round the clock and filled the room with as much furniture as it would fit, we could probably have done around thirty units a week. Maybe forty.'

They would need to produce at least twenty or thirty times that number each week to meet their commitments.

'OK. Anything else?' asked George.

Walters was openly laughing now.

'Well, the only other massive problem I can see is how labour intensive the process is. If we had a paintshop which worked, we'd just drop an entire batch on the conveyor belt in the morning, then stroll down after lunch and take it off. With spray guns it takes a hundred times longer, and you need care to get the finish right. We'd probably need to double or treble our staff just to do the painting. I can think of about nine or ten other problems, but they're minor by comparison. I expect you don't want the full list.'

George waited. Walters had finished. Darren too was silent. If he'd thought of anything else, he'd have chipped in by now.

'Good,' said George. 'Thank you. Here's what we'll do . . .'

13

Zack went straight from Ovenden House to Weinstein Lukes, arriving at eight o'clock on Sunday evening. He'd had two analysts work through the weekend to prepare for the week ahead. The two youngsters, a Brit and a Swede, sitting in their wasteland of cold pizza and discarded company reports, were nearly finished.

'How are you doing?'

'We've got to rerun some of the share price data.

The computers have been down. Apart from that we're done.'

'OK,' said Zack. 'Get on with that while I check this through.'

Weinstein Lukes is a banter-free zone. You say what you need to. You are polite and professional. But such is the pressure of work that unnecessary chat is squeezed out as surely as laziness.

Zack reviewed the work. It was basically fine, he saw with relief. He'd spent a weekend away from the office and it hadn't gone wrong. There were a couple of errors which needed correction and a bit of extra work to be done, but all in all, the young pair had done a good job. Another six hours this evening should finish it.

Zack broke the news. The young British analyst, a gangly ginger-haired chap called Smylie, was crestfallen. He had a receding chin and a protruding forehead. It looked like somebody had squashed his chin in making everything else bulge out, like a fat man on a waterbed.

'Actually, I'd been hoping to visit my grandmother this evening. It's her ninetieth birthday and there's a bit of a family get-together. I could come back in afterwards.'

'Where does she live?'

'She's in a nursing home in Surrey. I could probably be there in an hour. Spend an hour or so there and be back here by eleven or half past.'

'How much sleep did you get last night?'

'About four hours. We were cranking to get finished.' Smylie was hopeful.

'OK.' Zack was unmoved. 'You'd better stay and finish this stuff now. We've got a few hours more work to do and I don't want mistakes creeping in because of tiredness. You can see your grandmother tomorrow.'

Smylie nodded slowly. Tomorrow he was being taken off Zack's project to start on something else, something else with deadlines that couldn't wait, or wouldn't. Besides, the family would all be gone and he'd have missed her birthday. Still, he'd sent a card. He'd try to get down next weekend.

While the analysts went wearily back to their number-crunching, Zack settled down to work. But though he tried to concentrate, there was something on his mind, a little pulse of excitement, bugging him.

The weekend had been fine, very pleasant in fact. Lord Hatherleigh ('Call me Jack, for heaven's sake') had proved to be an excellent teacher of fly-fishing, and, to his surprise, Zack had turned out a fairly adept pupil. The two men got on well, and the following day Zack had been genuinely torn between whether to fish with the viscount or ride with his daughter. However, Zack was there for a purpose, and he let Sarah coax him on to horseback. Sarah had galloped around him, jumping home-made jumps with terrifying skill and making unhelpful comments to Zack about his riding posture. He scowled with frustration, trying to pummel his lethargic nag into something faster than a slow walk. Sarah's clear laugh rang out as she thundered past, inches away, spattering him with earth.

On horseback, her horsiness suddenly fell into place. She was strong, daring, athletic, in command. Out here, it wasn't off-putting, it was electrifying. By the time she'd dismounted and was standing beside Zack in the stable showing him how to undo the girth and remove the saddle, Zack was under her sexual spell as strongly as ever. He longed to touch her, but knew it was forbidden.

When he left for London, he told her he couldn't wait to be invited back.

'Don't be silly,' she said lightly. 'Old friends don't need invitations. Just let us know when you're coming.'

It had been a nice thing to say, but Zack didn't want to be thought of as an old friend. Had her body really gone deaf? Couldn't she hear his calling?

But it wasn't any of that which was on his mind right now. It was something else, something earlier, something only partially seen. Zack thought back, searching for the clue.

When he had crashed into Lord Hatherleigh's papers, he had looked groggily around at the debris as Sarah chased the two excited puppies round the room. Zack called up his mental picture of the scene, bringing it out of the shadows, sharpening the focus. In a remote part of his brain, the tiny pulse of excitement beat a little harder. The thing, whatever it was, lay here.

He scanned his mental image, reading the pages scattered on the floor. *Hatherleigh Pacific*. The name was everywhere. That was the family's Hong Kong holding company, source of all its wealth. It had been worth £30 million or so when Lord Hatherleigh inherited the stake from his father, but it was worth fifteen times that amount today. More than just a decent fisherman, was Jack Hatherleigh.

But the name didn't interest Zack. Hatherleigh's desk was bound to be spread with his own company documents. No. It was the others that Zack struggled to identify. He concentrated harder and the picture inched further into focus.

South China Trust Bank. That was one of the names alright. It was a middling sized Hong Kong bank, as far as Zack could remember. Why was Hatherleigh interested in South China Trust? Zack frowned. He'd been whacked on the head by a paperweight and the picture was blurred. But what was this? Sarah was fighting Bonnie for a sheaf of papers. The picture swayed to and fro as the contest raged. Zack froze the picture. Bonnie's drooping lip hid the crucial wording. Zack released the picture and let it run forward for a second or two. Stop. Sarah was winning and Bonnie's mouth was being forced open. Zack peered at the words visible through her teeth. There was some handwriting, hard to read. He grimaced with the effort.

Then he relaxed and smiled. He had work to do.

14

Founder's Day at work; a party in the evening; an excuse to dress up.

Josie hadn't been sure whether to go, worried about finding someone to look after her mother for the night, but in the end decided to go for it. She hadn't lost her taste for parties just because she'd lost her future, her wealth, her father and, in effect, her mother, all in a few horrible weeks last year. She'd go, get drunk, have a dance, do her best to have a good time.

It was a decision she regretted. Although she worked in the foreign trade department, she'd been seated on a table filled with computer types, a well-meaning gesture to seat her with people her own age. Their conversation was cyber-yak, computer games, and alcohol; their cheeks more accustomed to zit cream than the razor. Josephine sat in her designer gown, wondering whether to leave now or hang on for the dance.

Just then there was an eruption further down the table. A couple of geeks had produced pocket chessboards with magnets for chessmen. One of the older computer nerds, who must have been touching thirty, was protesting, but, to Josephine's accurate eye, was actually delighted by their appearance. There was a chant of 'Mik-los, Mik-los'. A jacket was pulled over his head and tied unnecessarily with someone's tie. The chessboards were set out, ready to play.

There was a complaint from inside the jacket. It appeared that the man within was unhappy at being prevented from drinking. There was some more cheering and the jacket was rearranged to allow him to drink while still unable to see. Further muffled sounds from inside the jacket. Josie didn't follow what was being said, but all of a sudden a space cleared opposite the man and Josie was being ushered into it.

'. . . play a beautiful woman,' she heard as she sat down.

'I'm no good at chess,' she said.

'I play without my horses,' said the Jacket.

'I don't have a chessboard,' said Josie, looking sideways at the two geeks who had first produced the boards. Neither of them looked like surrendering theirs.

'I play three,' said the Jacket, and too many helpful hands began tearing bits of paper and scribbling on them, until Josie was sitting in front of a paper grid with thirty paper chessmen ready to do battle. There were more chants of 'Mik-los, Mik-los'.

'We start?' he asked. 'Pawn to queen's four all three times.'

Josie studied her board. She wasn't much good at chess, but was mildly insulted at the suggestion that she could be beaten by a blindfolded man playing three games at once, drunk and missing two of his pieces. She moved her queen's pawn out and looked up, wondering whether they had to take it in turns to give their moves. They didn't. The two geeks, both of them more practised players, were singing out their moves and getting immediate responses from the Jacket.

'I've moved my pawn out,' said Josie. 'The one in front of my queen.'

'I am Miklos Kodaly,' he said. 'Pawn to queen's bishop three. It is my delight to meet you.'

A glass of wine moved inside the jacket and returned empty.

'Josephine Gradley,' she said. 'Nice to meet you.'

Other people's hands moved Kodaly's piece for him and suggested moves for Josephine to make. She complied, moving the piece and letting others translate what she'd done into chess-speak. Kodaly continued to play on three fronts, briskly moving through a well-memorised opening sequence with the two geeks, thinking longer with Josie, where his absent knights made things harder.

'I'm moving my bishop,' said Josie.

'Better to defend your castle,' said Kodaly. 'He's not safe.'

'I thought that was my castle. The paper's not very clear.'

It wasn't a great excuse to give a blindfolded man, but Kodaly waved his hand, as though permitting Josie another go conversationally as well as on the chessboard.

'Where did you learn your chess?'

'Bishop takes castle,' said Kodaly to one of the geeks. 'Check. I learned it at home.'

'Which is?'

'Székesfehérvar.'

'Not a Londoner, then,' said Josie. So far, she was less impressed by him than by his chess.

'Lake Balaton,' he said. 'Your move.'

'Can I castle?'

'No. My bishop checks your king. Hungary.'

'I've got your plate here if you want it.'

'No, no. Drink only. *Magyar vagyok*. I am from Hungary.'

'I'll take your pawn, then.'

'Better. Queen takes pawn.' Then to one of the geeks, 'Checkmate in three.'

'So what are you doing here?'

'I have three skills. Chess, alcohol, and computers. In Hungary, I am only the eighth player, one time sixth. In Italy, I would be champion, but Hungary . . .' he shrugged, still inside the jacket. 'Is not so easy to make a living playing chess or drinking.'

'So computers it is.' Josie sipped her wine. In the time it had taken her to drink half her glass, four glasses had disappeared inside the jacket. 'I think I'll take your castle.'

'Then I think I take your queen.'

Summer 1999

A tired old century ends with a whimper. A rainy summer fills photo albums with washed-out picnics, soggy weddings, and slug-eaten gardens. The mood is downbeat, uninspiring. It wasn't much of a century as centuries go, and at this rate no one'll miss it.

It is 19 June 1999. There are 755 days to go until Bernard Gradley's deadline.

1

Val began to load the dirty washing into the machine: her black knickers, his jeans, a few socks and some towels. With the jeans, she felt automatically in the pockets before shoving them in. Just as well. He'd left his wallet inside. She put it aside, added the rest of the washing and set the machine running, his wallet lying on top.

Although it was Saturday, George would be at the factory until tea time, walking the rain-swept buildings, obsessively doing whatever needed to be done. Once Val had arrived to pick him up to find him sweeping the factory's reception area. 'Looked a bit untidy,' he'd explained. 'Creates a bad impression.' George wouldn't need his money there. She got out a mop to wipe the kitchen floor, leaving the wallet where it was.

She wiped the floor, dusted the living room, cleaned the cooker, hoovered upstairs and down. The washing machine shuddered and finished. The factory was making money now, and George had started to pay himself a small salary, mostly so he could send Josephine some money each month. He didn't pay Val rent, but he was keen to contribute to household expenses and she needed a new hoover. She'd ask him that evening.

Val hung up the wet wash and loaded the machine with the whites. His wallet sat there, unmoved.

The next job was shopping, which meant a trip downhill into Ilkley. Val was low on cash and would need to go via the bank, unless she borrowed off George. She hesitated. His wallet was his, part of a man's private world. But then again, weren't they lovers? Why have secrets? Why should it seem so important that his wallet sit on top of the washing machine, untouched? Besides, it was raining and the walk to the bank would be a wet one. She picked up the wallet and opened it.

There was cash enough for the shopping. She could have taken what she needed and left the rest. But she didn't. They were lovers, after all. No secrets. She examined the wallet. There were some credit cards, a couple of receipts, boring stuff mostly. And there were some photos. Three in all, dog-eared and waxy with use. Two were of the French girl, Kiki, looking impossibly slim, young, tanned, flighty, attractive. She was posing on a beach somewhere, in bikini and sarong, looking straight at the camera and laughing, all white teeth and waif-like figure. The third photo was a group shot, George and Kiki beside each other in a group of their beautiful young friends. There were snowy mountains in the background, and piles of ski gear. George looked solid, plain, cumbersome. Kiki, as ever, pretty, alluring, one-foot-off-the-ground, desirable. On the back of the photo was scrawled, 'Georges, I had to send you this. You look so *adorable*, you big bear. *Gros bisous*, love Kiki.' Big kisses, love Kiki.

There were no photos of Val.

Val left the wallet and the money, went to the bank, did the shopping. That evening, she gave George a photo of herself, which he accepted awkwardly but with thanks. She didn't mention his wallet or the photos of Kiki. A week later she looked in his wallet again. The photos of Kiki were still there, facing the front, smooth with use. The photo of Val was there too, tucked away at the back. When Val pulled at it, it stuck to begin with, then, with another tug, the picture jerked itself free of the leather wall. It was the first time it had been moved.

2

Scott Petersen, now a government bond trader and, like Matthew, part of the smaller institutions group, crossed the trading floor. He was going to speak to Rick and Alan, as both he and Matthew did many times a day.

This afternoon, a third person sat in Alan and Rick's little alcove. She was medium height, thirtyish, thick dark hair framing a porcelain-perfect face. The face itself should have been beautiful – it was flawless, long, and elegant – but there was something missing: nothing to invite you in, nothing to make you feel welcome. She was in perfect shape, both in the athletic sense and in the sense that usually mattered to Matthew. It was clear from everything about her that she was in a position of authority. It was equally clear that that suited her just fine.

Petersen beamed his wide Pacific Ocean smile at Alan, Rick and the woman.

'Hi, Al, Rick,' he greeted his two colleagues. Then stretching his arm out to the woman, he introduced himself. 'Hi, I'm Scott from the government bond desk.'

His outstretched hand asked to be shaken. The woman looked at it, said nothing and continued her conversation with Alan and Rick. Petersen paused. Where he was brought up, people didn't behave like that.

'I hope you don't mind me interrupting for a second. I just want to confirm a couple of things with Rick here.'

This was standard. A trader needs to talk to his sales force continually. The etiquette of the trading floor recognises that, and nobody from the janitor to Dan Kramer himself could expect to hold a conversation uninterrupted. Rick and Alan made no move to help Petersen. Their eyes were on the woman, who stood up. The alcove where Rick and Alan had their desks was slightly raised above the surface of the trading floor. With the advantage given her by the step, she was almost as tall as Petersen. She spoke calmly.

'You may interrupt, but first you will kiss my feet.'

Petersen smiled. It was a reflex response when he was unsure of himself. People just didn't behave like that. He checked the faces of Alan and Rick, but they had turned completely impassive. No help there. He laughed.

'Sure I will,' he said. 'But I'll speak to Rick first.'

He made as if to step forward, but she blocked his way.

'I mean it. You will kiss my feet.'

What happened next, happened very fast. Petersen decided the whole thing had to be a leg-pull, besides which, what exactly was this five-foot-six woman going to do to prevent him? He put one foot up on to the step, intending simply to step round his adversary. But before he could even shift his weight, her hand darted down. She grabbed him hard between the legs and yanked him close.

'Kiss 'em.'

She twisted, squeezed and lifted. She was not strongly built, but her appearance of being in shape was accurate. Her knuckles whitened and the strength of her grip was unmistakable. Petersen's mouth moved, soundlessly to begin with. He just about managed to croak an 'OK' before he went back to an inarticulate groaning.

'So go ahead. Kiss 'em.'

She didn't move either foot, which lay about five feet below Petersen's gasping mouth. Neither did she release him, just squeezed a bit harder and lifted a little more. She began to jiggle him up and down, just a tiny bit – Petersen was a big lad, after all – but her victim was impressed by even a little jiggle.

His face went white beneath the suntan. Choking, he stooped as far as he could towards her feet. In order to make the last six inches, he virtually had to allow the woman to carry his weight in her clenched fist, as he pivoted his body down. He managed to land a just about adequate kiss on her foot and she let go at once, sending him crashing to the floor.

'Thank you,' she said. 'Please take your time with Rick.'

Petersen got to his knees, gasping. He didn't believe what had just happened, though if he'd been able to focus on the circle of traders watching the spectacle, he might have figured out, as Matthew had, that this was a fairly regular floorshow. Petersen recovered enough to walk, and limped off to the john to examine his hurts. The question he had for Rick could wait. Matthew turned to Saul Rosenthal.

'What the hell was that all about?'

Matthew had heard stories about all kinds of aberrant behaviour from the eighties, outrages permitted by the general flood of wealth and greed, with persecution of junior traders not merely commonplace but mandatory. But the nineties were meant to have changed all that. Firms were more disciplined, the courts quicker to jump on discriminatory behaviour.

'Ain't she great?' Rosenthal leered. 'Fiona Shepperton. One of the senior folk in sales. A real cutie. Management keep telling her to stop, but none of the guys ever presses a complaint, and the firm doesn't want to kick her out unless it has to. So she gets away with it.'

'Jesus Christ.' Despite himself, Matthew had folded his legs. Rosenthal saw him and chuckled.

'Come to think of it, she's Al and Rick's boss, so you need to get to know her. Believe me when I tell you she's all soft and squishy inside. Loves fluffy animals. Delightful to kids. Just has a thing about junior traders. But don't worry. She's never done any permanent damage so far as I know. She's good at her job too.'

Matthew didn't fancy testing out just how long-lasting any damage would be, but he also knew that Rosenthal was right. If Shepperton was responsible for Al and Rick, then he needed to meet her. And if he had to meet the ball-crusher, there was no time like the present.

He walked over to Al and Rick's alcove, bond calculator in one hand, a writing pad in the other. Shepperton was there, sitting as she had sat before. Matthew kept his expression completely unruffled. He wanted her to think he hadn't seen her recent performance. His advantage relied on surprise. On reaching the little group, he addressed Shepperton directly.

'I'd keep away from those doughballs if I were you,' he said, indicating Al and Rick. 'They don't have a clue.'

232

'And you do?' she asked without smiling. Even when you were prepared, she was unnerving.

'Sure I do. Pleased to meet you. I'm Matthew Gradley, trading corporate bonds on behalf of the Al and Rick comedy duo.'

He stretched out his hand. She didn't shake it. He asked if she minded him interrupting briefly. She smiled a tiny, tiny smile. Lucky twice in half an hour. She glanced downwards. His hands were full.

'Be my guest,' she said. 'But first kiss my feet.'

She stood on the step opposite him. He moved closer, until they faced off just a few inches apart. Matthew shook his head.

'No.'

She was fast, but he was faster. Her hand darted down to grab Matthew, but he had dropped his pad and seized her wrist before she found target. Her captured hand fought to get free. She was strong, but there was no contest. Matthew's grip held perfectly steady. She stopped trying.

Matthew took her other hand and locked it into the same grip. With his free arm, he picked up Fiona Shepperton, Managing Director, and bundled her down on top of Rick's desk. Lifting her weight reminded him of Sophie, and the memory washed through his body in a thin wave of pain. He put the thought aside.

'On second thoughts, I do want to kiss your feet.'

He made a mock bow, raised one of her feet towards him and blew it a kiss from a distance of several inches. Behind him, a ripple of applause spread round the room. Then ignoring Shepperton completely, he turned to Alan and began to discuss the trade. As they spoke, Shepperton interjected a couple of suggestions. For someone who had been away from New York for nearly a month, her grip of the market was remarkable.

It turned out that Alan liked Matthew's idea and asked him to price it up. Matthew took his leave.

'OK, Alan. I'll get you some prices right away.' Then, nodding towards Shepperton, he added, 'Nice meeting you. And thanks for your input.'

'The pleasure's all mine,' she said, smiling thinly.

Matthew walked back to his desk amidst ribald praise from his colleagues. His ability to produce children was intact, but he had no idea whether he'd impressed Shepperton or made an enemy of her. He'd find out.

3

Cabling for the electric lamps hung between the masts like rigging on a ship. It was night outside and a rainy one at that. But inside beneath the canvas, it was a dry, bright day. The drumming of the rain only intensified the activity below.

Men and women, children and pensioners moved amongst the furniture which sat everywhere on the sisal matting. One batch of furniture was being shifted out. In the last forty-eight hours it had been primed, painted, sealed and dried. Even in this strange setting it looked 'Bright and Beautiful' enough to live up to its name. As it moved out, another batch of furniture, this one untreated, was brought in. The baby trucks which moved heavy items around the factory couldn't move on the crowded and uneven floor of the tent. So it was pairs of men, rationing their strength with little puffs of effort, who cleared and refilled the space. Next to the vigorous colour of what had been there a moment before, the white pine boards and bare metal frames of the untreated furniture looked as 'naked as a Spice Girl in the shower', to use Darren's bizarre phrase. But the girl would not be uncovered for long. A group of workers, about half of them women, watched the new furniture as it came in. Behind them was a rough trestle table. Spread out on it were a tea urn, plenty of milk, some biscuits, and thirty-five spray guns, purchased new only a few weeks ago and already as battle-worn as a five-star general. Gulping down the last of their tea, flexing their fingers, and recharging their spray guns, the group advanced on the new furniture. Mostly it was tables and chairs – many of them kiddy-sized for final delivery to primary schools – but there were chests, cupboards, credenzas, lecterns, whatever.

Andrew Walters had been right. The process was very labour intensive. For the first thirty-six hours of the system, George had fussed around like a mother hen. Every surface had to be immaculate. A blemish anywhere, a dribble of paint on the inside surface of a drawer, and he would refuse to allow the item to be passed as finished. For about thirty-five hours, he drove everyone nuts, and it looked as though only a trickle of finished goods would emerge from the flood of raw material pouring into the marquee. But in the hour or so before George finally buckled with exhaustion and was driven home to bed by a determined Val, it all seemed to come together. Workers who had never used a spray gun before, became expert in their use. Tables shone like mirrors. The insides of drawers were dribble free. The Bright and Beautiful range was going to be a smash-hit, a bull's-eye, a chart-topper.

George had underestimated the volume of orders, but the system was coping. George's marquee was one of the largest available in the country, usually used for national agricultural shows, and at a stroke it had solved the problem of space. Meanwhile, Darren and Dave, scouring the DIY shops of Leeds and Manchester, had purchased enough spray guns to brighten up a battleship.

The labour force proved to be no problem either. George contacted all those he'd sacked back in the dark days before Christmas. He offered them a deal. The deal was: work night and day for three pounds fifty an hour, paid in cash. Once production levels had normalised, George expected to be able to rehire them or at least pay them the redundancy money they were owed. Everyone he spoke to accepted with pleasure.

But it wasn't only those he'd fired who helped. Sawley Bridge is a small community and everyone in it either worked at Gissings or had friends and relatives who did. The company's financial plight was no secret, and it was the main topic of discussion in the pub and village shop. The community rallied to the cause with a will. Wives dumped their kids with a neighbour and came on over to the factory. Kids without enough to do in their long summer holidays drifted around the plant, until someone noticed their empty hands and shoved a spray gun into them. Retired craftsmen, fed up with daytime TV and sodden allotments, came back to lend a hand. Even the vicar turned up one day and spent a couple of hours spraying varnish straight on top of some still wet undercoat.

In all, Val estimated that Gissings had a floating temporary workforce of more than two hundred people. Jeff Wilmot, the accountant, fussed about national insurance contributions, health and safety requirements and employers' liability. George doled out cash in brown paper envelopes and at weekends plonked barrels of beer next to the tea urns. He told Wilmot to record the outgoings as 'Consultancy Fees' and the beer as 'Client Entertainment Expenses'. Wilmot wrote a couple of strongly worded memorandums which George threw away, then did as he was told.

Deliveries to customers were ahead of schedule.

4

Walters looked glum, which was commonplace, but Darren and Dave looked like death, and George was alarmed.

'What's up?'

'Ye'd better come and see for yourself.' It was Walters who spoke.

They walked quickly from George's office to the museum which was being used as an overflow storage space. It was piled with furniture, most of it Bright and Beautiful.

'Take a look at this.'

George looked where Walters pointed. It was a Bright and Beautiful child's desk destined for a primary school somewhere in Scotland. It should have been shipped weeks ago, but the school had asked to defer delivery after the headmaster had gone AWOL with the PE teacher and the school's refurbishment budget. The desktop was painted in brilliant primary stripes, with a huge smiley face stencilled on by an ever-enthusiastic Sally Dummett. But the sealant, which should have been as smooth as glass, was wrong. It had begun to bubble and crack. Splits could be seen right across the surface of the desk. The smiley face was developing leprosy. George, his face like iron, dragged his thumbnail across the desk, leaving a furrow of splinters across the unhappy surface.

'What's the problem?'

'We've used two different kinds of sealant. This is the quick-drying stuff, which we started using about four weeks ago to save time.'

'How many are affected?'

'About half what we have in storage, but we expect

all of it to go too. Maybe a third of what we've already shipped.'

'What can we do?'

'Strip the sealant. Touch up the paintwork if we need to but not otherwise. Reseal with the right kind of sealant.'

'Do we know who's received this stuff?'

'We're working on a customer list right now. We'll get that to you by the end of the day. We'll also try to sort out a new production schedule once we know how much stuff will be coming back in.'

George nodded, grim-faced and in shock.

'Don't worry about this, lads. It's not your fault. I was on your backs to speed up the process and you did as I asked. I'm sure we'll sort something out.'

George wasn't being honest. They were at maximum production already. Already, George could see that the enthusiasm, which had let the impossible happen, was wearing thin. The pensioners were drifting back to their TV and allotments. The mothers and children were drifting back to their family homes. If they had to redo four weeks of production as well as meet their existing commitments – well, the thing was impossible. And the cost of doing it would blow all the profit they had earned since the trade fair. And if they failed to make money out of the trade fair, then they might as well forget the whole thing. George had no intention of struggling for ever with a giant loan, regarding each day lived through as a triumph to celebrate. He'd sooner earn his living as a belly dancer. He was getting the stomach for it.

Back in his office, Val was holding her hand over the mouthpiece of the phone.

'It's for you. It's a Mr Evans of Brynmawr Furnishings. He sounds cross.'

George took the phone.

'Mr Evans,' said George smoothly, 'thank you so much for taking the trouble to return my call.'

'I'm not returning your call. You haven't called me.'

This was perfectly true, but you wouldn't have guessed from George's demeanour.

'I certainly tried you earlier in the week. I left a message, but perhaps it didn't reach you. My fault, I expect. I'm always a bit hasty. But I'm pleased you called because I wanted to reach you urgently.'

'Oh. It's the paint surface, isn't it? That's why I was calling. A couple of the chairs you sent us are beginning to peel.'

'That's right. I don't know how to apologise enough,' said George. 'Our supplier persuaded us to change our brand of sealant and it turns out we were given a duff supply. I'm afraid it's more than just the chairs which will peel. The whole lot will go. What I had been calling to ask is whether we can bring the whole shipment back, at our expense of course. We'll redo it, good as new, and get it back out to you as soon as we can. And as a sort of apology, we'd like to give you ten percent off your next order with us and a guarantee that this won't happen again.'

'Oh, well, I suppose that's fair now.' Evans had clearly been expecting a row. Looking forward to it, in fact. Now that George had given him everything he had been going to ask for, he wasn't quite sure which direction to go. 'But I don't want to be left hanging around, mind.'

'Of course not. We'll give your shipment absolute priority when it arrives back here. We'll have it out to you just as soon as we can.' George sensed that Evans needed an outlet for his anger and supplied one. 'The real criminals are the bloody sealant suppliers. They lie through their teeth to sell you the product, then when it fails, they're nowhere to be seen. I don't know how any small businesses survive in this country.'

It was a lucky shot. Mr Evans had strong views about the treatment of small businesses in Britain. Twenty minutes later, George got off the phone, ears ringing with Mr Evans' complaints about the government, Europe and the world at large, but also equipped with Mr Evans' promise not to switch suppliers and the invitation to take as much time over the shipment as needed.

One down, forty-nine to go, thought George. But there was one call he had to make before any of those, the real make-or-break.

He called David Ballard, who, inevitably, was on his car phone. George wondered whether Ballard's insurance company knew about its client's habit of driving on winding Yorkshire roads at seventy miles an hour with one hand on the phone and one eye on the scenery.

'David? It's me, George. George Gradley.'

'George? Well, blow me. You're talking broad Yorkshire now. You should hear yourself.'

'Well, I'm born and bred Yorkshire, what d'you expect?'

'I expected an old Etonian, Giorgio Armani, year-round suntan, designer ponce, if you must know. But I prefer this one.'

It was a backward sort of compliment, but George didn't mind.

'Yeah, well, I wasn't phoning to get your views on my personal development, thanks all the same. I've got something to tell you.'

'Hang on.' There was a pause for a moment. George could hear a high-pitched squeal in the background. 'Sorry about that. Bloody lorry almost hit me on the bend just then. No consideration for other drivers. Lucky

I got back on to my side of the road in time. What were you saying?'

'David. Slow down to subsonic speed and listen. We aren't able to repay your loan. We're going under.'

There was a silence on the other end of the phone for a while. George wondered whether the signal had died. It's amazing how the two percent of the country not covered by the phone company always seems to be where people want to call from.

'OK.' It was Ballard, again, but solemnly this time. 'I've stopped the car and every slow-moving vehicle in the county is getting ahead of me again. So this had better not be a joke. What did you say?'

George repeated himself slowly. He explained the problem.

'I still don't understand,' complained Ballard. 'Take the worst-case scenario. Say you don't make a penny of profit this year. The company's beginning to live again. There's always next year or the year after.'

'Yes, but I won't stick around to watch. And if I'm gone, I wouldn't give all that much for its chances.'

'So why are you telling me this? D'you want me to call in the loan today? Put you out of your misery early?'

'Well, there is one thing you could do for me.'

George explained his idea in a few sentences. Ballard listened. A couple of times he asked questions which George responded to briefly and concisely. Eventually Ballard gave his verdict.

'As it happens, I'm off to see them in a week or so. They're one of my biggest clients, in fact. But they're a sharp bunch and I don't hold out much hope.'

'But you'll try,' said George. He was stating a fact not asking a question. 'That's great. And remember something, David. I've only got a quid invested in this company. You've got half a million.'

5

'Zack, for Christ's sake, you haven't bloody seen her for more than a month. She's had a complete nervous breakdown and you're never bloody here.'

'I'm busy, Josie. I'm literally averaging five hours sleep a night. I just don't have time.'

'So what's more important, then? Dicking around in the City or looking after your mother? Get your priorities straight.'

'My priorities are straight. I'm just doing the same as Matthew and George. We're working our butts off to save our inheritance. Once we have it, it'll all be different. Don't pretend I'm the guilty party.'

'Matthew's in New York. George is in Yorkshire. Matthew phones every weekend and George comes down every second or third weekend. George is as poor as a church mouse, but he still sends money every month, more than he can afford. You live a couple of miles away on some fat banker's salary and we never see you, let alone get money from you.'

Zack started to protest. He loved his sister and his mother at least as much as he loved anyone else, himself apart. But these three years were critical. Pissing around in Kilburn with a long face and a box of tissues wasn't going to make anyone happy. Not when thirty or forty million quid of their money went to endow some bloody children's home.

'Listen, Josie,' Zack began, but Josie had slammed the phone down. 'Yeah, I love you too,' he added sourly.

For now, Josephine could think whatever she wanted. Zack was busy. For one thing, he saw Sarah as often as he could. It wasn't all that often, but he hoped it was enough. He'd been down to Ovenden House a couple

242

more times, and last time had actually managed to stay seated as his horse went over one of Sarah's jumps, albeit on its lowest setting. She'd laughed her clear laugh at him and said he'd never make a horseman, though Lord Hatherleigh said he had 'the makings of a fine fly fisherman'. He still desired Sarah with gale-force intensity, while she remained apparently immune. Zack was in a frenzy of greed, frustration and desire.

Meantime, he was busy. He was working on three separate energy deals for Amy-Lou Mazowiecki. If each of them completed successfully, he'd have earned five and a half million dollars for the bank. He only had to find another half million dollars from somewhere and he'd have met his annual target for a first-year vice president. Mazowiecki was pleased with him and kept shoving good deals his way. He'd make the six million easily.

But Zack wasn't interested in making six million. He wanted to make partner, and for that he needed to make a splash. Mazowiecki had told him that the normal hurdle rate was thirty-five million, but that was for people the bank already knew well. If Zack wanted to make it to partner in the next twenty-three months, he'd have to blow their socks off. He wasn't aiming to make thirty-five million, but seventy. They couldn't refuse him if he made seventy.

This train of thought led him where it always did: to two names pinned to the noticeboard above his desk. He forgot about Josie and settled down to work.

6

Matthew filled out the last of his trading tickets. He made sure they were easily legible, as every screw-up in settling a trade could cost the bank five grand. What a day! What a week! The market had tossed around for five days and ended back where it started. Despite thin markets, Matthew had done more trades that week than in any other so far, but he was still down $20,800. Typical August trading, Rosenthal said.

He tidied his desk, grabbed his jacket and headed out. On the way, he passed by Alan and Rick's alcove.

'Coming for a beer, guys? I'm buying.'

Al and Rick were busy with some computer print-outs. Alan perspired as he always did, his dustbin overflowing with junk food wrappers. His bin was usually full, but not overflowing. He'd had a bad week too. Rick wiped his head with his sleeve. Maybe he thought he was pushing a hair back into place, but he had no hair. Maybe he was polishing.

'Buying a drink, huh, big shot? Don't tell me you've had a good week, 'cause I've seen your trading tickets. Sorry, pal. I've another hour's work here. So's Rick.'

Rick nodded. He didn't get chattier with longer acquaintance. Matthew was disappointed. On the training programme, he'd spent every spare minute either working or with Sophie. He had no friends in New York of his own, and he was finding it tough to make friends on the trading floor. He still missed Sophie too much to make a serious effort with other women, and that ruled out the sort of social interaction he knew best.

Scott Petersen left the room amidst a large and noisy group, mostly female. He'd recovered, then.

'Y'all have a good one,' he called.

Matthew and Alan called something back. Rick nodded and polished. The trading floor began to grow quiet, but it was Matthew's best friend in New York. He felt lonely.

A movement behind Alan and Rick alerted Matthew to somebody else's presence. It was Fiona Shepperton, who had been sitting down at a window, reading some documents. She stood up and handed something back to Rick when she noticed Matthew.

'Did I hear you offering to buy me a drink?' she said.

'Sure, if you like.'

'I'm tied up tonight, but I'm free tomorrow.'

'Certainly,' said Matthew, whose evenings were all too free these days. 'Where would you like to go? You name the spot.' An evening with the ball-crusher wasn't Matthew's idea of fun, but it beat microwaving a frozen lasagne for one.

'I'll have a think and give you a call lunchtime tomorrow.'

Matthew confirmed the arrangement and left the bank, feeling low.

7

David Ballard studied the figures in front of him. He had to admit they were impressive. He had to admit it to himself, that is. What he said was rather different.

'Your profit margins are coming under a bit of pressure, I see. And how do you explain the slowdown in domestic furnishings?'

Mike and Eileen Asperton looked at him startled. They were chief executive and chairwoman respectively of Asperton Holdings. Married for twenty-five years, they were alike as two peas, just as round and almost as small. Mike Asperton was never without a cigar, his wife never without a hanky to flap at the smoke. Their double act was famous throughout Lancashire, and a highly successful act it was too. Through two and a half eventful decades, the company had prospered. Ballard had long been an admirer of the company and had consistently supported its growth with loans and advice. His signs of doubt now were hard to interpret.

'Pressure? We've grown our sales by thirty-five percent,' said Mike Asperton, 'and our margins have slipped only one point three percent. Frankly, we're delighted with that performance. As soon as we slow down a bit, our margins will be back up. And as for the domestic furnishings – well, as you know, we've decided to concentrate on the office and light industrial markets, which is where we think our strength lies.'

Ballard looked dubious.

'Mmm. I agree that if you just look at the bottom line, these results are good, but I am worried about how you got there. Margins slipping with sales racing away – it's the classic recipe for cash flow crisis.'

Eileen Asperton, who had the sharper tongue of the pair, was annoyed. 'David, you know we've never had a cash flow difficulty in our lives. Our budgeting system is state of the art and we're in the middle of refining our projections even further.' Her husband's cigar prodded the air in emphatic support.

Ballard raised his eyebrows. 'You mean the projections in here?' he said, tapping the bundle of documents on his lap. 'These projections are only provisional?'

'No. They're hardly provisional.' Eileen was polite but only just. 'We just want to tighten them up further. You know our standards.'

Ballard frowned. The Aspertons wanted a loan of five million pounds to double their production area, a move which Ballard had been urging on them for some time. They would transform themselves into one of the country's largest manufacturers of furniture, and Ballard was confident they would succeed. Normally, he would have approved the loan without a second thought, but today his agenda was a little more complex.

'How long before you have final estimates?'

'These are final, David. It's just that we go on continuously refining. It's part of our culture here.'

'Well, maybe we should wait until you have your half-yearly numbers ready in another six months. That way we can see whether you're right about your margins, or whether I'm right to be cautious. To be honest, I'd be happy to chance it, but I have to get approval from my bosses. Credit committees and all that stuff.'

'For Christ's sake, man,' cried Mike Asperton. 'We want the cash now. What's to stop you waiting another six months come January?' His cigar was disappearing in rapid puffs and his wife's flapping had speeded up. Ballard studied his quarry carefully and pretended to study the figures again.

'I notice that your third-party income from the paintshop has fallen away to nothing. What's going on there?'

'Oh, we used to let out our facilities to other companies to help pay back our investment. We've discontinued that, as it didn't bring in a lot of money and we're not keen on helping our competitors.'

'Uh,' grunted Ballard. 'Stuff like that doesn't help my case. My credit committee always tends to interpret it as over-confidence. To be perfectly frank with you, your timing is a bit awkward. I got a call last week from one of your competitors. They were more or less throwing in the towel and declaring themselves bankrupt. And you know what committees are like. If I tell my credit committee as the first item of business that our loan to one furniture company has gone to hell, then asking them to lend five million to another is likely to get a bit of a belly laugh. That's why I think it would be better to wait.'

'Well, we're not waiting just so your committee can get its crying over and done with,' said Mike Asperton.

'You're not the only bank in town.' He was neither smoking nor waving his cigar right now. The tip was completely still and all his attention was with Ballard. His wife, too, had folded away her handkerchief and given up her normal background coughing.

Ballard raised his hands in a gesture of resignation.

'Maybe you're right. I shouldn't say that, of course. We want your business, but you're in a hurry and I've got a problem right now. But . . . well, never mind, it's up to you.'

Eileen Asperton wasn't one to let a comment like that slip away from her. 'What d'you mean, but? But what?'

Ballard hesitated.

'Look, just because there are loads of banks these days doesn't mean there's loads of competition. There are only a few banks who'll do these kind of loans and there are only a few people in those banks who are going to handle them. I know them and they know me. If you go trogging down the road to your friendly neighbourhood bank and ask for a few million quid, it won't be long before I get a phone call asking me if I've already turned you down. If I tell them I have, you'll get a lot of polite bullshit, but you won't get a loan.'

'So it can be our little secret then, David.' Eileen Asperton made it a statement, but all three of them knew it was a question.

'I'm not going to lie to another banker, Eileen. I can't do that. We've got a decent banking community up here, because we help each other out. If a couple of us have a loan out to a company in trouble, we sit down together and sort out what to do about it. Most often we agree to stand by the company. I couldn't do that if I was always worried that the other guy was going to cut and run, leaving me head-height in sewage. You understand.'

'Are you threatening me?' boomed Mike Asperton, over his wife's protests. 'Are you seriously telling me that either I sit tight for six months before you condescend to give me some money or you'll make sure that nobody in Yorkshire will lend me a penny?'

'I'm absolutely not threatening you, Mike. If you don't want to wait, then by all means go elsewhere. I won't get in your way. But if I get a phone call from a colleague, I'm not going to lie.'

Mike Asperton sat motionless, scrutinising Ballard. He noticed that his cigar had gone out, and in a frenetic burst of energy, he threw it away, pulled out another, lit it and puffed away until half an inch of ash lay beyond the glowing tip. Then he relaxed like a patient on oxygen therapy, while Eileen went back to coughing and beating at the air.

'Which company's going under, then?' she asked, in an apparent change of subject.

Ballard laughed. 'I can't really tell you that, now, can I?'

'It's Gissings, isn't it?'

Ballard made as if to deny it, but then shrugged. 'How did you know?'

'They've been waiting for the roof to fall in for years. There was an article in *Furniture Today* saying they'd been recapitalised, but we knew that was only a smokescreen. Recently they've been frantically trying to buy themselves space in our paintshop. We said no, they went bananas, then went out of radio contact. So they're finished now, are they?'

'Yeah. It was their paintshop which killed them. They couldn't meet their production commitments and – poof.'

Eileen Asperton leaned forward. She scented victory.

'Have they actually called in the receiver, or are they just about to?'

'No. Not yet. It was a courtesy call to let me know before the end.'

Mike Asperton had caught up with his wife's train of thought, and he leaped in enthusiastically.

'What if we let them into our paintshop? Just long enough to get our loan approved. We get clearance for our loan. Then we pull the crutches away from Gissings. Your credit committee may be upset, but by then it'll be too late. Eh? And you can tell them that with the revenues from the paintshop we'll have restored our margins to last year's levels. What do you say?' Asperton's enthusiasm was thicker than his cigar smoke. He was a good businessman but he'd play a lousy game of poker.

Ballard smiled. 'You're certainly a tough pair to do business with, you two. But OK. It's a deal. Just one thing.'

'Yes?'

'I know you can't wait for Gissings to roll over, but I've lent them a stack load of money. Give them six months in the paintshop. It won't save their life, but it will prolong it. And if they pay me a bit more interest before they cop it, I'm not complaining.'

Both Aspertons looked dubious. Eileen Asperton, the more cautious of the two, answered. 'Who's to say that six months won't throw them a lifeline? We're not in business to support our competitors. After all, they've got a new man in there. Bernard Gradley's son. There are big changes underway, we hear.'

'Yeah. That's right. But he's just a bloke, not the tooth fairy. He's cut jobs and wages. The workforce is thrilled because they think that if they endure the pain for a few months then suddenly everything will turn out rosy. But how long will their patience last? And what happens when it runs out?' The Aspertons were silent, and Ballard could see that his audience wasn't convinced. He dropped his final card, the ace of trumps. 'And you want to know a secret? Guess how much they owe me.'

Mike Asperton grinned. 'How much? Well, now. They're tiddlers and struggling tiddlers at that. Assuming you lent them the money when they were at their peak, I should think they would have been lucky to get two hundred grand. And if they still owe that much now, they're dead. Dead as doornails. OK. So that's my guess. Two hundred grand.'

'Higher.'

'Higher? Two fifty? Three hundred? Not three hundred, surely?'

'Five hundred grand.'

Mike Asperton's face worked briefly, then exploded. 'Five hundred! Half a million quid! Jesus Christ!' He was panting with laughter. His wife smiled, then chuckled. Both of them shook up and down and were turning red. Mike Asperton was beside himself. 'You lent them that much? You'd do better selling life assurance to dinosaurs. Ha, ha, ha. Jesus, David, I'm not surprised your committee is pissed off. God! I used to think you were good at your job. Ha, ha! Half a million quid! Just wait till I tell the board. Ha, ha, ha.'

'I gave you that information in confidence, Mike. Keep it under your hat.'

'Yes, yes. Of course. Don't worry.'

Mike Asperton was still doubled up laughing while his wife vibrated periodically as waves of laughter shook her. Mike's assurances to Ballard would be completely forgotten by the next board meeting, and David could picture the whole Asperton clan, sitting around collapsed with laughter as they thought of the doom waiting for old Tom Gissing's shop.

'Yes. Ha, ha. Of course they can have their six months in the paintshop. They can have twelve for all I care. But – ha, ha – but we'll take payment in advance.' Asperton doubled up again at his own crack.

After his laughter had subsided, his overstretched lungs exploded in a fit of coughing. Recovering quickly, he lit up another cigar, while his wife composed herself enough to start coughing and flapping. Mike Asperton waved his cigar at Ballard. 'Medicine, you know. Dreadful cough. Pardon me. Only thing which settles my chest.'

The remaining business was rapidly concluded. Mike Asperton would phone Gissings with an offer of the paintshop for twelve months, payment to be monthly in advance. David would wait for confirmation from both the Aspertons and Gissings, then recommend Asperton's loan to his regional credit committee in a fortnight's time. If everything was approved as expected, Asperton would get his money within three weeks.

On the road home, Ballard's car phone interrupted him in the midst of another hair-raising manoeuvre at speed on narrow roads. It was George.

'I don't know how you did it, David, but you've worked a miracle. Thanks. Now put both hands on the wheel and both eyes on the road. If you get here in one piece, I'll buy you a drink.'

8

At twelve o'clock promptly the phone rang. It was Fiona Shepperton.

'Hi. I've made all the arrangements. I'll come by

your place and pick you up. I'll be with you in ten minutes.'

Matthew was taken aback. He had assumed they were going out in the evening. Never mind. If he drank enough now, maybe an evening of frozen lasagne and old movies and trying not to think about Sophie wouldn't seem so bad. He ran a comb through his hair, thought about aftershave, then laughed at himself for the thought. This was the ball-crusher for heaven's sake, not a date. Ten minutes later the intercom buzzed and Matthew rode the elevator down to the street.

Fiona was waiting in a taxi. She was beautifully dressed in a short pastel summer dress and linen jacket. Her long hair flowed down in the glossy curls which were kept firmly tied back at the office. She looked unexpectedly feminine, and Matthew, who hadn't expected to find the ball-crusher physically attractive, found himself admiring her. He got into the cab. Like most New York cabs, it looked and smelled like something from the Third World, but there was a waft of perfume too, something clean and citrus smelling. Shepperton didn't strike Matthew as the perfume-wearing type, but he liked it. The driver moved out into the traffic, with the mandatory squeal of tyres and exchange of insults.

'Got your passport?' asked Shepperton.

'Sure. Can't get a drink in this town without one,' said Matthew tapping his pocket. With his fluffy blond hair and wide eight-year-old eyes, he looked young for his age and was well used to the sceptical enquiries of New York barmen. 'Where are we off to?'

'Place called Paradise Island. You'll like it. It's kind of old Colonial meets Caribbean.'

'You're dressed for the part.' She was too: light and informal. Matthew was dressed for the baking New

York weather, but he had opted for a more formal look: jacket, smart trousers, black shoes, starched cotton shirt. He even had a tie in his pocket in case.

They chatted about other things as the cab made its way out of town, heading for Long Island. Fiona Shepperton had no wedding ring, gave no signals of being taken and looked easily nice enough to meet Matthew's demanding requirements, but Matthew was disconcerted rather than intrigued. For one thing, he still missed Sophie and felt terrible about her. For another, Shepperton, despite her relative youth, was high up in the Madison hierarchy. And for yet another, Matthew still crossed his legs at the memory of their first meeting. Making a pass didn't seem like a smart career move.

The cab was following signs to Kennedy Airport. Matthew noticed the route, but assumed they were headed for Long Beach or somewhere on beyond the airport. But when the cab pulled off towards the terminal buildings themselves, Matthew intervened.

'Fiona, I think this guy's on autopilot. You want to set him straight?'

She shook her head.

'He's doing fine.' She leaned forward and spoke through the filthy glass to the driver, 'It's the American Airlines terminal, please.' Turning back to Matthew, she added, 'Paradise Island's just outside Kingston. It does wonderful cocktails and has a great sea view. I know you'll like it.'

'Kingston, Jamaica, right?' asked Matthew, but he already knew the answer.

Inside the terminal building, Shepperton mentioned that the plane tickets were reserved but not paid for and she politely stepped aside as Matthew paid. They were travelling business class, a nice touch. Matthew winced when he saw the price, but he signed without a murmur. This treat was on him, after all. His fault for offering to buy. He might have won the first round, but she had comprehensively outclassed him on the second. The best he could do was pretend he didn't mind.

'Sure you want to come back this evening?' he asked. 'Seems a shame to go all that way just for a drink. Let me get you dinner as well.'

She gave him a huge smile, as though the idea had never occurred to her.

'What a lovely idea. But of course we'd have to stay over . . .' She trailed off delicately.

'Of course we would. I'll book a couple of rooms somewhere. I bet you know some place comfortable.'

Her smile returned. It turned out she knew somewhere just beautiful and had taken the precaution of making temporary reservations on a couple of their best suites. The reservations would naturally need to be confirmed and paid for. The prices were eye-popping but there was no going back now.

'You're sure these suites are nice?' said Matthew stoically. 'These prices seem very reasonable. And do you have any ideas for dinner?'

One phone call later, Matthew had kissed goodbye to another fair-sized pile of hard-earned dollars. Even on his fat salary, he was going to be paying for this for months.

'What a great idea,' he said. 'I had a terrible feeling that you were going to take me to some drab little hole in Manhattan. It's so important to get out.'

They flew down to Jamaica, and stepped out into glorious Caribbean weather. Matthew's stiff city clothes felt instantly unsuitable in Kingston's more relaxed climate, and he dived into an airport boutique to buy some looser cotton clothes. The choice was poor and Matthew came away with a short-sleeved khaki shirt, some bright and baggy shorts and a pair of flip-flops, which he hated. Fiona, who bought a wide-brimmed straw hat at the same store, was a picture of cool elegance by contrast. They looked at themselves in a grimy mirror and laughed.

'I doubt if they'll let you into Paradise Island looking like that,' said Fiona. 'But I'll wave at you from the terrace.'

'No way. If your bar doesn't serve me, then the trip's on you.' He rumpled his hair, undid a few buttons on his shirt and leered at her. He looked like a tourist who'd been enjoying too much of the local weed.

Fiona laughed. 'We'll make it double or quits if you like.'

'Uh-uh. My wallet's in intensive care as it is.'

They bantered more on the ride to the bar. The road and the taxi were much the same as they had been in New York. The driver's English was better.

Beneath the sinking sun, the sea glinted pink and gold. The warm Caribbean breeze blowing in through the taxi windows reminded them how sweaty and grimy a New York summer could be. Fiona visibly relaxed and Matthew began to enjoy himself. Since learning of his father's will a little over a year ago, Matthew had buried himself in work. At least this crazy, expensive trip was a break.

Paradise Island lived up to its name. The wooden building was painted the very palest of pinks, with a wooden fretwork verandah wrapping right round the exterior, a fairy-tale cottage on golden sands. Inside, a courteous grey-haired waiter escorted Matthew and Fiona to a pair of deep wicker chairs by an open window. Beyond the terrace was the beach, beyond that only the glittering sea.

They ordered orange juice for their thirst, gin and tonics for their weariness. The two bankers clinked glasses, said little, and watched the last sailboats threading their way home.

After the first drink passed in companionable silence, Matthew ordered a couple more and asked Fiona about herself. She didn't tell him much that was personal. Her parents ran a large hog-farming operation in Iowa. She'd hated it and had wanted to work on Wall Street for as long as she could remember. She'd joined the bank eight years ago, making it to managing director last year, the youngest in the firm. Matthew told Fiona about his father's death and the training programme, but nothing about the will and nothing about Sophie. Partly, he still felt guilty and unhappy. But also, he was confused by this strange, attractive managing director. He'd hold back on the personal stuff till he understood where he was.

After an hour or so, Matthew noticed they were getting late for their dinner reservations. He offered to find a cab.

'Do you want to move?' asked Fiona.

'Not much, but I'll be hungry in half an hour.'

'We can eat here if you like. They do food, too. It's a bit more basic but much more fun.'

Matthew could imagine nothing better, and they walked out on to the beach. A short distance from the bar, a huge barbecue crackled away. Close beside it, in a bamboo beach hut, linen-covered tables stood heaped with salads and fruit. As in the bar itself, the patrons were mostly local Jamaicans, not tourists. They grabbed some plates and tried to choose what was best from the barbecue, but soon gave up and just let the chef pick out his own selection. They piled their plates high, turned away from the brightly lit eating area and sat on the sands eating with their fingers and looking out to sea. Above them, stars began to pick holes in the darkening sky.

'You seem so nice,' said Matthew. 'Why do you act the bitch at the bank?'

'Maybe I am a bitch and I'm just acting nice now.'

'Uh-uh. Bitches always use a knife and fork. You used your fingers before I did. So what's with the ball-crushing bit?'

'I don't see why you should have a problem with it, since you managed to escape intact.' Fiona's voice hardened and stiffened.

Matthew backed off. He wanted to spend the rest of the trip with the nice Fiona, not the bitch. He went to get more shellfish and scooped half his haul on to Fiona's plate with his hand. Peace was restored.

After some delectable fruit and coffee on the verandah, it was time to leave. Matthew found it hard to pay the bill. Nobody had kept any record of what they'd consumed, and nobody seemed anxious to take his money. But he eventually managed to settle up, the tally being about what he'd have paid for pizza and ice-cream in New York. At least one thing about this crazy trip was inexpensive.

The hotel was a couple of miles down the beach, and Fiona suggested walking. Half-way there, the temptation to take a swim overcame them. Fiona had a swimsuit in her bag, but, after a moment's hesitation, just stripped off. Matthew did likewise and they waded out into the warm water together. Fiona was an excellent swimmer, and, despite his strength, Matthew laboured to keep up. She let him come close, then dived away underwater, emerging in a burst of moonlit bubbles twenty feet away. Matthew approached again and this time she leaped at him and ducked him. He could feel her naked body sliding against his as he sank, but when he rose she had flitted away again, back to shore.

They wiped themselves dry on the beach using a hand towel from Fiona's bag. Seen by the light of the moon, there was nothing at all the matter with Fiona's figure. Just for a moment, Matthew forgot to miss Sophie.

The hotel consisted of a number of bungalows spread out around its expansive grounds. The two suites Matthew had reserved occupied the two halves of a bungalow, the two doorways separated by a sweet-smelling hedge of flowering tobacco plants. Matthew found his door and Fiona hers.

He spoke to her across the flowers. 'Thanks for a great evening. I've really enjoyed it.'

'Well, I should thank you, it's been your treat. Thank you.'

'Goodnight.'

'Yes. Goodnight . . . unless you'd like to come in here?'

There was no doubting what she meant. Matthew entered her room and before they'd even found the light switch, they were clasped round each other, damp body against damp body.

Matthew had never had sex quite like it. Fiona was athletic, passionate and demanding. There was no tenderness in her embraces, only a hunger which even Matthew was pushed to satisfy. When they were finally done, Matthew rolled on to his side, his arm around her.

'At times like this, I usually wish I was a smoker,' he said.

Fiona said nothing.

After a long pause, she said, 'You'd better go to your room now.' Something in her voice told Matthew not to argue. He left.

The next morning Fiona was friendly but distant. As they boarded their flight home, she stiffened further until, by the end of the flight, she was every inch a Managing Director of Madison. Matthew, the unregretful veteran of a hundred one-night stands, felt hurt by her indifference. It wasn't for this that he had given up his post-Sophie chastity.

At Kennedy Airport, she asked Matthew if he wanted to share a cab into Wall Street. Matthew thought she was joking and made some light-hearted response.

'I hardly think thorough preparation is something to be flippant about, especially from someone with your level of experience,' she said.

Without a kiss or any other goodbye, she got into a cab and drove off. But strange though she'd been, it wasn't her strangeness which preoccupied Matthew on the ride back to his apartment.

On the return flight, as Fiona dozed beside him, Matthew had noticed something sliding around beneath the seat in front. Bored with newspapers but not desperate enough for the flight magazine, he caught it with his toes and dragged it towards him. It was a spiral bound presentation booklet, of the sort that Wall Street produces in its thousands. Matthew dragged it closer towards him until he could read the lettering on the front cover. Then, impulsively, he dropped a magazine down on top of it and picked both up together, concealing the booklet inside the magazine. He went off to the toilet to examine his prize.

The presentation was addressed to Nicholas A. Draper, the well-known corporate raider. Draper had made his millions building up a successful engineering business; but he had made his billions pouncing on vulnerable companies and tearing them apart for profit. The 1980s had spawned many such raiders, but most of them had lost their way in the gentler climate of the nineties. Not so 'Black Nick' Draper. He was still active, still hungry.

The presentation – which bore a famous Wall Street name on its front cover – drew Draper's attention to a large Montana-based company, Western Instruments. The company was a tired old conglomerate, poorly managed and labouring under a huge pile of debt. Management was complacent, shareholders were fed-up, costs were high and the business decayed. The company was a classic takeover target, a textbook case. The trouble was, it had been for years and no one believed the story any more.

No one, that is, except the Wall Street bank responsible for the presentation. There were huge wodges of analysis which Matthew only partly understood, but the con-clusions were plain as day. The stock price had sagged so low, that if Draper chose, he could buy the company and do what he did best: slash costs and fire people. Two years of bloodbath, then, if the Wall Streeters were right, Draper could sell off what remained, doubling, maybe even trebling his money.

As far as Matthew could tell, the presentation was no-holds barred. There was a mountain of work behind it, work nobody would do unless they were convinced of getting a result. And what would Draper think of it, sitting in his luxury Jamaica home? What could he think of it? Two years, double your money. More if you were lucky. What better dinner for a hungry billionaire?

Matthew sat on the cramped airplane loo, hesitating. Should he keep the presentation or put it back? He wished he had Zack's photographic brain. But he didn't and the presentation needed thought. He kept it.

Matthew had a long list of bonds which he traded from time to time, most of them good solid corporate bonds, issued by companies with names you've heard of. But Western Instruments was on the list too. It was on the list for no other reason than nobody had ever bothered to take it off, but the bonds traded at eighty-two cents on the dollar. Matthew had never bought them, and no client of his had ever asked for them.

When the cab arrived at his apartment, he paid the driver absent-mindedly. Walking into the building's lobby, the presentation tucked firmly under his arm, Matthew was obsessed by the following thought.

If Draper was about to launch a bid for the company, every bondholder's dream would come true. When a company changes hands, its bonds fall due for immediate redemption. Not at the eighty-two cents trading price, but at face value of one dollar. If Matthew bought fistfuls of Western Instruments bonds, then when Draper launched his bid, Matthew would be sitting on a very fat profit indeed. If he wanted to make a splash in his first year, if he wanted to hoist himself into the realm of trading megastars, then here was the way to do it.

Matthew had long doubted that he could accomplish his Plan A. For a freshman to make a million quid in bonuses in just three years would be virtually unheard of, even on Wall Street, but his Plan B was difficult and dangerous too. If he wanted to run with Plan A, this was his chance.

9

Hal Gillingham, the tax partner, wrinkled up his eyes. His face was pitted and lined. He was forty-five but he looked nearer sixty.

That's unusual. Rich people look different. It's like they have an invisible coating which protects them, a layer of affluence stronger than any moisturiser. Their skins are tanned. Their complexions are good. Their shirts don't crease up the way normal shirts do. Their ties don't end the day stringy or crooked or stained. Their suits don't crumple or shine. They just look nice.

Hal Gillingham didn't look nice. He didn't even look average. His watery blue eyes had big bags underneath, which he rubbed despondently.

'Hong Kong. You know their tax rate is only sixteen and a half percent? Hardly worth dodging.'

'Sure,' said Zack. 'I also know they have some pretty tough anti-avoidance laws. So that's good news.'

'Why is that good news?'

'Because it means no one else will have come up with a way to save my client tax. That makes us look good when we do.'

'You're very sure we'll find a way.'

'Sure I'm sure. There's not a tax authority in the world who can draft a tax law without loopholes. We just find the loopholes, then figure out a way to pass over a billion dollars through the gap.'

'Hong Kong dollars?'

'No. Dollar dollars. American dollars. Real dollars.'

Gillingham rubbed his face again, but with interest this time, not weariness. Like nearly everyone in banking, Gillingham charged his clients a percentage of the deal. The bigger the deal, the bigger the fee. His percentage cut might only be half a percent, but half a percent of a billion dollars was five million. Even partners had their profit targets, and Gillingham sat forward.

'OK. I'm interested. What's the deal?'

Zack explained the deal, but when he was done, Gillingham looked disappointed.

'That's it? It seems very daring, and we don't even know if the client's interested.'

'I know the client. Personally. I know he's interested.

We just have to get the sums to add up. That's why you need to save him sixteen and a half percent.'

Gillingham bit down on his lip and nodded. Zack guessed he was unmarried. If he'd been married, his wife would have told him not to bite his lip. It exposed his teeth and gums, neither of which was pretty.

'OK. I don't know much about Hong Kong, but I did once have an idea that I didn't follow up.'

Gillingham dug out a book of Hong Kong tax law from his cluttered shelves and flicked expertly through the arcane pages.

'Capital gains. That's the answer. What we need to do is to find a way to convert any income into capital gains, then find a way to make sure we never crystallise the gains. The tax man can't get us, because we tell him, "Hey. You're going to get your money when we crystallise the gain. Don't be impatient." Then there's nothing he can do except wait. He'll wait until eternity, of course, but he's powerless. Now then, how to convert the income . . . ?'

Gillingham muttered as he searched through the impenetrable text. As he muttered, Zack began to realise why the guy had made it to partner. He realised how come Gillingham managed to stay a partner, when so many prettier bankers fell by the wayside. Gillingham was actually going to figure this thing out.

'Yeah. There's stuff here we can work with. We'll need to get legal help from Hong Kong. Maybe some accountancy advice as well. But we've got enough to work with.'

Gillingham dropped the heavy books on his desk and gazed sadly at Zack.

'That's great. Can we find a time to work on it? This evening, perhaps?' Zack was eager to get going.

'Not this evening. I have a meeting.'

'When does the meeting finish? I don't mind staying.'

Zack stayed most nights anyway. The only days he wanted to leave early – by nine in the evening, that is – were days when he was meeting up with Sarah. Tonight was free.

'Uh-uh.' Gillingham shook his head. 'The meeting's out of the bank. It's personal. It starts in three-quarters of an hour.'

Zack looked at his watch. It was only five-thirty now. Nobody left the bank by six. Gillingham was out of line.

'Hmm. This project is fairly urgent. I wonder if you could postpone your meeting? Maybe move it back by a couple of hours?'

Zack was way junior to Gillingham, but he was within his rights. The bank took priority over everything. Personal meetings couldn't get in the way of business. Gillingham smiled thinly.

'It's not that sort of personal. I can't move it.'

Zack stared at the older man. Zack wasn't backing down. Hong Kong closed for the evening soon after London opened in the morning. If he waited to meet with Gillingham until the next day, he wouldn't be able to talk to lawyers in Hong Kong until the day following that. Zack said nothing, but his face was stubborn. Hal Gillingham stared at Zack, then looked away.

'It's an AA meeting. Alcoholics Anonymous. Every Tuesday and every Thursday. I haven't missed one for six years, and I'm not going to miss one for you.'

Zack was astounded. He remembered Mazowiecki telling him that Gillingham had taken a break from the bank a few years back. It must have been to go and get dried out. Gillingham must be exceptional if the bank had taken him back after that.

'I'm sorry, I didn't know. Tomorrow's fine. Can we say tomorrow morning?'

'Sure. Eight thirty?'

They agreed the time and wrote it into their diaries. Gillingham's pencil still hovered over the page.

'Just remind me of the client? Who are we pitching to?'

Zack licked his lips. The moment of truth was inching closer.

'The client is Hatherleigh Pacific,' he said. 'We're pitching to the Chairman. Lord Hatherleigh.'

10

Well, he'd done it.

When Matthew got back to his apartment after his crazy Caribbean jaunt, he had spent five solid hours reading and rereading the presentation he'd found on the plane. The more he read, the more solid the case looked. Western Instruments was a lousy company and Draper just the man to fix it.

Matthew tried to see the presentation from Draper's point of view. He tried to pick holes in it. He tried to find flaws in the arguments or weak spots in the numbers. He found nothing. After five hours, he put the presentation aside, went out into the street and hailed a cab. He rode down to Wall Street and entered Madison at ten o'clock on Sunday evening.

On the trading floor he bumped into Fiona Shepperton, who was just leaving.

'I decided to take your advice and do some homework after all,' he said, remembering Shepperton's last caustic words to him.

She half-smiled, half-nodded, and began to stride off towards the elevators.

'The treat's on you next time,' Matthew called. He'd get her to take him to Timbuktu by private jet.

Fiona turned, smiled a twisted smile back at him, and hurried off. It was probably a 'Yes', but it was hard to tell. It certainly wasn't a 'Yes, with pleasure, just name the day'.

Bitch or sweetheart, Matthew wondered. On current form, there wasn't much doubting which, but stretched out on the Jamaican sands, eating platefuls of wood-smoked fish in her fingers and laughing up into the Jamaican night, she had been a joy to be with, and in bed, fire itself. Probably bitch, maybe sweetheart, Matthew decided. But he had bigger decisions to make.

He gathered a couple of things from his desk, then took the elevator up a few floors to the bank's research department. He wasn't very familiar with the research area, which was mostly there for those in corporate finance – people like Zack. Traders like Matthew got their information from Reuters screens and Telerate screens and morning meetings and screams echoing around the trading floor. Compared with those super-sonic thrills, a library atmosphere was decidedly low octane. But that evening, Matthew had research to do which the trading room could never provide.

There were research assistants on duty all night. There were also a dozen or so groggy-looking analysts who had clearly worked all through the weekend to complete some project for Monday morning. They looked like they still had a few hours work to do. A slogan had been taped up on the side of one of the data terminals: 'Definition of deadline – If it's not DEAD on time, your job's on the LINE.' Elsewhere another humorist had pinned up a note headed 'Lifecycle of a Deal'. Phase one was Excitement. Phase two was Disillusion. Phase three was Despair. Phase four was Failure. Phase five was Punishment of the Innocent and Reward of the Guilty.

Christ, thought Matthew, echoing the thoughts of countless traders before him, why the hell would anyone actually choose to work in corporate finance? Like them, Matthew could come up with only one possible answer. Corporate finance was for those who couldn't hack it on the trading floor.

But to work. With the help of a patient research assistant, Matthew dug out research reports on Western Instruments, press cuttings, stockholder reports, share price graphs, profit estimates, and anything else he could think of. He also built an impressive collection of cuttings on Nick Draper and his exploits. In the course of his career, he'd been nicknamed Black Nick, Nick the Knife, Vampire Nick and simply The Ogre. Matthew printed or copied everything he could, and, bundling his information together, set off home.

Once there, he opened the presentation again, and checked everything he could. Everything seemed to hold up. The presentation proved conclusively, as far as Matthew was concerned, that Draper stood to make a killing. And if Draper did decide to launch a raid, the bonds of Western Instruments would jump from being worth eighty-two cents to one dollar exactly, a rise of more than twenty percent. Those kind of returns simply weren't available on the bonds Matthew normally traded. But if he wanted to be king of the trading floor, make his million from bonuses, then those were the returns he needed.

By four in the morning, Matthew had made up his mind.

After two hours' sleep, he rose, showered, dressed, drank some coffee, and headed off for Wall Street. He attended the Monday morning meeting, greeted Alan and Rick, listened to Saul Rosenthal moaning about his weekend, drank more coffee, and went to work. As soon as the market opened, he began to buy Western Instruments bonds. He bought four million dollars' worth that day. Over the next week, he bought another sixteen million dollars' worth. The week after he added another five million. Twenty-five million all told, the maximum holding he was allowed under the bank's rules. Buying that much that fast was difficult, especially with a bond that was hardly traded. Matthew paid over the odds for the privilege, but, for once in his short trading life, he didn't especially care. The thing was to get the bonds before Draper attacked.

Nevertheless, Matthew wasn't exactly forgetful of the prices he'd paid. At the end of each day, every trader is forced to 'mark their portfolio to market'. That means looking at what you hold and comparing the prices you paid to the current market price. Matthew had paid an average of eighty-three cents on the dollar for his bonds, against a today's closing price of eighty-two. Building up his twenty-five million dollar portfolio had cost him two hundred and fifty thousand bucks, a loss that cancelled about half his trading profits in his brief career.

Matthew checked his monitors one last time that day for news. Nothing. There wouldn't be. Nobody launches a bid in the evening, something to do with the Protestant work ethic probably. He'd have to wait until the markets opened again on Monday. But as he reached to switch off the monitors, he noticed his hand shaking. His lips parted, in an almost silent whisper.

'Come on, big guy. Come on.'

11

'What's that, Josie? Looking for a job?'

'Oh, no,' said Josie, embarrassed. 'Just reading, that's all.'

She folded the bank's newsletter and thrust it away from her. It had been open on a page advertising internal vacancies. Apart from that, there had been nothing else to read.

'We wouldn't survive without you, you know.' Her boss smiled at her, meaning what he said. He was a nice man, not bureaucratic like some of them, and he added, 'I shouldn't really tell you this, but I've put you up for promotion. I know you're young, but the department depends on you.'

'Thanks,' said Josie. 'Thank you, really.'

'So you're not going to leave us?'

'No, honestly, I was just reading.'

Her boss turned to leave. He'd only been passing by. Josephine had turned red; red from her collarbones to her hairline; red as a beetroot with sunburn. She hadn't blushed like this, not even when he'd teased her about Miklos Kodaly, her tame computer nerd. And Josie hadn't just been reading. She'd had a pen in her hand and thought in the creases of her forehead.

12

On the far horizon, in the low-lying country around Leeds, the helicopter rose and flew a little further on, nearer to them this time. It descended once again, out of sight. George, Val, Darren and Jeff Wilmot, the accountant, noticed it, then ignored it. There was work to be done.

'Let's face it,' said Darren, 'the marketing boys keep getting decent crosses into the box, but we don't have a bleeding striker to convert the chances.' He stopped, thinking he had made himself perfectly clear, but George nodded at him to continue. 'What I mean is, we need a bigger production area and some proper kit. There's no point handing out brochures full of brilliant furniture

270

at brilliant prices, then telling our customers to sod off because we can't meet their orders.'

He was right. Sales were strong and rising. The Bright and Beautiful range was their bestseller, but all their products were doing well. George had started to insist that Gissings turn away new customers, in order not to disappoint existing ones.

'I understand your concern,' said Wilmot, 'but unfortunately these things need to be paid for. I'm afraid we don't have the cash to go and get the Alan Shearer of furniture factories.'

He looked around, wanting applause for his little joke. Everyone ignored him. Even accountants found him dull. Outside, the helicopter bobbed up again and drifted closer. It wasn't military and wasn't police.

'Remind us of the numbers, Jeff,' said George.

'Well, it's simple enough. We're making a decent profit now, but we still owe over four hundred and sixty thousand pounds. The bank will never let us borrow more, and if we spend all our profits on new equipment, then the debt will be hanging round our necks for ever. We just need to sit tight, pay off our debts, and then start thinking about investment.'

'How long will that take, Jeff?' muttered George. He was looking at the helicopter, which had apparently landed again. It wasn't more than two or three miles away now.

'If we keep on doing as well as we are now, then we'll be free of debt in less than four years. To be on the safe side, I'd say four to five years.'

George shook his head. In four to five years, he could pay off the debt. In another ten years, he might have collected his million pounds. By that time, Matthew or Zack would have been enjoying their father's money for the last twelve or thirteen years. They could sell off Bernard Gradley's beloved company and use the proceeds to buy themselves an island in the sun. They could have servants, yachts and cars. With thirty or forty million quid, they could buy a stackload of shares, pay as much tax as their lawyer thought prudent, and still have an income of a million pounds a year, every year.

The helicopter had risen again and was zigzagging across the sky like a drunk. It shot up into the air, hung for a moment, then dived down again. It had landed about half a dozen times since George had started watching, but never stayed put for more than a minute or two. George gazed at it gloomily.

'Jeff, we need to expand production. I don't give a monkey's about the debt. The only questions are, how much is it going to cost and where can we find the dosh. Do you have the latest cash flow forecast, please?'

The way he saw it, he hadn't a hope of making a million quid out of Gissings. All the same, he might as well try to build up the business, so he didn't have to feel ashamed when Matthew and Zack competed with each other to plonk the biggest pile of money on the table at the end of the three years. One of them would get their million, he was sure of that.

Wilmot and Darren started to argue again while Wilmot searched his fake leather briefcase for the cash flows. Darren wanted the biggest, shiniest factory they could afford. Wilmot wanted the smallest, oldest one they could get away with.

George liked Darren. You couldn't imagine Val or Wilmot having a good time with thirty million quid. Val would still be Val. She'd probably work at Gissings, the same as usual. Wilmot would take off to the Costa del Sol, but he'd still dress in cheesy little suits and still turn pink at the first hint of sun. Darren, on the other hand, would take his thirty million, spend it in a couple of years, then be back where he'd started, a scruffy young man with a big mouth and not a moment's regret for what he'd enjoyed and lost.

Darren and Wilmot squabbled, subject only to Val's quiet interventions. In blacker moods, George was amazed to find himself still shacked up with her, but she was of more value to Gissings than anyone else, bar none. Wilmot couldn't find the cash flows and went off to look for them.

The helicopter was right over Gissings now. It swooped down low and circled the factory. Glass rattled in the windows and the noise drowned out every other sound. It was just about possible to make out the faces of the pilot and passengers inside. George stared and stared again. His mouth moved but the din brushed his words away. And, as the helicopter prepared to land in the field adjoining the factory, George rushed from the room.

He burst out into the timber yard and ran across to the shed which used to be the factory sawmill. Red in the face, he clambered over the wire fence to reach the helicopter and its gradually slowing blades. From its side, a door swung open. A foot appeared; then a swirl of aquamarine silk; then, at last, whole and smiling, fragile and beautiful, Kiki emerged, blinking and clutching at her hat.

'Georges, sweetheart, we have had such a horrid time trying to find you. You are such a beast for hiding away.'

'Kiki, wonderful to see you,' panted George. He kissed her on the cheek and gave her a big bear hug.

'Georges, *sois sage*,' she chided. 'You are squashing my new dress and you are squashing me. You have got so big.'

'Kiki, why didn't you tell me you were coming? I'd have got things ready.' George gestured grandly around the timber yard.

'*Stupide*! I didn't know I was coming. But then I was going to this wedding in Scotland and I thought Yorkshire is on the way to Scotland, so I thought I would stop off and see you, because I miss you, but I didn't know that Yorkshire was so big and nobody seems to have heard of your factory and it was ages before I could find your address in my book and we had to stop and ask our way ever so many times and – *enfin*! – we have found you, but, Georges, I think you are ill, no?'

George was red in the face and almost trembling with excitement.

'No, Kiki, no. I'm fine. Just pleased to see you. Come on in. Or let me show you around?'

She shrugged.

'*Oui*. If you want. This is what you spent your money on, no? It is not very beautiful, I think, but I suppose factories are not so beautiful. I don't think I have ever seen a factory, unless you count the place where Papa puts his precious cognac into bottles. I went there once but it made me very ill with the migraine.'

She chattered on, as George barged through the heavy polythene doors that led on to the factory floor proper. You were meant to wear a hard hat, but George never bothered and somehow he felt that Kiki would be unlikely to let an orange plastic monstrosity anywhere near her carefully styled hair. So he let her keep her precarious blue-green hat, nodding with feathers and silk and strips of lace, and they moved out on to the factory floor.

George ushered Kiki along the yellow lines marking the routes where pedestrians were safe from hoists, forklifts, and the flying debris of the big cutting machines. He held a burly arm around her as she picked her way across the scurf and oil marks which covered the floor.

Usually, when George was showing clients or suppliers around the floor, he kept up a busy chatter, telling his companion about the plans for improvement, numerous little tricks of production, laughing at the antiquated equipment. This time, George was silent. For the first time since he'd come to Gissings, he became aware of the noise. Lathes, saws, drills, hoists, trucks, turning equipment, plane tables, electric sanders and god knows what else banged, whined and howled away. Workmen yelled, laughed, and pointed. On the breeze-block walls, the dirty calendars seemed as big as tarpaulins.

There was more to see, of course, but for Kiki a little went a long way.

'Let's go and get something to drink,' said George.

The lifts had been knackered for years, so they trudged up the two flights of stairs to George's office.

'It is always so noisy?' Kiki asked. 'I think perhaps I am not so *industrielle*.'

'Yeah, I suppose. You get used to it,' puffed George. He used not to be this unfit, but the daily fried breakfasts had gone straight to his middle. He looked more like Val every day. He should really join a gym or something and get in shape. The meeting was still going on when he got back.

'Would you lot mind clearing out, please. I've got a visitor.'

'There's something important you should know,' said Val, not moving.

'Yeah, well, it'll wait till later. Meanwhile, would you mind getting us some drinks? What do you want, Kiki?'

Kiki blinked like a bird.

'Some Badoit mineral water would be very nice, if you have it. Otherwise some Perrier would be fine. I like it with a slice of lemon, but no ice, please.'

Kiki smiled at Val. She was trying to be easy.

'It's tap water, tea or coffee,' said Val.

'Oh, I see, you are out of Perrier. I know. It's the same with me all the time, but luckily there is a dear little man who brings it to me when I run out. Some coffee would be very nice, instead. Espresso, please. I prefer cappuccino but it makes me giggle and I try so hard to be serious.'

The only coffee they had was instant, of course, and George intervened with a request for two teas. 'Not too strong,' he said, but he might as well have wished for world peace.

Val came back with two cups of tea, darker than a peat bog.

'There. Just the way you like it. I didn't know if you wanted sugar,' she added, for Kiki's benefit, 'so I put one in, just in case.'

Kiki stirred her tea politely until Val had left, then she pushed the mug away. George started to apologise, but she interrupted.

'Don't worry, Georges. I am not so thirsty and luckily there is a little bar on the helicopter if I get dry.'

She paused and George paused. Kiki perched on the edge of her chair. She had spread a handkerchief on the seat to protect her dress and was carefully keeping her arms away from the sides. She thought about taking her hat off, but looked at the table and thought better of it. Things were a little grimy, perhaps, George thought, greasy with long use. Val cleaned the place every now and then, but mostly just to keep the dust off things. No one would ever enter Gissings for a Factory Beautiful competition.

Kiki consulted her little jewelled watch.

'Oh, Georges, it took us so long to find you, now I don't have any time. But I see you are well. You are happy, I hope?'

George spread his hands. He had no idea.

'God, Kiki, this place is a different world. It's all changed so much since Dad died. Christ, I've changed. Sometimes, it's OK, but other times . . . other times, I miss it all . . . I miss . . .' He tailed off. He missed her, but couldn't say so. He longed to kiss her, but might as well have been a thousand miles distant.

He asked her about a few mutual friends, but the answers she gave were meaningless. He had lost touch with the friends they'd shared and, short of a miracle, he'd never mix with them socially again. What did he care if Xavier and Julia were engaged? Why should he mind how the von Hattenburgs disgraced themselves at Monaco?

She tried asking him about his life, but that was worse than useless. George's life was completely taken up by things of whose existence Kiki was completely ignorant. If he tried to explain, she would find it all *très désagréable* and sympathise with George for having to put up with such terrible things.

After twenty minutes of mutual discomfort, Kiki looked at her watch again. It was time to go. George escorted her back across the timber yard, offering her his arm and sympathising with her about the plight of her shoes. Her hat nearly blew off into a puddle of waste water and oil, but he caught it in time.

The helicopter took off. Kiki waved from the window until she was no more than a speck in the distance. George waved back, a heavy-built man in a dirty yard.

He stomped back upstairs. Val, Darren and Wilmot had regrouped, wearing long faces. Jeff Wilmot began to speak.

'Er . . . it has come to my attention . . . that is, I was looking . . . the cash flows appear to have been mislaid. Unfortunately, it seems that they were left . . . that is, I left them . . . inadvertently, er, in a non-secure location. It seems there is a risk . . . maybe a serious risk . . . that confidential data may have become available to – er – commercially hostile sources.'

What the hell was he talking about? There is nothing on earth more pompous than a guilty accountant. Val interjected.

'Wilmot went to visit an old friend of his in the Aspertons' finance department. He left a briefcase there with our cash flows inside. The Aspertons deny having found the case, but it seems virtually certain that they've found it and examined the cash flows under a microscope.'

There was a punch line coming, but George was slow to see it. Val helped him again.

'If they see how well we're doing, they'll stop us using their paintshop. If we have to rig up a paintshop of our own, we'll use up all the money you wanted to spend on expanding production.'

For a moment, George looked at the scene through Kiki's eyes. A grimy little room, sitting in a worn-out building above a tired and ugly old factory in a rainswept corner of England. Three people besides himself: an overweight woman without make-up, a scruffy youth dressed in whatever he found on his bedroom floor that morning, and a nondescript man dressed in nondescript grey, hiding a nondescript soul. And the fuss? The fuss was all about whether they could find a way to paint some furniture to sell to customers to make some money to give the bank. Make a million? He'd fly to the moon first.

'OK. OK. Please all get out of here. I need some time alone.'

Only Val hesitated before leaving. She wasn't just his secretary. She was his lover too. She didn't like the way the rest of the world became unimportant the moment a pretty little rich girl fell out of the sky in her helicopter. She'd talk to him about it later, but right now she'd let him be.

Val went off to eat her sandwiches with a couple of the girls from marketing and admin. They asked her about the girl in the helicopter, but Val said nothing. When she returned to her office, Gissings' only fax machine held a piece of paper in its out tray. It was a short note from the Aspertons. The paintshop contract would terminate after the stipulated one month's notice period. Wilmot was an idiot, but these things happened. What was needed now was a Chief Executive with his eye on the ball.

Val knocked on George's door and walked in.

George was gone. The van he drove was gone from the yard and there was no answer from Val's phone at home. He had left no indication of where he had gone or where he could be reached.

Val had been brought up never to swear, and years passed when she never once did. But if you had been able to see her lips move as she surveyed George's empty room, you would have seen her top front teeth briefly touch her bottom lip before her mouth opened once more.

It was a short word, and it rhymes with luck.

13

That day Zack had caught three trout, Lord Hatherleigh just the two. When the fish were grilled and brought to table, Zack laughingly offered to give Hatherleigh a fishing lesson. Hatherleigh took his revenge, imitating Zack's early attempts at casting a line. Zack claimed Smudge and Bonnie, the spaniel puppies, would make better fishing instructors than Hatherleigh, and proceeded to demonstrate why. The fish disappeared in a torrent of laughter.

For much of the main course Zack had been forced to excuse himself, as he took a phone call to work. A maid brought him a plate of beef to eat while he was talking, and he made it back to table in time for pudding.

The meal ended in a happy confusion of cheese, nuts, coffee, brandy, port and cigars. Only after midnight did the guests disperse. A local taxi firm ferried those who lived nearby back to their homes. The family, Zack, and the other house guests began to move upstairs to their rooms. Sarah walked up with Zack.

'You were really funny this evening,' she told him. 'You and Dad had everyone in stitches. Even me, and I've heard it all before.'

Zack found it hard to put all the Sarahs together. The Sarah of tonight, radiant in silk and pearls, easy and vivacious, always the centre of conversation and laughter. The Sarah of a few hours before, filthy and sweating, showing a new stable lad how to muck out a horsebox. The Sarah of London and Coburg's: professional, hard-working, tidy, self-effacing. Zack mentally added another Sarah to the list. Sarah unclothed. Sarah in bed with him. The Sarah knitted to him by a million strands of electricity.

'I love your dad. Your mum, too. I feel more comfortable with your family than I do with my own.'

Sarah stood slightly ahead of Zack on the great marble staircase. A Gainsborough portrait of one of the Hatherleigh viscounts gazed down on the scene impassively. For two centuries, he'd watched people come and go. The fashions changed, but people didn't. Sarah turned.

'You've changed so much. I can't believe it.'

Zack could smell Sarah. Not just her perfume, but her.

'I haven't changed as much as you might think,' he said softly.

'Oh, come on. A few years ago, you'd have wanted to turn Ovenden House into a shopping mall. Now I hear you and Dad discussing the best way to keep poachers out.'

'I didn't mean that.'

'What did you mean?'

Zack was silent, but his body was shouting. Why couldn't she hear?

'Oh, Zack. You aren't going to spoil things, are you? Don't you remember how much we hurt each other? I promised myself never again. You'll always be a friend, if you let yourself be.'

He shook his head. That, at least, was impossible.

'Sarah, I want you. I always have. I've never known another woman like you. If I can't have you, I'll die a bachelor.'

'Oh, Zack, you do really mean that, don't you?' Damp eyes searched his, but her heart already knew its answer. 'Dear Zack.'

Her arms were around him, her lips against his, their bodies once again as one.

From the turn in the stairs, the Gainsborough viscount watched the scene in silence. Pretty girls and handsome adventurers. He'd seen it all before. That night, Zack and Sarah made long, passionate and repeated love. And when morning broke in the room that the Duke of Wellington had once graced, it found them fast asleep in each other's arms.

Autumn 1999

The leaves are on the turn in Central Park and autumn colours fill the shops. New Yorkers leave the city to spend their weekends upstate, in the Shawangunks and the Catskills, there to watch the forests close down for winter. The leaves are good this year, but prices are high. This is the last autumn of the second millennium and holiday homes are booked solid.

It is 1 October 1999. There are 651 days to go until Bernard Gradley's deadline.

1

Matthew was worried. Had Draper gone soft? Had he lost his nerve like the rest of them? Had he given up?

Two months on and still Matthew needed a leap in the Western Instruments bond price, and still the price was depressed. So far, his paper loss amounted to a million bucks and, so far, the only direction had been down. If Draper didn't act soon, Matthew would have a miserable end of year, with no bonus at all and lucky to keep his job. The idea of earning a million pounds, Matthew's original Plan A, would be laughable; his Plan B quite impossible.

Though anxiety had become his bedfellow, today he had a more immediate reason to worry. That morning Saul Rosenthal had walked across to Matthew's desk. In itself that was remarkable. If the entire universe shrivelled up, leaving only Rosenthal's work station, the coffee shop and the john, he likely wouldn't notice anything amiss till he couldn't find the synagogue come Friday night. For him, the twelve-yard trip to Matthew's desk was a half-marathon.

'Hey, Matthew, you around this evening? We should talk.'

'Sure,' said Matthew. 'You want to talk about anything in particular, or you just want to complain about the Japanese?'

'Don't get me started, Matthew. Goddamn yen should be falling, but it's rising and my learned oriental friends keep jumping in to Uncle Sam's own glorious bond market. They should put some kind of reservation round it. I'll call myself a native American bond trader and apply for a subsidy. Stick feathers in my hair and live in a wigwam, if I have to.'

'Saul, is there anything particular on your mind?'

'Oh, sure.' Rosenthal recalled himself. 'Western Instruments. Management here has noticed you've been buying them like there's no tomorrow. We just wanted to have a chat about the situation.'

'Is there a problem?' asked Matthew, his voice rising a little.

'Is there a problem? We all got problems, Matt. I don't like wigwams. I'm allergic to feathers. I've been on the wrong side of the market for two weeks and you ask if I've got a problem.' Rosenthal tailed off, remembering that Matthew had asked a question. 'Just show up after the market closes this evening and we'll have a chat.'

Matthew tried to focus on other things, without much

joy. Matters weren't helped when Fiona Shepperton came by his desk.

'Can you meet this evening to talk about your position in Western Instruments?'

'Sure. Saul's already asked me.'

'That's OK then. I thought he might have forgotten what he came for by the time he reached you.' She paused, then added, 'I'm sure you know what you're doing, but it wouldn't hurt to think your arguments out in advance.'

Matthew took her hint. In between his other duties that day, he sketched out his thoughts on paper. He remembered his experience on the Euro summit with Pierre d'Avignon in Paris. Keep it short. Keep it clear. And, God, make it convincing. The very last thing he wanted was to be told to give up now.

By the end of a busy day, he had sketched out a six-page presentation and had it copied and bound. Busy with the presentation and still nervous, he had screwed up a few trades, giving him a daily loss of about sixteen thousand dollars, when he should really have been ahead by the same amount. Damn it. The sooner Draper rode into town, pistols blazing, the better.

Rosenthal had a disputed trade to sort out after the market closed, but by six forty-five he was done and came to get Matthew. They walked off to a meeting room, Rosenthal still muttering about wigwams and General Custer.

When they got there, the room was already mostly full. Fiona Shepperton was there. Al and Rick were there. Somebody else was there too. Someone talking on the phone with his back to Matthew, someone with a Scottish accent and a burly shape. Brian McAllister got off the phone and greeted Matthew.

'Nice to see you again.'

Matthew said something in response, but watched in alarm as McAllister moved to the door and swung it shut. Brian McAllister, who only closed his door when he fired people. Brian McAllister, whose piercing eyes could squeeze truth from a politician-turned-car-salesman.

The door hadn't been closed long when two more people entered. They introduced themselves as David Seymour and Jane Stalwitz from compliance.

Compliance officers are the policemen of modern banks. Their job is to make sure that all employees abide by the tangle of rules and regulations which bind the industry. Their job is to prevent insider trading; to prevent leaks of confidential information; to prevent breaches of rules so obscure that even the regulators can't make them out – to ensure, in a word, that the bank is free of sin. In a world where their colleagues earn salaries which sound like phone numbers, compliance officers earn salaries which sound like salaries. The job of a compliance officer is to say 'no' a hundred times a day, to be screamed at, abused, and then to say 'no' again. If your children want to make a career in compliance, dissuade them.

Matthew shook hands and sounded friendly, but his brain was working fast. The way he saw it, the presentation he'd found on the plane contained price-sensitive information: that is, information which, if publicly known, would be likely to affect the prices of the company's bonds and shares. By reading the presentation and then dealing on the basis of what he'd read, Matthew hadn't just committed a breach of etiquette, he'd committed a crime, the crime of insider trading. That's why the compliance officers were there.

Matthew repeated his golden rules to himself. Keep it short. Keep it clear. And, God, make it convincing. He turned down the cup of coffee offered by Saul Rosenthal and spoke to the room.

'How can I help?'

It was Rosenthal who answered.

'It's Western Instruments, Matthew. It's a dog. It's worse than a dog, it's a skunk. You're not stupid, Matthew. You must see that. But something's persuaded you to spend twenty-five million bucks of the firm's money on Western, while the poor old bank's gotta pay its heating bills, clean all these goddamn windows and hopefully find a nickel or two to reward its longest serving employees. We just wanted to know how come you've gotten so interested in canine protection.'

'Sure,' said Matthew uncertainly, and stared at the two people from compliance. They had lined yellow notepads and two biros each. They nodded and smiled at Matthew, but their hands were busily writing down everything that happened. Were they policemen on a routine patrol? Or policemen on the point of making an arrest? Matthew couldn't tell.

Jane Stalwitz, the senior compliance officer, set her pen down.

'You look like you're wondering why we're here. That's fair enough. We've been monitoring your activity and detected an abnormality. Usually you buy and sell on behalf of clients and do whatever you need to do in the market to meet their needs. You hardly ever speculate on prices, and when you do it's only for a few days at a time. Yet all of a sudden, you're making a giant-sized bet on a single company's bonds, you keep the bet standing not for days but for months, and even when the price goes against you, you hold steady. We're sure there's a good explanation. We want to hear it. That's all.'

Matthew licked his lips. It was as if he were a bank robber confronted by a ring of policemen saying, 'We notice that you have a smoking sawn-off shotgun in your left hand and a large number of loose bank notes stuffed into an unmarked brown sack in your right hand. We're sure there's a good explanation. We just want to hear it.'

Keep cool. Matthew handed out his presentation booklet.

'Great. This is a helpful opportunity to talk through my ideas. I realise that the trade hasn't yet worked out, but I believe in it. But there's a huge wealth of knowledge and experience at this table and I'd welcome everyone's input.'

Matthew started to talk through his presentation. He told the group that he had been looking for a way to add value to his normal trading routine and decided to do some deep research on a few selected companies in his bond portfolio. In the course of his research, which he outlined, he came to the conclusion that Western Instruments' bonds were likely to rise sharply as a result of a takeover, and he wanted to place a bet accordingly. That simple. Matthew had estimated it would take him six minutes to make his pitch, but he was nervous and repetitive and it took him eight.

Rosenthal and McAllister had a number of technical questions, which Matthew answered. As far as he could tell, his answers were sensible. Fiona stayed silent.

Eventually, Rosenthal said, 'OK. To begin with, I thought you must be delusional, but at least you've thought about it. More than most of our esteemed colleagues ever think about anything, 'cept maybe how to spend their bonus. But I gotta tell you, I don't like the trade any better now than I did before. The company stinks, Matthew, and all the analysis in the world won't take away the smell.'

McAllister nodded, but he didn't move his eyes off

Matthew. Fiona Shepperton could have been a statue. Then Jane Stalwitz leaned forward.

'I don't understand all this technical stuff, but you seem pretty well researched. Let me ask you this. How many companies did you need to research before you hit on Western?'

Jesus, that was a toughie.

'A few, I guess,' said Matthew. 'But I was lucky. I hit on Western pretty early.'

'Did you use this bank's research facilities?'

'Yeah, sure. I tried down the road at Merrill Lynch, but they wouldn't let me in.' It was a thin joke and nobody laughed.

'And over what period of time did you conduct your research?'

'A few weeks, I suppose.'

Matthew remembered reading somewhere that successful liars didn't lie, they just evaded, and when they couldn't evade, they gave the most imprecise answers they could. Most liars didn't have to sit a yard and a half away from Brian McAllister.

'Starting when and finishing when?'

Stalwitz was relentless, and her pen and her colleague's pen never stopped moving across their yellow pads.

'Well, I remember the night I really got excited about Western. That would have been the eighth of August. I'd probably been working seriously about four weeks by then, maybe four and a half.'

The pens scratched down the answer.

'And what companies did you rule out before you decided to run with Western?'

Matthew named a few random names from his bond portfolio, sensible names that anyone would research. The biros scratched out his answers.

'And what research tools did you use?'

Matthew stared blankly for a moment. What was the point of these questions? Why would anyone care?

Then he realised. You needed your swipe pass to enter the library. You needed a user identification number to access the data terminals. If you wanted help from the research staff, you needed to fill out a request slip. All these things left fingerprints. With the bank's huge data storage capacity, it was probably possible to crosscheck every inch of Matthew's story. But he couldn't back down now. Instead, he tried to evade.

'Oh, the usual stuff, I suppose,' said Matthew vaguely. 'Annual reports, press cuttings, published research.'

'Did you request the annual reports from the library or did you call them up on-line?'

Stalwitz was remorseless. Two biros stood ready for Matthew's answer. Damned in duplicate, he would be.

'On-line or from the library? I'm not sure . . .' Matthew tailed off. He had graduated first from Wall Street's toughest training programme. He had assembled a for-midable battery of arguments on Western Instruments. Nobody in the room was going to believe he couldn't remember how he got his annual reports. 'Uh, on-line, I guess.'

Stalwitz continued. The brokers' reports? Which ones? How many? What times had he used the library? The yellow pads filled with an ocean of detail, mapped out in pedantic blue ballpoint. Detail enough to drown Matthew. The questions continued. Which cuttings service? Which research system? How many requests did he file through the research staff?

Matthew was beginning to choke. He couldn't tell the truth. But every word he spoke took him further into the realm of the easily disprovable. When they came to check, all they'd find was a record of Matthew

Gradley bursting into the bank at ten o'clock one Sunday evening, and buying twenty-five million dollars' worth of Western Instruments bonds right away afterwards. Nothing, nothing on earth, could look less like the result of a well-disciplined and systematic research programme. Matthew could forget his father's millions. Right now he'd have swapped it all for a Get out of Jail card.

For the first time, McAllister's burning blue eyes moved off Matthew and faded out into the middle distance. He had made up his mind about something. Whatever it was, it could hardly be good news. 'You, Matthew, have used up your mistake.' Then a miracle happened.

Fiona Shepperton cleared her throat.

'Excuse me for cutting in, Jane, but perhaps I can speed things up. Matthew mentioned his intention to pursue this research to me and I encouraged him. Traders ought to know more about the bonds they're dealing in. I helped funnel a lot of the research stuff to him, using my head of group authorisation code. I doubt if you'll find most of the research requests listed under his name.'

Stalwitz was taken aback. Why would a high-flying managing director use her research privileges to help a junior trader whom she hardly knew? And why Fiona Shepperton, of all people? Even in the backwaters of Compliance, Shepperton's reputation was well known.

'Why did you help him out?'

'He had difficulty getting the right level of cooperation from the research staff on his first visit. It's a complaint I've heard often before. The staff give priority to managing directors and the junior analysts from corporate finance who pester them every ten minutes. If you put your request in in the normal way and if they're even half busy, your request never makes it to the top of the pile.'

Shepperton was utterly cool, utterly convincing. Here was a Get out of Jail card, embossed with a managing director's authority. Brian McAllister's eyes had shot back into focus after Shepperton began to speak, but now they were off into the distance again. He excused himself and got up to use the phone in the corner of the room.

'You're aware it's against bank procedures to let anybody else use your research authority?'

'Yes, I'm perfectly well aware of that. I will start to follow those procedures once the research department is properly staffed.' Shepperton was a managing director. Her breach of procedure was minor, even for lower levels of staff. Stalwitz was losing fast.

'So you're telling us we should check out all these information requests under your research code?' Stalwitz tapped her crowded pad.

'Sure, but you're not going to find a lot. Remember I have four research analysts reporting to me. All of them use my code. That's not even a breach of procedure.' Shepperton smiled at her little joke. 'All you'll find is an absolute mountain of data requests each and every week. I doubt you'll be able to separate out what came from Matthew and what came from my analysts.'

Stalwitz had stopped writing. She pushed her pad away from her a little.

'We can always check up on that, I guess.' She didn't sound enthusiastic.

'Sure. I think you should,' said Fiona. 'I think it's critical to pursue every avenue whenever you find something to cause you disquiet. Perhaps you can report back to me and Saul here over the next day or two.'

Stalwitz paused. She had been through this kind of investigation a couple of times before. The work was unbelievably time-consuming, riffling through innumerable request slips and computer print-outs to build up a picture of what had gone on. Tracking down requests for half a dozen or more companies over a four-week period would take ages. The last investigation had taken her and a colleague a full week of brain-thumpingly tedious work, and that had required searching a much smaller field. This could take the pair of them a month. It was part of her job, and worth it if the cause was important. But Shepperton had more or less guaranteed they would find nothing.

'Well perhaps we don't need to do all the work, if we're sure there's nothing to find,' Stalwitz ventured hopefully.

Shepperton looked at Rosenthal, who understood her look. He shoved away his coffee and sat as upright as he ever got, which wasn't very.

'No. I think it's always important to close off an investigation properly,' he said. 'I think we'd all be happier if we did our homework here.'

Rosenthal's private name for Compliance was the business prevention unit. As far as he was concerned, they might as well learn a lesson from this. Rosenthal wanted to encourage a thoughtful approach to risk-taking, not piss on it. Stalwitz nodded.

'Sure. I understand. It's going to take more than a day or two though. I'll try and get you an estimate of when we'll be done tomorrow or the next day.'

'Good,' said Fiona. 'Let's just keep it tight.'

Stalwitz had three kids, aged nine, seven and three. She had her normal work quotient to get done as well as this. There were going to be some long, long evenings ahead of her. Good job she knew a patient baby-sitter.

The meeting broke up, Rosenthal muttering none too quietly to Matthew.

'Don't worry about those neurotics from business prevention,' he said. 'They don't get paid enough and that gives them some kind of vitamin deficiency. Makes them tense and nervous. Jump at loud noises. I still hate your trade, though.'

'They're just doing their job, I guess,' said Matthew, watching Fiona walk away.

Bitch or sweetheart? She was neither. She was an angel sent down from God in heaven.

2

'Yes. This is my place.' Kodaly pushed at his living-room door, which was in danger of silting up from an accumulation of bottles, food wrappers, newspapers, chess magazines and old clothes. 'It's not so tidy.'

'No, it's not. It's disgusting,' said Josie. She exaggerated. She'd seen worse. Deduct five years from a man's chronological age to get his mental age, was her general rule, but Kodaly was a mathematician and a chess player, so she felt entitled to double the rule in his case. Knocking off ten years made him late teens, about right judging by the state of his floor. 'You'd better get it tidied up.'

'It's mostly rubbish. I throw it away.'

'And the clothes.'

'*Igen*, yes. And the clothes,' Kodaly muttered to himself in Hungarian as he shovelled rubbish into a black sack and kicked his clothes into a pile.

Josie sat on the arm of his sofa as he worked. There was a chessboard set out on the coffee table and a game in progress. In the corner of the room, a PC hummed with the monitor switched off. There wasn't much evidence of an active love life.

'Are you playing someone?' she asked.

He looked at the chessboard, his gaze drawn in to the pattern of pieces, the tense contest for survival. Calculations began to work automatically in his head as he replied.

'No. Is a game between Kasparov and Spassky.' He picked up a bishop and moved it. 'This is the move. Kasparov see it and win. Me? I see it now and understand . . . but in a game, with the clock ticking . . . This is why I earn my living with computers.'

He stood transfixed, though Josie knew he didn't need a chessboard to see the game.

'The rubbish, Miklos?' she said.

'Ah, yes, sorry.'

He turned his attention back to the sack of rubbish he carried and finished tidying the room. Magazines and books were stacked up, out of order, but neat. Clothes he swept into the bedroom, where he spent ten minutes energetically cleaning up. Josie ventured into the kitchen again and, avoiding excessive contact with the surfaces, made two mugs of instant coffee.

'It is done, all tidy,' said Kodaly at last returning. 'Next time I make it tidy before you come.'

Josie noticed his minute hesitation over the words 'next time'. It wasn't a question, more an acknowledgement that Josephine was a bit out of his league, a better catch than he was quite entitled to. Josie was happy for it to be that way. She wasn't, at eighteen, a virgin, but nor was she hugely experienced. It felt safer being in control.

'Thank you,' she said, smiling. 'I promise to appreciate it.'

'*Igen*. Please. Sit down. I move the board, in case I don't notice the beautiful lady.' He carried the chessboard to the corner of the room, eyes absorbed even as he walked. 'Kasparov is a great player. He is Beethoven,

Shakespeare. I play his games and I know . . . me, never . . . but I forget it. Now is all you.'

They raised coffee mugs to each other and drank, already on the verge of embarrassment. Kodaly's filmy eyes flicked leftwards to the shelf that acted as his wine cellar.

'So when did you start playing chess?' she asked.

Kodaly laughed. 'Inside my mother,' he said. 'My father was a good player, but he wanted me to be great. He made my mother play chess every night she was . . . big with me. Then when I was born, chess for me every day too. I learn to play chess before I speak. My first word was "king". I only learn "mother" after I can name all the pieces. Not joking, honestly.'

Once they escaped their initial awkwardness, conversation flowed quite easily. Kodaly had an unusual past and spoke about it interestingly, even wittily. Josie learned about the last years of Russian dominion in Hungary, Kodaly's career in the chess world, his behind-the-scenes accounts of major tournaments, his interest in computers and the bizarre world of East European computer hackers. 'In West, computers always get bigger, work very well, you don't need to worry so much about memory. In East, computers were very bad. You had to be very . . . very elegant. Worse the computer, better the virus must be.'

Josie spent two hours there. They did end up opening a bottle of wine, of which Kodaly drank nine tenths, but his ashen complexion suggested that his liver would consider one bottle a holiday. At length, Josie stood up.

'I should be getting back. I've had a neighbour round to look after Mum, but she needs to get home.'

Kodaly stood up too. 'Of course. Well, I hope . . .'

'It's been really nice, Miklos. I won't be able to come all that often, because of Mum . . . but maybe next week?

Thursday? I'll get a baby-sitter and maybe I can stay a little longer.'

'Yes, please. Flat will be very tidy. Maybe I cook. You like Hungarian food? Paprika?'

'That'd be lovely.'

There was no avoiding it now. They were on the landing at the door to Kodaly's apartment. They kissed on the cheek. Josie expected one kiss, Kodaly three. They laughed at the confusion and ended up with two, but Josie still had a hand on his shoulder. She smiled, pulled him towards her, and kissed him on the mouth, not firmly or long, but on the lips quite definitely.

'See you next week,' she said.

3

'Good morning, Zack,' said Lord Hatherleigh. 'Come in.'

Zack introduced the other members of his team: Phyllis Wang, a banker from the bank's Hong Kong office, and Hal Gillingham, the tax partner. Phyllis Wang was a tiny Chinese woman of indeterminable age. She had twenty years' experience in Hong Kong and knew pretty much everything that went on there. Hal Gillingham, who looked his usual careworn self, was there to provide the expertise on tax.

The viscount waved his guests over to a couple of large Chesterfield sofas.

'Do make yourself comfortable. I find you really need to slouch back,' he said, sprawling back himself. Despite his easy manner, he prickled with energy, as though his sinewy frame was too light to contain the motor within. Ever the good host, Hatherleigh asked Phyllis about her flight over and exclaimed with surprise that he'd never met her at the Hong Kong Jockey Club. But his chat was polite, not genuine. He wanted to cut to the chase.

Zack intervened.

'Perhaps we should get to the presentation,' he said. 'We've a lot of material to cover.'

Hatherleigh nodded and Zack handed out a spiral bound dossier to everyone in the room. Each copy was entitled *Hatherleigh Pacific – The Next Step*.

Inside, thirty pages of argument gave a bullet-point summary of a hugely complex financial analysis. On each page, headlines drew the eye to the main point, while beneath were charts, graphs, comparative data, maps, lists of issues, timetables, everything. Zack flipped to the first page and began to speak.

'Hatherleigh Pacific is a property and shipping company. It's got a lot of assets, basically office blocks and ships. When you became Chairman eighteen years ago, you saw that the company's assets weren't being used properly. The ships were chugging around half full. The office blocks were busily being refurbished and expanded. But nothing was making much money. You changed that. You cut costs. You found out what your customers wanted, then supplied it. Eighteen years later, you've finished what you started. Your coastal shipping service is the biggest and best there is. Your land bank is filled with state-of-the-art office blocks. Your profits are excellent.

'But where do you go from here? You can't expand the shipping side, because you pretty much own the markets you're in. Your land bank is full, and the price of land means it's tough to make a profit starting out from scratch again. You've got the management talent and ambition to do more. But how? Where next?

'We believe you need to think big. The smaller companies in Hong Kong are highly competitive. It's easy enough to buy them, but tough to improve on what they're already doing. But there are some bigger companies with plenty of fat. Companies like Hatherleigh Pacific was, eighteen years ago. Great assets, lousy managers. We think you have the chance to repeat your magic, but on a larger canvas. We've come to talk about those opportunities.'

Hatherleigh was absorbed. He crouched low over the table, studying the dossier intently, flipping forwards through the pages while Zack was still on the introduction. It was a good sign and Zack relaxed a little.

The first part of the dossier assessed the company's cash flows in detail. In a year or two at most, the company would hit a plateau. Hatherleigh Pacific would never be a bad company, but it might stop being an exciting one.

Hatherleigh scrutinised the figures. He became quickly frustrated with the charts summarising the analysis and asked for more detail. Zack hauled two heavy appendices from his case. Hatherleigh began to explore the vast and detailed spreadsheets, then paused to ask his secretary to cancel his next meeting. The viscount was intent. To a layman, there's nothing duller than huge volumes of financial analysis. But nobody in the room was looking at the numbers. What they saw was a company stripped naked and thrust beneath the lights. They weren't looking at spreadsheets. They were examining the company's soul.

Hatherleigh quizzed Zack on details. Once or twice, maybe, he wanted to know the answer. But Zack also guessed he was being tested. Did this young man really know his stuff? Or was the weight of numbers just for show? Zack's memory was flawless, his research immaculate. Without pausing for thought he recalled the tiniest detail. Why had they shown container flows at the Yang Sin terminal tailing off in 2001, Hatherleigh asked. Zack's response was instant. Some articles in the *South China Morning Post* and the *Hong Kong Coastal Shipping Bulletin* had mentioned a major redevelopment of the port scheduled for that year. Ships of more than a certain draught would not be able to obtain entry. Examination of the port's traffic statistics indicated that a thirty percent fall in container loads was likely. Hatherleigh was impressed. The conversation ran on.

Gillingham rubbed his ravaged face, and rested his eyes. He was feeling rough, had done ever since this project started. But he could handle it. He had stayed dry for six years, and, though it never got easier, he had got more practised at getting through the bad times. He'd been through worse than this. Gillingham took his hands away from his face and focused back in on the discussion.

Zack and the viscount finished with the spreadsheets and moved on to the guts of the presentation. What should Hatherleigh Pacific do? What should it buy?

Zack had a shortlist of six names. The first five were all medium-sized Hong Kong companies. All solid. All long-established. All sensible targets. The viscount continued to listen, but he flipped forward through the presentation a little too quickly. He was getting bored. Phyllis Wang and Hal Gillingham saw the symptoms. They'd pitched to enough senior executives to read the signs. Zack was losing this one.

Zack saw the signs too and was pleased. He wanted the right build-up to the final name. Not too slow, not too fast. He played with his audience, he spun things out, built up to a climax.

Finally, he judged that the moment was right. He'd proved his knowledge. He'd proved his understanding.

He'd talked about the other five names for long enough. Finally, Zack got to the last name.

The South China Trust Bank. The name Zack had seen emerging from Bonnie's teeth. The name which had been twice underlined next to a few words scribbled in the margin. Words which Zack had just about managed to decipher from a blurry mental image partly hidden by the drooping lips of a boisterous puppy. In his own handwriting, Lord Hatherleigh had written, *'We must have this company – but how?'*

Zack began the most important part of the most important presentation of his brief career.

4

'Come on you reds,' chanted Darren. He was lugging a pair of brilliant red chairs across the loading bay towards the exhibition hall itself. This was the Northern Furniture Industries Annual Show, the biggest trade fair for the industry aside from the British Showcase event in London. Months ago, George had booked a decent-sized stand and this time made sure they were well located.

Dave glanced across at Darren. Dave was bundling a bright blue shelf unit out of the van.

'Blue is the colour. Gissings is the name,' roared Dave. What he lacked in tunefulness, he more than made up in volume.

Val sat on an empty crate watching the unloading proceed. It was six in the morning and the air was chilly. She drank some tea from a Thermos. Things were running smoothly and she hadn't much to do.

Darren returned for a table with a sliding ledge for a computer keyboard. The table was yellow, with vivid markings of blue and red. Darren's flow of football chants was temporarily halted. Then, with a burst of inspiration, he hollered, 'We all live in the yellow submarine, the yellow submarine, the yellow submarine.'

Dave's next load was a low wooden cupboard, painted blue with huge white and yellow daisies. Dave didn't know any football teams with daisies on their strip. He was stumped. As he hoisted the unit on to his shoulder and began to trudge past Val in puzzled silence, she murmured, 'Daisy, Daisy.'

'Yeah. Good one,' said Dave. At the top of his unmelodious voice, he yelled, 'Daisy, Daisy, give me your answer do.' He knew some obscene lyrics to go with it and the whole loading bay got to hear them.

Val began to unwrap a couple of bacon sandwiches. She'd wrapped them in kitchen paper and foil before leaving home, and they were still warm. Perfect. George would have enjoyed them.

In the bay next to the Gissings' lorry, a larger truck drew up emblazoned with the Asperton logo. It reminded Val of the paintshop fiasco and her absent boss, and she sighed.

Darren and Dave collected in front of her. Could they have a bit of her bacon sandwich? It smelled so good and they'd forgotten to get anything for breakfast. Children, honestly, they were children. She gave them one of her two sandwiches to divide between them. They weren't having any of her tea, though. They stood munching, then, all of a sudden Darren leaped up.

'Bloody thieves!'

He jabbed his sandwich at the Asperton lorry.

Val and Dave turned to look. Two men, in Asperton company overalls, were unloading furniture painted in brilliant primary colours, styled and finished almost identically to the Gissings Bright and Beautiful. The display screens advertising the range were visible too.

'Welcome to the Asperton Brilliants!' they boasted.

'Functional and dazzling – and at prices you won't believe.'

Darren and Dave started to sing a football chant usually reserved for referees awarding the other team a controversial penalty in the ninetieth minute.

'Don't worry about it,' said Val. 'We always expected this to happen.'

It was true. There was no copyright in design and somebody was bound to copy the Gissings Bright and Beautiful range before long. It was only a pity that it should be the Aspertons who'd done it. They wouldn't just copy Gissings, they'd do it well.

The real shock was to come. When the show opened, Val sauntered over to the Asperton stand. She wanted a price list. Michael Asperton was on the stand, round and twinkly, with the inevitable cigar between his lips. He saw Val coming.

'Valerie Bartlett, isn't it? I remember you from the times I used to meet up with old Tom Gissing. Terrible shame about the old man, wasn't it? We sent a big bouquet to his funeral, you know.'

Tom Gissing had never liked or trusted the Aspertons, but he'd never been able to say no. Val didn't like them either.

'What can I do for you, my dear? Do you like our Asperton Brilliants? We're very pleased with them.'

He was chuckling and puffing and bouncing with delight.

'So I see. I was looking for a price list.'

'Prices, my dear? How very commercial! Old Tom Gissing would never have asked for prices before he'd looked at the product. Always liked to inspect the dovetails first. Still, you want a price list. Let me see if I remembered to bring any. Ha, ha. Yes, here we go. These are list prices only, of course. We're always happy to talk about volume discounts. Let me know if you're interested.'

Val took the list and walked off without a thank you or goodbye. The man was insufferable. Walking back to the Gissings stand, she opened the price list. If she hadn't felt sure that Michael Asperton's eyes were on her, she'd have stopped dead in her tracks. The prices weren't just cheap. They were giveaway.

Back on the stand, they assessed the damage. The Asperton range included a copy of everything in Gissings' own range. The prices were between twenty to fifty percent lower. Val also remembered Michael Asperton's crack about the volume discounts. That was his way of telling Val that if they needed to slash their prices even further to win business, then away they'd slash.

There was a decent press of potential buyers round the Gissings stand. They always had a good reception now. Nobody thought the firm was on the brink and it was developing a reputation for quality, innovation and service. But despite the interest, Val wasn't deceived. Polite words cost nothing, but orders wouldn't come until the buyers had checked out everything, and once they got to the Asperton stand, they wouldn't return to Gissings.

She was right. The morning grew quieter the longer it dragged on. It turned out that the Aspertons had slashed prices on a couple of other furniture ranges, close in style to Gissings' other ranges. They had held prices steady on their other stuff, aimed at markets Gissings didn't even compete in.

This was personal. This was war.

Over a dour lunch, Val, Darren and Dave discussed how to react. They were joined by Jeff Wilmot and Andrew Walters, whom Val had summoned from the factory. This was an emergency – or worse. It would have been an emergency if George had been there. As it was, he'd disappeared after Kiki had landed in Gissings' yard two months ago, and nobody had heard from him since.

'It's war, innit?' said Darren. 'We need to match their prices and knock another ten percent off if we have to. This is our idea and we can't just let 'em pinch it.'

Dave, predictably, agreed. Val was silent, but Wilmot and Walters formed a united front against price cuts.

'We simply aren't able to support any price reductions at present,' said Wilmot, speaking for the pair of them. 'Our costs have increased since – er – the paintshop contract was withdrawn –'

'It was withdrawn cos you handed them our profit figures,' said Darren.

'Well, er, the point is that our costs are higher than they were. Our profit margins are now around six or seven percent. If we take even ten percent off our prices we're into loss. If we take twenty to fifty percent off, we'll make a huge loss on every item.'

'Well, we're not going to sell anything with the Aspertons pissing on us.'

Darren's logic was hard to refute, but Wilmot persisted.

'Look. The point is that the Aspertons can't be making any money at these prices. They probably just want to ensure a good launch, before normalising their prices.'

'That's right,' said Walters. 'I'm absolutely certain we can produce more cheaply than they can. We've become very lean and mean these days. Any price that gives them a profit will give us a bigger one. I say we sit back and wait for them to come to their senses.'

Val shook her head.

'You're wrong. The Aspertons won't stop until they've

put us out of business. They've looked through the numbers which Jeff kindly left in their office and they've worked out that in a couple of years' time, Gissings might be a real competitor. They've also worked out that, although we've recovered fast, we're still close to death's door. They plan to just nudge us through.

'They copy our furniture, sell it at insane prices, and wait until we can't pay the bank. The second we give up and declare bankruptcy, Michael Asperton picks up the phone to David Ballard and offers to buy Gissings. We'll be bleeding so fast that Ballard will say yes. The price will be miserable, but he'll have to take it, because the longer he leaves it the bigger his losses. And the moment that Gissings is handed over, the Aspertons put their prices up. Overnight, Gissings becomes profitable again. And what will it have cost the Aspertons? Not much. They just need to put up with selling some unprofitable furniture for a few months. They'll recoup everything in no time.'

She was right, of course. There was no other explanation. Even Darren was silent. If George had been there, he might or might not have known what to do. But either way he'd have taken action, instead of letting the company drift rudderless towards annihilation. The outlook was bleak.

'How long have we got?'

Val was speaking to Jeff Wilmot.

'Until we need to declare insolvency? Er, well, I would need to develop some planning scenarios, and analyse the impact of alternative sales strategies – er, and obviously the important factor will be commercial judgement' – Wilmot meant that somebody else would need to take the blame if he were wrong – 'but I'd say we have about three months. Three months at the outside.'

5

Matthew crumpled his styrofoam cup and chucked it at a stained plastic dustbin. His shot struck the lip of the bin, the cup spun upwards, and a few drops of cold coffee splashed out on to his leg. His trousers were light tan and stained easily.

It was now just ten minutes before the plane was due to close its doors and there was no sign of Fiona Shepperton. Matthew needed to decide if he was going to go on to Vermont by himself or whether he should forget the whole thing and return to his apartment. Little as he fancied knocking around a luxury holiday cabin by himself, the thought of pacing his apartment was worse.

He picked up his holdall and boarding pass. He'd go.

Just then, the glass doors at the end of the lounge burst open. It was Fiona, arriving breathlessly. She was comfortably dressed in faded jeans and a flannel shirt, a picture of relaxed confidence, but her eyes were wide open and vulnerable. As she reached him, she coloured.

'Made it. Sorry.'

'Never mind. I'm pleased you came.'

He bent to kiss her, then, not quite sure how she would respond, pulled away to land a stupid sort of peck high up on her cheek. She was confused too, and gave him an embarrassed smile in return. What were they? Lovers? Colleagues? Friends? Conspirators? Matthew still didn't know why she had saved him during the compliance investigation four weeks ago, and since then, they'd hardly exchanged a word.

Matthew had tried to speak with her at work, but she oscillated between cold professionalism and embarrassed but not unfriendly efforts to change the subject. Finally Matthew, remembering their Jamaican trip, took the plunge and booked a superb holiday home in Vermont for a long weekend, paying top dollar for the privilege. He sent a handwritten invitation to her home address, saying he was keen to get to know her away from the bank. He booked two tickets and waited. After a week, when he still hadn't heard from her, he approached her at the bank and asked if she could come. She muttered that she'd like to but wasn't sure. So he mailed her her plane ticket and went to the airport not knowing if he was alone or in company.

The plane was delayed, but only after everyone had boarded, so there was an extra hour to endure the cramped seats. Matthew flicked through the in-flight magazine and Fiona dug through a pile of company research reports. A stewardess brought round coffee as feeble apology for the delay and managed to spill some on Matthew's other trouser leg.

At last, the plane was ready and taxied out for takeoff. Matthew threw his magazine on the floor and leaned across to his companion. He took all the company reports off her lap and out of her hands, and shoved them into the seat pocket in front of him.

'No more business of any sort until we touch down again on Monday evening,' he said.

Her face revealed a short struggle. Then she nodded submissively.

'OK.'

'And if you get withdrawal symptoms, you can ask special permission to spend an hour on bond analysis.'

She smiled and nodded.

'OK. Thanks.'

The further the plane took them from Manhattan, the more relaxed she became. By the time they landed, Fiona Shepperton, the hard-as-nails Managing Director of Madison, had been carried off and replaced by Fiona the human being.

They picked up a hire car at the airport and drove for ninety minutes into the wooded hills. They collected the keys from a nice old couple, who called them Mr and Mrs Gradley and insisted on their taking a basket of food 'to get them started'. Their home for the weekend was a traditional but luxurious log cabin, heated by an enormous log-burning stove and discreetly equipped with every modern convenience. Beyond the sundeck at the back of the house, a lawn stretched down to a private two-acre lake complete with rowing boat and jetty. The surrounding forest still sparkled with red and gold, but winter had long since begun to poke dead fingers through the golden canopy.

'Like it?' asked Matthew.

'It's fabulous. I love New England. I always tell myself I'll retire to a place like this in time.'

'You'd miss the city and be back the day after the first snow.'

'You couldn't be more wrong. I wouldn't relax until I'd been snowed in a couple of times.'

Going upstairs, they found that only one of the two bedrooms had been prepared for use. After all, why would a Mr and Mrs Gradley want anything more? Fiona unpacked her things while Matthew just dropped his bag in the hall outside. Later, as Matthew loaded the stove with logs, Fiona heated up stew in the kitchen. She brought it out with a hunk of warm bread and they sat on the rug in front of the stove and ate by the light of its flames. They drank some Yorkshire beer which Matthew had bought from a speciality liquor store in Manhattan.

Once the stew and the beer and the crackling flames had done their work, Matthew could wait no longer.

'Why did you lie for me in that compliance investigation?' he asked. 'I thought I'd had it.'

Fiona gazed into the firelight.

'I don't know for certain. I enjoyed our time together in Jamaica and I thought you deserved a second chance. Anyone can screw up once. But next time you see a presentation sliding around on an airplane floor, you leave it right where it is.'

'You saw the presentation? I thought you were asleep.'

'I saw it before I fell asleep. Some Wall Streeters trying to get Draper to step into the bullring again, right?'

'That's right. It still seems like a great idea to me, but I'm hurting badly. I'm more than a million bucks underwater. Right now, I'd settle for getting out in one piece.'

'Mmm.' Fiona frowned, thinking over the problem. 'Supposing you had no position in these bonds, and taking into account everything you know, what would be your best guess about how the bonds will trade?'

It was Matthew's turn to think. He turned everything over in his mind.

'Well, I guess the price could well fall further. The company's debts are getting on top of it, and there's still no sign of decisive management action . . . Yes. Unless Draper makes his move, the price will go on heading south. But on the other hand, if Draper goes ahead with the raid, I'll make a fortune.'

'How many presentations like the one you found would you guess Nick Draper receives each year?'

Matthew was taken aback.

'I don't know. Maybe two or three. There was a hell of a lot of work behind this one. It wasn't a shot in the dark.'

Fiona shook her head.

'The reason why our friends in corporate finance have

such a shit life is that every presentation to major clients has to have that much work in it. If it doesn't, the client throws it back at the bankers and never invites them back. That's why they all work twenty-three hours a day.'

'Well, this one had everything. Comparable company analysis, discounted cash flows, break-up valuations, funding scenarios. This was the full monty.'

'Matthew, Draper's worth two or three billion dollars. Would you go to see a guy like that if you hadn't done your homework? Especially when he's got a team of his own working on exactly the same kind of stuff.'

'I guess not,' said Matthew doubtfully. 'But if this was just a try-on, it was a hell of a good pitch. He can't see all that many ideas like that in a year.'

Fiona shook her head again.

'Every bank on Wall Street has teams devoted to churning out stuff like that. I once knew a chief financial officer of a company where there had been speculation about a merger with one of their competitors. He told me that they had received fifteen presentations from fifteen banks in the same year, all making the same recommendation.'

'Did they take it?'

'No way. The two Chief Executives hated each other. They wouldn't share the same room, let alone merge their businesses.'

Matthew thought for a long while. The fire burned low and he tossed some logs on to brighten it.

'You're saying I should quit?'

'I'm not saying anything. I'm giving you some information. You do with it whatever you want.'

'Well bang goes my bonus,' said Matthew. 'And bang goes my job, in all likelihood.'

Just then one of the logs popped, and a shower of

sparks leaped from the fire. A few of them fell beyond the hearth on to the wooden floor. Another dropped, still glowing, on to Fiona's thigh. Quicker than her, Matthew reached his hand out and swept it away on to the stone hearth. It was strange touching her. She was beautiful but unapproachable, a beautiful statue with stand-back eyes. Matthew still didn't know what to feel about her, and, as far as he could tell, she was confused in exactly the same way. She thanked him and they brushed the remaining embers from the floor.

'Don't get too worked up about a single bad trade,' she advised him. 'How have you done aside from your Western Instruments play?'

'I've done well. I'm up nearly eight hundred grand, which is good given that I'm still not allowed to play with much of the bank's money.'

'Yes. That does sound good. Well, you have to hope that the bank is smart enough to recognise that there's a good trader in you, albeit one who made one king-sized screw-up this year.'

'And do you think the bank will be smart enough?'

She shrugged.

'I don't know. But I'm chairing the PRC for junior traders this year.'

The Performance Review Committee had the annual task of assessing performances and handing out bonuses. Matthew smiled.

'Thanks a lot.'

'Don't thank me. I'll give my honest opinion. I'm never going to lie for you again.'

'Fair enough.' Matthew paused. Then he asked a question he had been burning to ask someone for a very long time. Now seemed like the right moment. 'Fiona, what is the very most I'm likely to earn at Madison over the next two years? Assume I'm the best trader they've ever had and I get all the recognition I deserve.'

Fiona laughed at him.

'You're not the best trader we've ever had. And you've made a pretty poor start.'

'Yes. But suppose I get everything right from now on. How much?'

'Well, you've heard of the rule of Wall Street, haven't you?'

Matthew hadn't.

'Well, the rule of thumb is a hundred thousand bucks for every year out of business school. You haven't been to business school, but you started straight in on the trading floor which is what counts. So, according to the rule, you'll get a hundred this year, two hundred the next, and three hundred the year after. Having said that, you're a trader, not a corporate finance guy, and you can earn more faster. Also, you're at Madison, which is one of the strongest banks on Wall Street, so that also translates into more money. So let's say we double the rule of thumb in your case, you'd get two hundred thousand bucks this year, four the next, six the year after. And if you really do turn out to be the best thing ever to hit the trading floor, then maybe treble the rule. Three, six, nine.'

'But I've blown the first year of that, right? Unless Draper comes charging to my rescue.'

'Right. And that'll more or less screw up any hope of getting six next year.'

So there it was. A million quid was more than a million and a half bucks. Matthew was a good trader, but not that good. Unless Matthew broke Wall Street records, he hadn't a hope of earning his way to a million pounds inside the three-year limit of his father's will. So it was going to have to be Plan B. That was no surprise. In his heart, he'd always known as much.

They spoke of other things until it was late. They damped down the fire, cleared away the dishes, and walked upstairs. Fiona went right on into the one usable bedroom. Matthew stopped at the door, where his bag lay.

'Fiona,' he said. 'You remember you said you would never ever lie for me again?'

'Yes.'

'Any chance of your lying for me right now?' He looked at the inviting double bed, heaped high with clean linen and feather quilts.

She smiled. Once again, ambiguity flickered in frightened eyes, but her answer was clear. She walked right up to Matthew and stopped a few inches from him. Her long dark hair fell around her shoulders, and her face was only inches from his.

'Kiss my feet, big boy.'

Matthew shook his head. Slowly, she moved her hand down between his legs. She grabbed him, firmly but not to hurt, and pulled him over to the bed.

'Kiss me,' she ordered again, and this time Matthew obeyed.

In bed, they had sex such as Matthew had experienced only once before. Their fires blazed high and long, until eventually and happily they sank back into quietness. Afterwards, as before in Jamaica, a change came over Fiona. Matthew tried holding her, she tried to let herself be held, but it was obvious to both of them that it wasn't working.

'Would you mind sleeping on the couch, please?' she asked, but it wasn't a question.

Matthew took a blanket and pillow from the oak chest beneath the window and took himself downstairs. He couldn't sleep and lay watching the dying fire. He thought about Western Instruments, and Nick Draper, and his bonus and his father's millions. He thought about his brothers, Zack and George, and he thought about Josephine and his sick mother. He thought about Sophie, the first woman he had ever really felt for. He thought about the enigmatic Fiona, wondering if they would ever pass a night in each other's arms. Over the lake and the wooded hills beyond, the starlit night paled at the first hint of dawn.

Just as Matthew had wondered for the hundredth time about Fiona, he heard the stairs creak. Fiona stood at the bottom, dressed in the long cotton T-shirt she used for a nightie.

'Are you awake?' she whispered.

'Yes.'

She came over to him and stood by the couch.

'I'm afraid I'm not great at intimacy. My childhood wasn't the easiest. But if you can put up with me, I'd like to try.'

Matthew held up a corner of his blanket. She crept inside and let Matthew put his arm around her. She was tense, but no longer running. Matthew opened his mouth to speak, but she raised her finger to his lips.

'Let's just lie quiet,' she said.

And as these two lovers watched the dawn gather slowly over the woods and rocks of Vermont, another dawn was breaking thousands of miles away, bringing sunshine once more to the warm blue seas of Jamaica.

Nick Draper, early riser and tireless worker, held a presentation in his hand. He'd studied it closely over the last couple of months – he'd had one of his best teams rip it apart and put it back together again. Western Instruments. What a company! It was crying out for a hatchet job. Logically, he should go for it.

But even with a man like Draper, logic carries only so

far. Western Instruments was headquartered in Sand-point, Montana, up in the mountains not far from the Canadian border. It must be cold as the devil in winter and none too fun in summer. Draper hated cold. That was why he'd moved to Jamaica in the first place. Spending two or three years kicking redneck ass in Montana wasn't his idea of fun. What was the point in being a billionaire if you couldn't have any fun?

Reluctantly, Draper took the presentation and, by the light of the swelling sun, dropped it on to his out tray. His secretary, Helen, would shred it on Monday.

6

It was one of those good news, bad news situations.

Looking on the bright side, the faxed confirmation note from the bank contained the information Val had long been waiting for: news of George. Val's anger at George's disappearance had long since turned to a cold and broody rage at his behaviour towards her, but she still had a loyalty to the company, and she knew that the company needed him to survive. So here was the good news: George Gradley was alive and well.

The bad news, however, was worse than the good news was good. The bad news was that George had taken it into his head to withdraw forty-five thousand pounds from the company's contingency reserve, leaving just fifteen thousand pounds. He was within his rights to do so. He was the company's Managing Director and sole shareholder. But his timing couldn't have been worse.

If Wilmot had been right before to give Gissings a life expectancy of three months, he'd need to slash his estimate now. Gissings had less than a month.

Zack was used to just a few hours of sleep a night, so the flight from Heathrow to Hong Kong seemed an eternity, and an eternity beyond the reach of mobile phones at that. Gillingham snored away beside him, his eyes even less attractive by night than by day. They watered in his sleep. Zack topped up his beaker of orange juice for him. He'd want it when he woke.

Zack had eaten, slept and was bored with the movies. The eastern dawn had already broken around the aircraft, hours before the same sun would wake the grey streets of London, but the little plastic shutters were all drawn down and the cabin was dark. Zack pulled out his briefcase and browsed once more through the documents. It wasn't necessary. He knew them by heart. He fidgeted on until breakfast was served.

On arrival, they passed swiftly through Kai Tek airport and rode a cab through Kowloon, under the tunnel, to Hatherleigh Pacific's offices on Wan Chai. Phyllis Wang soon joined them, followed a few minutes later by Lord Hatherleigh himself. Hatherleigh shook hands briefly and hurried them through the executive suite.

'We're in the boardroom today. Plenty of room to spread out and the view's quite something.'

So it was. Picture windows extended from floor to ceiling. Through them you could see the crowded seas of Victoria Harbour and the glittering cityscape beyond. In the blue distance beyond the towers lay the huge bulk of mainland China: communist, dictatorial, inscrutable. This was the very edge of the world, a fingernail on the unknown.

In the room, already seated, were two men. The first of them, with the auburn hair and freckles of the Highland Scot, rose, scarlet-faced.

'My name's James Macintyre, but ye needn't bother to remember that. I'm Scottie to my friends, Mr Scottie to the rest. I'm Chief Executive.'

He bustled over to shake hands, reaching Zack first. His grip was massive and Zack's hand ached. Zack hoped he'd go easy with Phyllis's tiny bones. She might want them again. After Scottie, Zack shook hands with the Chief Financial Officer, a neat Chinese man, Edmund Zhao. Zhao nodded and smiled like a glove puppet, but behind woefully thick glasses, an agile brain calculated.

The morning was spent in discussion of Hatherleigh Pacific's current situation. Scottie and Ed Zhao devoured the numbers as greedily as Hatherleigh had, and, if possible, with even greater attention to detail. Zhao smiled and nodded all the while. The red on Scottie's face grew ever deeper. Hatherleigh excused himself from time to time and left silently through a glass door at the end of the room. Zack and Phyllis Wang did the talking for Weinstein Lukes. Gillingham sat slumped with a coffee gazing out over the harbour, wishing he were somewhere else and a whole lot younger. Addiction nibbled at his soul and his soul was weary.

Eventually they were done. Zhao whispered something to Scottie, who nodded. Zhao smiled, nodded and left the room.

'We've been through your numbers in detail,' said Scottie. 'It's only fair that we show you ours.'

Zhao came back in with the Hatherleigh Pacific Strategic Plan. It's not just communists who draw up five-year plans. Companies do it too. Zhao spread out the figures for Zack to see. Turnover, operating profit, pretax profit, net profit. The numbers were extraordinarily close to Weinstein Lukes' own projections.

'We seem to have it about right then,' remarked Zack.

'Oh yes, pretty much right,' nodded Ed Zhao with a smile.

Zack and Phyllis exchanged glances. In the jargon of Weinstein Lukes, Hatherleigh Pacific had just dropped its trousers – revealed the most secret data in its possession. No company does that unless it trusts a bank completely. Zack and Phyllis knew that by the time they left they would be hired to do something. The only question was what – and for how much.

After lunch, Hatherleigh kicked off.

'I wanted Ed and Scottie to put you through your paces. They're as pleased with you as I was and we'd like to work with you further. Now, in London you showed me the names of six companies. We're interested in just one of them, the South China Trust Bank.'

Scottie took up the theme.

'Yes. The other names are sensible targets, but not thrilling ones. South China has everything. As you know, South China owns one of the biggest fleets of coastal ships besides ours. But whereas our fleet is completely containerised, South China's fleet is non-container cargo only. Coal, timber, cement, iron ore, oils, steel, you name it. It's a huge fleet with bags of potential and yet we believe they haven't made a profit for seven years. That's bad management, that is. The fleet's fine. We think the true value of the fleet is close to a billion US dollars.

'South China also owns some land, valued at next to nothing on their balance sheet, derelict land up in the New Territories. Well, we have a development scheme, which we believe we could pre-sell about eighty percent in today's market. We've got the scheme, the reputation, and the skills, but we don't have the land. South China would give us all we need and more. We believe the land alone could be worth two hundred and fifty million US dollars to us.

'And finally, of course, there's a bank there. Let me ask you this: how much do you think we'd need to pay to be sure of winning South China?'

Zack paused. He had pages of analysis on that. Loads of what-if analysis, tons of matrices. Scottie didn't look like a man for matrices.

'We reckon that one point two billion US dollars might buy it for you. To be sure, I think you'd need to pay a couple of hundred more than that. Say, one point four.'

Scottie nodded.

'That's what we think too. One point four. We think that in our hands, the land and fleet could be worth one point two billion. That means we'd be buying all the rest of South China for just two hundred million, virtually nothing for a bank that size. This could be a huge deal for us. Huge.'

'Which brings us to our final question,' said Zack.

'That's right.' Scottie smiled thinly, and Zhao for a moment stopped smiling and nodding. 'Where do we find one point four billion dollars? We can borrow a billion and that's stretching it.'

'More than that,' said Zack. 'We believe we can find investors in the US willing to lend you as much as one point one billion. Maybe, one point two if you don't mind paying a chunky interest rate. But that still leaves a gap. So you have two choices. The obvious one is to create some new shares and sell them on the stock-market.'

Scottie shook his head. Zhao smiled and shook his head. Lord Hatherleigh intervened.

'I'm afraid I've ruled that out, Zack. The family and I hold thirty percent of the company and we don't want our holdings to be diluted by selling shares. My mind's made up on that, I'm sorry, but you'll have to find another way.'

Zack nodded. He'd guessed as much and come prepared. That was why Gillingham was there.

'We have a second way on offer. We think you can raise the extra money from the taxman. Hal, do you want to explain?'

Gillingham sat up and began to speak. His worn-out face became animated, his voice commanding. Once again, the brilliance of the man who had been a Weinstein Lukes partner for more than a decade became apparent. He wasn't just convincing, he was mesmerising.

The concept was simple. The only reason why Hatherleigh Pacific couldn't borrow the full one point four billion was that some of its profits would be siphoned off by the taxman. If only the taxman would generously agree to stop taking anything in tax, the company should be able to borrow the one point four billion in full. And how could the taxman be persuaded into an unprecedented act of generosity? Gillingham had the answer. The scheme was simple in outline, complex in detail. It all had to do with the property portfolio and ways of shuffling it around. A clause in the tax law, intended to help property developers, had been turned by Gillingham into a scheme for avoiding tax altogether. It was brilliant.

The three men from Hatherleigh Pacific listened intently.

Zhao's understanding of the tax intricacies was excellent, and he quickly began to ask all of the right questions. Hatherleigh and Scottie were soon lost and they excused themselves as Gillingham, Zack and Zhao pored over some draft legal documents. After two hours Zhao was persuaded, and he brought his two superiors back into the room.

'We will need to check with our lawyers, of course,' said Zhao, 'but I understand this stuff better than they do. I am telling you, this scheme will work.'

He was emphatic and it was clear that his two superiors trusted him. The three men from Hatherleigh Pacific moved into a corner for a quiet talk. This was better than they'd dared to hope. In effect, the taxman would be paying for a big chunk of the deal, and Hatherleigh Pacific's potential profit looked enormous. The only thing that remained now was to formally hire Weinstein Lukes to advise them. The three men resumed their seats. Behind them afternoon light slanted across the waters of the harbour, lighting up ships, offices and banks: the fabric of Hong Kong, the fabric of the new Hatherleigh Pacific.

'Zack, Phyllis, Hal, I want to thank you all for a quite excellent presentation,' said Lord Hatherleigh. 'We would like to retain you to assist us in the acquisition of the South China Trust Bank. With whom should I discuss your fee?'

He still couldn't quite believe that Zack was in charge. He was so young, young enough to be his son. Good lord, if Sarah became serious about Zack, this young man might even be his son-in-law. But it was Zack who answered, blunt and direct.

'With me. Our advisory fee will be one percent of the eventual deal. Our financing fee for helping you raise the money will be another two percent.'

'Three percent? Of one point four billion? That's over forty million bucks!'

Hatherleigh's surprise was understandable. For large deals, fees are seldom more than one percent. Zack's response was cool.

'You're right, it's a lot of money. But remember. Without a way of avoiding taxes, you can't do this deal. We've shown you how to cut out the tax and that means that this deal becomes possible. That's why you're paying extra.'

Zack stopped, but his meaning ran on into the silence. Any investment bank could advise Hatherleigh on the takeover, but only Weinstein Lukes had the technology to make it work. Without Gillingham's tax scam, the deal was impossible.

Lord Hatherleigh tapped on the table in annoyance. His daughter's young boyfriend sat before him demanding forty million dollars, the politeness of the Ovenden House dinner table forgotten. But that wasn't the most annoying thing. The most annoying thing was that Hatherleigh was going to say yes. He had to.

Then Zack spoke again. He didn't even know what he was going to say before he said it.

'This deal could transform Hatherleigh Pacific. It won't be our skill that does it. It'll be your own management talent and energy. But we do offer you a key to the door. And . . .' Zack paused, then continued, 'and, hell, Jack, it would be fun, wouldn't it?'

Phyllis Wang, Hal Gillingham, Scottie and Zhao were dumbfounded. You don't say that. You just don't talk about launching a one point four billion dollar bid for fun. This young man had overstepped the mark and would surely be bellowed out of the door. All eyes were on Lord Hatherleigh. It was for him to pass sentence.

Hatherleigh too stared at Zack. It was an amazing thing to say. In all his years of business, he'd never heard anything like it.

'Fun?' he said. 'Fun?' He continued to stare, and as he did so, his thin aristocratic features warmed slowly into a broad smile. 'Yes, dammit, it will be fun.'

8

Blind and impenetrable stood the fortress. Off lime-stone ramparts, sunshine glittered and blazed. Beneath the ancient gate-tower, George stood drenched in clear autumnal light.

His hired two-seater Mercedes convertible was parked amidst a motley collection of Renault Clios, Fiat Puntos, and other small cars. George couldn't fathom it. Why would one of the most eminent families in France – Europe, indeed – put up with the discomfort of living in this forbidding castle? Where were the luxury cars, the great entrance, the gardens and the peacocks?

Still, his not to reason why, all he wanted was to track down his quarry after more than two months of fruitless pursuit. He pushed at the picket gate set inside the huge mediaeval doors and looked around for help. Inside, an old man in overalls was talking with a laundrywoman. A nasty, vicious little dog, ugly as a gargoyle, leaped to the end of its chain, barking and snapping.

'Excusez-moi,' said George, quickly coming to an end of his French vocabulary, 'I'm looking for – er – Kiki.' He used her nickname, as he had never mastered the correct way to pronounce her name and title. 'I'm expected,' he added lamely.

The man and woman looked at George, at his Armani suit and designer sunglasses and through the picket gate at his shiny black sports car.

'Kelso. Tais-toi!'

The man shouted at the dog to be quiet, but in vain. Then he spoke to George in rapid peasant French, waving his hands and shouting to drown out the barking dog. George understood nothing.

Finally, the old man changed his approach. He searched around for a word and said, 'Come.' The two of them crossed the courtyard in the shadow of the keep, then entered a hallway lined with bits of armour and rusting weapons. The man tapped a rough wooden bench running the length of one wall. 'Restez là. Stay.'

George stayed. The cool was welcome after the sun. He leaned carefully against the wall behind, hoping its rough plaster wouldn't come off on his new suit. Its careful cut struggled to hide George's increasingly corpulent figure. Despite the cool he was sweating. After a wait of ten minutes or more, a neat young man slipped through a doorway at the end of the hall and approached.

'Good morning. I understand that you have business with the family,' he said, in French-accented but immaculate English.

'Yes, please, I'm here to see Kiki. She's expecting me. I'm George Gradley.'

The neat young man hesitated briefly. He was wondering whether to correct George's use of Kiki's nickname, but decided against.

'Yes. I believe she was expecting you an hour or so ago.' That was true enough. George had got horribly lost and ended up crawling slowly behind a tractor which was also headed for the castle.

'I apologise that there was nobody to receive you,' said the neat young man without apologising. 'The old castle is for staff only. Guests of the family generally prefer to arrive at the north entrance.'

As he spoke, he escorted George rapidly down a series of dismal corridors until they arrived at a pair of nail-studded oak doors. They went through and emerged into a high light-painted hallway, with bright sunlight streaming through large and airy windows. The colours were pale pastels. The curtains were silk. Two uniformed maids were at work polishing a Louis Quinze table on which stood a pretty porcelain bowl. The neat young man lifted the lid to reveal a heap of chocolates and popped one into his mouth.

On they went. Up marble staircases, down more duck-egg blue corridors, eventually coming to a halt outside a pair of white and gilt double doors. The neat young man knocked out of politeness but swept on through. There, in the canary yellow room with its blue upholstered furniture and sky-painted ceiling, its tall glass doors flung open to welcome the sunshine and air from the gardens beyond, was Kiki.

She was dressed in pale olive linen trousers and a cream cotton blouse. She had been practising the flute and laid it aside as George entered.

'Georges, how nice to see you. Charles-Henri, thank you so much for rescuing him from the castle. I always get so lost in there. It gives me the terrors. And you will have his car brought round to the front, please?' Thus thanked and dismissed, the neat young man left. 'But you are a beast for being so late, Georges. There was nothing for it but to play my flute and that is so tiring, but so beautiful too, I suppose, so perhaps it's good.'

As she chattered, they kissed as friends kiss, and Kiki found George a seat amongst her litter of sheet music.

'It's really nice to see you again, Kiki. I've been looking for you for ages.'

'I know you have, you bad man. I had to run away to my friend Maria in Argentina. I felt like a fox that you English enjoy to hunt. I only came home because I thought "Poor Georges, he wants to see me very much, so I suppose I should see him, even though I have a funny feeling about it," but then of course you come so very late, so I have to play the flute until my lips are blue and I have to send poor Charles-Henri to rescue you from the dungeons over there.' She waved her hand vaguely enough that the old castle was probably included somewhere in the course of its long sweep.

'Kiki, why did you run from me?' asked George, as gently as he could.

'Oh, Georges, what have you come to tell me, that you have left your precious factory for so long?'

George's question had come first, but Kiki was the lady, so her question took priority. George knew what he wanted to say and cleared his throat. He spoke softly.

'Kiki, I love you. I have loved you as long as I have known you. When you kissed me last year at my flat, I knew that I couldn't stop loving you. When you came to the factory, I knew I couldn't be happy without you. So here I am.'

Awkwardly stooping on one knee, amidst the sheet music and the breeze from the open doors, George took out a small box from his pocket. He withdrew a simple diamond ring; a ring that had cost him thirty thousand pounds and maybe his factory as well.

'Kiki, will you make me the happiest man alive and agree to marry me?'

He looked up. Kiki's face was wet with tears. Her wilfully unserious manner was gone, but, amid her tears, her head was shaking. Wordlessly, she plucked at his sleeve and drew him outside to a terrace hung at either end with a long gilt-framed mirror. In the gardens beneath, peacocks called amongst the fountains and gardeners fussed over topiary and roses.

'Georges, I think you are the kindest, nicest man I know, and I am very fond of you, truly. But look at us. We are too different. If you marry me, you would hate me before we had spent a night together, and that would be too horrible.'

George stood in front of the mirror and stared. The Armani suit couldn't disguise the truth. He was his father's son. He had his father's bristling ginger hair, his father's piggy eyes, his father's heavy build. Of Yorkshire clay was George Gradley built and all the designers in the world would never be able to hide it.

And Kiki? He looked at her reflection next to his. She was trembling with emotion, as though the breeze from the garden was softly shaking her. She was all the things he was not. She was light, fragile, beautiful, rich. He was heavy, plain, thick-skinned, penniless. It was unimaginable that she should ever leave this world of hers, her golden cage. Gissings, Yorkshire, the factory would suffocate her in seconds. Neither could George imagine moving into her world. Christ, he hadn't even been able to find her front door. How would he cope living with her?

He looked for a long time. Kiki was the most desirable woman in the world, but she would be no wife for him. He nodded miserably.

'You're right, Kiki. I wish you weren't, but you are.'

'My dearest Georges. I am too fond of you. That was why I had to run away to Argentina. I couldn't bear to say no.'

She let him embrace her. They hugged for a long time. Eventually, she detached herself gently and kissed him, letting him dab clumsily at her tears with his handkerchief. When he'd finished, she silently completed the job with her own tiny scrap of cotton and lace.

'Georges, first you make me late and make me play my flute, and then you come and make me cry and spoil my make-up and just before lunch so Papa will want to know what's wrong and I shall have to lie to him and I cannot lie to Papa, because he always knows,' she chided, but her heart wasn't in it. She invited him to stay to lunch. For a moment George was tempted, but in the end he refrained.

'Thanks, Kiki, but I'd only be out of place. Besides, I'd best be getting back. My factory's probably missing me.'

'*Tu as raison*, Georges. You are right. Oh, and Georges,

this is a terribly sweet little ring, but I think it belongs to some other lady.'

She handed back the ring.

'Somebody else? Come off it, Kiki. It's only been you for years.'

'What about your lady – Valerie, I think she is called?'

'Val?' said George, bewildered. 'How do you know about Val? Anyhow, there's never been anything at all serious between us. How could there be?'

'Oh. *Pardon.* When I saw you with her, I thought, you must be . . . I thought you were together. That was the other reason why I ran away so hard. I didn't want to come between you and her. I hoped so much you would see that she was better for you.'

George took the ring back. Gissings wasn't doing so well that it could afford to waste half of its contingency reserve on an unwanted engagement ring. George put the ring in his pocket. He didn't feel brokenhearted but somehow purged, like when you cry a lot at the end of a weepie, before walking out into the street with your friends and feeling the world return to normal around you. He was pleased he had come, but now felt able to go.

George and Kiki walked slowly to the front of the house, into the grand hall, where there stood a bust of one of Kiki's ancestors, one of the most influential men in the history of France. His solemn features were crowned with a preposterous yellow hat.

'Oh! My hat! I have been looking for you.'

She put it on. In the enormous yellow shadow cast by the brim, George and Kiki kissed, fondly and sadly. Kiki's face was still a little damp.

'*Adieu, Georges,*' said Kiki. '*Bonne chance.*'

'Bye, Kiki. Don't forget me.'

George got into his Mercedes and headed for the

road to Bordeaux. For the past six weeks he hadn't been able to get Kiki out of his head. Whenever he'd thought of Val or the factory, he'd felt an almost physical sense of repugnance. But now, driving away, far from being heartbroken, he felt OK. And far from thinking obsessively about the woman he was leaving, he couldn't help looking forward to seeing Val again. He thought of her strong arms and cosy embrace, their ease with each other, their shared nights in bed, sex followed by steaming mugs of sweet tea, their shared passion for everything to do with the factory.

Val was the same as George. So close were they, she could almost be his sister. But she wasn't his sister, she was his lover. And George had an expensive engagement ring to dispose of.

9

Matthew touched a few buttons on his keyboard and his trading portfolio came up on screen. He hardly needed to look. All he cared about was the Western Instruments position and he knew that well enough. The bond price had rallied a bit, following some less-bad-than-expected results, but he was still heavily underwater. To sell or not to sell?

There wasn't a question really. He had lost his faith in Draper. Fiona was right. He must see a dozen opportunities like this every year, and he launched a bid only every four or five years. Betting on a takeover is like putting your money on the 30–1 outsider in a horse race: your odds of success are low, but the potential rewards are high. It's an attractive way to gamble, but a dumb way to trade.

The phone rang. It was a client interested in unloading some IBM bonds, 'in search of something with a higher yield'. As it happened, Matthew needed some IBM bonds to square out a trade from the week before, so he was able to quote a good price. The client hit his bid right away and Matthew began to scribble out a ticket.

'You're not interested in Western Instruments, are you?' he asked, before hanging up. 'I've got a position I need to unwind and I can let you have them at a quarter of a percent better than the market price.'

'Western Instruments? You're kidding. You're not? Let me have a think and I'll call you back.'

Fifteen minutes later the client called back, keen to proceed. Matthew confirmed the price and they did the deal for all twenty-five million. With a mixture of relief and pain, Matthew scribbled out the ticket.

He had sold his bonds at seventy-eight cents in the dollar, giving him a loss of one and a quarter million bucks. His first year in the markets was turning out to be a mess, but, on the positive side, Matthew had put an end to the fiasco and learned a lot in the process.

Now for Plan B.

10

Pale November sun tilted across the park. Behind him, Ovenden House glowed a rich gold, but Zack had no eyes for it. He stood by the archway leading into the rose garden and paused.

The arch was covered by a rambling rose of the palest pink. So late in the season, most of its flowers had long since turned into a litter of petals on the flagstones beneath, but a few late sprays still held their blooms. Feeling he should have something in his hands, Zack reached up to snap off a couple of tresses. But the old rose was unexpectedly resilient and it fought the attempt to steal its treasures. He persisted and ended up yanking off three decent sprays of roses, but at some cost to the plant. Where he had broken the tresses, the stalk was mangled and one entire section was ripped away from the arch. He patted it back into place and hoped no one would notice. He took the roses and went in search of Sarah.

He hadn't far to look. Sarah was kneeling beside a wooden arbour, planting a rose. On either side of her, yellow roses flushed with red sprang up, silent echos of the setting sun. Sarah looked up.

'Hello, gorgeous,' she said.

Zack kissed her and offered her the roses.

'What's this?'

'I'm giving you some roses.'

'You can't give them to me. They're mine already.'

'Eh?'

'This is my rose garden. Daddy gave it to me for my sixteenth birthday. And the rose you've got there was named after me by its breeder. It's the *Rosa* Sarah Havercoombe.'

'Oh. Sorry. I won't give you them then. I'll present them. To you, my dear.'

She took the roses briefly, before crying out.

'Ow! Damn!' she said, sucking her hand. 'You might at least have snapped the thorns off.'

Zack said sorry again and started to pick the thorns off the bouquet. It was rather prickly. The more he handled the roses, the more petals they shed. November roses are hardly the most robust of flowers, even the *Rosa* Sarah Havercoombe. By the time he had finished, the tresses had lost nearly all their flowers. It wasn't how he'd envisaged the scene, but romance wasn't his strong suit.

'We'd better go and have a look at the poor old rose. You should never just break things off one, let alone at this time of year. Frost can damage unprotected wood.'

Zack walked in Sarah's wake back to the archway.

'Oh, Zack. You've made a real mess.'

Sarah opened an unobtrusive green metal cupboard positioned just inside the arch. Inside, amongst other implements, were two pairs of secateurs. Sarah took one of them and began to tidy the plant.

'I haven't done any lasting damage, have I?'

'No, not lasting. Roses do shoot again after being pruned, you know. It's one of the magic things about them. But don't congratulate yourself on a job well done. This particular Sarah Havercoombe was doing perfectly well without your interference, thank you.'

Sarah finished snipping. She dropped the pile of rose clippings just outside the gate, where they would be collected for burning. She put the secateurs away and closed the cupboard. Peace was restored.

'Sorry about the rose.'

'It's OK. Forget about it. Next time do it properly.'

'There's something I wanted to say. It's the reason why I wanted to bring you roses. I want to marry you, Sarah. I mean, do you want to marry me?' Zack stopped. This proposal had been a mess from beginning to end. He took the threadbare roses from Sarah, dropped on to one knee, took her hand in his and started again.

'Dear, sweet, beloved Sarah, will you make me the happiest man in England, and be my wife?'

He offered her the bunch of roses, by this stage not much more than a bunch of sticks with the thorns picked off. She took them and her hand was shaking.

'Oh Zack, dear Zack! I will.'

11

Inevitably, the van broke down. George was no mechanic and, anyway, there were no tools. There was no garage nearby and if there had been, it would have been closed. It was ten o'clock at night and pouring with rain.

There was nothing else for it. George heaved the van on to the verge, took his suitcase from the back and began the five-mile tramp home. He'd be soaked before he'd gone a mile, but in a way it was a nice way to return. At the end of it, there would be a thick cup of tea, maybe some sausage and egg and, he hoped, the strong comfort of Val's embrace.

He trudged out of Ilkley along the country roads which would take him up the hill to Sawley Bridge. On either side, the wind moaned in the wet grass, and every now and then a horse or sheep ran startled away into the night. His suitcase was wet and heavy in his hand. All it contained was designer rubbish that he'd bought for Kiki's benefit. He wouldn't be needing it any more.

A little way off, a lake beat its waves in the blackness. From a ditch beside the road, he hauled a rock out of the sucking mud, opened his case and dumped the rock inside. He zipped the case up, squelched out into the field, and threw his case far out into the waters of the lake. The case bubbled and disappeared. Farewell Kiki. Farewell all that super-rich, French Riviera, your-chateau-or-mine world that George would never again enter.

Welcome Val. Welcome Yorkshire. Welcome Gissings.

By the time he arrived at Val's house, it was long gone eleven and he was soaked through and glad to be back. When he tried his key, he found the door bolted from the inside. His knock brought Val to the door in her dressing gown.

'Hi, Val. It's me.'

'So I see,' said Val, making no move to let him in.

'May I come in?'

She shook her head.

'No. I've decided to stop letting rooms. Just tell me when you want to come round and get your stuff. It's all in boxes in the shed.'

'Letting a room, Val? I thought we . . . I mean I'm sorry about buggering off like that. I really am. I've got so much to tell you. I . . . it was wrong, I know. It was something I had to get out of my system, but it's gone now. I promise. It won't ever happen again.'

'True,' said Val, making as if to close the door.

'Can't I even come in for a moment? There's something I have to say.'

He wasn't sure what he wanted to say, but the engagement ring in his breast pocket thundered against his heart. Val shook her head and the door closed further.

'Wait. I don't have anywhere to stay.'

Val shrugged.

'I think there's a hostel in Leeds if you're desperate.'

She closed the door. The centre of Leeds was a good fifteen miles away.

George spent the night at the factory. The place was all shut up and George didn't carry keys. Instead, he crept round to the old sawmill, which was left unlocked because there was nothing there. And on a pile of old lumber, wrapped in an oily tarpaulin pulled up over his Armani suit, George shivered and slept.

He woke early, walked back into Ilkley to get a proper breakfast and bought himself some decent clothes as soon as the shop opened. The sales assistant let George change into the clothes he had just bought and asked with a straight face if he would like his old suit folded or hung. George looked at the once lovely fabric, now soaked, torn and stained.

'Incinerated,' he said.

George arranged an indefinite stay at a local bed and breakfast, had a local garage come to pick up the van and meantime took a taxi in to Gissings. He plodded up to his office, feeling strange to be back.

A meeting was in progress. Andrew Walters, Jeff Wilmot, Val and a sulky Darren sat round the table. Andrew Walters, the acting managing director, was enjoying his turn in the seat of power, while Darren was sulking because he had no formal position in the company and, in George's absence, nobody paid him much attention. Everyone except the impassive Val was startled at George's arrival.

'Hello, everyone. Sorry I've been away. I'm back now. What's the news?'

Andrew Walters tried to tell the story of the Aspertons' attack on Gissings, the copycat furniture and the price war, but Darren kept interrupting to get George's attention. Wilmot weighed in behind Walters with his usual pomposity and Val, who could have summarised everything in a few crisp sentences, kept silent. Eventually George thought he'd got it.

'So the Aspertons have copied our stuff, chopped their prices and are waiting for us to bleed to death. Right?'

A babble of voices agreed in their different ways.

'And we are bleeding, are we?' asked George.

Wilmot responded acidly. The way he saw things, accountants should speak respectfully to their bosses. But then again, managing directors shouldn't disappear in the midst of the firm's worst ever crisis with a pocket full of the company's precious cash.

'I think you could say we are bleeding, yes. We've managed to survive as long as we have because we've been chasing customers to pay us and we haven't been paying our suppliers. As Mr Walters was saying just before you entered, we probably have about one week before we literally run out of cash. In my view, which I have made very plain, and, have indeed written a

number of quite forceful memorandums on the topic'
– he waved a wad of paper – 'we are on the brink
of insolvency and have a statutory obligation to cease
trading.'

'What?'

'We have no reason to believe that we can pay either
our suppliers or our workers, and it is illegal to continue
in business under those circumstances. In my memorandums, which you will find on your desk . . .'

'Yeah, OK. If we all go to jail, we'll have a whip-round
for you, Jeff. Thanks. You've made your point. Now,
what have we done in response?'

The answer was, precious little, but it took a long time
for George to establish the fact. A few costs had been
cut, an extra drive had been injected into the marketing
effort, but that was it. Their sales hadn't completely
dried up, but their order books weren't a pretty sight.

'OK. I get the picture. Can I have a look at the
Aspertons' stuff? We've got samples, right?'

'Er, not exactly,' said Walters.

'Well, I want to see it. Darren, go out right now
and spend this' – George tossed Darren a bundle of
notes – 'on the Asperton rip-offs. Come back as soon
as you can.'

Darren was out of the door before George had finished
speaking and had started yelling for Dave at the top
of his voice. A couple of minutes later, a Gissings van
sped out of the car-park, Radio One blaring from its
decrepit radio.

George filled in the next couple of hours going through
stuff that should have been attended to weeks ago. He had
a series of messages from David Ballard, the bank manager, which George tore up. Val spoke as little as she could
and avoided anything personal. George tried to apologise
for vanishing the way he had, but she cut him off.

'I don't think that that's got much to do with my job description, do you?'

'Oh, come on, Val. Let's talk, for heaven's sake.'

'I'm sorry. I have some filing to do.'

It was a miserable wait. Eventually, Darren and Dave returned, gleefully. The van was loaded dangerously full, both lads were smoking cigars and Darren was waving George's wad of money.

'Went to the Asperton factory outlet, called old man Asperton up from reception, and said we was from Gissings. Admired their bleeding furniture so much, we wanted to buy some samples. The bleeder came downstairs himself and gave us the van-load for free. He said not to worry about paying, cos furniture makers should stick together like brothers. Tosser! Idiot couldn't stop giggling. Dave managed to half-inch some of his cigars and I helped myself to a pile of their brochures.'

'Yeah,' added Dave. 'Darren wanted to slash a few tyres in the car-park but I told him not to be a plonker.'

Andrew Walters started to lecture the two lads on how every employee was an ambassador for the firm, but George just took his money and told Walters to forget it.

They lugged the Asperton Brilliants out of the van and into the old Gissings museum, which now stood empty. George summoned a couple of craftsmen and they started to rip the furniture apart.

They tried to identify the paint, the varnish, the wood, the preservative, even the metalwork supplier. They noticed where glue was used, where nails, and where jointing. They took precise measurements of every detail. They identified the types of hinges, brackets, handles and even screws. They sketched the designs and analysed the brochure.

337

Once they had done all they could, they started to cost out the Asperton range, aiming to calculate the production cost of each unit. The Aspertons' plan emerged clearly enough. They had produced a range of copycat furniture on the lowest budget they possibly could. At their rock-bottom pricing they were certainly making a loss, but they were cutting corners to keep their losses to a minimum. They wanted to bankrupt Gissings, but didn't want to pay too much for the pleasure. At two o'clock in the morning, George called a halt.

'Right, we know all we need to. Question is: What should we do about it?'

Wilmot, the accountant, was first to speak.

'Some elements of management and – er – non-management grades' – he glowered at Darren – 'have wanted to reduce our prices in line with the competition. I must caution you very strongly against doing so. Our losses will become dramatically higher if we sustain any further reduction in unit sales prices.'

'I agree,' said George.

Darren was stung. He had expected support from his hero and he leaped in fiercely.

'You can't score goals with ten men behind the ball. We're not selling anything with our prices stuck where they are. Doing nothing is suicide.'

George nodded. 'Yes, I agree.'

'I beg your pardon?' said Wilmot.

'Make up your mind,' said Darren.

'I have,' said George. 'We can't cut prices, but we can't leave them as they are either. So we'd better put them up. Twenty percent should do the trick.'

12

Josephine jiggled the mouse and the monitor shook itself

awake. The screen was filled with code, completely unintelligible.

'What's all this, Miklos?'

'This? Oh, it's nothing. My friend writes program to play chess. He want me to look at it.' He laughed. 'It's a very bad program. Also no point.'

'Why no point?'

'Chess is . . . chess is beautiful. Computers try to look into future. Always this move, that move, this move, that move. More and more times. This is not chess, this just big calculator. Good player look two, maybe three moves forward. Then ask, is this beautiful, is this good for me? Computers play ugly chess. No point.'

'Could you teach me?'

'You want to play chess?'

'No, computers, not chess. Programming, all that.'

'You? Programming?'

Kodaly wasn't being deliberately rude, but he still saw Josephine as a secretary, a beautiful and self-assured one to be sure, but still a secretary. And in Kodaly's world, there were whole layers of intellectual hierarchy between computer programmers and secretaries.

'Yes, me; programming. I want to learn.'

'What do you know already?'

'How to switch on. How to type.'

Kodaly puffed out his cheeks and blew.

'It's big job. Maybe a course . . .'

'I don't have the time or the money. Maybe my boyfriend could teach me.'

Kodaly puffed his cheeks again, but reached a book down from his shelves: *Pascal Programming 1.01.*

'OK. Computers are like chessboards: very simple, very complicated,' he began.

It was the first time she had called him boyfriend.

Winter 1999–2000

The end of a millennium approaches. The weather is sharp and cold. A tramp and her child are found in the park, frozen to death. The man who found her is a photographer and his photo splashes across the front pages: 'Still no room at the inn'. The self-righteous headline disturbs no one, at least not if the frenzy in the shopping mall is anything to go by. This is the last Christmas of the millennium. Got to have a new coat. Got to have a new dress. Can't start a century in last season's clothes.

On production lines in China and Korea, the fireworks are being bundled into boxes marked 'for immediate dispatch'. The pyrotechnic stockpiles, already at record heights, rise ever higher. The old millennium will pass away in a glory of gunpowder, and what better way to bid farewell to the tattered old thing?

It is 20 December 1999, five days before Christmas, eleven days from the century's end. There are 571 days until Bernard Gradley's deadline.

1

When Jesus said that rich men couldn't enter the kingdom of heaven, he lost the investment banking vote there and then. In banking, religious convictions are rarer than tattoos. But everyone has to worship something, and at Madison that thing goes by the name of EPAS – the Employee Performance Appraisal System.

EPAS is an Old Testament God, just and unmerciful. EPAS rewards the good and punishes the wicked. The favoured enjoy huge bonuses, promotions and giant salary increases. Sinners get small bonuses, sideways moves or the sack. The ordeal lasts all year, because as soon as one bonus is paid in January, evaluation of your performance starts again, ready for next year. But, though EPAS' shadow never lifts, it's in autumn that the pressure mounts.

Through autumn, everyone writes reviews of everyone. Bosses write about their subordinates. Subordinates write about their bosses. Colleagues, nervously competitive, write about each other. The appraisal forms are long, complex, and searching. The forms are written and sent in secret, and you don't know who is writing about you. Offend someone in February and the payback comes secretly nine months later, through a form you can't see, with lies you can't deny. No two bankers ever meet without knowing that any mistake, any word out of place, could come back to hurt them. EPAS is Big Brother turned capitalist, God turned spy.

In December, just before Christmas, the results are announced.

Matthew waited nervously outside Rosenthal's seldom-used office. Inside, Rosenthal was breaking the news, good or bad, to Scott Petersen. The sounds from inside the glass-walled room were muffled, and the Venetian blinds kept even the smiles hidden. Rumour had it that the bond department – Matthew's department – was being reduced in size, and Matthew hadn't had a great year. He fidgeted and waited.

Eventually, Rosenthal was done. Petersen had had a good year and he left Rosenthal with a smile wide enough to swim in. He stopped at the doorway.

'Thanks, Saul. Thanks very much,' he said to Rosenthal, then turning to Matthew, 'Hey, Matt. Hope it's OK.' He paused. He knew about Matthew's losses on Western Instruments and he knew about the downsizing rumours. Matthew was vulnerable. Petersen tried to compress his smile, not to look too happy. But he was no actor and his grin was back before he'd moved a yard. Matthew felt awful.

Still, his turn had come. He was about to tap on Rosenthal's door and walk on in, when a deep Scots voice behind him said, 'Hey there, Matt. How are you doing?' It was Brian McAllister.

'Yeah, fine, thanks,' said Matthew, giving the compulsory answer. 'I'm just about to hear the worst from Saul.'

'The worst, Matthew?'

'Well, you know, find out how I've done, I mean.'

'Why should that be the worst, Matt?' McAllister's pale eyes bored into Matthew, but it was a rhetorical question and Matthew didn't need to fumble for another answer. In the end, the Scotsman broke the silence, saying, 'I hope you've no need to fear, but if you don't mind, I'll sit in with you.'

Matthew was surprised. EPAS revealed its secrets in one-on-one sessions. They weren't a form of public entertainment. But Matthew knew better than to say no to Brian McAllister, and the two men went into Rosenthal's office together. Why had the Scotsman come?

Matthew, Rosenthal and McAllister squeezed round the fake mahogany table which was one of the rewards of making it to managing director. Rosenthal was a born trader, uncomfortable with anything to do with management. But he knew his duties, especially under McAllister's piercing gaze, and he plunged into his patter, doing his level best to sound like a responsible adult.

He talked about Matthew's team reviews, what people had liked, what they hadn't. The reviews had been positive, any criticism mostly constructive. Matthew wondered what Fiona had written about him, but Rosenthal's summary revealed nothing.

They discussed Western Instruments in depth. Rosenthal didn't like Matthew's losses and he didn't like it that Matthew hadn't discussed the gamble with anybody beforehand. As he put it, 'It was a horrible trade. Any time I'm feeling bad, I just remember your Western Instruments trade and it always brightens my day. But I'll say this, you put your tiny mind to work and your homework was first-class. This bank isn't in the business of penalising people for making wrong bets, just for incompetent ones – right, Brian?' Brian McAllister assented with a nod and Rosenthal continued. 'Next time, you do your homework just as thoroughly, but just remember to talk to uncle before you do anything further. And remember: bow wow. If it barks, it's a dog.'

Eventually, after twenty minutes, he came to the point.

'All in all, in its excessive wisdom and goodness, and don't ask me why, the bank's decided to give you a bonus. Don't go and blow it all on a soda before you get home.'

He tossed an envelope across the table to Matthew. Matthew tore it open, his hands slightly shaking. He hadn't been this nervous since the compliance interview.

Inside the envelope was a sheet of paper, headed 'Employee Compensation Award'. Beneath the heading there was Matthew's name and employment details, then a two line table showing salary and bonus. Matthew's salary was up fifteen percent. His bonus was a hundred thousand dollars.

'Thanks. Thanks very much.'

'Don't thank me,' said Rosenthal, 'thank the bank. Thank EPAS. Thank Dan Kramer. But well done, anyway. Someday, you'll be an all right trader.'

Matthew's sense of relief was so strong, it wasn't until later he noticed his disappointment. A hundred thousand bucks was OK for the first year. But it wasn't good. Petersen had probably made double that. If Matthew hadn't screwed up on Western Instruments, he'd have made as much as Petersen. If Matthew had got lucky on Western Instruments, if Draper had done what he'd been meant to do, Matthew could have been looking at a bonus with a three in front of it. If you translate a hundred thousand bucks into pounds, you have about sixty thousand pounds.

Some might think that sixty thousand on top of an already generous salary is good going for a youngster in his first year in a job and without even a college degree. But this was investment banking. This was Madison. This was the magical land where you win the lottery every year, year after year, and you bitch and moan if the payout is down on the year before. Matthew was entitled to feel bad.

'There's something else I wanted to tell you,' said Rosenthal. 'You've probably heard the rumours that the bank's cutting back in the bond department. Well, that's true enough.'

Matthew felt immediate panic. He wasn't going to earn his way to a million quid, that much was clear. But he knew how he planned to make a million, and that plan needed him to keep his job. Matthew's mouth went as dry as banknotes.

'Inevitably, when we cut back, the first people to go looking for a new desk are those who have just arrived. Unless, that is, they have done exceptionally well since arriving.'

Rosenthal meant Petersen. Petersen hadn't made a big bet which went bad. Petersen's dental-ad grin meant he was staying. And Matthew? What would he get? The regretful smile and a kick in the teeth? Here's your consolation prize, so sorry you can't stay. Never mind about your father's thirty million quid. We're sure it'll turn up. Matthew's mind raced as Rosenthal continued.

'But we don't want to lose our promising young professionals. And that's where Brian comes in. Brian?'

McAllister took over.

'We're setting up a new group in London, Matt, and I'd like you to be a part of it. The group's going to buy and sell distressed debt. European junk, if you prefer.'

Matthew knew what he meant. Say a company – Eurotunnel, for instance – borrows a lot of money. It hits bad times. The bankers and investors who lent to it realise they'll never get their money back in full. The loans trade, like the Western Instruments bonds, at big discounts to face value. Trading in these markets is a roller-coaster ride, for company and lenders alike. If you're smart, and you buy in the troughs and sell in the peaks, you can make a fortune. If, on the other hand, what you thought was the bottom turns out to be a brief respite before an even sharper collapse, then you can lose your shirt, collar and necktie, all in a sitting.

'The job needs trading sense, for sure,' continued McAllister. 'But it also needs intelligence, and the ability to do deep research on the situations that interest us. That's what made me think of you. I think you're a natural for this group, Matt, and I'd be delighted if

345

you wanted to join it. We're starting in the New Year, so you'd need to find yourself somewhere to live in London over the holiday if you can.'

McAllister went on to describe the job in more detail, but he didn't need to. Matthew was hooked. A job like this was perfect, just perfect, for what he had in mind. He was unhappy about his bonus, but the job was perfect. Perhaps Plan B would be possible after all.

The arrangement was quickly confirmed. Even if Matthew hadn't been keen, he'd have accepted. An offer is only an order in disguise, and Matthew's old job had crumbled beneath him.

There was only one problem and it was a big one. Fiona. As soon as Matthew had left Rosenthal's office, he hurried down the trading floor to Fiona's office. As he made his way there – passing the secretaries fighting with photocopiers, the traders bragging over their two-dollar cappuccinos, the mail men who serve the firm for fifty years never seeing a tenth of the bonus that had so disappointed Matthew – his mind was full of thoughts.

He was relieved to have a job. He was excited by the new position. He was pleased to get a bonus. He was pleased at the praise that Rosenthal and, more importantly, McAllister had offered him. He was disappointed with the size of his bonus, though he knew it was fair, generous even. But, most of all, as he hurried down the aisle, he realised he couldn't contemplate losing Fiona.

He burst into her glass-walled office.

He started to speak, but realised she was on the phone, using the speaker attachment instead of the receiver. He slumped into a chair and drummed nervously, waiting for her to finish. Eventually she was done and clicked the speaker off. As usual, she looked every inch the professional woman, glorious hair tied away so no one could see it, bone-perfect features, just a bit too much distance in the eyes and mouth. And, as usual when she first saw Matthew, her eyes betrayed anxiety.

'Bloody Chicago office,' she said. 'They need their hands held every second. Then by accident they make some money and it's all their doing and not a hint of thanks.' Then seeing Matthew's taut face, 'What's up?'

Matthew told her in a few words.

'So you're off to London in a couple of weeks,' she said. 'Sounds exciting.'

'I like the job, but what about us?'

'Us?' she asked. At the office, she mostly seemed to forget that they were together. 'New York to London's a fairly easy overnight flight. I'm sure we'll stay in touch.'

'Stay in touch? Bullshit. You know we'll never last like that.'

'Well, it seems like you don't have much option. There's nothing else on offer, is there?'

Only now did Matthew realise what he wanted to say.

'You're right. I do need to go to London. But I want you to come too. You're an MD. You've earned lots of brownie points for being a good girl here. You must be able to call in a favour and find something in London.' It was the most committing thing Matthew had ever said. 'Please.'

'You want me to chuck everything and come to London? Just to be with you?'

'Yes. It might turn out that we're meant for each other. I don't know for certain, but we need to give it a proper chance.'

'You think we might be meant for each other?'

Fiona turned her head so that Matthew couldn't read her expression. Her voice was toneless.

'Yes, I think we might.'

Fiona turned, frightened but resolute.

'I've got news for you. Brian McAllister was over here a month or two back telling me about this new group of his and how he planned to recruit you. I asked him who was going to head the group up, and he told me he didn't yet know. So I told him I'd do it. He agreed. In two weeks' time, I'll be your boss.'

Matthew was overwhelmed. That was probably the most committing thing Fiona had ever done in her life. They weren't exactly engaged but, as far as Matthew's romantic Beaufort scale went, this was pretty much gale force.

The glass walls of Fiona's office weren't all that helpful when it came to celebrating appropriately, and for a moment they just stood there smiling at each other. Then Matthew stepped close to her and with his left hand knocked a huge pile of papers off her desk on to the floor.

'So sorry,' he said, and bent down to pick them up.

She bent down too and in the secret corner formed by desk and filing cabinets, they kissed.

'Fiona,' said Matthew. 'Dearest Fi.'

2

Gillingham stared at the statute book. The print before his eyes blurred, then separated into two different strands of text. One phantom page moved upwards and leftwards, the other downwards and rightwards. The words were unreadable.

Gillingham closed his sagging eyes and rested them on his palms. It was only eleven thirty in the morning and he'd had an early night the day before. It wasn't just his eyes that were foggy, it was his brain.

He'd found his loophole back in the autumn before Zack had pitched the deal. It had been hard to find. Hong Kong law has a catch-all provision intended to eliminate tax dodging. The provision says, more or less, that if you do something to dodge taxes then that thing, whatever it is, can be ignored by the taxman when he comes to figure out your tax bill. For people like Gillingham, that kind of law can be a real party pooper. But, despite the fun-hating law-makers of Hong Kong, Gillingham found his loophole. He'd checked it with lawyers. He'd checked it with accountants. It worked.

But finding the loophole isn't the end of the story. It's the start. After that, you've got to start working out the detail. You've got to draw up the documents. You've got to fine-tune the wording. You've got to make sure that the deal doesn't look like a tax dodge, even though it is.

Once upon a time Gillingham had excelled at the detailed work. His reputation at Weinstein Lukes rested not just on his ability to discover the loopholes in the world's tax law, but on his ability to build solid and convincing transactions. His deals were robust. His legal documents had never been questioned. Taxmen wailed, but they stayed out of court. Laws had been passed to stop him, but none of his deals had ever been over-turned.

Or so it had been. But then a happy marriage had turned unhappy. Gillingham's wife had taken advantage of his long hours and big bank account to fall in love with a penniless college friend. Divorce followed, accusations, alimony, and rancour. Gillingham turned to whisky the way babies turn to comfort blankets. Heavy social drinking became heavier private drinking.

As he drank, his command of detail faded. One day, in a room full of lawyers, he made an error which almost blew a deal apart. He went out for a drink and wasn't sober again for eleven days. He wound up having his stomach pumped in a hospital ward reserved for winos.

Most people, the bank would have fired without a second thought. But Gillingham was special. People with a head for tax are rarer than diamonds and more precious. Gillingham could sit in London and direct tax schemes all over the world. He had enriched many of the bank's clients, and the bank's clients had paid well for the privilege. So he got a second chance.

The bank ordered him to dry out. If he did, he could come back without even losing his partnership. But if he so much as sniffed a drop of alcohol, he'd be out. It was a fair deal. It was more than fair in fact, and Gillingham was grateful.

As his fog cleared, his ability returned. If his former brilliance had gone, his mastery of detail was back in full. Once again, he was a man clients could trust.

Or at least, he had been. A couple of months ago, Gillingham had become aware of something. It was hard to describe what. It was like a man who, swimming in calm waters, feels a current pulling. It's not a strong current. If he didn't focus on it, he might not even feel it. But Gillingham had been dragged deep below the ocean once before, and he knew the feeling. There it was. Every day. A gentle current caressing his leg, urging him, entreating him to dip below the surface, just for a moment, just for one little drink. In his long recovery from addiction, Gillingham was well used to such eddies. But this time, six years after drying out, the current didn't go away. It stayed. And every day it grew a little stronger. It would be a difficult Christmas.

Gillingham was scared.

Thank God he had that man Gradley. Gradley was a

godsend. His memory was second to none, and he had a damn good brain as well. When Gillingham wrestled with the detail and came out the loser, Zack quietly got to grips with it. Gillingham watched the Hong Kong documents shape up under Zack's unobtrusive leadership and breathed a silent sigh of relief. Gradley was keen to help with Gillingham's other deals, and Gillingham was delighted to bring him on board. He had to ask Amy-Lou Mazowiecki for permission, but Zack made it easy for her to say yes. He worked like a Trojan, and willingly too. He worked seven days a week.

Thank God for Gradley.

Before switching his fogged attention back to some arcane points of Hong Kong sales tax, Gillingham rose. He walked over to Zack's desk which stood nearby. Zack was there making some changes to a draft purchase agreement. The two of them exchanged a few words about the deal. They didn't need to, they were just taking a break. Gillingham felt better for it.

Before returning to his desk, Gillingham helped himself to a long swig of orange juice from the bottle which always stood on Zack's desk. The orange juice was always freshly squeezed, chilled but not freezing. It had a tang you couldn't get from cheaper juice. It tasted great.

3

For once, Christmas is upstaged. Although turkeys are slaughtered in their millions, although crucified Father Christmases still hang over Japanese shopping malls, although kids still break their toys in minutes and burst into tears as their fathers drink more than they should while their mothers go spare in the kitchen – although

Christmas traditions are observed to the letter, for once, this isn't the big one. Even as the turkeys sit a-roasting, people's minds look ahead to the death of the century and the birth of the one to come.

The politicians are full of it. The churches are full of it. The talk shows and game shows, the shops and the streets – everywhere's full of it. The TV's never been tackier, the discussions never stupider. Doesn't matter. The stupider the better; people want to laugh and feel superior; don't make them think, now of all times. The old millennium passes out in a firework display stretching from Tai-pei to Tijuana, Petersburg to Jo'burg – a Mexican wave of gunpowder, a catherine wheel for Mars.

The politicians position themselves at the base of the biggest rockets, match in hand, and claim the coming thousand years as the conservative millennium, the people's millennium, the god-knows-what millennium. Cameras click, the smile vanishes, blue flame sparks a fuse and, on the stroke of midnight, rockets tear the sky apart in lightning and thunder. People drink themselves silly. Marital infidelity reaches an all-time high. Two hundred cultists kill themselves for reasons nobody much cares about. Across Asia and much of the rest of the world, computers silently freeze on the stroke of midnight, the first planes have fallen from the sky, and the biggest foreseeable disaster in human history is well on its way to unfolding, all because some spotty-faced computer geek in California couldn't count higher than ninety-nine. It's back to work when the hangover wears off. The twenty-first century and third millennium starts like most of the others, but this time blessed with Alka-Seltzer.

Matthew is in New York, seeing to the transfer of his trading portfolio and terminating the tenancy on his apartment. He and Fiona see each other most evenings, though she continues to be scared by the commitment. Matthew doesn't push her, letting her take things at her own pace. He regrets what he did to Sophie, he would never do it again, but he thinks that Fiona might be the grown-up relationship for the grown-up Matthew. Time will tell.

Zack is at Ovenden House. He and Sarah are happy together. Zack is pleased not to have to deal with his mother or Josephine, and is pleased too with the way his plans are shaping up. He has insinuated himself successfully into the Weinstein Lukes tax department. Gillingham can no longer do without him. Meanwhile, the Hatherleigh Pacific deal looks promising, and he is due to marry one of the wealthiest young women in England. Whether he will stay married to her beyond his father's deadline, he somewhat doubts, but Zack's not bothered. If he leaves Sarah, he will do so gently. She can keep her money and Zack will make sure they don't rush into kids. She'll be upset for a while, but she'll get over it. Meanwhile, Zack will have his father's fortune and may be a partner at Weinstein Lukes as well. The twenty-first century will be a good one for him.

George is in Kilburn with his mother and sister. Compared to last year's dismal celebrations these ones are OK. They forget about turkey and make do with chicken escalopes. Helen is thriving on the peace and attention. Her speech is slow but accurate and she's insisted on helping out in the kitchen – not much, to be sure, and her help isn't exactly helpful, but it's a wonderful sign. 'I still feel her condition has a lot of scope for improvement,' Josie tells her brother in a private moment. 'It's almost like she's nervous of getting better.'

353

George has been drawing a salary since the summer, and a big chunk of it finds its way into Josie's bank account each month. It's less of a struggle now finding daycare for her mum, though they could always use more help, and George and Josie talk about what else they should do. George issues a standing invitation for them to visit him in Yorkshire, but they both know that the effort to make their mother comfortable in a house not her own is more trouble than it's worth. Josie says that neither Zack nor Matthew are giving any money to help, and George asks her if she knows what they're up to. 'Behaving like spoiled little brats,' says Josie, and they both laugh.

'How's your factory?' she asks.

George shrugs. 'Just about solvent. We've got a maybe one in three chance of still being solvent in a few months' time.'

'That bad?'

'That bad.'

'So the million pound rescue act isn't going to come from you?'

'Not a chance, Josie. Not a chance.' He laughs.

They eat their escalopes and watch some telly. A game-show host is being dunked in some 'millennium custard' and they find a channel showing an old movie instead.

'How's your love life?' Josie asks.

'Flatter than our order book.' George tells his sympathetic sister about Kiki and Val, and how Val still refuses to talk to him. Josie can understand Val's point of view, but she gives her brother a cuddle.

'She's a good egg, she is.'

'I hope you're doing better than me on the romance front,' says George.

His sister blushes a bit.

354

'I am sort of seeing someone. A Hungarian chap at work.'

'Sounds good. Gypsy blood. Passionate temper and all that.'

'Not exactly. He hates gypsies.'

'Do I get to meet him?'

'I don't know. He's quite interesting, but . . . well, he's not very house-trained. I'm not sure how serious I am.'

Josephine isn't keen to pursue the subject, and George is sensitive enough to let it drop. 'Isn't it Mum's bedtime?' he asks.

They put Helen to bed. She wears incontinence pants these days, and George finds the whole business disagreeable, but he helps anyway. Helen says something, which George interprets as 'Sorry I'm so difficult', but it's the end of the day and her speech is quite badly slurred, so it's hard to be sure.

George and Josie go back down, watch more telly, and drink instant decaf coffee.

'How's your work and everything, Josie?'

'Not bad. I'm switching jobs in the New Year. I'm moving into the money transfer department. I'm going to be a settlements clerk.'

'More money?'

'No, less money actually, but I prefer the job. The bank advertised the vacancy internally. I applied for it and got it.'

George is a mite surprised. Josephine always complained about not having enough money and here she was taking a less well-paid job. Still, it was her life, and she was right to think that Zack and Matthew could easily pay for the care that Helen needed. Why should Josie make all the sacrifices?

'Good for you. What's a settlements clerk?'

'You know, sorting out money transfers and all that sort of stuff. It's admin work, quite dull really, but it needs to be done.'

'Could you see your way to transferring a few hundred grand into the Gissings' account? We could do with a leg-up.'

'I'll see what I can do.'

They finish watching the film, wash the coffee mugs, and go to bed.

There are 571 days to go until Bernard Gradley's deadline. That's half-way or near enough.

4

Zack left the canteen with a brown paper bag holding a croissant, a cup of black coffee and two bottles of freshly squeezed orange juice. Beneath his arm he carried a copy of that morning's *Financial Times*, and in his jacket pocket, a quarter bottle of vodka. He marched along the corridor, stepped inside the men's loo, closed the cubicle door, and sat down. He opened one of the two bottles of orange juice and swigged a couple of mouthfuls from it. He poured the vodka inside and shook it up. Vodka and orange is a nearly invisible alcoholic drink. You can't really smell it. You can't taste it. You might notice the slight dilution of the orange juice, but not if you were Hal Gillingham, and not if you'd been drinking gradually increasing amounts of the stuff for the past few months.

Zack was satisfied. Today was the day. He was disappointed that Gillingham hadn't cut his own throat. Many addicts only need a single touch of the ancient poison for all their addictive passion to come flooding unstoppably back. Not so with Gillingham. Zack had eagerly watched the developing contest, and came to have increasing respect for the older man. Gillingham was not only the most brilliant mind he had come across in Weinstein Lukes, he was a tough and persistent fighter too. It was a shame he had to go.

Zack left the loo and rode the lift upstairs. He bit into his croissant and walked to his desk. His route took him past Gillingham's office, and Zack walked in.

'Morning.'

'Morning, Zack,' said Gillingham waving a tax book. 'I had a great idea at my AA meeting last night. Great place to think. Want to hear it?'

'Sure. Here's your juice.'

'OK. Our Hong Kong tax scam is great but restrictive, right? It only really works for property companies and that sort of thing. To make real money out of the idea, we need something that every Tom, Dick and Harry can get his hands on. Preferably something where we don't need to spend ages tailoring the deal to the client, where we just have a standard product that we flog over the counter. With me?'

'Uh-huh. You're describing the Holy Grail, right? What every tax scammer in the world dreams of at night?'

'You got it.' Hal grinned. He liked working with Zack. Zack didn't have the originality to make it really big-time in the world of tax, the way he had. But the young man was brilliant with detail, quick on the uptake and very hard-working. He was a nice guy too. What a team! He swigged his orange juice. He felt zestful this morning and the juice slid down like nectar. Lovely stuff. He finished the bottle and continued talking. 'And to sell this miracle product, we don't want to create a whole sales team just for the job, we want to use a sales team which the bank already has.

Right? And what could be better than our derivatives sales team?'

Derivatives sound flash, but they're not too complex. If you think, say, that the Hong Kong dollar is going to rise against the yen, you could do one of two things. You could buy some Hong Kong dollars and watch them rise. Or you could make a bet that the Hong Kong dollar will rise. If you're right, you might double your money. If you're wrong, you lose your money. Compared with buying Hong Kong dollars, you're taking a bigger risk, but the rewards are bigger too. It sounds scary, but it's a scary world. Everybody does it. The bank which looks after your savings does it.

'You want to use our derivatives sales force to sell a tax dodge?' Zack wasn't questioning Hal's wisdom. He was almost breathless with admiration.

'You got it. And what's the dodge, you ask? Simple. It's our old friend the Hong Kong property tax scam, but with an extra twist to make it work for the whole range of derivatives.'

Hal talked on. It was complex, technical stuff, which even Zack was hard-pressed to follow. But he got there in the end and he was astounded. Gillingham was right. This was the Holy Grail indeed. And the real glory of it was that, on initial inspection, the idea looked like it would work right across East Asia. Hong Kong, Singapore, Taiwan, Malaysia, maybe even further afield too. What a concept!

They talked some more, until Gillingham started to fret. He should be feeling great, but he felt terrible. Addiction bit him harder than it had gnawed any time these last few difficult months. He felt ill. He felt drunk, for heaven's sake. What was wrong with him?

'Want me to get you some more juice?' asked Zack.

'Hey, that'd be grand. You're a pal.'

Gillingham looked gratefully after Zack, as his poisoner went to get more poison.

5

Mr Evans, proprietor of Brynmawr Furnishings, looked dubious.

'If you ask me, the Aspertons deserve their reputation for quality. They've never let me down and I haven't seen anything to make me change my mind.'

'That's the point, isn't it?' said George. 'You don't see anything. But ask yourself this. Why are the prices as little as half of what you would expect? Eh? The Aspertons have never been cut-price merchants before now, have they?'

'True. But it's a straight copy of your stuff. Can't tell it apart.'

'Oh, there's a difference alright. I'll show you. You have to admire the way they've done it. If we wanted to get into that end of the market ourselves, we could learn a lot from them.'

George escorted the reluctant Mr Evans to the revamped Gissings showroom.

'We'll see about that. To be perfectly frank, after I'd seen the Aspertons' prices I almost placed my order then and there. It was only because you acted decently over the peeling varnish fiasco that I – hello! Am I seeing double?'

George laughed at his visitor's reaction. 'Eye-catching, isn't it?'

It was like seeing double. An aisle ran down the centre of the former museum, ending at the foot of a broad velvet curtain. The Bright and Beautiful range was displayed on the left, the Asperton Brilliants on the right.

For every Gissings item, the matching Asperton twin stood in the same place opposite. The effect was remarkable, but it only emphasised that the two ranges were virtually indistinguishable. Indistinguishable, except for one thing. The Asperton range was half the price of the other.

'Eye-catching, I'll say,' said Evans. 'I normally only see that kind of thing after a few too many pints.'

'Their stuff certainly looks like ours. That's the point. They want the cachet we've built up, which we consider a compliment. But if you look closely at their products, you find everything is second-rate. See here, look at this paintwork.'

George took a cigarette lighter from his pocket, held it close to the brightly painted surface of an Asperton office desk, and lit the flame. After eight seconds the paint began to bubble and crack.

'Now that just won't happen with ours. Look at this.'

George held the lighter up against the identical Gissings product, and counted slowly to fifteen. He switched the lighter off. They'd done a hundred tests. On ninety-seven of those, the Gissings paint had lasted more than fifteen seconds. In none of them had the paint lasted more than twenty-five.

'They've used cheap paint which only just squeaks through the safety rules. And you can bet that it'll be chipping off before the year's out. That's why we always pay the extra for quality. But let me give you another example.'

George went to an Asperton cupboard and unscrewed the screws from the hinge. The screws were five eighths of an inch long. He repeated the experiment with a Gissings cupboard. The screws were a full inch long.

'The difference may look trivial, but believe me, the difference is between hinges which last a few months and ones that last for ever. We've never even thought about cutting the length of the screw to save money, but their range is all about cutting corners. Or look at their hinge compared to ours. Ours is strong. You'd never be able to distort it.' George twisted it around in his thick fingers to make the point, then picked up the lighter Asperton hinge for contrast. 'This tinny little thing will buckle the first time you put any weight on it. Fine for the showroom, terrible for life.'

George moved further along. He stopped at an Asperton chair, whose back legs had split from the seat.

'I'd ask you to guess what's wrong with this chair, except I've already given the game away. How come the legs split off? Answer: I made the mistake of leaning back when I sat down.'

This was true, although he omitted to mention that he had had Darren on his lap at the time, and Darren had had Dave on his lap, and all three of them had been bouncing up and down and laughing.

'Why did it break? I'll tell you. They haven't jointed the join properly, so all you need to do is tip back, and if you're any weight at all' – George patted his stomach – 'you'll end up on the floor. Compare that with our construction . . .' and George began to talk his guest through the elements of good chair design.

George continued his patter. Evans was absorbed. In reality, the Asperton products were a bit worse than the Gissings stuff, but the difference wasn't huge. The way George told it though, the Asperton Brilliants were just waiting to fall apart.

'What I don't understand is why the Aspertons would do this,' said Evans after a while. 'They've got a good name in the market. Why would they ruin it by selling rubbish?'

'Ha! The million dollar question. Let me ask you this:

have you heard the rumour about the Aspertons floating on the stockmarket?'

The rumour had been circulating for as long as anyone could remember, but Aspertons was still a hundred percent family-owned firm.

'That old chestnut. Sure I've heard it.'

'Well, ask yourself this. If you were getting ready to go to the stockmarket, not today perhaps, but in a year or so, what would you do?'

Evans looked blank.

'I'll tell you what you'd do. You'd bump up your profits as high as you could first. Then when you come to sell your shares, you get a great price, because people only bother to read your last set of accounts. And when profits hit the wall the year after, you don't give a damn, because you've sold out and it's some other poor sod who'll pay the price.'

Evans nodded sagely, looking as though he'd seen right through the Aspertons all along. George reeled him in further.

'The Aspertons have built up a reputation for quality over the last twenty years or more. Now they're cashing it in, to sell a range of nice-looking but trashy furniture. People wonder about the price, but think the stuff must be OK because of where it comes from. So sales go up. Profits go up. The Aspertons sell out. A year later, a load of dissatisfied customers are taking their business elsewhere or trying to get their money back. Profits are up the spout, and the company's reputation will take years to recover. But Mike and Eileen Asperton are in the Bahamas enjoying their well-earned rest, and they couldn't give a damn. Like I say, you've got to admire them.

'What I don't like so much is what they do to our business in the meantime. Or,' added George as a seeming afterthought, 'more to the point what they do to *your* business. If you start selling shoddy furniture to your customers, you're going to get the blame, no matter where the fault really lies.'

Evans was persuaded. It was time for the grand finale.

'Now, if you're interested in ordering more of our Bright and Beautiful range, we'd be happy to help you with whatever you want. We'll give priority to your order, so don't worry about delivery times.' This was an easy promise to make. Gissings was still running well under capacity. 'But since you're here, let me show you something really special.'

George walked to the curtain at the end of the show-room and pulled a cord. The curtains drew back and there, shimmering beneath halogen spotlights, stood a suite of superb designer furniture, glowing in a dozen lustrous colours. Panelling enlivened every empty surface, and every detail was picked out with a dab of vivid colour. Venetian reds were burnished with details of palest terracotta. Dutch blues were picked out in highlights of primrose yellow. Compared with the cheap and cheerful furniture they had just examined, this was a whole new dimension of quality.

'Welcome to Gissings Select,' said George.

The appearance of sophistication was, in fact, some-what justified. George and Sally Dummett had spent two long days going through a huge stack of interior design magazines. They looked at every feature and every advert. They were looking for something to copy as ruthlessly as the Aspertons had copied their own range. Every possible target they assessed according to a strict set of criteria, but all their criteria boiled down to three things. Could they build it fast? Could they build it cheap? Would it sell?

Eventually, they found what they were looking for. A famous New York designer had brought out a range of furniture in a palette of gorgeous but subtle colours. The basic furniture shells were remarkably close to the existing Gissings ranges. A few extra details were needed, of course: some fancy handles, a few bits of panelling. But it hadn't taken much. Most of the work had been put into getting the colours just right, but Sally Dummett was in her element, and she'd done a great job.

And that was it. The Gissings Select range was born. As George had promised, they slapped twenty percent on to the price, then thought better of it and added twenty-five.

Next, George turned to the showroom. He had it repainted, recarpeted and relit. Marketing literature was developed and printed. And finally, when everything was ready, the expanded sales team was permitted to call their clients to break the news of Gissings Select.

The overt purpose of the calls was to promote the new range of furniture. But as soon as the conversation loosened up, another theme became evident. Have you heard what the Aspertons are up to? Selling shoddy goods to make way for a stockmarket flotation. Tut, tut, tut. Oh, no. Don't worry about Gissings. Our sales are on the increase, if anything. No, it's the buyers we're worried about. Poor souls, buying cheap rubbish from the Aspertons in good faith, then looking bad when it falls apart. No way for them to behave, is it?

Soon the rumours about the Aspertons overtook anything that had been said by Gissings. Andrew Walters was told in confidence by a client that the Aspertons had already set their flotation date. Somebody else swore they'd seen a team of merchant bankers leaving the company. Yet another person said he'd heard that the

Aspertons were facing an unprecedented level of returns on their Brilliants range. And the Gissings people just listened and agreed and passed the stories on to their next caller.

Mr Evans was only the latest in a long line of clients who had walked with George around the showroom and watched disapprovingly as he revealed every flaw in the Asperton products. And at the end of every tour, the velvet curtain was drawn back to reveal the Gissings Select range, glowing and beautiful. George pointed out the highlights, but it was a soft sell. The furniture made the sale.

Like many before him, Mr Evans didn't leave before giving George a good-sized order for the Bright and Beautiful range and an even larger order for the Gissings Select. Gissings made a seven percent profit margin or thereabouts on the Bright and Beautiful. On the Gissings Select, the margin was closer to fifteen.

George walked Mr Evans back to his car for the long journey back to Wales. Mr Evans was still clucking with disapproval of the Aspertons, as George nodded in agreement. It was another triumph for Gissings and another step back from the brink of disaster. But George wasn't happy. He was miserable.

To his surprise, he didn't miss Kiki. He thought of her often, but with fondness rather than love. He hoped she was happy and hoped to hear from her again.

No. There were two reasons for his misery. The first and biggest was Val. She was still surly with him and he found himself missing his time with her more than he had ever missed anything or anyone. In George's playboy years, he had pursued pleasure in the places that pleasure was meant to be found. He had moved from ski slope to yacht marina, using his father's money as his passport, doggedly conforming to the standards of his class. Then, when he had been living with Val, all that had dropped away. They had worked hard and enjoyed it. They had relaxed together and really relaxed. They had made love – unflashy, unpretentious, unathletic love – and it had satisfied them both. She wasn't beautiful, but neither was George and anyway, he liked the way she looked.

Val was George's soulmate, and in his infatuation with the otherworldly Kiki, George had been too slow to see it. He had tried talking to Val, but got nowhere and soon stopped trying. She carried out her secretarial duties punctiliously, but refused to speak to him except on matters of business, and no longer acted as the company's brain and memory, as she had done before.

The second reason for George's misery was simple. Most people at Gissings thought he had saved the company a second time and were ecstatic. But George wasn't conned. The firm had a breathing space, no more. It was still head over heels in debt, and it still had a big rich competitor who wanted it dead. The Aspertons had failed with their first attempt. If they tried again, they would probably succeed. And what that would mean was almost too awful to spell out.

No Val. No Kiki. No Gissings. No money. No job. Nothing.

6

Zack closed Mazowiecki's door behind him. This was an American bank and her door was never closed, but Zack closed it.

'Amy-Lou. Can I have a word?'

'Sure. What's up?'

Zack sighed and ran his hands right back through his untidy black hair. He frowned with what was meant to be concern, but looked like a scowl.

'Amy, I hate having to say this, but maybe you can advise me what to do. I think Hal Gillingham is drunk.'

'Drunk? On alcohol? Oh Zack, I hope not.'

Zack didn't know it, and it wasn't widely known inside the bank, but Amy-Lou Mazowiecki and Hal Gillingham had had an affair with each other long years ago, before his divorce, before his addiction had overwhelmed him. They still had tenderness for each other, indeed Amy-Lou loved him still. But time had changed that love into something more like the love of a mother. She felt protective and fond.

'Christ, I hope I'm wrong. I haven't seen him drink or anything like that. But you know, he hasn't really been on form for ages, and this isn't the first time I've wondered.'

Amy-Lou nodded. Her office window faced south-east and light poured in behind her, hiding her face. She was pleased for the disguise, as tears trembled in her eyes. She shook her head.

'I've wondered too, Zack. I'm afraid many of us have. He hasn't been himself lately. And it's been widely noticed how much you've been doing for him.' She sighed deeply, and the light flooding in behind her couldn't disguise the sorrow in her breath. 'I'd better go and see him. But he'll have to take a blood test. The bank will insist.'

She went off to find Gillingham and fate took its course. Gillingham went down into the basement with Mazowiecki. He rolled up his sleeve for the nurse and watched impassively as the prick of the needle raised a blood-red pearl on his arm. The nurse swabbed away the blood and gave him a blob of cotton wool to press down on the injury. Gillingham did as he was told, then, when the nurse was finished, left again with Mazowiecki.

The blood test would deliver its result within hours. The bank carried out routine blood tests on all new employees, and had the facilities to conduct tests wherever drug abuse was suspected. Cocaine was the commonest problem, especially in New York, but the bank's medical service was geared up to test for alcohol too. Gillingham retired to his office with Mazowiecki to await the news. Zack stayed away. He had a sense of delicacy and, besides, he liked Hal and admired him. Gillingham was a great man and Zack was one of the few people in a position to really understand his greatness.

Inside his office, Gillingham abandoned any attempt at control. He blubbed like a newborn, while Mazowiecki cancelled her meetings, ignored her phone, and cuddled her disintegrating middle-aged baby.

'Oh, God, Amy-Lou. I can feel it inside me. I don't need a frigging blood test, I know I'm pissed. You know I really thought I'd beaten it. I used to hear these poor bastards at Alcoholics Anonymous talking about crawling out of the pit and you knew with some of them that they'd fall back in. Not once, but again and again. And I used to think, God, do you guys not understand what it means to fall back? Have you really forgotten the horror of that place? I knew I needed AA. I knew the craving was inside me for ever, but I really thought I'd never fall back. And the worst, the very worst of this thing is this: I swear to you, I absolutely swear that I don't remember taking a drink. Before, I used to lose my memory often enough, but at least I'd remember that there was a piece missing. I could feel the blank. I feel nothing like that now. I don't even know where I bought the drink. I'm a wreck, Amy. No wife. No job. No life. At least I'm fucking rich. I'll drink myself to death on twenty-year-old malts and be the sweetest smelling sinner at the Boozers Bar in hell.'

'Oh, Hal,' said Amy-Lou. There wasn't much else to say. She could smell alcohol on his breath and he was clearly tipsy to say the least. It didn't make much difference if he had had two sips or two bottles. The deal with the bank had been no alcohol, at all, ever. It had been a fair deal. She sat with the door closed and her arm around him. He sobbed, was silent and garrulous by turns.

Eventually, Amy-Lou had an appointment she couldn't defer.

'I need to go now, Hal. I'll be an hour. Will you wait for me here, please? Whatever the news is.'

Gillingham nodded. The deep channels in his cheeks at last served the purpose for which it seemed they were intended. Tears ran down the grooves, tickled the corner of his mouth, and splashed disregarded from his chin.

'Promise? You really have to promise me.'

'I promise.'

Amy-Lou was scared that Gillingham would go out on a binge when the bad news came. If she could save him from that, she might be able to save him from total ruin. She left for her meeting. Twenty minutes or so afterwards the phone rang. Hal picked it up. It was the nurse.

'We've had the results back, sir. I'm afraid the test was positive. I can give you the statement from our laboratory if you'd like. Or we can order a second test if you feel there's been a mistake.'

'No need. Thank you.'

Gillingham hung up. He needed a drink and he needed a piss. He'd promised Amy-Lou to stay put, but bars have drinks and loos. Addiction and his promise wrestled for his soul. He could always be back in time.

But the promise prevailed. The bar meant total destruction for him. Amy-Lou would take him home or, better still, to the clinic where he'd dried out the last time. She'd keep her eye on him and bottles away from him. He'd resent it, but he'd recover. Gillingham got up to go to the loo. He'd come straight back.

In the loo, he peed and rinsed his face. Alcohol surged through his bloodstream and laughed at the water splashing around on the outside. All the soap and water in the world can't wash away the drink. Next to him, he was aware of somebody crying, like him. A young guy. Ginger-haired, with a receding chin and a bulgy forehead. Gillingham had seen him around, working his knickers off for Zack, but he didn't know his name. That young, he must be an analyst.

'You upset too?' asked Gillingham.

The young analyst nodded, pleased to have his grief acknowledged.

'My grandmother died this morning. I've put off seeing her so many times because of work, and now she's dead. I feel awful. I feel like the worst guy in the world.'

It was nice to see somebody else's grief. Grief can be so lonely.

'We all make more sacrifices than we should. The bank insists on it. Don't beat yourself up just because you were the one left standing when the music stopped. We all do the same thing.'

The analyst, Smylie, smiled crookedly at Gillingham.

'God, that's a decent thing to say. Everyone else has just said, "tough luck, shit happens, and by the way how is that spreadsheet coming along?" and I end up feeling bad for even feeling bad.'

'Yeah, well, maybe you're a bit too much of a human being for this place. Coming from me, that's meant to be a compliment, by the way.'

Smylie looked at Gillingham, who looked pretty rough himself.

'I shouldn't really say this, but d'you want to come out for a drink? Just a quick one?'

For a long moment, Gillingham paused, but even as he waited he knew what he was going to say.

'Sure,' he said. 'Just a quickie.'

7

Matthew came home depressed from another grim visit to his mother and sister. Now that he was London-based, he could hardly escape these visits, but they left him feeling lousy every time.

His mother's state of dependence had an increasingly permanent feel to it, and once again he'd managed to squabble with Josephine before leaving. This time it had been about living arrangements. Josie asked Matthew to think about living with them in Kilburn so he 'could help out a bit'. Matthew told her some nonsense about needing to be close to work, but they both knew that for a lie. The truth was that he didn't want to live alongside his mother's neediness and his sister's saintliness; he didn't want the burdens of daily care; he didn't want the ugliness or economy or carefulness of his sister's frugal existence.

To make things worse, when he arrived back, he found a note from Fiona stuck under his door. 'Dearest M, I've gone to bed early – v. tired after work. Hope everything at home was OK. Breakfast together tomorrow? I'll be going in about 6.30. Love, F.'

Damn! He'd been looking forward to a cuddle with her, maybe more. That was the beauty of their current living arrangements. They'd both been too busy over the New Year to look for a place of their own, so the bank had put them both up in expensive but ugly service flats in South Kensington. His flat was across the hall from Fiona's, so they could be close when they wanted, separate when she needed.

Matthew had unravelled a little more of the mystery of Fiona's past, as much as he needed to know or was likely to. Her mother had abandoned her when she was four, and her father had for the most part regarded her as an annoyance to be ignored or got rid of, as he set about his drinking and womanising. Had it not been for a kindly old couple who had given the little girl every gift of love they could sneak past her savage and neglectful parent, Fiona would have grown up entirely ignorant of ordinary human love. Until her relationship with Matthew, she had had sex often and been intimate never.

Her wounds were deep and she still found intimacy tough, but, as she'd promised in Vermont, she was giving it her all. Quite often now, Fiona let Matthew stay in bed with her until morning, but when she found it too much, Matthew just slipped back across the hall. They ate together, worked together, had fun together. One day, Matthew believed and hoped, they would get married.

Although it was now gone eleven and he'd be getting up at six, Matthew didn't fancy going to bed. There was a wine bar down the road that served booze until midnight. He'd go there and try not to think about Josephine. That shouldn't be hard. With a string of phone calls to make the next day, he was on the brink of launching his Plan B.

The bar was called the Apollyon, done up in red leather and blackened oak. The effect was corny, but it apparently justified charging two pounds fifty for the cheapest bottle of beer. Matthew took a seat at the bar and ordered a Czech pilsner.

A few groups sat at tables. At the bar there was only Matthew and one other man, also in a suit. The man was short and extremely neat, the way short men often are. Maybe they think people won't laugh at them if their hanky is neat and matches their tie. The man was also drinking Czech beer. Matthew glanced at him and forgot him.

Despite himself, he began to think about Josephine and his mother. He wasn't going to change course now, but he knew that it was a struggle for Josie to make ends meet, even with the help that George gave her, and the knowledge made him guilty. He wondered whether to pay her something by standing order, but he knew he wouldn't. If he'd had a larger bonus, he might feel he had some money spare – but again, he knew he wouldn't. He'd be generous to Josie once he had made his million, or was sure he'd failed. Until then, every penny counted. The one thing he had agreed to do was get her a portable computer. 'It's a hobby,' she'd said. 'Maybe in time it might be a career. But for the moment, it's one of the few things I can do with my evenings, what with needing to be there for Mum and everything.' It was an easy enough request. Especially as Matthew knew the bank was replacing its existing portables, flogging the lot at bargain prices to anyone who wanted one.

Matthew sipped his beer and mused dejectedly. A voice at his elbow interrupted him.

'May I get you another?'

It was the neat little man. Close up, Matthew could see how ugly he was. At a distance, all you could see was neatness: folded hanky, immaculate parting, trim little suit, fat little knot on his silk tie. But near to, you could see his features were all wrong. His nose was too big, his mouth too small, his eyes too close together. He smiled almost all the time, but as Matthew got to know him, he realised that the smile was more like a sneer, almost a look of hatred.

'OK,' said Matthew. 'I'm drinking Budvar. Thanks.'

373

The little man got the drinks and introduced himself. His name was James Belial and he was to become a very important person in Matthew's life.

'Do you live round here?' asked Belial.

'Yes, for now at any rate. I've got a temporary flat just up the road.'

Belial raised his eyebrows, which were too hairy for his little face.

'Not Blenheim Court, by any chance?'

'Yes, actually,' said Matthew, surprised. 'Just until I find myself somewhere permanent.'

'Ah! I know it well. I spent a few months there once, when I worked in the City.'

'The City?' said Matthew, more interested now. 'Which firm?'

Matthew's question was not innocent. What he meant was: Did you work for a first-rate bank or not? He meant: Do I need to respect you, or can I continue to look down on you? Whenever two bankers meet and ask each other this question, the purpose is always to establish pecking order.

'Madison. Mostly based in Geneva, but in London for a while too.'

'Really? I'm with Madison. I've been in New York the past year and I've just started with a new group here.'

They exchanged gossip. It turned out Belial knew Brian McAllister well but didn't think much of him. 'Very judgemental. Jumps to conclusions. Bit of a god-complex.' Matthew told him about his new job trading distressed debt and Belial was interested. 'A very exciting area. Lots of opportunity for personal initiative.'

Belial now worked for a Swiss investment outfit called Switzerland International Capital Partners. He described himself as an investment executive and gave Matthew his card. Belial's hands were small and hairy and his neatly

manicured nails were thick and hard. There was really
something rather repulsive about him. Matthew stared at
the card. Switzerland International. The name and even
phone number were familiar to him. In a locked drawer
at work, he had a list of names and phone numbers,
beginning with this one. He had been about to start
calling them tomorrow, about to launch Plan B.

'Switzerland International,' said Matthew, trying to keep
his voice calm. 'I've been meaning to call. I wanted to find
a decent investment manager. Probably Swiss, but in any
event – how shall I put it? – somebody discreet.'

'Ah, discretion!' sighed Belial with pleasure. 'Yes,
we are very discreet. It's the reason why most of our
customers come to us. There's the taxman. There are
greedy wives. There are alimony attorneys. There are
business partners. There are regulators. There's police,
Interpol, vice squads, drug agencies, you name it. People
come to Switzerland for discretion, and you don't get
more discreet than us at Switzerland International.'

'And if I wanted to set up an account?' asked Matthew.

Belial took him through it. The minimum balance
was fifty thousand Swiss francs, but that would be more
than covered by Matthew's bonus. The commission rates
weren't cheap, but Switzerland International could deal
in anything that Matthew wanted to invest in. The
service was absolutely private. If Matthew preferred,
they wouldn't even mail him regular statements but
simply give him the balance by phone when he called.
Belial was very helpful and very encouraging. Matthew
could have his account opened within the week.

Matthew thanked him and left the bar. The ugly little
man watched him with a smile. And when Matthew had
collected his coat and could be seen walking away down
the darkened street, James Belial began to shake in sobs
of silent laughter.

Spring 2000

Snow still ices the Yorkshire hills, but in the valleys the snow is melting, and on the bravest trees, buds dare to show. It is the first day of spring, the first of March. The days are already longer, and in three weeks the clocks go forward. There are 499 days to go until Bernard Gradley's deadline.

1

George knocked on Wilmot's door and, without waiting for a signal, swept on into the accountant's meticulous office. A packet of biscuits was open on the table and Wilmot tidied it hurriedly into his drawer. He flushed slightly.

'I'll have a biscuit, if you don't mind,' said George, who enjoyed embarrassing Wilmot in small ways.

Wilmot got the biscuits out again, his blush more acute than before. George took one.

'How are we doing, Jeff? Do you have last month's profit numbers?' asked George. Val still wasn't talking to him, and he'd taken to wandering the building in search of company.

'Yes, indeed. Profit should come in over target at about seven thousand pounds after interest. At least something's looking healthy.'

'What d'you mean, "at least"?' asked George, whose grip of the company financials was only a little better than Kiki's would have been. 'We're making a profit, right?'

'Yes, but that's profit, not cash flow,' said Wilmot. 'Remember that we paid a lot of people late while you were, er, absent.'

'So what? We can pay them back now, can't we?'

'Well, not exactly. We need to pay our suppliers for those months, as well as pay for all the stuff we're buying now. What's more, most of our suppliers have shortened our payment terms, because we got into arrears previously. And we've got an interest payment date coming up. All in all, we have a bit of a cash-flow crisis.'

George could never understand the difference between profits and cash flow. As he saw it, his job was to increase profits, but whenever he did so, Wilmot usually started blathering about a cash-flow crisis.

'What d'you want me to do about it?' asked George shortly.

'Well, er, the very best thing would be a temporary cash injection.'

'What d'you mean?' George sounded cross, but he was impressed. By Wilmot's standards, this was assertive.

'Well, I couldn't help noticing, er . . . that is . . . during your absence, in your capacity as shareholder, er . . . you depleted the contingency reserve of certain funds . . . quite legitimate, of course, and um, understandable, but . . .' Wilmot wasn't finding it easy.

'I took forty-five grand out of the company,' said George.

'Exactly. Now if, er, you didn't have a compelling use

for those funds within an immediate time horizon, er, some restoration of the contingency reserve capital, if only for a brief – one might say interregnum – period, er . . .' He tailed off. He could go no further. He took another biscuit and nibbled at it furiously. A shower of crumbs fell from his mouth and he didn't even tidy them away.

'You think I should stick some cash into the company?'

Wilmot didn't look at George. He couldn't speak and couldn't nod. He hunched over another biscuit, hardly even daring to nibble. In Wilmot-speak, that was a firm yes.

'Well, I'd love to put some cash in, but I don't have any. When I do, I'll tell you.'

George was being truthful, but not honest. In his pocket, a diamond ring pressed against his heart. Thirty thousand pounds of ready money, if the hideously expensive shop in Bond Street would refund it. Even if he just sold it outright, he could probably get fifteen or twenty for it. But George said nothing and let the ring throb away in silence.

'Yes. Quite. I wouldn't have mentioned it, except . . . well, perhaps . . . I apologise, anyway.'

George relented a little. Just because he felt bad most of the time didn't mean that Wilmot had to.

'Don't worry, Jeff. You did the right thing. Anything which helps the company is allowed round here, even asking impertinent questions.'

Wilmot nodded his gratitude and began to round up the trail of crumbs.

'Now I've got a question for you, Jeff,' said George. 'If the Aspertons launch another attack on the company, how long could we survive?'

'Survive? How long would we survive?' Wilmot felt the pressure of the question. 'Hard to say . . . It would depend on a number of factors, primarily commercial . . . I could prepare some scenario analysis . . .'

He babbled away until George interrupted.

'OK. Let me put it another way. If we made a loss this month, instead of a profit. Say the Aspertons attacked us again and we lost ten thousand pounds after interest this month, next month, and the month after. Would we survive as long as the summer?'

Wilmot relaxed a bit. That was easy.

'Given our current cash position, there's no way we could survive for that long.'

George shook his head, but he was in agreement. It was as he thought. Gissings' health would remain precarious until the debt was paid off or until the Aspertons were called off for good. George looked at his watch. It was one minute past two.

George had just opened his mouth to ask Wilmot another question, when a clatter of feet coming down the passageway outside interrupted them. It was Darren and Dave with a group of their workmates, from the sound of it just back from a long and enjoyable liquid lunch. The group stopped outside Wilmot's office, to get some crisps and drinks from the archaic vending machine which stood outside.

'No. You don't need to put any bleeding money in,' screeched Darren. And, as George watched through a glass pane in the door, Darren wiggled a key around in the coin slot while thumping the machine with his fist. A scream of triumph greeted the first can of Coke to tumble. Darren immediately started instructing the others in how to repeat the trick.

'Better watch out for the guv'nor,' said one.

'Watch out for Georgie Porgie?' laughed Darren. 'I don't think so. With his gut, you'd hear him coming a mile off.'

Darren pulled a fire blanket off the wall and stuffed it up his T-shirt. He puffed air into his cheeks and scrunched up his eyes.

'Hello, lads,' said Darren, imitating George's heavy tread and uneven Yorkshire accent. 'Stealing crisps from the vending machine again? I wouldn't mind a few dozen packs myself.'

The drunken group sniggered. It wasn't a bad impression, though not exactly complimentary. Darren enjoyed the impact he was having and cast around for ways to keep the laughter going.

'I know, how about this?'

He tore the ring pull from the Coke can and shoved it up his nose to make a nose ring. He assaulted the vending machine for a liquorice wheel, uncurled it and stuck it into the back of his trousers, a curly black pig's tail.

'I'm Georgie Porgie,' puffed Darren in his George accent. 'Getting a bit porky. Must be all those crisps I'm stealing.'

George watched the scene with tight lips. Wilmot, who could hear everything, was frozen with embarrassment. Outside, Darren was getting down on all fours, patting his fire blanket belly and oinking. The laughter was unstinting but nervous, but Darren had lost all sense of caution. He was on a roll. Then George opened the door.

The group fell silent. Darren was the last to see anything, but when he looked up, he stayed where he was.

'Hi, George,' said Darren.

'You're fired,' said George.

Darren's departure was swift and final. Pink with anger, George virtually dragged him from the building and ordered him never to return. But though gone, he was not forgotten. Dave mooned around the building like a teenage lover. There was muttering on the shop floor, where Darren had been popular. Even Andrew Walters drew Sally Dummett and Jeff Wilmot into his office to discuss the incident behind a tightly closed door.

The consensus of opinion was that Darren had been out of line, but George's reaction had been unforgivable. You couldn't just sack somebody for one incident like that, especially after all the devotion that Darren had shown. There was a mood of creeping hostility but, typically, the only person to speak up about it was Val, for once stepping out of her self-appointed role as silent secretary.

'How dare you? How dare you fire that young man for taking the piss?'

'I didn't fire him for taking the piss. I fired him for stealing company property, for vandalism to important safety equipment, for exceeding his authorised lunch hour and for being under the influence of alcohol while on duty.'

'What?' Val was briefly nonplussed. She hadn't heard about any theft or vandalism.

'Darren stole from the vending machine and showed others how to do it. He took a fire blanket from the wall and clearly had no intention of replacing it.'

Val breathed out deeply. So it was just as she had thought.

'You are the most self-righteous self-centred bastard I've ever met. I can't believe you would be willing to wreck that young man's future just because he once took the mickey out of you and I hate the fact that you have to lie about why you sacked him. I think it's despicable.'

She had started to cry. George took a handkerchief from his pocket and twisted it in his hands. He wanted to offer it to her, but knew she would reject it.

'Val, listen –' he began.

'No, you listen to me. After you came back from chasing your French princess or whatever she is, I vowed I would never have anything to do with you again. But I admit – dear God, I can't believe it – I admit I had started to waver. I really was making up my mind to give you another chance.' Val was weeping profusely now. George's watching face bore the conflicting emotions of concern, hardness and love, but Val wasn't looking. 'But now you do something like this. It's so unbelievably petty. I realise you really don't give a damn about anything in the world except yourself. And I will never, never, never allow myself to come close to you again.'

George opened his mouth to say something, but thought better of it and bit his lip instead. The conversation was over.

2

Zack climbed the spiral staircase running up the tower. The old steps looked like they were melting in the deceptive April sun, sagging where centuries of feet had worn them down. They were polished and slippery and Zack ascended carefully.

The door at the top was closed but not locked, and it swung open at the push of Zack's hand. With a sudden rush and lift, the stifling darkness gave way to the airy brightness of day. A flight of birds dived past his shoulder as he tiptoed gingerly out, shading his eyes to see where he was going. His leather-soled shoes were precarious on the leaded roof and, for the first time in his life, Zack felt a touch of vertigo. It was said that from the top of Ovenden House you could see the sea on a clear day, but Zack left the sea to its own devices and focused on finding the viscount without falling over.

After an increasingly giddy traverse, he found two men leaning over the parapet at the end of the west wing.

'Jack! I thought I'd never find you.'

'There you are, Zack. Glorious day, isn't it? We'll see the sea if the cloud lifts over there. Let me introduce you to Jimmy Glass. Jimmy looks after our buildings for us.'

Jimmy Glass, the servant, and Zack Gradley, the future son-in-law, shook hands. It appeared that the stonework on the parapet was worn in places and Hatherleigh wanted it restored or replaced throughout. Glass promised to get some estimates, but offered his own guess of about eighty thousand.

'That little?' said the viscount. 'Perhaps we should think about seeing to the front at the same time. No point getting people in, if there's nothing for them to do.'

Glass walked off across the roof, promising to think about other jobs that needed doing, and Hatherleigh turned to Zack.

'Splendid view, isn't it? I keep meaning to get a telescope fitted up here, but I forget as soon as I come down.'

'Yes, wonderful,' panted Zack, hugging the parapet and looking anywhere but the sunlit lands rolling away into the distance.

'This is a good spot to plan your wedding reception from. Over there's the village church. We need to use that one, the house's own chapel isn't big enough. You'll drive back here. Sarah insists on using her great-grandmother's horse-drawn carriage. My grandpa swore Grandma wanted a Rolls, but there's no telling that to Sarah. The carriage will bring you back to here,' Hatherleigh pointed to a spot at the end of the west wing, 'and we'll have the receiving line in Sarah's rose garden or the ballroom if it's raining.

'We'll put a marquee on the lawn there and serve a decent dinner with a band and dance floor for later on. We've never had a dance after a wedding before, but it seems a good idea. A rare case of the younger generation improving things. By the way, when you and Sarah want to leave, you may as well borrow my helicopter. It'll save time.'

'Thanks, yes,' said Zack. Right now, the thought of being airborne just added to his giddiness, but he clutched the parapet and imagined himself face down on the great lawn, breathing the cool air between the grass, with nowhere to fall.

'And family, Zack. We must meet your family. I know they're not used to all this,' Hatherleigh waved his hand over his house and grounds, and the woods and fields beyond, 'but don't let that put you off. Or them. We're more democratic now than in the old days, and any family of yours is our family too. No exceptions.'

'You're very kind.'

'Cobblers. That's elementary courtesy, but I mean it. We mean it. Zack, my boy, I regret sometimes that I don't have a son to carry on the title, but Elizabeth and I never wanted to go on chugging out babies just to hang on to it. All I've ever really wanted is to make sure that the next generation to look after the house and estate is competent to do it. Happy and competent. Sarah's a bloody good girl, but I haven't always gone for her suitors. That chap Leighton, I never really liked and I'm pleased he's a goner. And frankly, Zack, I'm pleased she's settled on you. She's very happy, plus you bring a bit of commercial blood into the family. I'll feel happy trusting you and Sarah with all of this. I think you'll do a bloody good job.'

Hatherleigh had enough of the traditional aristocrat in him to find this kind of speech difficult, and his blue eyes dug into the distance throughout. But as he ended, his eyes came to rest on Zack and his lean face nodded approval of his words.

'Thanks. I couldn't be more pleased with the family I'm marrying into either,' said Zack, with truth.

He might have added, though he didn't, that he was becoming pretty impressed with his future father-in-law's commercial acumen as well. Hatherleigh was convinced that things were going to get worse for South China over the next year or so. Instead of plunging right in with a bid, Hatherleigh wanted to hold back and wait for the price to fall. So far the share price had dropped just half a dollar to forty-six dollars a share, but Hatherleigh and Scottie were adamant that the price would come down more. And Zack was forced to do nothing, whilst ensuring that his team was in a continual state of red alert. If it were possible for anyone to get their money's worth from forty million bucks, then Hatherleigh was the man.

'There's one other thing I ought to mention. Money. Sarah's a rich girl. As far as I remember, she holds about fifty million pounds' worth of shares in Hatherleigh Pacific. Up to now, she's chosen to reinvest the dividends to build up her stake, but when you're married the two of you can do whatever you like.

'There are just two things in particular I wanted to say. The first is, when I die, Sarah will get the house and a trust fund for the maintenance costs. There's plenty of money there, but it takes desire too.'

Hatherleigh's words made a statement, but his sideways look, almost shy, asked a question.

'Of course,' said Zack. 'Sarah's passionate about the house and I've come to love it too. We'll care for it as it demands to be cared for.'

Zack was surprised by his own ardour. He really spoke for a moment as though he expected to be here still in decades to come, lord of all he surveyed. But he didn't really believe that. Sarah was a nice girl, but deep down he and she were very different, weren't they? Zack reminded himself that this was a marriage with a limited shelf life.

'The other thing I wanted to say was this. When I settled the Hatherleigh Pacific shares on the two girls, I made it a condition that they enter into a prenuptial agreement before marriage. It sounds terrible, but I'd like you to sign something which says that Sarah's money stays with her if you two split up, as God forbid you should. And for the first five years, all the money and all the shares stay with Sarah. No joint accounts, nothing like that. I don't want to seem suspicious, because I'm not. But our wise old family lawyer made me promise him that I'd do it, because he knew I'd chicken out if I got the chance. So I promised and, after all, there's no harm in taking precautions.'

'None at all. Quite right. Of course, that makes sense,' gasped Zack.

His dizziness leaped up like a wave of nausea and he had to press himself into the parapet to avoid shaking like a leaf. The air, birds, sun, tower, the great house itself, all swung wildly about his field of vision. Had all this been for nothing? All the flowers, the dinner parties, the romancing, the wedding? Even in his giddiness, Zack would have volunteered to walk tightrope between the wings of Ovenden House rather than sign a prenuptial agreement, but he had no choice. Short of calling the wedding off then and there, he could only nod his assent.

'You really don't mind?'

'Really not. If you hadn't mentioned it, I was going to bring it up. As your financial advisor, I'm obliged to keep your financial interests uppermost in my mind.'

The viscount chuckled as he walked back with Zack towards the tower. He couldn't have hoped for a better son-in-law. Zack wondered how soon he could get to a loo. He needed to vomit.

3

Ed Deane was a keen trader, but a passionate gardener. His desk, like Matthew's, was devoted to trading: phones, computer screens, research reports, spreadsheets, yellow post-it notes, coffee cups, sandwich wrappers. His filing cabinets, however, supported a different landscape. Amidst the surrounding mayhem, a bonsai forest grew. Bending down and staring horizontally, you could almost believe that miniature birds were about to fly from bonsai oak to bonsai elm. At night, you half-expected tiny squirrels to forage crumb-sized acorns among the twisted trunks.

Deane was fiercely proud of his creation and he tended it with as much love as he did his trading portfolio. But the centrepiece of his collection was not a bonsai, but a dwarf apple tree. It had full-sized leaves, bore full-sized fruit, but it stood no more than three feet high. Matthew had watched it blossom, form tiny hard green apples, and watched those apples grow larger and redder as they slowly gained in ripeness. Unfortunately, despite the bank's puritanical air-conditioning system, a disease had crept in and blighted the fruit. Deane had sprayed, fed and cleaned to no avail. Five apples had been lost, as Deane anxiously cut off the diseased stalks and dabbed tenderly at the wounds with plant antiseptic.

Only one apple was left, intact and healthy. And Deane watched it lovingly as it slowly developed into a perfect fruit.

Ed Deane was the third member of Fiona and Matthew's trading group. He was a little senior to Matthew and had proved to be an outstanding trader and a sure judge of company prospects and problems. Matthew realised that McAllister had picked some of his most able traders for the group and he felt complimented at having been chosen. A couple of months into the group's existence, McAllister had come clean about his ambitions.

'The bank doesn't want to run this group like a normal trading operation, a glorified bureau de change. We want to invest our own money in large amounts. We want you to bet big time and win big time. I've told my bosses to expect returns of thirty percent a year. But I'm telling you that I won't be satisfied with less than fifty.'

They had started work in January, in their own private little room some distance from the main trading floor. They were special and what they did was secret. The information systems had been ready in February. In March, they had gone live with their first trade. And from March to April they had slowly but surely grown in confidence as their experience of the market grew. As their confidence grew, so did the size of their trading activity. Earlier, they had been happy to buy small stakes and watch to see if their guesses about the market had been right. Now they were sure of their judgement and were increasingly ready to go in big time.

The group researched companies which had hit bad times, companies whose share prices had gone from being measured in pounds to pence. Anyone who had lent money to these companies in their good times was terrified now that bad days had come. And anyone in a state of terror was a perfect candidate for the kind of therapy offered by Fiona, Ed and Matthew.

In their best deal to date, they had called up one of

the big high-street banks, which had lent fifty million pounds to a fashionable menswear retailer. The chief executive had turned out to be a crook, the company's accounts turned out to be fairy tales, and the share price had nosedived.

The high-street bank was convinced it would never get a penny back on its loan and the executives who had authorised the deal were in despair. Then a very professional woman from Madison called up. Fiona Shepperton. She offered to buy the fifty million pound loan off the bank for twenty million. The bank would be getting forty pence in the pound, which was pretty bad – but, hey, anything was better than nothing. The despairing executives agreed gratefully. The deal was closed within a matter of days.

But Matthew and Ed had done a mountain of research. The research told them that things weren't as bad as they seemed. New cleaned-up accounts due in October promised to show the company had recovered further than anyone had thought possible. Already they reckoned their twenty million pound stake was worth twenty-five million. They were confidently expecting to sell out for thirty by the end of the year.

And, just as the group had grown in its confidence, Matthew had grown in his. He had his account with James Belial at Switzerland International. He was ready, mentally and emotionally. At long last, Plan B could begin.

First, though, Fiona, Ed, and Matthew needed to finalise a decision of their own.

'OK,' said Fiona. 'Cobra Electronics. We've done the research. We've discussed it for hours. We think that the market has, if anything, improved. Are we ready to go ahead?'

Cobra Electronics was a defence company which had

invested too much in a new missile. The missile looked great but it didn't work. The company wasn't too sure what was wrong. It hadn't even come up with an estimate of how long or how much it would take to fix the problem. Meanwhile, the company had lost a few important contracts, and its future looked perilous. Bankers and investors were running for cover.

Ed Deane went first in answer to Fiona's question.

'Yes. There's nothing new on Cobra itself, but over the last few weeks I've noticed that the decisions on three important missile contracts have been deferred. Saudi, Indonesia, and Malaysia, to be exact. Most people have taken that as bad news for Cobra, but actually I think it's good. People had been expecting Cobra to lose anyway. If the decisions have been deferred, then maybe Cobra has some good news that the missile buyers are taking time to evaluate. There could be a great surprise around the corner, and even if there isn't, it's no worse than we're expecting anyway.'

Fiona nodded.

'Good. Matthew, how's the loan market?'

She looked into his eyes. There was nothing but cool professionalism in hers, nor would she see anything else in his. Romance has no place on the trading floor, but out of the office their relationship went from strength to strength. They were in love.

'Good news,' said Matthew. 'The price of the loans has been falling. Cobra is asking its banks for more money. In effect, it's saying "If you don't give us more cash now, then everything you've lent is going down the pan". The banks don't really believe that, but there's no organised resistance. So the company will probably get the extra cash and the banks are nervous. Given everything, I think we'd be able to buy thirty or forty million pounds' worth of the company's loans at forty pence in the pound.'

'Excellent,' said Fiona. 'I say let's do it. Right?'

Matthew and Ed nodded. This was the biggest deal they had yet attempted and the boldest too. Fiona wanted to buy ten percent of the company's loans. Once they had that, they would have a blocking vote over anything the company wanted to do. Cobra Electronics was in for a shock.

'Yes, let's do it,' said Matthew hoarsely. 'I'll go get some cappuccinos, and we'll get started.'

The others agreed with pleasure. The Blue Mountain Coffee Boutique coffees were from heaven, just the way to start a raid. Matthew put on his coat and left the office.

In his coat pocket were two mobile phones. One belonged to Madison. Its number was in the bank's internal phone directory and anyone could reach him on it. The other phone was Matthew's own property. Only one person knew he had it, and that person lived in Switzerland and was very keen on keeping secrets.

On his way to the coffee shop, Matthew ducked up a side alley, away from the noise of the street and the passing crowds. The alley led up to a small garden, surrounded by offices on three sides and a pub on the fourth. This early in the day, the pub was closed and the benches standing beneath an elderly fig tree were empty. Matthew sat on a bench, his back to the tree, pulled out his phone and dialled.

James Belial answered the phone. Matthew imagined the ugly little man moistening his lips as he said smoothly, 'James Belial, at your service.'

'James, it's Matthew Gradley. I've a trade I'd like you to execute.'

Matthew described it briefly. He wanted to buy bonds in Cobra Electronics. He wanted to invest everything

391

he had – his bonus, plus any accumulated interest. He wanted the trade done instantly.

'If you wish,' said Belial. 'But you do understand, don't you, that this is a risky situation? You're buying into a company widely seen to be on the brink of disaster and you're investing everything you have.'

'I understand. I've evaluated the risks.'

'I'm sure you have. We'll be delighted to execute this trade on your behalf. Would you like me to mail you a confirmation slip? I could fax something through to you at work, if you'd like it immediately?'

'No. Absolutely not. I'll call you later on for the information. Don't ever fax anything to me at work. Don't even call me. I'll call you.'

'Ha, ha! Of course, of course. Madison can be very old-fashioned at times. Better to keep these things discreet. Mum's the word.'

Matthew rang off. It was difficult to like Belial.

4

Darren hung around Sawley Bridge for a while, living with his mother. It was common knowledge what had happened, and village opinion was generally behind him. People thought that he'd behaved like an idiot, but that George had gone too far in dismissing him. It wasn't as though George had been much of a disciplinarian before.

Darren was in the pub pretty much every night, where his former workmates never allowed him to pay for a drink. He made the most of the free beer, developed his pool game to new heights and never got out of bed before midday. He was endlessly bitter about George's treatment of him, and grumbled to anyone who would listen.

Eventually, the joys of free beer and endless pool wore off. Darren rowed with his mum one afternoon. He got drunker than usual in the pub that night and became unusually argumentative and belligerent. He told the landlord that he was off to 'get even' with George, and stumbled out into the night. The landlord was concerned enough to call George in Ilkley, who thanked him and promised to be on the lookout for trouble. As it was, Darren didn't show up at George's lodgings, though Darren's mum said he wasn't home until gone four in the morning. When he got up the next day with a temper as bad as his hangover, he stuffed some clothes into a backpack, and left.

Darren's mum thought he was off to stay with a friend in Skipton, but wasn't sure. At twenty-two, he was old enough to look after himself. The news reached Gissings as the factory began to close up for the day, and was met with a general sense of relief. Although his workmates were sympathetic, Darren's incessant moaning had become hard to take. 'He'll be alright,' said Dave. 'At least he's getting on with his life.'

Dave might not have been so philosophical had he known where Darren actually headed. He didn't go to Skipton. In fact, he hitched a lift south with a lorry driver heading into Bradford. From Bradford, he caught a ride south on the A641, then hitched a ride into Halifax, and left on the A646 heading west towards Burnley. By seven in the evening, he had reached the outskirts of Stirby. It would be dark in an hour and the weather was rainy with a gathering wind behind it. Darren had forgotten to pack any rain gear when he left, and he shivered inside his denim jacket.

The van driver who had given him a lift dropped him at a petrol station just outside town. Darren waited until the driver had set off again, then started to walk the half mile north-east to the town's industrial estate. There were other firms on the estate, but one company dominated. As the sign at the gateway put it: 'Asperton Holdings Ltd – Quality Furniture Nationwide'.

Darren found the Asperton car-park, now mostly empty. Among the few cars present was a black 5-series Mercedes with a recent registration plate. Darren dropped his backpack on the wet tarmac by the car's boot and sat on it, his back against the rear bumper. He dug some headphones out of the side pocket of his pack, but the drawstring hadn't been pulled tight and the Walkman itself was missing. He swore and threw the headphones away. He did manage, however, to light a damp cigarette with some damp matches and puffed away and waited. He'd only started to smoke tobacco since getting the sack. 'No smoke without a firing,' he said.

Time passed. Darren got wetter, and colder. He chain-smoked his remaining cigarettes, because the matches were now too wet to use. The wind blew harder, whipping up spray from the growing puddles.

Eventually, the neon lamp at the car-park entrance betrayed two figures, walking hurriedly. Bundled in wads of cashmere and hunched beneath a pair of wind-blown umbrellas, the couple approached the Mercedes. When they were close, Darren called to them.

'Hi there.'

The pair halted, alarmed. The slightly less short of the two figures bustled about for a while in the depths of his coat, while the shorter figure, a woman, tried to hold his brolly for him in the snatching wind, scolding him for his tardiness. Eventually, the man found the torch he had been searching for and pointed it at Darren.

'Who are you? And what do you want?' asked Mike Asperton.

'I'm Darren. I used to work at Gissings, but I don't

work there any more. I was wondering whether there might be anything on offer around here.'

Darren gestured around the car-park with his cigarette. He was still sitting on his pack, with his back against the car.

'Well, I'm not sure if there's anything suitable. But you need to apply in writing, we can't just give you a job here and now.'

The Aspertons weren't sure whether Darren was harmless or not. For the moment, they would treat him with care. They stood their distance and continued to prod the torch beam into his eyes.

'Well, it's not quite like that,' said Darren. 'I wanted to speak with you, you see.'

Eileen Asperton took the torch from her husband's hand. She approached closer, using the torch as a shield, while the wind tugged and snatched at her umbrella.

'There's nothing you can say to us that can't be said better in writing, young man. You have no business to be in this car-park. Now, please move aside.' She flicked the torch beam away into the night to show him what she meant. Then the light moved back, full square on Darren's face.

Darren didn't move. He dragged on the last of his cigarette, burning the tobacco right down to the filter. He dropped the butt on the ground, where it was immediately extinguished in the rain.

'Well, you see, what I was going to say was, I used to be George Gradley's golden boy. There's nothing that went on at Gissings that I didn't know about. I thought it was better to come and see you personally, if you know what I mean. Sorry about scaring you and everything, but I thought I wouldn't get to see you if I just came and banged on the front door.'

The Aspertons didn't move, but their posture subtly changed. They weren't scared any more, just interested. Mike Asperton made a sudden gesture of recognition.

'You were one of the lads who came to buy some of our Brilliants, weren't you?' He started to explain to his wife, who cut him short.

'Why did you leave Gissings, if you were so close to Gradley?' she asked.

'He caught me taking the mick and he fired me. Without even a thank-you after all I'd done.' Darren spat, something at which he excelled.

'What did you come here to tell us?' asked Eileen Asperton. 'You didn't just come to ask for a job.'

'Well, Gissings ain't as bleeding holy as it makes out,' said Darren. 'They get up to stuff, just like everybody. Difference is, I know what stuff.'

'Unsubstantiated allegations are of no interest to us. If that's all you've come about, you may as well leave right now.'

But she wasn't dismissing him. She was waiting. Darren patted his backpack.

'I've got everything in here. Everything you could want. Copies, not originals, so they don't even know they're missing.' Both Aspertons stared greedily at the filthy pack. 'And you don't need to worry, cos I've put them in a plastic bag, so they won't even be wet. Unlike me,' he added, hinting.

Muffled in their cashmere coats and scarves and hats, and bobbing gently beneath their tugging umbrellas, the two proprietors of Asperton Holdings stood and drooled. Eileen Asperton dropped the torch beam away from Darren's face on to the ground, then from the ground to the shiny black car.

'You'd better climb in,' she said.

5

'I'll go get the celebration coffees,' said Matthew.

'Champagne, more like,' said Fiona. But she was joking, of course. This was Madison. Alcohol was no more acceptable than trading losses. Coffees it would be.

They had plenty to celebrate. They had successfully bought eleven and a half percent of all outstanding bank loans to Cobra Electronics at an average cost of forty-three pence in the pound. Last week, they had issued a press release announcing the size of their holding. They also mentioned their intention to block the company's proposed refinancing plan.

There followed a week of frenzy. Cobra's first response was not far short of hysterical. It accused Madison of being a 'self-centred American bank with no understanding of the complexities of the industry'. It said that if Madison blocked the refinancing, the company might go bankrupt 'by year end'. It called all of its other banks in a rush of indignation, only to discover that they were all quietly delighted at Madison's leadership.

Cobra called on its merchant bankers, who broke the truth. The company didn't need more money; it needed competent management. The quickest way to get it was to dismember the company and sell the pieces to the highest bidder. The management resisted, but not for long. With Madison preventing new money from coming in, the company had no choice. A fortnight after Madison had issued its press release, Cobra issued its own, announcing that the company was putting itself up for sale.

The stock price exploded into life, doubling on the first day, then doubling again over the next three days. The price of the loans also rocketed, giving Madison a paper profit of near enough seventy percent. Brian McAllister was ecstatic. He got an e-mail from Dan Kramer congratulating him, and he passed the note on to each of Fiona, Matthew and Ed. Fiona had a dozen picture nails banged into her office wall. She framed the note from Dan Kramer and hung it from one of the hooks. The other eleven stayed empty. This group was going to stay hungry.

Matthew put his coat on.

'Cappuccino for you, Ed?' he called to Ed Deane, who was fussing over his bonsai forest.

'Coffee? Yeah, OK, whatever. But can you go by the florist's and pick up some plant food? My apple's developing a blemish. I think it's magnesium deficiency.'

Deane pointed out a minute black speck on the last of his prized apples. The speck looked suspiciously like dirt to Matthew, who didn't know too much about magnesium deficiencies. He poked the speck with his finger and it moved. Deane wiped it away with a soft cloth he kept ready.

'I'll go by the opticians, if you want,' said Matthew, but his joke was lost on Deane, who was spraying distilled water on the apple in his relief.

On the way to the coffee shop, Matthew ducked into the little side alley that led up to the garden and the pub. The square was quiet again. The only people there were a couple of tourists trying to find an obscure Christopher Wren church. They asked Matthew's assistance but he couldn't help. They left. Matthew pulled out his phone and dialled.

'Matthew! How nice to hear from you,' said Belial, once he knew it was Matthew. 'I had a funny feeling you were going to call.'

'Yeah,' said Matthew, who didn't enjoy Belial's innuendoes. 'I want to sell out of my position in Cobra Electronics. Completely.'

Belial said it would take a few minutes but that Matthew could call back to find out exactly how well he had done. Matthew agreed and went off to get the coffees. Once back in the little square again, he called Belial.

'Congratulations. We've sold everything. You've made a seventy-two percent profit on the deal, after commissions and everything. Your balance with us is now £109,000 sterling. I must say, you did strike lucky. Just imagine Madison marching in the very same morning you made your investment with us! I bet you were pleased.'

Matthew rang off. He could just imagine the tidy little man, his ugly little face screwed up in laughter. He was unpleasant, but useful.

Matthew went back to the bank, coffee in his hand and joy triumphant in his heart. Plan B was rolling into action.

With Cobra, he had done particularly well, because of the company's vulnerability and the way Madison had been able to take advantage of it. But even when Madison was just buying on the basis of long-term research, Matthew could profit. The market for company loans and bonds is very thin. Big trades will push the price up or down by a long way and almost overnight. Just knowing that Madison was going to make a trade was information that Matthew could profit from. Even if prices moved by just ten percent, he could make an overnight profit of ten thousand pounds. Even five percent was a huge move – as long as it happened overnight, and as long as, like Matthew, you knew which night was the night. And each time his capital increased, his scope for profits increased too. He'd do it. He now really believed, perhaps for the first time, that he'd do it. He'd get his father's millions.

But in amongst the joy, there was also shame. Insider trading is deeply illegal. It carries a maximum of seven years in jail. Everyone who respected him at Madison would despise him if he were caught. And, above all, if she knew, Fiona would never speak to him again. She mustn't know.

He got back to his desk. Fiona and Ed were somewhere else, in a meeting probably.

Matthew took the lid off his cappuccino and drank. God, it was good. He couldn't just sit down at his desk and begin to work again. He was too keyed up. He strolled up and down drinking his coffee.

He thought about George and Josephine and his mother. He'd send Josephine a present of some money. Not much, but something. Whatever he did, he wouldn't jeopardise his chance of making the million now.

He thought about his shame. He told himself that insider trading is a crime without victims, but he knew it was a lie. When he bought his bonds, somebody else was selling them: an investment manager maybe, or a pension fund perhaps. If they hadn't sold, somebody's pension would pay a little more, somebody's savings would be that little bit more valuable.

He shook off the uncomfortable logic, and thought instead of his father's company, about how much it was worth and how long it would take to sell. Matthew hadn't decided how much of his father's cash he'd give to his family. Maybe a quarter to Josie, and a million or so to each of his brothers. The world was all before him and he'd aim to be generous.

As Matthew drank his coffee and mused, he saw an apple in front of him. He reached for it absent-mindedly and bit into it. It was bitter and unripe.

As he put it aside, he suddenly saw what he'd done. He had picked Deane's last, precious, forbidden apple.

The bonsai forest and the dwarf apple tree at its centre looked reproachful, menacing even. Matthew picked up the half-eaten apple and wandered guiltily away.

6

The building was a manor house auctioned off by its original, posh but penniless, owners shortly after the roof had sprung its first major leak. The building had been purchased, tidied, prettied. Tall iron gates operable by remote control sprang up at the entrance. Local girls were interviewed for menial positions and the prettiest ones selected. Soft-spoken doctors with mediocre qualifications and a melting bedside manner swished in and out in their discreet German cars. It was unflashy, but immaculate, a clinic where the sick rich are gently reminded that wealth is always to be preferred to health.

Behind a high mahogany desk in the front hall, a white-suited receptionist icily surveyed the two newcomers: a pretty young woman, not especially well dressed, and an older woman, obviously frail and in need of treatment. The receptionist was unimpressed. The cab that had brought them had been local, meaning that the new arrivals must have arrived by train, and no one who travels by train is wealthy enough to obtain treatment here.

'You're here for a consultation, are you?' she enquired with freezing politeness and indicating the older woman with a tiny flick of her chin.

'No, no. I haven't come about my mother,' said Josephine. 'I've come to visit one of your patients.'

'Ah.' The receptionist eased up. Even wealthy people have poor relatives. 'Of course. Who was it you wished to see?'

And Josephine told her.

Summer 2000

Summer is here, the first of the millennium. It is hot and bright. The water companies are moaning, the newspapers mutter about climate change, and the skies are already scorched by holiday jets heading south.

Summer is a time for young men's thoughts to turn to love, but right now some young men are preoccupied. It is 16 June 2000, and there are 392 days to go until Bernard Gradley's deadline. That's little more than a year.

1

'How are you, Zack, you revolting sod?'

Dixon Banderman was in a good mood. He made a habit of swearing at Zack whenever they met as a reminder of their first encounter, screaming at each other on the zebra crossing outside Coburg's. Zack, naturally, reciprocated.

'Not bad. How about yourself, you repellent old fossil?'

'Good, thanks. You want a bonus this year, or do you want to give it to the Partners in Hardship Fund?'

Zack gave the matter some thought. 'Well, I'm the first

to help the needy, Dixon, but the partners are such an ugly bunch and dishonest as hell from what I've heard. I'll take the bonus.'

Dixon grinned. He liked Zack.

'Fair enough. God knows it's small enough.' Dixon's face changed and his voice grew businesslike. 'Amy-Lou has given you the rundown on strengths and weaknesses and all that?'

'Yeah. My strengths are that I work hard, my work is always top quality, and I've made plenty of money. My weaknesses are that I'm a bit arrogant, a bit insensitive, and a bit hard to work with.'

'A *bit* arrogant?'

'Amy-Lou might have used a stronger term, it's true. I do think I'm smarter than most people I work with, but then again, I am smarter than most of them. So what am I meant to think?'

'There's more to this game than brains, Zack. You won't work well in this organisation if people don't like you, and the same goes for our clients.'

'Fair enough. I'll be sweet as a kitten from now on.'

Banderman held Zack's gaze a moment longer, then picked up an envelope and handed it over.

Zack tore it open. The slip inside told him his bonus was two hundred and fifty thousand dollars plus a salary increase which Zack didn't register.

'You should feel pleased with that. That bonus puts you into the top twenty percent of your peer group, which is a tremendous achievement for your first year. You'll have a good career here, if you want it.'

Zack was pleased, but not over the moon. Unlike Matthew, the bonus didn't play a big part in Zack's plans for the future. Either Zack was going to make partner, or he would find a way to Sarah's money, or both. Either way, a quarter of a million dollars didn't make a lot of difference. This was just spending money. Still, it was nice to have. He could buy something for Sarah, maybe for her parents too. And Josie. She should have something. He could get her something from Aspreys perhaps, a necklace or something. She always used to love jewellery.

'Thanks,' said Zack briefly.

Banderman smiled internally. Zack probably meant it when he said he'd try to be nice, but he didn't stand a chance. The young man didn't even realise when he was being rude.

'OK. You can probably guess why I wanted to have this chat.'

'It's to do with finding a replacement for Hal Gillingham, right?'

'That's right. As you know, we've had our head-hunters searching for a replacement and we've all been grateful to you for holding the fort in the interim, especially since I know that you've still been working hard for Amy-Lou.'

'It's been my pleasure.' That was kind of true. Zack worked hard because he needed to. On the other hand, Sarah was beginning to wonder who exactly she was engaged to: a future husband and father, or a workaholic business machine. They hadn't rowed about it, exactly. Sarah was uncommonly mature about these things, and Zack had managed to stifle his natural impulse towards aggressive sarcasm. But it was an issue, like sand in the folds of their clothes, that chafed constantly and wouldn't disappear.

Banderman nodded. He could imagine the conflict. Most partners at Weinstein Lukes were divorced, or else their spouses had long since decided to remain wedded to the bonus cheques while looking elsewhere for love and sex. The relationships that worked best were those where both partners worked crazy hours for American banks and left the kids to be brought up by a succession of motherly British nannies. It screwed the kids up – but, hey, at least when they grew up they'd be able to afford the therapy.

'What I wanted to ask you, Zack, is whether you felt able to take over Hal's role permanently. We'll find somebody else to take over the projects you're doing with Amy-Lou, and you can devote yourself to tax stuff. Full-time, your show entirely.'

'My show entirely? Gillingham's job?' Zack was delighted. If he had to choose between the Gillingham job and the quarter of a million bucks, he'd have chosen the tax job without a second thought. The quarter of a million was neither here nor there. The tax job was Zack's passport to partnership and the key to his father's fortune. 'That's absolutely fantastic, Dixon.'

'D'you think you can handle it?'

'Handle it? I've handled it for the last four months, haven't I? Even when Hal was still here, I was running things. He showed up at the office, but it was me that ran the deals. Of course I can handle it.'

'Good. In that case, I'd like you to start transferring all your remaining non-tax-related assignments to other people. I want you full-time on tax.'

'Excluding Hatherleigh Pacific, right? I get to keep the Hatherleigh Pacific deal?'

'Is that still alive? You were hired back in November as I remember.'

'Yes, of course it's alive,' snapped Zack. 'The company wants to wait for the price of South China to fall before going after it. They're expecting bad news on the shipping market to depress the price.'

'And has the price fallen?'

'Not yet. It's at forty-five bucks, and they want it to go to forty.'

Banderman raised an eyebrow. He didn't believe the deal would happen. Zack breathed out through his nose and made an impatient gesture.

'If they say it'll go to forty, it will. These guys are very smart and they know their markets better than anyone. They'll do the deal and they'll do it with us.'

Banderman shrugged. He didn't care. The Hatherleigh Pacific deal bore all the signs of an entanglement which would cost the bank a mound of work and bring in nothing at the end of it. But if Zack wanted to keep it that badly, then he could. It'd be something for him to learn from.

'This guy Hatherleigh, he's your father-in-law to be, right?'

'Right.'

'OK. Keep the deal. I wouldn't want to spoil your family get-togethers.'

'Thanks. There's just one other thing,' said Zack.

'Yes?'

This was the moment Zack had been waiting for: the moment when Gillingham's job was finally, definitely, irrevocably, his. Gillingham's last great idea, the idea he'd had that sad morning when alcohol had finally mastered him, the idea that Zack had stolen with a smile before flinging its creator to the ocean floor – the idea's time had come, with Zack secure in the knowledge that the glory would be his and his alone.

'It's to do with an idea I've had. Gillingham's ideas were always tailored to suit each particular client. That was great for the client, but a lot of work for us. It would take us a day to think of an idea, a month to work out the details, then three months or more just to negotiate the contract. I want to get away from that. I want a tax idea which will fit everyone. I want to move from *haute couture* to ready-to-wear. I want to make a tax dodge so uniform that we just roll the contracts off the photocopier. I want the idea to be so simple that every salesman in the bank can sell it to every client.'

'Ah! The Holy Grail, right? Hal used to talk about that too. He said there was a goldmine there, if you could only find it. Don't spend too much time looking, Zack. Hal never found it, and he searched long and hard.'

'Dixon, I've found it.'

'You've what?'

'I've found it, Dixon. There's still a lot of legal work to be done, but I know it'll work. The idea came to me in Hong Kong . . .'

And Zack began to explain. The idea wasn't his. It was Gillingham's. It was a brilliant concept, a Holy Grail worthy of the name. But Gillingham wasn't there to claim the glory. Gillingham had gone off on a four-month blinder, which had brought him once again to the verge of liver failure and an early grave. The threat of death had induced him to check into his old clinic, but recovery would be slow, and his stamina was less than it had been. Nobody would doubt that the idea was Zack's.

Banderman was soon lost, but the details were immaterial. The important point was easy. Zack had found a way to let gamblers make a one-way bet. A certain type of financial bet – called a derivative – is like a bet on a horse race. If you win, you can double your money, or even more. If you lose, you lose. What Gillingham had found and Zack had stolen was a way to swing the odds in favour of the gambler. If you placed your bet through Zack's tax loophole, your winnings would be tax-free, while if you lost, your loss could be offset against tax. Through this loophole the taxman would unwittingly subsidise gambling, and the bigger the bet, the bigger the subsidy.

Zack was talking about a completely legal tax dodge that could be sold through salesmen across the Far East to literally thousands of potential clients.

'You got a name for this product?'

'I call it ROSES,' said Zack. 'It stands for –'

'Don't tell me what it stands for. But I like the name.'

'Dixon, I need you to make sure the bank throws its weight behind ROSES.'

'Have you had the lawyers test to see if this dodge is solid?'

'I've got opinions to say it's bomb-proof in Hong Kong, Singapore, and Malaysia. I've got lawyers looking at the concept in six other Pacific Rim countries. So far, they've come up with no major objections. I expect the idea to work in every territory.'

'Bomb-proof, huh? You send your legal opinions to our corporate lawyers in New York. If they're happy, I'm happy. This has got to be squeaky clean, but as soon as our lawyers tell me it works, you'll have my support. We'll push your ROSES so hard, we'll be growing 'em on the moon.'

Zack grinned. Banderman was the head of corporate finance in Europe. He wasn't just a partner, he was one of the most powerful partners in the bank, and he never exaggerated. If he said the moon, you'd find ROSES on Jupiter.

'Thank you,' said Zack earnestly. 'Thanks a lot, dungbrain.'

2

Another conference. Another yes decision.

This time it was a leasing company, Albion Leasing.

It had borrowed a ton of money to buy equipment to lease to people, thus allowing it to borrow another ton of money to buy more equipment to lease to a whole lot more people. The game of musical chairs had been wonderful while it lasted, but one day the company's salesmen ran short of sales, while the company's accountants discovered that the mountain of debt had developed a nasty overhang. The inevitable happened. The debt mountain went into avalanche. Banks demanded their money. Albion couldn't pay. Customers heard about the problems and took their business elsewhere. The trouble got worse.

Right now the Bank of England was banging heads together, trying to sort out a rescue plan. But meanwhile, true to form, the courageous banks were selling off their loans at huge discounts to anyone brave enough to buy. And, true to their form, Fiona, Ed Deane and Matthew scented a profit and were sniffing around.

There wasn't any magic in their game plan. The Bank of England negotiations were going through a particularly fraught couple of weeks and some of the banks had lost their nerve. That's common enough. Unlike the swashbuckling investment banks, high-street banks contain some of the world's most timid people, the sort of people for whom adventure means a brightly coloured tie. When the going gets tough, these heroes squeak with fright and run for shelter. And, as they run, they lose all sense of proportion. They're prepared to sell for forty pence in the pound what ought to be valued at sixty. Just because a loan's gone bad doesn't mean it's worthless.

So Fiona, Ed and Matthew went mouse hunting. They called around town, seeing who squeaked loudest. They tossed out bits of cheese – letting it be known that they were interested in buying loans to Albion Leasing – and watched to see who came nibbling at their door.

Out came the mice, whiskers twitching. Different mice placed different values on the loans. Some wanted seventy pence in the pound. Others had no price in mind, they just wanted whatever they could get. Fiona, Ed and Matthew watched the rodents come and go, meanwhile conducting their own intensive research.

Right now, they needed to come to a decision. They agreed that the real value of the company loans was around fifty pence in the pound. If the Bank of England negotiations went well, the loans could be worth sixty. Meanwhile, they knew they had mice willing to sell out for between thirty-five and forty pence. The maths was simple and the team agreed without difficulty. They'd go for it. As usual, they wanted to bet big time to profit big time.

But first, Matthew had a call he needed to make, part of a well-practised routine.

'Coffees?'

'Great,' said Fiona.

'And an apple,' said Deane. He still hadn't forgiven Matthew for eating his last apple from his bonsai forest, and he took care to remind Matthew of it about twice a day, every day. Matthew had grovelled profusely, bought Deane a second dwarf apple tree, complete with half a dozen ripening apples, and by now considered himself entitled to ignore Deane's grumbling.

'You're nuts,' he said. 'Isn't he nuts, Fiona?'

'He's nuts . . .'

'There you go, you're nuts . . .'

'. . . but you still shouldn't have eaten his apple.'

'You're nuts too,' said Matthew and went out for the coffees.

The streets were hot. Most people, like Matthew, were in shirt sleeves, their hot grey jackets, relics of a Victorian dress code, left behind them in the office. Matthew

410

walked quickly. He came to the little alleyway and looked furtively around. He saw no one he recognised, though the streets were crowded and it was hard to tell. He ducked up the alleyway and came out into the little garden. It was nearly lunch time and the pub was already filling with people. Everywhere in the sunshine, office refugees sat on benches with sandwiches or stood round drinking under the tree.

Matthew hesitated. He preferred to be alone. However, it would be hard to find anywhere completely private and he needed to make his call fast.

He dialled the well-known number.

'Good afternoon, James Belial speaking. How may I be of service?'

'It's Matthew Gradley. I want to check my account balance.'

'Ah, Matthew, my dear fellow! One of my most fortunate clients! Truly blessed with the golden touch. Let me see.' Matthew caught the sound of Belial hitting a few computer keys to get the right screen up. 'Yes, indeed. Lady Luck rides with you, my friend. Your modest portfolio of sixty-eight thousand pounds has grown to a remarkable two hundred and eighty thousand in just a few months. Is it luck, or do you have a secret formula?'

Matthew ignored the obnoxious little man.

'I want you to invest everything in Albion Leasing. Bonds not shares.' Matthew gave a few more precise instructions. It is difficult for individuals to buy bank loans, but easy for them to buy bonds. There are a few exceptions, but generally speaking if bank loans go up in value then so do bonds. Matthew gave Belial detailed instructions. The ugly little man on the other end of the line repeated the instructions back clearly and precisely. Nobody was more disagreeable, but Matthew had to admit that his service was impeccable.

'I must warn you, as always, that the investment you want to make carries an extremely high level of risk –'

'I know. Just do it. I'll call you back to confirm the trade in a couple of minutes.'

Matthew cut off Belial's snickering voice, bought the coffees, phoned back, and got the confirmation he wanted. Switzerland International charged painfully dear commissions, but its traders seemed to be excellent and succeeded in buying whatever they needed to buy at a rate which was always fair and sometimes exceptional. This time, they seemed to have done their usual good job. Matthew barely thanked Belial and walked quickly back to the office.

'How are our mice doing?' he asked when he arrived.

'No responses yet. They're probably all out to lunch,' said Deane.

'You're telling me.'

'Now then, don't be nasty.'

The afternoon drew on. Fiona repeated her calls. Still no answer. That was odd. Mice don't generally take long lunch breaks, and right now there was an epidemic.

Eventually, at quarter to five, one of their chief mice called back. Fiona explained that Madison was willing to buy a substantial chunk of Albion debt at thirty-five pence in the pound. The offer, as always, was conditional on Madison having access to all the information that the existing lenders enjoyed.

From previous experience, Fiona expected to have her hand virtually nibbled off. Instead, she discovered that her mouse had turned into a tiger.

'Thanks for the call. Unfortunately, you're too late. Once you've heard today's news, you won't be interested. It turns out that there was a substantial fraud on top of everything else. It's too soon to say, but the debt's probably worth ten pence in the pound, if that. We've just taken the decision to write the debt off completely. If we recover anything at all, we'll treat it as a bonus.'

'Fraud, huh?'

'That's right. On a big scale. It should have been spotted sooner but wasn't. I sure wish we'd sold out to you guys a couple of days ago.'

'OK. Well, thanks for being straight with us.'

'No problem. You'd have learned about it before closing the deal anyway.'

That was true. By the time Fiona had come off the phone, Ed Deane and Matthew were clustered round their Reuters terminal. The headline spoke volumes: 'Bankers announce fraud at Albion Leasing'. Beneath it, the article went on to describe the fraud. The company's shares were suspended. The bonds were trading at five to ten pence in the pound, but in practice no deals were being done even at that rock-bottom price.

'Damnation,' said Deane. 'We'll have to find some other mice to hunt.'

'It's good news, really,' said Fiona. 'We'd have lost a heap of money if we'd made our offer a day or two sooner.'

Matthew said nothing. He just stared at the screen and punched buttons to get whatever information there was. At this stage, there wasn't much. There'd be more over the next day or two. But information wouldn't save him. Matthew had invested two hundred and eighty thousand pounds in bonds which had collapsed in value. He had bought them at around forty pence in the pound. Assuming he was able to sell at all, he'd probably get between five and ten pence for them now. That would give him between thirty-five and seventy thousand pounds before Belial's fat commissions.

Just a few hours ago, his father's millions were getting so close he could wave. Now they had become more distant than the stars. He was back to square one, or worse.

3

The editor looked at the mock-up. Beneath the regular *Furniture Today* masthead stood a red-highlighted headline in 30 point type: 'RIP-OFF! Our exclusive report reveals the cheats some manufacturers get away with'. Then, in smaller print, 'Story on page 14'.

Furniture Today was a trade magazine, not a beacon of investigative journalism. Its stories dealt with new techniques for steam-treating pine and the latest design award-winners. The magazine had no budget for lawsuits and no appetite for libel.

In the end, though, the editor had run out of excuses. The evidence damning Gissings was as robust and complete as could be imagined. The editor had not only seen the evidence himself, he had copies of it in the office safe. He had spent a long time interviewing a disgruntled ex-employee of Gissings and had the whole interview on videotape. He'd had a journalist, undercover, check out the Gissings man's story, and every word of it could be corroborated. The young man had been close to Gissings' boss. He had been sacked and humiliated. He had hung around bitter and vengeful, until an idea had struck him. He'd turned up on the Aspertons' doorstep the very next day.

But better than any of this, the editor had a letter from Eileen Asperton herself. The letter promised that all the allegations made were true, and indemnified the magazine against any lawsuits. If the magazine was sued for libel, the Aspertons would pick up the tab. The editor sighed. They must really hate Gissings.

The editor spoke with his owner. The owner spoke with his lawyers. And the lawyers, owner and editor all agreed. They'd go ahead.

The story ran as follows:

Exclusive!

GISSINGS CONS CUSTOMERS WITH EMPTY PROMISES

Investigation reveals unsafe paints and poor quality materials

Ever had the experience of buying something that looked great in the showroom only to find that it falls apart within days? Well, you may not just be the victim of your own careless buying. You may be the victim of systematic fraud.

Furniture Today has conducted a lengthy investigation into one long-established firm, Gissings Furniture Ltd, and is able to reveal some of the tricks in its carefully planned campaign of deception.

Suspicions were first aroused when Michael and Eileen Asperton, proprietors of the well-known Asperton Holdings Ltd, started to pay close attention to a new segment of the furniture market, dominated by the Gissings 'Bright and Beautiful' range. As Mike Asperton says, 'We were doing our own research into the area, when Gissings produced their range. When we looked at the quality standards which Gissings claimed to meet, we were very sceptical. We couldn't see how it could be done with the technology we knew they had.'

The Gissings marketing literature claimed to use 'top quality paints with excellent durability'. In fact, a joint investigation by *Furniture Today* and Asperton Holdings indicates that paints have regularly been sourced from an East European supplier, whose products contain dangerous levels of lead and other toxic substances. Brian Conway, Health and Safety Consultant to the British Furniture Council, commented, 'Use of such lead-based paints is in clear contravention of British and European safety standards, and could result in criminal prosecution.

What's worst about this kind of practice is the risk of potentially fatal health consequences, especially in young people.'

Eileen Asperton comments, 'We were shocked. We felt it essential to hurry out our own range of furniture to offer customers a real alternative. Meanwhile, we've done everything we can to expose this dreadful practice as soon as possible.'

But Gissings' efforts to cut costs at customers' expense haven't stopped there. The marketing material described the wood used in the product as 'high quality fully treated Scandinavian pine'. In reality, our investigation shows the wood is reject material from a Scottish sawmill, which in most cases hasn't even been treated. Mike Graham from the Asperton Holdings technical department comments, 'They were claiming to use some of the best softwood materials on the market. In fact, they were using wood of such poor quality that warping and distortion is almost inevitable. The only wonder is how long they've got away with this kind of practice.'

Other tricks include using high quality fittings such as knobs, handles and hinges on showroom models, and replacing these with the cheapest available lookalikes on the goods shipped to customers. Nor was it only the customers who paid. Important VAT returns were sent to the revenue authorities deliberately incomplete, in order to delay payment for as long as possible.

Gissings was recently acquired from the well-respected Gissings family by George Gradley, son of the self-made Yorkshire millionaire, the late Bernard Gradley. It is thought that – contrary to claims made by its proprietor – Gissings is highly indebted. In Mike Asperton's words, 'Perhaps they thought it was OK to cheat customers to stop the firm from going to the wall. But in this business, the only thing that can save you is hard work, and honesty. Unfortunately, under the new management, Gissings seems to lack both.'

We invited Gissings to comment on our investigation, but all we received was a terse 'No comment'. The documents collected by the joint *Furniture Today* and Asperton Holdings investigation have been passed to the police. Meanwhile, Asperton Holdings has set up a Free*fone* helpline for customers fearing that they may have bought sub-standard products.

The magazine usually had a print run of eight thousand copies. This time, the print run was to be thirteen thousand copies, as the Aspertons had ordered five thousand additional copies for 'promotional purposes'. Apparently, they had prepared a customer mailing list of five thousand names, each of whom would be sent a copy of the magazine with a covering letter from Mike Asperton. The aim was to make sure that nobody in the country ever bought a piece of Gissings furniture again.

Gissings, of course, subscribed to the magazine. Everybody in the industry did. And when, on Friday morning, Val opened the mail, the red headline on the front cover caught her eye. She turned straight to the article and read it in a state of mounting shock. She didn't know what to make of it. She assumed it was rubbish, of course, but it looked like lethal rubbish. And there was one thing that bothered her. She remembered George once insisting on sending in incomplete VAT returns during one of Gissings' perennial cash crises. What else had he been doing that she didn't know about? These days, it seemed, there was nothing he wouldn't be willing to do.

She dropped the magazine on George's desk before walking out wordlessly. George read the article once, then reread it, slowly and carefully. He wondered what the Aspertons would do to take advantage of it – but it hardly mattered. The article alone was designed to kill

417

Gissings. He ran his fingers through his short ginger hair and breathed out heavily.

'Game, set and match,' he murmured.

4

What better time to be married than this first high summer of the third millennium? And what better place than the magnificent grounds of Ovenden House? And what finer couple in England today than the young, brilliant, acerbic Zack and his rich, lovely, undeceiving bride? There may be marriages where the motives are a little purer, on the side of the husband at least, but what you don't know can't hurt you, and under the brilliant sunshine, in her billows of lace and ivory silk, trotting away from the village church in a carriage drawn by four white horses, next to the only man she has ever truly loved, Sarah lives in bliss and ignorance.

The wedding service had been perfect. Five hundred people crammed into the village church and the windows rattled with their singing. Sarah wore a traditional full-skirted dress of ivory silk satin trimmed with old lace, that everyone said looked lovely and meant it too. Lord Hatherleigh gave her away with dignity, a happy man. Unlike most fathers of the bride, he felt he was gaining a son, not losing a daughter.

Lady Hatherleigh was kind enough to sit next to Helen Gradley, who was quite well by her standards. She was attentive and alert, though she needed reminding that it was Zack who was getting married to Sarah, not, as she kept thinking, George to Val.

Bride and groom spoke the vows loudly and clearly, looking into each other's eyes. Zack had remembered to comb his hair and managed to avoid rumpling it a few moments later. He looked darkly handsome, even dashing: a wonderful match for a wonderful bride. The couple spoke their vows as if they meant them, sang the hymns as if they liked them, and kneeled in prayer as though they did it all the time.

Ceremony over, the congregation poured out into the village churchyard to watch the happy couple step into their waiting carriage.

The horses had been woken early to have their coats groomed, their tails plaited, their manes ribboned, and their hooves oiled, and they had waited a lot longer than they wanted outside in the bright sun. So, when Zack and Sarah climbed aboard and the coachman shook the reins, they trotted off brightly, looking forward to an afternoon of snoozing, nosebags and sweet summer grass. So sweetly did they canter, that Sarah, on a high of happiness, but never happier than when her pleasures involved horses, insisted on looping the long way round by the lake and taking the reins herself for the long gallop through the woods. Zack, too, was as happy as he'd ever known. Prenuptial agreement or no, this was a huge step in the right direction for him, and he genuinely did like his wife a very great deal – just a little bit less than she might have imagined. When, finally, she reluctantly let go the reins and dropped back into the carriage, filled like cherry blossom with her skirts, she and Zack began a kiss which didn't end until the sweating horses, doubly impatient now, drew up to cheers and confetti on the gravel drive.

The receiving line stretched through the rose garden. Zack and Sarah, Lord and Lady Hatherleigh and Josephine and Helen Gradley offered hands and best wishes to the long procession. Josephine had been very nervous of how Helen would manage, but she sat like royalty in a wicker armchair, shook every hand that was offered and mumbled her pleasure and thanks.

Everyone was there. Helen Gradley's parents had come, as had Bernard Gradley's mother, Peggy, teetotal now after ferocious warnings from her doctor. A few of Zack's aunts and uncles – a random selection of Bernard Gradley's numerous siblings – had come, and stood around now, awkward as pigs in a synagogue, but pleased to be there.

To George's astonishment, Kiki was there as well, disappearing beneath an enormous scarlet hat.

'But of course I am here,' she said. 'My family and Sarah's family have known each other for generations. I think it was my great-great-grandmother who married the fourteenth viscount, or something. Anyway, Sarah and Kate used to come to my house in France every summer when they were babies.'

George was thrilled, and he and Kiki spent much of the day together. She asked him where Val was. He shrugged unhappily and told Kiki the story.

'But I think it will turn out right in the end, Georges. I think she must love you and if she is in love then she will not stay angry for ever.'

George was pleased that she thought so. But then again, Kiki kept nothing in her head for more than a minute or two, and so probably wasn't the best guide to the course of anger in strong-willed Yorkshirewomen. George loved spending time with Kiki, but his infatuation had gone. She was a good friend, but would have been a horrendous wife. Besides, Kiki had started to date a good-looking Italian, and gave George all the details. 'I tell you as my friend, Georges, if he gets his horrible old *palazzo* tidied up, I think I will marry him.' George was genuinely delighted and hugged her as close as she and her hat would permit.

The wedding reception passed in a happy daze. Champagne was poured in abundance, but the glasses didn't stay full for long. The great marquee buzzed with laughter, and at the head of it all, Sarah sat, glowing with pleasure and beauty. Only Matthew, Zack's best man, was glum. Fiona had been invited, of course, but she'd ducked out at the last minute for fear of being introduced as Matthew's girlfriend to all his family. He missed her and, what was worse, he had his speech to get through.

Lord Hatherleigh was first to speak, welcoming, genial and witty. He was warmly applauded, an encouraging sign. Zack went next, ticking off a long list of thank-yous and handing out a number of presents. With every present and every thank-you there was a little joke and a ripple of laughter. Matthew got a sterling silver billfold – a coded sneer, meaning 'I've just married fifty million quid. How's *your* million coming along?' Matthew shoved the gift into his pocket. He'd throw it away later. Zack finished the thank-yous and launched into an impromptu description of Sarah taking the reins in the carriage that afternoon, standing up in her wedding dress and geeing up the galloping horses. The audience's laughter rose into guffaws. Then Zack added a few very warm words about Sarah and her family. More applause. Matthew's turn.

He drew out his notes and set doggedly out. Six minutes his speech would last. He had nine principal jokes and a few minor ones. He marched from one to another, halting briefly at each punch line before striding off once more. The audience tittered obediently, but without mirth. He sat down to polite but modest applause.

Zack leaned across to thank him, but his eyes were cold. Both brothers knew that this wedding was just another gambit in their three-year contest. One year to go and Zack had married money. All he had to do now was get it into his pocket. Zack's eyes boasted victory, while Matthew's flashed back his unbroken resolve. Even if Zack won, Matthew wanted to prove that it was he, and he alone, who could make the million the way their father intended, through his own solitary effort. Zack knew what Matthew was thinking and returned his gaze unflinchingly. Millimetres beneath the surface, hostility flickered.

The party dispersed into the gardens, while the marquee was cleared and refitted for the evening's dance. Lord Hatherleigh's helicopter sat ready on the lawn. George and Kiki spent as much time as they could together. Helen Gradley had got hold of some champagne and the alcohol had knocked her for six. Josephine let her snore peacefully in a deck chair and meanwhile began to enjoy herself. She liked Sarah, her sister Kate, and Zack's new parents-in-law. She also had a long and enjoyable chat with Arabella Queensferry, Zack's oldest friend, analysing his past and his future, his strengths and the weaknesses in exhaustive detail.

As often happens, the bride and groom saw relatively little of each other. There were five hundred guests, and each of them wanted to tell Sarah how beautiful her dress was or Zack how lucky he was. The happy couple circulated, repeating the same conversation five hundred times, but (at least in Sarah's case) enjoying it every time. The weather was fine, the mood was good and the bride glowed.

Matthew, however, was preoccupied. He had recently lost upwards of two hundred and ten thousand pounds and, for all his recent posturing, his prospects of making a million seemed remote. He wandered the happy scene alone, gloomily inspecting the guests.

Beneath a spreading chestnut tree to the side of the

main lawn, a crowd of Sarah's colleagues from Coburg's laughed and drank. A bunch of equity traders from the sound of it, with the inevitable shop talk. Matthew pulled out his phone and held it to his mouth.

'Do we have to do this now? I'm in the middle of my brother's wedding . . . Oh, OK, I see.' Matthew sauntered closer to the tree. He could hear the conversation of the Coburg's people loud and clear: office politics and drinking stories. He spoke a little louder.

'Someone's bidding for Albion? Seems unlikely . . . Oh, I see. Well, they've certainly got the money for it . . . Yeah, I can see that . . . Have they put a number on the table? How much? Jesus, that's going it some. After the fraud on top of everything . . .' The Coburg's people weren't talking as loudly now. Matthew ploughed on. 'Oh, I see . . . Yes, that does explain it . . . Who'd have thought Albion would find a white knight at this stage! What's our strategy?'

He got up from his bench and walked away, still talking. The Coburg's people watched him leave, then resumed their conversation. When he was out of earshot, Matthew put his phone away, back in his pocket. It hadn't been switched on.

The wedding ended as all things must. As darkness fell, and the wedding guests began to yawn and think about the journey home, Zack and Sarah dragged themselves away. They would spend the night in a five-star Buckinghamshire hotel, then fly to Tuscany for a fortnight's sun, swimming and sightseeing. And, yes, Zack had checked, and there was horse-riding available in the wooded hills nearby.

They made their way to the waiting helicopter. It was decorated with ribbons and a sign in the window read, 'Just married'. Sarah began to say goodbye to everyone important, until Zack stopped her. They'd be there another hour otherwise. They climbed on board and pulled the door shut.

Zack gave a sign to the pilot, who motioned the crowds to stand well back. Lord and Lady Hatherleigh stood with their arms around each other, watching. Josephine and Helen, George and Matthew were all there. All their other friends, relatives and well-wishers stood in a big circle spreading out into the darkness. The heavy blades began to turn. More waving. The blades swung faster, disappearing into their own movement. The waving reached fever pitch. Sarah blew kisses from the window, Zack's face darkly visible behind. Then, without appearing to move, the helicopter no longer rested on the ground. It rose steeply, banked and flew off into the night. On the ground, the wedding guests watched and waved, until the tail lights were swallowed by the billowing midnight stars.

5

Matthew came in to work on Monday. He was earlier than usual, but couldn't concentrate and Fiona and Ed teased him for his absent-mindedness. He bantered back, but his mind was elsewhere. When the bond markets opened, his hands turned to his keyboard. There was no price quoted for Albion's bonds. Time for coffee.

From the deserted garden, Matthew called Belial.

'I want a price to sell my Albion Leasing bonds. I'll hold while you get the information.'

Matthew held. Belial seemed to be gone for ever. Eventually, the familiar obsequious voice came back.

'Interesting news, my friend. The bonds are up to thirty pence in the pound. There's a rumour in the market that someone's foolish enough to make a bid. The equity desk at Coburg's seems to be behind the rumour and they've bumped up all their prices accordingly. Everyone else is following suit, because they assume Coburg's knows something they don't.'

'I want to sell everything.'

'Sell everything at thirty pence, my friend? Am I right in remembering you've only just bought them at forty?'

'Just sell them.'

'Very well, my dear chap. We're here to serve. Curious that your usual good fortune deserted you on this occasion. Or perhaps I should congratulate you that a market rumour is saving you from very much worse trouble.'

'Just sell them.'

'Consider it done.'

Belial sold the bonds. Matthew had lost twenty-five percent of his investment in just a few days. He had gone from being worth two hundred and eighty thousand to two hundred and ten thousand. He wasn't unhappy. He was ecstatic.

The game he played was high risk, but when his luck had turned, he'd salvaged something from the wreckage. That was something to be proud of, something to celebrate. Any fool can make money when times are good. It's holding on to your shirt in a hurricane which takes skill.

Albion Leasing heard the rumour floating around the market that day. The following morning it published a brief statement, saying that the company was not involved in any talks with potential bidders, nor did it expect to be, given the circumstances. The statement killed the rumour and the bond price slumped back to seven pence in the pound. The talk in the wine bars that week was that Coburg's had lost a million pounds backing the Albion rumour with its own money. If so, that was hardly Matthew's problem.

Back from honeymoon, a suntanned Zack stood at the walnut podium and looked out over his audience. There were only about twelve people physically present, including the ever-distinguished Dixon Banderman, but cameras and microphones beamed Zack's presentation to his real audience in Hong Kong, Singapore, Tokyo, Sydney, Seoul, Tai-pei and Manila. ROSES was a very, very sophisticated tax concept, but it wouldn't survive the more advanced tax codes of Western Europe or the US. ROSES was strictly for the Far East, where Zack's kind of tax avoidance is virtually unknown. Some Asian finance ministers were in for a shock.

'Welcome,' began Zack. 'I'd like to introduce you all to a new product which we are formally launching next week. It's called ROSES . . .'

He ran through his pitch while behind him a projector flashed up slides. The first slide was entitled 'ROSES – heads you win, tails the taxman loses'. The title was set over a background picture of pale pink roses sprawling over a pretty stone archway: the *Rosa* Sarah Havercoombe at the entrance to the Ovenden House rose garden. Zack was pleased with the touch. The slide combined two of his favourite ways of making money: ROSES and Sarah Havercoombe. All the slide needed was something to represent Hatherleigh Pacific, and the holy trinity would be complete.

'ROSES is a fairly complicated idea, and I'd encourage you to keep your clients focused on the central point: namely, you can use ROSES to bet on pretty much any financial market in the Far East. If you win, you win. The taxman doesn't claim any of your winnings. If you lose, though, you don't quite lose. The taxman comes to the rescue and makes up for your losses. He doesn't make up all your loss, of course. You're still taking a risk. But the odds have shifted in your favour. It's like playing roulette, where instead of the house taking a cut, the house is paying a subsidy and not a bad subsidy at that. The more you play at this table, the more you can expect to take home.

'We've made a complicated idea as simple as we possibly can. We've supplied a totally uniform set of contract documents, so every deal you do with your clients is standardised. If they want anything tailored to their own specific circumstances, then the answer's no. We're selling a mass-production car here, not a custom-built vehicle. We've also delivered a mountain of marketing material to every office in the Far East. Please use it. We've worked very hard to make it simple, understandable and compelling.'

Zack ran on. He explained the idea behind the tax dodge briefly and simply. He wasn't going to get into the real complexities, as it would put too many people off. After twenty minutes he was done. He used the remote controller to flick the projector on to his final slide. The photo of pale pink roses came up again, along with the ubiquitous slogan 'Heads you win – tails the taxman loses'. You can't repeat the key message too often: the golden rule of marketing.

'Any questions?'

The faces in front of him shook their heads. The people from London office had mostly been involved in developing ROSES into a saleable product, and they already knew the spiel. There were a couple of questions from Korea, where a faulty video link had played havoc with the transmission. Apart from that, the presentation appeared to have gone down well. Finally, as Zack was about to wind up, there was a question from an American salesman based out in Manila.

'Zack, I just want to be very clear about something here. Your ROSES idea is a sweet way of taking money from the taxman, but you can still lose your shirt with it, right? I mean if you bet heavily on the financial markets and those bets go sour, you lose, don't you? I know the taxman makes good part of the loss, but you still pay most of it? This isn't a licence to lose our heads and bet for the sake of it.'

'That's right,' said Zack, a bit less than thrilled to have the point made quite so graphically. 'If you bet wrong, you still lose. You just don't lose as much as you would have done otherwise.'

Then Dixon Banderman stood up and walked to the front of the room. He made sure that the videos and microphones were picking him up properly, then addressed the invisible audience.

'You put your finger on a very important point. We're all excited about ROSES and we want to make sure all you guys sell it hard. But remember, this firm is a hundred years old and some of our client relationships are a hundred years old too. We don't want to sell our clients anything which is bad for them, however much cash we make from it in the short term. If you see a client going barmy with this product, then stop selling it to him. There are responsible uses of derivatives and irresponsible uses. We don't want to be caught selling this stuff irresponsibly, however greedy our clients may wish to be. I hope that's crystal clear.'

Dixon Banderman gazed into the lens of the camera. With his piercing blue eyes and silver hair he was the picture of a responsible banker. The audience didn't reply, but it didn't need to. Rumour often identified Banderman as a future senior partner of Weinstein

Lukes worldwide. If you wanted to get on, you did what he said.

Next to him, Zack soberly nodded his approval. He didn't mean it, though. He couldn't give a damn if clients killed themselves with ROSES. The more they bought, the better his chances of making it to partner. The marketing packs were stuffed full of advice on how best to sell ROSES to clients for whom dodging tax was likely to be a novelty. There were diagrams, charts, graphs, examples. Every pack was covered with photos of the lovely pink rose sprawling over the stone archway and the heads-tails slogan was everywhere too. Everything was in full and beautiful Technicolor, with translations into every language you could think of. It was a monument to the art of the graphic designer and the advertising executive.

But in the whole mountain of marketing stuff, there wasn't a single word about responsible salesmanship. Not a word.

7

The Aspertons did what they had to do. They popped five thousand magazines into five thousand envelopes. They added a covering letter full of heavy-handed regrets for 'the damaging practices of some firms within the industry'. They listed the terrible things that Gissings had got up to and included the phone number of their own sales hotline. The super-low prices on the Asperton Brilliants and a couple of other furniture ranges were to be held for a few months longer, as a result of an exceptional response from their client base. The letter and the copy of *Furniture Today* went to every name on the Aspertons' nationwide database.

The knockout punch was felt by everyone at Gissings.

People stopped calling the sales department. Phone calls to clients weren't answered. Requests to call back were ignored. The shop floor went quiet as machines fell idle and workmen huddled over copied pages of the magazine, spelling out the murderous accusations. This would never have happened in old Tom Gissing's time.

8

A Weinstein Lukes salesman shifted from foot to foot. He was visiting the group treasurer of a Singaporean multi-national, one of his best clients. The treasurer hadn't yet arrived and the salesman was nervous. He gazed out of the window at the throng of shipping and the stacks of containers waiting to change ships, to move on east or west around the globe. The density of shipping was reminiscent of Hong Kong, but not the port or city around it. Hong Kong is busy, dirty, noisy, tatty; an Asian New York. Singapore is quiet, clean, efficient, authoritarian; an Asian Frankfurt. What the salesman had come to offer his client today was not very Singaporean, and he felt uncomfortable.

The deal he had come to pitch was a new gimmick invented by some tax whizz kid in London and christened ROSES, not a great name for Asian tongues. ROSES looked like an unbeatable way to take money from the government's pocket, but it was hardly the kind of thing to go down well in Singapore. In Singapore, companies and their government were close. The sort of things you could do in more dissolute countries like England or America would not be acceptable in this island state. Still, the big boys in London were pushing their precious ROSES hard and every salesman in Asia had to pitch it. The salesman hoped the meeting would be short and painless, and enable him to return to normal as soon as possible.

His client walked in. With him were three other gentlemen: the Chief Financial Officer, the Chief Counsel – the company's top lawyer – and the company President himself. The salesman bowed and nodded effusively. This was a bad sign. They would only have brought this much corporate fire power if they wanted to give him a really major rollocking. He'd blame everything on the London office and try to salvage what he could.

No tea or coffee was offered: another terrible sign. This was Asia, where politeness, even politeness to your enemy, is paramount. The company President took his seat and brusquely gestured everyone else to take theirs. He looked impatient. There were no how-are-yous, none of the normal greetings. This was the last time the salesman was ever going to pitch ROSES to any of his clients. Ever, ever.

The President spoke.

'So your bank is trying to sell us ROSES?'

The salesman bowed his head, a bow of assent, a bow of submission.

'We love your ROSES. We want to buy a whole garden full.'

The salesman's mouth dropped open. The President laughed at his joke and repeated it. 'We want to grow a garden of ROSES.'

The salesman laughed, a laugh of relief. The President laughed louder. The Chief Financial Officer laughed because the President was laughing, the Chief Counsel laughed because the Chief Financial Officer was laughing, and the Treasurer laughed because everyone else was. The room hooted with laughter.

Autumn 2000

The cultists were wrong. Eight months of the new millennium have come and gone without incident. The world has not expired. The apocalypse has not arrived. Armageddon has stayed at home.

It is 4 September, warm and summery in feel. Women still wear cotton dresses and eat ice-cream in the street, but cooler autumn weather will arrive any day now. Matthew is confident. Zack is expectant. George is without hope. There are 312 days to go.

1

The famous libel lawyer took his seat. He tweaked his jacket sleeves to make sure that just the right amount of cuff was exposed: a glimmer of white, a twinkle of silver cuff links but no more. He cleared his throat unnecessarily, but loudly, until everyone else in the room was silent. Harry Cunningham, London's most famous libel solicitor, was satisfied.

He was a big man. Tall and broad, white-haired already at fifty, he dominated almost anywhere. Right here, right now, he hadn't much competition. He took the business card given him by the man opposite. Cunningham didn't offer one of his own. He scowled as he looked at the card.

'Addison, Steele, de Coverley,' he read. 'I don't recall hearing the name before. Have you been long established?'

'About thirty-five years,' said Dick Steele, the likeable Yorkshire lawyer who had handled the Asperton account for the last fifteen years.

'Oh, I see,' said Cunningham. 'A newish outfit, then. Do you handle a lot of libel business?'

Steele was uncomfortable. Addison, Steele, de Coverley was a decent firm with a good reputation in the county. But the work they did was generally mundane stuff, and the last breath of a libel case they'd had was eight years ago, which had folded long before it came to court.

'A little bit,' said Steele. 'Less than you, of course.'

Cunningham ignored the last part. 'A little bit?' he repeated. 'I'm not sure I remember reading about any of your cases. Curious. I usually have a good head for these things.'

'None of our cases has got as far as court,' admitted Steele.

'Ah!' said Cunningham. 'You've kept your cases away from the court. Quite right! They say a good libel lawyer is one who avoids the courtroom. You've got a good lawyer there, Mr Asperton, Mrs Asperton.' He winked in turn at the two Aspertons and laughed his famous booming laugh. 'I'm afraid my own track record isn't so good. My clients have been in court rather too much recently. Ha, ha! Still, they usually win when they get there. Ha, ha, ha! That's the important thing, isn't it?'

Cunningham had been in the press quite a lot that

433

year. He had represented a pop star, an oil magnate and a TV actress. He had won all three cases and won very substantial awards. He was expensive and worth it.

'Now, let's turn to business, shall we?' said Cunningham. He and George were sitting in the Asperton company boardroom across the table from Mike and Eileen Asperton and their lawyer, Dick Steele. Business etiquette would normally dictate that one or other of the Aspertons chaired the meeting, but Cunningham wasn't one for etiquette. First, he asked Eileen Asperton to pour him some coffee. Next, he asked Mike Asperton to put his cigar out or smoke outside. Then, ignoring Mike Asperton's spluttering protests and his wife's silent fury, he continued.

'As you know, we've come about an article which appeared in a journal called *Furniture Today*.' Cunningham took out some wire-rimmed glasses and perched them precariously on his massive face. He took George's copy of the magazine and studied it as though for the first time. '"Rip-Off." Hmm. That's on the cover, I see. Story on page fourteen.' He leafed through the pages. 'Page fourteen. Here we are. "Gissings cons customers . . . Systematic fraud . . . campaign of deception . . ." Strong stuff, eh? The magazine tells us you've endorsed this story. You must be very sure of your ground.'

'We are sure of ourselves, thank you,' said Mike Asperton, thumping a file in front of him. 'We've got letters. We've got contracts. We've got invoices. We've got sworn evidence. You name it, we've got it. The story's true and I'm proud that we've revealed it.'

Dick Steele and Eileen Asperton glared at her husband. The first rule of dealing with lawyers is to say nothing, except via your own lawyer. It's an expensive

434

form of communication. You can talk to your friends in Australia for less. If you had friends on Mars, you could talk to them more cheaply. But you do tend to stay out of trouble.

'Good,' said Cunningham. 'Excellent. That's what I like to hear. Ha! If I'm on the defendant's side, I mean. Ha, ha! Good written evidence. Just the stuff. Now, for instance, I expect you'll have evidence linking Gissings with this supplier of lead-based paints. Eh? That would be a fine start in your defence.'

Before Dick Steele could intervene, a yellow invoice slip floated across the table to Cunningham. Mike Asperton, who had dug it out of his file and thrown it across, looked triumphant. Cunningham took it, and inspected it carefully.

'Tremendous. Thank you.' He beamed at Mike Asperton, who beamed back. 'Here we have it. An invoice for so many litres of paint, in such-and-such colours. Specification attached. That'll be all the poisons they have to add, I suppose. Ha, ha! Lead paints never did me any harm. Can't be as bad as they say, what? Ha, ha, ha! Amount owing. Payment details. Blah, blah.' His index finger traced across the sheet as he spoke, then came to rest in the bottom left-hand corner. He tapped it twice. 'And here we are. A phone number for the good old Czech manufacturer, Praha Fabriky Zdenikova. That's quite a mouthful. The name, I mean, not the paint. Let's try it, shall we?'

He reached across to the phone which stood on the desk. It had a speaker attachment, allowing everybody in the room to hear the call. Cunningham dialled the number. The phone rang a few times, then a woman's voice answered in Czech.

'Good morning,' boomed Cunningham. 'My name's Harry Cunningham and I'd like to buy some paint, please.' Then in a quieter voice he added for the benefit of the listeners in the room only, 'Lots of lead in it please. Eh? Ha, ha!'

The woman on the other end said something in Czech, then tried again. Then she gave up, and said in German, 'Warten, bitte.'

Cunningham wiggled his eyebrows at the room and waited as he had been asked. Presently, a young man's voice answered the phone again, speaking reasonable English.

'Good morning. May I help you, please?'

'Yes, indeed. My name's Harry Cunningham of the well-known English furniture company, Cunningham Furniture.' He winked at his listeners. 'I'd like to buy some paint, please.'

'Yes, unfortunately we do not have an export business with England. Only with Germany and Austria at the moment. Maybe next year.' The voice at the other end was firm.

'Well, perhaps we could work out a special arrangement. I have a very specific requirement for some lead-based paints. I'd like to place quite a substantial order and I'd pay a bit extra for delivery.'

The voice at the other end became very precise and emphatic.

'You must be aware, I think, that the use of lead in paints is prohibited by European regulations. In the Czech Republic now, we are meeting the Euro standards for many years already. It is not possible for us to supply any other type of paint. If you have a requirement for our other range of paints, we might be able to quote if your order was substantial.'

'No. I definitely want a lead-based paint,' pursued Cunningham. 'I know you produce it, because one of my friends here placed a large order with you. Gissings

Furniture. I have an invoice from you dated November 1999.'

'That is not possible,' said the voice. 'We do not have an export business with England. We have not heard of any Gissing company. We do not produce or supply lead-based paints.'

'And who am I speaking to, please?'

'My name is engineer Jaroslav Svejk. I am export director.'

Cunningham thanked him and hung up. He looked at Mike Asperton in astonishment.

'Eh? That's a bit of a blow, isn't it? Perhaps you checked with somebody else? Did you speak to the managing director? These Eastern bloc firms, you never know quite what's going on.'

Mike Asperton was ashen-faced and took another cigar from his pocket. Cunningham raised his shaggy eyebrows and glowered at the company director. Mike Asperton put his cigar away. Even the more controlled Eileen Asperton was visibly upset. Dick Steele watched his case sliding away from him. Damage limitation would be the order of the day.

Cunningham read the faces over the table.

'What? You didn't speak with anyone else there? But how could poor old George here' – he thumped George sympathetically – 'have covered his furniture in these terrible paints, if the dear old Czechs won't sell them to him. Eh? You can't go round saying these things if they're not true.'

'We've conducted a thorough chemical analysis of his furniture. It does have lead on it.' Mike Asperton was sulky.

'Ah! Now that's better. Good old chemistry, eh? Never did get far with my chemistry set as a nipper. When I ran out of smells and bangs, that was that, eh? Ha, ha!

Where did this deadly table come from then? You can prove it came from Gissings, can't you?'

Nobody answered. Darren had produced a suite of furniture which was certainly identical with the Gissings range. The analysis of the paint had been definitive, but where he had got it from nobody exactly knew. But that wasn't the worst of it.

The worst of it was that Darren had disappeared that morning. He hadn't come in to work as usual. He had gone from his bedsit in town. He had left no contact address, no message, nothing. The mainstay of the Asperton case had vanished as miraculously as it had appeared.

Cunningham looked at the faces ranged opposite him. He didn't need to labour this point any further.

'Let's leave the paints. Let's have a think about this timber, instead.' Cunningham twisted his wire spectacles back on to his face and peered again at the article. '"In reality, the wood is reject material from a Scottish sawmill",' he quoted. '"Warping and distortion is almost inevitable". Eh, George? What d'you have to say to that? Had many complaints?'

'No,' said George, speaking for almost the first time since entering the room. 'We've never had a single complaint.'

'Do you know of any complaints?' Cunningham asked the Aspertons.

Their blank faces told him the answer. Dick Steele opened his mouth to speak, but Cunningham interrupted him with his booming laugh.

'Ha, ha! I can see what you're about to tell me. No complaints proves nothing. Maybe they're all about to pour in. Maybe people don't bother to mention it when their furniture falls apart. Quite right. Quite right. Keeping me on my toes, eh? Alright, maybe we should

438

have a look at your documentary evidence. I see you have a great stack of it there.'

Cunningham nodded at Mike Asperton's thick folder, but this time Steele managed to restrain his client.

'I think we should reserve our evidence at this point,' he said.

'Quite right, of course. Best policy. But maybe your evidence includes the following document,' and Cunningham tossed a piece of paper across the table to Mike Asperton.

Asperton looked at the paper. He said nothing, but he didn't really have to. His face could be read as easily as a pre-schooler's picture book. His face said: 'Yes. The piece of paper you have just handed us is one of our key bits of evidence. And something tells me you are about to demolish it.' Cunningham smiled. He enjoyed this kind of meeting. It was a relaxing change from his normal arduous cases and just as well paid. He'd take his time.

'Now what I've just given you,' said Cunningham, 'is an invoice from the Strathclyde Sawmill Limited. The invoice contains details of a shipment of goods, which is described as untreated timber, with "quality as found". I understand that means the timber is pretty much rubbish and the sawmill is disclaiming any responsibility for it. Am I right?'

George nodded. The invoice had come from the Gissings company files. It was legitimate in every way.

'So, George, you plead guilty to buying the lowest grade of timber possible from this sawmill?'

George nodded again. Cunningham flashed a brilliant smile at the Aspertons, as though to encourage them.

'And, George, can you tell me your reason for buying this timber?'

'Yes,' said George. 'When we build prototypes of our new designs we make them out of the very cheapest materials available. This invoice relates to timber for our prototypes.'

'Have you received any other invoices for this kind of timber?'

'No. When we buy in stock, we buy enough to last ourselves two years or so. It's cheaper to buy it that way. This is the first and only time we've used the Strathclyde Sawmill.'

'So any additional evidence that you've been buying more low-grade timber from this sawmill would be very bad indeed for your case. Any evidence such as this, for instance.'

Cunningham tossed another piece of paper across the table. Mike Asperton read it and passed it to his wife. She read it and passed it to Dick Steele. Steele just glanced at it and listened to Cunningham. The piece of paper was a letter written on the Strathclyde Sawmill Limited writing paper. It read as follows:

Dear Mr Gradley,

We are delighted that you have agreed to purchase further timber supplies from us. We have never had such a large order for our reject timber and we look forward to doing business with you for many years into the future. We would stress, however, that on no account can we give any guarantees as to quality of material and that additional prices would be charged should you want the timber treated with preservative.

Yours sincerely,
Hamish Campbell,
Managing Director

The Aspertons waited, puzzled and nervous. They didn't actually have a copy of this letter, though they did have something fairly similar in the pile of documents Darren had given them. But somehow, nobody believed that Cunningham was giving away a prime bit of evidence for free. Cunningham smiled.

'I've got another letter from the company that you might enjoy.'

He tossed another letter across the table. This one read as follows:

Dear Mr and Mrs Asperton,

As agreed we are sending you a whole lot of appalling rubbish for you to use in ripping off your customers. We guarantee that the timber will buckle and warp within hours.

Yours sincerely,
Hamish Campbell,
Managing Director

Cunningham smiled again. The faces on the other side of the table were grey as ash.

'Spot the deliberate mistake. Eh? Eh? Ha, ha, ha! The letter's nonsense, of course. Wrote it myself. Ha, ha! I just took a letter they sent to George here. Any letter, doesn't matter which. I cover up the text, so all I have is the letterhead. Then I run it through the photocopier as often as I want. Lo and behold, I have some blank writing paper.

'Next, I write myself a letter. I wrote both of these letters. I could have written anything I wanted. I added a signature just by photocopying the signature and sticking it on. I pass the whole thing through the photocopier again, and bingo. Any letter I want. You can tell that it's a copy of course, because you can't see the pressure of the pen on the signature. But let me guess. I guess you have a copy of the letter in your file, not an original. Am I right? Eh? Ha, ha!'

Cunningham drenched the room in his laughter once again. It wasn't just victory he wanted. He wanted unconditional surrender. His brief from George wasn't just to win the argument. It was to pulverise the opposition. Harry Cunningham was enjoying himself.

'Now let's turn to the remaining items, shall we? Knobs and handles, eh? Dodgy tax returns, eh? Perhaps we should interview your ex-Gissings employee? But Mr Asperton, you're looking ill. Do you need some water? Eh? Or a good smoke? Maybe you'd like to step out and get some fresh air?'

It was true Mike Asperton was looking ill, and his wife wasn't exactly blooming. Dick Steele called a halt.

'I think perhaps it would be useful if I had some time alone with my clients,' he said.

'Quite right. No one like a lawyer to help with a giddy spell. Now I notice that there's a fine church in town. Norman font. Stained glass. Well worth a visit, I'm sure. George here doesn't get out as much as he should. Too busy working. I'll take George to have a look at the jolly old font and take a turn about the churchyard. I usually manage to find a gravestone that's good for a chuckle. Eh? We'll be back in an hour.'

So Harry Cunningham and George walked into town and spent an hour wandering around the churchyard. They didn't spend much time discussing the stained glass. They did spend a bit of time talking about what they hoped to get from the Aspertons, but they had already prepared their list of demands and didn't have much to add. Cunningham insisted on slashing away with a stick at the long grass around the tombstones, but he didn't find an inscription to satisfy his sense of humour. After an hour they walked back.

442

Mike Asperton was still looking ill, although calmer. Eileen Asperton was sombre. Dick Steele opened the discussion.

'This morning's review of the evidence has been most helpful,' he said smoothly. 'My clients have considered the new facts you've brought to light and are prepared to concede that an honest mistake may have been made. We'd like to discuss ways in which we can help resolve any difficulties the article may have caused.'

Cunningham grew serious. He stood up, and allowed his massive frame to fill the room.

'No. That's not enough. Your clients, Mr Steele, attempted to destroy my client's business with malicious falsehoods. I don't care whether they made them up or whether they just wanted to believe what an ex-employee with a grudge chose to tell them. Either way that's not an honest mistake. It's an irresponsible attempt to ruin a decent and properly run company. George Gradley's property was at stake. The livelihoods of dozens of people were at stake. The law does not permit that kind of behaviour and it is right that it should be punished.'

Cunningham strode around the room. He was now standing behind the Aspertons, who cowered like naughty schoolchildren.

'The first thing that we require is an outright apology. Now.'

The Aspertons glanced meekly across at Dick Steele, who nodded them permission. Mike Asperton cleared his throat.

'Sorry,' he said, looking at George. Eileen Asperton's lips agreed soundlessly.

'A proper apology,' boomed Harry Cunningham, towering above them.

'I am – we are – deeply sorry for this article. We made

an awful mistake. It's all the fault of that wicked young man Darren. We apologise,' said Mike Asperton.

'Whose fault is it?' thundered Cunningham. 'Whose fault?'

'Our fault. Sorry. It was our fault. We should never have believed him.'

Mike Asperton hunkered down like a schoolboy before a spanking. Cunningham caught George's eye and winked broadly.

'That's better,' he said. 'The next thing that we need is immediate damage limitation and some assurances as to future conduct.'

Cunningham drove on. He and George had rehearsed the list of demands and Cunningham had insisted on George making it as full as possible. Cunningham was determined to secure every item on it. The rest of the conversation lasted five hours. Dick Steele attempted to negotiate each point, but the threat of court action overwhelmed him each time. If this case ever came to court, there's no telling how a jury would react. But damages could be monumental and the legal costs horrific.

By the time George and Harry Cunningham left the Aspertons they had everything they wanted. A visit to *Furniture Today* the following day would secure everything else.

The Aspertons had agreed to write to every single one of their customers, retracting in full the statements made in the magazine article. They would immediately withdraw their Asperton Brilliants from the market and all other furniture ranges which overlapped with Gissings products. They would hand over all of their existing orders to Gissings. They would undertake not to compete against George in these areas for a ten-year period. They would use their marketing network to sell Gissings products alongside their other products for the next two years. There would be Gissings staff seconded to Asperton Holdings to ensure that the deal was complied with to the letter. They would agree to pay in full any costs or shortfall in sales that Gissings might encounter as a result of the magazine article. There were a few other points of detail that George didn't care too much about, but Cunningham did.

As they left the building, Cunningham clapped George on the back.

'Well done. We'll get a full retraction from the magazine tomorrow plus a few years' free advertising. Like anything else?'

George shook his head. He was happy. Gissings was safe. He was looking forward to seeing Darren again and congratulating him on his performance.

'Well, then. Game, set and match to us, eh?' said Cunningham.

George nodded. 'Yes. Game, set and match.'

2

In time it had come to seem unnecessarily arbitrary that programming lessons should always take place in the living room and sex always in the bedroom. They had experimented with sex in the living room, but a floor is never satisfactory for long, and so they moved back to the bedroom taking the computer with them. They lay at the wrong end of the bed where there was no headboard, with the computer on a low table immediately in front of them. They could make love and write program code all without changing position.

Josephine's homework that week had been to write a program which moved a knight around a chessboard, respecting the edges of the board and the placements of existing pieces. She inserted the disk and called up her homework. 'Run, little knight,' she said, and the symbolic knight on screen began to hop around as commanded.

Kodaly watched for a few moments, checking her work. It was fine.

'It's very good,' he said. 'I have people in my department who would make a mess up of that.'

'I must be a genius,' said Josie.

'You must have very good teacher, I think.'

The computer knight continued to hop, as the computer-in-the-bedroom concept gave a further proof of its merits. After a while they rolled over on to their bellies again and Kodaly reached for the keyboard to give the knight a rest.

'Homework next week must be harder. Maybe plant a virus in the White House. Or tell Pentagon to invade Canada.'

'You always talk big, Miklos, but I've never seen you do anything like that.'

'*Igen*. Now I am on side of enemy.'

'You're not at work now and you don't work for the Pentagon.'

'Pentagon is too difficult. I can't get into Pentagon.'

'Typical man,' said Josie. 'All mouth.'

'No, not all mouth. Just not Pentagon. Department of Immigration, maybe? Internal Revenue Service?'

'You can get into the American IRS?'

'*Igen*. Maybe. Don't know. I haven't tried for long time. But first wine.'

'And nibbles,' called Josie to her man's retreating bottom. 'I'm starving.'

'Food. Wine. Then hacking.'

They didn't get into the IRS that night, nor did they the week after that. But Kodaly's blood was up, and on the third week he marched Josie straight into the bedroom and, before she had even removed her clothes, his hands had typed the sequence that gave entry to the IRS system.

'IRS system for you, beautiful lady.'

'How long did it take you to crack that one, Miklos?'

Kodaly said nothing, but his grey skin was greyer than usual and his eyes wearier. A tab in the bottom left-hand corner of the screen was labelled 'Security level: One'.

'Is security level one the highest or the lowest?'

'Is lowest,' said Miklos. 'But hardest thing is always getting in at all.'

'Typical man. Mouth, mouth, mouth,' said Josie. But she was laughing as she slipped naked beside him into bed.

3

'Coffees?'

'Yes, please.'

'Please, yes.'

It was a formality now, the question and answers. When they decided to place a bet, Matthew went out for coffees. It was a ritual, like wolves licking before the hunt. This time the hunt concerned a duff transport company, EuroRoad Haulage and its unhappy banks.

On with his coat. It was late September and the weather offered a preview of the London winter: wet, drab, windy, chilly. Down the lift, out on to the street. Up the road to the coffee shop. Then, a few yards before the mouth of the alley, stop and look around. No one? OK. Proceed. Turn into the alley. Go up into the garden. Sit under the tree. Phone. Wait until the odious little man answers. Don't mind him, just do what you need to do. You have two hundred and forty thousand pounds in your account. You've quadrupled your money since starting this game: three big wins, numerous smaller gains, one bad loss. You've only got to quadruple it all again, and your million's in the bag. After that, you never need to talk to the obnoxious little creep again.

'Good morning. James Belial speaking. How may I be of service?'

'Matthew Gradley here. I'd like to buy some bonds.'

'Matthew, my dear fellow. What a pleasure to hear from you.'

Matthew could almost see the ugly little man sitting up straighter in his chair and smirking down the telephone. Matthew quickly described what he wished to do. From past experience, Matthew reckoned that this deal should be a five percenter. Maybe less. Only when Madison did something really dramatic could he expect more.

Belial, as ever, was crystal clear about his instructions and he relayed them back to Matthew virtually word perfect. Belial and the rest of the crew at Switzerland International were good at their jobs. Matthew was always impressed by their trading skill, finding low prices to buy at and high ones to sell at. On a deal like the one today, that kind of skill probably translated into a two percent advantage, which may not sound a lot, but if your objective is only to make five, then you're already nearly half-way there. If Belial weren't obnoxious and Matthew weren't a crook, this would be a beautiful partnership.

This time, however, Belial didn't get off the phone right away.

'May I make a suggestion, my dear friend? It's a little impudent of me, in view of your remarkable eye for a winner, but I fancy there may be a way for you to increase your winnings even further.'

'Yes?'

'Well, in the past, you've always purchased the bonds of the companies you're interested in. Your returns have been good, but they've seldom been more than a few percent. The trouble is that bonds aren't really volatile enough. They don't go up and down in price all that much. If you want real action, you need to buy equities – in short, you need the stockmarket, my friend.'

'Well, I'm not sure . . .' said Matthew uncertainly. The thought had occurred to him a number of times, but he knew the bond market and was comfortable with it. Bond trading was his living, after all, while shares were unknown territory.

'Consider this, my dear fellow. Your first trade through us was with Cobra Electronics. You made seventy-two percent on the bonds more or less overnight. That's by far your best deal to date. But if you had bought shares instead, you'd have quadrupled your money with a single trade. In eighty percent of your other deals, the shares have moved by more than the bonds. I calculate that your portfolio could now be worth close to one million pounds if you had consistently invested in shares instead of bonds.'

'One million pounds . . .'

'That's right. And I confess I'm a little surprised that someone as gifted as you should overlook the opportunity.'

Matthew hesitated, but his greed was greater than his fear of the unknown. It's true. Bond prices don't move around nearly as much as share prices. You make more money with shares, but you need stronger nerves. Matthew hadn't done the calculations Belial was talking about, but he guessed that Belial's answer was pretty much right. In the end, there could be only one answer.

'OK,' he whispered. 'I'd like to buy shares. Invest everything in EuroRoad Haulage shares.'

'Excellent,' said Belial happily. 'The shares are trading at about three pence each. We'll see what we can pick up.'

'Thanks. I'll call back.'

4

One thing about buying companies is different from buying cars. If you want to buy a car, you're not allowed to go up to anything you like the look of, haul the driver out by his collar, stuff a wad of banknotes into his pocket, and drive off. You can certainly try it, but you'll soon be wearing stripy pyjamas and regretting your new-found social life.

But that's cars. In business, not only are you allowed to behave like this, the chances are you'll be revered for doing so. It's as though, instead of negotiating with the driver, you negotiate directly with the finance company which finances the vehicle. If you persuade the finance company to accept your bid, then the car is yours and the driver is left stunned in the street.

In business, the finance company is the stockmarket, and to appeal directly to it, over the heads of the company management, you make a hostile bid. The bid says, in effect, 'These useless drongos who manage your company are making a hash of things and you poor shareholders are suffering. We, on the other hand, are offering you thirty percent (or forty or fifty) more than the current market price for your shares. If you say yes, we'll write you out a fat little cheque, sling out the existing management and the company will be ours. If you say no, we'll go home, and you can spend the next few years repenting your decision.'

Unsurprisingly, a lot of hostile bids are successful. And, unsurprisingly, the management of the company being bid for tends to be a lot less than thrilled with the whole idea.

After an agonising year for Zack, watching the South China share price rise and dip and rise again, the thing that Lord Hatherleigh and Scottie had predicted came to pass. The South China Trust Bank shipping side sailed into trouble and was eventually forced to reveal its woes to the stockmarket. The market, which thought little enough of the stuffy old bank as it was, punished it by knocking its share price down from forty-four dollars to thirty-nine.

Hatherleigh had always said that forty dollars was the magic threshold, and, the same afternoon that the price sank below forty bucks, he called an extraordinary meeting of the Board. The subject matter was not to be disclosed until the day of the meeting.

At nine in the morning, Lord Hatherleigh and Scottie presented their plan. Their argument was simple. If Hatherleigh Pacific was to go on growing, it needed more scale. South China provided that scale in one simple step. The bid would cost one thousand three hundred and fifty million US dollars, of which they proposed to borrow every penny. What was more, to get the numbers to add up, they were going to employ a tax scam on a scale never before seen in Hong Kong. The plan was breathtaking in its audacity, monumental in its ambition.

Zack sat in a room with his Hong Kong colleague, Phyllis Wang. They were eight yards away from the boardroom and they had no idea what was going on. Zack had drunk four cups of coffee, Phyllis two. They had both called the office and dealt with their voice-mails. They had chatted about the weather, the bank, and Hong Kong, but neither of them wanted to chat and the conversation lapsed. It was now one o'clock.

It should have been a slam-dunk. Lord Hatherleigh and Scottie were enthusiastic supporters of the plan. Hatherleigh controlled thirty percent of the company and Scottie another one or two. In most such companies, the Board is a rubber stamp whose role is to con smaller shareholders into believing that their interests are being looked after. Not so Hatherleigh Pacific.

Lord Hatherleigh got some of the toughest and most independent-minded businessmen in Hong Kong to sit on his Board. He made sure they owned a big enough chunk of the company to care about the share price. Then, when he called on them to debate something, they usually did. Just before going into the meeting, Hatherleigh had cornered Zack.

'You'd better wish me luck, young man. I've no idea how the buggers will vote.'

'Good luck, Jack. Tell 'em that if they say no to South China, you'll be forced to go after the Hong Kong and Shanghai instead.'

Hatherleigh grinned. The Hong Kong and Shanghai Bank was worth a little over seventy-five billion dollars. Not even Zack's tax dodging would be able to come up with that kind of money.

'Hey, why didn't you suggest that sooner? We don't want to play in the minor leagues all our life.'

That was four hours ago. Since then, a secretary had come in once to ask for a document which Zack had in his briefcase. Somebody else had come in to put a fresh pot of coffee on the table in place of the old one. Apart from that, nothing. The Board might at this moment be finalising the price at which to launch the bid, or it might be thumping the final nail into the coffin of an overambitious idea. There was no way of telling.

The boardroom had a glorious view over Hong Kong

harbour, but the room Zack sat in had no windows, just a couple of tedious little prints of Hong Kong in the 1920s. Zack thought about pouring himself another coffee, but decided against. He picked up the *Asian Wall Street Journal* again, then tossed it down. What did he care about Tokyo steel stocks?

At half past one, a secretary knocked on the door and asked if Zack or Phyllis could get the current stock price of South China. Zack and Phyllis leaped into action, pleased to have something to do. The stock was thirty-eight and a half dollars, down half a dollar since the evening before. The secretary left again with the information. Zack caved in and had another coffee.

A quarter of an hour later, someone brought a tray of sandwiches, and Zack and Phyllis tucked in out of boredom. Phyllis called her office again. She was lucky. Her office was open. Zack had to wait hours before his would leap into life. He drifted over to the coffee pot and poured himself his sixth cup of coffee. At two thirty he called Sarah, six thirty in the morning London time.

'Hello?' Sarah had been asleep and her voice was bleary.

'Hello, darling. It's me. I thought I'd be your alarm clock this morning.'

'Oh, Zack. Hi, darling. How's your big deal?'

Sarah knew Zack was in Hong Kong working on something big, but she didn't know what. Absolute secrecy was the rule and neither Hatherleigh nor Zack had mentioned anything of what was afoot.

'I don't know. All the action's taking place without me. How are you, sweetheart?'

'Missing you, my love. This bed seems awfully lonely with just little old me in it, lying here in just the teeniest scrap of a nightie.'

Zack heard Sarah moving in the bed. He could imagine her stretching out towards him, her smell, her sleepy kisses. This was a time of morning when they often made love. Zack knew that when he wasn't there she preferred wearing thick flannel nighties from M & S, not the little satiny slips she wore for him. But he didn't allow reality to get in the way. He moved as far away from Phyllis as he could in the tiny room and talked low and quiet to his wife.

Too soon, their conversation ended and Zack was at a loose end once more. The day wore on. Zack called his office as soon as it was open and spent half an hour on the phone. ROSES was selling like cold fizz in a heatwave. Just keeping on top of the flow was a full-time job in itself. Zack did what he could by phone, but he needed to be in the office really. God knows how he was going to manage the Hatherleigh Pacific deal as well, but he needed both. He guessed he needed seventy million dollars for his partnership, and if Hatherleigh Pacific was bringing in forty, then ROSES had to manage the remaining thirty. Zack got off the phone and drummed his fingers.

Three o'clock came and went. Zack picked up the *Asian Wall Street Journal* again and this time read every word about the progress of Japanese steel stocks. He tried to do the crossword, but he wasn't good at them and he didn't like things he wasn't good at.

He called Josephine.

'Hello, Transfers and Settlements Department,' she said.

'Hello, Transfers and Settlements. It's your big brother.'

'Hey, Zack. So you're still alive. I'd been wondering.'

'Well, don't sound too pleased. I might get the wrong idea.'

'I am pleased actually. And I was really touched to get the invitation as well. We'll definitely come.'

'Eh? Come where?'

'To Ovenden House. For Christmas. I got a letter

454

from Lady Hatherleigh this morning. I assumed you had suggested the idea or at least approved of it.'

'Well I do. It's a great idea.'

'You knew nothing about this, did you?'

'No, but I'm delighted. Will you be able to find someone to look after Mum?'

'What d'you mean, "look after Mum"? I'll look after her. You can bloody well look after her.'

'You mean –' Zack broke off, but too late.

'Christ, Zack. You weren't thinking of leaving her in a home for Christmas, were you? It's a good job Lady Hatherleigh didn't consult you, or we'd never have got the invitation, would we? I'm going to reply right away and invite ourselves down there for the whole bloody week. I'll leave Mum's incontinence knickers at home and I'll spend every minute moaning to your wealthy in-laws about how you don't contribute a penny to looking after her.'

Josie slammed the phone down, leaving Zack to feel vaguely nauseous. Christ! Was it any wonder he didn't spend more time with Josie, when this was how she behaved? Something had better change or he'd have to find an excuse to work right through the Christmas week.

Four o'clock came, more sandwiches and a pot of tea. Zack switched from coffee to tea and chatted more with Phyllis. Still the Board was in the boardroom and not a word came out.

Five o'clock passed. From the boardroom, you'd be able to see the western sun bouncing off the channel, light glinting from the skyscrapers opposite. Hong Kong was part of red China now. If this was what it felt like to live in a one-party police state, it didn't seem so bad. What the hell was happening in there?

At ten to six, the door opened. Lord Hatherleigh strode

in, Scottie not far behind, and behind him, Zhao the finance director. All of them were smiling.

'We've got unanimous approval. The deal's on.'

5

Madison had moved in on EuroRoad Haulage. Once again, there was no dramatic putsch planned. It was just a case of intensive research convincing Fiona, Deane and Matthew that there was an undervalued company out there, whose loans were worth more than the market judged. Madison bought heavily.

As usual, the scale of Madison's purchases made a big difference to a thin market. The market price of the bank debt rose by about five percent. The market price of the bonds rose by about four percent. The company's share price rose from three pence to three and a half pence. That half a penny rise doesn't sound like much, but it's one sixth of the original share price. Seventeen percent, as near as dammit. After Matthew's costs buying and selling, the seventeen percent became a more modest twelve, but still he was ecstatic. He'd got treble the return he'd have got on bonds. He would make his million more quickly in shares and he'd make it more safely too. Better returns meant fewer trades. Fewer trades meant fewer opportunities to get caught.

There was only one fly squirming around in the ointment.

When Matthew had stumbled out of the little alley-way, fresh with the pleasure of his success, who should he have stumbled into but Brian McAllister?

'Bit early for a pint, isn't it?' asked the Scot, nodding up the alley in the direction of the pub.

He'd meant nothing by it. It's just the sort of thing you say when you bump into someone in the street. But

Matthew floundered. He groped for words. He waved his hand around – his hand that still held his portable phone. He opened and closed his mouth.

'Been waiting for a friend,' he said, at last.

It wasn't such a stupid thing to say, but his way of saying it couldn't get much stupider. McAllister nodded slowly, as though Matthew had just unveiled a great mystery, then smiled and walked on.

Nobody, but nobody, played a better game of read-my-soul than Brian McAllister, master of the trading floor. What had he seen? What had he seen, as he looked so piercingly into Matthew's stuttering, awkward, guilty face?

6

The price of South China Trust Bank shares had nudged down to thirty-six dollars. Over the week it had come down a full two dollars fifty, another six and a half percent fall. That was good news for Zack, Scottie and Phyllis, huddled round their coffees in the uneasy dawn. It was five thirty in the morning and once again they were gathered in the Hong Kong offices of Hatherleigh Pacific. Lord Hatherleigh was in England, but insisted that they call him at any time of day or night to let him know their decision.

'Why d'you think the price has come down so far? This is more than just the bad news on the shipping side,' said Scottie.

They'd been through this many times, but some people get nervous before spending 1.35 billion US dollars.

'We don't know exactly. Probably no one does. What's clear, though, is that banking stocks as a whole are down three or four percent. South China is worse hit because it's a worse bank.' It was Phyllis Wang speaking. She was the Madison expert on the Hong Kong market and she spoke with authority. 'But we're not aware of anything which should cause you to hesitate at this stage.'

Fingered by the grey light of dawn, Scottie's ruddy face glowed a dull pink.

'Only our company's future,' he whispered.

Zack and Phyllis smiled. What Scottie said was true. Bankers flit from deal to deal like birds in the wood. The company executives who actually do the deals have to live with them, the successes and failures, for years. A bad deal can set a company back five years or more. A good one can skyrocket it to a level of success impossible by any other means. And Scottie was justifiably nervous. South China was nearly as big as Hatherleigh Pacific itself. Not only did Hatherleigh aim to swallow something its own size, it wanted to do it all with borrowed money. By any standards, that was hugely risky. And despite all their homework, there was always the risk of something they didn't know.

Zack and Phyllis waited calmly. There was only one decision Scottie could come to. He was welcome to take his time.

'There's no chance that the stock price falls further? If it does, we'd pick up the company cheaper.'

'Of course it may fall some more,' answered Phyllis. 'Equally it could rise. We can't predict that. But you have your borrowing facilities in place. You have a company you like, at a price which is excellent. You know of no reason for delay. This is as good as it gets.'

'You'd better be right, guys.'

Scottie owned about one and a half percent of Hatherleigh Pacific. He would be responsible for seeing the deal through, for shaking up South China and turning it into a money machine. If he succeeded, he stood to double his fortune and consolidate his reputation as one of the most daring and effective businessmen in

458

all Hong Kong. And if he failed – well, failure was not to be contemplated. Across the harbour, a molten sun lifted above the grey rim of encircling sea and glimmered lividly beneath the cloud. Scottie glanced at it, and shook himself.

'You guys think we should bid forty-five dollars?'

'That's right. You need to pay something over the existing share price, otherwise no one will be interested. You could try to low-ball it, but the chances are you'd need to raise your price later on. We reckon that at forty-five dollars you stand a chance of taking the company out in a single punch.'

Scottie pondered. The sun struck a thousand orange flames from the skyscrapers opposite. It looked like an advert for hell: 'Come to hell – it's flamin' pretty'.

'OK. Let's go for it. Forty-five dollars it is.'

'You're ready?' asked Zack. 'We launch the bid? You understand that there's no return?'

'Yes. I understand. You can go ahead.'

Phyllis moved towards a phone. She had her team on stand-by to issue a press release, which would formally state that Hatherleigh Pacific was bidding for South China. Within a couple of minutes, Hatherleigh Pacific's takeover of South China would be public – and irreversible. In Weinstein Lukes' dealing rooms the share traders would start to buy stock in South China at any price up to forty-five dollars.

Scottie now had a couple of calls to make. One was to the Chief Executive of South China. It was just a courtesy call. What he'd say, in effect, was: 'It's nothing personal, but we've just bid for your company. If we win, you're sacked. And in the course of the takeover campaign, we're going to say lots of nasty things about you, to convince your shareholders that you're useless. I just wanted you to make sure you heard it from me first.'

It's a bizarre form of courtesy, but it's standard practice. The other call was to Lord Hatherleigh, now fretting the evening away in his Chelsea home. He'd be pleased. And excited.

Scottie moved towards a phone, while Phyllis stood in the corner talking into her mobile. The orange light which filled the harbour disappeared as quickly as it had arrived. The sun, now lifted clear of the grey sea beneath, rose into the suffocating embrace of the covering cloud and the world grew dark again. Phyllis clicked her phone to off. The press release was issued. The bid was launched.

7

When George had said 'Game, set and match', he might have added the word 'tournament'. Things were going outrageously well. *Furniture Today* had written the most grovelling apology conceivable, and included a long and flattering article on the 'Gissings miracle' with extensive colour photos of all their product ranges. Full-page colour ads would appear for free for the next two years. Plus, of course, the Aspertons' war on Gissings had been thrown violently into reverse. The Aspertons had sent out letters to all their customers retracting the libel. Their order book for the Asperton Brilliants had been passed over to Gissings, and the mighty Asperton marketing department was now selling Gissings furniture as though it was their own. The volume of orders was so great that Gissings was working at full capacity and work was even having to be subcontracted to other manufacturers. The prices were good, too. Without the remorseless competition from the Aspertons, and with the huge flood of positive publicity, Gissings could sell as much as they wanted at the prices they wanted.

Everyone whom George had fired when he first took charge of the factory was now back on the payroll. Salaries had been restored to previous levels, plus a generous allowance for inflation. George had even insisted on paying a bonus to all employees, despite a muted protest from Jeff Wilmot. The mood on the shop floor had never been better.

They were making money, too. If they kept sales up at this rate, they'd be producing three million pounds' worth of furniture a year, and selling it at a ten percent profit margin. That was three hundred thousand pounds in a year. The money would go towards repayment of the debt, of course, but Ballard hinted that Gissings could keep at least some of it towards completing the long-delayed expansion of their production area.

'Don't tell me you're about to start being generous now that we don't need you to be? Typical bloody banker,' said George.

'Not at all,' said Ballard. 'The moment when a company's in profit and growing fast is exactly when it needs money. You'll get some use from it now. Before it would have just disappeared up the chimney.'

'Yeah, well, we could use some cash to expand our production area and save ourselves having to subcontract. Bloody subcontractors eat up half our profits.'

Ballard's moustache muffled his smile, but his eyes twinkled with laughter.

'What are you laughing at?'

'You. You should have seen yourself when you first arrived up here. You looked a right sight, all designer shades and flashy car. And now you've turned into an out-and-out Yorkshireman and a bloody good businessman at that. Better than your dad.'

'Better than Dad? You're joking.'

'No. He was an exceptional entrepreneur. He'd have

made money in a prison camp, he would. But running a big business was never his thing. He always got in everyone's way and ended up making things worse. You get the best out of people. Old Tom Gissing would be proud of you, really proud. Just remember: if you want to, you can take this firm all the way to the top.'

'If I want to?' echoed George. 'What d'you mean "if I want to"?'

Ballard looked sharply at the younger man.

'Well, there's your dad's will, isn't there? I assume you're still aiming to make your million.'

'There's no way on earth I can make a million in time, David. With a bit of luck we'll make three hundred grand this year and maybe even more the next. But by the time we've paid off your bloody loan and invested in the production area and stuff, it'll be years, absolutely years, before I can get a million pounds out of the place. Maybe five years' time, more likely seven or eight. That's better than I ever expected, but I'll have missed Dad's deadline by years and years. You know that as well as I do.'

Ballard's smile had completely vanished. His smiling, pudgy face focused intently on George's, his shrewd eyes searching there for an answer to something. At length, the veteran banker spoke again.

'You're right, George. If you stay at Gissings, re-invest your profits sensibly and keep your eye on the long term, it'll take you at least five years to make a million. As you say, it'll probably take longer. You'll expand your production area, then you'll add to your product range, then your marketing people will do their stuff again and quite soon your production people will be clamouring for more toys. So it might be five years, it might be ten. All you can be certain of is that Gissings will grow, and prosper, and enrich you and all those who work with you.'

Ballard paused again, unsure whether to continue.

'Yes?' George prompted. Ballard continued to hesitate, but then appeared to make up his mind.

'But that's not your only option. You can sell the company. It's making three hundred grand profit before interest. You should be able to sell it for six to eight times that amount. If you're lucky you may even fetch ten times. You'll need to knock something off that for the debt, of course, but you should clear two million. Possibly more.'

George was astounded. Never once in all this time had this thought occurred to him. He had assumed he would come third out of three in the race to the million. He guessed that Zack and Matthew would each make their fortune, and his best hope had always been not to be ashamed in front of them when the contest was settled. And now . . . now Ballard was suggesting he could actually come first. Make his million – his *two* million – and scoop his father's jackpot. Thirty million quid, or more. Just imagine the look on Zack's face! And Matthew's if it came to that. He'd feel damn sorry to say goodbye to Gissings, to the whole bunch of them who had helped him turn the company around – but it was hard to argue with thirty or forty million quid.

'But who would buy it?' he asked lamely.

'If you want to sell it, tell me. I can probably find you buyers if that's what you want. But think about it, George. Think about it hard.'

8

You're in your car, driving peacefully along. You stop at some lights. A bloke comes up to you and says: 'Please get out of your car and give me the keys. I've just offered the finance company ten grand for the car, and they're inclined to accept.' What do you do?

Well, let's assume you succeed in refraining from violence. Let's assume you manage to think calmly. The first thing you might do is get on the phone to the finance company. Don't waffle on to them about ties of obligation, your long-standing relationship and all that blah-blah. Instead, say this: 'Ten grand? Are you crazy? This is a genuine low-mileage vehicle, immaculate paintwork, engine as clear as a bell. Don't even think about accepting such a ludicrous offer.' Be convincing. Be clear. And if you feel you have to, there's nothing wrong with a little bit of personal abuse directed at the person making the hostile offer.

OK. That's your turn. Now it's his go. What does he do? He does the same. He gets on the phone too. 'Low mileage? Yeah and my aunt's the Pope. That car's higher mileage than the bleeding space shuttle. The only thing holding the body together is the paintwork, and as for the engine . . . all I can say is, don't sneeze when you've got the bonnet up. Ten grand is five more than it's worth. Take the money and scarper.' Most likely, this bloke is stung by the nasty things you said about him: all that stuff about his parents' marital status and his personal hygiene habits. He probably feels that now would be a good time to add a word or two about your own less pleasing personal characteristics.

Good. Now it's your go. Your go, his go, your go, his go. The war of words continues for a while. If you begin to bring the finance company round to your way of thinking, the bloke's got a choice to make. He can raise his offer, or hope to swing it with the cash he's already put on the table. It's a tough call, but either way a bit more personal abuse won't go amiss.

And this was the stage that Hatherleigh Pacific and

the South China Trust Bank had reached. South China had just fired off its latest broadside at its shareholders. Now it was Hatherleigh's turn.

Zack and Lord Hatherleigh were in Hatherleigh's Pall Mall offices, hunched over a speaker-phone on a conference call with Scottie and Phyllis Wang in Hong Kong.

They had all been impressed by how hard South China was resisting their attack. The beleaguered management seemed to have shaken off its lethargy and come out with all guns blazing. The battle swayed from side to side. Hatherleigh attacked South China's abysmal record. South China attacked Hatherleigh's bid for being opportunistic and cheap.

'What do you people make of their latest document?' rasped Scottie.

'Eight pages of abuse. Eleven pages of stuff they've already said. One page which matters,' said Zack.

'Page three, right? The new profit forecasts?'

'Correct. They claim that their profits this year are going to be thirty percent higher than the stockmarket was expecting. If that's true, then, on the face of it, we should be offering thirty percent more than we are.'

'And d'ye believe they can make these profits? They've never managed that kind of increase in the past.'

'Yes and no. They're not allowed to tell out-and-out fibs, so they must be pretty sure that they can achieve these profits. But –'

'What?' Scottie roared in, without waiting for Zack to finish. 'Are you saying we've got to pay another thirty percent? We don't have that kind of money.' Scottie's excitement threatened combustion. Zack could imagine his red face almost bursting with the pressure.

'Wait a minute, Scottie.' He glanced sideways at Hatherleigh, expecting a smile from the more self-contained aristocrat. But Hatherleigh wasn't smiling.

465

This was too serious. 'If you look carefully at these profit forecasts, you can see that all the extra profit is coming from financial trading. Buying and selling foreign currency, that kind of stuff. Now South China's markets haven't suddenly gone through some kind of boom. We know that, because our own Far Eastern dealing rooms have been quiet. And that means only one thing.'

The silence was audible. Zack continued.

'They're making more profits because they're speculating more. Gambling. They've nothing to lose. If they make money, they boost their profits and stand a chance of keeping their independence. If they lose money – well, hell, they were going down anyway.'

'So before we were buying a bank. Now we're buying a casino?' The question came from Lord Hatherleigh.

'Yes. But you can close down the casino part as soon as you take control.'

'Can we walk away? Can we walk away from the deal now?' Lord Hatherleigh asked the question so quietly the listeners in Hong Kong could barely hear him.

'Why would you want to walk away?'

'We wanted to buy a bank, not a casino. Can we walk away?'

Zack paused. He hadn't expected this.

'No,' he said. 'You're not allowed to drop your bid. If South China had revealed some huge hole in its accounts, it would be a different matter. But the authorities won't let you abandon your bid, just because the target company had made unexpectedly large profits. That would be unheard of.'

Hatherleigh drummed his fingers softly on the lacquer coffee table. It was the only sign of excitement in his whole lean, thoughtful body.

'How do you feel about running casinos, Scottie?'

Scottie laughed, a laugh that was more like a bark.

'I just do what you tell me, boss. You tell me to run a casino, I'll run a casino. You tell me to run a brothel, I'll run a brothel.'

'We can close the gambling rooms as soon as we get control, right?'

Zack nodded. 'Yes.'

Hatherleigh drummed his fingers and pondered. He and his family owned thirty percent of Hatherleigh Pacific. Zack had married Sarah, who owned a big chunk of it herself. Just for once, here was a banker with almost as much to lose from a wrong decision as the company executives themselves. Hatherleigh had an old-fashioned distrust of financial speculation, and steered clear of it wherever he could. But this was a short-term thing, wasn't it? And all the fundamental reasons for buying the company were still intact.

'OK. We'll compromise. We'll put out a document blasting away at these new profit numbers. Make it as strong as you can, right, Zack? And we'll add just $1 to the bid price. We'll go with $46. That's our final offer. Make that clear. I don't want to overpay just because some young fool with stripy braces has made a couple of good bets.'

Zack nodded. 'OK.' Hatherleigh looked at him approvingly. God, what a good son-in-law he was. He was proud as hell of Zack's performance right through this whole bid. Zack would produce a document so scathing of South China's new profit forecasts, the company would feel shamefaced for making them.

Zack's calm nod concealed tension, though. Thanks to him, Hatherleigh Pacific was winning the shouting match, but in the end money counted more than words. They would be cutting it fine, very fine. The bid was wide open now. His forty million dollar fee was wide open. His partnership prospects and his key to his father's millions. Zack was gripped with anxiety.

Scottie and Phyllis signed off from Hong Kong, and the phone went silent.

'Good luck,' said Hatherleigh to Zack.

'Yes, likewise, Jack,' said Zack.

They were more than chairman and banker now. They were father and son. Roped together by Sarah, the wedding, their family company, the shared ordeal of the bid. If this were a movie, they'd have hugged.

9

It's accountants who run hospitals these days, but even if the place had been run by a choir of angels, the doctor would have been forced to question the value of continuing.

'I'm not sure that our recent progress really justifies us in carrying on,' he said. 'Sometimes the patient makes further gains once they're completely removed from a hospital environment.'

Helen's chart had been flat for a year or more. Speech therapy, physical therapy, occupational therapy had all brought about some early improvement – then nothing. Josie could see the chart, but she didn't need it to know the truth.

'If you mean we should stop coming, then I agree,' she said.

'I think we should continue with medications aimed at treatment of anxiety and depression,' said the doctor. 'Particularly if you feel your mother continues to suffer from lifestyle stress.'

It was a bizarre phrase to use. Nursed by her daughter every evening and weekend, looked after by care assistants at all other times, you could hardly call Helen a victim of classical stress. On the other hand, the doctor was right. Bernard Gradley's will had laid a curse over the family, and Helen was its principal victim. Her sons were fighting each other for money, her daughter struggled with scant resources of time and income, while the fortune that Helen coveted seemed likely to disappear for ever. She was anxious; and anxiety made her prefer the shelter of a muddled head to the clear and cold realities of a difficult world.

'Say goodbye to the nice doctor, Mum,' said Josephine. 'We shan't be coming here any more.'

Helen scowled in concentration, forcing her lips to pluck words from the babble. Eventually they came, slow but perfectly distinct.

'Thank God for that.'

Winter 2000–2001

Christmas is coming, the goose is getting fat, please put a penny in the old man's hat. If you haven't got a penny, a million will do. If you haven't got a million, then who needs you?

It is 15 December 2000. There are 210 days to go, and for the first time, each of the brothers is hopeful.

1

Matthew tapped at Fiona's door.

'Coming,' she called, and a moment later stepped out into the hall.

She was wearing a full-length cashmere overcoat with a woollen scarf at the neck. Matthew noticed she had touched up her make-up for the evening instead of removing it completely as she usually did. They walked to the lift together and rode down to the joyless lobby.

They were still living in their pair of serviced flats in Blenheim Court. They were stuck, no longer because work took up too much time, but because they simply didn't know where else to go. Matthew wanted to live with Fiona. Properly live with. One front door. One living room. One bedroom. But he was worried that asking Fiona to live with him would push her away, and that would be unthinkable. And, though Josephine was keen for him to move back to his mum's house in Kilburn, nothing could appeal to him less. After a long day's work, coming home to find your disabled mother sitting up in the dilapidated front room of her shabby little house and feeding her mashed up food when she was unable to feed herself? No thank you.

Fiona, for her part, liked their current arrangements. She still needed space. She still needed to be able to ask Matthew to leave the bed after sex, even though she seldom did now. He didn't have a key to her apartment and she still occasionally needed whole weekends, even weeks, of separation from him. But despite her reflexive need for an escape route, Matthew knew she needed him as much as he did her.

The bank's admin department had tried hard to get them to find their own accommodation. Fiona had stalled them, gaily using her managing director's prerogatives to get her way. But even an MD can't stall for ever. The bank would stop paying the rent on 31 December and after that they were on their own. Fiona said she'd stay on in her impersonal little suite and pay the outrageous rent herself. This wasn't an option for Matthew, though, and he had pondered the alternatives long and gloomily.

They walked out of the lobby on to the chilly street. It was a frosty night and above the neon glow, a caffeine stay-awake for the elderly city, stars glittered. They walked a couple of blocks to Gianfranco's, their favourite restaurant and a fashionable haunt of the affluent residents of South Kensington.

Although they ate there often, tonight was special. The EPAS system had ground through another annual cycle and bonuses were announced this week. Matthew's boss was, of course, Fiona, and it was her duty to break the news. They had agreed to do it away from the bank, and tonight was the night. In her pocket was an envelope. Inside the envelope, a couple of short lines would tell him salary and bonus. This year there was no blot on his copybook, no repeat of the Western Instruments fiasco. The group had made a stackload of money and Matthew had contributed fully to the achievement. McAllister was pleased. The bank was pleased. Matthew was giddy with anticipation.

At Gianfranco's, in front of the cloakroom tended by a succession of young Italian women of plentiful bosoms and limited English, Matthew helped Fiona off with her coat. It slid off to reveal her in a red evening dress, which Matthew had never seen before. She kissed him.

'Surprise,' she said.

It was a surprise. Matthew had never see her wear anything but office clothes or casual outfits. Everything was always excellent quality and well chosen – but it was relentlessly unsexy. At work, she was professional. At home, she was comfortable. Short skirts and extravagant dresses were unknown to her wardrobe.

'You look wonderful, absolutely wonderful. I never imagined I was going out with a beautiful woman,' said Matthew.

She pinched him lightly for his cheek.

'What's the special occasion? I thought you said bonuses weren't all that important.'

She shrugged. Her shoulders lifted the dress and let it drop back again. The fabric moved and fell as only very expensive, very well tailored fabrics do.

'Bonuses aren't,' she said. 'You are. Very. I sometimes worry I don't tell you that enough. This has been a wonderful year for me.'

Matthew nodded.

472

'For me too. At least,' he added, crassly joking through nervousness, 'I think it has. It depends what's in that envelope.'

'Idiot,' she said. She was hurt that Matthew ended the moment with a needless reference to money. He was obsessed by it. She always told him to relax, but he never did. With a gesture of annoyance, she picked the envelope from her coat pocket and walked on into the restaurant.

They ordered without needing to look at the menu. The waiter brought them a basket of warm ciabatta and a dish of olive oil, and Fiona began to dunk the bread in the oil. Matthew normally joined in, but not tonight. She sighed.

'I guess we'd better cut to the chase or you'll ruin the evening.'

She put the envelope down on the table, but with both hands on it. She looked even lovelier by candlelight than she had done beneath the overhead lights in the hall. Matthew's eyes, though, rested not on her, but on the envelope. She noticed and was saddened.

She pushed the envelope across the table.

'You're a very good trader. You work very hard. You've made a lot of money for the bank. Here's your reward. Congratulations.'

Matthew ignored the bitterness in her voice. He ripped open the envelope.

His salary had been increased to sixty-five thousand pounds. He was promoted to vice president, another of the bank's meaningless titles. His bonus was three hundred and seventy-five thousand dollars.

Matthew calculated rapidly. That was getting on for two hundred and fifty thousand pounds. A quarter of a million pounds. Earned honestly, through talent and hard work.

Oh, boy. Through his insider trading, Matthew had

grown his first bonus to a grand total of three hundred and four thousand pounds. With this bonus on top, Matthew was worth close to five-fifty. In eight months' of insider trading, Matthew had grown his paltry sixty thousand pounds by five times. All he needed to do now, in the seven months remaining to him, was to double what he had. That was a piece of cake. And now he was enjoying the fatter returns from investing in shares instead of bonds, he'd get there even quicker.

He wouldn't try to get more than the million, though. As time went by, he had become more nervous, not less. He hated Belial's crooked, self-satisfied chuckle. He hated the fear and deception and the criminality. He hated the little square garden with the benches under the tree. He hated the fact that he was scared of Brian McAllister and of everything around him. He wanted out.

'That's great. That's absolutely great,' said Matthew. 'Thank you.'

'Don't thank me. Thank EPAS,' she replied automatically. 'Do you want to know all your strengths and weaknesses and all that kind of stuff?'

'Yes, I suppose. But not now. Not tonight.'

Matthew looked again at Fiona. She was radiant and he was blissful, and the combination made her irresistible.

'Has my bonus obsession been annoying you?' he asked.

'I swore I'd never wear a nice dress again unless you looked at me properly. You did, but only with about a minute to spare.'

'I'm sorry. I promise you that I won't be like this next year,' he said, then broke off. It had been an unwritten rule of their relationship that they never spoke of the future more than about a month ahead. Fiona was so quick to feel suffocated, it worked better to keep things low-key. 'You do look fantastic,' he added. 'I've never seen you look better.'

Fiona smiled a half-smile. It was her way of telling him that she'd noticed his reference to next year, but that it was OK. She wouldn't freak out and start behaving like she didn't know him.

'Thanks,' she whispered.

Matthew paused. He had an envelope in his pocket too. He hadn't been sure whether to hand it over. But he decided to chance it.

'Fi, you realise that in a few weeks we're not going to be living next door to each other any more, don't you?'

She nodded, but she was already tensing up.

'Aren't you going to miss that?'

She nodded again.

'Wouldn't you like to do something about it? Take some positive action?'

Fiona waited, saying nothing. On the trading floor, she was decisive, swift and level-headed. In anything to do with the relationship, she was almost incapable of action.

'Fiona, my love, I'd like to live with you. Share a house with you.' Fiona's tension visibly mounted, and Matthew was quick to throw her the lifeline she needed. 'I know you need your own space. I know there will be times when you need to be able to live separately from me. But take a look at this and tell me it's not perfect.'

He tossed his envelope to her across the table. She reached for it and opened it.

Inside the envelope was an estate agent's blurb describing a mews house set in a tiny dead-end road in the heart of Chelsea. Surrounded by imposing four-storey houses, the least of them worth very well upwards of a million, the mews houses stood at a lowly two storeys, like the stables they once were. Number 11 stood at the end. The main house comprised a couple of bedrooms, each with its own bathroom, a small kitchen-cum-dining room, and a large and delightful living room. At the back was a tiny brick-paved courtyard, with a fountain in the middle and a hundred terracotta pots which overflowed with scent and flowers in summer. But the real jewel, the feature which first attracted Matthew's interest, stood at the back of the courtyard. A long, low building had been converted from an artist's studio to a self-contained flat. Anyone living there would have no need of the main house – not even for access to the street, which was available through a gate in the courtyard.

Fiona looked through the blurb, quickly at first, then, once she had understood Matthew's intentions, more slowly.

'We'd buy the house together, but the flat would be yours. I wouldn't have a key to it. I wouldn't even set foot in it. You could have your own phone. Your own bed. Whatever clothes you wanted. It would be Fortress Fiona, there for whenever you needed.'

She nodded. Though they had been going out for eighteen months, every step forward still seemed sudden to her. Dangerously rushed. But she knew herself well enough now to do battle with her first impulses. She gave a brave smile.

'It does look interesting. Perhaps we should take a look at it. Some weekend soon. I'd like that.'

She was trying her hardest. Matthew smiled at her.

'I've already looked round. It's beautiful. You'll love it.'

Matthew paused. Fiona was swallowing, trying to master her fear. The next bit would be the hardest.

'Well, perhaps we should think about making an offer,' she said. 'Just to hold off other buyers, till I've had a chance to see it.'

Matthew nodded and leaned forward.

'I've put in an offer. It's been accepted. Of course you need to see it, but we can do that any time. We can do that tomorrow lunch time. I know we're busy,' he added quickly, forestalling objection, 'but we're always busy. We could make excuses until someone else has bought the house. But let's not. Let's really try to buy it.'

Fiona took a deep breath. She looked at Matthew, then down again at the photos of the house.

'This is very sudden.'

'Yes. But it's no easier for you when you have more warning. You just have longer to think up reasons to say no.'

Fiona hesitated. She sat very still. The only movement visible came from the candlelight flickering over her arms and shoulders. Then she sighed and nodded.

'OK, let's look tomorrow. If it's nice, we'll go ahead. And I won't raise problems where there aren't any. And thanks. It's a great idea.'

Her words were brave, but she was shivery with fear. Living with somebody was as scary as it could get. Though her past had grown less terrible with distance, she was its prisoner still. She bit her lip.

'Remember. Fortress Fiona will be yours, and only yours. You won't need to see me for months on end if you don't want to.'

She squeezed his hand across the table.

'Thank you. Don't ever ever let me down. I wouldn't be able to bear it.'

'It's OK. I won't.' Easy to say. He knew he wouldn't be unfaithful. He wouldn't drink too much or beat her up or stop loving her. But what if he were sent to jail for insider trading right under her nose? It would destroy her. Another reason not to get caught.

They kissed and talked more about the house. The

price was six hundred thousand pounds which should have been exorbitant, but this was Chelsea. Fiona insisted that she would pay for Fortress Fiona by herself, while they would go halves on the house itself. They decided that that meant Fiona paying four hundred thousand, while Matthew would put up the balance. She would pay cash, of course. If you've been in banking for ten years, as Fiona had, you certainly don't need a mortgage. Matthew, naturally, would borrow to make up his share. He certainly wasn't going to dip into his funds at Switzerland International.

As they talked, Fiona felt a surge of nervous relief. She laughed lots, drank plenty and flirted outrageously. She looked gorgeous and knew it. Matthew was mesmerised by her, as he had been once on the Jamaican sands, as he had been in Vermont and as he had been so often this year. He couldn't wait to get home to fulfil the passionate promise of her eyes. She saw his impatience and teased him. She ate her pudding slowly, then wanted coffee, then more coffee, then got deep into conversation with the waiter about his family back in Genoa. All the while her eyes darted fire at Matthew and her leg nuzzled his beneath the table.

Eventually she relented and, as they left, she allowed Matthew to put his arm around her. She swayed into his embrace, letting him know her promise held good.

They made their way to the cloakroom booth. Except for the red glow of a smoke alarm, the room was dark and the buxom Italian had disappeared.

'Don't worry. I'll just hop over the counter and get the coats myself,' said Matthew.

'No need,' said a man's voice from within. 'I'm just rummaging round for mine.'

The figure approached the counter, where the light in the hallway provided some brightness. With a rush of horror, Matthew recognised him. It was Belial.

Looking as neat as ever, in a snug little dinner jacket, the repulsive man pumped Matthew's hand.

'Matthew! How good to see you! And who's this very lovely lady, may I ask? Let me introduce myself. I'm James Belial,' he said, turning the attentions of his hairy little handshake to Fiona.

Belial grinned at Matthew, squeezed Fiona's hand too tight and too long, then bounded around the interior of the cloakroom looking for their coats. He insisted on wriggling back over the counter with the coats, kicking with his absurd short legs to lift himself up.

'Pardon me. Pardon me. This counter's not designed for the smaller gentleman. There you are. Let me help you with your coat.'

Before Matthew's appalled eyes, the ugly little man helped Fiona on with her coat, his thick brown nails grazing the back of her neck. All the while he chattered away, unstoppably.

'Sorry, I didn't catch your name? Fiona? Fiona Shepperton. Pleased to meet you. No, no. Matthew and I are just business acquaintances, eh, Matthew?' Belial gave Matthew a leer and a wink. 'Yes, I'd quite forgotten you lived in this part of town. Still up at Blenheim Court, I suppose. Yes, I always come here when I'm in London, which is quite a lot, you know. All my best clients live here. Splendid restaurant, isn't it? One of my favourites. Used to come here lots while I was at Madison. You work there too, Miss Shepperton? Or should I say Ms? You American women are so formidable. Yes, I enjoyed working there, but I'm happier where I am now – let me give you my card, there you are. Yes, I meet a much better class of person, now. Ha, ha.'

Eventually, Matthew was able to tug Fiona away. Belial stood at the door and watched them go. He bobbed up and down on his stumpy legs, a dapper little figure with a twisted face.

'Who the hell was that?' asked Fiona.

'Forget him. Just a guy I met at a conference once, who kind of glued himself on to me. Wanted me to invest some money with him.'

'And did you?'

'Think I'd give him my money? Not likely.'

They spoke no more of it, but Matthew was horrified. Throughout the year he had succeeded in keeping Belial and Switzerland International totally away from Madison. And now this repulsive man had barged in on his girlfriend and boss, shoved a card in her hand and made out that he and Matthew were practically bosom buddies. Fiona believed Matthew's denials, he was sure of that. But all the same, before this evening, the dark side of his life had dwelled in its own world, unseen. Today it had erupted, leaving a huge ugly thumbprint on the part of his life Matthew most wanted to keep pure.

They got back to Fiona's flat and made love. It was pleasurable, of course, but Matthew was upset by the encounter with Belial and Fiona felt it. What should have been a perfect end to the evening was spoiled.

Three or four more trades with Belial. Five or six if necessary. Then that was it. For ever.

2

It was half past midnight as the taxi drew up outside Zack and Sarah's Chelsea home, a two-storey, three-bedroom apartment in a quiet street near Sloane Square. The lights were still on, and Zack walked upstairs and let himself in.

He expected to find Sarah curled up on a living-room sofa, ready for bed and smiling welcome, but the room was empty. He walked on into the kitchen. Perhaps she was there, making bed-time decaf. She was there, but not making coffee. The kitchen was L-shaped and in the long arm of the L, a cream-panelled dining area stretched away from the pots and pans of the kitchen. The mahogany dining table was usually swathed in felted tablecloth, to protect the polished surface beneath, but not tonight. Sarah had stripped it away, laid the table with glass and silver and fine crockery. The stumps of two candles guttered in silver candlesticks. Two platefuls of Sarah's cooking at its most elegant lay disregarded and cold on a tray to the side. Sarah had changed, not into her normal jeans and T-shirt, but into a blue silk blouse, long velvet skirt and pearls. Her face, normally so spring-like, was dejected.

'Hello beautiful. I'm so sorry. I had no idea you were doing this,' said Zack.

'You told me you'd be back at nine.'

'Did I? Hell, you're right. I'm afraid something came up right after that and I've been ploughing away at it ever since.'

Dejected or not, Sarah in silk and velvet attracted Zack as strongly as Sarah in jodhpurs and a sweaty T-shirt, or Sarah in pretty much anything, or nothing if it came to that. Zack didn't mind missing dinner, but he felt an urgent desire for his favourite after-dinner pleasure.

'Can we rescue anything?' he asked. 'Do you want a brandy?'

She shook her head and tucked her hair behind her ears, both ears. That was a pretty much fatal sign. If her dark blonde hair covered both ears, she was feeling relaxed and warm, with sex only a short nuzzle away. If one ear was uncovered, there was hope. But if both ears peeped out, it was hopeless. Zack went to the fridge for a beer and sat down opposite his wife. It had been another long day at work and, used to it though he was, Zack was weary. His dark, angular face always seemed darker and narrower when he was tired, and a full day's growth of stubble and the creases of a hard day's work marked him.

'What's up? It's more than just me being late, isn't it?'

Sarah nodded. Her blunt chin was manlier than many men's and her frankness likewise greater.

'I'm not angry. You had work to do, so you did it. You forgot to phone, but I could have called you. You didn't know I was planning a surprise dinner. It's just . . . well, it's just where does this end? When are our lives going to stop being like this? When was the last time we had a proper dinner together during the week?'

Zack swigged his beer, and dropped his jacket over the back of his chair. Without the padding in the shoulders, he looked more round-shouldered, like the sedentary man he was.

'It's extra bad at the moment. There's your dad's takeover of South China which is taking buckets of time. Then I've got my big tax project going full steam ahead at the moment. Then there are lots of other bits and pieces. It all mounts up. But once I finish your dad's deal, things will settle down again.'

'Don't kid yourself. Once you complete the South China deal, there'll be another. Then another after that. That's the way Weinstein Lukes works. It's the way Coburg's works too, except we knock off at nine in the evening, not midnight, and we try not to work weekends.'

Zack sighed. She was right, of course, and they both knew it.

'Well, short of quitting, I don't see what option I have. They won't take any notice if I say I'm doing too much.'

'I know. Do the senior guys work less hard?'

'No. Just as hard. Just as much travel.'

'Oh, God, the travel! Don't even remind me.'

What with the Hatherleigh Pacific deal and the ROSES tax gimmick, Zack was travelling to the Far East once a fortnight or more. Because the flights to Hong Kong were often full, Zack had had his secretary book him on the Sunday evening flight every week for the next twenty weeks. If he didn't need the booking, he didn't turn up.

'What do you want to do?'

Sarah tucked her hair behind her ears again, though it was already quite well tucked.

'I don't know. All I know is I don't want us to be one of those awful banking couples who never see each other. And when we have babies, I don't want to chuck them at a nanny and reintroduce myself when they've graduated from college.'

Zack's lust had ebbed away, dampened by the message from Sarah's hair and by his own tiredness. But now he felt something unexpected. He realised that Sarah was one of the most straightforward, honest, easy to live with people he had ever met. How many other women would have picked a fight with him over the spoiled dinner, instead of simply tackling the issue they both faced? Zack tuned out from her words and sat mesmerised by this vision of her.

'I love you, Sarah. I think you're an amazing person and I'm delighted to be married to you.'

Sarah leaned forward, one wing of her bob falling away from her ear and hanging loose again. She laughed her clear healthy laugh at him.

'What on earth made you say that?'

Zack shrugged. 'I thought it, so I said it.'

'What a strange man you are.' Sarah smiled at him,

her eyes tracing a path up and down the outline of his face. 'So what are we going to do?'

'Well,' said Zack, 'I promise that I'm not going to stay at Weinstein Lukes for long. I enjoy it, but I don't enjoy it enough to do it for ever. I'll hand in my notice when you produce your first baby.'

That was an easy enough promise to make. Zack's banking career didn't need to last beyond winning his father's money. As for babies . . . well, they might feature in Sarah's life-plan, but they weren't a part of Zack's.

'What about now? These are meant to be our best years and we're not even seeing each other.'

'I'll try to work fewer weekends.'

'You already try.'

Sarah's hair was entirely free of her left ear, and was beginning to struggle free of the right one. She was still in silk and velvet and Zack's feelings for Sarah started to take a more familiar turn. He reached over the table and clasped her hands.

'Sarah, I don't want to give up on Weinstein Lukes yet, but I'm no more a career banker than you are. I want to finish your dad's deal. I want to finish my big tax project. I might want to do another two or three years after that, but no more.'

Sarah played with Zack's hands across the table.

'Why did you become a banker, sweetheart?' she asked.

'Had to do something after Dad died. And I wanted to prove that I could make the grade. I don't know what I'll do afterwards. Maybe go back to philosophy.'

'Don't do that. I hated you as a philosopher. You've been as sweet as a teddy bear since you started banking.'

Zack smiled back at her. However in the end he

extricated himself from this marriage, he would do his utmost not to hurt this wonderful woman. 'How come you went into banking?' he asked.

'That's easy. I knew Dad would love me to become involved in Hatherleigh Pacific in some way, even if it was just to sit on the Board after he's moved on. I wanted to learn what I could about business to prepare myself. But I'm not wedded to it either.'

'Sounds like we were made for each other,' said Zack. His hand massaged hers, with strokes which became slower and deeper. Her hair was free of both ears and her face was no longer dejected. She saw the question in his eyes.

'It's a bit late for that,' she said.

'Best get started, then,' he said.

3

One Monday morning, nine months after his departure from Gissings and three and a half months after his disappearance from the Aspertons, Darren turned up at work. His former workmates crowded round him, shaking his hand and clapping his back like a celebrity on walkabout. Dave leaped for joy, turned the radio up to full volume and started to dance round like a lunatic. A thousand questions greeted the returnee. 'Have you made it up with George, then?', 'Where've you been all this time, mate?' and 'Are you back for good now?'

Darren didn't answer in detail. 'I got bored pissing round, so I called George and said sorry. He said I could come back, so here I am.' And that was all anyone was ever to get out of him.

Apart from George and Darren himself, the only other person who knew more was Jeff Wilmot. Going through the accounts a few weeks previously, he had discovered that George had been making a series of payments to Darren ever since his departure. Wilmot brought the matter up. 'I hope that we're not employing Darren in some – er – informal capacity,' he said. 'We would be in very serious breach of our obligation to pay national insurance, to make deductions for income tax, to apprise him of pertinent health and safety requirements, to . . . well, many things. I hope, I mean . . . it would be quite improper . . . we should . . . at once,' he stopped, aghast at George's complacent criminality.

'Don't worry about it, Jeff,' George had said. 'Just mark it down as research and development and let it be.'

Wilmot had gone straight back to his office, eaten three biscuits one after the other without so much as tidying the crumbs, and fired off a strongly worded memo. George threw the memo away. Wilmot was too nervous to gossip, and that was all that concerned George. He didn't want the Aspertons to reconsider their generosity.

The only other person to put two and two together was Val, who had happened to see Darren being mobbed by his crowd of well-wishers. She strode upstairs. It had been raining outside and Val's heavy brown shoes scattered water in her wake. At the top landing, just before turning into the grandly named management suite, she shook her black umbrella out with needless energy. She seemed perturbed. Since George had left Gissings in his wild goose chase for Kiki, she hadn't spoken a civil word to him except on routine business matters. It was time to break her own rule.

'George, excuse me.' She was nervous about this, actually nervous. Her voice hardened as she continued. 'Darren's disappearance, this libel from the Aspertons, you stuffing the libel back down their throats, Darren coming back – it's all connected, isn't it? The whole thing was a set-up.'

George nodded. Val sounded angry to him, but she'd been angry ever since he'd run off. Still, however much she knew, she'd never say anything which might put Gissings at risk. He could trust her with the secret. He bit his lip and nodded. 'Yes. Start to finish. My idea. Darren's flawless execution.'

Val breathed out deeply. 'Then I owe you an apology. I owe you . . . Well, sorry. Sorry for the things I said.'

George watched her. She obviously found it hard to apologise. She must still be furious with him, and George was hurt. Ever since Kiki had helped him find his own feelings for Val, they had grown inside him with every passing day. Doubt had given way to certainty, or almost certainty. But for all the change that had taken place in him, it seemed as though Val was as changeless as the Yorkshire gritstone.

'Yeah, well, we need to keep it quiet,' he grunted. 'The Aspertons won't stay tame if they get wind of what happened.'

'I understand. But I do apologise. I think you did a wonderful thing. I'm sorry if I made it harder for you.' Val's deep-set blue eyes were looking down and away from him. Anywhere but into his eyes. Her mouth was trembling.

George reached out a hand towards her. He longed to touch her, to draw her into his arms and comfort her, but he held back. He tried to help her with his words.

'Thank you, Val. I . . . I knew you wouldn't have been angry if you'd known. And I certainly did make myself look a bit of a bastard.'

She looked up, her lips still quivering. Like this, tearful and emotional, George saw a Val which few had ever seen. Her broad, slightly crooked face, her deep intelligent eyes, her boyish ginger hair – to George, they were all entirely beautiful.

'Val . . . I . . .' he began and broke off.

Val stood there, not moving away, but not approaching him either. How was he to read this?

'Val,' he said, 'I know it was awful of me running away from you like that. You deserved, well you do deserve much better than that. But is it possible for you to give me a second chance?'

She struggled with herself.

'We were living together, George. We were lovers.'

'I know.'

'You hurt me so much. I swore I would never forgive you.'

Ever so gently, George lifted Val's chin until her swimming eyes gazed straight into his.

'I know how much I hurt you. I've grown up since then, grown up a lot. You wouldn't have to pardon me, just give me a second chance.'

Val stared ahead of her, fear and hope struggling in her face. Kiki had phoned her in the summer, after George's brother's wedding. Kiki had told Val that George really loved her, that she should give him a second chance. Val's pride and her anger at George's treatment of Darren had kept her aloof, but it had been hard. What was she to make of this man?

She reached out to George's jacket. She felt in his pockets until she found the weight of his wallet, and she picked it out. She opened it up. Inside were some credit cards, a couple of receipts, boring stuff mostly. And there were some photos. At the front of the wallet, framed in a clear plastic panel, was the photo of Val which she had given him that summer when they were first together. There was also a passport photo which George must have swiped from her desk drawer at some point. She hadn't missed it. There were also the photos of Kiki which George had long kept in his wallet. They were tucked away at the back. When Val pulled at them, they came unstuck with a jerk. They hadn't been moved for months.

Val didn't say anything, couldn't, just nodded. He reached for her, she for him. They embraced with the intensity of prisoners finding freedom. They kissed again and again until they'd had enough to pause awhile. Val sat on his lap, each of them giving or receiving kisses as they felt the need.

'I've missed you so much.'

'I hated not speaking to you. I knew I had to be firm with myself, because I'd be putty in your hands otherwise.'

'God, I wish I'd known. It would have made waiting easier.'

'Oh, George.'

Neither of them yet dared call the other what they wanted to: sweetheart, darling, my love. They were reunited, lovers again, but were they more? Neither of them had ever spoken deeply about their relationship while it had lasted, and they hadn't spoken so much as a word since it had ended. Where did they stand now? All this time, George had kept a ring tucked away against his heart and now it clamoured out its question, like cathedral bells.

'Val,' said George. 'If it's too soon, if you need more time, then . . . then, it's OK. I still want whatever you feel alright with, but . . . is it possible? . . . will you marry me?'

Her mouth was wordless, but her eyes said everything. He hugged her. 'Val, dearest, dearest, Val.'

Eventually they pulled apart. She was still on his lap and there they sat: a plain, ginger, overweight pair. George pulled the ring from his breast pocket.

It's hard to pay thirty thousand pounds for a ring.

Diamonds big enough to be worth that much look like high-class knuckle-dusters on the finger. George had managed to find a genuine pink diamond which had once belonged to a movie star and that had pushed the price up. All the same, the stone was large for any woman. On Kiki's tiny hand, it would have looked ridiculous. Val looked at the ring, the big stone on the little gold band, and tried to squeeze it on. She got it as far as the first joint of her ring finger. She turned her hand, catching the light, watching the precious reflective magic inside the stone, and smiled.

'Have you been lugging this around with you all the time?'

George nodded. 'Every day.'

'It must have cost you an arm and a leg.'

'More than that. It almost cost the bloody factory.' And George explained when he had bought it and why.

Val stared into the ice-cold heart of the ring.

'To be honest, George, I don't want Kiki's cast-offs. I'd sooner have something which is more me.'

George nodded.

'It is a bit big,' he said.

'And a bit flashy.'

'Yes, that too.' George sighed. 'I didn't really think you'd want it, to be honest, but I offered it to Kiki, so I owed it to you to offer it to you too.'

'Maybe we could drive into Leeds together tomorrow. Look around for something there,' Val said as she kissed her fiancé.

He smiled. 'Let's do that, my love.'

4

Christmas has come. The goose has grown fat, and heads for the oven with all the other birds who wish that Christ

490

had never bothered.

Josephine and Helen spend Christmas week at Ovenden House. Because Helen is there, George and Val, and Matthew and Fiona come to visit as well. Lord and Lady Hatherleigh are perfect hosts. They welcome their new family as their own and aren't put out in the slightest by Helen's disability. What's more, Josie can't help noticing that, as before at the wedding, Helen is very well here. Something about Ovenden House comforts her. Her speech is slow but distinct; she walks strongly, albeit slowly; her stamina is better than it ever has been at home. When she does tire though, her understanding fades. She persists in forgetting that Zack and Sarah are married, but she believes that George and Val are, and she likes that. She calls Val, 'Val', and she calls Sarah, 'that girl'. Fiona she doesn't mention at all.

Zack and Josephine declare a kind of truce. She doesn't complain about his stinginess or neglect in front of Sarah or her family. She's also agreed to leave her beloved portable computer at home. To everyone's surprise, she's showing every sign of turning into a computer nerd, something no one could have imagined three years ago. For his part, Zack marks the suspension of hostilities with politeness, and by doing his fair share of looking after Helen. He's not very good at it though, and his stints often end in tears, which only Josephine or Val are competent to deal with.

Val feels out of place, despite the warmth of her welcome. She doesn't have a posh dress to wear at the black-tie dinners, and, despite Sarah's offers of help, she doesn't have a hope of fitting into even Sarah's loosest frocks. So she puts on the best thing she's got, sits in the candlelight by George and looks at the pearls and diamonds all around. Something like this used to be George's scene. It's a bit posher and a bit more British.

However, he's outgrown dinner tables like this one, and even though he knows which way to pass the port, he feels out of place too. He and Val will be pleased to get back to Yorkshire.

Matthew is comfortable enough. He likes the affluence that surrounds him: the immaculately kept house and gardens, the litre bottles of Penhaligon's aftershave in the bathrooms, the genial assumption that money and wealth and family will just go on and on for ever. This is what motivates him. This is why he trades on the inside and jeopardises his wealth, his relationship and even his freedom. His father's fortune wouldn't buy wealth of the kind that Lord Hatherleigh so effortlessly commands, but it would be plenty. Matthew's not greedy.

Fiona, on the other hand, is as brittle as glass. She's stranded in the bosom of her partner's family. Matthew's eldest brother is married. His brother is engaged. Fiona feels as though the world's looking at her and Matthew, waiting for them to tie the knot. What's more, she has to share a room and a bed with Matthew. They do most nights now anyway and they'll be moving into their new home soon as well – but she likes to have the option. She likes an escape route, which Ovenden House, for all its rooms, can't provide. She is distant, strange, hard as nails. She leaves as soon as she can, before Matthew's ready.

It's not a great Christmas, but not too bad. Josephine has a real holiday and her mum feels relaxed and easy. The three brothers all have business matters to worry about and all three scoot back to work while the rest of the country is still regretting last night's turkey curry and making short-lived resolutions to drink less. This is the last Christmas before Bernard Gradley's three-year deadline. Next year, everything will be different.

5

The strange battle is drawing to a close.

For months now, the two contestants have done their worst. Hatherleigh Pacific has slagged off South China. After reading one of Zack's masterpieces, you wondered how South China's management managed to get to the bathroom on their own, let alone run a company. But South China hasn't been idle. They've hit back as hard as they can, and their new-found profitability is certainly eye-catching. Where does the profit come from? Hatherleigh Pacific calls it 'dangerous speculation which the current management is ill-equipped to handle'. South China calls it 'years of investment bearing fruit'. Who do you believe? It's time to decide. The shareholders must vote, and the day for voting is today.

Once again, Zack, Lord Hatherleigh, Scottie and Phyllis Wang were gathered in Hatherleigh Pacific's Hong Kong boardroom. Through the windows, a three-masted wooden-built sailing ship was gliding up Victoria Harbour, heading east. Tugboats and fire-fighters danced around it, pumping jets of water up into the midday sky, celebrating something.

The four executives watched it idly. There was nothing for them to do. The deadline had passed. The votes had been cast and were now being counted. All they had to do was wait.

'You're sure your phone's switched on?' asked Scottie.

Phyllis nodded. 'My team will call me as soon as they get the message through from the count. If for any reason they can't get through, they'll call Zack. And they know where we are, so they can come through the switchboard if they have to.'

Scottie nodded. He knew all that anyway. 'I don't

understand how you folks do this for a living.' His crimson face had burned brighter with every day of this takeover battle. The end wasn't coming a minute too soon for his blood pressure.

In the corner, two bottles of champagne shifted in their ice buckets as the ice melted into water. The count was running behind schedule. Scottie drifted back to the plate-glass windows to watch the sailing ship, when Phyllis's phone rang. She leaped to it.

'Phyllis Wang here.'

She listened for a moment, then shook her head. 'They haven't heard anything.' She went on talking in a low voice. Just because one deal was coming to a close, didn't mean she didn't have other things to be getting on with.

The other three lapsed back into expectant silence. Phyllis wound up her call. The sailing ship came to the eastern end of Victoria Harbour and began to head for the narrow strait of Lei Yue Mun and the sheltered waters of Junk Bay beyond. Zack's phone rang.

'Gradley,' he barked. His voice was snappish and his dark face was broody and drawn with tension. He was acutely nervous. Lord Hatherleigh thought it was the Hatherleigh family fortune that Zack cared about, but the thought hadn't crossed his son-in-law's calculating mind. Zack was concerned about his forty million dollar success fee. With the success fee and the ever-increasing success of ROSES, came his partnership.

'Hi, darling, it's me.'

'Sarah! Hi. We haven't heard anything yet. We're all here, still waiting.'

'I thought you were going to hear by eleven at the latest.'

'Yeah, I thought so too. It's gone twelve here now.'

'Is that a good sign or a bad sign?'

'It's a sign we should have chosen someone else to run the count.'

'Anyone ever tell you that you're very sexy when you're grumpy?'

'You do quite often.'

'Your fault for being grumpy so often. Well, I'm going back to sleep. It's five in the morning here. Ring me when you hear anything, and good luck.'

'Thanks, I will.'

Zack rang off. Sarah sounded calm, like she didn't have fifty million quid invested in the outcome. The four executives watched the clock and waited. The sailing ship was now almost out of sight, only its stern still visible amongst the jumble of traffic and the dancing light on the water. Phyllis's phone rang once again. She leaped to it and listened.

Her face broke into a smile of joy and her little hand clenched into a fist, thumb up.

'Fifty-two percent,' she said. 'We won with fifty-two percent.'

6

Val wasn't keen to make a fuss, but George insisted. 'It'll be fun,' he said.

His first move wasn't all that smart, recruiting Darren and Dave to help with the preparations. He told them to close the museum-turned-showroom and clear it of furniture, except for a few tables and chairs at one end. He also gave them five hundred pounds for 'refreshments and stuff', which in Darren's hands bought a surprisingly large amount of alcohol, no food at all, and the hire of a sound system which would have caused hearing loss on the far side of Leeds.

George persuaded a deeply sceptical Darren that the

showroom's own music system would be adequate and coaxed Val into spending another £200 on nibbles at the nearest Waitrose. By this time, all effort at secrecy had vanished and it was a matter of open speculation what the fuss was about. By five o'clock, the shop floor was pretty much empty, despite Gissings' groaning order book, and knots of workers milled around outside the showroom waiting for George to tell them what was happening.

'You'd better go and tell them,' said Val, peering out of an upstairs window.

'You'd better come with me.'

'I'm not coming out there. I'll die of embarrassment. I'll come down after you've told them.'

George took his fiancée's hands. They had chosen her an engagement ring, but it had to be sent away for fitting and her hands were bare.

'There's nothing to be embarrassed about. Unless you mean me, of course.'

'Do I look alright?'

George looked at her, up and down. 'You look absolutely beautiful.' He meant it.

'Idiot.'

'Well, why ask?'

Still nervous, Val walked downstairs after George. Before they went out into the yard, George tried to take her hand, but she shook free. George walked in front of her over to the showroom.

'Come on in, then, you lot,' he said, and everybody flooded into the familiar room.

At the far end, there was a platform where the Gissings Select products usually sat, and George climbed up. Val stood close to him, but down a step, with everybody else. The crowd fell completely silent, waiting.

'Thanks for coming. I've got a bit of an announcement,'

he said, suddenly embarrassed himself. He glanced down. Val was half smiling to support him, half longing to be somewhere else. 'I've got some good news,' he said. 'I'm – er – well, Val and I are engaged, engaged to be married, that is. And –'

Anything else he was going to add was drowned out in a din of cheering and stamping, started by Darren and Dave, but immediately filling the whole room. Before either Val or George could react, Val was being bundled up on to the platform and Darren had started yelling a chant of 'Kiss, kiss, kiss.'

George turned to face his now truly blushing fiancée. He brushed a strand of hair away from her face and drew her close. 'I love you,' he said, and kissed her. The cheering and clapping and stamping continued. George, too, was as red as a beetroot, and over the swelling chorus of 'For they are jolly good fellows' he yelled, 'Now sod off and get something to drink.'

As Darren's investment in alcohol began to bear fruit, George and Val were repeatedly touched by the number of people who came up earnestly offering them their delighted congratulations. In a rare quiet moment, Val turned to George.

'I've never been so embarrassed in my whole life, but I'm pleased you made me do it. It's been amazing.'

He was about to reply, when Jeff Wilmot, drunk already on two glasses of white wine, came to add his goodwill to the mounting heap. George listened patiently to Jeff, while Val was ambushed by some girls from marketing who wanted to hear all about the proposal, the ring and the wedding plans. David Ballard came along too, having been invited by George to drop in if he could.

'I can't stay long. I've got a dinner to go to in Leeds.

But I wanted to give you both my very best. Val's a smashing girl, you couldn't have done better.'

'Thanks, David. Is that a personal opinion, or a professional one?'

'Both actually, but I meant it personally. Here, come outside a moment, I've something to give you.'

George walked out into the dirty yard. The Gissings Transit van he'd once lived in was there, now restored to its proper use. Three other vans stood alongside it, all of them busy now, six days a week. George felt a glow of pride, at his factory, his success, and, inside the crowded showroom, at his soon-to-be wife. Ballard's BMW flashed and clicked at their approach.

'Picked up another fine on my way over. These bloody cameras don't give you a chance.' Ballard opened the front passenger door and searched around inside the glove compartment. He pulled something out and handed it to George. By the light from the car, George could see what it was: an old-fashioned die-cast model of a forklift truck, mounted on a black plastic pedestal.

'I'm touched, David, but –'

'Look underneath.'

George looked underneath, where an engraved brass plate was glued on. The engraving read, 'To David Ballard. With thanks for your help on the Harrogate deal, Bernard Gradley, October 1976'.

'Your dad gave it to me after I helped him buy a dying plant-hire company in Harrogate. I think you should have it now. You're the businessman of the family.'

'Yeah, well my brothers are probably happy just being the millionaires of the family.'

The older man looked at the younger. George Gradley was the spitting image of his dad, but a much nicer man. Ballard felt paternal towards him. He jerked his thumb in the direction of the noisy showroom. Noise and light was spilling out. The shadows against the windows were moving faster, as Darren did what he could to test the limits of the showroom's sound system.

'If either of your brothers went into their place of work and announced their engagement, do you think they'd get that kind of reception?'

'Probably, if they'd spent as much on booze as I have.'

'That's bollocks and you know it, Master Gradley.'

George shrugged. He looked towards the showroom again. Val was in there somewhere, explaining for the hundredth time about the engagement ring and promising to show it off as soon as it came back from the workshop. He longed for her, longed to be alone with her.

'All the same, David, I'll take you up on that offer you made. About finding people who might be interested in buying this place. I just want to test the possibility, you know. I'm not committed one way or the other.'

'Have you talked to Val about this?'

'Not yet. Been too busy with the engagement and everything.'

Ballard raised his eyebrows, so George added, 'And anyway, nothing's definite. Obviously, I won't do anything without her on board, but before I do that, I'd like to know if it's even realistic.'

'OK, George. I promised you help if you wanted it, and I'll stick to that. I'll phone you with some names and numbers in a week or two.' The two men closed up the car and walked back towards the noise and light of the showroom. Just before re-entering, Ballard tapped the toy truck on its black pedestal, which George still carried in his hand.

'When your dad did that deal, George, I remember him telling me that he couldn't understand anyone who sold their business, whatever state it was in. He said to me he thought he'd sooner die than sell his.'

George sighed and walked inside.

7

Brian McAllister had a meeting in Frankfurt that afternoon. As usual, he was late to leave. The taxi outside already had twenty pounds on the meter. His secretary had moved from impatience to despair and began to look up the time of the next flight. So far, so normal.

Eventually he was ready. He marched out of his office, briefcase in hand. He grabbed a blue woollen coat from the cupboard by the exit and headed out. He jumped into the waiting taxi and set off. The taxi driver refused to believe McAllister could make it. McAllister refused to believe he couldn't. So far, so normal.

McAllister looked at a string of e-mails his secretary had printed off, and a couple of research reports predicting meltdown on the Hang Seng. But bankers don't read in taxis, they talk. Planes are for reading. He reached into the inside coat pocket, pulled out a phone and dialled his secretary. She would act as a switchboard for the next hour or so, until he was walking down the gangway on to the plane. So far, so normal.

When he got through, his secretary sounded surprised.

'You've left your phone here on the desk. Has the driver lent you his? Anyway, I've arranged for you to collect a rental one on arrival in Frankfurt.'

It was McAllister's turn to be surprised.

'No. I'm using the phone in my coat pocket.'

McAllister looked at the phone. A printed label told

him that it was the property of Matthew Gradley at the London office of Madison.

'Damn. I've pinched young Matthew Gradley's coat. Can you tell him I've got it? Say he can take mine if he needs one this evening.'

He turned to business and started to dictate replies to his e-mails, until the traffic heading west out of London threatened to end his hopes of making the flight. He ended the call temporarily and dropped the phone back into Matthew's coat pocket. He gave the cabbie detailed instructions on how to avoid the traffic on the Cromwell Road, then reached back for the phone. He hit the redial button and waited for a connection.

The number rang, then connected. The rings sounded different from the tone at Madison, but McAllister wasn't really listening. Then a male voice answered.

'Good morning. This is James Belial at Switzerland International. How may I be of service?'

'I'm sorry. Who am I speaking to?'

'James Belial,' said Belial, speaking clearly. 'Who's calling, please?'

'It's Brian McAllister, James. But I'm afraid I have a wrong number. Very wrong.'

McAllister hit the off button. He explored Matthew's coat more thoroughly. Matthew carried two phones, both Nokias, nearly identical models. The phone McAllister had just used had no identification on the back, not even a note of the phone number.

The burly Scotsman drummed on his briefcase, lost in thought. His mouth told nothing, but his blue eyes had turned to ice. Then he took out Matthew's work phone and hit the redial button again. This time he got through to his secretary.

'Put me through to Fiona Shepperton, please,' he asked.

8

Josephine enjoyed the lines of computer code. Its exactitude was pleasing. A well-written computer program could run for thousands of lines and the outcome would be precisely known, plotted to within nanomillimetres by the intricate structure of logical commands. Tonight, she was setting herself the biggest challenge so far; one that Kodaly himself would be impressed by.

It had been a good evening. Her mother was as well as she had been for ages and was now happy to doze a little in front of the telly. Josephine sat beside her mother, giving her a gentle shoulder massage to let her know that she was there. In her half-sleep, Helen Gradley sighed. Foggy though her world had become, with her daughter by her side, it was a safe world, even pleasant.

Josephine began to work. When she needed to pause, she stretched out, found her mother's hand and began to rub it, eliciting further sighs of contentment. Josephine would never have chosen this way of life, nor would her mother ever have chosen the treacly slowness which had been poured into her mental gearbox. All the same, the pair of them had discovered things they would never otherwise have known. Josephine had learned the pleasure of giving love in a place where words didn't matter, and Helen had learned, perhaps, that it was possible to trust and feel held, however keen her earlier disappointments.

Josephine went back to her program code. Instructions flitted noiselessly down the modem, exchanging words with other computers somewhere in the London darkness outside. An answer came back and a new screen unfurled, awaiting instructions from its human mistress.

Josephine stared at the screen. It took her a second to realise what she was seeing. Then, 'Eureka!' she murmured, as her hands floated back to the keyboard. She remembered the lessons Miklos had taught her. She'd need to go carefully now.

9

Ten days after the party, Ballard phoned back.

'Still want the names?'

'Yes,' said George, pleased that Val was out of the room.

'OK. I've got three possible buyers for you. You won't like the first one, but they're by far your best bet.'

'If it's the Aspertons, then no,' said George.

'They're the most obvious buyers. They've got the cash. They know your business. You've chucked them out of a whole slice of the market that they'd love to get back into. They'd be ideal.'

'Yes. But it'd be like Everton selling out to Liverpool. I can't do that.'

'Right, but selling Everton to Man United would be fine, would it? Or Juventus?'

'Skip the lecture, David. The answer's no. Just no.'

'Right you are. The next possibility is a German outfit. Gundrum Möbelsgesellschaft GmbH, München. Something like that. I can't pronounce it. GMG, anyway. I spoke to one of our German corporate staff from head office. He says GMG are dying to get away from German wage costs and want a base in what he called the low-wage periphery. That's us apparently. Gissings might be perfect.'

'And they've got cash, have they?' asked George morosely.

'Plenty. The only difficulty would be getting them to

part with it. They've never made an acquisition before and their only country of operation outside Germany is Austria. Yorkshire's on the dark side of the moon as far as they're concerned and my friend tells me that they're a bureaucratic, slow-moving lot.'

'In other words, don't count on them.'

'There's always the Aspertons.'

'No.'

'OK. My last offer is an American group, Oregon Furniture. They're a tough bunch. They make decent products. They make 'em cheap. And when their competitors start to buckle at the knees, they leap in and buy them up for a song. Then they slash costs and repeat the process. They've cleaned up in the States. Now they're looking to repeat the formula in Europe.'

'How d'you know all this?'

'Head Office. They do a lot of business with Oregon in the US. Oregon phoned them up to ask for the names of acquisition candidates in Europe, and Head Office sent the word out to the regions. I haven't answered yet. I never do. At least, I only do if a client asks me to.'

'Have they got the money?'

David chuckled down the phone.

'The stockmarket reckons they're worth four billion dollars. They have unused bank facilities of half a billion. The only question is whether Gissings would be big enough to whet their appetite.'

'And these guys could act fast if they had to?'

'They buy companies for a living, George. They make thirty acquisitions a year.'

'OK. Phone number, please.'

David gave it to him.

'Are you going to get advice? You know, lawyers, accountants, all that.'

'No,' said George. 'I hadn't intended to.'

'It could cost you, trying to do things on the cheap.'

'That's not the point, though. I don't need the last penny from the sale, as long as I make enough to pick up Dad's legacy. Besides, I want the whole thing done as quietly as possible. I don't want squads of suits charging round upsetting everyone.' ·

'Anyone in particular they might upset?'

'I haven't told Val yet, David. But I don't need your sniping. This is my bloody factory, isn't it?'

'Yeah? What about "All that I am I give to you, all that I have I share with you"? That excludes furniture factories, does it?'

'We're not bloody married yet.'

The two men rang off, angry with each other. But George was also upset. For all his outrage, George knew that David was absolutely right about Val.

She lived in a tiny working-man's cottage, worked as a secretary in a small provincial furniture company, and she was about to marry the boss. Even if George never got a sniff of his father's cash, Val was going to be richer than she had ever imagined. Val couldn't care less if Bernard Gradley's cash fell into a black hole and never came out, but she'd be livid if George betrayed her precious Gissings.

David hadn't asked George the question directly, but he hardly needed to. It was there all the time. If George sold out, would Val still marry him?

10

McAllister's first call from the taxi had been to Fiona. He asked her whether she was aware of any contact between Matthew and James Belial.

'Yes, as a matter of fact, they do know each other,' Fiona had said. 'I was eating out with Matthew one night and we bumped into this Belial character. A creepy little guy. He greeted Matthew very warmly. Claimed they were business associates. Matthew said they had met once, but that was that.'

'Are you aware of any reason why Matthew should have called Belial from his own personal mobile phone?'

'His personal phone?' asked Fiona. In her year and a half of going out with Matthew, she didn't even know he had a second phone. 'No. I don't know. What's all this about?'

'I'm not quite sure yet,' said McAllister. 'But I know two things. First, the Stock Exchange is conducting a couple of insider trading investigations at the moment. They're looking into some trades made just before some of the big deals you and your team have pulled off this year. And secondly, James Belial is a crook. He used to work with us until we caught him selling our trading strategies to a competitor. We didn't have enough evidence to convict him of anything so we just fired him. Last I heard he was working for some dodgy Swiss outfit. You know the sort of thing. They pretend to have a client list which includes half the royal families of Europe, but in reality they spend their time laundering drugs money, assisting tax evasion, and all the rest of it.'

Fiona didn't say anything to Matthew until they got home in the evening. They faced their normal dinner time decision: eat out, microwave something from the freezer, or scrambled eggs. Matthew favoured eating out. Fiona, this evening, insisted on bunging something into the microwave. She wanted to talk with him in private.

'I got a call from Brian McAllister today.'

'Uh-huh,' said Matthew. He had been worried about McAllister finding his phone, but as the day passed without event, he had begun to relax.

'He asked me whether you knew a chap called James Belial and I said you did. I told him what you said to me at Gianfranco's that night: that you knew him, had considered investing with him, but had decided against. Then he told me that the last call you made was to Belial.'

'Uh-huh,' said Matthew again, his belly suddenly diving to somewhere below floor level.

'Apparently McAllister fired Belial some years ago. Belial had his hand in the till and was lucky not to be prosecuted. McAllister thinks that Belial's current outfit, Switzerland International, is up to its neck in drugs money.'

Fiona spoke these words gazing steadfastly away from Matthew, out of the window, but at the end of the speech she turned to look him full in the face. It could not be, it could not possibly be that the man she was slowly daring to trust with all her soul could be an insider trader. If Matthew let her down, she would never, never, never risk involvement again. But there was more to tell, and she owed it to him to tell it.

'And one more thing,' she said. 'The Stock Exchange is nosing round a couple of our deals. There were some suspicious trades just before a few of them and an inquiry is underway.'

Matthew stared at Fiona across the table. Oh, Jesus. Oh, Jesus, Jesus, Jesus. Was this how it felt? Was this what Al Capone had felt when the court summons for unpaid tax first fluttered through his letterbox? All those corporate crooks of the 1980s – Ernest Saunders, Mike Milken, Ivan Boesky – was this how they'd felt, when the first sign of trouble had wafted across their desks like the first snowflake of winter? Exposure had ruined them. They'd lost reputation, money, even their freedom. If they'd had women as special as Fiona, they'd have lost them too. Oh, Jesus, Jesus, Jesus.

Matthew yelled at his brain to keep cool. Insider trading carries a maximum seven-year jail sentence in Britain, but not many people get convicted. Think. Think. The first rule is to go slow.

'So what does McAllister think I've been up to?'

'He has no fixed ideas. I think he called me soon after finding out you knew Belial. He's obviously worried about the connection. And I think he believes that Belial would certainly be a willing collaborator on any insider trading scam. It does look bad, you know. You know Belial. You've got all the insider knowledge of our deals. And . . .' She trailed off. The next bit was hard for her to admit, even to herself. But it had to be said. 'And, Matthew, you told me you had nothing to do with Belial, yet you call him. And I've spent a year and a half with you and you've never told me you had a second phone.'

Her face was strained and white. She looked worse than he did. There was one extra fact, which lay unspoken between them. Matthew had already tried to trade on the inside. The whole Western Instruments fiasco back in New York. Fiona knew all about it and had rescued him from the consequences. He had promised her never again, and she had put the episode down to youth and foolishness. Once might be unfortunate. Twice would be unpardonable. 'It does look bad.'

Fiona almost whispered the words. My God, how she wanted Matthew not to prove a villain. Her pain made it easier for Matthew to do what he needed to do. He took her hands in his. He would be as truthful as he could be. Not for the sake of honesty, but because little lies were easier to maintain than big ones.

'My love, it's OK. I did tell you a fib about Belial,

because I was so ashamed when he popped up like that at the end of the evening. I watched him pawing you when he helped you on with your coat and I was embarrassed to admit that I'd trusted him with my money. Because I did invest my bonus with his firm. He sold me a story about the prestige of having money at a Swiss bank and I was naive enough to believe it. I gave him my bonus to invest and that's all.

'As for the phone, that's simple. I've been worrying more about my mother, and bought a phone for Josephine to call me on if there was ever a problem. My work number's engaged so often, I thought it was safest to have a special hotline.'

Fiona relaxed a bit. It was so much easier to believe that Matthew was really the loyal, supportive, loving man he seemed to be. It would blow her world apart to find he wasn't.

They spoke about it some more, and both grew calmer. Eventually, they relaxed enough to decide to hurry across to Gianfranco's to fit in some pudding and coffee. They shared a half bottle of some quite excellent German dessert wine and their mood lifted. They got to the cloakroom before the buxom Italian had disappeared and Belial's alarming presence was nowhere to be seen.

Matthew was still deeply worried, but he hid it successfully. Convincing Fiona of his honesty was the easy bit. Persuading McAllister would be much tougher. And a Stock Exchange board of enquiry could be terrifying. He'd have to cooperate in full. If he didn't, Madison would fire him. And if he cooperated, there was no limit to what they might find out.

But there was something else on Matthew's mind. Nobody at Madison knew that Fiona and he were lovers. They had kept it secret, partly to keep their working relationship smooth, and partly to help Fiona by avoiding any public commitment. McAllister would never have called Fiona with his suspicions if he had known that her strongest loyalty was not to the firm but to Matthew. Fiona was a spy inside McAllister's camp and she could be of untold value as things developed.

But she was also exposing herself. If Matthew was caught and Fiona's conflicted loyalties emerged, it would look terrible for her. She would look like Matthew's accomplice, and even if she kept her job, her career would be deader than the dinosaurs. For her, the only safe thing was to tell McAllister about their relationship.

Matthew wanted her on his side as a spy, but he wanted to protect her more. Matthew remembered Sophie and, for once, to his credit, he didn't even hesitate.

That night, as they lay together in Fiona's bed, he stroked her cheek.

'My love, I want you to do something for me,' he said.

'Anything, big boy,' she answered lazily, stroking him beneath the covers.

He moved her hand.

'I want you to talk to Brian McAllister tomorrow morning. Tell him that you and I are in a relationship. Tell him that we intend to move in together as soon as our house purchase completes. Ask him to keep you out of any decision-making as far as it affects me. Tell him that, of course, you will tell him anything he needs to know. You've got to stay out of this and that's the only way to do it.'

Fiona tensed up again. Matthew knew she would and cradled her in his arms.

'You need to do it,' he said. 'I know it's tough for you, but only McAllister needs to know. We don't have to broadcast it round the whole office.'

'I don't see why we should worry. It's working so well keeping things quiet. Don't forget that I can help if I know what McAllister's thinking.'

'And that's exactly why you have to tell him. What will he think of you if he finds out you've been murmuring all the secrets of any investigation into my ear? You have to tell him. If you don't, I will.'

Fiona snuggled up closer to Matthew. He could feel her warm body lying alongside his, from his feet to his shoulder. Their faces were close and warm on each other. She was trying to evade him.

'Say you'll do it,' he ordered her.

She moved away slightly, but still in his arms. She nodded, her submissive little girl nod.

'OK.'

'Good.'

'And, Matthew, don't . . . don't let me down.'

'I won't.'

The next day she told McAllister. The big Scotsman was surprised, but not alarmed.

'I'd never have guessed it, though now you mention it, I fancy I've seen a new twinkle in your eye this year. You did the right thing to tell me. And you're a good judge of character. If you trust young Gradley, then I'm a bit more inclined to do likewise. But you'd better ask him to step this way all the same.'

Matthew went. As he went, he prayed for a miracle. He didn't see how the miracle could happen, but he prayed anyway. Matthew closed the door behind him. McAllister was friendly and congratulated him on his alliance with Fiona.

'I've always believed that there's been a first-class woman lurking somewhere inside the first-class banker. I hope you're happy together.'

'I don't know if she mentioned it, but we're very keen

511

to keep our relationship private. You're the only one in the bank who knows.'

McAllister nodded.

'She didn't mention it. But I wouldn't have told anyone anyway. That's up to you. But you'd better tell me all about how you got mixed up with Belial. Tell me everything.'

So Matthew told him the story, as he'd told Fiona the night before. McAllister nodded encouragingly.

'OK, Matthew,' he said. 'I don't think we should have any problems here. You didn't know about Belial's track record and there's no reason why you should have done. You'd better transfer all your investments away from Switzerland International in double-quick time and you'd better tell me once you've done it.

'Meanwhile we need to deal with the London Stock Exchange. They were aware of some suspicious trading in the bond markets earlier on last year, but couldn't do much with their suspicions. As you know, most bonds are unregistered. They're like cash, where there's no central record of ownership. Shares, on the other hand, are registered, which makes it a whole lot easier to chase up insider dealing. When they started to see the same pattern of trades on the stockmarket, that's when the enquiries got underway properly. They've been asking me to make sure that our traders are clear of suspicion. For obvious reasons, the prime suspects are you, Fiona and Ed Deane.

'Personally, I doubt if we'll have any trouble. The Exchange often follows up on suspect trades and most of the time, they either discover nothing or just find an investor who got lucky. I don't see you, Fiona, or Deane as being likely to abuse your positions.

'The first thing is to clear up your investment track record. If that's fine, then I doubt the Stock Exchange will need to go further. What you need to do now is give me all your records of your dealings with Switzerland International, your account balance, what you've invested in, what stuff you've bought and sold. The lot. Bring me every document in your file. Assuming there's nothing suspicious, I'll make a report to the Stock Exchange and I'd expect that to be the end of the matter.'

Matthew nodded and said something. He couldn't even remember what. His stomach felt as though the floor of the world had fallen clean away. The miracle hadn't happened.

He could ask Belial to send him accounts, no problem. But the accounts would be damning. They'd prove he had traded on the inside, aggressively and with all his money, whenever he'd had good quality inside information at his disposal. The accounts would send him to jail quicker than you could sing 'the Bells of Old Bailey'. In six months' time, he wouldn't be counting up his father's millions. He'd be sitting in a cell counting the days until his release. Seven years is the maximum sentence, and Matthew couldn't think of a single reason why he'd get a day less.

He walked to the loos and vomited, not once, but again and again and again.

11

'Zack, you snotty-nosed creep, do you have a minute?'

'Sure. I'll come up, you miserable old slimeball.'

Zack picked up a pad of paper and a pencil and walked up the couple of floors to Banderman's office. Banderman welcomed him inside with another insult. Zack took his seat with an equally colourful greeting.

'I wanted to get an update on ROSES. You must be thrilled with the way it's taken off.'

513

Banderman had become Zack's boss. Zack was making too much money and was too important to the firm to report to anyone more junior. The two men liked and respected each other. But, despite his flippant manner, Zack knew that his chances of making it to partner depended crucially on the older man's support, and he was very careful in what he said.

'Yes, it's been amazing. After one month, I was nervous. We'd only made a couple of million bucks and I was worried that ROSES was just too sophisticated for the Asian market. But then a couple of well-known names decided to trust it, so then their competitors had to, so then everybody had to. No one wanted to be the only kid on the block not to make money out of it. Our monthly revenues are now fifteen million dollars and rising.'

'It's one hell of an achievement. How long d'you reckon you can keep it up?'

Zack shrugged. 'Not long. Our competitors are trying to muscle in, but we can handle them. The real problem is the tax authorities. The smart ones are already taking steps to plug the loophole. The dumb ones haven't yet woken up, but they will do as soon as they see how much money is escaping. And once they've plugged the loophole, then that's it. ROSES will be dead.'

Banderman nodded. Zack was right. ROSES would fade as all roses must. But before they did, they'd make a serious amount of money.

'We'll make a hundred million bucks before we're done,' said Banderman. 'That's an amazing start to your career as Gillingham's replacement. Absolutely amazing.'

Zack's narrow mouth broke into a wolfish smile. He could scent his partnership. He'd made forty million bucks on the South China deal. He'd make a hundred million or more out of ROSES. A hundred and forty

514

million bucks was four times the threshold needed to make partner.

'Dixon,' he croaked. 'I take it I'm going to be under consideration for partner this year?'

'Partner?' Banderman was taken aback. 'You want to be put up for partner?'

'You bet. I've made a hundred and forty million bucks for the bank. I've proved I can do Gillingham's job at least as well as he ever did it. Gillingham was a partner. I don't see why I shouldn't be.'

Banderman's face grew grave. Weinstein Lukes isn't like any normal company. Weinstein Lukes isn't owned by a pack of anonymous shareholders, or a tycoon and his family. It has nothing to do with government, or trusts, or mutual societies. Weinstein Lukes is owned one hundred percent by its most senior employees, its partners: a workers' cooperative – socialism in action, if not quite as Marx envisaged.

To become a partner is a rare and tremendous privilege. It's the financial equivalent of making it to saint. To be elevated to that rare height, to be told that you too may own a piece of this great company, you have to prove yourself beyond the tiniest tremor of a fraction of a shadow of a doubt. The fairy-tale princes forced to slay dragons, flatten mountains and swallow oceans were not more rigorously tested than are the would-be partners of Weinstein Lukes. And Zack Gradley, aged twenty-nine, an employee for just two years, was asking for admittance.

'It's unheard of,' said Banderman softly. 'You realise that. No one has ever made partner that quickly. No one.'

'Dixon, I've made more money this year than any one of the existing partners. You know I can go on making money for the firm. Maybe not on this scale, but on a very large scale. You know you want to keep me.'

Dixon raised his eyebrows. 'You're thinking of leaving us?'

Zack knew the right response to this question and he gave it.

'No, Dixon, of course not. But headhunters have been calling me twice a day ever since ROSES took off. So far I've just said "not interested" and left it there. But I've been assuming that Weinstein Lukes would value my contribution the way I think it deserves to be valued.'

Zack spoke the truth. Headhunters flock to success like paparazzi to a princess, and Zack was seriously successful. Banderman understood the threat latent in Zack's remarks and knew better than to regard the threat as a form of betrayal. Bankers play hardball for a living. They do it for their clients, they do it for themselves. Banderman was perfectly used to employees demanding things from him: bonuses, promotions, jobs.

'Your contribution is valued, Zack. And you'll be rewarded this year, don't you worry about that. I can promise you a fantastic bonus. I'll see to it myself. The only question is whether you make partner right away or not.'

'Dixon, the bank owes me a partnership as well as a bonus.'

'I can't promise you a partnership. It's not in my power. The Board decides who gets partnerships.'

'I'm not asking you for a promise. I'm asking you to support me. I'm asking you to do what you can.'

Zack was calculating correctly. A partnership would guarantee Zack a million pounds, because it wouldn't just bring him his bonus, it would bring him a share in all the firm's profits. And though Banderman's say wouldn't be decisive, his voice would carry a lot of clout. Banderman looked at the arrogant young man. Gradley's confidence knew no bounds, but his ability seemed beyond question.

'I'll support you, Zack. I really will. But no promises, OK?'

'OK.'

'And keep telling those headhunters to jump in the lake.'

'I will.'

It wasn't a promise, and both men knew it. Bankers worship at the altar of the market, and there's a market for bankers just like there's a market for everything else. And if there's one belief common to every banker in the world, then it's the belief that markets should be allowed to find their own level. Zack got up to go.

'Thanks, Dixon, you bonehead.'

'Go to hell, pipsqueak.'

Zack was almost out of the door when Banderman called after him.

'Oh, and Zack. I've been looking through a list of our ROSES clients. Your old friends at South China sure seemed to have an appetite for ROSES. They've been one of our biggest buyers.'

'South China? Really? They loaded up, did they?'

'You bet.' Dixon quoted some figures. For a bank of South China's size, they were certainly going it some. 'They had a real splurge.'

Zack blew out through pursed lips.

'Well, it makes sense. They were bringing out these amazing profit numbers throughout our takeover campaign. They had to come from somewhere. Now we know where. Jesus, though, Dixon, it sounds like they were speculating till kingdom come. Thank goodness they came out on the right side, otherwise they could have blown their legs off, tax dodge or no tax dodge.'

517

'Well, as it is, your father-in-law should be pretty pleased with you. First you buy him a nice new company, then you add to its value by selling Roses to it hand over fist. Maybe you should ask him to increase your fee.'

Zack laughed.

'I don't think so. He wanted to buy a bank not a casino. At one stage he even thought about pulling out. I think I'll just stay very, very quiet.'

12

Matthew walked out into the stadium. Forty thousand people were already there and the first few chants already echoed across the ground. It was a freezing February evening. A heavy grey mist hung over the stadium and swirled round the banked floodlights. The referee and a couple of ground staff came out on to the pitch to check visibility. Kickoff was running late and the crowd was impatient.

Matthew checked his ticket again and walked down the imposing North Bank to locate Belial. It was a good choice of venue, thought Matthew. He'd told Fiona he was watching the match with a friend of his from university and no one from Madison was likely to be there to spot the fib. Though Belial had responded with his usual offensive courtesy to Matthew's urgent request for a meeting, Matthew was still deeply nervous about the favour he had to ask.

Belial was easy to find. He was probably the only person on the whole of the North Bank to be wearing a newly pressed navy-blue suit complete with silk shirt, hand-made silver cuff links, pale pink silk tie and matching handkerchief, cashmere overcoat, cream silk scarf, and gleaming English brogues.

'Good evening, good evening,' said Belial. 'You cut it a little fine, but you're in time.'

'I just hope they play. The mist looks heavy.'

'Oh, they'll play all right,' said Belial as though the decision were up to him.

He was right. A few moments later, the players trooped out, kicked around for a while and took up their positions. The referee blew his whistle for kickoff and the match began. From the very first kick, Belial focused on the game with incredible intensity. It was as though the pitch, the game, the players, the crowd, even the famous stadium itself would stop existing if his concentration flickered for even a moment.

They watched ten minutes of the match in silence. Leeds had come looking for a draw and played a lone striker in front of a massed and physical midfield. Arsenal, seeking to play a more fluent game, was unable to find a way through, and a couple of times resorted to punting long balls upfield to their outnumbered strikers. The North Bank did its job and threw a wall of noise forward into the fog in an effort to lift the team. But the fog muffled the sound, and the noise and players remained muted.

Neither Belial nor Matthew joined the chants, but Belial's face quivered and frowned with every tackle, pass and kick of the game. He smiled just once, when the Arsenal captain brought a Leeds player to a halt with a juddering tackle that left both players temporarily winded. The referee booked the Arsenal player to boos from the crowd.

During a lull, as a Leeds player received treatment for a gashed leg, Matthew broached the subject that burned inside him.

'As I mentioned on the phone, I've a favour to ask.'

Belial's attention was as firmly fixed on the injured

player as it had been earlier on the football. Without moving his eyes, he replied, 'Please ask. All of us at Switzerland International are at your service.'

Matthew hesitated. Unless he could show Madison a set of investment accounts proving he was clean, he would certainly lose his job and risk conviction for insider trading. Favours didn't come more important than this.

'For reasons which I hope we needn't go into, I'd like to have a set of statements from Switzerland International which show me holding a conventional investment portfolio. I'd like to be able to show that I invested my bonus last year in well-known UK stocks and shares. Maybe some British government bonds. That sort of thing. Obviously, the portfolio won't show much of a profit. Nothing compared with what I've actually made. But that's fine. I just want to be able to show somebody – er – a more conventional-looking port-folio.'

Matthew paused. It was hard to go on without so much as a glance from the other man. Belial heard Matthew out. The injured player was running back on to the pitch, to a scattering of applause. A Leeds player positioned the ball ready to restart. Belial watched, then turned to Matthew with a smile.

'Of course we can do that. No problem at all. You invested sixty thousand with us in January. You bought stocks and shares in good solid companies. Your port-folio is now worth, say, seventy thousand. You'd like a set of statements putting all of that in writing. No prob-lem at all. It's a service we're quite used to providing, to be quite honest.'

Matthew was shocked and relieved. He knew Belial was happy to associate with clients of questionable ethics, to say the least, but he hadn't guessed how matter-of-fact Belial would be about such blatant deception. Matthew's relief was enormous. It washed through him like a huge cleansing flood. He felt lighter than he had done at any time since he and Fiona had bumped into Belial at Gianfranco's. This was it. He'd be in the clear. He'd have a clean set of accounts for Madison. Brian McAllister would tell the Stock Exchange that Matthew was clean as a whistle. He'd walk away scot-free – and what's more, he could finish off the job in hand, which was to make his million. Matthew's delight knew no bounds.

He began to thank Belial, but the game had restarted and Belial was intent once more. Matthew watched the rest of the first half without taking anything in. The freezing fog closed in and lay clamped down over the ground. The Leeds midfield successfully squeezed all life from the game and both sides resorted, gratefully it seemed, to a more physical style of play. A penalty appeal was turned down for the home team and a goal disallowed for offside. Four players were booked for fouls, all of them purposeless tackles in the centre of the park.

The first half finished goalless and the shaven-headed Arsenal fan sitting to Matthew's left predicted the game would end that way. It didn't seem to bother him that he was paying good money to freeze outside for a couple of hours, while twenty-two millionaire athletes chose to kick each other rather than the ball. Belial wasn't bothered either. In fact, he grinned with pleasure and his eyes shone.

'What an excellent match,' he said. 'The English game has so much to offer.'

Matthew began to disagree, but Belial ignored him. Instead, he unbuttoned his overcoat and withdrew a manila envelope. He handed the envelope to Matthew.

'When you asked for this meeting so urgently, I guessed what you might have in mind. I prepared these for you in Geneva this morning.'

Matthew tore open the envelope. Inside was a dream come true. There were about two dozen documents all told. He had a letter acknowledging his account had been opened and was in credit to the tune of sixty thousand pounds. He had contract notes, indicating the timing and amounts of his fictitious purchases. According to the statements he had bought shares in British Airways, Marks and Spencer's, Unilever, Glaxo Wellcome, Lloyds TSB and a handful of other impeccable British companies. He had quarterly statements showing the progress of his portfolio. He even had a couple of phoney letters about a mislaid share certificate. Everything was dated, signed, and printed on Switzerland International's stationery. It was perfect.

'I can't thank you enough,' said Matthew. 'This is absolutely perfect. I can't believe it.'

'It's our pleasure,' said Belial flatly. 'I should warn you, however, that we do charge a fee for this service.'

'Of course, I quite understand. That's fine.'

'Perhaps you misunderstand me. The fee is quite substantial.'

'I'm sure it's fine. How much is it?'

'Half a million pounds sterling.'

Matthew was blown away. He asked Belial to repeat the figure, but he had heard perfectly. Belial's words were unmistakable. He wanted to believe Belial was joking, but he knew he wasn't.

'Half a million quid? For producing a few bits of paper? You're joking. I could get a whole set of accounts made up at a printer's for a few hundred.'

Belial's eyes were on the far end of the stadium, where

there was some stirring amongst the travelling Leeds fans. Black-coated policemen were moving to the scene.

'You could go to a printer's. The forgery will probably be obvious immediately, but it will certainly be obvious if your boss bothers to check with us. Your boss, or the Stock Exchange, or your partner, or the Fraud Squad. Or whoever you are seeking to hide the truth from. If you do not accept the fee, then we shall tell the truth to whoever makes an enquiry of us. If you accept the fee, then the full resources of Switzerland International will be deployed to corroborate your story. The choice is yours. Personally, I'm quite indifferent.'

The mêlée at the other end had abated, but the police presence had noticeably thickened, like the fog.

Matthew felt violently sick. The freezing air felt oppressive and there was a rushing sound in his head. Half a million pounds. That would leave him with about seventy thousand, round about one quarter of his last legitimately earned bonus. Matthew felt faint and put his head between his knees. He thought he would vomit.

He sat out the ten minutes of half time racked by waves of nausea, but not indecision. Belial's trap was perfect. He could send Matthew to jail with the tiniest effort. He could also save him with an equally small effort and with complete certainty. If half a million was the price, then Matthew would simply need to pay up.

The players came out on to the pitch again, and took up their formation. Before the whistle blew, Matthew tucked the envelope into his pocket. He was chilled to the bone and damp with it.

'It's a deal.'

'Yes. You may rely on our complete support. We will deduct the funds from your account at the commencement of business tomorrow.'

Matthew nodded. His father's millions had evaporated beyond reach. The whole effort, the lying, the fear, the whole desperate battle had been worthless. He stared blankly ahead into the fog.

The second half of the match made the first look scintillating. Tackle after tackle thudded heavily into flesh while the ball scampered away ownerless. Seven more yellow cards were given, and two players, one from each side, were sent off for second offences. A fist fight broke out among four of the players, but was unseen by the referee who was chasing an infraction at the other end of the pitch. For some unknown reason, the Leeds manager took off the only player in his side who had come close to scoring and brought on instead another defender with a reputation for toughness. More scuffles broke out amongst the fans and the police surged in once again.

Belial was thrilled with the way the match was going. Every clattering tackle, every yellow card, every sign of aggression delighted him. He leaned forward, his face contorted with pleasure. The Arsenal fans lining the North Bank had long given up hope of a goal and contented themselves with yelling insults at the referee and everyone with anything to do with Leeds. One player was struck on the head by a missile thrown from the stands and came off the pitch to get medical treatment. Matthew had had enough of Belial's entertainment.

'Thank you for the documents,' he said hoarsely. 'I'm going to make my way home now.'

Belial turned in surprise.

'Leaving already? Just as the game's warming up? Oh – of course – pardon me. You're feeling upset about our little fee. Perhaps I should have waited till the end of the match before mentioning it.'

Matthew had started to leave, when Belial plucked at his arm.

'If you're really upset about that fee, I know an excellent way for you to recoup the money. It's remarkably swift and easy.'

Matthew sat back down. Little as he liked or trusted Belial, he had to hear this. Belial's attention drifted back to the game. Another player knocked to the ground by a late tackle, another caution, another wave of booing from the crowd. Another free kick, incompetently taken. Belial's lips were parted in pleasure and flecks of spittle hung in the corners of his mouth. The game resumed and he turned back to Matthew.

Belial explained his idea clearly and effectively. He sounded as if he were making a business presentation to a trusted client. In fact, he was making a completely illegal and outrageously dangerous suggestion to a man he scarcely knew. The depth of Belial's willingness to associate himself with crime once again stunned Matthew. There was not a flicker of emotion, not even excitement in his face as he talked through his proposal.

Matthew left immediately afterwards, while the game was drawing to its ugly close. As he left the turnstiles at the exit, another wave of booing hinted at another foul. He made his way rapidly to the tube station. While most fans stayed till the bitter end, a few had left early like Matthew. They hung about the empty streets in groups, avoiding the lamplight, dark as clots of blood. At the far end of the road the first fight was breaking out, to a tune of breaking glass. He hurried away.

Belial's idea was mad, wrong and dangerous, but Matthew couldn't get it out of his head. Whenever he closed his eyes, he could see Belial's twisted face grinning at him.

'Have you heard of vault duty?' it asked.

Spring 2001

You know the feeling, everyone's had it. Maybe it was an exam, or a speech, or dinner for your girlfriend, which you left too late. You were busy doing other things, then you looked up to find that time had caught you napping and left you for dead. The months of revision had to be crammed into weeks. Your plans for duck's breast *à la* tickle-my-fancy flew out the window, and instead you were opening tinned vegetables and swearing at your freezer for the wonderful food it didn't contain.

Three young men named Gradley have that feeling now. None of them has his million. None of them has anything that vaguely resembles a million, not unless you count it in roubles. Their father's fortune hangs plump and heavy on the tree, but it won't hang there for ever. It is 5 March 2001 and there are 130 days until Bernard Gradley's deadline.

The feeling's gut-wrenching and it never leaves. You must know it. Everyone's had it.

1

There are lots of ways to make money in this world.

One old-fashioned technique is to make things. You buy something that folks don't want, say wood, then you turn it into something that they do, say tables. Then you sell the things you've made and use the money to buy more wood. Next time, you try to make your tables a little better and a little cheaper and you aim to sell a few more. You do that each year, until by the time you retire, you are making and selling an awful lot of tables, your profits are fat and you are the toast of your local Rotary Club. The annual challenge cup at the local golf club bears your name and your wife is named president of the village horticultural show.

Recently, other techniques for making money have been invented. Instead of buying wood and selling tables, for instance, you can buy companies, fix them up and sell them. With the profit you've made, you can go and buy a bigger company, fix it up and sell that at an even larger profit. You can go on doing that until you're buying companies worth several billion, and making profits of a billion or more on each sale. There are disadvantages to this way of doing business. People tend to dislike you, for one thing, and nasty things are written about you by an embittered and envious press. On the other hand, you are now happily retired in your twelve-bedroom home on Mustique, your mistress living quietly nearby, or perhaps you have your own island somewhere in the neighbourhood. In those parts, people tend to ignore the spiteful chatter of journalists. And if it really bothers you, you can buy your own newspaper to set things straight. You wouldn't be the first.

What kind of businessman was George to be? For most of his life he had assumed he would be a third type of individual, namely the type that inherits money from his dad and passes his life finding ways to spend it. Then, since his father's death, George had begun to think he might be a businessman after all: the first type, who makes things and sells them, makes things and sells them. But now Ballard had put an idea into his head. If he sold Gissings for a couple of million, and claimed his father's estate, who knows what he could go on to achieve? Gradley Plant Hire Limited was still there, in trust, making money but in need of leadership. None of the three brothers had given the company a second thought. They'd assumed that if they collected under Gradley's will, they'd flog the company and keep the money. But now George had another dream. What if he became his father's successor? If he'd turned around Gissings, which was extremely unpromising material, what would he be able to do with Gradley Plant Hire? On the other hand, if he sold Gissings to a bunch of hire-and-fire Americans, what on earth would Val think?

George clasped a beer in the seventeenth-century coaching inn and waited for his guests to arrive. Under his chair, behind his legs, a fat briefcase pressed into his calves. It was to see that the contents of that briefcase that David Thurston and Kelly O'Shea had flown in from the Cascade Mountains of distant Oregon. Would he recognise them, he wondered, as he sipped his beer.

He needn't have worried. The old oak door creaked admittance to two newcomers, a man and a woman. He was tall, fit, clean-cut, tanned, perfect teeth, perfect suit, crisp white button-down shirt, dark red tie. George knew from the sight of him that he worked out, had quality time with his kids, ate a low-fat, low-salt, high-fibre diet, attended church on Sundays, and played a mean game of golf. And as for his partner – well, she'd have turned heads at the Oscars. She, too, was tall, fit, tanned, perfect teeth, perfect sand-coloured suit, crisp white shirt – plus, she had the face of a movie star and

528

the billowing auburn hair that usually only lives in cosmetic ads. George didn't need to ask to know that she graduated with honours from a good Ivy League school, that she believed women were entitled to careers and kids, that she jogged every morning, and was up with current affairs and probably flossed her teeth too. George stared like a street kid at a peepshow. Then he shook himself. He could recognise them, but they had no way of distinguishing him from the other jacket-and-tie Yorkshiremen in the bar. He rose and went over to the two Americans.

'Mr Thurston? Miss, I guess I mean Ms O'Shea? I'm George Gradley.'

'Hey, George, nice to meet you,' said Thurston, gripping George's hand like something in a gymnasium. 'Please call me David.'

Thurston quit mauling George's hand, which wasn't delicate but still felt ragged. George turned to Kelly O'Shea. Close up, she was dazzling. George went weak at the knees, in a way he hadn't done since he was fifteen. She took his hand. It was a firm grip for a woman, but next to Thurston's, it was rose petals.

'Kelly O'Shea. Pleased to meet you,' she smiled at him. Her smile lingered for the amount of time prescribed by the best business schools: use your assets, but respect yourself; don't flirt.

They took their places at the table. George's briefcase still sat beneath him. Inside were management accounts, statutory accounts, tax filings, product brochures, customer analyses, cash flow forecasts, design prototypes; everything. A waitress came to take their orders. George ordered shepherd's pie and another beer. Thurston asked for lasagne with a big mixed salad and orange juice. His partner asked for the same but with mineral water.

'So, George, you have a pretty nice business, we hear,' said Thurston with a perfect smile.

'I hope so. We've put in a lot of work over the past couple of years. Brought the company back from the brink.'

Thurston nodded, like a therapist listening to some childhood trauma.

'That must have been a whole lot of hard work, right? But pretty satisfying, I'll bet.'

'Do you mind?' asked O'Shea as she got a portable computer from her bag. 'I put all my notes on here now.' She laid her mobile phone beside the PC, 'In case I need to download stuff from head office.'

'Go ahead,' said George. 'First, maybe, you could tell me a bit about Oregon Furniture and your interest in coming over to Britain.'

'Sure, George, I'd be glad to do that. Have you had the chance to review any of our corporate documents? Annual report and review, corporate profile, our "what the press says" brochure, 10-K filing, 10-Q? You'll see they each carry our mission statement on the inside cover.' Thurston began to lay a bunch of glossy brochures one on top of the other in front of George, who leafed through them aimlessly. Thurston began to recount the company's story, from its humble beginnings to its current dominance of a swathe of the US furniture market. 'Our research indicates we have the opportunity to replicate that success in Europe, and that's why we're here, George.'

At this point, the waitress returned with the orders. Thurston's orange juice came from one of those irritatingly small bottles they still serve in pubs, poured into a wine glass over a rapidly melting ice cube. The mineral water was similarly small and warm and the mixed salad wasn't mixed enough, or green enough, or something, for Thurston. He began to give rapid instructions to the waitress on how to remedy the situation. She listened wide-eyed and dived off to get her manageress, who listened impassively as Thurston explained what he wanted. To pass the time, meanwhile, O'Shea gave George a smile which made his knees wobble. 'David's very particular,' she explained, then frowned as someone at a next-door table lit a cigarette.

As Thurston's attention returned to the matter in hand, George took charge of proceedings.

'How much do you know about Gissings?' he asked.

'Not nearly enough,' smiled Thurston.

George dragged out his briefcase and started to stack his own piles of documents on the table. 'I didn't know exactly what you wanted, so I copied the lot,' he said. 'If there's anything additional you want, then you should ask, and if we've got it, you can have it.'

Thurston's hand hovered over the pile. 'Did you want us to sign a confidentiality agreement?'

George was thrown by the question. 'Er, no, that's OK. I mean as long as you're not going to post this stuff on the Internet or something,' he said nodding at O'Shea's computer.

'Ha, ha, ha! The Internet!' Thurston laughed, and nodded at O'Shea who laughed as well. The laughter was careful, like the laughter of missionaries. 'Very good, George. The Internet! No, seriously though. You're quite right. We take business integrity very seriously. It's right up there on the mission statement. We won't misuse this material, you have our corporate word. Right, Kelly?'

'Right.'

Thurston's hovering hand dived into the pile. He began identifying the documents in the pile and Kelly began to tap the titles into her computer. The waitress returned with the orders as amended by Thurston. The manageress stood behind her in silent support.

'This is the freshest orange juice you have?' he asked.

Waitress, manageress and George nodded.

'OK. Fine then. Thank you.' He sipped it, as though testing for contamination, but it appeared to pass. The mixed salad was still the same mixture of iceberg lettuce, supermarket tomatoes and cucumber, but it had grown to fill a large mixing bowl and Thurston passed it without comment. George happened to catch O'Shea's eye and she wrinkled up her eyes at him, flashing him another my-dentist's-more-expensive-than-yours smile. Her auburn hair tumbled in cascades down on to the gleaming white collar of her blouse and shone there like coils of copper. George dug into his shepherd's pie and burned his tongue.

Lunch proceeded with a detailed examination of the documents George had brought. Thurston and O'Shea were both very complimentary.

'You've lifted sales a long way in a short time,' he said.

'And good margin improvement too. Nice!' she said.

They looked at the product brochures.

'Nice design concept,' he said.

'Yes, really neat,' she echoed. 'Like our own Blue Mountain range, isn't it?'

They passed on pudding. There was no decaf coffee available, so Thurston ordered a herb tea which the pub by some miracle had available, while O'Shea risked a normal coffee.

'We can take these documents away with us, can we, George?'

'Sure.'

'That's great.' Smile. 'Get us crunching numbers early, eh? This is really very interesting, very interesting indeed.'

O'Shea leaned forward. 'Tell me, George, why are you

keen to sell now? Not that I think it's the wrong thing to do – not at all – I'm just interested in your motives.'

'Quite right,' said Thurston. 'We're sure you're doing the right thing. The industry's consolidating fast. Economies of scale, one-stop shopping, retail power, national marketing. Things are going to get tough for the little fellers, right, Kelly?'

George shook his head. 'Gissings is doing just fine. It's got years of profitable growth ahead of it as an independent manufacturer. I'm not selling out of fear. I'm selling because I want the money. That's all.'

'Ha, ha! Right, the money. Well, that's the best reason there is. Right, Kelly?'

They began sorting themselves out to leave. George called for the bill but Thurston beat him to it.

'No, no. We absolutely insist, George. It's been a great pleasure, even if next time we have to bring our own juice. Ha, ha. Only kidding, honestly. It's a neat place. Seventeenth century, right? My wife'll go bananas when she hears. She loves historic things.' The pub wouldn't accept Thurston's corporate Amex card, and he paid with dollops of notes, counting them out like a five-year-old with Monopoly money.

'We'll take it as far as we can with what you've given us. Kelly's our spreadsheet genius –'

'Oh, I wouldn't say that –'

'No, really, she is – and we'll do our crunching as fast as we can and kick the idea round at head office. If we need any more information, Kelly'll give you a call. I'll keep my eye on her, though, make sure she doesn't ask you for too much. Always the perfectionist, right, Kelly?'

'Oh, I wouldn't say that –'

'All being well, we'll call you in a couple of weeks to sort out a site visit and maybe start to negotiate ourselves a deal. OK? How does that sound, George?'

'That's fine. But the fact that I'm considering a sale is very confidential. Nobody except for me knows about it, and for the moment that's how I want to keep it. If you want to call me, that's OK, but just pretend you're a friend of mine. Don't let my – er – secretary know that you're calling about a business matter.'

'You want confidentiality, George. Sure. We understand that.' Thurston was very earnest. 'You're not alone in that. Many of the companies who have joined the Oregon family have had similar considerations, and we do our best to respect that. We believe that honouring confidentiality is a key part of ethical business behaviour. Kelly, you and George are old friends, right?'

'Sure. Right.' Another big smile made its way down George's spine and lodged like jelly in his knees. 'I'll be very sensitive to that.'

'And one other thing,' said George. 'I assumed you would want a site visit at some stage and that's fine. But if you could make yourselves as inconspicuous as possible when you come, it would really help. I don't want your visit to upset my workers.'

'We'll be so inconspicuous, you won't even notice we've been.'

George shook hands, and made ready to leave.

'Nice to meet you,' he said.

'Great meeting you,' they said. 'And see you again soon.'

George watched them leave. A billow of late spring rain coming in from the west washed across the grey pub car-park. George drove away, feeling depressed.

2

A moral conundrum. How far would Matthew go for his million?

Insider trading was somehow OK. He hated the fear and the risk and the lying, but it was only the risk of getting caught that perturbed him. If he could be a hundred percent sure it was safe, he'd do it all day every day, make his million and as much more as he could, until his time ran out:

Betray Fiona? No. That he wouldn't do, not after Sophie. He knew that his insider trading had taken risks with Fiona's trust that weren't his to take, but all the same she was more precious than a million pounds and all his father's money. She was off-limits.

But between the black and the white, there lie a million greys. Dove, silver, ice, ash, steel, slate, charcoal, gunpowder. What Belial suggested wasn't at the nearly-white end of grey. It was up there with the gunpowder and charcoal. It's true, no individual would be obviously hurt by it, but all the same, even as Bernard Gradley's son, you couldn't help but learn some basic rules. And the rules were explicit. What Belial suggested was wrong.

Would Matthew do it? The rules were clear, but his mind was not. He didn't know. He honestly didn't know.

3

'Sorry you had to trail all the way out here,' said Lord Hatherleigh to his son-in-law. 'Parking's getting so damn difficult these days.'

The service elevator dropped them at the top storey, leaving them to walk the last bit up two flights of concrete stairs. From the windswept roof of the office block, the dense heart of London stretched away to the south. West of them, Hampstead Heath spread like a dark island in the neon tide.

'I love this thing. Saves hours, despite the trouble parking. Elizabeth's none too keen on it though.'

Zack wasn't all that keen on 'this thing' either, but he didn't like to seem wimpish in front of his father-in-law, and he climbed resolutely into the small helicopter. As Lord Hatherleigh checked his instruments and established radio contact with Central London flight control, a spatter of rain fell across the windscreen. Zack looked at the rain and found himself wishing he had been able to join Sarah and Elizabeth on the train down to Ovenden House a few hours earlier. When he was at work he hardly thought about Sarah. He had a job to do and he got on with it. But at other times he resented time spent away from her. It wasn't that he was in love, he insisted, just that in one package Sarah supplied him with all the things that an eighty-hour week at Weinstein Lukes deprived him of: relaxation, fun, sex, warmth, laughter. He was looking forward to seeing her this evening, and he let his mind skip over the two hundred dark miles that lay between them.

Hatherleigh was done with his checks. 'All set?' he asked, and started the engine.

Above their heads, the drooping fins began to turn. As they increased in speed, something in the feel of the helicopter changed. Before it had sat heavily on the concrete roof, a thing of metal, clumsy and dead. Now, life vibrated through it, standing as a dancer stands, lightly. Before Zack even noticed movement, the helicopter was six feet off the ground, the lovely safe roof below unreachable, and all those windy miles ahead.

Both men were silent as Hatherleigh took the 'copter up to small aircraft cruising altitude, across the great city and out beyond Heathrow's thundering airways. A late-arriving jumbo from the States passed close by, leaving Zack feeling like a pedal-cyclist on a motorway.

He knew a few rules about helicopter flights for the nervous. Don't look down. Don't think of where you are. Never remember that you're in a tiny glass egg, a transparent bubble, a speck of foam with only air to lean on.

Zack broke the first rule soon after the passage of the jumbo. And in the giddiness of seeing suburban London spread like a map beneath him, he broke the second rule too. He tried to think about Sarah instead, or about the forthcoming weekend, or about his father's cash, and the certainty that it would soon be his. None of these comforting thoughts helped, and a buffet of turbulence, which lifted then dropped the little craft, emphasised all too strongly the extent of Zack's dependence on the unreliable skies.

'OK?' asked Hatherleigh, into quieter airspace now and able to relax.

Zack nodded. He didn't like talking in the helicopter, yelling above the blades, but Hatherleigh always enjoyed it and Zack needed anything to take his mind off his fear.

'I'm fine,' he yelled. 'How are things going at South China?'

It had now been two months since Hatherleigh Pacific had enjoyed control of South China, and Hatherleigh and Scottie had been busy whipping their new acquisition into shape.

'Good. Shipping side is amazing. There's a whole damn goldmine there and the lazy sods before us never even bothered to dig. Scottie's fired all the existing bunch and brought in the best of our own managers from Hatherleigh Coastal. In a couple of years, we'll be making more from South China's ships than from our own.'

'That's great.' Zack's conversation wasn't too clever when he was frightened.

Hatherleigh's route was simple. He picked up the M3 motorway out of London, then, just after Basingstoke, he'd follow the A303 west all the way to Devon. The lighted canal of traffic below at least gave something for Zack's eyes to hang on to in the luminous dark. The shower of rain which gusted over them in London had returned in company and a series of squalls pitched into the helicopter. Hatherleigh made constant minute adjustments to keep on course. Basingstoke passed beneath them and Hatherleigh skipped the southward bulge of the road, to rejoin it somewhere over Andover. Beyond Andover lay Salisbury Plain and the dark pillars of Stonehenge.

'How about the property side and the bank itself?' bawled Zack.

'Property's great. Land slap-bang where we want it. Our property guys are delighted. Bank's a different matter. It'll take time to get it sorted, but we don't see too much of a problem. So far, we're all very pleased.'

The helicopter sped on into the thickening night. The weather was getting worse and Hatherleigh ducked lower to keep his eyes on the landmarks beneath. To Zack's inexperienced eyes, the traffic on the A303 looked very thin or perhaps the falling rain simply swallowed the lights. In any case, it felt a dangerous and friendless journey. Every now and then, Hatherleigh spoke to air-traffic control, requesting and obtaining permissions, soliciting and passing information. To them, this was just another rainy Friday night, nothing to be upset about.

'Be entering a front, soon. May be a bit bumpy.'

Zack only caught the last couple of words. He didn't know if Hatherleigh was warning him or just passing on routine information. Zack assumed it was routine, but his pulse rate accelerated anyway. It'd be nice to see

Sarah again, to share a hot bath with her. Outside the rain increased. The helicopter left the A303 and headed west across the Vale of Somerset towards the distant fires of Taunton. The wind was strong and gusty, and Zack felt the metal cage around him ride the gusts like a boat on the open sea. They passed over Taunton and the M5, the last bright lights they'd see. As they headed over the Brendon Hills to Exmoor, there'd be a few clusters marking villages and scattered dots for farmhouses; otherwise only the endless sighing black of forest, night, and open moor.

Ovenden House lay south of Exmoor, but Hatherleigh always enjoyed spinning over the moor before wheeling south to Ovenden. Tonight was no exception despite the weather, and Hatherleigh focused furiously on the dark land below. If he strayed too high, he risked losing visibility in the low-lying cloud; too low and the lightless peaks of Exmoor could rise to meet him.

'Did you find out where South China's extra profits were coming from?' yelled Zack, desperate to keep his brain occupied with anything except where he was.

'Yes. From the roulette wheel, every penny.'

'Speculation?'

'Yes. They played a pretty dangerous game from the look of it. Loaded up on some tax gimmick – ROSES it's called – that your crowd is pushing hard at the moment. Is ROSES one of your brainwaves?'

'I had some input,' said Zack, not wanting to take the credit for something that Hatherleigh would be certain to disapprove of.

'Yes, well, it certainly encouraged South China to take risks that they shouldn't have taken.'

'At least they came out on the right side.'

Hatherleigh glanced sideways at Zack. It was old-fashioned of him, he knew, but he didn't like the culture of instant wealth, and he had a hunch that Zack had more to do with ROSES than he let on. Hatherleigh's glance found Zack, lit up by the instrument panel, pressing his angular frame into the padded seat. He looked nervous. Hatherleigh looked ahead again, eyes raking into the darkness ahead, fingers sensing every tug on the helicopter's frame. He nodded.

'River Exe below us now. We'll follow it south to Ovenden.' Then turning his attention back to business, he added, 'Yes, we've closed down the casino, but apparently we can't shut down the trading rooms altogether, much as I'd like to. You'd understand all that better than me.'

There was a sudden flash, which Zack, in his fear, immediately assumed came from some major fault with the helicopter. He would have leaped from his seat, except that his seat belt caught him. As a second flash lit the sky, he realised without much reduction in his anguish that the helicopter was fine, but the rain clouds were producing bolts of lightning and hurling them in fiery poles to earth. Zack was sitting amidst the fireworks of giants. By now, he was in a state of naked terror. He would never, ever travel this way again. He'd sit in eternal traffic jams if he had to. He'd walk if he had to. He'd cross England on a pogo-stick. The helicopter followed the rushing river below, chased by the fury of the thunder and the screaming lightning. Zack wanted to continue talking, anything to distract his attention.

'You've checked their books carefully have you? I know our guys were surprised at how greedy South China seemed to be.'

Hatherleigh's eyes strayed once again from the unmarked way ahead to Zack's taut face.

'Yes. We've checked their books.'

540

Zack nodded. He felt like vomiting. Hatherleigh glanced again. Was Zack worried by something? Something apart from the lightning, that is?

'You could ask your guys to send us a list of transactions,' said Hatherleigh. 'That way, we could check off what you sold us against what South China bought. Seems like a sensible precaution to take. Good idea.'

Zack nodded in feeble assent. He could imagine the bitching and moaning that that kind of request would cause on the Weinstein Lukes trading floor, but a client was a client and he'd get Hatherleigh what he wanted.

Just then a flash of lightning seemed to explode directly in front of them. Simultaneously, a downdraught of wind snatched the helicopter and threw it down, causing Zack to lose his belly somewhere in the blackness above. The black lift shaft carried them on down, until Zack's fingernails cut into the seat cover. Another dart of lightning lit up a bristle of treetops at what seemed no distance away. If they'd been rocks on a lee shore, Zack couldn't have been more frightened. In his terror, he almost felt the first branches sweeping against the base of the helicopter, sucking them down into certain death. They were still moving downwards fast.

'Look out!' he cried.

Hatherleigh didn't take his eyes from the rain-blotted screen. But with his right hand he thumped his passenger and pointed. In the midst of the Ovenden House woodland, a white-painted H was lit up. Hatherleigh dropped the helicopter on to the landing pad with the gentlest of impacts.

'We're here,' said the viscount. Beneath the feeble shelter of Zack's city raincoat, the two men ran across the grass to the welcoming stones of Ovenden House.

4

Matthew entered the lift. It had a corrugated rubber floor, metal walls and a rubber buffer running right round the compartment at waist height. The compartment was perhaps twenty feet long, ten feet wide and twelve feet high. A plaque on the wall indicated a maximum carrying capacity of thirteen thousand five hundred kilos. Thirteen and a half tons. Two hundred people.

'Get a lot of elephants down here, do you?' asked Matthew.

The security guard shook his head.

'Bullion. Gold and silver. The loading bay's not a secure area. That means that whenever we need to transport anything, we take an armoured truck downstairs. It uses this lift.'

A security camera in the ceiling winked as Matthew looked at it. The security guard pressed the down button on the lift and spoke simultaneously into a video intercom. Unseen colleagues in the control room verified his face and voice. They released a lock on the lift and it moved slowly down. It was six twenty-two in the morning.

The Madison offices in London are architecturally unremarkable, except for one thing. They are nearly as deep as they are high. There are seven storeys above ground, four larger storeys below.

The first underground level is dedicated to the canteen, a gym, some storerooms, the mailroom, a sickbay. A few other bits and bobs. Nothing exciting.

Below that level, there's a floor devoted to mainframe computers, back-up phone switchboards, emergency generators, data storage, and tapes of all trading-room phone calls. The entire level is capable of being sealed off in the event of fire, flood, or terrorist attack. The floor is important, but, important as it is, the next two floors below ground hold something of far greater worth.

Madison boasts the world's largest custody business. The idea of custody is simple. If you buy a few bars of gold, you don't want to dig a hole in the ground to store them, but you don't want to leave them knocking around your desk either. So you come to somebody – Madison for instance – and ask them to look after your gold for you. Madison is happy to oblige. They charge you a fee. Pop the bullion in their vaults and everyone's happy.

The third floor below ground is given over to the admin staff who look after the vaults. But Matthew was headed for the floor below that. The vaults themselves. Belial had been right. There is a well-kept secret at Madison, and Matthew had only just been inducted.

The vaults are guarded by a single door. The door is guarded by a triple lock. Each lock is released only when a certain combination has been correctly inserted. One set of combinations is passed from security guard to security guard on a fortnightly shift pattern. The second set of combinations is passed between police officers belonging to the Metropolitan Police Force's Valuable Commodities Unit, known as ValCom. The police officers also change on a fortnightly basis, but the shifts are out of sync with those of the Madison security guards. The third and final set of combinations is passed down amongst Madison vice presidents on a weekly basis. All three sets of combinations are changed every six weeks, but again, out of sync, so that one combination is altered every second week.

Matthew's promotion meant he was down on the vault duty rota. He would be on duty for a total of four weeks this year. This week. Again in about a month's time. Then again, a couple of times in autumn, after his father's deadline had expired.

Belial's suggestion was madness, but Matthew couldn't get it out of his head. He wasn't going to do anything today. Nothing this week, even. Nothing at all, except look and listen. Belial's suggestion was almost certainly insane, but there was nothing illegal about looking.

Four floors below street level, the lift came slowly to a halt. The security guard pressed the intercom again and asked for the doors to be opened. The control room verified his request and released the doors.

There wasn't much to see. A concrete passageway, wide enough for a lorry, ran from the lift to a corner about sixty feet away. The passageway was lined with foil-insulated pipes and festoons of cables, a metal cupboard housing some kind of electrical control station. In the ceiling, cameras blinked on and off, monitored from the control room upstairs. All pictures were recorded and stored for a minimum of six months.

The security guard with Matthew didn't pause at the view.

'The vaults are through here,' he said, pushing his way through a small door in the main passageway. 'You need to report down here at six thirty every morning this week and seven o'clock every evening. Don't be late or get hit by a bus, because we can't open or close the vaults without you.'

The passageway ended in a circular glass booth. The guard pressed a green button set into a control panel and the glass wall on their side slid open.

'This is the vault-user identification chamber. You step inside. The door will close. There'll be a flash, which means it's taken a photo. Then you press the grey wall panel with your right hand. The panel will record your fingerprints, then let you out. Oh yes, and you'll be weighed as well. If you walk out of here with a bar of gold stuffed up your trousers, we'll know all about it.'

Matthew stepped into the booth. The glass wall closed. There was a flash. He held his hand out against the grey panel, and in a second or so, the opposite glass wall hissed open. He waited on the other side for his companion. The security guard followed, and escorted Matthew down the final stretch.

Punctual to the minute, at six thirty exactly, they arrived at the north end of the vault. Two people were waiting, deep in conversation. One was dressed in the grey uniform of the Madison security staff, the other dressed in a nondescript grey suit. He must be the ValCom policeman. Matthew's escort reminded him of the way out, then left.

Everyone was present. It was time to open the vaults.

The doorway was closed by a green-painted steel door. The door had three dials on it, each one numbered from one to a hundred. In the centre of the door was a glass panel with a liquid crystal timer unit set above a few controls. Below that, there was a metal wheel like a steering wheel.

When the vaults were closed in the evening, the timer was set to six twenty-eight the following morning. Even if you had knowledge of all three combinations, you couldn't release the door until the time on the timer had expired. A green lamp indicated it was OK to proceed.

The security guard went first. He flicked the top left dial expertly round, first clockwise, then anticlockwise. Each time he went slowly as he came to the exact number which made up the combination, then once he had positioned the dial exactly, he flicked it back round to find the next number. Six times in all. When he found the last number, the dial locked into position. Now it was the policeman's turn.

The man from ValCom was just as speedy as the security guard, and just as accurate. The upper right-hand dial also locked into position. Matthew's turn.

Matthew had been given the combination by his predecessor, a vice president in the equity research department. Matthew was allowed to write down the combination, but only once and only on condition that the codes were disguised. Matthew had written them down like a phone number in his address book. If it were lost or mislaid at any point, he needed to call the Head of Security. The combinations would be changed immediately.

Matthew twirled the dial. The dial worked a heavy drum inside the door, but the balance was so perfect that the motion was very easy. Matthew almost overshot his first number, sixty-two anticlockwise. When he found it, there wasn't the tiniest click to tell him he was right, just the same oiled silence as there had been with all the numbers. He twirled the dial back the other way. Eighteen clockwise. By his fourth number, Matthew became confident, but as a result, he overshot on his fifth twist and ended up at forty-five anticlockwise, instead of forty-four. He needed to start again from the beginning.

Eventually he got it. The third and last dial was locked in position. The security guard turned the big circular wheel. As he turned, a hum became audible. The hum turned into a whistle. The whistle turned into a deep roar. The guard and the policeman made no move to open the door.

'What's that?' asked Matthew.

'Once the door's shut, it's airtight. Any temperature

difference between the inside and outside creates a pressure difference. The wind is just balancing out the pressure. You can't open the door till the pressure's balanced.'

Sure enough, the wind began to subside. The guard pulled at the wheel, and the door swung easily open. It was perhaps eighteen inches thick, its sides studded by steel rods each an inch and a half thick. When bolted shut, the rods fitted snugly into bolt holes all round the frame of the door. You could put a barrel load of explosives against that door and you'd only dent the paintwork. You wouldn't have much joy with the surrounding walls either. Sheets of steel ran right round the entire area and every inch was wired with anti-tamper sensors. The Bank of England has some pretty secure hidey-holes, but for purpose-built modern technology you don't get safer than the vaults of Madison.

The security guard, the policeman and Matthew walked on in. It was a regular part of vault duty. You opened the vault, then made a brief tour of inspection. Belial had been right about that, as he had been right about everything else.

First, the bullion vault. Beneath cold overhead lights, on a thousand steel racks, the wealth of nations lay gleaming. Bars of gold, silver and platinum lay stacked, orderly and dead. Gold is easy stuff to look after. It's not like books which mustn't get damp. It's not like wine which mustn't get cold. It's not like paintings, which mustn't get damp, or warm, or cold, or dry. Gold just sits there, ready for when you want it.

'Jesus Christ,' whispered Matthew. 'How much is that lot worth?'

The security guard was unimpressed. Everybody seeing the vault for the first time said that.

'I don't know, mate. But put it this way, when we

moved to this building ten years ago, it took fifty-four lorryloads to shift it all. We've got a lot more now, mind you.'

Matthew was sceptical. There was a lot of metal here, but not that much.

'It doesn't look that much to me.'

'Have you tried lifting one of these babies? Fill a truck with them and you'll break both axles. Little by little, that's the only way to do it.'

As they spoke, they walked quickly round the three chambers which formed the vault. Matthew wanted to stop and touch the gold, feel the weight of a bar, feel the chill of it against his cheek, see if he could dent it with his teeth. But they hurried on. Nothing was awry. Routine stuff.

If Belial was right, there was one more vault to see, the exciting one. Matthew followed his two escorts through the next door.

They emerged from the bullion vault into a general office area. There were desks, phones, computers, calendars, coffee machines. It was like any office anywhere. A few billion dollars' worth of gold next door didn't make it interesting. They walked through another door, into an anteroom containing a steel cutting table and circular saw. A stack of cardboard-wrapped spare blades lay next to the machine. Next to an Air France calendar, open on the wrong month, was a rack of safety goggles.

'What on earth is that for?' asked Matthew, who already knew. Belial had mentioned the saw and why it was there.

'Coupon cutting. We could do it with scissors, but it would take for ever.'

The security guard pushed at a final door as he spoke, and they walked on into the last vault. The Eurobond vault.

It was a large tatty-looking room. Ceiling tiles were missing in places. The carpet tiles on the floor were worn and stained. Tinny metal racks stretched from floor to ceiling, reminding Matthew of his college library. The racks were labelled the same way too. Someone had written out some signs in black felt-tip, then Sellotaped the signs to the racks. The signs ran A–B, C–E, and so on.

The racks weren't full. They probably weren't more than a third full. Bundles of paper sat there. Some of the bundles were wrapped in cellophane. Others were tied together with plastic strips. Some just sat loose. Some of the piles were fat, others thin. In one corner of the room, a neon light flickered annoyingly. It didn't look like much.

It didn't look like much, but here was wealth beyond the dreams of princes. Matthew stepped forward in awe and walked reverently down the aisles.

As he walked, he looked at the names on the bundles of paper to either side of him. Ford, France Telecom, Fuji, General Motors, Generali, Hoechst, Honda, IBM, ICI, Japan Airlines, J.P. Morgan, Kodak, Krupp. The names were a directory of the world's most powerful companies.

Then Matthew let himself glance at the numbers. Fifty thousand dollars. A hundred thousand Euros. Twenty thousand pounds. Two hundred thousand francs. Not each bundle. Each bit of paper. Matthew stopped at the IBM bundle, which stood about twelve inches high. Each bit of paper in the stack had a face value of fifty thousand dollars. Matthew guessed there must have been a thousand bits of paper in the bundle.

These bundles explained the saw outside. Every Eurobond has a certain number of coupons attached. Each coupon entitles the holder to claim one interest payment, usually every twelve months. Unusually, in this world of computers, it's the physical bit of paper which you need to claim interest. No bit of paper, no payment. Madison used saws to clip the coupons.

Matthew walked on. As he stepped into the next aisle (Lloyds TSB, Lufthansa, Microsoft, Motorola) he banged up against something standing in the way. He felt a searing pain in his knee and foot.

He had walked into a librarian's trolley standing in the middle of the aisle. The trolley, like the shelves, was piled with bundles of paper. Matthew looked down at it. There was some miscellaneous stuff on the upper shelves – Ericsson, Electricité de France, Glaxo Wellcome. The lower shelf was solid with a General Electric bundle so big it needed to be split into five piles. Each bit of paper in those piles was worth a hundred thousand bucks.

Matthew had stubbed his toe on a billion dollars.

Eurobonds are the world's way of borrowing money offshore. Don't be fooled by the name. They're called Eurobonds just because the marketplace is situated in Europe. But everyone uses it. American companies. European ones. Far Eastern ones. You can borrow pounds or euros if you want to. You can borrow dollars or yen. If your name covers the globe from Kansas City to Kyoto, you can borrow what you like and as much as you like.

So popular is this method of borrowing, the entire Eurobond market is now valued at over four trillion dollars. Madison looked after about seven and a half percent of all Eurobonds in issue. Seven and a half percent was three hundred billion dollars. Matthew was standing in the presence of three hundred billion dollars.

There's another thing about Eurobonds which Matthew knew. He knew it anyway, but Belial had taken great pains to emphasise it. Eurobonds are bearer instruments. That means there's no central record of ownership, no company register recording who owns what. A Eurobond is like a banknote. If it's in your pocket, it's yours. You don't need to ask permission to exchange it or sell it. You don't need to say where you've got it from.

Eurobonds are the highest denomination currency in the world.

The security guard and policeman were bored. They hung around by the door waiting for Matthew. First-timers were always like this. Gobs open in awe. Silly, really. It was only paper. The guard and the policeman wanted to get back for a cup of tea.

Walking towards the way out, Matthew bent to tighten a shoelace. As he did so, he swept the floor with his eyes. He didn't know what he was looking for, but he looked anyway. The floor was tidy. There was a loose ventilation grille in one corner. Apart from that, nothing at all. The ceiling had a couple of security cameras that he could see, but there might be others that he couldn't.

'Are we done?' asked Matthew.

'Yup. Till this evening. Back seven o'clock tonight. Don't be late.'

They left the way they'd come.

5

'Goodbye Atomic Energy people,' said Kodaly, as Josephine exited from the Atomic Energy Authority's highest security system. 'Thank you for your secrets.'

The screen cleared and a cursor blinked, awaiting its next mission with a steady heartbeat. Internal Revenue Service? The AEA? A well-known bank, whose security measures had caused Kodaly to snort with contempt and send rude e-mails to its head of IT? The cursor had been there, done that, would have got the T-shirt if it had found one skinny enough to fit. Josie logged off and Kodaly powered down, finishing the last of the wine as he did so.

'Next week maybe go to Hungary. Play with Central Bank accounts, see if anyone notices.'

Josie had rolled out of bed and was getting dressed.

'I won't be coming next week, Miklos.'

'Not coming? Not find anyone to look after your mother?'

'It's not that. I just think it's time we had a break. We're not really going anywhere together.'

'Having a break? This is the same as break-up?'

'What do you think? You're a part of the decision too.'

Miklos spread his hands, but he wasn't genuinely uncertain. Josephine had been coming pretty much every Thursday for eighteen months now. They had fun, had sex, played with computers, and that was that. Neither of them had really expected to move further forward together. An end had always been inevitable.

'I think I maybe return to Hungary,' said Kodaly, for whom the thought was about five seconds old. 'It's good money in London, but if I marry . . . I marry Hungarian lady.'

Josephine was dressed now, ready to leave.

'I hope you find her. I've enjoyed being with you.'

'Yes. *Igen*. Me too.'

'Bye, Miklos. Thanks for everything.'

'*Szervusz*, beautiful lady. *Csó kolom*, I kiss your hand.'

6

A Ford Puma in metallic silver and the latest registration plates swept into the yard. A man and a woman stepped out. They were both tall, fit and tanned. He was good-looking, but she was exceptional, her flawless face surrounded by abundant auburn hair. He held a briefcase, she carried a portable computer. Both wore brand-new navy boiler suits and carried unused yellow helmets under their arms. They locked the car and walked over to the reception area.

The receptionist gawped at the two strangers. Beneath their overalls, they wore expensive office suits and nice shoes.

'Can I help you?' she asked.

'Sure,' said the man with a smile. 'Please tell Mr George Gradley that Mr Thurston and Ms O'Shea are here to see him.'

'Certainly. May I ask you to sign in?'

Under 'company name' Thurston wrote 'Oregon Surveying'. A gold Rolex peeped from beneath his disguise. The receptionist called George's office, while trying to memorise everything she could about the two visitors. It would be valuable gossip come lunch time.

George scuttled down as quick as he could. The sooner this was over the better. He'd got rid of Val for the day, sending her to keep an eye on Andrew Walters as he negotiated timber prices with their main supplier. Walters was always enormously pleased with his own efforts, but George had noticed that sending Val along as well was equivalent to an extra five percent discount. When he saw Thurston and O'Shea in their spotless boiler suits, George's heart sank. They stuck out like royals in a soup kitchen.

'Morning.'

'Morning,' said Thurston, before adding conspiratorially, 'we've introduced ourselves as surveyors. That way we can look around and nobody will suspect.'

'Good idea. But you might want to remove those tags from your cases.'

'Oh, sure. Good catch,' said Thurston as he and his partner scrambled to remove their gold-card frequent-flier tags.

As O'Shea perfected her disguise, she shot one of her big smiles at George. A month ago in the pub, his knees had reacted like jellies, but today the missile seemed to have lost its power. Maybe it was that O'Shea had called George twice a day with finicky questions about the numbers he'd handed over, or maybe it was George's embarrassment with the visit. Either way, he smiled back, his knees as solid and stiff as ever.

'Let's get going, then, shall we?'

Kelly O'Shea coiled her hair into a chignon and fixed it with a pin. Her hard hat sat on top, plausible as a politician's promise, and George led them out on to the shop floor. He had expected them to look ignorantly around and move rapidly on, but not a bit of it. They had seen a lot of furniture factories in their time and their scrutiny was detailed and insightful.

They asked about the dilapidated plant. They asked about throughputs, and scheduling, and worker training, and safety records, and factory layout and investment plans. They even examined some of Darren's more inventive repairs, and, rather than being shocked as George had expected, were impressed. 'Neat cash conservation technique, huh, Kelly?' Thurston commented. Their tour of the shop floor lasted two hours plus forty minutes or so in the paintshop. They spent a further hour and a half in the showroom, and even managed to find things to do for thirty minutes in the warehouse. When they were done, they removed their hard hats, O'Shea released the pin from her hair, letting it tumble down in undiminished splendour, and they all went up to George's office.

'Many thanks for the tour, George. It's a very impressive facility you have here.'

'No one's ever called it that before. Clapped out, yes. Archaeologically interesting, yes. Impressive, never.'

'But seriously, George, we admire your low-cost, low-investment production techniques. Why spend money if you don't have to?'

George shrugged. He didn't feel the need to argue.

Thurston continued. 'Actually, we see plenty of possibilities. We centralise all our design work in Oregon and our customised information systems have the potential to shave costs from your marketing, purchasing, and financial units. Then there's the advantages of centralised purchasing, our financing costs are way lower than yours – I guess your British banks must be greedy, right? – and, oh, a lot of things.'

He stopped short abruptly. His evangelical fervour had carried him further than he had intended. If Thurston thought Gissings' potential was as great as all that, then logically Oregon Furniture should be willing to pay top dollar for it. 'Of course, there are negatives too,' he added, 'but we prefer to dwell on the positive.'

'Would you anticipate a lot of lay-offs?' asked George.

'Well, George, we can't be sure of anything until we've put our own people in here and developed a business plan. But remember that our aim is to build a European-scale business here. Gissings would only be a first step in a much broader vision. And, in any case, we will always protect the employment rights of every employee.'

'We're proud of our record on employee empowerment,' chimed O'Shea. 'Our mission statement draws attention to that.'

That was true. But the story told by the annual reports and the press clippings and all of the other documents that had landed on George's lap in the pub left no room for doubt. Oregon took over smaller companies. It taught them how to do things the Oregon way, then fired everyone who was no longer needed. Much as George wanted to believe that things would be different, he knew he wasn't handing the company over to a bunch of sweet-natured philanthropists. And the Gissings name would go, of course. His last obligation to old Tom Gissing would be violated.

'Are you going to make me an offer, then?' asked George.

'Well, George, we can't commit to that right here. We'll have to defend any recommendation of ours at our monthly strategy committee, which usually throws it back at us with a whole bunch of questions. Right, Kelly?'

'Right. We have to present a rigorous business plan, which they'll do their best to beat up on. It's a very thorough procedure.'

'But that means that you will be putting forward a recommendation?'

Thurston was taken aback by George's bluntness. 'We haven't discussed price, yet, George. Or terms and conditions. I guess if we get a provisional go-ahead by the committee, we'll be back with our legal team and see if we can negotiate ourselves a deal. If we manage to reach agreement with you – and let me be up-front with you, George, we can be pretty tough; tough but fair – then we'll put forward a recommendation. If we get the committee's final say-so, then we can close the deal.'

'How long does all that take?'

'Well, if you give us everything we ask for, we can move pretty fast, right, Kelly?' Thurston laughed excessively at his own joke. O'Shea smiled and nodded. Her smile could have sold toothpaste to the toothless, but George's knees were immune. Maybe he'd gone off pretty women. Thurston continued, 'But if you insist on negotiating, George, then I'd say the whole process would last around four months.'

'That's too long.' George took out two copies of a document from his desk drawer. It was a contract for the sale of Gissings drawn up by a local solicitor, the same one who had drafted the contract when George had bought the place. This time, the contract was drawn up to be one-sided in favour of the seller. 'Here's a contract. There are two blanks in it. One is for the date. One is for the amount you guys are paying. You can have a good read of this contract, take it to as many committees as you wish, then send it back to me. You can make changes if you want to, but if I don't like them, I won't sign. You can put in whatever purchase price you want, but if I don't like it, I won't sign. There's not going to be any negotiation. You just have to name your best price and see if I like it. You won't get a second chance.

'That's one thing. The other's this. The business has to be sold by July the thirteenth. That's when I need your cash in my bank account. If there's any delay, even a day or an hour, then we don't have a deal. That gives you a full three months, so I can't see you having any problem. Do I make myself clear?'

Thurston picked up the contract uncertainly. They didn't teach this kind of negotiation in business school. 'You're very clear, George, but I'm not sure that the process you've outlined is going to lead to an optimal issue resolution matrix. There are some pretty complex issues to think about here.'

'That's fine. You do your best. But if you can't meet my deadline, then I swear to you we don't have a deal.'

'You must really want the money on that date, George. What's happening? Want to put the money on a horse race?'

557

'Maybe.'

Thurston remained uncertain. He looked at O'Shea for help, but she didn't understand what was going on either.

'Help me out here, George. Any clues what price you're looking for?'

'Oh, I know what price I'm looking for,' said George, tapping a sealed white envelope on his desk. 'It's in here. And if you're even one penny lower, or if your lawyers start playing games with the contract, then it's no deal. Am I clear?'

Thurston nodded. 'Couldn't be clearer,' he said.

There didn't seem to be much point in hanging around to make conversation, so Thurston and O'Shea gathered themselves up to go. Thurston tucked his papers into his briefcase, O'Shea closed up her laptop and tucked her phone back into the pocket of her ridiculous boiler suit. A tag from the store where she'd bought it still hung from the collar. They stood ready to leave.

'Great to see you again, George.'

'Yes. It's been a great pleasure to see your facility here. We've been most impressed.'

Thurston's iron handshake, O'Shea's cooling clasp.

'Thanks for coming. I suppose I'll be hearing from you.'

Thurston's eyes strayed one last time to the white envelope on George's desk. 'You don't want me to post that letter for you, George? Huh? Ha, ha.'

Thurston's nervous laughter and O'Shea's brilliant smile walked off down the hall. George watched from the upstairs window as they made their way out into the yard, took one last look around and drove off in their hired sports car. Gravel spurted from its tyres as it accelerated away from the factory gates. George wondered whether he'd put them off for ever by his unconventional negotiating stance, but he wasn't sure he cared. He'd miss Gissings.

A clatter of footsteps on the stairs and Darren's noisy panting recalled him to reality.

'Who the friggin' hell were they? They were unreal. We tried to have a poke round in their car, but it was alarmed and we couldn't see anything lying about anyway.'

'They were surveyors.'

'Yeah, well if they were surveyors then I'm the bleeding King of Spain, I am. But don't worry, I'll grab Val when she gets back and get her to dish the dirt. You're not keeping secrets from me, Georgie.'

'We'll see about that, your highness.'

7

The first two dials were locked into position and Matthew stepped forward. A month had passed since he'd first come here. This was the first day of his second spell on vault duty, and his last chance to do as Belial had suggested.

He rotated the dial quickly to begin with, then let it slow as the first number of the combination moved into sight. He found the right number and twirled the dial back the other way. Inside the steel door, an oiled drum moved round, counting off the numbers.

Matthew found the last number and locked the dial into position. Overhead, a camera watched him do it and sent the silent pictures upstairs to be recorded and stored. The security guard put his hand to the wheel and began to open the door. Wind howled for a moment as the pressure equalised, then the gale subsided. The vault fell silent. They walked in.

Matthew had two rubber bands round the ankle of

his left leg and a plan in his head, but he didn't know if he was going to put his plan into action. He'd recently escaped a jail sentence for insider trading at the cost of half a million pounds. Only a lunatic would try to burgle the safest bank vault in England. Was Matthew a lunatic? He didn't yet know.

The party of three walked round the vaults. The bullion sat in the bullion vault, as precious and as lifeless as ever. The offices just looked like offices. The circular saw on the cutting table was sheathed and silent, but a shower of paper dust hadn't been cleaned up from the day before, and the Air France calendar had been turned forward to the right month. Cameras watched as the three of them inspected.

They went into the Eurobond vault. The Eurobond vault is more alive than the bullion vault. Gold is eternal. Gold doesn't pay interest and doesn't get repaid. Gold could sit in the vaults at Madison for ever, while a million owners bought and sold, won and lost, made their fortunes or ruined them. Eurobonds aren't like that. Coupons need to be cut. Interest must be claimed. The bonds need to be repaid and the certificates destroyed before companies borrow again to stock the vaults with new bundles of their invaluable paper.

Every day, the bond vault looked a little different, as bonds were taken out, coupons trimmed, old bonds destroyed, new ones filed. As they entered, Matthew looked round to locate the librarian's trolley. The trolley was in the centre of one of the aisles furthest from the two cameras that Matthew could see. There could well be others. He mustn't make assumptions. But it was a nice start. Better still, the trolley looked well stocked.

The three men walked round the room, looking for anything amiss. The neon light which had flickered a month ago, still flickered. It was irritating but irrelevant.

On their way back towards the door, Matthew let the security guards walk down aisle T–U. He took the slightly longer route down aisle V–Z. The librarian's trolley was in the middle of the aisle.

When he got to the trolley, he stooped down. His right shoelace had come loose. It was loose because Matthew had loosened it. He knelt down to tie it, leaving the shin of his left leg at about forty-five degrees to the floor. His trouser leg hung open about eight inches from the trolley. Round his ankle, the rubber bands squeezed his leg. 'Will you or won't you?' they asked. 'Dare you or daren't you?'

Positioned as he was, Matthew could see the ventilation grille he had noticed the month before. It was still loose.

'Hey,' he called. 'Is that grille meant to be loose over there?'

Matthew pointed. The guard bent down.

'Doesn't look like much,' he said grumpily, and straightened again.

The policeman had a look too. He bent down, then got down on his hands and knees to get a better look.

The security guard hesitated, then knelt down too. It was just a loose grille. It wasn't a tunnel. But still. The coppers from ValCom looked down on security guards. Thought they weren't fully trained. Not real professionals. That's what they thought. The security guard lay on his belly and pulled himself underneath the rack to get at the grille. Not to be outdone, the policeman pulled out a pocket torch from his trouser pocket and got down too. The rubber bands cut into Matthew's leg, and sang their question again. 'Dare you or daren't you?'

His head didn't know, but his hands replied.

The middle shelf of the trolley contained a few bundles

of miscellaneous bonds. Matthew's hands skimmed over the bundles taking just a few papers from each one. He was almost perfectly silent. Over the past four weeks he had spent an hour practising every night. First with the lights on. Then with the lights off. He had taped himself and timed himself. He was very fast and very silent.

He had about twenty or thirty sheets of paper in his hand. The policeman was pulling himself out from underneath the rack. It was only a dodgy grille. Something for the maintenance men to look at. Nothing for a copper to worry about. Typical overreaction from the security people. The policeman began to stand up.

Matthew had the sheets of paper inside his left trouser leg. He pulled up the first rubber band over the bonds to mid-calf height. They sat snugly against his leg like a shinpad. He tried to get the second rubber band over the bonds as well, but fluffed the first attempt and decided against trying twice. He pulled his sock up over the bonds and straightened up.

His left trouser leg fell cleanly to the floor. It looked just the same as his other trouser leg. The policeman was standing, waiting, by the door of the vault. The security guard was calling from a wall phone to the control room to report the ventilation grille. The control room sounded bored. Matthew followed the guard and policeman out of the vault.

As they walked back the way they had come, Matthew excused himself and nipped into the loos. He closed the door and checked the ceiling for cameras. No sign of any, but it was foolish to take chances. He went into the urinal and peed. He had drunk a litre and a half of water before leaving the house that morning and now the water was dying to come out. It was a long pee.

Probably long enough, thought Matthew. The vault-user identification chamber weighed him on entering and leaving the vault. He didn't even want to be one gram heavier on his way out than on his way in. People don't get heavier for no reason. People get heavier because they're taking things they shouldn't. But if he came out lighter than he went in – well, that could hardly arouse suspicion.

Matthew felt the rubber band slipping a bit. He thought about securing both bands properly round the bonds but decided against it. In the vaults, there were likely to be cameras everywhere. He might have evaded observation first time round, but there was no reason to chance it twice. He washed his hands and left the john.

The policeman, the security guard and Matthew, the thief, left the vaults.

With every step, the bonds inside Matthew's trouser leg pressed against the rubber band and complained. Matthew's sock loosened and the rubber band slipped a bit further down his leg.

Matthew thought of stopping to pull up his sock, but he'd already stopped twice. Once to do up a shoelace and once to go to the john. A third time would look excessive. If he'd wanted to adjust anything, he should have done it in the loo.

They walked on. They came to the lift, which was still there, Level Minus 4, waiting. They got in. As Matthew stepped in, he bent his knee just a little too much, and the rubber band pinged down his leg. The bonds collapsed forwards. They were still held securely at the bottom, but at the top a semicircle of accusation had formed below his left knee. A ring of paper, pressing through his trouser leg, calling him to jail.

Matthew froze.

The guard called the control room, needing authority to rise again to ground level. The intercom blinked on and off. The control room checked the video picture and the voice and released the lift. The huge lift slowly, slowly began to climb. In the ceiling, the inevitable camera blinked on and off, on and off, watching Matthew, watching his rising perspiration. One day they'd invent one which could see fear itself.

The guard and the policeman paid no attention. They leaned against the steel walls and chatted. The head of security in every bank is an ex-copper. The job is dull compared with the thrill of the force, but the pay is double or treble. When you're passed over for that final career-completing promotion, you start to think about the private sector. You take the money, but your heart stays with the force.

The policeman knew that. He wasn't yet senior enough to worry, but it was a rule amongst the ValCom policemen to cultivate their contacts at the banks. You never knew when you might want them.

The lift climbed, and Matthew fought to come to a decision. Risk tucking the bonds in again, three feet away from two pairs of eyes and right underneath a security camera? And a camera which the control room might still be actively monitoring, for all Matthew knew. Or risk walking out of the lift, the paper ring begging for him to be arrested?

In the end, it was no contest. Wise or not, Matthew couldn't stand the suspense of walking out of the lift, with the evidence pressing forward out of his trouser leg. Hi. I'm a thief. Spot the deliberate mistake. It's a fair cop, guv. Did people really say that? What would Matthew say?

He bent down, hitched up his trouser leg and rolled the rubber band tightly up his shin again.

If the copper or the guard had turned, Matthew would have had years of leisure to repent his decision. But they didn't. They went on chatting.

The lift stopped. The guard requested authority to open the doors. There was a delay.

Was it that they were even now deploying a ring of guards around the lift doors, ready to pounce? Or was it that the chap in the control room had left the monitor, gone away for a pee, while Matthew's crime revealed itself on screen in glorious Technicolor?

The intercom clicked on. An unseen hand released the doors. The doors slid open.

No ring of guards. No accusers. Freedom.

'See you guys this evening,' grunted Matthew and walked carefully away.

8

In a mahogany-panelled boardroom on the fortieth floor of a Wall Street skyscraper, the Chairman of Weinstein Lukes – Seth Weinstein III – calls the meeting to order. It is afternoon. The great men have eaten lunch: a light meal of smoked trout followed by grilled chicken and green salad. No wine was served, and for pudding only fruit. Beyond the double doors, a pair of secretaries wait in silence, their task to prevent interruptions. Multi-billion dollar deals may hang in the balance. Financial markets may totter and crash. But the rule is final and absolute. The committee is not to be disturbed.

'Gentlemen, let us move to our next candidate. Please take out your papers for a Mr Zachary Gradley, known as Zack, head of tax in our London office. As you can see from your papers, Mr Gradley is twenty-nine years of age. He has been with the firm for two and a half years. He is currently a vice president only, but it is proposed that he should skip right over the senior vice president bracket and be entered on our roster of partners.'

Seth Weinstein is a quiet, formal man. He does not

have the roar of Dan Kramer, head of Madison and Lion of Wall Street, but in his own way Weinstein too exudes power, authority and charm. In annual surveys of the most admired bosses on Wall Street, sometimes Kramer wins, sometimes Weinstein. Hardly ever is it anyone else.

Weinstein's summary is carefully neutral. You would not be able to guess from his voice whether he approves of Gradley or hates him. Weinstein forces everyone to make their own judgement and to defend that judgement as best they can. Jorge Esparza, the bank's treasurer, whose job every day is to choose where the bank's billions should rest, speaks.

'This guy's young, isn't he? He's been with us for a couple of years. Before that he spent a few months at Coburg's, the British bank. Before that, a few months at some accountancy firm. Before that, he got part-way through a PhD, then chucked it in. We're not used to handing partnerships out to kids right out of school, however hot they are.'

Esparza speaks his feelings as they come to him. As treasurer, he has an uncanny knack for keeping the firm's money in the right currency and the right securities at the right time, but a great thinker he is not. Weinstein sits quiet. He won't speak again until the end. Lars Anderssen, an Americanised Swede, is next. Head of corporate finance in the US and softly spoken, he speaks so quietly that everyone must strain to hear.

'You're right, Jorge. None of us wants to hand out partnerships without reason. But this kid has achieved a stunning amount. In a single year, he's made as much money for the firm as Gillingham did in three. We all liked Gillingham. We stuck by him when he first admitted his alcoholism, something we wouldn't have done for everyone. Yet the signs are that Gradley has something even more special than Hal. We've all worked with these tax guys. They tend to be a bit weird, a bit unconventional. They have to be, to do what they do. To me, it's very important we don't take a cookie cutter approach with Gradley.'

Alan Carmichael is next. He is lean and sunburned, a strip of sun-dried beefhide. But despite his rodeo looks, which come from excessive exposure to Alpine ski slopes and summer visits to his native Kenya, he has been the partner in charge of Weinstein Lukes' European business for five years. He is Dixon Banderman's direct boss, and the two men have spent hours discussing Zack's prospects.

'I agree. Gradley's achievements since joining us are quite remarkable. He arrived on our doorstep with an unconventional and brilliant deal with Tominto Oil. He was hard-working and effective on a series of other energy deals with Amy-Lou Mazowiecki, one of my senior vice presidents. Then he brought in and executed a stunning deal for Hatherleigh Pacific. He launched a successful takeover bid for the South China Trust Bank – a company almost as large as Hatherleigh Pacific itself – and funded it with a brilliantly imaginative tax gimmick. The client –'

'His father-in-law, no?' challenges Esparza. The notes they have before them are extremely detailed.

'Yes, Lord Hatherleigh, Gradley's father-in-law is Chairman of Hatherleigh Pacific,' continues Carmichael. 'To me, that is of no consequence. Hatherleigh wouldn't have done the deal if it wasn't sound. And he forked out forty million dollars for it. Not only did Gradley have the guts to ask, he had the wit to realise that Hatherleigh had to say yes or forfeit the opportunity. That shows brains and nerve, a winning combination in my eyes. But all of this is less important. Gradley may be an extremely capable all-rounder, but the reason why we're considering him for partnership is his tax ability. And let's be quite clear. Gradley didn't just find a tax dodge, Roses, he found a way to sell it to everyone in Asia. Demand was so strong, we had people biting off our hand for it. We did business with companies we'd never even spoken to before. We now have thriving relationships with companies who didn't even let us through their front doors. It's not just money that Gradley made. It's reputation.'

Carmichael ends his speech on the word reputation. He knows – everyone knows – that Seth Weinstein would sooner dump half a billion dollars into the sea than damage the bank's reputation. 'It took us a century to make,' he'd whisper, 'but it would only take a minute to lose.' And what Carmichael said was true. Zack's Roses had given Weinstein Lukes a prominence in Asia that nothing else could have done. An Nguyen, the head of Weinstein Lukes in Asia, nods his vigorous assent.

'I agree, I agree. Recently, our reputation's relied on Roses. Client relationships have really rolled.' Nguyen pronounces his Rs and his Ls the same way, but everyone knows what he means.

'OK, so he's had a great year. Can he do it again? How do we know?' Esparza growls the questions.

Carmichael had had a long talk with Banderman before flying across for this meeting, and he knows the answer to this question.

'Yes he can do it again. Dixon Banderman, who most of you know, knows Gradley better than any of us. Dixon tells me that Gradley is possibly the most talented individual he's seen in all his time in the firm. Gradley may not bring us Roses again, but he'll bring us as much as Gillingham ever did, more in fact. He's hard-working. He's ambitious. He's razor sharp. He has a superb commercial instinct. I think we can rely on these judgements as solid fact.'

Esparza doesn't have anything against Gradley, but he doesn't much like Carmichael. He finds Carmichael patronising and cold. Esparza rumbles belligerently on.

'So he's a good guy. But where does his heart lie?' Esparza thumps his chest. 'Does he love this firm?'

The question is addressed to the room in general, but the management committee waits to hear Carmichael's answer. Carmichael, however, is silent.

'Alan, can you answer this?'

This time Esparza is more direct, and this time Carmichael opens his mouth to respond.

9

'Matthew Gradley? Main reception here. There's a bloke down here for you. Says you've got a package for him.'

'That's right,' said Matthew. 'I'll be down.'

He took a large manila envelope from his desk drawer. It was addressed to Helmut Zeithammer, an investment manager at one of the biggest Swiss banks. Down in the Madison lobby, Matthew handed the envelope to the courier, getting a receipt in return.

This was a same-day service. You actually had your own guy jump on a motorbike, scream across London to Heathrow, and jump on the first plane out to wherever the destination was. He handed the package over to a local representative and the thing was delivered literally as fast as you could get it there yourself. It wasn't a cheap way of doing things, but Matthew wasn't too concerned.

Inside the envelope was a packet of Eurobonds, worth about $8 million. It was eight o'clock in the morning.

Matthew worked hard that day, but he kept an eye on the clock. At midday, Fiona and Ed Deane went out to get lunch. They invited Matthew to join them, but he refused. He'd get a sandwich later.

The call came at twelve forty. It was the courier company's Zurich office. The envelope had been delivered half an hour ago. Matthew thanked them and rang off. Time for coffee.

On the way to the coffee shop, he passed the familiar little alley and ducked up to the little garden. Beneath the tree, crouched low over his usual bench, he made a couple of calls. His first call was to Helmut Zeithammer.

'Have you received my bond portfolio?'

'We have indeed, Mr Gradley. We have deposited the bonds in our vaults pending your instructions.'

Zeithammer was no Belial. His was a bank which did not deal knowingly with criminals and it carefully researched the background of potential clients before accepting them. Zeithammer's research had been reassuring. Matthew Gradley was one of the sons of the late Bernard Gradley, an English self-made millionaire. Zeithammer's sources suggested that Matthew Gradley's share of his father's fortune would be in the region of ten million pounds, though the sources admitted they didn't have any specifics on the will itself. Gradley was now working at Madison, one of the very best American banks. Zeithammer was happy. Gradley was clean, a welcome new customer.

'Excellent,' said Matthew. 'Do you have a current market valuation of the bonds?'

'Yes. Current market valuation is eight million two hundred and thirty-seven thousand three hundred and eight dollars.'

'And you can lend me up to seventy percent of market value?'

They had discussed this many times. Zeithammer's bank would hold the bonds in its vaults and extend a loan to Matthew, using the bonds as security. If Matthew didn't repay the money, the bank would sell the bonds and repay itself from the proceeds. As far as the bank was concerned, it was a risk-free transaction.

'Correct,' said Zeithammer. 'I have authority to lend you five million seven hundred and sixty-six thousand dollars immediately. I am awaiting instructions about where to transmit the money.'

'Good. I'd like you to transfer the money today to an account at Switzerland International.' Matthew gave the account number and a couple of other transfer details.

'Switzerland International?' Zeithammer's intake of breath was audible, but he kept his thoughts to himself. 'I will organise it immediately.'

The next call was to Belial. And for this call Matthew needed another piece of equipment. A pocket dictaphone. He switched it to record, checked it was recording properly, then made his call. Matthew trusted Belial considerably less far than he could throw him.

'Matthew Gradley! How very nice to hear from you,' purred Belial, as soon as he heard Matthew's voice. 'I felt sure you would be in touch again soon.'

'Yeah, I'll bet. You'll be pleased to know that I've followed your advice.'

'My advice, Matthew?' Belial tittered. 'What advice would that be? Was it something to do with skincare? I myself am always careful to use a moisturiser with sun block.'

'You know perfectly well what I'm talking about. I'm worth about six million dollars more than I was the last time we spoke.'

'Six million dollars? Congratulations! But may I enquire the source of your good fortune, my friend? Not the National Lottery, I expect. Ha, ha.'

It was second nature to Belial to keep his guard up. Matthew needed to shock him.

'I nicked the bonds from the Madison vault exactly as you suggested. I sold them this morning. I'm having the money wired to you as we speak.'

'You've done what?' cried Belial, alarmed. 'You've sold them? Who with?'

Matthew gave him the name of the big Swiss bank. Belial repeated the name in shock.

'You're mad. I told you quite explicitly you had to sell them through us. Madison will find the theft sooner or later. They'll put out an alert and the sale will be traced. Discretion, Matthew, discretion is the watchword. We could have sold the damn things so they'd never be traced. You're a bloody fool.'

No wonder Belial was appalled. He was sure that Matthew's folly would lead to him being arrested and convicted for one of the most audacious bank robberies in history. If Matthew were tried, the publicity would be enormous. And Switzerland International needed publicity the way Barings needed Nick Leeson.

Matthew listened to Belial storm away. Then he interrupted in a quiet voice.

'Haven't you forgotten something?'

Belial was silent.

'I think you may have forgotten to deny that the robbery was your suggestion,' said Matthew. 'That's always a mistake when your conversation is being recorded.'

Matthew replayed the last few seconds of conversation to prove to Belial that he was telling the truth. Belial was silent. Matthew switched back to recording.

'And what do you propose to do with this tape, my friend?' asked Belial after a long pause. 'You've incriminated yourself too, you know.'

'I propose to keep you honest. If you do as I ask, then any relationship between us will be completely finished by the end of this week. I will keep this tape in a very, very safe place, along with a complete statement recording the history of my dealings with you. There they will remain, hopefully for ever. But if I should ever come to court, for any reason at all, the tape and the statement come out and I shall do everything I can to see you convicted too.'

'And did you sell the bonds this morning?'

'That's none of your business.'

Belial began to recover his composure.

'My dear friend, I'm sorry to hear that we shall be losing you as a client after this week. Is there nothing we can do to tempt you to stay with us? But you may be sure that we will look after your interests with all possible care and attention.'

'I'm sure you will. My interests and yours have grown remarkably close, wouldn't you say?'

Then Matthew told Belial what he wanted. Belial grasped the instructions quickly and promised to do as Matthew asked. Matthew would call in a day or two to check progress. It was now two fifty on Monday afternoon. Everything had to be finished by Friday lunch time at the very latest. It wasn't long.

Matthew rang off. He would deposit a copy of the tape and a signed statement at his bank later that day. Then he walked briskly out of the garden, bought some coffees and headed back to work. The group had a big deal brewing and they were due to launch their raid the very next morning. Everything had to be ready.

10

The management committee has considered and made its views known to the board. The board listened, deliberated and decided. Now the board has spoken and it is time to break the news.

Since daybreak, Carmichael has been in meetings with would-be partners. Some leave elated, others in despair. Some leave the room as partners of the firm, others are told to wait. Still others are told that Weinstein Lukes' sharp-topped pyramid no longer has room for them and they are to leave the firm with immediate effect. Compassion? Leave it at the door. There's no place for it here.

All morning, Zack had been totally unable to work. He drank coffee. He bugged Sarah with phone calls. He paced up and down his little office. He leaped to the phone when it rang, thinking it might be Carmichael's secretary, then leaving it when the display indicated a different caller. He drummed his fingers and twiddled his thumbs. He paced the room and bit his nails. He sat down, stood up, moved to the window, moved away. He was in pain with tension.

A hundred and forty million bucks he'd made for the firm that year. One hundred and forty, and money from ROSES still poured in, month by month. There couldn't be any doubt, could there? Could there?

Again, the phone rang. Zack leaped to it. The extension flashed up: 3153. Carmichael's secretary. Zack snatched the receiver.

'Yes?' His voice was a rasp. What came out was hardly even a word. But Carmichael's secretary knew why and was unperturbed.

'Mr Carmichael is ready to see you. Perhaps you could make your way upstairs.'

Zack croaked something. It wasn't lack of fluid that glued his tongue to his palate. He'd been swallowing coffee all morning. He was rolling on a tide of caffeine. But for all that, his mouth was drier than a tax opinion. He raced upstairs. He was outside Carmichael's office in no time at all.

'Mr Carmichael will see you in just a moment. He's

had to take a phone call first.'

Zack nodded. No point even attempting speech. He groaned with tension. He ached with it. He went to the window and looked out, a view across the City of London, dominated by St Paul's famous outline. Sunlight glittered from the dome. It meant nothing to Zack. He hardly saw it. If some joker had painted it pink and green overnight, Zack wouldn't have noticed. The view and the caffeine and the tension gave him a stab of vertigo and he staggered back. The roof of Ovenden House and Hatherleigh's helicopter had given him an aversion to heights he'd never had before.

Eventually, the thing Zack had awaited so long happened without him even noticing. Carmichael's office door swung open, the great man came out and was standing at Zack's shoulder.

'Shall we go in?' Lanky, brown and wizened, he looked baked: a sun-dried banker.

Zack leaped in surprise and whirled around, clumsily knocking against Carmichael, his boss's boss and master of his destiny.

'Sorry.'

'Don't worry,' smiled Carmichael and waved Zack on into his office. 'Zack, let me start by congratulating you.'

Zack heard these words from the far side of a rush of images. He saw his father, he saw Earle reading the will, he saw Sarah, Lord Hatherleigh, Gillingham, his mother, Josephine. Congratulations. Zack was in such a whirl that he'd lost the exact meaning of this moment. All he knew was that it was good. Congratulations. Zack may or may not have said something, and if he did, it may or may not have made sense. He was beyond knowing.

'Congratulations on a fantastic year. We've all been absolutely delighted with your performance, and the way

575

in which you picked up the reins from Hal Gillingham so effectively.'

Zack nodded. The whirl was beginning to subside. He paid attention. As far as he could tell, Carmichael hadn't yet mentioned the word 'partner'.

'There's no doubt in my mind that you have a brilliant career ahead of you as partner of this firm and that is the firm view of all my colleagues in top management.'

There it was. There was the word. But Zack was listening carefully now, his mind now crystal clear. Carmichael still hadn't said what he needed to say. Say it, damn you. Say it now.

'In view of that belief, it is my pleasure to tell you that the Board of Directors of Weinstein Lukes has agreed to promote you with immediate effect –'

There it was. This was it. So sharp was Zack's mind now that time had slowed right down. A second lasted a minute. A minute took an hour. In this mood, Zack could have seen a midge land on the dome of St Paul's. He could have told you if the midge's necktie was spotted or striped.

'– to the position of senior vice president, on the understanding that another satisfactory year will see you appointed to the rank of partner.'

What? How could this man deliver this news in this way? How dare he think this was a matter for congratulation? My God, Weinstein Lukes babbled on about making money for the firm and rewarding merit, then you make a pot full of cash for them, more money than anyone in the firm in fact, and they crap on you. It was unbelievable. Zack was appalled, but he still couldn't take in the fact that he was snookered. No partnership and a prenuptial agreement which meant Sarah's money was hers not his. He'd lost and he hadn't yet clicked.

Zack moved his mouth but nothing came from it.

'I hope you are not excessively disappointed. The fact is that almost nobody in senior management knows you directly. Perhaps Dixon Banderman and I should have forced you over to New York a little more to meet the top guys. But the truth is, I think we've been right to hold you back. A partnership is coming to you and there's not much to be gained by haste. In any event, you should be delighted that you have made such a powerful impression on this firm in such a short space of time. I believe your promotion to SVP is fully merited.'

Zack was listening with only half his brain. Things were beginning to click. He hadn't made a million. He wasn't getting his dad's cash. My God, he might actually be beaten by Matthew, even George. Jesus, suppose he was the only one not to make the million. The humiliation! Zack was choked. Carmichael continued his monologue.

'We have also decided, in view of your exceptional year, to award you a very substantial bonus. With the exception of a handful of options traders and the like, this is the largest bonus award in the firm outside of the partnership tier. We've decided to give you a bonus of three million dollars. And again, my congratulations, for you've deserved every last bit of it.'

Three million dollars. Divide by about one point six to give a sterling amount. One point eight million pounds. Knock off forty percent UK tax to give an after-tax amount. One point one million pounds. One point one. That was right. One point one million pounds. That was less than he'd have got through a partnership, but plenty enough all the same. A million pounds. Nought to a million in three years. That was the challenge. That was what he'd done. His relief was enormous. It would have filled St Paul's and lifted the dome off its stanchions. He could kiss Carmichael.

The sunburned partner stood up to indicate the end of the interview and he handed Zack a letter with the bonus and all the rest of it. Zack didn't care. One point one. One point one. He said something, he didn't know what, and walked away. As he headed back down, sunlight bounced off the dome of St Paul's as it had done all morning, as it would do for centuries to come.

Zack walked downstairs, accepted the congratulations of his colleagues, and rang Sarah at once to share the news with her. Only then did he turn his attention to the letter that Alan Carmichael had given him.

The letter confirmed the award of three million US dollars. All bonuses were converted by the firm into the employee's local currency, in this case sterling. In sterling, the three million dollars were worth exactly one million eight hundred and forty-eight thousand pounds, plus a few unimportant hundreds. In Britain, income tax, payable at forty percent, is withheld at source. So, cutting the numbers once again, Zack's bonus shrank to just over one million one hundred and nine thousand pounds, still plenty more than his father's million pound cut-off.

But Weinstein Lukes, like all investment banks, has a policy whereby bonuses are split between an upfront element and a deferred element. The bigger the bonus, the greater the deferred portion. The idea is that if you quit to take up a job elsewhere, some of your past bonuses are forfeited, in an effort to promote loyalty. Zack knew this perfectly well. But he'd forgotten it. Carmichael's letter reminded him of it in plain, clear, black-and-white. Zack would be issued a cheque right away for seven hundred and seventy-six thousand three hundred and forty pounds. The remaining three hundred and thirty-three thousand would be payable in three years' time. Zack would be entitled to interest on the amount withheld.

He had made his million, but he couldn't collect it for three years. He had won and he had lost. He could hear his father guffawing from the grave.

11

Meanwhile, in Oregon, a committee is meeting. Two of the firm's most able employees are to give a presentation. They think they've found an appropriate launch-pad for their European operation. The committee has high hopes for Europe. It's a fragmented, high-cost market, ripe for consolidation. Oregon has the cash, the technology, the know-how and the drive to start from behind and wind up ahead. The Chief Executive says he wants a hundred million bucks in revenues from Europe within five years, and ten times that amount in another five. But we all know the Chief. He talks big, but he delivers bigger. If he says five years, he means four. It'll be interesting to see what the project team has to say.

Outside the room, David Thurston and Kelly O'Shea look at each other. He has a dozen bound copies of his presentation. She has her portable computer to plug straight into the big-screen TV. If the committee wants to hit the numbers hard, she'll be ready. Both of them are looking a million dollars. They want to impress.

'Good luck, Kelly.'

He gives her a smile so big you'd need two men to lift it. She smiles back. It's a smaller smile, but nicer: the sort of thing to put on your mantelpiece and spend a while looking at.

'Yes. Good luck,' she says.

*   *   *

12

Josephine sat on one side, Matthew on the other, their mother in between. Helen was half-asleep, tired from the small excitement of Matthew's visit.

'How's Mum?' he asked.

'I worry about her. I think she's sinking into her depression. I've tried upping the dose of antidepressants, but then she copes badly with the side effects. I'm not really sure what to do.'

Throughout her little speech, Josie stroked her mother's hand and the older woman relaxed deeper into her armchair.

'I don't know either, Josie, but I've brought something which may help. I'm sorry it's been so long coming.'

Matthew handed his sister an envelope.

'What's this?'

'It's a small part of what I owe you for these last three years. There's more to come, but it'll have to wait a while longer.'

Josephine looked searchingly at her brother and opened the envelope. Inside was a cheque for ten thousand pounds, signed and dated by Matthew.

'Does this mean you've made the million? Or have you given up?' Josephine scrutinised Matthew's face. 'You've done it, haven't you? My God, you've actually done it. You've actually done it.'

Matthew couldn't conceal his joy any longer. He threw his arms round his sister and kissed her.

'Oh, Josie, I'm so pleased. I'm pleased for myself, of course, but you as well. Dad's will was so unkind to you, and then these last three years . . . You've been a saint. Soon you can be whatever you want to be. We'll make sure Mum gets the best care money can buy and you can go to university, or move to the south of France, or what-ever you want. The cheque's just an advance instalment.'

Josephine looked at it, eight months' salary on one small slip of paper.

'That's great. Thanks. And congratulations.'

'My pleasure . . . Are you OK? You look upset.'

Josephine held the cheque between finger and thumb, looking at it like some kind of rare curio. And Matthew was right. Behind her eyes, tears were pricking.

'It's just . . . you would have helped me more by giving me less sooner.'

'I know it's been hard, Josie. But we've got the rest of life to worry about now. You won't worry so much about the last three years, after you've been enjoying the freedom of Dad's money for a while.'

'It won't be all that free, you know. You want to give Mum the best care money can buy? Well, the best care is the kind of care that money can't buy. It's my care and your care, and George and Zack's care. She needs her kids, Matthew. You can be as rich as anything, but you can't get away from that.'

'I know, but money will help. Lighten up. You can quit work tomorrow. Go on holiday, do whatever the hell you want.'

'Oh, I'm not quitting. Not yet, anyway.'

'What? Why not? What's the point? I know there's only ten grand there, but you'll have a quarter of every-thing in a couple of months.'

'Maybe. But pitiful as it may seem to you, I actually have a career to think about.'

'A career? Why would you want to do computer programming for a tiny wage while you have a fortune sitting in the bank? Don't tell me you're going to be like one of those lottery winners who stay with their job cleaning windows.'

'I'm not a computer programmer. That's just a hobby. What I do is –'

'OK, but still, why work?'

'You'll go on working, won't you?'

Matthew shrugged. That wasn't a question he'd thought about much. He'd always assumed that he'd buy a yacht, and bob around the Caribbean for a year or two, but as the day grew closer, he thought about that less. He wouldn't want to give up Fiona, and he couldn't see her wanting to give up work. And he enjoyed his work too. He'd enjoy it even more now that he didn't need to obsess about making the million. He probably would continue working, but that was a question for another time. Right now, he just wanted to enjoy his achievement.

Matthew had every right to feel pleased. Everything had gone according to his plan, mad though it had been.

Nicking the bonds from the vault had been the scariest part, but after that it had been plain sailing. Getting the loan had been simplicity itself. Taping the conversation with Belial had been a masterstroke. Matthew had been deeply worried about Belial double-crossing him, but after that taped phone call, Belial was as tame as a lamb.

Matthew had asked Belial to invest the borrowed money in shares on the London stock market. The company was called Hippety Hop plc – a toy manufacturer. The company was struggling, nearly drowned by excessive borrowing. It was currently locked in negotiations with its banks, trying to sort out a rescue plan which would avert catastrophe. The management was lacklustre, its banks jittery and disorganised. For most people, it would be an insane place to invest every last penny they possessed. Not so for Matthew.

He made his investment shortly before the market closed on Monday. On Tuesday, the Madison Distressed Debt Group launched a raid on the company's loans. Once it had secured twelve percent of the total loans outstanding, the group issued a press release, noting the size of its investment, and stating its intention to 'use our influence to unlock the undoubted value in Hippety Hop's portfolio'. The language was coded, but everyone knew what it meant. Madison had enough votes to hold the debt negotiations to ransom. If the company management didn't do what Madison wanted, there would pretty soon be some new managers, who would. The loan market was excited by the news. The stockmarket, too, reacted favourably.

Matthew had bought his shares at eleven pence each on Monday. He sold them on Thursday at an average price of thirteen pence. His five and a half million pound investment showed just over a million pounds of profit.

Matthew asked Belial to transfer the funds back to the big Swiss bank, and then to close down his account for good. Belial objected, but had no alternative.

Matthew then phoned Zeithammer. Matthew had changed his plans, he said. He wished to repay the loan and take back control of the bonds. He would have his million pound account balance wired to him in London.

Zeithammer had been puzzled, but not excessively so. Taking a loan out for three days is a strange thing to do, but strangeness is one of the privileges of wealth. Zeithammer arranged to return the bonds to Matthew. It was now Thursday evening, too late to get the bonds out of the vault, but Zeithammer promised to have them couriered first thing the next day.

Friday morning dawned. Matthew had to have the bonds that day to avoid disaster.

It was misty in Zurich, and for the first two hours, nothing took off or landed from the fogbound airport. Matthew's gut knotted with tension. Then the mist started to lift, enough to clear a single runway. The courier was booked on a BA flight, but the plane was pushed to the back of the queue of aircraft trying to leave. Matthew spent half an hour on the phone to the courier company. They had to get the courier on to the next flight out, whatever the cost. The company complained, but managed it. The courier flew business class to Amsterdam, then switched to BA for the hop across to Heathrow, where he landed at two in the afternoon. He passed the bonds to a motorbike courier and Matthew had the bonds in his pocket by two forty-five.

Matthew was not a diligent worker that afternoon. At six o'clock, he went into the loos, and taped the bonds to the inside of his calf. Securely this time. They weren't going to slip. At seven o'clock, it was time to close the vaults. Matthew walked through the underground chambers a pace or two behind his escorts. The gold glittered at him as he passed. 'Feast your eyes,' it murmured. 'You too are one of the golden children. You too are rich.' The bonds inside Matthew's trouser leg fitted snugly and securely.

In the Eurobond vault, things were fairly simple. Matthew just walked down a different aisle from the other two. He stopped to tighten a shoe lace and yanked the bonds from his leg. It wasn't a brilliantly subtle manoeuvre, but what the hell. You couldn't be arrested for bringing bonds *into* a bank vault. Matthew shoved the bonds on to a shelf any old how. They were in the wrong place, out of sequence and jumbled. They'd be found on Monday and cause puzzlement. Bonds weren't meant to be out of place. But they'd count the bonds and find everything was there. They could make all the enquiries they liked, but the only thing wrong would be some bonds on the wrong shelf.

Matthew closed up as usual, twirling the metal wheels for the last time, locking the doors on the impregnable vaults. The vault-user identification chamber clicked and flashed as usual. The huge lift rolled slowly upwards as before. This time when the doors opened, there was no threat of encircling police, no danger of jail and failure.

Matthew walked out of the loading bay a millionaire, standing to inherit many millions more in just a few months. No more insider trading. No more theft. No more worries. He had a lovely house and a beautiful partner. Fiona was getting closer than ever to him, trusting him more and more. He hoped that, before long, they'd be married.

Matthew was very, very happy.

He wanted to rush out and buy things. A car for him. A diamond necklace for Fiona. But he held back. Zack might always have his million too. A few thousand quid was unlikely to make the difference between them, but there was no sense in taking chances. A cheque for Josephine would be the only exception: an exception he knew she deserved many times over. He smiled at his sister. He had smiles enough for the world.

'What will you do with your money?' he asked her. He liked talking about money.

She shrugged.

'Haven't thought about it. What about you? Are you going to give Zack and George their shares?'

Matthew was embarrassed by the question. He wouldn't mind giving Josephine her share. She deserved it, if anyone did. But George and Zack? The way Matthew saw it, this had been a race. The prize was for the winner. If George and Zack had ever intended to slice the pie four ways if they came out on top, then they hadn't bothered to mention the fact to Matthew.

Besides, if Matthew only kept his quarter, around ten million or so, he'd spend about four or five on houses and stuff and have five or six left to live off. That sounds a lot, but it's not really. Say you invest five million pounds at eight percent. Knock off three percent for inflation, because you don't want your capital to shrink over time. So you've got five million invested at five percent. That's two hundred and fifty grand a year before tax. One hundred and fifty after tax. That's nice, but not a fortune. That's what you can earn as a top accountant, or a middling barrister, or an unsuccessful banker. Matthew hadn't done all that he'd done just for that. He'd hand out some big presents, but he'd look after himself too. You could hardly call him stingy.

'I'll sort something out,' he said. 'But you'll get your share, Josie, I promise.'

Helen Gradley was dribbling in her sleep, a consequence of poorly controlled facial muscles. A column of spit threatened to splash down on to the envelope with Matthew's cheque still inside it. Josephine gently wiped away the spit and patted her mum's hands. The frail woman tensed for a moment, then sighed. Somewhere inside her troubled head, she knew her daughter was with her.

Josephine waited until Helen was quiet. Then, softly, with her left hand, she reached for the envelope and tucked it away inside her trouser pocket.

Summer 2001

Who cares about the weather? Who cares about cricket? Who cares about the century that lies ahead?

It is 3 June 2001. For more than a thousand days, Bernard Gradley's fortune has hung in the balance, luscious, golden, and out of reach. For 40 more days, it will hang there still. On the fortieth day, on the stroke of midnight, it will fall, unstoppably, irrevocably.

Who will catch it?

1

David Thurston's Strategy Committee didn't hesitate long. It liked Gissings. It was low-cost and could be made lower-cost. It had good products. It had a national marketing effort. It would be a cheap bridgehead for Oregon's conquest of Europe.

George's unconventional negotiating strategy was a problem, of course. Oregon had a deep-rooted aversion to signing contracts which were fair to the seller, and they hated paying top dollar. But as Thurston and O'Shea argued, this was an exception, the first purchase on European soil. Once they knew their way around the market better, they could play their normal games, but Gissings was a small bite anyway. Oregon's shareholders wouldn't even notice the purchase price in the small change of their annual accounts. So it was agreed. Thurston called off the lawyers in the two thousand dollar suits and made a few changes to the contract to produce something genuinely fair to both parties.

And as for the price – well! Thurston wished more than once for a peek inside that white envelope of George's. In the eight months since the rout of the Aspertons, Gissings had made a profit of two hundred thousand pounds before interest. Over the next twelve, they expected to make at least three hundred and fifty thousand pounds. More if they could expand their production facilities fast enough.

Oregon knew that this profit would take another leap forward if they got control. Even if they only cut ten jobs, and they were sure they could do much better than that, they should save a hundred and fifty grand a year. That would take Gissings to half a million profit in its first year in Oregon's hands.

So what price was fair? Usually, Oregon got away with paying around six times profit, sometimes eight. On the other hand, Oregon's own stockmarket value was more like fifteen times profit, so they could afford to pay more and still keep their shareholders happy. The committee argued to and fro. You couldn't try to read George across the negotiating table, because there wasn't a table and there wasn't a negotiation.

Eventually, they settled on a number. They decided to offer ten times the profit that Oregon reckoned it would make. That made a nice round number: five million pounds. Normally they'd knock off something for the money Gissings owed to the bank. But this was exceptional: the first foot on European soil. So they offered a full price. Five million British pounds sterling. If George wanted more than that, he was being unrealistic. Thurston worried that they were overpaying, but there was no way to tell, and Oregon was keen to get started.

The Committee agreed. The Chief agreed. So Thurston and O'Shea wrote the number into the amended contract and sent it FedEx to George. Then they sat back and waited. How would he respond?

2

There was nothing else for it. Zack, the proud, the arrogant, was forced to beg.

One Saturday morning, just four weeks before the deadline, Zack and Sarah were lying together in bed. Zack needed to go into the office and Sarah had some chores to do in London, so neither of them was heading down to Ovenden House. They could have a lie-in and breakfast in bed, rare luxuries both.

They celebrated by making love, of course, not the urgent passionate love of their evenings, but the lazy, sleepy love of first waking. Zack was unusually attentive, Sarah more than ever in love.

'You're gorgeous,' she told him. 'We should have more mornings like this.'

Zack swung his legs out of bed and began to pull on his trousers.

'You shower if you like, or just go right on lying. I'll go and get some breakfast.'

His young wife nodded at him happily. She knew Zack still had a long hard streak of arrogance, even cruelty, in him, but since they had started going out again, years after their long college affair, he had never once hurt her with it. His hardness, it seemed, was reserved for the rest of the world. She was happily married and believed that

589

he was too. She stretched out full length in the luxurious bed. She wouldn't shower yet. She'd eat breakfast next to Zack, both naked, snuggled up against each other, sharing food and warmth and company.

Zack came back soon enough. He'd been to the café across the road and had a cardboard tray loaded with coffee, fresh orange juice, scrambled eggs and bacon, and two croissants, still warm from the oven. Sarah watched him unload it.

'Did I remember to tell you that you're gorgeous?'

Zack smiled at her. 'You'd say anything for a warm croissant.'

She bared her teeth, rolled on to all fours, and snatched a croissant from the tray with her mouth. She growled at him like a tiger, daring him to take it off her. Zack looked at the familiar face. Sarah's chin was much broader than women's chins are meant to be. It was broader than Zack's own angular jaw by some distance. But it was typical of her. She was frank, open, forceful; as strong in her way as Zack was in his own more cunning way. He admired her. He growled back, threw off his clothes and climbed on to the bed.

Sarah taunted him with the croissant, waving it in front of his nose, then pulling back as Zack grabbed for it. They were both on all fours now, the bedclothes all in a heap. Sarah was much more athletic than Zack, and though he wouldn't get the croissant off her by skill, he could by force. He leaped at her, threw both arms round her, bound her legs with his and ended up with his mouth closed over the croissant. She continued to growl and wouldn't release it, so he began to gobble at it, trying to eat it faster than she could gulp it. Between them, they devoured the croissant in a few seconds flat, a shower of golden flakes falling all over Sarah's naked body and the white sheet beneath.

590

'Now look what you've done,' she panted, laughing and choking with the same breath.

'Easily fixed,' said Zack, who began to pick each golden flake off her with his tongue. He took his time and was easily distracted with other local amusements. She let him wander and stray as he pleased. When he was done, she brushed the remaining crumbs from the sheet and restored some order to the bedclothes.

'Where's breakfast then? I'm starving.'

They ate happily, squeezed so tightly together that Zack, who lay on the left, could only use his left hand to eat with, Sarah only her right.

'Darling,' said Zack after a while, 'I have a confession to make and a favour to ask.'

'I love confessions. Will you be kneeling for it?' Sarah's words were joking, but she tucked her dark blonde hair behind her ears in readiness for a more serious conversation.

'I'm serious, sweetheart. It's quite a big confession and quite a big favour.'

'OK, my love, I'm listening.'

So Zack told Sarah. Not the whole story, of course, he could hardly do that, but he told her enough. He told her about the terms of his father's will, his efforts to make partner, his shattering disappointment that his bonus wasn't enough to swing it. He told her of the deadline now only a month away. Sarah listened in serious silence, her face grave and attentive.

'Why didn't you tell me any of this before?' she asked when he was finished.

'I couldn't. I couldn't bear it if you thought I might have married you for your money. I wanted to make my million by myself, release Dad's cash from trust, then tell you everything. That way you couldn't possibly doubt my motives.'

591

Sarah gazed at him. 'I don't think I'd have worried. They say that a man who marries a woman for money ends up earning it. But it was sweet of you.'

'Well, whatever I'd wanted to do is beside the point now. The fact is I don't have my million, and I'd like to ask your help.'

'You want me to make up the few hundred thousand you still need?'

Zack nodded and put his hand to his wife's cheek, softly stroking it.

'And when you get the money, you'll share it with your family, I guess? It's not as though we need it.'

Zack nodded dumbly again. This was why he had racked his brains for weeks since hearing the bad news from Alan Carmichael. He knew that if he simply threw himself on Sarah's mercy, she would calmly ensure an equal division of the money, assuming all the time that Zack's intentions were equally generous.

'Mmm, I see,' continued Sarah. 'If you divided your dad's money into quarters, then everyone would be really well provided for.'

'Yes, quarters, that's right. A quarter each for George, Matthew, Josie and –'

'– and your mum.' Sarah finished Zack's sentence for him. 'That's so sweet of you, darling. But you should keep something for yourself. Buy something to remember your dad by.'

Zack was gobsmacked. He hadn't possibly imagined that Sarah would assume he'd give all the money away. He had thought that, by grovelling, he would get to keep at least a quarter of his dad's wealth.

'Well, I'm not sure. Mum's not well enough to have money of her own. I was thinking of keeping a quarter of it for myself and obviously we'd all take care of Mum. That way you don't need to worry about me financially.'

'Don't be silly.' It was Sarah's turn to stroke Zack's cheek. 'I don't worry about you. There's plenty of money to go round.'

'But the prenuptial agreement . . .'

'Don't worry about the prenup. We're married, aren't we? It <u>would</u> be silly to hold on to money that your brothers or sister might have a better use for, just because of the prenup.'

'Well, anyway, I'm sure we can sort something out,' said Zack grumpily. He would not, *would not*, end up winning all the money out of his dad's will just for his brothers and sister to benefit. And what if – or when – he and Sarah split up? It just wouldn't be right that he should be the only one to lose out.

'I'm sure we can,' said Sarah, kissing him. 'Anyway, how much do you still need?'

'Three hundred and fifty grand.' Zack added an extra hundred grand for luck. He wanted to make sure of beating Matthew.

'Well, I'm not sure you've done anything to deserve it,' she said, putting her breakfast things away and slipping down in bed again. Her hair had fallen free of her ears.

'What would I need to do for it?' said Zack, rolling on to his elbow.

'Well, I'm not sure exactly. But I know I'd need to be in a good mood.'

'Just how good exactly?' Zack had moved his hand to her neck and rubbed slowly, moving his hand down in slow circles.

'Oh, very good, I'd say. Very good indeed.'

Zack's hand moved lower and Sarah's mood improved and improved, until, three quarters of an hour later, they were both sitting up in bed again, drinking more coffee and discussing how to get the money into Zack's bank account.

3

On that very same Saturday, one scant month before the deadline, Matthew rolled over in bed and gazed up at the ceiling, his arm around Fiona. Sunbeams poured through the little windows of the mews house, playing hide-and-seek among the broad yellow stripes of the wallpaper. Outside, the street was quiet except for a pair of pigeons cooing on the window ledge. And in one short month, Matthew stood to inherit a fortune.

Happiness doesn't come much better.

It was Saturday morning. He and Fiona had made love when they went to bed the night before, and again this morning when they woke up. Their lovemaking had become less passionate than it had been those first nights, first in Jamaica, then Vermont, then sporadically in New York. But Fiona the fiery had given way to something that Matthew preferred: Fiona the tender lover. She looked at him during sex and kissed him, and spoke to him with love.

'You're getting very middle-aged,' said Matthew. 'No nails gouging into my back, no rolling all round the room, no screaming. Not as much screaming, anyway. I think I'd better find a younger woman before you start going to bed with curlers in your hair.'

She bit him gently on the arm.

'I can gouge you anytime. Doesn't have to be during sex. Just say when and I promise to draw blood.'

She ran her fingernails across the plain of his stomach leaving four parallel tracks etched in red. Matthew lifted her hand away and drew her closer.

'Don't worry. I can live without being gouged. I'm getting middle-aged myself, anyway. I used to think that any relationship which lasted more than a week was past its sell-by date. Now, I find myself planning where we're going to go on holiday next year and where the year after that. I swear to you, before I know it, I'll be thinking about which schools our kids should go to.'

And it was true. The fact was that Matthew was already thinking about engagement rings and weddings, kids and grandkids – everything once guaranteed to scare Fiona off for ever.

She turned over on her side, and her grey eyes stared into his. He brushed a long dark curl away from her cheek. Matthew had once judged his women's beauty with a kind of ruthlessly detached objectivity. He really believed that men who claimed to have eyes for only one woman were either liars or low on testosterone. He had changed now. In his eyes, Fiona really was the most beautiful woman in the world.

'And what have you decided about our holiday next year?' she asked.

'Mustique.'

'And where the year after?'

'Mustique again.'

'And which school are our kids to go to?'

'Eton or Winchester for the boys. Saint Paul's for the girls.'

'What makes you think we're staying in this country? Perhaps I'll want to return to my hog farming roots in Iowa.'

'Well, in that case, I'll get myself some gum boots and come tagging along to Iowa.'

'You will? I expect I could make a decent hog farmer of you.'

They gazed at each other. This conversation wasn't exactly like getting engaged, but by Fiona's standards it was like agreeing to get surgically attached at the hip.

'I've been thinking myself,' she said.

'That's a first,' he said, as she bit him again. They cuddled and played for a while. It was easy, tender, shared time.

'Seriously, though,' she resumed. 'I think it's time we made a change in our domestic arrangements.'

Matthew raised his eyebrows. She wasn't going to propose to him, was she?

'My little flat at the back of the house. Fortress Fiona. I haven't slept there for a month and I realise I just don't need it any more. I'd like us to share everything. That included.'

'Hey, that's wonderful. That's absolutely wonderful.'

They kissed passionately and cuddled ever closer. Matthew's happiness expanded another notch. He didn't know life could be like this. This was the first time ever that Fiona had proposed a step forward in their mutual commitment. And giving up Fortress Fiona too. That was incredibly significant for her. Now she had nowhere to run away to, even if she wanted. Fiona was saying she no longer needed to run. As ever at times like this, there was fear in her eyes, but the fear was no longer her master, merely an annoying and lifelong companion, to be lived with not obeyed.

Matthew rocked her in his arms and was happy. In a few weeks, he'd have inherited his father's millions. At this rate it wouldn't be long before he got engaged to the woman he loved. What could be better?

'So you agree?' Fiona persisted.

'Agree? Of course I do you nincompoop.' It was Matthew's turn to bite Fiona's ear. She nuzzled him back.

'Good. Well, we should do it properly. Your share of the flat is £100,000. And you're a lucky man because I won't charge you for all the improvements I've made.'

'Yeah. Like fixing up a new shower curtain.'

'Hey. I had a fax line put in and two new plug points. So don't quibble, or I'll put the price up. Anyway, I guess you should be able to get the money together by the end of the week, in which case we can have a house-warming on Friday.'

In the warm bed, bathed in sunshine, Matthew grew cold.

Fiona meant it. To her orderly financial mind, a deal was a deal. You share the house, you pay your way. You don't pay, you don't share. And she was right about the timing, of course. Matthew could theoretically write out a cheque for her there and then. There wasn't a problem with that. None at all, except that he wouldn't be left with a million quid.

But he couldn't tell her that. He couldn't tell her the truth, because he'd be exposed as the worst kind of criminal in banking. He couldn't borrow the money, because he was at his limit as it was. And he couldn't pretend he didn't have the cash because it was she who had given him his bonus. She knew he could afford it.

'I'm not sure,' he stuttered. 'I might need a little longer.'

'Why? A week gives you masses of time.' Fiona pulled away from Matthew, her body tense.

'Fiona, please. It's not like that. I'm keen to buy the flat. I just need some time to sort out the money.'

'What do you mean? What precise exact steps do you need to take to get the money?'

Fiona was frozen on the edge of the bed, her voice high and brittle.

'Just . . . just it may take time. But there's nothing to worry about. I want –'

But Matthew broke off. Fiona was out of bed now, getting dressed in a frenzy. She was shaking all over. This was the first time – the first time ever – she'd been the one to move the relationship forward on to a whole new level of commitment. And immediately, not waiting a day, not even a minute, Matthew was backing off. She recognised the signs. She had been a fool to trust him. She shouldn't trust anyone ever, but especially not men. She had been cruelly hurt and rejected as a child and all her injuries flooded back, a tidal wave to smash anyone too slow to outrun it.

Fiona would do her best to outrun it. She'd do her best, even though the wave was inside her and could never be outrun.

'Fiona, stop it!'

Still racked by violent shudders, she turned to him. 'I swear to you,' she said. 'I swear that if you play games over this flat, then I'm leaving. I can't handle it, Matthew. You know I can't. I'm going back to New York, and I swear – I swear – I'll never speak to you again. I knew I shouldn't trust you. I knew I shouldn't trust anyone.'

She was three quarters dressed now and was shoving clothes randomly into a bag.

'Fiona, it's OK. I'll get the money. I didn't mean that. I didn't mean anything. I'll get the money to you right away. I want you. I love you. I want to live with you. I didn't mean anything by what I said. It's OK. No one's betraying anyone.'

Matthew caught Fiona by both arms and forced her to sit beside him on the bed. Her body was still victim to huge surges of anxiety, but her breathing began very slowly to normalise. She let herself be held and forced herself to listen to Matthew's voice. 'No one's betraying anyone. I'll get the money. There's no problem.' She panted, recovering her breath.

'You promise?'

'I promise. There's no problem.'

'You'll get the money?'

'I'll get the money.'

They sat a few minutes more.

'I'm sorry to react like that. It's just . . . you know. It's the first time I've ever . . . you know, committed to someone. It felt like you were backing off.'

'I'm not backing off.'

'That's good. But I do mean it about getting the money. I need it to feel OK. I know I'm nuts, but that's how it is.'

'That's OK, sweetheart. I can write you out a cheque right now.'

And he did.

4

The garden of the Inner Temple is pleasant at any time of year, but maybe its best time is early summer, when the great plane trees are decked out in green and the garden blooms in youthful ignorance of drought, decay and season.

Josephine took a turn about the grounds before leaving. She wiped her eyes, wondering if her make-up had run, but not caring excessively. Her tears had surprised her. She had never had the gift of easy tears, but just when they were most needed, they came, softening the elderly lawyer's heart. 'I'm sorry, dear girl,' he had said. 'There are certain uncomfortable facts we simply can't overcome.' It was then she'd felt her rush of grief. Her father's death, her mother's illness, the meanness of two of her brothers and the outright contempt of one of them; all that plus the daily grind of earning a living, caring for her mother, keeping house on a tiny budget. Overwhelming her for a moment, her tears had come, and with them, charity. 'I'll see what I can do,' said the lawyer, back-pedalling fast.

5

Val came into George's office waving a purple and white envelope.

'Mr Gradley?'

'Yes, Miss Bartlett?'

'You have a package from Oregon Furniture Incorporated.'

'Thank you, Miss Bartlett. You may open it.'

She knew everything now. There hadn't been any possibility of disguising things from her, not after the two totally unsurveyor-like surveyors had set everyone in the factory speculating about who they were and what they were doing. Val had confronted George and George had told her everything. He told her about the will, about why he had come to Gissings in the first place, about his brothers, about the conversation with Ballard which first opened his eyes to the possibility of selling Gissings. He told her about his meetings with Thurston and O'Shea. He even told her the truth about what he thought Oregon would do to Gissings.

Val had been angry with George's deception at first, but she had sympathy for him too. Val was deeply attached to Gissings and she assumed that George had an equal or greater attachment to the company his father had founded. As she saw it, it was natural for George to do all he could to keep his father's company in the family. They talked about what to do all evening and much of the next day.

A couple of weekends later, Josephine came up for a visit, bringing Helen, and the three of them discussed the problem while Helen watched intently, almost appearing to understand what passed. After a while, they came to a conclusion. Everyone was satisfied and the topic was dropped. They all knew what was to be done, so there was no need to worry further.

As Val ripped open the FedEx package, George raised his eyebrows.

'What d'you reckon they're offering then?'

She shrugged and passed him the contract while she skimmed the covering letter. They each found the crucial number at about the same time.

'Well, well, well,' he said. 'Five million quid. And from the look of it, they haven't dicked around with the contract too much either.'

'Can they get the money to you in time?'

'Oh sure. These guys are made of the stuff. That's no problem.'

Val smiled at George. Her deep-set blue eyes were alight with humour and warmth.

'Well, fancy you being worth five million,' she said. 'I'm certainly marrying up in the world.'

George tossed the contract down dismissively.

'Don't sell yourself cheap. Five million's neither here nor there. Just wait until you're Mrs Gradley Plant Hire Limited.'

Val smiled at her boss.

'I have a favour to ask, Mr Gradley.'

'Yes, Miss Bartlett, what is it?'

'A minute of your time, please, Mr Gradley.'

'By all means, Miss Bartlett.'

They drew together and kissed with passion.

6

Just one last thing to do, and that was to finish making his million. It had taken a while to arrange an exemption from the prenup, but everything had been sorted out in time. Sarah kept all her money in Hatherleigh Pacific shares, so she simply transferred a million pounds' worth of shares into her husband's name. That had been much more than Zack needed, but Sarah said he could keep the extra.

Zack called his stockbroker and gave instructions to sell all his newly registered shares. Altogether Zack would have around one and three quarter million pounds in his account.

The stockbroker read back Zack's instructions for confirmation and promised to call back in a few minutes as soon as the trade had gone through.

Zack went to get a coffee, swung his feet on to his desk and gazed out of the window. He had a pile of work to get on with, but it could wait. A holiday. That was the first thing he needed: a proper holiday. Every break he'd tried to take with Sarah had been invaded by the long arm of Weinstein Lukes. Well, he didn't need to worry so much now. With his share of his dad's cash, he could think about quitting the firm, or perhaps stay for a few years, make it to partner and build up some cash of his own. And Sarah? He'd need to make up his mind. He couldn't imagine life without her, but he still felt too young to be married. Probably he'd stay with her as long as he carried on enjoying it, and as long as she wasn't talking about having kids. Kids he could live without.

The phone rang again. Zack stretched out to answer it.

'Zack Gradley speaking.'

'Mr Gradley? This is Jason Armitage from your stock-brokers. I'm afraid there's a problem.'

'A problem?' Zack gripped the plastic receiver so hard it creaked.

'It appears that Hatherleigh Pacific made an announce-ment early this morning. To do with some financial irregularity. The shares have been suspended. I'm afraid the sale can't go through.'

'Suspended?'

Zack dropped the receiver and leaped to the Reuters news terminal which stood in the corner of his room. His experienced fingers tapped in the code for Hatherleigh Pacific. The screens blinked for a minute, then unscrolled their wicked news.

An audit of The South China Trust Bank, now wholly owned by Hatherleigh Pacific, has revealed a huge hole in its accounts. While investigators are still working to get to the bottom of the problem, it appears that in the course of the takeover bid, South China gambled massive amounts of money on the financial markets. In particular, South China put huge quantities of funds into a product called ROSES, heavily marketed by Weinstein Lukes, the investment bank. The gamble went sour. Instead of admitting the error, South China management shuffled the losses into a secret account, and creamed off any profits into the public accounts. During the bitterly fought takeover campaign, they boasted of increased profits, when in fact they had made losses big enough to sink the whole company. It is now unclear whether Hatherleigh Pacific itself will have the resources to survive. Meantime, Hatherleigh Pacific's shares have been suspended with immediate effect and can be neither bought nor sold.

It was the biggest financial story in the Far East that day, and Reuters devoted a large number of pages to it. Zack didn't read them all. He staggered away from the screen and fell into his chair. His face was white as a sheet, blank as the empty grave.

The Ending

1

Three years and eight days ago, Bernard Gradley, father and millionaire, ran his car into the stone wall that ended his life. Eight days later, his family heard his final wishes in astounded silence. The fortune they had expected to shower down upon them was, they learned, to hang suspended, in sight but out of reach.

Three years have now passed. The race that Bernard Gradley set running that day is finished, his last joke nearing its punch line. It is midnight in the City of London, Friday night tipping over into Saturday morning. Three bank accounts – in the names of Zachary, Matthew and George Gradley – lie quiet. It is too late now to add more money, cheat new people, earn more cash. The last deposits have been made. The final transfers requested, authorised and executed.

As the bells of London peal midnight to the empty city, a coded impulse leaves those silent accounts. Down the wires it travels to a central computer. A printer chatters briefly and is silent once more. The chit of paper lies unmoving in the dark office. When morning breaks, a clerk will come in, stamp and sign the piece of paper, add a certificate of confirmation, and have them couriered to a solicitor in Leeds.

Everything has been carefully arranged. Josephine's job in the Transfers and Settlements Department has made her expert in these matters. Much to Augustus Earle's relief, she has supervised all the arrangements and is sure there will be no slip-up. It is her job to be sure. Alone of Bernard Gradley's children, Josephine sleeps peacefully in her bed this night.

2

And now, at last, the great day dawns. It is perfect summer, cloudless and hot. Up and down the country, brides-to-be are throwing back the curtains and exclaiming for joy. Children wake early and burst in on their sleeping parents. Pilots and rock-climbers, balloonists and fell-walkers see the sunshine and rush to be outside. Today, from the skies and the cliff-tops, the world will lie unfurled, every last chimney pot distinct as a pinprick in the clear blue heat. This is no day to be in bed.

The sons of Bernard Gradley are also excited. They throw back their curtains and greet the sun, blood thrilling through their veins. Each one knows the riddle of his fortunes, but the others are secretive. Has anyone made his million? Who has made the most? Time will tell. The fortune is falling and someone must catch it.

Each must shower, shave, dress as though this were a normal day. But it is no normal day. Sarah laughs as Zack catches himself with a razor. 'Good luck, you clot,' she says, handing him some cotton wool. She's having a bunch of college friends round to drinks that evening and will travel on down to Ovenden House late that night, where Zack plans to join her. They are cordial with each other, but strained and careful. They still need to talk about the calamity which threatens Hatherleigh Pacific and with it the entire Hatherleigh fortune. They still need to tackle head-on Zack's role in the whole disastrous mess. Lord Hatherleigh will be there too, fresh from crisis meetings in Hong Kong. No doubt he will have some views of his own. But now is not the time for such thoughts. Zack is anxious to be off. Sarah teases him for his impatience. At the door, she kisses him on the cheek. For the last three nights they haven't made love, which, for them, is a record.

Matthew should be calmer. Are his nerves not steeled on the trading floor? Is he not used to gambling millions on the turn of the wheel, winning or losing with equal composure? Is this the same Matthew Gradley? It is one and the same, but Matthew's nerves are shot to shreds. Fiona sees his anxiety, but he brushes it off. She doesn't mind. He is welcome to be nervous if he wishes. He is welcome to have mysterious appointments in the north of England. She, Fiona, is happy. She has a wonderful job, plenty of money, and a partner who has all but soothed away her fears of intimacy. Matthew had been a bit funny about paying for his share in Fortress Fiona, but he'd done it and they were as happy together as they'd ever been. Fiona watches her partner leave, then climbs back into bed for a lazy morning with *Cosmo* magazine. The glossy pages fall open at a feature on wedding dresses. Instead of turning hurriedly away, Fiona lingers. They are nice, some of them. She leafs through the pictures, feels the fear, but knows she can handle it.

George and Val eat their usual breakfast without hurrying. Leeds is only a few miles away. They can take their time. Val will come to the solicitor's with George. No reason why not. Val washes the dishes, George dries. They are still both living in Val's tiny house. Will they move? They have talked about it and would like somewhere larger, especially as they both want kids and dogs, and Val has her heart set on a larger garden. George breaks one plate, then another in his anxiety. Val takes the drying-up cloth from his hand and makes him sit down. She'll get him there on time, she says, but she'd sooner he didn't break any more of her crockery.

And Josephine. Josephine attends to herself first, then wakes her mother and gets her ready for the day. Helen Gradley won't accompany her daughter to Leeds. She copes badly with travel and she'd only get stressed. At eight thirty, a care assistant arrives, a nice Kiwi girl with whom Helen gets on well. Josephine gives her her instructions, and steps out into the hall. She picks up a plain manila envelope from the foot of the stairs and walks outside to a car she has hired for the day. She gets into the car and sets off. In the back of the car are two large suitcases. Anyone would think she was off on holiday, but she points the car north and gets on to the M1, headed for Leeds. She too will be there on time.

3

Augustus Earle paces about his office, remembering the scene three years before. He is nervous, and nervousness makes him fussy. He shakes curtains into shape, shifts chairs, flicks dust from his polished desk. It is ten to twelve. Gradley's children should be here in ten minutes.

Suddenly, something catches his attention. Or rather, it is nothing which catches his attention. His grandfather clock has fallen silent and its heavy ticking no longer sounds out across the thick carpet. The spring has wound down; he must have forgotten to wind it. Earle puts a hand to the glass front to open the door, to wind the spring, but he is too late. Gravel crunching outside and a crashing at the door drag his attention back to the matter in hand. The clock must wait for now in silence.

Earle answers the door himself. It is a Saturday and he is the only person present in his office. There on the door-step stand not one but all of the Gradley children. They must have gathered in town and come on together.

'Come in,' he says, 'come in.' His voice is fluty and tremulous with excitement.

Zack, Matthew, George, Val and Josephine walk down the thickly carpeted hall into Earle's own immacu-late room. It hasn't changed from three years before: broad windows which let the universal sunlight come streaming in; Earle's grand walnut desk, with a smaller table, leather-covered, beside it; shelves solid with law books; on a side table, a sherry decanter and glasses. The five young people take their seats without needing to be invited. The room is filled with tension. People smile and are polite, but the anxiety is thicker than syrup.

'Is it a little bright for you, sitting in the sunlight, there?' Earle asked Josephine gallantly. She had been most helpful in sorting out the many annoyances to do with the banks and, as promised, he had received the account details and confirmation certificate in plenty of time that morning. Earle had examined the documents, but only to check their authenticity. Everything was in order, as it should be, as he knew it would be. But he hadn't looked at the account balances themselves. Even he was nervous.

Earle drew the heavy red curtains across the window, reducing but not cutting out the sunshine that poured into the room. Josephine's head now swam in darkness, her feet on a sea of gold. 'Is that better?' he asked.

'I'm fine,' she said. 'Thanks.'

'Sherry, or shall we get started right away?' Earle remembered the children's capacity for rudeness, Zack's especially, and he wanted to avoid unpleasantness.

Matthew, a handsome young man, though with something childish in him too, answered for them all. 'Let's cut to the chase, please, Augustus.'

Earle winced. Nobody used his christian name like that, not even his wife, who always called him darling. But Matthew wasn't being rude, just American. Earle did as he was told and cut to the chase.

'Right. You all know the rules. Bernard Gradley's estate has been placed in trust over the past three years. As you know, the estate mostly comprises Gradley Plant Hire, which has had an excellent three years. Profits for the year just ended are almost seven million pounds before tax, and the acting general manager tells me that a reasonable stockmarket valuation of the business would be in excess of fifty million pounds. In other words, the value of the legacy has increased substantially since your father's death. The acting general manager also tells me that in his view prospects are as strong as they've ever been.

'All of this, of course, belongs to whichever of you had the most money in their bank account at midnight last night, as long as that person has a minimum balance of one million pounds sterling. I don't need to stress, of course, that the money must be yours and only yours. It can't be borrowed or anything like that. Is that completely understood and agreed?'

The three brothers nodded, throats too dry to speak. Even Val and Josephine were drawn into the swelling tension and they too nodded silently.

'I have here,' continued the solicitor, 'confirmation from the bank, received this morning, of your account balances at midnight last night. I have also received the certificate guaranteeing the authenticity of this confirmation.'

He passed the stamped and signed certificate around the room. The paper was headed with the crest of one of Britain's biggest banks and the signature and stamp were clear and untampered with.

'Very well,' said Earle. 'I shall now reveal your account balances as they stood at midnight last night.'

Earle drew the second piece of paper from the envelope, the one he hadn't yet read. Even now, he forced his eye not to jump down the page, to leap ahead to the end of the story. He would reveal everything in due order.

'First,' he said, 'Mr George Gradley. Account number 7089030. George, can you confirm that your account details are correct?'

'Yes,' rasped George. 'That's correct.' God knew why he was so nervous. He knew the answer.

'The balance in your account last night was – was –' Earle gripped the paper more tightly as the unexpected number jumped out at him from the page '– the balance in your account was exactly nothing. No pounds and no pence. Do you dispute that?'

'No, that's quite correct.'

George's face was white. Beside him, Val squeezed his hand. Zack and Matthew's hearts leaped up. Both of them had secretly been worried that perhaps, after all, George could have pulled off a miracle at Gissings. But, it seemed, he had failed. George didn't have his million and there was no point putting less than that into the competition. Nine hundred and ninety nine thousand pounds was failure just as surely as nothing at all. Zack and Matthew breathed out through their mouths, looked sideways at each other and shifted in their seats. The competition amongst the three of them had narrowed to a competition between the two of them.

But this was and always had been the real contest. The movement in the room subsided and Earle continued.

'Therefore, George, you will not be entitled to claim your father's estate. Do you dispute that?'

'No. That's quite correct.'

'Very well. The next account on the list here is yours, Matthew. The account is in the name of Matthew Gradley. Number 4456723. Are those details correct?'

Matthew nodded. He couldn't speak, and yet he too surely knew the number which was about to be revealed.

'The balance in your account last night – at midnight – was –' Earle gripped the paper tightly once again. He forced his old eyes to make out the digits clearly, to make no mistake. For some reason, the silence of the grandfather clock, the emptiness of the room without its constant ticking, forced its way into his mind. He shut it out and made out the digits once again. 'The balance in your account last night was exactly nothing. Zero pounds and zero pence. Is that correct?'

The room spun before Matthew's eyes. The golden sunlight on the floor, the deep pools of shade cast by the red velvet curtains whirled around his rushing brain.

'No,' he cried. 'That's absolutely not correct. There's a million pounds there. More. I made more than a million.'

'I'm afraid it was not in your account last night.' The solicitor spoke with certainty. 'Are you sure you've given me the correct account number? If you have two accounts, there could be a confusion.'

'No. That's the right account. I know the money's there. I checked it yesterday at close of business. I swear to you –'

He didn't know what he was swearing. The money had been there. At four thirty, he'd called the bank and asked them to confirm the balance in his account.

A clerk had sent him a faxed confirmation. He pulled the fax out and showed it to Earle. The solicitor took it and examined it, but his examination was polite and sympathetic rather than professional. The fax wasn't authenticated or stamped. And besides, even if it carried the Royal Seal of the Queen of England, it wouldn't have mattered. What mattered was not the funds present at four thirty in the afternoon. What mattered was the funds present at midnight. And Earle knew what those funds were: zero pounds and zero pence.

'I'm sorry,' he said, handing back the fax. 'If you believe the bank has made a mistake, you can take the matter up with them. If there has been an error, despite the confirmations' – Earle indicated the certificate – 'then, of course, we will accept whatever the correct amount actually is. But, as I understand, mistakes of that sort are not common . . .'

He trailed off. He was right. Banks get your account balance wrong often enough. It's a foolish person or a rich one who doesn't check their bank statement each month. But this was different. The bank's central computers had been consulted. The records had been checked by a senior clerk, signed, stamped and delivered. This wasn't the bank's ordinary shoddy treatment of its run-of-the-mill customers. This was serious.

As Matthew's stomach plummeted into the abyss, his head told him what the matter was.

Belial. Belial had stolen the money, in revenge for Matthew's treatment of him. How he had done it, Matthew had no idea, but the truth was that he had no real concept of what Belial could and couldn't do. But he should have been suspicious. Belial had been a willing partner in Matthew's insider trades. His half million pound fee for the phoney account documents was blackmail, neither more nor less. He had promoted the idea of robbing one of the world's most heavily protected bank vaults. He would have sold the stolen bonds without a qualm. What on earth had made Matthew believe that he wouldn't be up to stealing from a perfectly ordinary British high-street bank account? Christ, Belial even knew the bloody account number from the days when Matthew had had an account with him. Matthew hadn't just made it possible, he'd made it easy.

This was an awful ending to a story which should have been so happy. Matthew had paid Fiona the money she wanted. He truly believed that she would leave him if he didn't and he wasn't sure he could ever persuade her back. So he had paid up, knowing after his bitter experience with Sophie that his happiness depended more on Fiona than on his father's cash. He had paid up, but not given up.

After paying Fiona, Matthew had nine hundred and thirty grand in his account. He had one month to make up the remaining seventy grand. He knew he couldn't make it through insider trading. To risk another encounter with Belial at this point would be madness, and he didn't dare try it with a more honest broker. So he would have to make his money honestly, the only way he could: by trading. Trading not with illegal insider knowledge, just with three years' worth of experience and judgement.

He couldn't afford to be cautious. He had to make around seven and a half percent on his money in only thirty-two days. That's equivalent to a hundred and forty percent a year. He needed to place his bet, spin the wheel, and stand back as the gods decided.

For three days and the best part of three nights, Matthew researched the markets. He looked at bonds, exchange rates, stockmarkets, everything. He worked night and day, barely resting. Eventually, he thought he'd found what he was looking for. He didn't find it anywhere obscure. On the contrary, he decided to settle on the dollar–euro exchange rate, the most widely traded exchange rate in the world. Everybody had been saying for months that the dollar had to fall. The trouble is, everyone had been saying it for months and the dollar had kept on inching up.

So why did Matthew stake everything on this one chance? He could have given you an answer to do with political pressures, G7 summits, economic realities, institutional requirements – but in the end that was nonsense. Matthew's head absorbed the information, but his gut gave the orders and his gut said: the rate had to change.

So Matthew made his bet. He called an honest London broker and explained that he wanted to bet on the dollar–euro exchange rate. He wanted to invest nine hundred and thirty thousand pounds exactly. He wanted to make his bet using short-dated currency options.

The broker hesitated. Was Matthew sure he knew what he was doing? Options are to normal investing as Russian roulette is to normal behaviour. Options aren't safe. They aren't sensible. If you're wrong you lose everything.

But Matthew was sure. He convinced the broker that he knew what he was doing. He insisted on making the trade. The broker obliged. Matthew had nine hundred and thirty grand riding on the fate of the world's largest currency market. Nothing that Matthew could do now could alter the course of events.

He prayed.

He prayed and he watched the market like a hawk. For twenty-seven long days, the dollar held steady. A couple of times it seemed ready to dive, but then some invisible force caught it and held it steady again. Matthew watched the market intently, but without panic. If he lost, he lost. There was nothing he could do. So he just watched the market and prayed.

Then, on the twenty-eighth day, just three days before the deadline, just as he was beginning to give up hope, it happened.

The dollar inched down, not far, but it did move down. This time, instead of encountering that invisible resistance, it found nothing to hold it and it inched down some more. It was a small movement, but nothing had intervened to block it. The talk in the market overnight was that the European Central Bank would step in to halt the move, but it didn't. The next morning the dollar moved down by inches, then by whole feet. Matthew's bet came good.

He quit. He could have stayed in for the two days that were left. He could have gambled on making a little more, hoping to outdo Zack, but he'd had enough. If he stayed in and the dollar went back up, he could lose everything. So he quit. He phoned his broker, sold out of his position, and collected his money: his original investment of nine hundred and thirty plus his profits of seventy-three.

He took the money and plonked it in his bank account. One million and three thousand pounds. He had two days to spare.

He'd done it. He'd met his father's challenge, not just once but twice. Once illegally. The second time legally. And now Belial, the cursed, evil Belial had taken not just the million, but Bernard Gradley's everything as well.

'I – I don't know,' said Matthew hopelessly. 'There was a million in there when I last looked. I'll check with the bank, obviously. I'm sure it'll be OK.'

His words fooled no one. Matthew looked defeated, devastated. Suppose Belial had stolen the money, and suppose Matthew could prove it – so what? Matthew could no more put Belial in a dock than vice versa. They were roped together now, jail for one would mean jail for both. Matthew's face was as white as ash. There was no more to say.

That left Zack. Zack who sat darkly forward. His turn. A wolfish smile began to spread across his narrow face. Two down and one to go. And may the best man win.

'Finally, Zack,' said Earle. 'Your brother wishes to check his account balance with the bank and, of course, he's perfectly entitled to do that. Therefore any conclusion we reach here today will, of course, be provisional. We will need to wait for final validation of Matthew's account. Do you understand that?'

Zack nodded and licked his lips. He was a wolf and he could smell blood.

'Very well then. Mr Zachary Gradley. Account number 7763421. Zack, can you confirm that these account details are correct?'

'That's correct.' Alone of the three brothers, Zack's voice worked perfectly at this point.

'The balance in your account at midnight last night,' said Earle, turning back to the numbers on the sheet in front of him. This was it. This was the final answer. The round number leaped out at Earle from the page. It was unmistakable, but like a good solicitor he double-checked his facts before speaking. 'Zack, the balance in your account was also zero. Zero pounds, zero pence.'

'No!'

Zack's cry split the room. He leaped from his seat and tore the paper from the older man. Zack took the page in at a glance. Zack, Matthew, George. All zero. No pounds. No pence. Three years and nothing to show for it. Zack snarled with disgust and hurled the paper from him.

'This is bollocks. They've screwed up. Josephine, what

the hell have you been doing? I thought it was your fucking job to sort out stuff like this. This bit of paper is complete cobblers. Matthew, how much did you have in your account?'

'A million.'

'A million exactly? How much?'

'One million and three thousand. Plus some hundreds, I can't remember how many.'

'George, how much did you have?'

'Nothing.'

'Nothing? So this is correct?'

'Yes. Absolutely correct.'

'Right. Well, unfortunately boys and girls, I have one million and ten thousand pounds. So I win. I'm sorry, Matthew, but it's mine. We'll call the bank on Monday. We'll get them to give us the proper account balances and finalise it all then. But when we do, I'm afraid you'll find that the money belongs to me, just as I told you it would.'

Matthew's emotions took another loop-the-loop ride. If the bank had screwed up Zack's account balance as well, then it was all just a clerical error. Not Belial at all. Once the error was sorted out, the million would be sitting there, as fat and happy as ever. That was the good news. The bad news was that Zack had won. After three years and a million pounds apiece, Zack had won by just seven thousand pounds. Seven thousand quid, when Matthew had give Josie a cheque for ten. It was a joke, really.

Matthew sat slumped in his chair. He didn't know now whether to be relieved or disappointed. By rights, he should be upset. He'd come hoping to win and now found that he'd lost by the smallest of margins. Yet, astonishingly, he wasn't unhappy. He had his million. He'd proved to Zack and to George that he had what it took. More to the point, he'd proved it to himself. He had Fiona. He had a job that he loved. He had as much money as he wanted for now; and if he ever wanted more, he'd earn it. He was a damn good trader and he could earn a lot in his lifetime. With Fiona's earning power as well, they'd never be anything but exceptionally well-off. And the best part was this: no more Belial, no more secret phone calls, no more theft, no more anxiety sitting in his stomach with its whispers of capture, jail and disgrace. Matthew was happy as the summer sun.

'Is it possible that there's been a mistake?'

Earle addressed the question to Josephine. She replied quietly.

'Yes, I think there has been a mistake.'

'Is it possible for you to get it sorted out on Monday?'

The solicitor was gentle. He intensely disliked Zack's violent outburst towards his sister and he tried to make up for it by being the pattern of old-fashioned courtesy himself.

'I hope that we can sort it out right now,' she said.

'Excellent. Do you need to use the phone?'

'No. There's no need.' Josephine opened the manila envelope which had sat by her side all this time. She withdrew two sheets of paper. 'May I present you with my own statement of account? As you can see, I held over two million pounds in my account as at midnight last night. I also attach a certificate of authentication.'

Earle examined the documents, completely bewildered now. They seemed to be all in order.

'I'm very sorry, Josephine. I really don't understand. I'm afraid that the will doesn't – um – extend the same offer to you as to your three brothers.'

Earle was flummoxed. As far as he knew, Josephine had spent the last three years taking care of her mother and working as a secretary in London. How she had come by two million pounds was beyond him. Not so Zack and Matthew, who were staring open-mouthed at their sister. She spoke again, so quietly that her listeners had to bend into the silence to hear her words.

'I think you'll find it does.'

She was completely calm. Hadn't she – a girl not out of her teens when all this began – coped for three long years with an ailing mother and too little money? What was before her today that was harder than that? She could be calm. She could have fun.

'Josephine, I'm very positive that the will was drawn up to benefit your brothers only.' Earle was insistent.

'Then can you please tell me what words are used in article seven of the will.'

Earle found his copy of the will on his desk and turned through the dense pages. Article seven was the bit which dealt with this very moment: measuring the accounts and releasing the estate from trust. Earle mouthed the legalese as he read. 'If the Account Balance of any Child contains the Requisite Amount at midnight on the Third Anniversary of the First Disclosure of this Will . . .'

The words ran on, but one stood out. *Child*. It said *Child*, not *Son*. Josephine was Gradley's child.

'Josephine, I see your point. The article says child. But, I don't think . . . I mean, it's clearly against the intention of the will . . . I'm afraid it's just a typo, an error . . . your father's intentions were absolutely clear.'

Josephine rose and stepped forward into the pool of light on the floor. Her head was in the light now and she was illuminated from head to foot, as though picked out by a ray from heaven.

'I'm afraid I don't care about my father's intentions. I care about what the will says.'

'The letter,' gasped Earle. 'The letter to you all. Bernard

wrote a letter to you. In it, he said that you, Josephine, should have the money for secretarial college and all that. And it was for your brothers that he set up this awful challenge. I'm afraid in any dispute over interpretation, that letter will carry a lot of weight.'

Josephine nodded.

'And do you remember the critical paragraph of that letter?' she asked.

Earle looked around his desk for the letter. It would be there somewhere. But Josephine beat him to it.

'The letter says: *If more than one of you kids has come up with the million, then the one with the most gets everything. I like winners, not runners-up.* You're welcome to check, but that's what it says. He used the word *kids*, not *sons*, not *boys*, not anything like that. And I am Bernard Gradley's kid alright.'

Earle was dumbfounded. Josephine had an argument, of course, but surely it didn't stand up. He couldn't yet see the flaw, but it was there, he was certain of it.

'And one other thing,' said Josephine. 'I have a legal opinion you may be interested in.' She tossed a document across the table to Earle. He picked it up and flicked through it. He didn't take much of it in, except the ending. The last sentence began, 'I would emphatically support Miss Josephine Gradley's entitlement to compete for the estate on equal terms . . .' And at the bottom, the unmistakable signature belonged to one of London's most respected barristers, well known for his expertise on matters to do with wills, and equally well known for his fondness for the courts.

'I don't know,' said Earle. 'I really hadn't expected . . . I'll look at this carefully, of course. But I'm afraid I can't promise . . .' He trailed off.

He couldn't find the mistake in what Josephine was saying, and Earle knew full well that the legal expertise of the barrister she'd consulted was much greater than his own. It really seemed as though Josephine might be right.

Josephine saw his hesitation and decided to help him along.

'Let me be quite clear,' she said. 'I believe in my case and my lawyers believe in it too. If you try to obstruct me, I shall be forced to go to court, where I am confident of success. That would be a difficult, painful and costly way of doing things, but I'm quite prepared to do it if need be.' Her tone was hard, but then she mellowed and floated a warm smile across the room to the elderly solicitor. 'And besides, I don't see why you should wish to get in my way. I know that the way my father drew up his will was very painful to you. If you do need to use your discretion, I'm sure you'll use it to benefit the family that you've served so well and for so long.'

Augustus Earle was charmed. He mumbled something. Something to do with due consideration, consultation with his fellow executors, needing to come to a sensible agreement – but everyone knew what he meant. Josephine had won. Gradley's millions were landing up in the one place that no one had predicted.

'You won't get away with this,' hissed Zack. 'That's not your money and you know it.'

'I'm sorry,' said Earle. 'What are you alleging? Are you saying –'

'I'm saying that Josephine stole the money from my account and Matthew's. She's a bank clerk isn't she? She knows all about these money transfers. She knows the ropes. That's what's so bloody great about being a bloody settlements clerk.' Zack was spitting his words now. 'But it won't wash, Josie. It's not your money. And I – I mean we, me and Matthew – will sue you for our money. And I'll sue you for Dad's estate as

621

well. You stole my money and you're not entitled to the estate.'

'Josephine! Is this true?'

'It's perfectly true. I stole the money. It wasn't quite as simple as he makes out, though. It was a lot of hard work hacking into the bank systems and authorising the transfers. It's a good job I've spent the last year and a half practising.'

Earle was dumbfounded once again.

'But, Josephine, you can't just steal money. Zack's perfectly right, you know. He and Matthew can just recover the money and the estate too.'

'I understand that. But I don't think that Matthew or Zack will wish to sue. In fact, I rather think they'll wish to let me keep the money.'

She looked squarely around the room, inviting challenges. George and Val sat there, like two plump Yorkshire chickens, impassive. As Earle looked at them, he suddenly wondered if they'd known all this in advance. Was that why there had been nothing in George's account? Forewarned and forearmed?

George's calmness couldn't have been more of a contrast with his two brothers. Zack was standing up, quivering with fury, anger concentrated in his dark eyes and outraged mouth. Matthew was white, standing behind his brother. He wasn't sure whether to be angry or not, but his mouth was screwed into a petulant sulk. Josephine looked at Matthew first.

'Well, Matthew. Are you going to sue?'

Matthew licked his lips. He couldn't sue anyone or anything. He couldn't sue Belial. He couldn't sue Josephine. He could no more withstand scrutiny of his financial affairs than a vampire could garlic. He shook his head.

'I'm not suing, Josie.'

She smiled at him. 'No, of course, not. How about you, Zack. Are you suing?'

'Of course I'm suing, you fool. How on earth did you think you could get away with a stupid schoolgirl game like this? I'll sue you for every penny.' Zack was incandescent with anger. He shook his finger at her, furiously adding, 'I swear to you, Josie, after I've got my money back and Dad's too, you'll have to crawl on your belly from here to London before you so much as smell a penny of it.'

'You're so kind,' said Josephine. 'It's always nice to know where one stands.'

'It's mine, Josie. It's all mine.'

'Of course,' added Josephine, musing, 'if you did sue me, certain facts might get revealed.'

'What facts are those?' Zack snorted. He didn't know why Matthew had backed down, but he sure as hell wasn't going to.

'Well, at your wedding, I had a most interesting chat with your friend Arabella Queensferry. She was telling me all about a certain ball a couple of years back. You remember the occasion, I'm sure. You knocked out Sarah's fiancée and had Arabella set him up. Arabella didn't know what she was doing and spoke to me because she was concerned about it. I told her not to worry, but Sarah might feel differently. You never can tell how people react to these things.'

Zack hesitated, but he was so incensed at Josephine that any hope of balanced judgement was gone. Sarah, for the time being, was nothing to him, nothing except another stepping stone on the road to his fortune. Zack hesitated, but not for long.

'I'll kill you if you tell her anything, but you're not going to stop me getting my money.'

'Really? And what about poor old Hal Gillingham?

623

What a coincidence that he should find himself an alcoholic again, when he never even remembered touching a drink.'

'What the hell do you know about that?'

'Well, you told me about your promotion and the reason for it. I felt Hal was probably short of visitors so I decided to track him down. I rang round the most exclusive clinics in Britain and, lo and behold, there he was, being looked after for a few hundred quid a day at a posh clinic in Kent. I went to visit him. We became friends – he's quite a nice man, actually – and he told me his life story. The bit involving you had a terribly familiar ring to it. I didn't tell him anything about you, but I could. He's getting married, by the way. Fell in love with a pretty nurse and seems happy as a songbird.'

'I don't care what he knows,' rasped Zack, but his voice was unconvincing even to himself.

'No, I bet you don't. But your employers? Oh, I know I can't prove anything, but things don't work on proof in your world, do they? You have to be whiter than white or they'll drop you quicker than hot coal. Conning your wife into marrying you, nudging your boss into alcoholism – well, they'd be nuts to let you continue, wouldn't they?'

'Why would I care about them? I'll have the money, won't I?'

'Really? You won't mind losing wife and job and reputation just for the sake of Dad's fortune? Are you sure?'

Zack wasn't sure. Everyone in the room could see he wasn't sure. But he hated losing, and losing publicly he detested.

'Damn right I'm sure. It's not your money, Josie. It's mine.'

'Well, maybe you're right. Maybe you really won't

mind hugging your fortune to yourself and ignoring the whispers which say, "There goes Zack Gradley, the man who swindled his way to a fortune".'

'Don't push it.'

'On the other hand, maybe you wouldn't even get the money, after all.'

'What the hell do you mean?'

'Well, Dad's will is pretty clear on this point, Zack. You have to have made the million pounds outright. You can't owe any of it to anyone.'

'It is mine, you idiot. The million pounds is mine. I made it. It's mine.'

'Really? Well, do you know what, as I was hacking my way through the bank's computer systems last night, I got curious. I decided to have a look at the recent transactions on your account. That's the beauty of hacking, Zack. You can see whatever you want. I must show you some time. I think you'd enjoy it.'

'What about my account?'

'Oh yes, sorry. Well, I noticed something rather peculiar. I noticed that until the day before yesterday you only had seven hundred and seventy-six thousand pounds in your account. That's well short of a million.'

'So what? That was the day before yesterday.'

'Well, the interesting thing to me was where the missing two hundred and thirty-four thousand pounds came from. It was a direct transfer from an account at another London bank. I guessed that would be Sarah's account, in which case there wouldn't be a problem. After all, there wouldn't be anything peculiar about a wife giving her husband money. Now, it was naughty of me, I know, but I just thought I would take a look at that other account. And what do you think I saw? It wasn't Sarah's account at all. I'm sure she'd have given you the money if you'd asked for it, but then I remembered that you'd all but bankrupted her and her family. Maybe she had a hard time scraping together that kind of money. Or maybe she was feeling peeved with you. I don't know, but anyway, that's not the point. No, the interesting thing was that the missing money came from a chap called Dixon Banderman, who seems to be a Weinstein Lukes employee, judging by the monthly salary payments into his account. I think I remember you mentioning that he's your boss.'

'So what?' said Zack, sneering. 'Dixon gave me the money, because Sarah was hard-pressed to find it at short notice. Who cares who gave it to me?'

'Gave it, Zack? Gave it? Are you sure he gave it? I can understand your wife giving you money. That's the sort of thing that wives do. I could even understand it if your father-in-law, Lord Hatherleigh, gave you the money. God knows why he should after what you've done to him, but he seems like a nice chap. But Dixon Banderman? Your boss? Why on earth would he *give* you nearly quarter of a million pounds?' The room was silent, waiting for her conclusion. She let the words tiptoe out into the deafening quiet. 'Are you sure it wasn't a loan?'

'It was a gift.'

Everyone knew what they were talking about. The will was absolutely clear. The million pounds had to be made without borrowing. If even a penny of the million pounds was borrowed, then none of it was allowed to count. Josephine continued.

'It was a gift, I understand that. Your boss just decided to say, "Hell, I love this chap Gradley so much I'm going to give him quarter of a million without expecting a penny of it back". I believe you. After all, you're my brother. But what do you think they'll make of that in a court of law?'

'There's nothing written. You can't prove anything.'

That was true. Zack had told Banderman enough of the story to persuade him to come up with the cash. Zack had said that there had to be nothing in writing, nothing at all to document the fact that the money was a loan not a gift. Banderman had agreed. But even as he picked up the phone to authorise the transfer, he said, 'We won't put this into writing, but you and I both understand that this is a loan. If you don't pay it back, then I will personally come and murder you. Got that, scum-face?' Zack had agreed, of course. He hadn't imagined any possible comeback. But what if Banderman were dragged on to the witness stand? What would he say? Weinstein Lukes prided itself on the integrity of its employees, and Banderman would no more lie under oath than he would commit burglary. Josephine resumed, dreamily.

'No. I doubt if I'll be able to prove anything. Perhaps I can. Perhaps Dixon Banderman will tell the full story. But to get the money, you would have to demonstrate to the satisfaction of the court that the money was not borrowed. And that would be pretty tough, wouldn't it? Be pretty tough to get a jury to swallow that one.'

She trailed off. Zack's face was white and his lips moved in silence. She was right. Even if Dixon were to pretend the money was a gift, who on earth would believe him? Banderman was a wealthy man, but no man, no matter how wealthy, just gives away quarter of a million pounds to an all-but-new employee. One inch – no more – separated Zack from his father's fortune, but try as he might, he couldn't find a way to cross that last tiny distance. His lips worked in silence. He was beaten. The inch was wide as the Pacific, high as the Himalayas.

'I can still make you give back my million even if

I don't try to claim the estate.' Even in defeat, Zack couldn't concede. His voice was petulant now, spiteful and bitter.

Josephine watched him for a moment impassively, then answered him.

'Of course, you could make me give your million back. After all, you'll need to find at least two hundred and fifty grand with which to pay back Banderman. But before you try, just consider this. If you sue me, then I swear that you will never see a penny of Dad's money. If you don't sue, if you leave me with the million I stole from you, then I might decide to give you some of it. I'm not saying I will. I'm just saying you have a chance, depending on how I feel. It's up to you.'

Zack was unable to speak, and Matthew spoke the question uppermost in his mind.

'What are you going to do with the estate, Josie?'

She looked at him sharply. She was in complete control of the room now, all the cards in her hand.

'Well, I haven't quite decided on everything,' she said. 'But whatever happens, I'm not going to sell Gradley Plant Hire. I'm going to run that as a business and I have every expectation of doing extremely well with it. I've already found myself an excellent managing director.'

'Eh? Who?'

Josephine indicated George with a tiny wave of her hand. George received Matthew's glance and nodded in confirmation.

'You? What's going to happen to Gissings, then?'

'Oh, I shan't sell Gissings. I'll just ask somebody else to run it, and as a matter of fact I've already found myself an excellent managing director too.'

George indicated Val with a tiny wave of his hand, and Val smiled at Matthew in embarrassed acknowledgement. Matthew stared at Josephine, George and

Val. So they'd all been in on this, had they? George got to keep his precious little factory, while simultaneously stepping up to the big time with Dad's old company.

'Congratulations,' he said. 'I'm sure you'll do a good job – both do a good job, I mean,' nodding to include Val. 'And what about – I mean, Josie . . . are you going to keep all the shares to yourself or will you share them out?'

Josie shrugged. 'Oh, no. I shan't keep them all. George will get a quarter. After all, I want my managing director to have some incentives.'

'And us, Josie, what about us?'

Matthew indicated himself and Zack. Josie stared at them like they were zoo animals. She shrugged.

'I don't know, Matthew.' For the first time, a tremble entered her voice and the dazzle of sunlight on her face told of emotion in her eyes. 'What I do know is that while I struggled for three years to look after Mum, George was the only one of you who did right by her. When I was really struggling, he emptied out his wallet to give me literally his last money in the world, even though he'd been living in a van, and even though he hadn't drawn so much as one penny in salary. I know that he visited when he could, that he phoned every week at least, that he sent cards and presents and money, that he and Val treated me and Mum as welcome guests not as embarrassing intruders. I know that he deserves every bit of good fortune now. And as for you two, I honestly don't know. You, Matthew, tried to be nice, but in the end the thought that Zack might beat you to the million stopped you every time. And as for you, Zack, your performance just now shows where your heart really lies. Right now, I haven't made any decisions. I'm off on holiday. With Mum, to the Caribbean. George and Val are coming too. We'll be there for two weeks. Maybe when I come back,

I'll have simmered down a bit, but then again, maybe I won't. You'll just have to wait and see.'

Nobody answered her. There was nothing much to say. Augustus Earle, who had vanished off into a world of his own amongst the papers on his desk, suddenly sprang back to life.

'Zack, Matthew. I have a question to ask each of you. Do either of you dispute Josephine's right to the money she – er – transferred from your accounts last night?'

'She hadn't any right,' muttered Zack.

'That's not what I mean. I mean do either of you now contest that the money is hers? Will you seek to reclaim it?'

The two brothers shook their heads.

'Good. Now, Josephine, I've been rereading the will, and this legal opinion you've given me. I believe you're right. I believe we can justify an interpretation along the lines you've talked about. Frankly, it's a stretch. It's not what Bernard intended and you know that as well as I do. But I don't want to stand in the way of justice, and I'm sure my fellow executors won't want to either. So far as I can see, the only major stumbling block would be if any of your brothers chose to contest your entitlement in court. But I take it that none of them will do that. Am I right?'

The two brothers nodded in silence. George sat motionless. His opinion was already fairly clear.

'Excellent. And you will be willing to confirm all this in writing?'

They nodded again. Earle noticed that at some point, he hadn't noticed when, the old grandfather clock had found new life in its springs and was beating out time across the carpet as before.

'Then, Josephine, I shall call a meeting of my fellow executors immediately. I am confident that we shall be able to release the estate into your hands within a matter of days. May I be the first to wish you my heartiest congratulations and to wish you an extremely pleasant holiday.'

'Thank you,' said Josephine, making ready to leave.

And as she did so, the old clock paused for breath, began to whirr, then rang out the noonday chimes, an hour or so late, but sweet and clear as ever.

Epilogue

1

And so it was. Bernard Gradley's estate passed in its entirety to his only daughter. Her first act on taking possession of the company was to call a meeting of the board, at which she installed herself as chairwoman and her brother George as managing director. George was to receive a salary of eighty thousand pounds, modest by the standards of a large company, and he was entitled to no bonus, no share options, nor any other perks. But Josephine also transferred into his name a parcel of shares which, as promised, gave him one quarter of the whole company. That was incentive enough.

George spent his first three weeks buried in the company records. He read the accounts, he tried to understand the business, he went on site tours and interviewed his principal managers. At the end of it he was breathless with excitement. 'There's no stopping us, Val,' he confided to his fiancée. 'This company's got bags of potential, and for once it hasn't mortgaged away its future. The sky's the limit here.' Val was pleased for him, of course. She knew that George's ambitions wanted a bigger arena than Gissings could now provide, and she saw his excitement and encouraged him. But she was pleased for other reasons too. They were soon to be married and there was joy for Val in every detail of the wedding preparations. They were looking round for a new home and had already seen a number of gorgeous houses with room for kids and dogs aplenty. George wanted a big dog: a Labrador perhaps, or a collie. Val wanted something smaller: a spaniel probably or maybe even a terrier. But there was no hurry. They'd choose in their own good time and Val knew she'd get her way.

And then there was Gissings. They called a board meeting there too, at which George resigned as managing director and appointed Val in his place. Val would have to make do with the meagre salary that George had put up with, but she too was given an incentive. George transferred half of Gissings into her name and – most important of all – wrote out a cheque which completely cancelled Gissings' debt to David Ballard.

'Congratulations you two. Don't you lose touch just because of this,' said Ballard, waving the cheque. 'I'm not going to retire happy until I've seen you, Val, buy out the Aspertons and you, George, notch up your first fifty million profit. I tell you, there'll be no prouder man in heaven tonight than your late father, George, my lad.'

George wasn't sure that Bernard would be too fussed. If he'd managed to barge through the pearly gates at all, he'd be too busy establishing his harp rental business to think about the family he'd left behind. If he had taken it into his head to look, though, he'd have liked George's new desk ornament. In the centre of George's impressive desk (a special order from Gissings, of course), there stood a black plastic pedestal bearing a die-cast model of a forklift truck. Like his father, George would sooner have died than sell his shares in the company he now managed.

Val normally didn't go in for trifles, but she too had a memento she was reluctant to throw away. It was a fax from David Thurston and Kelly O'Shea. When George had rejected their first offer, they'd reported the news to their Strategy Committee, which was astonished by the rejection. The Committee approved a higher offer, contained in the fax, which valued Gissings at six million pounds exactly. George hadn't responded despite a series of increasingly frantic phone calls from across the Atlantic, but Val had kept it. Up in heaven, there was another ex-businessman keeping a watchful eye on his former baby. Tom Gissing would have been astonished and proud to know that anybody valued his business as highly as that, and he'd have been equally astonished to see its new managing director. Val was determined to make it worth even more in the future and, free of debt, began to concoct plans for a major overhaul of the ailing plant. Andrew Walters had mentioned his intention to take early retirement and Val chose Darren to take the lead on the plant renovation.

2

Matthew was happy too. He'd come home from work one day to find Fiona radiant in one of her rarely seen evening gowns. No sooner had he come through the door than she grabbed him gently between the legs and drew him after her in to their living room. The room was filled with flowers: white ones, lilies, roses, gypsophila, carnations, anthemis, orchids, white lilac; flowers in every vase, jug and bowl the house contained; flowers on every table, every shelf, on the arms of the chairs, on the sofa, on the floor. The air was thick with perfume and Matthew's nose tickled. On the living-room

table was a small box, bearing the signature of Asprey &
Garrard, the queen's jewellers.

'I'm ready, Matthew. I'm finally, genuinely ready,'
she said.

Matthew took her hand and dropped to his knee.

'Dearest Fiona,' he said, 'will you marry me?'

She didn't answer him directly, but by the time they
were done kissing, a diamond ring had made its way
out of the little box on the table and on to Fiona's ring
finger. They were engaged.

Matthew had lost his million and lost his claim on his
father's wealth. He regretted this, but not excessively. He
was glad beyond words not to have to deal with Belial
any more, glad too that he had no secrets from Fiona
or from Madison, glad to have proved something in the
process. He would earn more bonuses. He was a good
trader and now that his attention was focused entirely
on the bank's business, he'd do better yet. In time, he
hoped to become a managing director alongside Fiona
and they'd have money enough to bathe in. In time, he
expected Josephine to relent. She'd give him back his
million and maybe even some of her shares, in which
case they'd have enough to swim in. Time would tell.
Matthew wasn't in a hurry.

3

Then there was Zack. He didn't travel back up to London
after the final climactic scene at the solicitor's. He got into
his car and drove round the country trying to make sense
of what had happened. He thought about Sarah and the
calamitous state of Hatherleigh Pacific. He thought about
Weinstein Lukes, about Dixon Banderman, and about
the quarter of a million pounds which he owed and
didn't have. He thought about Robert Leighton and Hal

Gillingham. He thought about his sister, brothers, father and mother. He drove randomly until nightfall, finding himself finally a short distance north of Oxford. He drove there, banging on his old tutor's door at half-past ten.

Ichabod Bell opened the door to his former star pupil, and welcomed him in. Bell lived alone with his books and was glad to see Zack. Zack told his story, not quite truthfully but almost, and listened to Bell's quiet commentary. Bell didn't pass judgement, but didn't conceal his opinions either. He was a good listener.

Zack and the philosopher talked till half-past four that morning. Then at nine, Zack got up, climbed into his car and began to nose out of Oxford on the Wiltshire road, heading for Devon to face the wrath of his ruined wife and father-in-law. But before he got on to the main road proper, force of habit made him dial into his voice mail at work.

There were two messages. The first was from Banderman: 'Call me immediately you get this.' The partner left a few phone numbers where he could be reached, but didn't once insult Zack. A bad sign. He surely couldn't want his quarter of a million back already, could he?

But the other message was worse; far, far worse. It was from Arabella Queensferry of all people. As an old friend of Zack's and a college acquaintance of Sarah's, she had been at Sarah's party the evening before. Her message ran as follows: 'Zack, it's me, Arabella. At the party last night, I heard Sarah talking about your father's will and about how you'd asked her for the money to make up your million pounds. That's when it clicked. That's when I remembered who you were with that night at the ball. I asked Sarah who Robert Leighton was and she told me the whole story, about how she was engaged to him, then broke it off because of that incident. So I told her everything. I had to. I would never have done

636

what you'd asked if I'd known you could be so low. I mean, I knew you were low, but not that low. Sarah was furious, beyond furious really. If you've got anything to say in your defence, you'd better start saying it now. As for me, I'd sooner not hear from you again. I'm sorry, Zack. Bye.'

Zack sat frozen, forgetting to turn the phone off, not hearing the 'End of messages' announcement repeat every few seconds. He was like an ardent football fan, needing only a draw from an important game, watching ninety minutes go by goalless and tame – and then, an error, a slip, a moment's inattention, hardly noticeable in the ordinary run of play. Yet almost without build-up, without preparation, before you've got your bearings, the ball is crashing against the back of the net, the wrong net, the net's ballooning out, the scorer's breaking away with arms aloft, and the game's lost, the final whistle now only seconds away. The first emotion is disbelief. But there, already lurking beneath the denial, is the knowledge that the very worst thing has happened, the one thing which had not to happen, has really taken place. The images are simultaneously vivid and disconnected – the flash of the ball, the goalie's dive, the billowing white of the net, the roar of opposing fans – but everything points to the one terrible and irrevocable truth.

Somewhere, Zack knew all this. Losing his father's money had been bad, but this was shattering. For the last three years his life had been two things only: work and Sarah. The work had been for nothing and now Sarah – what would she think? How could she possibly do anything but turn her back on him for ever? If Zack had all the money in all the world clipped neatly into a billfold, he'd have tossed it aside without a second thought for the chance to undo his wife's terrible discovery.

In shock as he was, his agony was still numb. He moved mechanically. He dialled Banderman first.

'Dixon, it's Zack.'

'I want you to come in to the office at once.'

Banderman hadn't insulted Zack. His tone was awry. Somewhere Zack registered these facts, but his mind wasn't working.

'Is there a problem?'

'There is, yes.' Banderman was grim. 'We're being sued by Hatherleigh Pacific. They're claiming our sales-manship of ROSES to South China didn't meet due stand-ards of responsible marketing. They're trying to shift the losses on to us.'

Zack's mind lagged a long long way behind.

'What? Hatherleigh Pacific? Can they do that?'

'Don't know. Our lawyers say they may have a case. I've been going through the marketing materials you put together, and there's not a word about responsible salesmanship. That isn't going to help us. We'll probably need you to appear in court.'

Zack's wife had found him out for a cheat of the worst sort. His father-in-law was suing his employ-ers. His employers would soon find out, if they didn't already know, that Zack hadn't spent a single minute encouraging responsible salesmanship. Zack promised to come in right away and rang off. He was in a mounting daze. Sarah. He had to speak to Sarah. He wouldn't even mind her anger, he wouldn't mind anything so long as he could speak to her. He dialled her number.

The number was unobtainable. He redialled carefully. Unobtainable. The long whining signal told him what he didn't want to know. Sarah had changed their phone number. He called directory enquiries. The new number was ex-directory. Zack's numbness spread through his body, but his mind still clicked forwards. If she'd bothered to change the number, chances were she was still in London and hadn't gone down to Devon.

Zack turned the car round and drove east into London. The Saab must have guided itself down the M40 because though Zack was at the wheel, it wasn't him making the decisions. He drove, not to Weinstein Lukes, but to his flat – Sarah's flat – their flat, their home. He tried his key, but he already knew what he would find. The lock had been changed. He thought of dialling Ovenden House, but he hadn't the nerve to speak to anyone there.

A piece of paper caught his eye. Paper addressed to him. He opened it and read the familiar handwriting. Handwriting which should have said something ordinary, something to do with popping out, lunch in the fridge, see you later. It didn't say that. The note told Zack that Sarah was having his possessions packed up and moved into storage. The location and the key would be mailed to him at Weinstein Lukes. He should not try to contact her, now or ever.

There was nothing to do. Zack believed Sarah was inside the flat, but she wouldn't answer his knock, wouldn't answer him if he called. He waited a moment. He was suddenly sure that she was standing on the other side of the door listening, knowing he was there. He wondered whether he should say something, but what would he say? 'It's true. I married you for your money, and now I've lost your money, my money, my father's and your family's. I can't even pay my boss what I owe.' Or should he just say what was in his heart. 'I love you, I adore you and I've found out too late'?

He hesitated in front of the door, arm raised, ready to knock. For fully a minute, he stood there motionless. Then he stepped back and dropped his arm.

'I'm sorry, my love,' he whispered, so quietly the

sound barely carried, then he turned and left the building.

His daze carried him to Weinstein Lukes. Banderman was in command of a huge legal operation, which snowballed by the hour. Lawyers came and went. Papers mounted up. Legal secretaries filed and indexed each new document. Mounds of paper were copied and dispatched by courier to Hong Kong, Singapore, New York; cost no object. Never in its history had the firm been forced to defend such a costly action.

'Come in,' said Banderman. 'We've work to do.'

For one week, Zack stood at the centre of the whirlwind. Legal strategies were explored, debated, refined. Documents corroborating each individual point were located, scrutinised and reinterpreted. To the thousand bucks an hour suits, this was playtime, and despite the fundamental truth of Hatherleigh's complaint, Weinstein Lukes grew increasingly confident of total success. Zack's numbness wore off and his pain mounted.

At the end of the week, he left the office at lunch time and walked briskly to Pall Mall. At Hatherleigh Pacific's offices, he asked to see the chairman. After a brief wait, he was shown up to the viscount's room. Zack, feeling lower than the mould which feeds off gutter slime, walked in.

The viscount nodded, but didn't offer his hand.

'Well?'

Zack swallowed. He had rehearsed something before coming, but he couldn't remember a word of it. He shook himself and began.

'I won't apologise, because there isn't an apology in the world that's big enough. All I came to say is that I think there's merit in your action against Weinstein Lukes. But you won't win the case by yourself. They've got too many defences. You need an insider, someone at the centre of the whole ROSES thing, someone who knows their legal strategy. I know I'm the last person on earth you must want to work with, but I think I can save Hatherleigh Pacific.'

'You'll not get Sarah back.'

'I know. I know I've lost her and I'm afraid she's better off without me. But at least I can save something from the wreckage – Hatherleigh Pacific, I mean. If you'll allow me.'

The viscount allowed him. Zack quickly inserted himself at the heart of the Hatherleigh litigation. He knew which witnesses should be called, what questions to ask them, what documents to demand. He tore up one set of arguments and rewrote them. He developed entire lines of questioning for key witnesses. Eminent barristers sat meekly as Zack took charge. The case as Zack presented it would be witheringly destructive – and at the heart of it all would be Zack's own evidence: how he personally, the inventor and organiser of the whole ROSES effort, had never for a moment considered his clients' best interests.

There were some personal costs in all of this for Zack. He lost his job, of course. He had been forced to tell Banderman that he couldn't repay his quarter of a million, and personal bankruptcy seemed assured as Banderman opened proceedings against him. What's more, to fight the case, Weinstein Lukes needed a tax expert to rely on. With Zack gone, that only left Hal Gillingham, who agreed to offer his services as a consultant. As Gillingham began to master the details of the case, he discovered, inevitably, that the tax scam at the heart of it all was his own idea. Right away, he told Banderman, who looked quizzical initially, but when Gillingham managed to produce some notes and doodles from that evening long ago when he'd had his brainwave, Banderman was convinced. Weinstein Lukes' busy lawyers began to take time out to explore whether they could sue Zack to recover the bonus they'd paid him when under the impression that ROSES had been his idea.

But none of this Zack minded. He had lost Sarah and all the money in the world wouldn't make good her loss. Just two days after getting the terrible news, he'd written to her, confessing everything, apologising and wishing her the very best for her life from now on. He had enclosed his wedding ring and promised that he would do everything to facilitate a divorce the moment she was ready. His relations with Lord Hatherleigh, meantime, were strictly businesslike.

The case settled out of court. Hatherleigh Pacific didn't get everything it wanted, but the settlement was as good as they'd hoped. The company's shares resumed trading on the Hong Kong exchange, battered by the experience, but not crippled. The Hatherleigh Pacific board meetings once again focused on the future, and Scottie could once again turn his attentions to fixing up South China.

By this time, Zack was legally bankrupt. If Josephine, one day, condescended to give him his million back, he'd have to hand it over to Banderman and Weinstein Lukes. He didn't mind. They were welcome to it. He was back in Oxford now, living in a freezing attic on the Cowley Road, once more living for philosophy. He had resurrected his old thesis, which had more life in it than he'd thought. He was excited by its potential and hoped to have it ready quickly, then maybe develop his ideas further, write a book perhaps. Ichabod Bell was encouraging.

In all this time, Zack had neither seen nor spoken to Sarah, but on his desk he had a huge photo of her in her wedding dress, and some snapshots of her on his mantelpiece. Apart from heaps of philosophy books on every surface, there was no other decoration in his single-room flat. He wasn't happy, in fact, his misery could scarcely have been more intense, but with Sarah gone, philosophy seemed the only thing worth living for.

And then one day, eight months or so after the whole hideous tragedy had unfolded, there was a ring at his door. He pressed the buzzer to let his visitor up and, a moment later, there in his doorway stood Sarah, heavily pregnant.

The blood dropped from Zack's face.

'Sarah!'

'May I come in?'

He nodded, not able to speak. There was only one chair in the room and Zack thrust it at her, himself sitting knees drawn up on his untidy bed. They stared at each other in astounded silence.

'You're pregnant,' he said. 'Is it . . . ? Is it . . . ?'

'She's ours, Zack. That's right.'

'And . . . do you . . . I mean, have you . . .' He couldn't finish.

'I'm not sure why I've come. I was passing, so I thought I'd drop in.' She stopped. 'But I do know that this child would be better off for having a father.'

'But Sarah, you can't . . . you can't want me after what's happened. Find someone else for heaven's sake. Someone who'll be good to you.'

'Is that what you want?' she asked in a whisper.

Zack's mouth worked, but no words came out. He felt that, if he only had one last wish on earth, it would be to protect Sarah against the worst of all fates, that of being married to him. But now it came to the point, his mouth was unable to form the words that would save her. His lips struggled soundlessly, till he gave up and shook his head.

Sarah stood up. Her belly billowed out, the largest

thing in the room, the centre of the universe. Inside was life; tiny, wriggling life.

'Zack?'

'Sarah!'

He was holding her now, desperate to kiss her, but not kissing her.

'If you want, we could try working something out.'

He nodded dumbly.

'Just for a trial period.'

He nodded again.

'I suppose you'll want to go on living here?' She shivered. It was March and the attic wasn't insulated or heated.

'I suppose so, but –'

'Good. Then you can live here during the week and we'll see each other at weekends to begin with. See how that goes. You can come up to London or down to Ovenden House if I'm there.'

'But your father . . . how will he feel? Maybe I should stay out of his way.'

'If you want to work something out, you'll come to Devon. My family will let you back in if I do.'

Zack nodded. 'OK.'

'So it's agreed?'

'Yes, my love. Agreed.'

4

And Josephine? She is a rich woman now, but that doesn't mean that the cares of the world have left her. She has given up her job, of course. There are worse things in the world than being a settlements clerk and a well-liked one at that. But, all the same, there aren't many settlement clerks who own three quarters of an expanding company worth fifty million quid or more, and Josephine isn't minded to break the rule.

So she's a free woman. She always assumed she'd go to university, and perhaps she will. She can afford to choose a subject that she's interested in and pursue it for its own sake. Afterwards, whatever kind of work she does – if she chooses to do any at all – she can do also for its own sake. Will she be an active chairwoman of Gradley Plant Hire? Perhaps. David Ballard told her that her brother George was one of the best businessmen he'd ever seen, and Josephine wouldn't need to worry about leaving the business in her brother's hands. But she has to do something and perhaps her destiny, like George's, is with the company her father founded. All of this, however, lies in her future. Right now she's a free woman and that's enough.

She'll also need to come to a decision about her money. Does it rightfully belong to her, or should she share her wealth with Matthew and Zack, the two brothers from whom she stole so much? She's still angry about their treatment of her, and though they've apologised (sincerely in Matthew's case, and with surprising grace in Zack's), she doubts that anything would change if the whole business started back from the beginning again. In her heart, she knows she'll give them each back the million she stole, but she is genuinely unsure about giving them a share of their father's wealth. For now, she accepts their apologies and keeps the money, except for a plump six-figure cheque which finds its way (very much to his surprise) to a little-known Hungarian chess player, now returned to the land of his birth. Meantime, George is keen to reinvest profits in the company, which, he says, has an amazing future ahead of it. So the money's not going anywhere. Later on, if she chooses to share things out, the shares will be worth more than they're worth today.

Right now she has her own life to get started and her mother's to watch over. She has bought her mother a cottage in the Cotswolds. The cottage has a rose-covered porch and a bungalow at the bottom of a big garden, where an old couple live. The woman looks after Helen and the man looks after the garden, which has some wonderful fruit trees and its own small stretch of stream. Matthew and Fiona, George and Val, and Josephine herself are frequent visitors. Even Zack comes up from time to time these days.

Unbelievably, Helen Gradley is recovering a bit. Not all the way; probably she never will. But somehow, something inside her has sensed that the world has become a safer, kinder, more comfortable place, and the distress which has been with her so long has lifted. She's re-entered physical therapy, and this time she attacks it with a will. Her speech is better, her coordination very much improved. She'll remain disabled, of course, and she'll always need help with the day-to-day business of life, but to see her walking in her garden, you wouldn't dream of thinking her unhappy.

What's more, if you were to see her walking there, you would most likely see her in the company of a retired gentleman, a former major in the Royal Greenjackets. He's not the best-looking gentleman in the world, not even for his age, and his brain is a little scrambled too (the result of honourable service, no doubt). But the two of them seem to like each other – at any rate, he makes a point of calling frequently and Helen always seems pleased to see him. And if, one day, he should lift his tattered Panama hat and propose – why, the chances are, she'd say yes.

And that would be the happiest of endings.